JUDGE DREDD

DREDD VS. DEATH · BAD MOON RISING
BLACK ATLANTIC · ECLIPSE

Mega-City One – a massive urban sprawl that is home to 400 million citizens, each one a potential criminal. Spread down the Eastern coast of what was once the United States of America, unemployment is endemic, boredom is universal and crime is rampant. Using the powers as judge, jury and executioner, only the Street Judges can prevent total anarchy!

I Am the Law collects together four original novels in the Judge Dredd series (*Dredd vs. Death, Bad Moon Rising, Black Atlantic* and *Eclipse*).

In the same series

KINGDOM OF THE BLIND
THE FINAL CUT
SWINE FEVER
WHITEOUT
PSYKOGEDDON

Judge Dredd, Judge Giant and Galen De Marco
created by **John Wagner & Carlos Ezquerra**.

Psi-Judge Anderson, Chief Judge Hershey and
the Four Dark Judges created by **John Wagner
& Brian Bolland**.

Novelization based on the PC/PS2/Xbox game
"Judge Dredd: Dredd Vs Death". Script by **Tim
Jones, Kevin Floyer-Lea & Paul Mackman**.

I AM THE LAW

THE JUDGE DREDD OMNIBUS

Gordon Rennie, David Bishop, Simon Jowett,
Peter J Evans & James Swallow

A Black Flame Publication
www.blackflame.com
blackflame@games-workshop.co.uk

Dredd vs. Death Copyright 2003. *Bad Moon Rising, Black Atlantic* and *Eclipse* Copyright © 2004 Rebellion A/S. All rights reserved.

This omnibus edition published in 2006 BL Publishing, Games Workshop Ltd., Willow Road, Nottingham NG7 2WS, UK

Distributed in the US by Simon & Schuster, 1230 Avenue of the Americas, New York,. NY 10020, USA

10 9 8 7 6 5 4 3 2 1

Copyright © 2006 Rebellion A/S. All rights reserved.

All 2000AD characters and logos © and TM Rebellion A/S. "Judge Dredd" is a registered trade mark in the United States and other jurisdictions. "2000 AD" is a registered trade mark in certain jurisdictions. All rights reserved. Used under licence.

Black Flame and the Black Flame logo are trademarks of Games Workshop Ltd., variably registered in the UK and other countries around the world. All rights reserved.

ISBN 1 84416 412 8

A CIP record for this book is available from the British Library.

Printed in the UK by Bookmarque, Surrey, UK.

CONTENTS

DREDD vs. DEATH

BY GORDON RENNIE

MEGA-CITY ONE, 2112

It was the smell from the rotting corpses of his wife and daughter that finally forced Vernon out of the apartment he had shared with them for the last five years.

He wasn't sure how long he had been in there with them. Time seemed to have altered its flow in the days since the whole of Mega-City One had fallen into this place, which must surely be something close to Hell. The perpetual gloom that cloaked the city and enveloped the tops of the highest city blocks made it difficult to tell day from night, but by his reckoning it could only have been a few days since reality, as the citizens of Mega-City One had known it, had simply ceased to exist.

Just a few days. Not long enough to account for the rapidity with which the city had fallen apart. Not long enough to account for the overwhelming stench of weeks-long decay emanating from behind the closed door leading to the small apartment's bedrooms. But more than long enough to account for the growing sensation of gnawing hunger in his stomach.

The city's power supply was intermittent now, but even that couldn't account for the speed at which the food in the icebox had rotted away. There was something in the air that seemed to seep into absolutely everything, bringing festering decay in its wake. Even the contents of the packets of synthi-stuff in the kitchen cupboards had become mouldy and rotten, and Vernon hadn't been able to keep down more than a few mouthfuls of the raw synthi-noodle flakes he had tried to eat.

All he could do was sit there in the semi-darkness of the apartment, shivering against the unnatural cold that seemed to creep right into his very bones, listening to the terrible sounds that echoed through the deserted street-canyons outside – and wonder when it would be his turn to meet the awful, shapeless source of those sounds.

The stench got worse every day. It touched something deep inside Vernon, something dark and growing. Finally, he found the courage to flee the apartment and venture into the terrible, frightening world outside before his sanity finally gave way, before the terrible, groaning hunger within him caused him to look at that closed door and think of the bodies festering away behind it with something other than revulsion and a distant, mournful despair.

He stepped out into the corridor, closing the apartment door silently behind him, leaving behind forever the life he had lived there. The flickering corridor lights illuminated a scene of derelict decay. Slime dripped down cracked walls onto mildewed floors. Strange patterns of mould and moss crawled across walls and ceilings, finding nourishment from ultra-synthetic surfaces that should have provided none.

Just a few days, Vernon reminded himself. All this has happened in just a few days.

Most of the apartment doors that lined the corridor were closed. From behind some, he heard a few faint sounds of life: sobbing or weeping, or disjointed, mumbling words that may have been snatches of some half-remembered prayer. From behind one – 78/34, the Kirschmayers, he remembered, and Mr Kirschmayer was a deputy lieutenant in the block's Cit-Def unit – he heard a broken, maniacal cackle. From another, a few doors along – 78/42, Mr and Mrs Voogel, who had been friendly with him and his wife – he heard eager, hungry, scratching sounds.

One door at the end of the corridor stood open, with the welcome, reassuring sound of a voice on a tri-d coming from within. Vernon found himself running eagerly towards it. Tri-d at least meant some kind of normality, a reminder of what had until recently been a huge part of everyday life in Mega-City One, when the city's thousands of media outlets poured out a brain-numbing torrent of game shows, vidverts, chat shows, info-blips, newscasts and shock jock tirades into the over-saturated minds of the citizens. Someone talking on a tri-d meant that maybe someone was explaining to them the cause of the madness that had engulfed the city – and that maybe, just maybe, someone somewhere was doing something about bringing an end to it all.

"Good morning, citizens," hissed the eerie, sibilant voice on the tri-d. "Once again, a sinister black pall has settled over the entire city, blocking out all light and hope, while the temperature will be somewhere round about zero, meaning that you can leave the corpses of your friends and loved ones to fester for a while longer yet. If you are foolish or brave enough to venture outside, remember that the curfew is still in force and that you will be shot on sight... which would be a real pity, since we have provided so many other more interesting and painful ways for you to die."

Vernon was at the door, staring in at the figure suspended from the ceiling, hanging from the synthi-leather belt wrapped round its neck, the other end attached to the lighting fixture in the ceiling, and at the figures – a woman and two children – all dead from single gunshots, lying sprawled on the floor beneath its dangling feet. But it was the ghoulish, cackling apparition on the apartment's tri-d screen that monopolised his attention.

"Although, really, we should be grateful to you all," it continued to hiss in its monstrous voice. "Many of you have already given up hope and lost the will to live. Some have already begun to starve, and disease is spreading rapidly throughout all parts of the city. Faced with this, many of you have already chosen to take your own lives rather than await your fate at the hands of my brothers and their servants."

The creature broke off, laughing shrilly to reveal an animal-like mouth crammed with sharp-fanged incisors. With a start, Vernon realised that the thing on the tri-d screen was actually female.

"All this pleases us very much,' the monstrosity continued. 'Your help in achieving our great work is very much appreciated. Even now, our brothers work tirelessly to bring justice to you all, but they are few, and you are so many. Be patient, remain in your homes and they will get to you in time."

The creature's voice was rising, moving swiftly towards a shrieking crescendo: "It is a momentous task we have set ourselves. To purge this city, to cleanse all of you, its teeming millions. To grant you eternal absolution from the greatest crime of all... life itself!"

Vernon started to run, fleeing from that voice and from the terrible, awful things it was telling him. Even as he fled down a stairwell choked with corpses, climbing over the bodies of neighbours and strangers, he could still hear the final words of the inhuman, mocking creature on the tri-d pursuing him.

"With your help, we will turn this city into a monument to justice, a home fit only for the innocent. Where the only sound will be the blessed silence of the grave, and where the only sign of life will be the flies crawling amongst the vast mounds of your rot-bloated corpses. With your help, all this will soon come to pass... TOGETHER, SINNERS, WE WILL BUILD OUR GLORIOUS NECROPOLIS!"

He never could remember how long he had wandered the city for, or how he had managed to survive. He imagined he must have found food from somewhere, scavenged from the many derelict city blocks or shopping precincts, for the hunger pangs were not such a problem anymore. Deep down, he knew he had probably gone mad. But what did it matter, he reasoned to himself, when the whole city had also gone mad?

He glimpsed other wanderers like himself, other survivors and scavengers, but warily stayed clear of them. Several times, he saw larger groups of survivors, on one occasion several hundred strong, but he always hid until they had passed by. One of these groups spotted him and called out to him, urging him to come back and join them, but he kept on running. They were doomed, he knew. They had the invisible mark of death upon them – he had seen it clearly in the faces of the nearest of them – and he had no wish to join their fate.

On another occasion, a Judge patrol spotted him. Vernon didn't know why, but he knew that the Judges were part of what was going on in the city. He had taken off running as soon as he saw them. The Judges had chased after him, firing at him with their Lawgivers, but Vernon had managed to lose them somewhere in the darkness of the Hel Shapiro Underway. Bored with the chase, the Judges had given up and gone into the nearest building, looking for easier targets. Even from several kilometres away, Vernon had heard the gunfire from their weapons as they roamed at whim from apartment to apartment and level to level within the massive city block.

On that occasion, he had been fleeing from gunfire, but it would be the same kind of sound that ultimately led him to the moment of glorious rebirth, when he was to discover where his own new destiny lay.

He heard them from afar: rippling bursts of gunfire, tight and coordinated. There were always plenty of gunfire sounds in the city, but something about these seemed different in a way he could not explain. Carefully, going against every new instinct he had developed surviving on his own on the city's devastated streets, he crept towards the sound, drawn in by something invisible yet undeniable.

He found his destiny in Whitman Plaza. The surface of the square had been violently ripped up, transformed into a series of giant craters, which were now being used as mass graves. There were Judges everywhere, herding in groups of citizens in their hundreds, barking harsh orders at them, lining them up in neat rows at the lips of the craters and then sending their lifeless corpses tumbling down into the burial pits amidst crashing volleys of Lawgiver fire. Some of the people in the mass graves were still alive, and an occasional laughing Judge would fire into the pits with rippling bursts, making the corpses piled down there dance and jerk as the high-velocity Lawgiver bullets tore through them. Those they missed were left to die, suffocating beneath the weight of the new layers of corpses that soon fell down to join them.

Vernon picked a path across these burial pits, drawn inexorably towards something in the centre of the square. Judges were all around him, but none saw him. Death was everywhere around him too – in the dismal, tainted air he breathed, in the lifeless, bloodied mass of flesh he crept across – but something or someone had decided that he was to be spared from it all. Taking up a position at the edge of one of the craters, crouching down to stifle the dying moans of one of the bodies he was standing on, he looked upon the figures that had drawn him on to this place.

They were standing in the centre of the square, surrounded by their Judge servants. Hover vehicles known as H-wagons, restless and lethal, circled overhead, standing guard over the new masters of Mega-City One.

There were four of them, and Vernon knew instantly who – what – they were, as soon as he saw them.

Death. Fear. Fire. Mortis.

The four Dark Judges. Creatures from another dimension, the news-vid reporters had said, with a thrill of fear in their voices. Twisted, evil entities who had decided that all crime was committed by the living, and that, hence, the greatest crime of all was life itself. They had wiped out all life on their own world and had then discovered a means to cross the dimensions to find Mega-City One. Twice before, the city had come under attack from them, with thousands of citizens losing their lives, but each time the human Judges of the Justice Department had fought back and defeated them, seemingly destroying them for ever.

But, like creatures from an old horror-vid, the Dark Judges refused to die and would return again, each time seemingly more deadly than ever. Now they were back once more, and this time killing not thousands but millions. The entire city was theirs, and they would not rest until they had killed every living thing in it.

Judges, seemingly under some kind of twisted mind control, were moving amongst the columns of captured citizens, randomly pulling people aside and herding them forward to be personally judged by the four creatures. Terrified citizens were herded in groups of a hundred or more into a smouldering crater, where Judge Fire immolated them en masse with blasts of lethal, supernatural fire from his burning trident.

His three brothers stood waiting as their Judge servants brought their unwilling subjects forward to them. The creatures had been busy, Vernon could see. Pairs of Judges carried off the lifeless remains of those who had been selected to be personally judged by the Dark Judges, and the pits set aside for each of the Dark Judge's victims were all nearly full.

Pleading and sobbing, each citizen was brought forward in turn to meet his fate at the hands of one of the Dark Judges. The Judges attending Mortis wore their helmet respirators down, Vernon noticed, to fend off the decayed stench from the rot-corrupted flesh of his victims, while even from this distance he could clearly see the frozen looks of sheer terror on the unnaturally twisted features of the victims of Judge Fear.

But it was Judge Death above all who captured Vernon's attention.

He stood like some regal overlord, his Judge servants making his victims kneel before him as they were brought forward to be judged.

'Rejoice, sinners! Soon you will be free from the crime of life, and the burden of your terrible guilt will be gone!' he hissed as each was made to kneel before him, before reaching down almost as if to bestow a blessing upon them. His claw-like hands melted seamlessly through flesh and bone, passing mysteriously through organs and innards until they unerringly found the heart, before those same long, inhuman fingers closed around the vital organ and squeezed all life from it.

The victims fell dead at his feet, the same look of horror and fear stamped into all their faces. Instantly, each corpse was picked up and tossed into the nearby pit, before the next victim was dragged forward to meet the same fate.

Vernon was awestruck by what he saw. Here was something far more than a supernatural bogeyman, the extra-dimensional fiend of the old news-vid reports. Here was a creature beyond life and death, an unholy, blasphemous god; terrible in his glory, undying, immortal, a taker of lives and guardian of the secrets of what lay beyond death. Had Vernon been one of those the Judges were bringing before Death, he would have fallen to his knees willingly and without being forced, in voluntary submission to this most glorious and terrible of creatures.

Death paused in his work, looking up as though suddenly sensing something amiss. From behind the iron grille of his helmet, undead eyes gazed out in search of what it may be. He gave a low hiss of irritable displeasure as his gaze picked over the thousands of corpses in the craters surrounding him. He did not like to be disturbed in his work, not when there were still so many sinners waiting to be judged.

Vernon cringed in terror, pressing himself into the tangle of cold, lifeless flesh beneath him as he felt Death's eyes searching him out, inexorably finding the spark of treacherous life amidst the otherwise pleasing landscape of death. The icy grip of fear took hold of Vernon's body as Death's gaze fell upon him and, horribly, he felt the creature's long, cold fingers picking through his mind, almost as if he were physically kneeling before him to receive the Dark Judge's lethal blessing.

His body convulsed and the beating of his heart slowed... and stopped. For a moment, he knew what it was to stand on the very edge of the abyss of death, and then the fingers withdrew, and the gaze of Death was lifted from him. Whatever Death had found in the mind of one helpless and terrified human had pleased him.

Death withdrew his deadly tendrils from Vernon's soul with a long, low hiss of satisfaction and turned his attention back to the business at hand. "The crime is life... the sentence is death," he ritually intoned and, seconds later, another corpse joined the thousands of others in the burial pits.

Vernon crept away, still only dimly aware of the significance of what had just happened. Death had found him, had judged him – and had found him worthy of something other than extinction.

There was something more though, something the Dark Judge had left within him. If he closed his eyes and concentrated, Vernon imagined he could just see it, a slick, hard, black pearl planted amongst the living tissue of his brain.

He had been marked by the Dark Judge. Marked not for death, but for life. For a purpose that was yet unknown to him, but which he already knew he would faithfully and devoutly carry out when the time came, for he knew that if he did Death's bidding, then he would be suitably rewarded.

"I don't want to die," he intoned to himself as he crept away again. "I don't want to die. Not now, not ever. I don't want to die."

MEGA-CITY ONE, 2122

ONE

"Anything happen while I've been away?" Burchill asked, helping himself to a few generous gulps from Meyer's cup of now lukewarm synthi-caf.

Meyer sighed in unhappy resignation. Being a Judge-Warden wasn't exactly the most exciting duty in the Justice Department, and keeping watch over the things they kept down here in the Tomb wasn't exactly the choicest duty posting in the Division, but it was having to work with jerks like Burchill that was the worst thing about this job. Worse even than the mind-numbing boredom and the extra creep-out factor of the nature of the... things encased within the crystalline cube-prisons only a few steps from where Meyer sat at the duty-console.

"Nothing much," she told the smug Psi-Judge. "You're welcome to watch the vid-logs, if you want. We've got the whole of the last eighteen months since you were last here still on file. Not much to see, I'll grant you, but I think maybe Sparky might have done something like blink or change the flicker pattern of his flames a month or two ago."

Burchill snorted into the cup of synthi-caf. "Sparky! It was me that christened him that, you know that? Sparky, Spooky, Creepy and Bony, that's what I called 'em one night, a year or two ago. Glad to see it's caught on while I've been away."

Meyer bristled in irritation again. Psi-Judges were notoriously highly strung, and other Judges were expected to cut them a little extra slack, but Burchill was just an annoying creep. Duty regs said that there must always be a Psi-Judge on duty in the Tomb, to protect against any dangerous psychic activity from the things imprisoned down here, but the Psi-Judges selected for the job were rotated every three months since there were concerns about the effects on a Psi's mind of long-term exposure to the creepy vibes generated by the four detainees held in the Tomb. It had been a year and a half since Burchill had been on Tomb duty – or "spook-sitting", as he called it – and Mayer didn't think that was nearly long enough.

"Yeah, ain't you just the Department comedian?" she commented, the sarcasm bare in her voice. "And, hey, by the way, feel free to finish the rest of my synthi-caf, why don't you?"

"Thanks. Don't mind if I do," laughed Burchill, draining the last of the contents of the plasti-cup.

"No! Don't you d–" began Meyer, way too late, as the Psi-Judge casually flipped the empty cup over his shoulder, throwing it towards the thick red warning line painted on the floor behind him, which divided the underground room into two distinct halves.

On one side of the line were the duty-consoles for the two Judges – one experienced Judge-Warden and one Psi-Judge – which Tomb regs required to be at all times on duty here, as well as the elevator entrance back up to the surface. On the other side of the no-go line were the four entities imprisoned within the Tomb.

Even before the plasti-cup had crossed the line, hidden sensor devices buried within the walls of the chamber had detected the movement and were tracking the object's progress. As soon as it entered the no-go area marked by the line, multiple sentry guns placed at various points around the chamber opened fire, using precise telemetry data fed to them by the room's remote sensors.

The cup was instantly vaporised, struck by several laser beams simultaneously. All that remained of it was a fine residue of ash, which drifted slowly down to settle on the ground on the forbidden side of the red line.

Meyer cursed, and punched a button to open up her duty log. "Thanks a lot. Now I'm going to have to make a report on that."

Burchill laughed, and settled down into his seat in his duty-post across from her. "Hey, look at it this way: at least I've given you something to do now, which makes a change down here."

From behind the substance of the crystalline barrier, from behind the walls that had imprisoned him and his brethren for too long, Death watched his captors. The failure of their great work, the collapse of their grand vision of the Necropolis, had been a galling experience. And defeat at the hands of their old enemies, Dredd and Anderson, had been even more so. The destruction of their physical bodies, the entrapment of their ethereal spirits within these crystal prisons, where they were almost completely cut off from each other and unable to plan the continuation of their holy work, all this was bad enough, but worst of all was seeing sinners so close by – sinners guilty of the worst crime of all, the crime of life – and being unable to bring due punishment upon them.

Although Death could not actively commune with his brothers, he knew that they felt as he did. Within his prison, Fire blazed with angry, vengeful rage. Next to him, Fear writhed in agitation, his spirit twisting in on itself. On his other side, Mortis's restless spirit-shape formed and reformed itself, prowling round the borders of its prison, endlessly testing the strength of the walls and psychic wards that had been put in place to contain him.

Of them all, only Death was at relative peace. While the others raged and turned their anger on themselves and the seemingly unbreakable walls of their prisons, he watched. And waited.

And now, perhaps, his patience was being rewarded.

Death recognised their new gaoler, the Psi-Judge. He had been here before, and Death, probing subtly and tentatively at the edges of the man's mind, had sensed the interesting possibilities within. There was weakness within this one, Death understood, weakness that could be exploited to his advantage. The man had gone away again, as they always did, but Death had waited patiently for his return, silently laying his plans.

In the city beyond were the special ones, the ones who knew the Dark Judges for what they truly were – liberators, come to free all from the sinful burden of life – and who were eager to help Death and his brethren in their glorious task. Death had encountered several such special ones, and had put his mark upon them, knowing that one day he might have need of them. That day was soon, he knew now, and his call had already gone out to them.

Secret acolytes in the city beyond this place, and now a weakness here amongst their guardians. Yes, now he had everything he needed.

Patience, brothers, he whispered silently to the occupants of the other three cells. Soon we will be able to begin our great work anew. Soon, Necropolis will be ours once more.

Eyes, red and hungry, blazed at her from out of the darkness. She tried to move, to draw her Lawgiver, but the darkness around her was a living, sentient thing. It wrapped itself around her, snagging her limbs, dragging her down.

She felt herself falling, down into the dark. From above her came the angry, cheated snarl of whatever had been pursuing her.

She hit the ground with a clattering impact. She felt dust on her face, smelt withered, ancient decay and felt something dry and brittle beneath her fingers. Opening her eyes, she saw she was lying on a carpet of bones. Raising her head, she saw the litter of bones – human remains, she noticed, seeing identifiable skulls and bone shapes amongst the graveyard detritus – stretching out as far as she could see. The vague tombstone shape of vast buildings, cracked and ruined, loomed up out of the surrounding gloom. There was something horribly familiar about the whole scene.

Deadworld, she wondered to herself, remembering her past experiences in the nightmare world that had given birth to the Dark Judges?

Or Necropolis maybe, she asked herself, noticing with growing disquiet how much the surrounding buildings resembled the familiar outlines of Mega-City One?

No, none of these things, something whispered inside her. Not something from the past. Something from the future, something dreadful that had yet to happen.

Pulling herself to her feet, she heard a chorus of menacing growls from the nearest of the buildings. Backing off, she heard more of the same sounds from the buildings behind her. And from those to her left, and then her right.

Surrounded on all sides, she checked the ammo counter on her Lawgiver and waited for whatever was out there to come to her.

She didn't have to wait long. From out of the buildings they came, a black wave of shadow figures, snarling and hissing at her in hungry anticipation. She opened fire with her Lawgiver, firing off quick controlled bursts as per Academy of Law standard training. The bullets tore into the ranks of the shadow things, giving rise to an outraged chorus of howls of pain and anger. A dozen or more of the things tumbled to the bone-littered ground, to be fallen upon mercilessly and ripped apart by the others swarming close behind.

Despite the carnage, the others came right on at her, swift and relentless. As they closed in on the Judge, heedless of the Lawgiver bullets tearing through unnatural flesh, they merged into one great shadow-shape, a black and red collage of maddened, hunger-filled eyes and crimson-dripping fangs.

They bore down on her, dragging her to the ground, and the last conscious thing she remembered before the red veil descended was the sensation of talon-like fingers raking into her and sharp, needle-like teeth worrying at her flesh.

After that, there was only the darkness, and the overpowering smell of freshly spilled blood.

My blood, she thought, awakening with a shuddering start. The thin synthi-satin sheets of the bed were soaked with perspiration; the short vest she wore – definitely not Department-approved, which was probably why she wore it – clung to her sweat-soaked skin.

Coming out of the nightmare, it took her a moment to remember where she was: the small and predictably Spartan temporary quarters assigned to her within the dorm-wing of Psi-Division Headquarters. Closing her eyes, she received a few brief but gruesome mental after-images of the nightmare she had just experienced.

"Grud on a greenie, that was a doozie," she murmured to herself as she leaned forward to flick-activate the intercom control on the panel set into the wall beside the bed. Instead, she hit the wrong switch, and made the room's small tri-d screen activate into sudden and noisy life.

"...it's Fluffy, darling... he's dead!" bellowed the voice on the tri-d, making Anderson look up with an involuntary start. She saw a husband-and-wife pair of citizens, both of them straight out of the usual dumb vidvert central casting, by the looks of things, crying and cradling the white-furred corpse of something she assumed was supposed to be a dead rabbit. At that moment, the vid-generated background of an ordinary city block apartment wiped away, and a tall, rather intense-looking man in a spotless white lab coat stepped into shot, smiling in a supposedly disarming but actually rather scary manner at the camera.

"Dr Dick Icarus, chief scientist from EverPet! What are you doing here?" exclaimed the wife character in a way that probably made the vidvert director wish he'd gone for digitally generated actors after all.

"I'm here... for Fluffy!" declared the freaky mad scientist type, brandishing a syringe filled with an alarming-looking, glowing green liquid, and quickly injecting the noxious stuff into the dead pet. Almost instantaneously – because vidvert airtime didn't come cheap, naturally – the animal sprang back to life and went hopping off out of shot.

"He's alive! But HOW???" shrieked the wife-actor in amazement, no doubt seeing a dazzling career ahead of her in walk-on roles in middle-of-the-night graveyard slot soap-vids.

"It's all thanks to this," boasted the wacko in the lab coat, holding the syringe and its contents up to camera. "EverPet's revolutionary new Pet Regen Formula. That's right! Now there's no need for death to part you from your most beloved animal companions. For only a small monthly fee, and regular injections of Pet Regen, EverPet can bring your furry little family members back to life. So dial 555-REGEN and resurrect your pet tod–"

"Bringing dead pets back to life... only in the Big Meg," Anderson muttered, hurriedly switching off the tri-d before what was shaping up to be a predictably dumb and irritatingly catchy musical jingle started playing. Second time lucky, she activated the intercom.

"Psi-Control – Anderson. Just picked up something. Could be a pre-cog flash, maybe a big one."

The answering voice on the radio-link was politely sceptical. "You sure about that, Anderson? We've got more than thirty other Psi-Judges asleep in the dorms, not to mention the full-time pre-cogs down in the Temple, and none of them are interrupting my duty shift to report on picking up anything. You sure it wasn't just some REM sleep phantom bogey stuff?"

Anderson fought to keep her temper under control. "You know my rep, Control. You're not talking to some rookie Psi straight out of the Academy. I know the difference between a nightmare and a genuine pre-cog flash."

"Okay," sighed the voice of Control. "You want me to log this as a possible pick-up. We both know the routine. Tell me what you thought you picked up, starting with surface impressions first."

Anderson closed her eyes, bringing her psi-powers to focus on the images still burning in her brain. A moment's concentration, a careful sectioning off of the various areas of her mind to prevent random and subconscious psi-spill from polluting the memory of the images she had picked up, and then she was ready to replay the nightmare she had just experienced.

"I see blood, Control. Lots of blood."

"I mean, just what the drokk is it with these so-called 'Church of Death' freakoids, anyway? The Big Meg is what I like to call a broad church, with room for all kindsa wackos, freaks, gomers, spazheads and nutjobs, sure, but there's still gotta be some limits, ain't there? Now, all you regular listeners out there know that good ol' Drivetime Sam ain't no bigot – except when it comes to muties, Alientown freaks, Juggernaut fans, stuck-up Brit-citters, assorted Euro-cit trash, those big-mouthed domeheads from Texas City, Luna-cit weirdos and especially those dirty Sov-Blockers – but usually I say 'live and let live'. Except in the case of these Death cult creeps.

"You know the freaks I'm talking about, right? Loons that paint their faces like skulls, dress up like it's Halloween and worship – yeah, you heard me right, I said WORSHIP – Judge Death and his three fellow extra-dimensional freakshow buddies? That sound SANE? That sound LEGAL? That sound like the kind of thing we should encourage our innocent young people to get into, when they could be out there getting into juve gang rumbles, taking illegal narco-tabs, setting fire to winos or doing any of the other traditional things the juves of today get up to?

"'Of course not, Sam,' I hear you say, 'that's why the Judges are rounding these freaks up as soon as they appear.' Which is fine by ol' Drivetime Sam, but I say we should all be doing our part too. You know

any of these wackos, you think some of your neighbours might be per-
verted sickos who have a shrine to the Dark Judges hidden in their
apartment, then there's only one thing to do. Let the Judges know about
it. Dial 1-800-KOOKCUBE, and tell 'em Drivetime Sam told ya to do it.

"Okay, so that's the Rant of the Hour slot and our statutory public
information obligations taken care of for the time being, so now it's
back to our usual mix of travel-time news, made-up stuff about the private lives of vid-celebs and phone-in chat with you, the dumb,
feeble-minded and pathetically attention-seeking ordinary cits of Mega-
City One. First on the line is Chuck Cheedlewidge, who we understand
is some dweeb who wants to tell us that the weird growth on his neck
has started channelling the spirit of the late Chief Judge Goodman.
Ooowww boy, now where did I put that kook cube num–"

Galen DeMarco switched off the radio with a curse that would surely
have earned her a verbal reprimand from any of her old Sector House
shift commanders. Like millions of other citizens, she couldn't stand
arrogant, opinionated shock jock creeps like Drivetime Sam. Then
again, like millions of other citizens, she also couldn't help tuning in to
hear what he was going to say next.

"So much for all those dull citizenship classes they made me take,"
she said to herself. "If I really wanted to blend in with the rest of the
population, all I had to do was listen to the meatheads on talk radio."

She looked out of the series of wide bay windows that lined one
entire wall of her apartment, relishing the spectacular view it gave
her across the central core sectors of MegEast. In the distance,
behind the towering bulks of Sax Rohmer Block and the DaneTech
Building, one could just catch a glimpse of the Statue of Judgement
standing guard near Black Atlantic Customs and Immigration, while
off to the east the afternoon sun reflected brightly off the gilt-
metalled giant eagle facade of the Grand Hall of Justice. Clustered for
tens of kilometres around it were a host of other Justice Department
ancillary facilities, including the Academy of Law, Psi-Division HQ
and the Tech 21 labs, as well as City Hall, the glittering stratoscraper
headquarters of nearly every giant mega-corp company worthy of the
name, and several of the most elite and exclusive luxy-blocks and
conapt buildings in the entire city. When foreigners thought of Mega-
City One, this was the sector they thought of: the soaring, gigantic-
beyond-belief buildings, the colourful, teeming millions of citizens
and the seemingly never-ending number of fads and crazes which
these citizens invented to occupy their time, and the dominating and
ever vigilant presence of the Justice Department. Right outside her
window was a snapshot of all the allure, glamour and splendour of

the biggest, craziest and most powerful Mega-City on the face of twenty-second century Earth.

The reality, DeMarco knew, was nowhere near so exciting and exotic. Over on the West Wall, on the city's border with the Cursed Earth, the Department fought what was practically a non-stop war against the hordes of muties who tried every night to get into the city. There were areas of the city, most notably parts of City Bottom or some slum sectors such as the notorious Pit, where the Judges had all but ceded control to perp gangs that were more like small standing armies than criminal groups – not that anyone in the Department would ever officially acknowledge this. Eighty-seven per cent of the population was unemployed, and too many of them chose some form of lawbreaking as an alternative pastime. The cits invented new crimes faster than the Judges could pass laws to deal with them. The city's iso-cubes were full to bursting, the kook cubes even more so.

Statistics said that sixty per cent of citizens were likely to suffer some form of serious mental breakdown some time in their lives, mostly due to the pressure of twenty-second century life as it was lived in Mega-City One. They even had a term for it – Future Shock Syndrome – and the kook cubes were full of the plentiful evidence of its virulence and widespread adoption.

Statistics said that fifty-three per cent of citizens were afraid of being murdered by their neighbours. Maybe with good reason, though, since another survey also suggested that seventy-seven per cent of citizens – including, simple arithmetic suggested, many of the respondents from the other survey – actually had given serious thought at least once to the idea of murdering whoever was living next door to them.

It was the Big Meg, the craziest and most violent city on Earth, home to four hundred million citizens, every one of them a potentially violent criminal, and Grud help her, she loved every over-populated, crimeridden, polluted and blood-stained square metre of it.

Looking down from the penthouse level of the two hundred storey apartment block, she could see the stacked snarl of megways, skeds, overzooms, underzooms, pedways and shoppo-plazas that passed for the Mega-City One street system. It was times like this that she missed those streets the most, missed being a Street Judge and being out there on patrol, dealing with all the madness and mayhem the city had to throw at you.

Boredom was the biggest problem for her now. More than twenty years with the Department, and every minute of that time she had always been busy doing something. She had money, of course – the fortune she inherited from her father more than ensured that, unlike the rest of the ordinary cits, she'd never have to worry about where her next cred was coming from – but like a lot of other cits she had had to deal with the boredom.

Setting herself up as a Private Investigator after she had left the Justice Department hadn't been her idea, but she had to admit that it was a gruddamned good one. Her connections within the Department gave her more leeway than that afforded to others in her profession, and, while it would never beat the buzz of having to quell a full-scale block war after pulling an energy sapping, sixteen-hour double shift of street patrol, it was better than sitting in your luxury apartment all day painting your nails and watching the tri-d, which is what she figured most of her neighbours seemed to do.

Since she didn't have to work for the money, she tried to pick and choose her cases, sifting through the run-of-the-mill surveillance, insurance fraud and employee-vetting jobs that came walking in through her office door. She passed a lot of these kind of jobs on to some of her competitors, only keeping on the cases that interested her. The ones that involved the stuff that slipped through the cracks of the Justice Department's attention, the ones that made her feel she was still doing some good for someone. She had an office downtown, close to City Hall, but a lot of the time she preferred to work out of her apartment.

That was what she was supposed to be doing now, she reminded herself guiltily as she called up a number on her phone. It rang, and was immediately answered by an auto-message program. DeMarco gave a silent prayer of thanks. As a Judge, the security of the badge and uniform had always allowed her to erect a professional barrier between her and the cits she dealt with. As a cit herself, she was still learning about how to deal with people in emotional distress.

"Hello? Mrs Caskey? It's Galen DeMarco. As I promised a few days ago, I'm calling to give your progress report on what I've found so far. I've talked to some of Joanna's friends at her college, and, according to them, she had got involved in some college fringe society that calls itself the 'Friends of Thanos'. I did a little digging on these creeps, and found that…"

She checked herself here, trying to work out an easy, sympathetic way to tell a mother that her daughter had probably run off to join a cult of death-worshipping loons.

Damn it, she thought to herself. Why did the Academy learning program have more than fifty compulsory courses on combat techniques and only one brief one on Cit Relations?

"Well, uhhh… I have reason to believe that they're maybe connected in some way to a group you might have heard about on the vid-news recently, a group called the Church of Death. I'm not sure, but it's possible she might be with them... It's possible some boy she met might have persuaded her to join. I'm looking into it now, and I've already got a few leads I want to follow up about this cult, maybe even be able to track them down. Don't worry, Mrs Caskey, whatever you've heard on the tri-d about these people, it's probably just the usual exaggerated vid-news stuff. I'll contact you in a few days, by which time I'm fairly sure I'll have some good news about your daughter."

She hung up, thinking that maybe the Academy of Law training wasn't so bad after all, since at least it taught you how to lie with conviction to the cits. She had some leads on this Death cult all right, but her gut feeling was that these Church of Death creeps were a cut above your usual Mega-City One lunatic fringe/apocalypse cult bunch of wackos.

She had a lot to do now, she knew, but she couldn't help looking out of the window at the city again and wonder, for what was maybe just the twentieth time that day, where Dredd was, and what he was doing right now.

TWO

Judge Dredd's fist smashed into the perp's face, spreading most of his nose across his face and making a trip to the iso-block med-unit for some dental reconstruction surgery a likely event in this creep's immediate future.

One of the perp's buddies used the moment to his advantage, slipping around Dredd and trying to blindside him. The Judge turned and pivoted as the perp came at him with a pig-sticker blade. Dredd swung his daystick twice, swiftly. One sharp crack of reinforced plasteel on bone broke the wrist of the creep's weapon-hand and sent the knife skittering across the rough rockcrete surface of the alleyway. The second caught him neatly on the top of the skull and booked him a place in an iso-block med-unit alongside Creep Number One.

Creeps Number Three, Four, Five and Six looked slightly disconcerted about this. They hung back for a moment, weighing up the odds. Creep Number Four, with slightly fewer disfiguring facial tattoos than the rest of the gang, was maybe the brains of this particular outfit, and the others seemed happy for him to do all their collective, half-witted thinking for them.

"Don't matter what the name on that badge says!" he shouted, weighing up the odds, doing all the necessary mental arithmetic and still coming up with very definitely the wrong answer. "There's one of him and four of us, and he can't take us all. Get him!"

They rushed at him together. Dredd's Lawgiver was in its boot holster, within easy reach, but he made no move to draw it. None of these punks were packing guns, and so far there didn't seem to be any just cause for the use of deadly force against them.

Besides, he thought to himself, it had been a slow day so far, and he could probably do with a workout.

Creep Number Five hit the ground first, taking a plasteel-reinforced Judge's boot to the groin and a daystick blow to the temple. Creep

Number Three followed swiftly, courtesy of a knock-out punch to the jaw. Creep Number Four drew back, looking like he was having second thoughts about the whole thing. Dredd gave him something else to think about instead: a daystick jab to the solar plexus which sent him reeling to the ground, winded, the follow-up kick from a boot swiftly reintroducing the perp to the violently regurgitated remains of his synthi-fries and Grot Pot lunch of only a few hours ago.

If Creep Number Four was the brains of the outfit, then Creep Number Six must have fancied himself as the brawn, throwing himself at Dredd with a savage roar. Dredd bent slightly, caught him in the ribs with the hard edge of his eagle-shaped shoulder pad and used the creep's own momentum against him, judo-throwing him over his shoulder and sending the perp face-first into the surface of the wall behind him. The pattern of the rough brickwork, now stamped deep into the skin of the unconscious thug's face, made an interesting new addition to the mosaic of ugly tattoo markings already there.

With the six perps lying unconscious or groaning on the ground around him, Dredd finally relented and lifted his foot from the back of the original perp – Creep Number Zero, he supposed he should call him – who had been lying there helpless, hands cuffed behind his back and pinned to the ground by Dredd's foot, during the entire fight.

"Control – Dredd. Seven for catch wagon pick-up, Mohammed Alley, just off Spinks and Foreman."

"Wilco, Dredd," came the crackling reply over his helmet radio. "What are the charges?"

Dredd looked at the seven subdued figures around him. "Six of them on Attempted Judge Assault – five years." Dredd paused, looking at the six groaning, bleeding perps lying around him. "Tell the catch wagon crew there'll be no problem figuring out which ones they are. The other one..."

Dredd looked round at the colour-splashed and still-wet graffiti wall decor behind him.

"Scrawling – one year's cubetime."

Scrawling was a common enough Mega-City crime, Dredd knew, and Sector House Chiefs were required to order regular crackdowns on it in some of the worst-hit areas. Dredd had made thousands of arrests for scrawling in his years on the streets, and this one had at first seemed no different from the rest when he had come across an illegal scrawler – Creep Zero – still at work on his latest graffiti masterpiece at the mouth of the alley.

What had been unusual, though, was when Creeps One to Six turned up to dispute Dredd's arrest of their buddy. Scrawl wars were common amongst the city's street gangs, with gangs leaving provocative scrawl-tags on their rival's turf and then protecting their own gang territory – often with lethal force – from reprisal scrawl attacks in return. Gang members protecting their gang's scrawl artists wasn't that uncommon, but what was very much out of the ordinary was a gang willing to do the same thing if it meant attacking a Judge.

Especially if that Judge happened to be Judge Joe Dredd.

Dredd looked again at the scrawl design the scrawler had still been working on when he arrested him. He saw a cartoon depiction of a familiar-looking ghastly figure, a figure which Dredd knew all too well, but which the scrawler would only have seen in brief and heavily Justice Department-censored news-vid images. The figure, a grinning ghoul wearing a crudely imagined parody of a Judge's uniform, was surrounded by a chemically treated fluorescent paint halo of glowing black energy. Written beside it, in large and still unfinished letters, was a single stark message: "DEATH LIVES!"

Despite the cartoon crudeness of the thing, despite the mundane setting of a typically grubby and garbage-strewn Mega-City alleyway, there was something strangely unsettling about the image, almost as if the scrawler had subconsciously tapped into some greater hidden reservoir of fear and dread.

Sensing he was onto something, Dredd bent over the nearest prone body, ignoring the injured perp's groans of pain as he quickly searched him. Like all the other gang members, the perp's clothes were uniformly black, but, beneath the fresh dye marks, Dredd could still see the evidence of the ganger's original and quite different gang colours. Likewise, while his arms bore traditional juve gang tattoos – Dredd recognised them as belonging to the Sid Sheldon Block Big Spenders Crew – the ones on his face were most recent, and different from the gang tattoos. Flaming skulls, vampire bats, clawed hands coming out of graves and similar cartoon-gothic imagery seemed to be the predominant style here.

Standing back up, he reactivated his helmet radio link.

"Control – Dredd. Extra to that last call: possible evidence tying my perps into these Church of Death creeps."

"That's a check. We've been seeing more and more of this amongst the sector juve gangs. Could just be the latest passing street gang fad."

"Or it could be something else, Control," growled Dredd. "Fads don't make gangers attack Judges the way these punks tried to attack me. Slap a mandatory extra five years onto all their sentences for membership of an illegal organisation, and have them all run through the interrogation cubes to find out what they know. It's time we came down hard on these Death cult freaks."

"Wilco, Dredd," responded the voice of Control, before suddenly assuming a more urgent tone. "Just got something coming in. Armed assault at the Bathory Street med-supply warehouse. Judge Giant on the scene and requesting assist from any nearby units!"

Dredd looked at the seven subdued perps around him. Bathory Street was only five blocks from here, just off Ingrid Pitt Plaza, and it would take him less than a minute to secure his perps for catch-wagon pick-up. Cuffed together, and with most of them already beaten unconscious, he didn't figure it likely they would be going anywhere before the catch wagon crew arrived.

"Wilco, Control. On my way."

Judge Giant didn't believe in vampires.

Which was not to say he'd not witnessed some freaky stuff in his time as a Judge, of course. Even as a cadet, during the darkest days of Necropolis he'd faced off against no less a creep than Judge Mortis. And then there had been the whole Judgement Day thing, with the dead – yeah, the freakin' dead – rising from the grave and forming into one big zombie army to try and destroy everything and everyone. Since then, he had seen or heard about all kinds of weird stuff – tribes of werewolves in the Undercity, alien monsters with acid for blood attacking the Grand Hall of Justice – but he still didn't believe in vampires.

Which was perhaps a pity, since "vampires" seemed to be exactly what he was faced with right now.

He'd already pumped six Lawgiver rounds into one of the freakers, but now here it was again, popping up from behind the cover of those crates of med-supplies to take another shot at him. It didn't look much like what Giant thought of when he thought about vampires – no fancy burial suit, no black cape lined with red synthi-satin, and so far it hadn't turned into a bat or a plague of rats, or anything really freaky like that – but the fangs, the pale, dead-white skin pallor, the superhuman strength and the blood-crazed hunger all seemed to be present and correct.

And guns? Vampires weren't supposed to fire guns at you, thought Giant, ducking back round the corner as the hail of bullets from the thing's spit pistol popped holes into the surface of the doorway beside him.

A security guard's corpse, throat brutally ripped out, lay in the corridor behind him. The perps' means of entry into the building had been anything but subtle. The building was closed to the general public and its doors and windows were impressively secure, considering the

amount of proscribed drugs kept in the place for use by the city med-
units, they would have to be, but the perps – Giant knew there were an
even half-dozen of them – had simply ripped through the front door to
get in.

Yeah, with their bare hands, Giant reminded himself, remembering
seeing what had looked unpleasantly like claw marks gouged into the
metal of the door.

After that, they had gone on the rampage through the building, brutally killing everyone they found in the place before breaking into the
large central room they were in now, where the repository's main med-
supplies were kept.

Arriving minutes after the break-in had been reported, and moving
through the building in the perps' murderous wake, Giant had automatically assumed that they must be stimmed-up hypeheads, breaking
into the place in a desperate need to feed their narco-addiction. Professional perps would have been long gone so many minutes after the
alarms were first tripped. These creeps might be vicious – Giant had
counted seven corpses on his way in here – but they were also amateurs, and now he had them trapped in the main storeroom.

Like juves in a synthi-candy store, he had thought to himself. Probably too busy getting stimmed-up to even remember that the Judges were
coming to throw their punk-ass butts into a Detox Cube if they didn't
get out of here fast.

He'd pretty much abandoned the hypehead theory, though, when he
came across two of the things feeding on the dead security guard. The
creeps were hunched over the corpse, lapping eagerly at the blood pouring out of its ruined throat, too busy in their meal to register the Judge's
approach at first.

They'd looked up at him in fury at having their meal interrupted as
he aimed his Lawgiver at them and called out a warning. They'd hissed
at him in raw anger, baring their teeth and showing him their fangs –
and then reached for their own weapons.

He'd shot both of them, quickly and expertly, putting them down with
a piece of clinical precision marksmanship worthy even of Dredd himself. Then they had got back up, run into the cover of the main storage
area and started firing back at him.

Giant took stock of the situation, trying to evaluate what he'd seen
with what he still thought was impossible. A glance down at the dead
security guard – throat savagely laid open, eyes wide in disbelief at the
circumstances of his death, killed by vampires right here in the biggest
city of the twenty-second century – told him that the impossible was
what he was dealing with right now.

Well, if it looks like a vampire, acts like a vampire and tries to rip your throat out just like you'd expect a vampire to, then... thought Giant, deciding it was time he took the fight back to these things.

He darted out from the corner where he had been sheltering, heading for deeper cover inside the storage room. The move instantly provoked a hail of bullets from the two perps, but luckily any kind of marksmanship ability with automatic weapons didn't seem to be such a high agenda item with the undead.

The warehouse space was divided into a maze of wide aisles separated by pallets of med-stuff, and row upon row of storage shelving which stretched all the way up to the building's high ceiling. Giant ducked into the first aisle he came to, which seemed to be solely devoted to the storage of artificial cybernetic limbs. There were thousands of the things there, bionic arms and legs stacked floor to ceiling, everything from the cheap and basic models that any cit could get on the City Mega-Care program to the high-performance, top-of-the-range bionic-enhancement deluxe jobs favoured by the top professional athletes and sports celebs. Giant wondered for a second if someone knew something he didn't, and was stocking up in advance of some forthcoming rerun of the Apocalypse War, before returning his attention to the problem at hand.

He heard fast, eager footsteps behind him, and turned to see one of the perps following him in, charging down the aisle towards him. No sign of a weapon, but from the way it bared its fangs at him and flexed its talon-fingers in keen anticipation, he figured it had other ideas about how it was going to kill him. He fired instinctively, pumping three Lawgiver rounds into its chest. Three heart shots, each one a perfect ten score. The vampire staggered a little, and the change in pitch of its snarling seemed to suggest that this had hurt it some, but it was still on its feet and coming at him.

Department regs didn't allow Judges to carry religious ornamentation, so the idea of waving a crucifix at it was a complete non-starter, and only Psi-Division had access to the exotic stuff like silver-bladed boot knives and holy bullet Lawgiver rounds – so just how the hell was he supposed to kill the drokking thing?

Giant remembered Judgement Day, and Dredd's sanguine advice when they had been the first to encounter the zombie menace while on a Hotdog Run out in the Cursed Earth: "Pick your targets and shoot for their heads."

It had worked for zombies – and so had Hi-Ex and Incendiary too, though the latter only worked if you had the luxury of enough time to wait for the things to burn to death – so just how much difference was there between vampires and zombies?

Giant got his answer soon enough, firing off another burst of shots as the thing leapt at him. Its head exploded in a bloody pulp, and he hurriedly stepped aside to avoid its flailing corpse as it flew past him to land on the floor behind him, where it continued to twitch spasmodically.

Giant was just beginning to congratulate himself on his new-achieved status of vampire-slayer, when the next one stepped out at the opposite end of the aisle from the other one. And this sucker was a lot closer and a lot angrier-looking.

"Hold it right there, freak! You're under arrest!" Giant barked, aiming his Lawgiver right at it, wondering as he did so if the undead were entitled to the same Justice Department regulation warning as living perps.

It leapt at him, faster and more agile than the first creature. Giant, following years of drilled-in Academy of Law training, put three textbook shots into its chest before amending his aim in light of what he'd just learned, and snapped off another three at its head.

It twisted out of the way, tucking its head down protectively, although one of the shots drilled through its cheek and blew away its lower jaw. This only seemed to make it even madder, Giant noticed.

The monstrosity crashed into him, slashing at him with its claw-like nails, tearing rents in the bullet-resistant material of his uniform. Giant fell, taking the vampire with him. He dropped his gun, unable to bring it to bear on the squirming thing clinging tightly to him, and used both hands to try and tear the thing off him.

Its strength was incredible, even more so when Giant realised that his attacker was a young girl, probably no more than about twenty years old. Her shrieks of rage were shrill and hellish and she seemed possessed by a frenzied, almost superhuman strength and tenacity. Her head darted down towards his exposed throat, elongated fangs eager to bury themselves in the soft flesh there. Giant desperately blocked the attack with his arm, and she sank her teeth into the tough material of his Kevlar-lined Judge gauntlets, chewing into it to get at the meat beneath. If she could bite through the stuff his gloves were made of, Giant didn't even want to think of what kind of quick work she would make of his jugular vein, and his efforts to get away from the thing became all the more frantic.

His heart sank as he heard more footsteps running along the corridor behind him. If it was another one of these things, he knew he was doomed.

"Out of the way, Giant. Give me a clear shot."

The voice was authoritative and unmistakable. Suddenly, Giant was pretty sure he wasn't going to die anymore.

"Dredd!" he called out. "I know it sounds crazy, but they're vampires. You need to…"

There was a sound of a Lawgiver shot, and the thing on top of him was snatched away, the top of its head blown clean off.

"Shoot them in the head," finished Dredd with typical steely calmness as he stood over Giant, offering a hand to help him to his feet. "Figured that was the best way to go, soon as I saw it."

Dredd looked down at Giant, at his torn uniform, unsure whether the copious amounts of blood splattered across it belonged to Giant or to his attacker. "You injured?"

Giant climbed to his feet and recovered his Lawgiver, for the first time getting a good look at the thing that had almost just killed him. Scratch twenty. That thing had been no more than seventeen, tops.

"Only if you count my pride, I guess."

"How many more of the creeps are in here?"

It had been Dredd who had rescued Giant as a juve, keeping him on the straight and narrow and enrolling him in the Academy of Law, making sure that his life would have some real purpose. Dredd had been a permanent fixture in Giant's life for almost as long as the younger Judge could remember, and was the nearest thing to a father he would ever have, even if neither him nor Old Stony Face would ever admit it.

Still, no matter how long he had known Dredd, Giant would never fail to be impressed by the way Dredd dealt in the same stoic and matter-of-fact way with absolutely every freaky and weird thing the city had to throw at him. Whether it was vampires, zombie armies, extra-dimensional superfiends or apparently indestructible Cursed Earth headbutting cyborg maniacs, it was all just another day on the streets for Joe Dredd.

"Security cams picked up six of them when they broke in, so I figure that means four of them left. Watch your back – some of them are armed with more than fangs and bad breath."

"So am I," said Dredd, bringing his Lawgiver up to bear. "Let's go find them."

It wasn't too hard. The creatures had left a trail of destruction through the interior of the warehouse, randomly smashing every-thing and anything along the way as their frustrated search continued for whatever it was they had come here to get. That search had apparently ended at one of the refrigerated storage rooms off the main warehouse space. The thick metal door had been ripped off its hinges. Hungry snarls and chill, refrigerated air drifted out of the room beyond. Dredd silently motioned with the barrel of his Law-giver towards the sign beside the entrance to the room: Synthi-Plasma Storage.

"Figures, when you think about it," said Giant. "What else would a bunch of vampire perps pull a heist job for?"

Both Judges tensed, automatically bringing their Lawgivers round to bear as another one of the vampire creatures shambled out of the freezer room, its face dripping with bright-red synthi-plasma, its arms laden down with packet after packet of the stuff. Gorged on the blood substitute, almost drunk on the taste of it, it stared in stupefied surprise at the two Judges. Finally, something within its brain clicked, and it made to unsling the stump gun it wore over one shoulder.

"Picnic's over, freak. Hi-Ex!" barked Dredd, giving the command to his Lawgiver's voice-activated shell selector, aiming his gun at the target's central body mass.

Both Judges ducked as the area in front of the entrance to the freezer room was suddenly painted bright crimson as the vampire and the twenty-eight one-litre plasti-packs of concentrated synthi-plasma blood it was carrying exploded under the impact of the Hi-Ex bullet.

Giant recoiled back, splattered with the stuff. Some of it had got into his mouth, and he spat it out in disgust, revolted by its taste. If he ever turned vamp, he figured he'd probably end up starving to death, if that was the only kind of chow he was expected to go for. His vision was a red smear, and he was still wiping clear his helmet's face visor when he heard Dredd's Lawgiver firing again.

The remaining three vamps were holed up in the freezer room, prob-ably armed and ready to blow away anyone who tried to storm in there after them. Which Dredd wasn't about to do – not when his Lawgiver had everything he needed to encourage them to come out to where he was instead.

"Ricochet," he ordered, firing off a brace of shots through the freezer doorway. He hadn't bothered taking aim, and couldn't even see the tar-gets he was firing at. With Ricochet rounds, though, he didn't need to.

The rubber-tipped titanium bullets weaved a deadly pattern in the close confines of the freezer room as they bounced off metal walls, bursting the racked packets of synthi-blood by the dozen and biting into vampire flesh. In seconds, the floor of the room was centimetres deep in blood spilling out from the bullet-exploded storage packs.

Possibly more enraged by the destruction of their food supply than any damage caused to them by the bullets, the vampires charged out wildly to face their attackers. Lawgivers at the ready, Dredd and Giant were more than prepared for them.

Dredd shot the first one with an Incendiary shell. Howling in agony as its body exploded into flames, the creature threw itself back into the freezer room, rolling and splashing about on the blood-covered floor in a vain attempt to put out the volatile and hungry phosphor fire that ate relentlessly into its undead flesh.

Taking a cue from Dredd, Giant picked off the next one with a Hi-Ex shot, splattering its shredded remains against the nearest wall. This was going to be a messy one for the clean-up crews, Giant guessed, and he hoped the Tek-Judge forensics squad that was soon going to be crawling all over this place were packing spatulas and scraping tools with their tech-kit, to gather up all the evidence now sliding down the walls.

Dredd coolly took care of the third creep as it leapt at him with apparent lightning speed, claws and fangs ready to tear him open. It was fast, but not fast enough. For a moment, it seemed to almost defy the laws of physics, hanging suspended in mid-air as Dredd's rapid-fire spray of bullets struck against it. Then it was moving again, hurled backwards by the relentless force of the shells still being fired into it. A final burst decapitated it as it struck the far wall. Head and body fell to the ground several metres apart.

Yes sir, a very messy one for the poor slobs in the clean-up crews, thought Giant.

Dredd took in the aftermath of the brief but spectacularly gruesome fight, casually prodding the remains of the nearest vamp with the toe of his Judge boot.

"Creeps don't seem in too much of a hurry to turn into dust when they're dead either, or whatever it is they're supposed to do in the horror stories."

Giant bent down to study the scraps of the one he had tagged with the Hi-Ex shot. It had been wearing what looked like ordinary citizens' clothes. No fancy evening suits. No red synthi-satin lined opera cloaks. "You think we're looking at something normal here, not necessarily supernatural?"

"Bloodsucking freaks that shrug off standard Execution rounds aren't exactly what you'd call normal, even for this city, but I'd rather look for some rational answers before we call in the Psi-Div spook chasers," Dredd said.

He shifted impatiently, re-holstering his Lawgiver. Giant sighed inwardly. He knew what was coming next.

"Meat wagons and clean-up units are on their way," said Dredd, already moving to leave. "Stay here and supervise, Giant. I want full forensics backup on this one. Let me know what they find. Anyone wants me, I'll be finishing the rest of my patrol shift."

Giant watched him go. No, Old Stony Face never changed. Vamps, freaks, muties and weirdoes Dredd took in his stride, but every chance he got, he always pulled rank and left someone else to deal with the paperwork.

THREE

It was the paperwork Hershey hated the most.

Well, she also hated the meetings, the drafting of minutes, "resolutions" and "mission statements", the inane photo-op PR events, the occasional obligatory chat show appearance to show the citizens the allegedly friendly face of the Justice Department, the mind-numbing meet-and-greets with foreign dignitaries and ambassadors, the endless briefings from her policy advisors on a thousand different and tediously uninteresting but vitally important subjects.

But, most of all, she decided, she hated the paperwork. It was only now, two years after being elected Chief Judge of the most powerful city in the world, that she fully appreciated why Joe Dredd had turned down the post on several occasions in the past, when it would otherwise easily have been his for the asking.

"My place is on the streets," Dredd had always said.

"Yes, Joe," those within the Justice Department who, like Hershey, knew him best, could always have silently added, "because that's where you're the furthest away from the drokking paperwork."

Not that she blamed him, really. Sitting here in the Council of Five chamber within the Grand Hall of Justice, listening to Judge Cranston of Accounts Division making his quarterly budgetary report to the Council, she wished with all her heart she was out there with him, putting down a block war or two, or even re-fighting the Apocalypse War all over again.

Grud, even the time she had been kidnapped, completely paralysed and almost tortured to death by Fink Angel had almost been preferable to this.

"Furthermore, looking at our overseas balance of trade figures for this current fiscal quarter, and taking into account our projections for the next fiscal quarter, as well as the standing moratorium on non-essential trade with the former Sov Blok cities and the ongoing renegotiation with Sino-City as regards their Most Favoured Nation trade tariff status, we can predict with some modest confidence that, as far as the budget deficit for both this quarter and the next two is concerned–"

"Thank you, Judge Cranston," Hershey interrupted with what she hoped was the correct amount of tact. "Unfortunately, I have several other pressing appointments following this meeting, so thank you, but we'll read and review your budgetary report and recommendations later, and let you know our decision before the end of the week."

She kept on going before the flustered-looking elderly Accounts Division Senior Judge could protest. "Moving on to the next item on the agenda: the rise in incidents involving members of the so-called 'Church of Death'. Hollister?"

Judge Hollister, the Council's only member who wasn't already a Justice Department Divisional head, had been assigned to brief the rest of the Council members on the problem. Hershey was amused to see that, for once, Hollister had actually turned up for a Council meeting in proper Judge uniform. As a senior member of the Wally Squad, she had occasionally attended meetings in various kinds of civilian attire, some of them downright scandalous. Hershey wondered what Silver, one of her predecessors as Chief Judge and a notoriously prudish stickler for the rules, would have had to say if one of his most senior Judges had turned up for a Council of Five meeting wearing the fishnet tights and low-cut halter top outfit of a common slabwalker, as Hollister had once so memorably done.

"Most Sector Chiefs are reporting a rise in crimes associated with the cult. Up until now, it's been relatively small-time stuff; pro-Death scrawl-graffiti, juve gangs swapping their gang tags for cult symbols, the occasional case of pet animal sacrifice."

"And now?" said Hershey.

"Now we're seeing a sudden spike in these crimes, not just in number, but also in terms of their seriousness," replied Hollister. "Juve gangs claiming an association with the cult are banding together to start violent rumbles with the other gangs. Street preachers claiming to be pronouncing the 'Gospel of Death' have started appearing – we're picking them up as soon as they appear, of course – and some of them have even taken to the airwaves on illegal pirate radio stations to spread the word even further.

"My anti-pirate monitoring units have already tracked down a number of these illegal broadcast stations, and identified and arrested those responsible," interjected Tek Chief McTighe testily, keen to counter any suggestion that his Tek-Judges weren't already on top of the situation."

"Granted," agreed Hollister, "but what we're dealing with here is something more than a few pirate broadcasters. We're looking at Death cult-related crimes all across the board. More worryingly, we're seeing a noticeable rise in missing persons cases. We believe the cult may be tied into a lot of these."

"You think they've maybe graduated from pet sacrifice to something more serious?" asked Judge Niles, head of the Public Surveillance Unit and, in Hershey's opinion, probably the most astute mind in the room.

"Human sacrifice? The cult grabbing victims off the streets?" answered Hollister. "It's possible, but we think it's more likely that a lot of these are simple runaways. Juves or dropouts running off to join the cult."

"So they're actively recruiting now?" noted Buell, the gruff and no-nonsense head of the Special Judicial Squad, the division of the Justice Department charged with rooting out corruption within the force itself. "If they're recruiting, they must be organised. Do we have any idea of the kind of numbers they might have, or how they're organising or funding themselves?"

Hershey nodded in silent agreement. Typical Arthur Buell, his question cutting right to the heart of the issue.

"Nothing so far," admitted Hollister. "Grud knows we've rounded up enough of these loons, but the ones we're seeing so far are strictly small fry, lone kooks picking up on the Death cult vibes on the streets at the moment, or loosely associated local groups like street gangs or the odd kook collective. If there's a central leadership or organisation to the thing, we've yet to see any real hard evidence of it."

Ramos, the head of Street Division, shifted impatiently in his seat. "We've seen this kind of crap before, surely?" he said, with typical Street Judge bluntness. "Last month it was half the juves in the city painting red stars on their foreheads, calling themselves stuff like the 'Sons of Orlok', pledging their undying allegiance to East Meg One and swearing to avenge its destruction. This month it's worshipping the Dark Judges, and next month it'll be something else. Sick as it is, it's probably just another fad. Maintain control of it, round up a few of its most visible proponents and make examples of them, and it'll soon blow over, just like that whole 'Kool Kommunista' thing did."

Several heads round the table nodded in quiet agreement. Hershey looked towards the man sitting on the far side of the room, seated beside Cranston and amongst the other non-Council member divisional heads. Even though the accountant and these others had no right to a vote when it came to making Council of Five decisions, Hershey still welcomed the opinions of her divisional chiefs, especially when it came to matters relating specifically to their own division's field of expertise.

Like now, for example. When it came to anything to do with the Dark Judges, Hershey didn't believe in leaving any possibility unconsidered.

"Psi-Chief Shenker, Death and the rest of his super-creep buddies are supposed to be your bailiwick. What does Psi-Division have to add to everything we've heard so far?"

"Nothing much, Chief Judge," came the Psi-Chief's answer. "Whatever this supposed cult's activities involve, it doesn't seem to have generated any significant psi-presence to be picked up over the psychic white noise thrown out by a city of over four hundred million human minds."

"Nothing at all, then?" asked Hershey, aware of the thinly veiled sharpness in her voice. Psi-Division's success in predicting city-threatening disasters had been less than stellar, most notably in the case of the so-called "Doomsday Scenario" event of the previous year, when organised crime group the Frendz almost seized control of the entire city. Like many others within the Justice Department, Hershey's faith in Psi-Division's effectiveness had been severely tested by such events, which went a long way to explaining why Shenker had swiftly lost Psi-Division's long-held seat on the Council after Hershey's election to the position of Chief Judge.

The Psi-Chief, a quiet, slightly fussy man, paused, looking vaguely uncomfortable, before venturing an answer. "We have had one unsubstantiated pre-cog warning in the last few days, relating to a possible supernatural threat against the city, Chief Judge, although as far as we can tell, there's nothing in it yet to suggest any connection to the Dark Judges or this Death cult phenomenon."

"Just one?" queried Hershey, puzzled and slightly irritated. Whenever possible, Psi-Division policy was to cross-check possible pre-cog warnings from any of its operatives with any secondary visions picked up from other Psi-Judges, especially those amongst the Division's supposed powerful and specially trained pre-cogs. Usually, it took verification from several other Psi-Judges before the alarm bells would start ringing loud enough to be heard here within the Grand Hall of Justice.

"Who did the pre-cog warning come from?" asked Hershey, suspecting she already knew the answer.

"Well... Anderson," said Shenker reluctantly.

There was a series of muted sighs from several Judges in the room. Although no one questioned Anderson's psi-abilities – she was without doubt Psi-Division's top operative – her reputation could only be described as... troublesome, at best. She could be irreverent, highly strung, insubordinate, even downright mutinous at times, and was becoming increasingly questioning of Justice Department methods and policy. That was Anderson all over, and Hershey knew that she wouldn't be the first Chief Judge to have problems with Psi-Judge Cassandra Anderson.

Nevertheless...

It had been Anderson who had dealt with Judge Death the first time he had ever appeared in Mega-City One, trapping his spirit within her own mind at a cost to herself that few here within the Council of Five chamber could ever possibly imagine.

When the other three Dark Judges had struck, freeing Death and slaughtering the inhabitants of an entire city block, it had also been Anderson who, along with Dredd, had stopped them. The pair had followed them back to the ghastly netherworld where the fiends had originally come from, and apparently destroyed them for good.

They had returned once more, though, tricking Anderson into unwittingly bringing them back to life, but she had redeemed herself for that terrible mistake, devising a way of trapping them forever in extra-dimensional limbo. Or so it had seemed at the time.

Then, in the nightmare that had been Necropolis, it had been Anderson who had enabled Dredd to deliver the killing blow, destroying the power of the twisted beings known as the Sisters of Death and allowing the Judges to take control of the Mega-City back from Death and his foul kin.

Every time the Dark Judges had struck, Anderson had been instrumental in stopping them. There was no denying that Anderson had a special link with Death, almost certainly down to having the creep taking up joint residence in her brain for over a year, so Hershey wasn't about to ignore any chance, no matter how slight, that there was any threat to the city involving Death and the other Dark Judges.

"There's a cult dedicated to the worship of Death on the rise in the city, and Psi-Division's top telepath has a vision about a possible supernatural threat. Coincidence?" asked Buell, making Hershey wonder if her SJS Chief didn't have a few mind-reading powers of his own.

"Let's assume not, at least for the time being," replied Hershey, looking to Shenker. "Have Anderson brought in. I want a full face-to-face briefing from her on what it was she thought she picked up."

"And the Church of Death?"

"As you suggested," she told Ramos. "We come down hard on them, right across the board. Brief all the Sector Chiefs to round up any and all Death cult agitators in their sectors. Any of them who look like they might know anything get a full tour of the interrogation cubes. Until we know anything better, we assume there might be more to these munceheads than just another passing fad. Agreed?"

There was a brief show of hands round the table. Unanimous agreement.

"Very well," Hershey began. "Next item on the agenda, the increase in illegal alien smuggling at the spaceports. Judge Blunkett of Immigration Division will give us his report."

Cowed and fearful, cringing and repentant, the vampires bowed in submission before the angry figure on the altar's vid-screen.

"With so much at stake, at this late hour, you fools couldn't contain your blood thirst for a day or two longer?"

Hissing in fear and contrition, the vampires grovelled even closer to the stone floor, afraid to even glance up at the figure on the vid-screen before them.

"Your children grow hungry and impatient," said the priest, shuffling forward in his dark green and amber cult robes to address the hidden speaker on the vid-screen. "Impatient at having to remain in hiding for so long, impatient for the glorious moment when the Dark Brethren are at last released from their imprisonment and we, their children and faithful servants can come out from the shadows and finally claim this city as our own."

There was a keening of agreement and anticipation from amongst the congregation of vampires, some baring their fangs in murderous and barely restrained blood hunger at the thought of the slaughter to come.

Many kilometres away, secure in his own hidden sanctum, the figure on the vid-screen sighed in thinly veiled irritation. They had their uses, these things, but ultimately they were at best a mistake on his part, yet another failed experiment on the route to his ultimate goal. Like these Death cultist fanatics whom he had found and with whom he shared at least some beliefs, he would use them to his own ends. And then, when they were of no use to him any longer...

He broke off from that distracting, if not entirely unpleasant, train of thought, reminding himself that there were still important matters to be attended to first, and that these creatures he had created and these ignorant fools he had gathered to him were still the only tools he had at hand to carry out those matters.

"Believe me," he told the coven, the more conciliatory and understanding tone in his voice evident even over the static interference of the heavily code-scrambled vid-link. "I understand your impatience, and there is no one more eager to see our Dark Lord and his Holy Brethren returned to us, but there is still work to be done first, and we cannot afford any more mistakes. If the Judges discover our plans, everything we've worked for up until this moment will have been pointless. You understand me? The Dark Ones will remain held prisoner by the unbelievers, and you will have failed them in the holy duty they have asked of us."

"I... I understand," the Death cult priest said, bowing his head in fearful contrition.

Fear and religious awe, the figure on the vid-screen marvelled to himself. That's how to make these fools do as you want. Keep them properly subdued, remind them who it is that they believe speaks through you and dress up everything you say in the right amount of portentous-sounding quasi-religious gobbledygook, and you can get them to do just about anything.

Even die for you, he thought with a smile. As would be amply demonstrated soon enough.

"Excellent," he said aloud. "Contain your hunger and impatience just a little longer, my children. I know the serum I provide you with is not enough to satisfy you, but I promise blood enough to feed the hunger of all of you, just as soon as the psi-witch is no longer a danger to us."

"Anderssssson..." Her name was a collective hiss of pure hatred from the members of the coven.

"Yes, Anderson," affirmed the figure on the vid-screen, further stoking the fires of the vampire coven's hatred. "The witch who has defied our masters time and time again, the one who has always been there to lead the Judges against them. The one who has even foolishly believed that she had actually succeeded in destroying that which cannot be killed!"

The coven snarled and hissed in rage at these reminders of past transgressions against their holy masters. The figure on the vid-screen waited a few moments for the sounds of their anger to abate.

"You still have her under surveillance?" he asked the priest, who nodded eagerly. "Then do our masters' bidding – and kill her!" commanded the figure on the vid-screen. "This time, when the Dark Judges are set loose to continue their holy work, Judge Anderson will not be there to stop them!"

Sitting there secure in his hidden sanctum, he leaned forward, hitting the switch to kill the vid-link, cutting off in mid-snarl the coven's predictable sounds of enthusiastic and bloodthirsty approval.

He tapped his fingers lightly on the console keyboard, calling up the floor plans, which it had cost him much effort and money to secure from the supposedly impregnable Justice Department computer files.

He looked over the precious schematics for perhaps the thousandth time, mentally tracing out the pre-planned entry points, his eyes automatically seeking out those vital places, which a hundred or more

detailed computer simulation assaults had shown to be the most tacti-
cally vital or weakly defended. There would be casualties during the
attack, of course, but that wasn't really going to be too much of a problem, was it? Not when he had a small army of death-obsessed fanatics
and bullet-resistant vampire servants at his disposal?

Allowing himself a small smile of satisfaction, he closed his eyes and
thought of the glorious transformation that would soon be his.

He was so close now, so close, and, the blundering incident at the
med-supply repository aside, everything was going perfectly to plan.

"So much for that plan," muttered DeMarco to herself, drawing herself
further into the shadows of the doorway from where she had been keeping hidden watch for most of the last few hours.

Another vehicle drew up, depositing a further group of figures outside
the seemingly derelict dockside warehouse, which she now knew to be
the headquarters of the Church of Death.

In truth, the place wasn't much to look at, just another run-down old
pre-Atomic Wars building in a street full of similar abandoned heaps in
a neighbourhood almost completely derelict due to the pollution over-
spill from the lethally toxic waters of the nearby Black Atlantic shore.
Then again, DeMarco reminded herself, if she was setting up a secret
and highly illegal cult dedicated to the worship of a mass-murdering,
extra-dimensional super-freak, wouldn't this be exactly the kind of gen-
erally forgotten place she'd choose to hide out in too?

Her original plan had been to sneak into the place and reconnoitre it,
to discover if it really was the cult's headquarters and see if she could
find any clue about the whereabouts of the Caskey girl.

The constant flow of people in and out of the building – she had
counted over fifty people arriving or departing in the last hour alone –
had swiftly put paid to that idea.

"Grud, this place is almost as busy as Remembrance Square on Apocalypse Day," she muttered to herself again, as the warehouse's loading
doors screeched up noisily and a medium-sized hov-truck slid forward
into the street outside. Its rear panel doors were still open, and DeMarco
saw a small platoon of figures in the now-familiar garb of the Death cult
scrambling aboard. One of them suddenly looked round, straight
towards where she was hiding, and DeMarco hurriedly pressed herself
deeper into the shadows of the doorway.

Still, the brief moment she had seen the cultist's face was enough time
for her street Judge-trained instincts to get a glimpse of the creep, and
she registered a shockingly pale and gaunt face with fierce, red-rimmed
eyes and...

"Fangs?" she breathed to herself, wondering just what she had gotten herself into. She was also pretty sure that almost all of them had been armed with a mixture of firearms: stump guns and automatic spit guns, the weapons of choice amongst most of Mega-City One's criminal fraternity.

She supposed that this was the point when she should do what any good cit was required to do, and call in a crime report to the Justice Department. Leave it to the Judges, that's what ordinary citizens were supposed to do. There was just one problem with that theory: Galen DeMarco didn't consider herself to be just another ordinary cit. She was an ex-Judge – she had been a Sector Chief before she left the Department, for Grud's sake, in command of a force of hundreds of Street Judges and responsible for the safety of the millions of inhabitants of an entire city sector – and she still had an experienced Judge's training and instinct, so no way was she just going to turn and walk away and leave it for someone else to deal with like a good little cit was supposed to.

Besides, she reminded herself, she was a Private Investigator, and she had a job to do and a responsibility to her client. And to her client's daughter, the still-missing Joanna Caskey.

DeMarco had gone to town on one of these "Friends of Thanos" creeps at Joanna's college, and, after searching his apartment (illegal entry: minimum five-year sentence, the Judge part of her mind dutifully reminded her) and finding a large stash of highly illegal narc-stims there (failure to report a crime: automatic minimum five-year sentence) she was fairly sure that the girl was here, and probably being held against her will. Apparently, her unwilling informant had told her, there was something special about the Caskey girl's aura, and she had been chosen for some unspecified "special purpose".

None of which DeMarco much liked the sound of at all. She told herself that even if she called it in now, the Judges might still not arrive in time to stop whatever was going on in there.

No, she decided, she had to get in there herself, find the girl and discover what exactly these creeps were up to. Then, she promised herself, she'd put in a call to the Judges, once she had done her duty to her client and got the Caskey girl safely out of there.

There was a guard left at the still-open loading doors. He was wearing robes with identifiable Church of Death markings (membership of an illegal organisation: five years), was openly carrying a well-worn pump-action stump gun (possession of an illegal weapon: two years) and, even as DeMarco watched, paused to light up a cigarette (illegal smoking in a public place: one to three years mandatory).

"Creep sure is racking up the crime count," DeMarco murmured to herself. "At this rate, he'll probably be catching up with me soon."

The guard was standing with his back to her now, looking along the street while taking a long draw on his cigarette, although DeMarco wondered why he even bothered smoking the thing down here. If he wanted to dramatically cut his lifespan and pollute his body with lethally toxic substances, then a few good big lungfuls of the stuff that passed for air down here would do the job just as easily.

Reaching into her pocket to make sure that her pistol with its add-on stun beamer (unregistered modification of a licensed firearm: six months to a year, that little Judge voice reminded her) was still there, she slipped quietly from her hiding place and began sneaking across the street towards the guard's unprotected back.

The first plan had been a bust, she told herself, so let's see how this one worked out.

FOUR

Anderson was revving up her Lawmaster, before pulling out onto Tinto Brass Memorial Expressway for a long, looping, random patrol circuit of the inner sectors of MegEast, when her bike radio crackled into life.

"Anderson – Control. Chief Judge Hershey wants to see you. Report your position; we're sending an H-wagon to pick you up and take you to the Grand Hall of Justice."

"Not necessary, Control. I'm a big girl now, I can get there on my own."

She broke off communications before she received Control's no doubt exasperated repeat of the instructions they had just given her. Even though she was a telepath, she didn't have to be a mind-reader to know what was probably going through the mind of an anonymous Comms Judge back at the local Sector House Control.

'That Anderson. Always making trouble, always thinking that normal regs don't apply to her. Grud knows why she's still even a Judge.'

To be honest, Anderson asked herself the same thing a dozen or so times a day at least. She thought she'd left the Justice Department and even Mega-City for good before – "Cassandra's little hiatus away from us" was how Psi-Chief Shenker referred to that period, with a wry smile – but, despite herself, she had eventually returned, called back by something inside her.

She loved Mega-City One, but she hated it too. She had hated being a Judge, had hated and fought against the monolithic authoritarian weight of the Justice Department and much of what it stood for as well, but still she had come back, realising that this was all she knew and was where she was needed most.

Like now, for instance. The last time she had come back it was because, even from halfway across the galaxy, she had sensed a premonition that the Dark Judges were going to strike once more, and she had arrived back on Earth just in time to stop Death and his three super-creep amigos from escaping again.

And this time? What was the source of the vision she'd had, and that growing, creepy feeling at the back of her mind? Was it linked to the Dark Judges in some way?

Anderson didn't know, but she intended to find out and, while the immediate prospect of an audience with the Chief Judge didn't exactly thrill her, she hoped that it would go some way to putting her mind at rest. Death and the other Dark Judges might be contained under the highest security in the Tomb level beneath Nixon Penitentiary, but, as the Justice Department had discovered to its cost too many times before, imprisonment or even their apparent destruction hadn't been enough in the past to reduce the deadly threat they represented to every living soul in Mega-City One.

Checking the non-stop flow of Traffic Division info-updates scrolling across the screen of her bike computer, Anderson saw that Tinto Brass was severely congested at a point a few kilometres ahead, with serious delays at the Brucie Campbell Interchange caused by fans travelling to the smashball game at the nearby Juggernauts stadium and the aftermath of yesterday's brief block war spat between the Kylie and Dannii Minogue twin conapts.

"Grand Hall of Justice – best alternative route from present location," she barked to her bike computer in the approved Justice Department tone of voice.

"Wilco. Please stand by," responded the onboard computer in a voice Anderson had long come to call Justice Department Techno-Soulless. She'd heard that some of the younger Judges coming out of the Academy these days liked to have bike computers with a selection of changeable audio circuits. Apparently some bright spark at Tek Division had even made it possible to have your bike speaking to you in a synthesised version of Dredd's own unmistakably terse and no-nonsense tones. Anderson grinned at the thought – Grud only knows what Dredd thought of that. Then she smiled to herself again at the realisation that, to many of the younger Judges hitting the streets these days, she must seem almost as much a piece of Justice Department legend – "relic" would be the more unkind term they used amongst themselves in the sector house locker rooms – as Old Stony Face himself.

A moment later, the screen on the compact instrument panel in front of her displayed the requested map route, with secondary and even tertiary alternatives suggested as optional extras. Anderson selected the main route and guided her Lawmaster away from the expressway and onto an off-sked ramp, keeping one eye on the scrolling flow of traffic data as she did so. Like any good Judge, she knew the city's main roadway map by heart, but the day-to-day traffic situation was so chaotic, affected by everything from freak Weather Control mishaps to major block wars, and not forgetting the seemingly random basis on which the planners down at City Hall decided to carry out roadwork repairs and construction projects, that any seemingly simple trip from A to B could end up taking in unplanned detours to C, D, E and F along the way.

She hit the off-sked ramp at an easy 150 kph, turning onto it in a casual manoeuvre that would not have met with approval from any Bike Skills tutor at the Academy of Law – and which would have quickly drawn angry beeps and honks of protest from the vehicles behind her, had she been anyone other than a Judge.

Three lanes back, unnoticed by Anderson, the hov-truck which had been following her jumped lanes to match her manoeuvre, drawing a chorus of complaint from the motorists around it. Anderson, speeding off and accelerating up to 200 kph, didn't notice as the vehicle slid onto the sked ramp behind her, bringing its own speed up to catch her.

She was on Joey Ramone Undersked, travelling east towards Sector 44. From there, she would cut off at Linneker Junction, catching the Tushingham Expressway for half a sector until she hit Slab 12 with its For Justice Department Use Only express lanes, which would allow her to open up the throttle and cruise all the way to the Grand Hall at a cool 350 kph. In less than fifteen minutes, she figured, she'd be pulling into the Grand Hall's motor pool levels.

When it came to beating the big city traffic, Anderson mused to herself, there were times when being an agent of a rigidly authoritarian law enforcement regime definitely had its advantages.

A juve skysurfer swooped in low above her, buzzing the speeding traffic below him and briefly mooning a party of outraged-looking elderly Brit-cit tourists sitting on the top deck of a strato-bus. He laughed at their reaction and briefly posed theatrically for the cameras of the delighted party of Hondo-cit tourists sitting behind the more uptight Brit-citters, and then hit the uplift throttle on his board, zooming back upwards and making the complex task of juggling high-speed aerodynamics with balancing the requirements of the skyboard's notoriously delicate and unreliable anti-grav field look as easy as riding an escalator.

Anderson supposed she should call the incident in to Control and have an aerial unit pick him up. Grud knows a stickler like Dredd would already have done it as soon as he spotted him, probably with good justification. Pulling illegal low-level flying stunts like that, the juve was a danger to himself and others, and maybe a few months in the Juve Cubes would cool his heels a little and do him some good.

On the other hand, she thought, watching the skysurfer accelerate away, dodging with masterful skill through two lanes of aerial traffic and then gliding gracefully up across the strong thermal updrafts from the stacked rooftops of the giant city blocks below, Anderson couldn't help but marvel at the momentary illusion of complete freedom the juve seemed to represent.

"Enjoy it while it lasts, kid," she murmured to herself. "Trust me, the rest of life in this city is all downhill from where you are now."

Distracted by her thoughts and the skysurfer's antics, she didn't even notice the hov-van pull almost level with her in the lane opposite. It was the psi-flash, screaming through her brain with nerve-shredding intensity, that warned her scant moments before the panel door at the side of the van nearest her slid open and a hail of automatic weapons fire was blasted out at her at near point-blank range.

Anderson swerved.

And braked. Hard.

She ducked too, leaning forward fast and hugging the chassis of her Lawmaster as a hot stream of bullets passed through the space where her head had been a brief moment ago.

The gunfire raked down the side of the bike. Anderson's violent swerve manoeuvre took her away from most of it, but she still heard shots ricocheting off the bike's armoured bodywork or shattering its sidelights. Something punched into the calf of her leg, while another red-hot shell tore painfully into the tough, bullet-resistant material of her Judge boot.

No biggie, she thought to herself. I'm a Judge. I've been shot plenty of times before.

She veered away from the van, into the next lane and the path of traffic flowing in the other direction, forcing her to violently swerve again to avoid smashing into oncoming vehicles. A bright red Foord Strato screamed by, passing close enough for Anderson's Lawmaster to leave scrape lines along the length of its gleaming paintwork. Anderson caught a lightning-speed glimpse of the horrified expressions of the car's occupants – mother, father and their population regs-permitted two juves – and then they were gone before they could realise just how close they came to having Psi Division's top telepath smeared all over the front of their family car.

She was behind the van now, wondering how long it would be before back up might arrive, wondering if she could stay alive long enough for it to matter. By now, some of the cits in the passing cars might be making emergency calls to the Justice Department. Roving spy-in-the-sky anti-crime surveillance cams might already have picked the incident up, beaming the images of it back to the local Sector House Control, while the Traffic Division cameras would surely have picked up something of it, although, unless a human supervisor was present, it might take the autobot programs that each monitored the images from thousands of such cameras some time to realise what was happening.

A personal heads-up call from her probably wouldn't do any harm at this point either, she thought.

"Control – Anderson. Am under attack, Joey Ramone U-sked, between Fred Fellini and Pete Bogdanovich Interchanges. Perps are driving a black, late-model Kryton-Skesky hov-truck. Am in pursuit and still under fire."

Right on cue, she was reaching for her Lawgiver even as the rear doors of the van burst open. She saw her attackers clearly this time. Four of them, wearing familiar-looking green and amber robes, and aiming their weapons at her.

Death cultists, she realised with a chill. In her book, at least, the Church of Death had just become something much more than another passing craze amidst Mega-City One's usual quota of harmless loons and jaded thrill-seekers.

She swerved again as they opened fire. What they lacked in accuracy, they more than made up for in sheer ferocity of firepower. Spit shells smacked into the rockcrete surface of the sked, gouging huge chunks out of it, or smashed into the front of her Lawmaster, shattering against its array of powerful headlights or ricocheting off its densely armoured eagle badge facade. One lucky shot drilled through the armoured casing of her bike computer and the thing died with a noisy electronic squawk, cutting off any reply that she might have been expecting to hear back from Control.

Stray shots flew everywhere, causing mayhem amongst the traffic behind her. She veered off again to a position directly behind the hov-truck, drawing her attackers' fire directly back upon herself and away from the other vehicles on the road. She wasn't in a hurry to get killed today, but she didn't want innocent cits to get hit by any bullets meant for her.

In doing so, she caught an unexpected break. Her attackers had completely emptied their magazines and were now struggling as fast as they could to reload their guns.

I'm being attacked by a hit-squad of amateurs, she thought to herself. If these creeps kill me now, I'll probably never live it down.

She could see them clearly. The hood of one of them slipped back, and she saw a shockingly pale face, a pair of red eyes staring at her in hatred, a mouth snarling open to reveal...

Fangs, she wondered to herself, remembering the things from her psi-flash nightmare?

The cultist raised his reloaded spit gun to fire at her again.

"Not going to happen, freak," Anderson said, beating him to the punch, as she raised and fired her Lawgiver at him.

As was normal with Psi-Judges, she wasn't the greatest shot the Justice Department had ever seen. The extra-intensive psi-training at the Academy of Law came at the expense of some of the other regular skills taught to all Judge cadets, and she was never going to be able to beat someone like Dredd on a sector house firing range – but, nine times out of ten, her Lawgiver shots went exactly where she wanted them to. This time was no exception.

The two shots punched into the white-faced freak's chest, knocking him backwards. A second later, though, he was back on his feet, reaching for his dropped weapon and snarling in even greater hatred.

Body armour, thought Anderson. That's what he must be wearing under those robes. There's a couple of light and flexible armour types – stuff like the new shokk-hard jackets favoured by Mega-Mob blitzers – that can stop anything up to a Lawgiver AP round.

Then Anderson saw the freak's face again, felt for a moment the burning hatred in those unnatural red eyes, sensed the awful hunger behind that hatred, and suddenly knew that, no, there was no armour hidden underneath those robes. She had just put two shots straight into this freak's chest cavity, and it hadn't even phased him.

The other three were getting ready to fire again too. One of them was fumbling with an object in his hand, and Anderson got another psi-flash as, in her mind's eye, she saw the object leave the cultist's hand; saw it explode against the front of her bike; saw both her and the Lawmaster burning furiously, wreathed in unquenchable flames. Saw herself falling screaming from the saddle as she burned alive in agony, her body smashing into the surface of the road and then lying there lifeless and yet still burning. By the time the nearest backup unit arrived a few minutes later, there would be hardly anything left of her to scrape up and deliver to Resyk.

Phosphor bomb! her mind screamed to her in warning at the weapon in the cultist's hand.

Her own hand stabbed the handlebar-mounted fire control switch for her Lawmaster's main armament, sending out a long, roaring stream of shells from the twin-linked cannons on the bike's front. Large-calibre shells raked the rear and interior of the hov-van, ripping through metal bodywork and human flesh with equal ease. The phosphor grenade, blown out of its owner's hand, exploded inside the van with devastating effect, and Anderson had to manoeuvre hard to avoid the ferocious fireball that suddenly burst out of the vehicle's open rear doors.

Its whole interior ablaze, including its driving compartment, the vehicle swerved violently across the lanes of the sked. A flailing figure covered head to toe in flame fell out of the still-open side door and hit the surface of the road with a sickening crunch. Anderson followed the vehicle on its careering course, hitting her bike sirens to alert all oncoming traffic of the danger, although the sight of the fiercely burning and out-of-control vehicle was surely enough to make the driver of any oncoming vehicle sit up and take notice.

Suddenly, without warning, something detached itself from the flame-filled furnace that was now the van's rear compartment. It was a human figure, covered in fire. It leapt – flew, almost – from the rear of the van, covering the nearly ten-metre gap between the burning van and Anderson's position in an astounding feat of strength, landing on the bullet-scarred front of the Lawmaster with a bone-jarring impact.

Anderson recoiled back in her saddle in disbelief, finding herself staring into the inhuman eyes of the thing as it launched itself upon her. Most of its clothes were burnt away by the fire that crawled over almost all of its body, and Anderson could clearly see the gaping holes on its torso from the wounds inflicted by the bike cannon shells and her two Lawgiver shots. It was the same freak she had already shot twice in the chest.

It leapt across the front of the bike at her, forcing her to relinquish control of the bike's handlebars as she brought an arm up to block a lunging bite from that fang-filled mouth. With her onboard computer knocked out by a lucky bullet hit, the Lawmaster was now effectively out of control.

The monstrosity locked its hands round her throat, pressing forward eagerly towards her. Her nostrils were filled with the stench of burning meat, and she could feel the heat from the flames starting to blister those portions of her skin that weren't protected by the fire-resistant material of her uniform.

The thing's face – Anderson no longer thought of her attacker as being anything remotely human – loomed up in front of her, only centimetres away from her own. Its red eyes bored into her with a terrible intensity. For a moment, Anderson involuntarily brushed minds with the thing, tasting the hunger and hatred that consumed it. There was something else there, something hidden at the back of its mind.

She focused her psi-talent, pushing violently through the repellent barrier of the creature's hunger-thoughts and into the remnants of the ravaged mind beyond. In that briefest of moments, she plundered what she could from the creature's own memories. She saw the gleaming antiseptic surfaces of a high-tech laboratory... a dingy warehouse front, possibly somewhere down at the Black Atlantic docks, judging by the pollution haze hanging in the air.

She pushed in still further.

Some kind of religious ceremony, heads bowed in fear and awe before some kind of altar... A figure speaking on a vid-screen, its face hidden from view, its voice sending a thrill of fearful obedience through the mind of the thing.

Further. Still further. Not memories now, images of events still to happen.

Doors opened to reveal huge caches of weapons, eager hands reaching in to snatch up what they can... Dozens of creatures identical to the thing Anderson was now fighting crammed into the compartments of hov-transporters, a sense of almost unbearable hunger and eagerness running through them as they neared their destination... A set of schematics marked with a 'Justice Department: Highly Classified' security notification... Guard tower points, security bypass procedures, level after identical level of corridors lined with small cube-like rooms... Cells... An iso-block?

With a sickening realisation, Anderson knew in an instant what these freaks were up to. She broke off the psi-contact, snapping back to the reality of what was still happening to her right this moment. The sucker's hands were still around her throat, burning into the material of her uniform, strangling her. She felt herself start to black out. From somewhere far away, but somehow coming swiftly closer, she heard an urgent roaring sound.

She threw herself backwards off the saddle, taking her attacker with her, hurling them both off the Lawmaster a split second before it crashed into the front of the huge jugger-transporter, the sound of the impact as the Lawmaster was smashed apart momentarily drowning out the blaring roar of the giant vehicle's batteries of warning horns.

Falling backwards at a 100 kph or more, it was times like this Anderson wished she had paid more attention to the Department regs about the compulsory wearing of helmets. She desperately twisted in mid-air, putting her attacker's body between her and the road surface now rushing up towards them, figuring she might as well let him hit it first.

It worked, mostly.

They hit the ground and rolled for fifty metres or so, the rough surface of the sked making them pay for every bone-breaking, skin-shredding metre. The creature took the worst of it, as Anderson had hoped, but at least it didn't have to worry about being on fire anymore. Not when most of its burning skin had been scraped off along the way.

Anderson fared better, her uniform and protective pads saving her from the very worst of the variety of injuries on offer.

She came to rest on the edge of the sked's hard shoulder, still conscious, and started counting the damage. A couple of ribs were gone, and she suspected one of them might have punctured a lung, judging from the white-hot spears of agony she felt every time she took a breath. Her left leg was bent back at a decidedly unpleasant angle, and she didn't need to try to pick up any pre-cog visions to see some serious time spent hooked up to a speedheal machine in her immediate future.

The pain was bad, real bad. She knew some psi-tricks to block a lot of it out, but they would have to wait. The most important thing now was to let everyone else know what it was she had seen inside the mind of that creature.

She was just reaching down for the communicator stored in her utility belt when the hand, charred and almost fleshless, reached out to grab her.

The creature, incredibly, was still alive. Its body was smashed, its skin was burnt away from it in huge, terrible patches, yet it still wouldn't accept the inevitable and just roll over and die. It was crawling up the length of her body, making a horrible, hissing, gurgling sound from its ruined throat.

Pinned to the ground, weak from pain, Anderson was helpless to stop it. Her Lawgiver was long gone, knocked from her hand as they fell from the back of the bike, and probably now crushed beneath the wheels of the jugger-transporter. Which only left her with...

Ignoring the screaming pain from her broken leg, she reached down for the boot knife secreted there. Her hand found it just as the creature pressed itself down at her throat. Its mouth hung slackly open, revealing the jutting fangs there. Anderson's hand flashed up, stabbing the knife's blade right between the thing's open fangs.

Psi-Judges were equipped with silver-bladed boot knives as standard these days. Anderson didn't know what this fiend was or where it came from, but she was pretty hopeful that this might finally be enough to kill it. Silver blade or no silver blade, ramming the point of a boot knife right through the roof of its mouth and straight up into its brain was sure to have some kind of effect.

It did. The creature gave a choking cry and fell forwards across her, its fangs closing around the hilt of the knife still gruesomely jutting out from between its clenched jaws.

Using almost the last of her rapidly failing strength, Anderson painfully pushed the thing off her and reached in desperation towards the communicator lying on the ground nearby.

A black, nauseous wave of unconsciousness rushed up towards her. She struggled to hold it off for a few more precious moments. She had to radio in what she knew... Had to let the rest of Justice Department know what was about to happen.

Had... to...

She heard sirens in the distance, coming closer. Her fingers brushed against the hard casing of the communicator. Her vision swam. And dimmed.

The backup squad found her less than two minutes later. She was unconscious, lying in a spreading pool of her own blood. The first Judge on the scene gingerly knelt over her, feeling for a pulse and relieved to find one, weak though it was.

"Control – Varrick. Med unit urgently required down here on Joey Ramone. Alert anyone who needs to know – Psi-Judge Anderson's down and in a bad way."

"Wilco, Varrick. Med assist on its way."

"Hold on, Anderson. Help's coming," Varrick said gently to the near-comatose Psi-Judge. Two years ago that had been him, lying bleeding into the ground of a block plaza after being caught in the crossfire of a juve gang rumble, and he knew from experience how much it meant to hear a friendly voice or just to know somehow that someone's there with you, watching out for you, while you're lying there helpless and injured.

He reached down to take her hand, noticing as he did so that she had her backup communicator held in it. Her finger was on the call switch, although she'd passed out before she could activate it.

FIVE

"Hey, what was that?"

Burchill looked up in irritation from the book he was reading, his concentration broken by the sudden sound of Meyer's voice. Dull as it was, Dredd's *Comportment* was supposed to be required reading for any Street Judge.

Despite the mood of breezy nonchalance Burchill affected whenever he was on duty down here, he hated this posting, and seriously resented having to come back to the Tomb for another three months of sitting here doing nothing.

Which was why he had put in a request for permanent reassignment to something a little more interesting than guard duty in the Tomb, once this latest three-month stint was up. Something like open patrol assignment, say, maintaining a visible Psi-Division presence on the city streets and giving psi-specialist backup to the ordinary Judge on patrol.

Which meant he'd have to undergo a series of re-evaluation tests at Psi-Div HQ, to see if he was suitable for more responsible duties.

Which meant having to brush up on his knowledge of Street Division and the way the Street Judges operated.

Which he couldn't do, if Meyer kept on drokking interrupting him.

"What?" he said testily.

Meyer indicated the instrument panel in front of her. "The needle on Containment One. Did you just see it move?"

Sighing in undisguised irritation, Burchill laid down the book and looked at the matching instrumentation on his own duty station. There were huge and expensive batteries of delicately calibrated electronic sensor devices trained on the four containment capsules on the other side of the no-go line. Much of it was designed to measure or detect any kind of psi-activity on the part of the four beings imprisoned in those capsules. If Spooky, Creepy, Sparky and Bony were up to anything, it was supposed to register on these instrumentation panels.

Which it never did, because nothing – absolutely nothing at all – of any interest ever happened down here in the Tomb.

"Nothing here," he answered. "You sure you didn't just imagine it?"

Meyer didn't look amused. "Check the log record," she ordered. "You know how the regs work."

Burchill punched up the sensor readings for the last few minutes, giving an unimpressed grunt in response to what he saw. "Okay, so there was a tiny micro-spike on One, forty-three seconds ago, but nothing to get your panties wound up about. Less than point-three of a psi-joule. Despite what the Tek-heads say, you know how random some of this junk is. One of the perps in the cells a hundred levels above has himself a real hot erotic dream one night, and sometimes the instruments down here pick it up. Satisfied?"

"Not yet. You still know what regs say. I need you to do a psi-check."

Now Burchill was getting really irritated. Despite the flippant names he gave them, the four things in those containment cells seriously creeped him out sometimes, and he really hated having to do what he was now required to do.

He sat back in his chair, closed his eyes, doing his best to empty his mind of the usual mental clutter as he brought his psi-abilities into focus. He reached out, overcoming the instinctive mental recoil from the sheer evil power of the things on the other side of the no-go line and, for the briefest possible moment, scanned the psi-activity within the chamber, looking for anything out of the ordinary. He hated doing this. What made it even more unnerving was knowing that Meyer, sitting across from him, had her hand on the grip of her Lawgiver, ready to draw it and put a Standard Execution round through his brainpan at the first sign that he had become possessed or psychically controlled by any of the occupants of the containment units.

After a few moments, he opened his eyes again, seeing Meyer looking at him intently.

"Anything?" she asked, the tension clear in her voice.

"Not a thing," he replied. She stared at him hard for a few moments more – like maybe she's expecting me to start spouting tentacles or levitate into the air with my head spinning round in circles on my shoulders, he asked himself, incredulously? – and then visibly relaxed, bringing her hand up from under the desk where her Lawgiver was secured.

"With these creeps, it's always best to be sure," she said, perhaps by way of partial apology.

"Whatever," grumbled Burchill, going back to his book again.

"A Judge's first weapon is not his Lawgiver or his boot knife or his day-stick," he read. *"It is his Judge badge, and the natural authority it gives him."*

Oh brother, Burchill thought to himself. Old Stony Face might still be Mega-City One's greatest lawman bar none, but when it came to writing, he'd all the slick prose style of the late, great Mayor Dave the orang-utan.

Within his prison, the spirit of Judge Death hissed to itself in silent pleasure. Yes, this one was pleasingly weak, not even aware of Death's growing control over his deep-buried subconscious. He saw only what Death wanted him to see and nothing more.

Death was pleased. Equally pleasurable had been the event he'd just detected from afar. Since the time he had first come to judge the sinners of this place, his fate and that of the psi-witch Anderson had always been intertwined. He still rankled at the memory of his imprisonment within her, trapped by the frightening power of her mind, unable to escape her comatose body, the two of them put on display together in a museum, of all places.

The memory of that first defeat, that first humiliation, still fuelled his hatred against this city and the sinful life that teemed within it. It was this connection between them that had allowed Anderson to defeat him and his brothers several times since, but that connection worked both ways. Just as Anderson could sense him, so too was he sometimes psychically aware of her, even while he was imprisoned down here, weakened and disembodied.

Her aura was like a distant glimmer of light in the darkness of his thoughts, torturing him with the knowledge that she still existed, despite all his attempts over the years to extinguish that light forever.

Now, though, the light was faint, barely perceptible and unusually dim. She was not dead, he sensed, or at least not yet, but her life force had been seriously diminished. Perhaps for good, he hoped.

His servants in the city beyond this place had done well. Anderson was no longer a threat to him and his brethren, which meant that those same servants were now ready to take the final step.

The spirits of his foul companions writhed in psychic restlessness, demanding to know when they would be free.

Soon, brothers, he whispered to them in a voice that only those who had passed beyond life and death could ever know. *Very soon now. I promise.*

* * *

Hershey resisted the urge to yawn. They had almost reached the end of the Council session, which was traditionally Kook Time, when the Council discussed what Hershey secretly called AOOC.

Any Other Outstanding Crap.

Last on the Kook Time agenda was a concern about some new bio-product that had come onto the marketplace a few months ago. Med-Division had given it a clean bill of health and approved the patent, but there had been a number of complaints about it from the citizens. For reasons that Hershey still wasn't quite sure about, no one at Justice Central had been able, or perhaps cared enough, to make a decision about what to do, and so the case had gradually risen up through the hierarchy of the Department until the Council of Five, which regularly debated issues vital to the security and existence of a city of over four hundred million people, found itself now arguing about a novelty medical treatment for raising pet animals from the dead.

Only in the Big Meg, thought Hershey, using a Street Judge's customary dismissive opinion on all the weirdness and craziness that passed for daily life in Mega-City One.

"After the events of Judgement Day, we're aware of many citizens' objections to the idea of a product that brings dead flesh back to life," Hershey said, gesturing towards the computer file compilation of the several tens of thousands of complaints they'd received from the citizens about the EverPet adverts that had been running for weeks on the tri-d networks, "but we have Med-Division's most stringent assurances that the treatment only works on the simpler nervous systems of animals like common household pets, and definitely not on human beings."

"Quite so," nodded the representative from Med-Division. "We went down to Resyk and pulled dozens of corpses off the conveyor belts there and dosed them with increasingly huge quantities of the Pet Regen formula. We got nothing so much as a twitch from any of them. And besides," he added a hint of a smile, "a chemically reanimated cat, budgerigar or goldfish isn't quite in the same league as an army of millions of flesh-eating zombies knocking on the gates of the West Wall."

"My thoughts too," agreed Hershey, glad that the issue looked like it was going to be quickly resolved. "Any other comments?"

"Well, there are the fiscal benefits to consider too," volunteered Accounts Judge Cranston, pouring over the tables of carefully prepared statistics he'd brought with him. "Besides the standard twenty-five per cent sales tax charged on the product, there's also the extra income we'll derive from the necessary re-issuing of new pet licences."

"Meaning what, exactly?" Ramos asked, showing the same kind of impatience as Hershey.

Cranston shuffled through his beloved piles of paperwork. "Well, the cost of a general pet licence is one hundred credits, with some of the more dangerous or alien pet types also requiring an annual additional inspection fee on top of that. In all cases, however, a pet licence becomes legally null and void when the animal dies. If a pet owner then wants to use this product to bring their beloved creature back to life…"

"Then they'll have to buy a new licence," Niles smiled, instantly seeing where Cranston was going. "And the Department in effect will receive double the licence money for the same animal."

"Indeed!" beamed Cranston, making quick-fire calculations on his desktop analyser. "So, with fifteen million, three hundred thousand and twenty-seven pet licences currently issued, and assuming that at least ten to fifteen per cent of pet owners might take advantage of this product, we can probably expect to accrue additional revenues somewhere in the region of…"

Hershey, however, had already heard all she needed or wanted to. "Enough to settle the issue, I imagine. Unless anyone has any other points, we'll assume the Pet Regen product is allowed to remain on sale – for the time being?" She looked around the room, seeing only nods of agreement and gratefully brought the Council meeting to an end for another week."

"Very well, then. If there's no other business to be discussed…"

"Just one item," interrupted a new voice from the other end of the room. All heads turned to see Dredd standing in the council chamber doorway. The Council of Five meetings were supposed to take place in closed session, with no one permitted to enter without the Chief Judge's permission. A guard of armed Judges was posted in the corridor outside, to make sure of this. Dredd, however, was always a special case. There seemed to be an unofficial and unspoken understanding, established many administrations ago, that Dredd had automatic and unrestricted access to the Chief Judge whenever he required it.

When Dredd spoke, Hershey knew from long experience, it paid for Chief Judges to pay attention to what he had to say. She sat back in her chair, signalling for her old street patrol partner to continue.

"What's the official Department policy on vampires?" he asked.

SIX

Anderson struggled and fought against the darkness that surrounded her. She was back in the nightmare world she had seen in her earlier precog vision – only this time it was much, much worse.

She was running through the empty streets of the city again, her feet crunching gruesomely on the carpet of bones that littered the ground. From all around her, she heard the growling and snarling of the vampire creatures. At first she thought they were hunting her, but then she realised they had no interest in her.

There were thousands of them, maybe even tens of thousands. The vampires were flooding through the city streets like a living tide of darkness, converging on one central point. In the distance, Anderson could see their destination: a vast prison tower, forbidding and impenetrable. The teeming creatures threw themselves at its walls, tearing at the seamless stonework with their claw-like hands, gnawing madly at it with their bare fangs. Teeth shattered against dense, unyielding stone. Taloned fingers were shredded down to the bone, but still the creatures persisted in their crazed task.

Their toil and mindless sacrifice finally paid off. A crack appeared in the blood-smeared surface of the wall, then a second. The creatures redoubled their efforts, tearing eagerly at the weakened stonework with a renewed fervour. The cracks widened and vast blocks of masonry tumbled out of place.

There was a scream of hellish triumph from within the breached prison tower, echoed a moment later from the snarling throats of the thousands of creatures gathered around its base. A wave of darkness poured out through the breach, accompanied by the overpowering stench of pent-up decay and corruption.

There were presences within that darkness, the fetid feel of their psychic auras so sickeningly familiar to Anderson. Four voices, so terribly familiar also, hissed in unison: "At lassssst. Now the great work continuessss. Thisss time, there will be no esssscape for thosssse guilty of the ultimate crime – the crime of life!"

The brief but urgent series of beeps from the devices monitoring Anderson's vital signs was enough to bring the med-bay orderly over in a hurry to where the unconscious patient lay on the bed of the speedheal machine. Anderson was out of danger now, but her body still needed time and rest to allow the speedheal procedure to go to work on her injuries, and so she was still under sedation.

The orderly leant in close to study the readings on the monitor beside the bed. She frowned, seeing a sudden momentary spike in the patient's brain activity. That shouldn't be happening, not with the sedatives that had been administered, and under the technology the speedheal machine used to accelerate the body's own healing processes. Still, she thought to herself, Anderson was a Psi-Judge, wasn't she, and who knew what went on in the minds of those frea–

She jumped back suddenly, dropping the tray of instruments she had been carrying, as Anderson's hand snatched out and grabbed her by the wrist.

Anderson's eyes fluttered open, which should have been nearly impossible, considering how much sedation she was under. She locked eyes with the Med-Div auxiliary, her grip tightening on the frightened woman's wrist. Using strength she shouldn't by any rights have at the moment, she pulled the orderly closer, her lips forming half-mumbled, slurred words, every one of them taking a supreme effort of will to get out as she struggled against the black walls of near-unconsciousness that still pressed in on her from every side.

"Nixon Penitentiary... D-Dark Judges... Tell Dredd, warn the Chief Judge... before it's too late."

"Vampires?" asked Hershey doubtfully, looking at the naked corpse of the thing lying on the autopsy slab in front of her.

They were in a forensics lab deep within the Grand Hall of Justice. This was where Dredd had had the remains of the perps from the Bathory Street med-repository attack brought for examination, and whatever the Forensics Teks had found had been enough for him to bring the Chief Judge down here in person.

The corpses of the perps killed by Dredd and Giant were spread out on various autopsy slabs around the large room, with various combined teams of Tek- and Med-Judges working over them. Hershey had received Dredd's verbal report of what happened down there on Bathory, and had heard all about how hard it had been to truly kill any of the perps.

Hi-Ex, Incendiary and rapid-fire had been the order of the day, it seemed. The corpse on the slab in front of her, the top half of its skull clinically removed by a Standard Execution round from Dredd's Lawgiver, was definitely one of the more presentable pieces of evidence that Dredd had given the lab technicians to work with.

"Yes, most assuredly. Not that they seem to be the kind of things that sleep in coffins and have any kind of unlikely aversion to sunlight, garlic or random religious symbols – but they're definitely vampiric in nature," Tek-Judge Helsing beamed, using a forensics tool to proudly show off the most interesting details of the specimen on the slab in front of them. Helsing was a typical forensics Tek, probably more at ease poking through the innards of some horribly mutilated corpse than in talking to real, live people. His complexion was only a ghost of a shade darker than that of the bloodless thing on the autopsy slab, and he looked like he probably spent his every waking moment under the thin, antiseptic light of the windowless forensics labs.

"Look here," he indicated, drawing back the corpse's lips to reveal its unnaturally long and sharp fang teeth. "And here too," he added, lifting up one of the corpse's hands and displaying the long, cruel talons that passed for the fingers there.

"Plenty of Bite Fighters get fancy dental work jobs like that, to give them an advantage in the ring," noted Hershey, "and we've seen the combatants in underground bash'n'slash fights coming back from the Hong Tong chop shops with surgically altered hand weaponry just like that."

"These aren't surgical alterations," said Helsing. "They're the result of some kind of massively accelerated bio-evolutionary change."

"Mutants, then?"

"Of a sort, but these things didn't evolve naturally. They were deliberately created. Probably as recently as a few short months ago, they were still ordinary human beings."

"And now?"

"Bio-engineered vampiric creatures, their body chemistry altered to an extreme degree by massive infusions of a gene-reprogramming retrovirus. Their systems are saturated with the stuff, although unfortunately we haven't been quite able to identify it yet."

"What are its effects?" Hershey asked, staring in mild disgust at the thing on the slab. In twenty years on the streets, she had seen countless thousands of dead bodies, had attended Grud-knows-how-many forensics examinations like this, but there was something uniquely disquieting about the corpse in front of her.

"Unnaturally high levels of strength, almost superhuman resistance to physical injury–"

"Giant and I can vouch for that," grunted Dredd.

"So that the only way to put them down for sure is to inflict massive physical trauma to their central nervous systems," Helsing concluded.

"Blow them up, set them on fire or just shoot 'em through the brain," commented Dredd. "It worked during Judgement Day and it works with these creeps too."

"So far I'm only wondering why we aren't pumping our personnel full of the same stuff," quipped Hershey. "I assume there's some drawback to it."

"Alterations in brain chemistry probably cause violent psychosis and, in the long term, true death or complete derangement, but the main immediate and adverse side-effect is this–"

Helsing deftly slit open the arteries of the creature's wrist, and pressed down with his fingers. Hershey wrinkled her nose in distaste as a milky and pale pink liquid wept out of the wound.

"The retrovirus consumes the haemoglobin in the body's blood supply at a quite astonishing rate. Combined with the psychotic effects, anyone infected with the retrovirus will be consumed by an overpowering need to find fresh supplies of haemoglobin to keep the virus's long-term side-effects in check."

"Blood thirst," noted Dredd dryly. "Now we know why these creeps were raiding a blood bank."

"You said a *retrovirus*," said Hershey, picking up on the unpleasant implications of what she was hearing. "These creatures can kill by biting their victims, and traditionally the victims of vampires are supposed to rise from the dead and become vampires themselves. What are the chances the victims of these things might become infected by the virus too, and turn into yet more vampires?"

"We've already thought of that," Helsing smiled cadaverously. "The bodies of the victims from the Bathory Street massacre are being transferred over from Resyk. We'll give them full tests for any signs that they might be infected with the retrovirus."

Hershey nodded in approval. After Judgement Day, another outbreak of the dead coming to life and attacking the living was the last thing the city needed.

Or almost the last thing, she thought to herself, remembering the news that had come in about Anderson shortly after the Council of Five meeting had broken up. The implications of that weren't too thrilling either, not with her best Psi-Judge unconscious in a med-bay when trouble relating to the Dark Judges was maybe on the agenda again.

"And we're sure that these were the same things that attacked Anderson?" she asked Helsing.

"The report from the clean-up crew at the attack scene indicates they might be," answered the forensics specialist, "but the ones in the truck are too badly burned to do anything with. There's one specimen on its way here. I'll get to work on it as soon as it arrives."

"The clean-up crew say the thing they scraped up had fangs and had taken enough damage to kill maybe a dozen Kleggs," pointed out Dredd, with his customary impatience. He gestured to the half-dozen charred and exploded corpses in the room around them. "Sound familiar? We know now why the creeps Giant and I met were robbing a blood blank. Big question is: why were they so keen to see Anderson dead?"

The question was a troubling one, the possible answers to it even more so, thought Hershey. "Something she knew? You think this is all connected to that precog vision she had?"

"Too much of a coincidence to be anything else," said Dredd with trademark certainty. "Anderson gets a psi-flash of a possible supernatural threat to the city. Next thing we know, she's been jumped by a bunch of wannabe freaks from an old cheapo-horror vid-slug."

He gestured at the thing on the slab. "These things didn't fly over the West Wall on bat wings. Someone created them. So: who, and why?" He looked at Helsing. "We got an ID on any of them?"

"Not yet," conceded the Tek-Judge unhappily. "The massive genetic changes caused by the retrovirus have so far made identification by DNA match impossible, and the physical changes to their facial features and hands is making slow work of any attempt to identify them by normal fingerprinting or photofit ID methods. If they're on the citizens register, we'll find out who they are eventually, but it'll take time."

Hershey considered what they had so far, and wasn't pleased with the answer she came up with. "What we really need is more information, and fast. As soon as Anderson's conscious, I want–"

As if on cue, Dredd's helmet radio crackled into life.

"Dredd – Med-Judge Caley, head of Med-Div operations, Sector House 42. Got a message for you from Psi-Judge Anderson. She says you've got to get down to Nixon Penitentiary fast. She says the Church of Death and some bunch of vampire creeps are about to try and bust out the Dark Judges!"

Dredd and Hershey looked at each other in alarm. It was Hershey who replied to the voice on the radio: "Anderson's conscious? How does she know this? Why isn't she reporting this to us herself?"

Over in the Sector House 42 med-unit, Caley blanched as he recognised the voice now interrogating him over the radio link. Talking to

Dredd made him nervous enough, but now he had the Chief Judge on his back too.

Unhappily, he glanced over at the now-empty bed of the speedheal machine.

"That's just it, Chief Judge. Anderson's gone. None of us could stop her. She just got up and took out of here running, just a few minutes ago!"

Anderson exited the turbo-lift, still jogging. Her barely healed leg, the one that had been badly broken only a few hours ago, hurt like hell. So did her ribs. But only every time she took a breath, she reminded herself with a smile.

In fact, most of her still hurt like hell. She stuck a few more stim-tabs into her mouth from the bottle she'd grabbed on her way out the med-bay. They took the edge off the pain, and allowed her to overcome the effects of the sedatives that had been pumped into her, but mostly she was running on pure psi-fuelled adrenaline. Properly trained Psi-Judges could turn their psi-ability in on themselves, using it to push their body often well beyond normal human endurance limits. It wasn't recommended, though. The comedown, when their reserves of psi-power finally ran dry, could be brutal, sometimes even lethal.

Anderson figured that was a problem she was just going to have to deal with when it came. Of course, considering what it was she was just about to do, and who she was just about to go up against, she might be dead long before then.

That's it, Cass, she reminded herself. Just keep looking on the bright side of everything.

She arrived at the Sector House's motor pool level, sprinting across a maintenance bay towards a line of parked Lawmasters. The instrument panels of several of them showed a green light on their status panels. All systems running, and engine refuelled and ready to go. Better still, they all had scatter guns locked into place too, which was a relief, since she had lost her Lawgiver back there on Joey Ramone and hadn't had any time after her escape from the med-level to stop by the sector house armoury and pick up – you mean "steal", Cass, she reminded herself ruefully – a replacement for it.

She jumped onto the nearest of the bikes, slipping her Department-issue ID card into the slot and punching in her personal recognition code. The bike computer screen blinked into life in acknowledgement.

"Hey! You can't just take one of those," shouted a Tek-Judge, running towards her from the motor pool admin office. "I need to see something from the Watch Commander before I can let you ride that outta here!"

"Anderson, Psi-Division!" she told him, waving her badge at him. "Sorry, friend, but the paperwork's going to have to wait for another time."

What the hell, she thought to herself. I've only broken about half a dozen Department regs in the last few minutes. Stealing a Lawmaster is just adding one more to the list.

The Tek-Judge's protests were drowned out in the powerful roar of the Lawmaster engine as Anderson gunned the thing into life and headed at speed out of the motor pool.

A few seconds later, she was out of the Sector House and lost amongst the seemingly never-ending flow of the city's traffic. She looked around her, getting her bearings. She was on Megway 126, heading east towards the core sectors of MegEast. If she stayed on this route, it would eventually take her to Sector 57, where Nixon Penitentiary was located.

On the other hand, the turn-off for the McFly Spiral was just coming up, which would take her to the Black Atlantic dockside sectors.

Much closer, she thought to herself. 57 was way too far away, and she'd never get there in time. Dredd would have to deal with whatever was about to happen at Nixon Pen without her. In the meantime, she had urgent business down at the docks.

She hit the accelerator controls, abruptly changing lanes and taking the turn-off for McFly. She realised then that she still had her uniform tunic and utility belt gripped in her hand. She would just have to finish getting dressed on her way to the docks, at least it would give the citizens some unexpected entertainment.

After all, it probably wasn't every day they saw a half-dressed Psi-Judge struggling to put on the rest of her uniform while riding a Lawmaster at high speed along the megway.

SEVEN

Being an iso-cube guard sure could be boring, Judge-Warden Kiernan grumbled to himself. Nixon Penitentiary was a maximum-security facility, maybe the most impregnable iso-block in the entire city. Some of the most dangerous perps on the Justice Department's files were kept under lock and key here, and that wasn't even counting the four... things they had locked away down in the basement, he reminded himself. But it still didn't make guard duty here nearly as interesting or exciting as it maybe sounded.

Mostly, his duties involved patrolling the prison building's eighty levels of iso-cubes, or closely monitoring the prisoners' activities during the few hours a day they were actually allowed out of their iso-cube cells. Over fifteen thousand perps were held here, with several hundred arriving or being released every day, and Kiernan reckoned he'd seen just about every kind of perp there was, everything from the ordinary cit doing a six-month stretch for Jaywalking, Littering or Slow Driving, to the hardened lifers who were never going to see the outside world again: the Mega-Mob blitzers, responsible for dozens of gangland hits and carrying sentences totalling hundreds of years; the Judge killers, whose crime carried an automatic life sentence in a justice system where life imprisonment meant exactly what it sounded like; the juve gang thrillkillers, who would spend most of the rest of their young lives in here in payment for those few hours of murder-spree fun.

You name it, thought Kiernan, if there's a law against it, then there was someone in Nixon Pen who had been locked up for doing it.

And then there were the four monsters in the basement, but no one really liked to talk or even think about them. As dull as iso-block guard duty sometimes was, Kiernan would much rather be dealing with all the freaks, psychos and stone-cold killers in the main population levels than the creepshow inhabitants of the Tomb.

Kiernan shivered involuntarily. Sometimes he swore he could sense the vibes from that place, feel them creeping up from deep underground below the prison, subtly affecting the minds of everyone inside it. Psi-Div said that was impossible, that the prisoners in the Tomb were under full containment and that there was no possible chance of any psi-radiation leakage, but Kiernan and the rest of the Judge-Wardens in the Pen weren't so convinced. Vividly macabre nightmares were a frequent complaint amongst both guards and inmates and even for a max-security facility holding so many dangerous perps the Pen had much more than its fair share of fights and violent disturbances among the prisoners.

Everyone's on edge round here, thought Kiernan. It's this place, and it's not just the creeps in the cubes who want to get out of here.

His radio buzzed. "Thinking about that transfer to a West Wall guard duty assignment again?" laughed the voice of Sprange, his partner on this duty shift. "Mutie raids, rad-storms blowing in from the Cursed Earth, dodging the falling crap from low-flying dog-vultures? You don't seriously think any of that is better than this?"

Kiernan laughed in return, and looked over to where his opposite number was stationed. The two of them were on the prison's H-wagon rooftop landing pad, manning the two gun turrets positioned there to defend the facility from aerial attack. The airspace around Nixon Pen was restricted, strictly forbidden to civilian traffic, and the only flyers that came near the place were Justice Department H-wagon transports, delivering high-risk category prisoners who were too dangerous to be conveyed by ordinary catcH-wagon road vehicles.

As guard duties went, this was one of the dullest, but at least it got you outside.

"Hey, at least on the West Wall, your job's to stop creeps breaking in. All we do here is–" began Kiernan, only to be cut off by Sprange's alert-sounding tone.

"Hold it, Solly. You picking this up?"

Kiernan glanced at the scanner screen in his turret console, and looked up into the darkening evening sky for confirmation of what the scanner showed him.

"Check. A hov-transporter, a big one judging by the scanner readings, inbound our way. We expecting any more perp deliveries tonight?"

"Not according to what I know. Hold on, I'll check with Control. Those muncheads in Perp Transfer are always doing this to us. You ask me, they're the ones who should be finding out what it's like to go on West Wall duty, not chumps like you."

Kiernan waited, watching the hov-transporter coming towards them. It was in restricted air-space now, and this was just about the point when it should be hitting its retro-jets to slow down to land while signalling in to them with the correct recog-code.

It was doing none of these things. Instead, if anything, it seemed to be increasing its speed. And so were the two identical craft coming in right behind it, on the same approach course.

"They're not Justice Department flyers, and they're not responding to hails!" warned Sprange, bringing his turret round to bear.

Kiernan fumbled to do likewise, losing precious seconds as he got the unlock code wrong on his weapon's auto-targeter. By the time he had got his weapon activated it was too late. He looked up in horror as the first hov-transporter came straight at him. Whoever was in the cockpit must be some kind of madman, Kiernan realised, because the pilot wasn't even trying to bring it in on retro-jets; instead, he was simply going to crash-land the transporter on the roof. Kiernan's last act was to press the firing controls on his turret weapon, sending a long line of explosive shells into the nose of the lumbering hov-transporter, raking the cockpit and blowing apart anyone seated there.

It didn't matter, just as Kiernan had already sickly realised. Gravity and the vehicle's own momentum would finish what the pilot had started.

The transporter hit the roof of the prison in a shower of sparks and screeching metal, belly-flopping right across the wide area of the landing pad and smashing into Kiernan's turret, ripping it right off its mountings and hurling it over the far edge of the roof.

Sprange, in the other turret, fared better, at least for a while. He concentrated his fire on the second flyer coming in, riddling its cargo compartment with armour-piercing shells and destroying a power-feed to the underbelly grav-lifters. Stricken, the transporter dropped out of the sky on a downwards trajectory that ended with it pile-driving itself into the body of the iso-block some thirty levels below. Amazingly, many of those creatures inside the transporter would survive the impact. Unfortunately, the more human occupants of the hundreds of iso-cubes on those levels would not, and many were crushed or burned to death as the transporter's engines drove it deep into the structure of the building.

Alarms were going off all over the building. Up on the roof level, the third transporter was coming in to make the same kind of makeshift landing as the first. Sprange concentrated his fire on it, aiming for the engines and trying to cripple or destroy it before it could land. He was still firing when he noticed the dark figures streaming out of the wreck of the first craft down. He didn't know who these freaks were or why they were attacking a heavily defended maximum-security iso-block, but he was just about to show them what a dumb proposition that was.

He spun the gun turret round towards them, bringing his targeting scope to bear and switching the fire selector on both guns to rapid-fire wide dispersal. These babies could cut up armoured steel like it was synthi-cheese, and Sprange couldn't wait to show these chumps what they could do to a packed mass of human bodies.

Before he could fire, however, the door behind him was wrenched off its hinges and dozens of clawed hands reached in to violently pull him out of the gun turret. He was borne aloft into the midst of the baying pack of creatures there, screaming as he realised what was about to happen to him.

The monstrosities descended on him eagerly, claws and teeth hungrily tearing into his flesh. They had been waiting a long time for this. The serum the master provided staved off the worst of the blood thirst that consumed them, but it was nothing in comparison to a taste of the real thing.

"Rocking Jovus, what was that?!"

Mayer and Burchill had felt the impact of the transporter crashing into the iso-block, although this deep underground it had registered as little more than a faint rumbling tremor. Even that, however, had been more than enough to break the eerie, perpetual calm of the Tomb.

Seconds later, alarm lights started flashing on their consoles. Mayer flicked switches on her comms board, trying to raise someone in the prison levels above to find out what was going on, but no one seemed in too much of a hurry to answer. She flicked through channels, getting back only static in answer to her calls. Finally, she found an open frequency – someone's helmet radio was broadcasting, even if they themselves weren't talking – and she could pick out identifiable sounds. What she heard didn't exactly thrill her.

It was gunfire, and the frantic sounds of human panic.

She drew her Lawgiver. "Stay alert," she told Burchill, "I think there's some sort of prison riot going on above."

She locked her gaze on the thickly armoured slab of the sealed elevator door, the only means in or out of the Tomb. You needed about ten different security codes to even begin to think about getting into that thing up there on the surface, never mind starting it up and using it to come down here. As added security backup, every metre of the elevator shaft was monitored, and anyone trying to climb down it surreptitiously would trip a dozen or more alarms and run into a seriously nasty surprise at a point about halfway down, where the hidden robot sentry guns were located.

"Stay alert," she repeated again to Burchill. "Until we know what's happening up there, we assume anything coming out of that elevator is going to be bad news."

Burchill barely heard her. The Psi-Judge's attention was fixed on the four containment cubes on the other side of the line, and he stared at them in unnatural concentration... as he listened to the voices whispering inside his head.

The recently deceased Judge-Warden Kiernan would have been very unhappy if he could see the events unfolding throughout Nixon Penitentiary at the moment. However else you might want to describe it – chaotic, gruesome, a murderous bloodbath – you certainly couldn't describe it as being boring.

Senior Judge-Warden Scholker and his riot squad, en route to the rooftop H-wagon landing pad, would be the first to agree with that. As far as Scholker was concerned, all hell seemed to be breaking loose inside his beloved Nixon Penitentiary. Some kind of large flying vehicle had crashed into the iso-block, causing several fires and major casualties on levels 54 to 57. The impact and subsequent fires had also damaged the security systems in the prison, and Scholker was getting confusing reports about armed perps being loose on some of those floors, although where these perps came from, no one could yet figure out, since they didn't seem to be inmates. He had been on his way to the section affected by the crash, with the firm intention of busting heads and restoring order, when he got the call to head to the roof level instead. The turret crews there had reported engaging incoming aerial targets, but nothing had been heard from the Judge-Wardens on duty up there since.

Scholker fumed in impatience and tightened his grip on the stock of his scatter gun as he watched the level numbers tick past on the elevator control panel display. No creep was going to get away with mounting a mass break-out attempt – if that was really what they were dealing with here – on Nixon Pen. Especially not on his shift.

"Get ready," he growled to his squad. "Whoever's up there, we'll give 'em–"

That was all he said, before the doors rumbled open and the tide of vampire creatures that had been waiting for the elevator's arrival swept in at them with a howl of ecstatic glee. Scholker's finger couldn't even close on the trigger of the scatter gun before a vampire ripped his throat out with one sweep of its claws.

With Scholker and his squad obligingly bringing the large transport elevator up to where they were lying in wait, the vampires now had a means of entry down into the rest of the iso-block. They swept into the place, more than two hundred of them, shrugging off Lawgiver bullets and scatter gun shots, killing everything in their path. Some, overcome by blood-thirst and the temptation of having so much prey trapped helplessly all around them, broke into cube after cube, feeding on the defenceless and terrified inmates they found inside. Most of them, though, retained sufficient self-control and presence of mind to follow out their master's instructions.

Guard points were overwhelmed, control rooms seized, security systems destroyed or sabotaged. As they were slaughtering their way down through the levels of the prison, those vampires, which had been aboard the second hov-transporter and had survived its crashing impact into the building, were doing likewise.

In a way, Sprange had done the Church of Death a big favour. Starting from the levels where the transporter had hit the building, they were able to reach the iso-block's main control centre on level 45 far quicker than had been anticipated. After breaking into the place and killing the command staff there, they were able to bypass the security codes and open every iso-cube door in the prison at a point far earlier than had been expected, way back when this crippling attack had first been planned.

Sherman "Sharkey" McCann didn't like being locked up. In truth, he didn't like most things, but most of all he didn't like Judges, which was why he had kept killing them. He'd killed six of them – although a couple of them had been those wannabe Judges who drove the catch wagons and did all the cleaning up after the real Judges had finished doing their law stuff, so Sharkey wasn't too sure if they really counted – before the drokkers caught up with him.

Sharkey hadn't liked getting caught, and had liked being shot even less. He'd taken three Lawgiver shots, one in the arm and two through the chest, and the Med-Judges had fitted him out with a crappy paper lung after one of those shots in his chest had royally messed up one of the perfectly good human lungs he'd had all his life. Still, Sharkey took quiet pleasure in the fact that the Judges hadn't been able to kill him, not even with three Lawgiver slugs. Better still, it had been Dredd himself that had pulled the trigger on those shots. Sharkey knew that the rest of the Judges were secretly afraid of him, 'cause otherwise why would they have had to call in their top lawdog to bring him in?

Yeah, he took three shots from Dredd, and he still wouldn't lie down and die for them.

Not that Sharkey liked Dredd much either. Dredd had shot him. It was because of Dredd that he was in here, with this crappy paper lung that didn't work properly, that gave Sharkey a pain in his chest every time he took a breath, never mind what the Med-Judges said about the pain all being in his head. Sharkey knew the pain was real, and every time he took a breath and felt it cutting into him, it made him think of Dredd.

Oh man, but there was one lawdog Sharkey would like to add to his score. He fragged Dredd, and he knew he wouldn't ever hear any more sniggering behind his back from the other cons about how he wasn't really such a big, bad Judge-killer 'cause some of the badges he scragged weren't real Judges.

This was what Sharkey was thinking, and wasn't really that much different from what Sharkey was normally thinking, when the hov-transporter had hit the iso-block about ten levels above where his cell was. Sharkey's cube didn't have a window – like everyone knew, only narks or rich creeps who could bribe the Judge-Wardens got cubes with windows – so he didn't see the rain of burning wreckage from the crash tumbling down the outside of the building. But he sure felt the impact and he sure heard every gruddamned alarm in the place going off right afterwards.

After that there had been a lot of screaming and shouting, and then a heap of gunshots, and then just a whole lot more screaming. Looking out of the tiny aperture in his cube door, Sharkey hadn't been able to see or figure out much of what was supposed to be going on, even if he did fleetingly see some freak in a Halloween monster mask run down the corridor outside, which just didn't make much sense at all to Sharkey.

It was a little while after then that there was a familiar-sounding clunking noise, and Sharkey's cube door swung open. Sharkey stepped forward and peered cautiously out into the corridor. It turned out that Sharkey's wasn't the only cube door to have been opened, 'cause there was everyone else in the corridor standing there and peering out just like Sharkey was.

Best of all, the only guard in sight was the dead one slumped against the wall at the end of the corridor. Sharkey moved fast, getting to the Judge stiff before anyone else and helping himself to whatever he had.

Sharkey knew enough to leave the stiff's Lawgiver in its holster – try pulling the trigger on that sweet little package and you can kiss your flipper goodbye – but he was happy to help himself to the scatter gun.

Satisfying himself that the weapon was in working order – Grud, but it felt good to have a gun in his hand again after all these years – Sharkey looked up, seeing the faces of his crew looking expectantly at him. Some of the other cons, the ordinary Joe cits doing the kind of joke cube-time that you counted in months instead of years or even decades, stayed in their cubes, too afraid of what was happening, but Sharkey's crew knew what the score was.

"Find some more weapons," he told them. "We're gonna bust our way outta here and maybe have some fun while we're doing it."

"There's serious trouble at Nixon Pen. Let's roll!"

The message crackled through the helmet radios of more than eighty Judges, all of them mounted on Lawmasters and heading at speed out of Sector House 57. The call had come in only a few minutes ago. Nixon Penitentiary was under attack, and every Street Judge in the sector house had been scrambled in response. Off-duty Judges were rudely roused out of dorms or sleep machines, Judges who had just come in from an eight-hour duty shift immediately got ready to hit the streets again. Emergency response units were being pulled in from other sectors, and more units from their own sector house – pat wagon crews, riot squad teams, even sector house admin and auxiliary staff to plug the holes in the ranks of the Street Judges – would follow them up soon enough, but these would be the first Judges to arrive at the scene and bring the situation at Nixon Pen back under control.

They were travelling along Minnie Driver Megway towards the prison, bike sirens blaring en masse, when the ambush happened.

A juggernaut-transporter jackknifed on the road ahead of them, over-turning and completely blocking the road, crushing half a dozen other vehicles and their occupants in the process. At the same time, ten or more roadsters travelling along behind the Judge convoy suddenly skidded to a halt, blocking off the road behind the Judges and cutting off their escape. Hidden snipers on the block plazas and pedways on either side of the road opened fire at the Judges below. Seconds later, their comrades at the road-blocks in front of and behind the Judges joined in too.

Corralled in, the Judges took cover behind their Lawmasters, return-ing fire at targets whenever they presented themselves. It didn't take them long to identify their attackers; their coloured robes and the way in which they fought with almost suicidal abandon soon gave the game away.

"Death cultists!" shouted a senior Judge, picking off a black-cloaked, skull-tattooed sniper perched on top of a Sump Industries advertising billboard overlooking the roadway. "And if it's death these freaks are looking for, then today's their lucky day!"

"It's happening everywhere, Dredd. We're getting reports of attacks and violent disturbances involving Church of Death cultists all across the board!"

Dredd studied the tactical display on the H-wagon's control console. A pattern quickly appeared to him.

"They're centred around Sector 57, and Nixon Pen. Every incident is either designed to cut off one of the main routes to Nixon or tie up units that would otherwise be sent to deal with the trouble there."

"That's a roj," said Hershey's voice over the radio link. "These Death cult kooks are coming out of the woodwork everywhere. They're doing everything they can to keep us away from Nixon Pen. There's thousands of them, but at the rate we're mopping them up, they'll all be either in the cubes or on their way to Resyk by the end of the night."

"If we don't get more units into Nixon fast, the whole city might be following those creeps along the Resyk conveyor belts," Dredd said grimly.

He'd commandeered the fastest H-wagon available at the Grand Hall of Justice as soon as Anderson's warning had reached him, but it had barely even taken off before the news of the attack on the prison had come through. Anderson's warning had been passed on too late, and the Death cultists had already made their move. It was minutes after that, as the H-wagon sped across the sky, that the first reports started coming in about the other Death cult attacks.

Like Hershey said, the Church was coming out of the woodwork, throwing everything they had into slowing the Judges down. Small groups of heavily armed Death cultist commandoes were on the loose in several sectors adjacent to 57. A human wave of unarmed, chanting cult members had blocked off Bachman-Turner Oversked, cutting off yet another approach to Nixon Pen. Lone cultists were going on killing sprees in crowded plazas and ped-precincts, and a report had just come in that a Death cult suicide bomber had detonated herself in the lobby of Sector House 58. Several block wars had suddenly flared up – the ever-feuding Minogue twin conapts had been the first, eagerly renewing simmering hostilities once more – and it seemed too much of a coincidence for the Death cult's involvement not to be suspected.

Dredd had intended to rendezvous at Nixon Pen with the local Judge units already at the scene there and then take command of the operation to restore order in the prison. At the moment, with roads blocked off and most of the available reinforcements tied up in dealing with the Death cult attacks, he was going to be the first unit to reach the place. He needed more Judges, and he needed them now. He activated his helmet radio.

"Giant – Dredd. Where are you?"

"About twenty minutes behind you," came the reply, "with four H-wagons' worth of riot squad units and a couple of heavy weapons teams. There's another ten wagons of the same taking off now, about another ten minutes behind me. We'll rendezvous with you at Nixon Pen, and–"

"No time," growled Dredd. "These Death cult creeps are trying to bust out the Dark Judges. The whole city's at risk."

Dredd could see Nixon Pen through the H-wagon's cockpit window; a dark, forbidding-looking tower standing starkly against the illuminated backdrop of the city's spectacular skyline. Part of the building was burning, and even from this distance Dredd felt a sense of the chaos that had suddenly enveloped the place. Grud only knows how bad it was inside.

He signalled for the H-wagon pilot to begin his approach. "I'm going in on my own right now," he told Giant. "I'll meet you inside."

Two minutes later, the H-wagon touched down briefly on an emergency landing platform on the side of the prison building, then at Dredd's signal took off almost immediately afterwards. There were probably hundreds, if not thousands, of escaped and dangerous perps on the loose inside the prison, and Dredd had no intention of leaving an H-wagon sitting there on the landing pad for any of them to try to seize and make their aerial escape in.

Dredd was left standing alone on the landing pad, with the door into the main prison levels in front of him. He deactivated its coded locking mechanism with his override card, drew his Lawgiver and stepped into hell.

EIGHT

The Hi-Ex shot caught the vampire in the midsection, blowing it and the one next to it apart in the same single, bloody blast. The third creature leapt over their smoking remains, fangs bared in anger.

"Hungry, creep?" Dredd asked it. "So chew on this!"

He fed his Kevlar-reinforced fist into the creature's mouth, feeling its fangs break against the armoured material of his Judge glove. Two Law-giver shots into its chest gave it something more to howl about. Dredd knew the shots wouldn't kill it, but they would keep it distracted for a few more seconds – and a few more seconds was all he needed.

Grabbing it by the shoulders, he hurled it backwards, smashing its head into the cell door opposite and then, before the creature could recover, he propelled it in the other direction across the narrow corridor, throwing it through the broken doors there and into the elevator shaft that dropped through fifty levels of this section of the iso-block building.

The vampire fell, uselessly flailing its limbs and howling in equally useless fury. Dredd didn't know if the fall would kill it – as he had been finding out ever since the battle at the Bathory med-repository, these creeps took a lot of killing – but he was fairly sure he wouldn't be see-ing that particular example again in a hurry.

He continued on, following the route down to the next level. Power to the elevators and grav-tubes was gone, possibly as a built-in security measure when the alarms had first gone off, possibly as a result of dam-age done to the building's power supply either by the impact of the crash or sabotage by the rioting prisoners. Either way, the only way down through the building was on foot.

Dredd was heading for level 10, where the elevator entrance to the Tomb level was located. So far, he'd managed to fight his way down through twenty-six, with another twelve still to go. His combat responses had fallen into a pattern on the way down through those twenty-six levels.

Vampires got Standard Execution rounds to the head, or Hi-Ex or Incendiary shot special deliveries. Any armed perps he came across – and there were thousands of them loose within the prison – and who were dumb enough to get in his way got the Standard Execution treatment, no more questions asked. Everyone else got a single warning and, if that didn't work, they got a brief but efficient first-hand demonstration of Dredd's unarmed combat ability and renowned daystick head-busting skills.

It was a crude but effective system, designed to get him to where he wanted to go with the minimum of delay and using the minimum of ammunition. Even so, in the twenty-six levels he'd covered so far, he'd still managed to go through four whole Lawgiver magazines, and his supply of Hi-Ex and Incendiary shells was now at a premium.

At the moment, nothing else mattered other than getting to that express elevator to the Tomb, and Dredd was forced to press on, going against his every instinct by ignoring all the other law-breaking going on in the prison around him. If the Dark Judges escaped, the chaos happening now in Nixon Pen would be as nought compared to what could result across the entirety of Mega-City One.

Giant would be touching down with his riot squad reinforcements soon enough. Dredd had been in constant radio communication with him, giving him updates on his progress so far. Thanks to Dredd, when Giant and his squads stormed into the place, they would already know where the worst trouble spots were, and where to apply the most force to swiftly bring order back to the prison.

He found the stairs from the level below and was down them in seconds, applying his daystick to the two shiv-armed escaped perps who stepped out of the shadows halfway down, demanding that he first pay the "entrance toll" to the next level. Dredd left them where they fell, unconscious and bleeding.

"Giant – Dredd. Two more for you, level 22, bottom of Stair B. Attempted Assault on a Judge: five years apiece onto their sentences, on top of the general counts for Rioting and Attempted Iso-Cube Escape."

Level 22. Twelve more levels to go.

Level 19.

Turning a corner, he ran into a mob of fifty or more escaped perps, all of them armed with a variety of makeshift weapons, all of them doing their best to slaughter each other. Freed from their cubes, and with no sign of any living Judge-Wardens, the prisoners had so far been at liberty to pursue their own violent agendas. Many of them, like the fifty creeps here, were using the opportunity to reignite some ancient gang feuds.

Dredd didn't have time to deal with a distraction like this. A precious Hi-Ex shot into the ceiling stopped the fighting and grabbed their attention. Two more Standard Execution rounds into the heart of a perp – probably one of the gang leaders – who tried to fire a stolen scatter gun at him grabbed their attention even further.

Fifty pairs of hostile eyes regarded him with sullen hatred, fifty hands grasped the handles of makeshift clubs or shivs, fifty minds imagined how good it would feel to bring those clubs down hard on that helmet or bury those shivs hilt-deep into that chest. Dredd coolly stared down every one of them, daring any of them to make their move. Not one did.

"Lay down your weapons and return to your cubes," Dredd commanded, bringing his full, natural authority to bear in what could almost have been a textbook moment straight out of his own Comportment. "Wait there – and don't even think about leaving them again. Judges will be here soon enough to deal with all of you."

"Drokk that!" shouted some big creep who had stripped off to the waist, his filed teeth and scar-crossed skin marking him out as a former bite-fighter. It was time for the classic equation. "There's one of him, and–"

He never got to finish it. Dredd's Lawgiver sounded once and the perp hit the floor, a Standard Execution round drilled through the centre of his forehead.

The other creeps took the hint. By the time Dredd reached the end of the corridor, there wasn't one of them left in sight.

Level 16.

"Giant – Dredd. Make sure someone picks up the four creeps in the Level 16 med-bay. Life sentences all round – murder of a Med-Judge. Any problems finding them, just look for the four perps with my Lawgiver slugs in each of their kneecaps."

Level 15. He was getting close now, and running into more vampires along the way. Some of them were sluggish and bloated from feeding on the plentiful supply of unwilling blood donors they had found in the iso-cubes around them. Some of them weren't, but sluggish or still hungry, they all went the same way.

By the time he found the way down to the next level, he had taken care of another eight vampires, at the cost of most of another Lawgiver mag and an extra minute's delay. It was time Dredd knew he didn't have to spare.

* * *

"Gruddamnit, what's keeping them up there?" cursed Mayer, frustrated at her attempts to raise anyone on her console radio. "Why isn't there anyone there to tell us what's happening?"

"Yessss. Do it now."

The sound came from behind her. It was Burchill's voice, but at the same time it wasn't. Mayer spun round, seeing Burchill standing right in front of the no-go line and staring in what she could only describe as mesmerised adoration at the things imprisoned on the other side of it.

Being chosen for Tomb duty meant that she was no shrinking violet, and was more than capable of taking the kind of swift and cold-blooded decisions necessary for keeping the four most dangerous beings in Mega-City One safely under lock and key. She didn't hesitate, snatching for the Lawgiver stored in the specially built holster under her console desk. She had seen Burchill's combat scores, and knew that she was both quicker on the draw and a better shot.

She shot him four times, just as he drew his own Lawgiver, hitting him three times in the stomach and once in the chest. Each time she hit him, his body jerked weirdly, as if it was suspended on strings.

Also like a puppet on strings, it refused to fall down, no matter how hard it was struck.

Burchill continued moving as the bullets pummelled into him, drawing his own Lawgiver with a horrible, awkward slowness, a gruesome rictus grin fixed on his face which only seemed to grow wider as each bullet tore through him.

Finally he raised it to face her and returned fire, even as Mayer's fifth shot hit him in the throat in what should have been an instantly lethal wound. His own shot took her through a lung. She dropped to the floor, coughing blood.

She heard his weird, shuffling footsteps coming towards her across the room, heard the blood from the four or five fatal wounds she had inflicted on him pumping out of him and splashing onto the ground. She stretched out to reach for her Lawgiver, almost managing it before his boot came down hard on her fingers, breaking them all.

She sobbed in pain as he reached down to grab her under the arms, dragging her roughly across the room. She tried to struggle, but could not. She tried to call out, maybe hoping desperately to be able to reason with whatever remnant of Burchill remained in the thing that had hold of her now, but all that emerged was a choked and bloody cough.

She groaned again as he took even firmer hold of her, lifting her bodily up with a strength that he simply shouldn't have had. She saw where they were now, right at the edge of the no-go line, saw the four things in the crystalline containment cubes looking at her as their possessed servant displayed her to them, almost as some kind of offering. She felt herself being lifted up higher, suspended high above Burchill's head – and suddenly she knew what was about to happen to her.

He threw her. She suddenly found her voice again and screamed, although the sound was abruptly cut off a moment later amidst the hissing chatter of the sentry lasers as her hurled body sailed across the no-go line and was instantly cut apart in the bright tangle of laser fire.

The alarms had started going off as soon as the hidden sensors in the room had registered the sound of Lawgiver shots. A whole chorus of further, more strident ones went off now, as Burchill's body jerked round to open fire at the two control consoles, riddling them with rapid-fire Standard Execution rounds. Hi-Ex rounds unerringly found both the sentry gun sensors and then the hidden guns themselves.

Now that it was safe to do so, Burchill stepped forward to stand before his masters and do the final things necessary to release them. The alarms kept ringing, both in the Tomb and in the prison above, but Burchill knew that there was no one left up there to hear them.

Level 12. Almost there.

The bloodsuckers had been through this level like an impossibly virulent plague, and many of the corridors were choked with the corpses of their victims. Dredd heard screams from an open iso-cube door ahead. Approaching it at a run, he glimpsed in and saw a prisoner being attacked by one of the vampire creatures, the vampire pinning down its victim and biting bloody chunks out of his neck and shoulders.

Dredd raised his Lawgiver and shot the creature through the back of the skull as he ran past, never even breaking stride. The victim was still, weakened by shock and blood loss, and looked in a bad way. Dredd didn't know who he was or what his crimes were, but even as an iso-block inmate he was due the same cold, dispassionate mercy accorded to every citizen of Mega-City One.

"Giant – Dredd. Vamp victim in urgent need of med-treatment, Cube 47, Level 12. If he's still alive when you get to him, put him into med-unit quarantine until we find out what effects there might be from a bite from these things. Same goes with any other vamp victims you find."

Sharkey couldn't drokkin' believe it! Him and his crew were down on Level 10 somewhere, heading downwards all the time. They'd lost a couple of guys along the way – Long Louie had got shivved in the riot they'd had to blast their way through up in Level 33 and good ol' Marv had been jumped by one of those bloodsucker freaks somewhere in the 20s, and, boy, was Sharkey not in a hurry to run into any more of those freaks – but they were still in pretty good shape and on course to reach one of the lower level exits outta the Pen.

They had just shot their way through a security point down here – two Judge-Wardens had tried to stop them, but Sharkey and a few scatter gun blasts had nixed that idea – when Sharkey caught sight of him on one of the vid-monitor screens.

Dredd! Right here in the Pen, running along a corridor somewhere.

Sharkey glanced at the monitor reading. Level 11, Sub-section 4A, it said. Sharkey grinned. That was only one level above them, and, better still judging by the direction he was heading towards the level exit drop-tube, Dredd was heading straight this way.

Sharkey wasn't big on all that Holy Church of Grud prayer-mumbling stuff, but he decided there and then that someone up there must like him. First of all they get him sprung from his cube, and now they obligingly drop Dredd right into his lap, and if that wasn't just too sweet, then Sharkey didn't know what was.

Of course, he'd added to his Judge-fragger score a couple more times today, but all the ones he'd killed had been Judge-Wardens, and Sharkey didn't really think they rated that much higher than those other kinds of phoney Judges who drove the med-wagons and handed out the parking tickets.

But Dredd... Well, he was the biggest, baddest Judge of them all, wasn't he? So fragging him would make Sharkey the biggest, baddest Judge-killer of them all, wouldn't it? Then there wouldn't be anyone laughing behind his back at him no more, would there?

Besides, Sharkey reminded himself sourly, thinking of that paper lung in his chest and the pain it caused him every time he breathed, him and Dredd had some history together, and he still owed the lawman some payback, didn't he?

He picked up his scatter gun and checked its load. Plenty of shells left, more than enough to take care of business, even with a tricky drokker like Dredd.

"Gonna be a change of plan, boys," he told his crew. "Got some unfinished business to settle up before I get us out of here."

Burchill's hands moved over the small control console, their movements stiff and awkward. The four shadowy beings in the crystalline containment cubes focused their powers more heavily upon him, redoubling their efforts to remain in control of his mind and body. The material their prisons were composed of blocked virtually all their powers, and the vassal's body had sustained too much damage to allow them to keep it alive for very much longer.

Time was running short, but they were too close now to even think of the possibility of failure.

"Release us!" hissed the voices in Burchill's head, forcing his body to carry out the Dark Judges' bidding.

He hit the final command key and a robot arm unfolded from its cradle in the chamber roof, smoothly snaking down towards the four crystals held in their heavy mechanical restraints. The restraining grips holding the crystal cubes in place were built into the deepest foundations of the iso-block building, and were designed to survive even a major earthquake. Nothing had been left to chance that might allow the creatures held here to be accidentally released, but it had always been hoped that sometime in the future a means might be found to destroy the Dark Judges' disembodied spirits once and for all. With that in mind, there had to be a way of opening up the virtually indestructible crystals to get to the things contained inside them, since the crystals protected the Dark Judges from harm just as much as they protected the city from their escape. The holding chamber's designers had no doubt imagined the deliberately engineered release of the creatures taking place under carefully controlled conditions, with a large number of Psi-Judges on hand to keep them under psychic control. What was happening now was probably beyond their worst nightmares.

A lance of stellar-hot laser energy shot out from the las-drill attachment on the end of the robot arm, cutting into the ultra-dense material of the nearest crystal's surface with a piercing sonic shriek. In just over a minute, its work was done and it was already moving on to the next crystal in line as a thin stream of what looked like greasy smoke poured out of the tiny, centimetre-wide hole that had been las-drilled through the wall of the crystal.

As the other three Dark Judge spirits writhed in impatience, the smoke from the first crystal coalesced in mid-air, slowly re-forming itself into the familiar visage of the greatest enemy Mega-City One had ever faced.

"Freeeeeeedommmmm!" Judge Death hissed in triumph, over the shriek of the las-drill and the continuing chorus of warning alarms.

KOOM!

Dredd rolled for cover as the scatter gun spoke loudly again. The desk he had been sheltering behind just a moment ago exploded, throwing shredded paperwork and a spray of cold synthi-caf into the air around him.

"Remember me now, Dredd? Thought you'd seen the last of Sharkey McCann, didn't you?" called the voice from up the corridor. "You made a big mistake last time we met, lawman. Shoulda made a better job of your aim last time you pulled a trigger on me. You only get one chance with a guy like Sharkey!"

Sharkey McCann? Who the drokk was Sharkey McCann, Dredd wondered? He'd put tens – Grud, maybe even hundreds – of thousands of perps into the cubes in his time. His ability to recognise perps from memory alone was legendary within the Justice Department, but even he couldn't be expected to remember every two-cred punk and small-time jerk who had crossed his path during his forty years on the streets.

Still, at least all this dumb creep's jawing had allowed Dredd to get a good fix on his position.

"Ricochet!" he commanded, firing a single shot up the corridor. It hit the far wall of the foyer area at the end and rebounded back at an angle. He heard a choked-off scream of pain and surprise, followed by the sound of something hitting the floor.

"Sharkey!" The call came from one of the other armed perps, who came popping up from behind the overturned desk he had been sheltering behind. Dredd wasn't about to pass up the gift of a free target, and sent him sprawling back behind the desk again with a single shot.

Another creep broke cover from behind a doorway off the foyer, firing two shots with his scatter gun. The weapon was set on wide spray. Dredd ducked as he felt the sizzling flurry of hot lead rip through the air around him. He tracked the target, manually adjusting his shell selector setting as the creep ducked behind the open, heavily armoured door of a high-security interrogation cube. The creep might have thought he was safe from harm there, but the Armour Piercing shell that Dredd put through the thick metal slab of the door said otherwise. A second later, there was the sound of another body hitting the floor.

Dredd strode forward out of the abandoned Judge-Warden duty station area where the perps had thought they'd had him bottled up. He hadn't killed them all, but experience told him he'd more than made his point. The three remaining, terrified-looking perps standing there waiting for him with their hands in the air and their guns dropped at their feet obviously agreed.

Dredd glanced down at the corpse of what he assumed was Sharkey McCann on the ground at his feet, noting the surprised look on the creep's face and the bullet hole dead centre in his back, which had gone through to find the creep's heart.

"How's my aim this time, creep?" he asked the corpse as he tossed three sets of handcuffs to the three surrendered perps.

"Cuff yourselves to the wall over there," he commanded, gesturing towards the holding bars on the side of the room. "Judges are on their way. If you're not here when they arrive, I guarantee I'll come looking for you."

Dredd ran on down the corridor. He was halfway down it when his memory put the name and face together. *Sherman "Sharkey" McCann: sentenced to life back in 2016, for the murder of a Judge.*

A Judge-killer, then. So no big loss there.

Still, the incident had been yet another troubling distraction along the way. A delay that might yet cost the city dear.

The scream of the las-drill died away as soon as its job was done, and the robot arm glided smoothly on to the last of the crystal containment cubes. The same stream of foul smoke poured out of the hole to coalesce into shape beside the other disembodied Dark Judges.

The spirit form of Judge Fear took his place alongside Death and Fire, as the drill went to work on the final crystal containing the spirit of Judge Mortis.

Now that it was no longer needed, the lifeless body of Psi-Judge Burchill lay discarded on the ground nearby, like a puppet with its strings most definitely cut.

The late Judge-Warden Mayer had been right in thinking that anyone wanting to access the Tomb level from the main prison building would have needed ten different security clearances even to make it to the elevator entrance. Sometimes, though, there were exceptions.

"Dredd, alpha red priority!"

The double set of thickly armoured blast doors obediently rumbled open before him and he ran through them without breaking stride. The sentry guns lining the corridor beyond submissively swivelled away as he approached and then swivelled back after he had passed, guarding his back. The Tomb and its entrance level within Nixon Pen had their own independent power source, and so were unaffected by the damage inflicted on the iso-block's security and power systems. The computer controlling them was now responding to the order, the combination of Dredd's name and voice recognition pattern, together with the command code he had given it, all combining to override all other considerations.

"Activate elevator!" he barked while still a good ten paces away, making it through the heavy blast doors just before they rumbled shut, saving himself a few more precious seconds.

The ride down was a speedy one, considering how far below ground the Tomb level had been buried. For Dredd, with the safety of every citizen in Mega-City One at stake, it still seemed to take forever.

He squeezed himself through the doors as soon as they began to open again, his Lawgiver held at the ready. He took the situation in at a glance, seeing the two dead Judges, the bullet-riddled control consoles and the disabled security systems. The las-drill he destroyed with a single Hi-Ex shot, but it was too late, because its work was already done, and the stream of spirit matter was already flowing out through the fissure that had been cut into the material of the crystal.

The spirit of Judge Mortis coalesced alongside those of its brethren, the four Dark Judges hissing together in shared triumph.

"Free at last," they exalted. "Free to continue our great work."

The atmosphere inside the Tomb was charged with dark psychic power. Even Dredd, who was double-zero rated for psi-sensitivity and thus mostly immune to any kind of psi-attack from the Dark Judges' spirit forms, could feel it, like a pressure between his temples. There was a foulness there too, a creeping sickness, the sense of something tainted hanging invisible in the air of the place. The Dark Judges were toxic, completely poisonous to everything around them. Even in spirit form, their deadly, corrupting power could still be felt.

They began to flow through the air of the chamber, heading towards the metal grille openings of the chamber's air-conditioning system. Dredd instinctively opened fire at them, spraying a dozen or more Lawgiver rounds into them, knowing just how futile the gesture was even as the bullets passed harmlessly through the creatures' insubstantial forms to strike the walls of the chamber.

They flowed with ease through the grilles and into the narrow conduits beyond. Dredd knew that the air-conditioning was supposed to be secure, with dozens of fail-safes built into it to prevent anything – even something gaseous – making it in or out of the Tomb, just as he had no doubt at all that the Dark Judges would find a way to elude all such safeguards. They were too cunning, too dangerous, to allow anything as mundane as air filters or vacuum-sealed plasteel slam-barriers to stop them.

The others were gone, but the Death spirit lingered for a moment, floating tauntingly in the air before him. Dredd stared dispassionately at the leering visage of what was probably his oldest and greatest enemy.

"Patience, sinner," it grinned at him. "Your time to be judged will come soon enough."

Dredd raised his Lawgiver to give Death his reply, but the spirit-thing was already gone, flowing into the grille after the others, leaving behind only the mocking echo of its chilling laughter. Dredd activated his helmet radio to deliver the bad news to the rest of the Justice Department.

"Alert the Chief Judge. Tell her we were too late. The Dark Judges have escaped and are loose in the city."

NINE

Just as night fell, disembodied, invisible, the spirit-forms of the four Dark Judges passed across the face of the vast, teeming future city that had once come so tantalisingly close to being theirs forever. The city bustled with life as day turned to evening. The bars, clubs, restaurants, hottie houses, shuggy halls, vid palaces, juve joints, poseur parlours and all-nite shoplexs were starting to fill up with the night's customers, and the zoom trains were running at double frequency in the busiest central sectors, bringing in millions more citizens to the bright lights of the city's main attractions. It was Sunday night, which meant that the familiar phenomenon known to the Justice Department as Sunday Night Fever was just beginning to bite. Countless millions of citizens went out to drown their sorrows or vent their anger and frustration against the fact that the following morning would bring nothing but the prospect of another long week of unemployment, boredom and poverty.

This was also the time when the tour party flyers took to the city skies in droves, each one packed full of foreign tourists who gawped down in stupefied amazement at the ocean of light that was the Big Meg by night. For these visitors, no matter how large they had previously thought their own mega-cities to be, there was no sight like it. Light and life stretched out everywhere below them; giant city blocks clustered together to form bright, glittering constellations, vehicle-filled megways threading between them and looking from this height like living rivers of light; the spaceports and strat-bat ports were blazing galaxies of light, throwing out the comet-like engine trails of craft blasting off for somewhere new every few minutes. Few ordinary flyer vehicles were capable of ascending to the height necessary to see the city in its entirety, where it stretched from the shores of the Black Atlantic in the east to the sullen, ominous darkness of the Cursed Earth rad-wastes to the West, so for those looking down on it from the tour flyers, it seemed as if Mega-City One was all there was to the whole world.

For these sightseers, the sight was simply amazing. For the spirits of the Dark Judges, moving invisibly amongst the drifting flyers, it was simply hateful and frustrating. So much despised life teeming beneath them, so many sinners waiting to be judged.

They were travelling at great speed, riding the invisible currents of psychic power that flowed across the face of the city, drawn inexorably towards a point somewhere just over the horizon. They were being called, they knew, and allowed the call to carry them to their ultimate destination.

A summoning spell, they realised. Their followers were calling the Dark Judges to them, to a place that had already been prepared, where Death and his brethren would be garbed in flesh again so that they could continue their great work of eradicating the crime of life from this world.

Passing unseen amongst the tourist flyers, Death amused himself for a moment by plucking thoughts from the minds of those sinners within the craft. He had always known that there were other cities in this world, other clusters of pestilent life waiting to be judged, but the number and variety of them, which he found within the minds of those sinners, surprised even the Dark Judge.

Brit-Cit… Simba City… Banana City… Hong Tong… Hondo City… Oz… Cuidad Espana… Cal-Hab… Puerto Nova… East-Meg Two… Sino-City Two. So many different places. So much disgusting life. So many guilty souls awaiting judgement.

"Patience, sinners. Your time will come," gloated Death to himself, deliberately echoing what he had told Dredd earlier, thinking now of all the glories that still awaited even after Mega-City itself had fallen to him and his brothers.

There was still much to be done here first, of course. Their old enemy Dredd had arrived just too late to stop their escape, and he and the rest of his troublesome kind were still a danger to Death and his brethren at this early stage of their escape. Clearly something must be done to distract Dredd and those like him, while the Dark Judges and their servants prepared for the next stage of the great work.

Death could sense the one who had set all this in motion. He was one of those few sinners whom Death had allowed to live long ago, choosing him for some greater task and setting his invisible mark upon him. That mark was there still, like a hard black stone planted within the mortal's mind, and the chosen one had passed it on to the things he had created, the Hungry Ones. And they, in turn…

Death hissed in pleasure to himself, seeing a sudden opportunity to keep Dredd and the others from interfering in their plans for a little longer.

"Concentrate, brothers," he told the others. "Focus your energies. Let us put one more obstacle in the path of those who would try to stop us completing our work."

"For Grud's sake, will someone go and see what that banging sound is?"

Unlike their colleagues in Street Division or on general Sector House assignment, the specialist staff of the central tek-labs didn't work in shifts, and many of them were off-duty, leaving the labs mostly empty for the night. That suited Helsing just fine. He didn't like noise and he didn't like company, at least while he was working, and the few other Judges and auxiliary staff still on duty in the labs knew to keep their distance and give the Forensics Chief some space.

Helsing picked up the las-scalpel again and bent down over the corpse to take another tissue sample from its inner organs. The results of the last few sample tests had been inconclusive, but he felt sure that he was getting close to what he was looking for. Despite its startling gene-altering properties, there was something tantalisingly familiar about the chemical composition of the as-yet-unidentified retrovirus. The Justice Department computers still hadn't found a match for it yet anywhere in their mind-bogglingly huge file repositories, but Helsing trusted his own instincts more than any computer, and felt sure he had seen a protein chain profile much like it before – and recently too. If only he could get a better idea of the way it reacted and replicated, then perhaps–

The sound occurred again, breaking his concentration. A dull booming noise coming from somewhere at the back of the labs, near the refrigerated mortuary rooms where specimens and evidence still awaiting analysis were stored. The corpses of the victims from the Bathory Street massacre had arrived just after Hershey and Dredd had left the lab, and–

The sound came once more, louder and more insistent. A hammering, drumming sound, like fists pounding on metal.

Laying down his las-scalpel with an exaggerated sigh, Helsing went to investigate. The lab was deserted and he seemed to be the only one here. Acting on a vaguely disquieting afterthought, Helsing went to his desk and retrieved his Lawgiver from one of the drawers. As a Tek-Division lab specialist, he had never fired the weapon in anger – the closest he ever usually got to actual perps was when they turned up as evidence on his autopsy slab – but Justice Department regs required him to attend marksmanship courses at least once a year at the Grand Hall of Justice's firing range.

He walked towards the source of the sound, which was definitely coming from one of the locked mortuary rooms. Even as he watched, he could see the metal door shaking on its hinges, as something or some-one relentlessly hammered on it from the other side. By the looks of things, the lock on it would only last a few moments more, and then there was the matter of the angry, animal-sounding, growling and moaning noises coming from whatever was on the other side of the door.

Calmly and methodically, Helsing reached down for his belt radio handset. "Control – Helsing. Unidentified intruders in the Forensics lab. I need some backup down here as soon as possible."

He had barely finished speaking before the door lock gave way with a scream of snapping metal. The occupants of the mortuary chamber beyond tumbled out, snarling and hungry as they quickly spotted Helsing and started shambling eagerly towards him.

Helsing had lived through Judgement Day and knew what zombies looked like. How these zombies had come into being, whether the corpses of the vampires' victims had been reanimated by scientific or psychic means, these were questions the forensic scientist in him would have to wonder about later, assuming he was going to live through this. Right now, the only part of him that mattered was the Judge part, and his reactions were textbook perfect.

He brought his Lawgiver up to bear, drawing a bead on his first target and fired. The zombie's head exploded and it tumbled soundlessly to the ground, where the others trampled over it in their mindless, stumbling rush to get to Helsing.

Helsing took aim at the next nearest one, wondering if his first shot was a fluke, since to be frank his marksmanship scores on those annual firing range courses were barely above the Department required minimum.

One way or another, he figured he was soon going to find out. The zombies were almost upon him, and there was still no sign of that backup.

"Say that again, Giant?"

"It's happening all over the prison, Dredd. Corpses are coming back to life again. Anyone who was killed by the vampires' bite is getting back up again as a zombie."

Grud almighty, that's all we need, Dredd cursed to himself. Vampires, Death-worshipping freaks, the Dark Judges and now the walking dead. This case was turning into a real late-night vidshow horrorfest.

"You able to handle things at your end?"

There was a pause on the radio link. Dredd could hear screams and Lawgiver fire in the background. Giant's riot squads had touched down a few minutes ago, and were methodically working their way down through the iso-block from its uppermost levels, rounding up escaped perps and gunning down any of the vampire things still on the loose. More H-wagons full of reinforcements were on their way, and it was confidently expected that Nixon Penitentiary would be back under full Justice Department control before dawn the next day.

Of course, that was before they had found out about the zombies, Dredd grimly reminded himself, listening to the dead air over the radio link with Giant.

"Giant?"

He heard a chorus of snarling sounds over the radio link, coming from somewhere close to Giant, followed by a series of rapid-fire Lawgiver shots. A moment later, the Judge came back on the radio.

"Sorry, Dredd. For a moment, a couple of the things got closer than they were supposed to. Yeah, no problems here. Zombies I can handle. I was there with you for Judgement Day, remember? It's Death and those other three creeps I'm worried about."

"Same here," answered Dredd. "Everything else they're throwing at us is just a distraction to keep us busy while they make their next move."

He was in the elevator now, travelling up from the Tomb to rejoin the effort to take back the prison. Might as well make himself useful, he thought, until they got a fix on the Dark Judges' position. To do that, of course, they really needed...

"What about Anderson?" he asked, knowing that Giant would easily pick up on the note of anger in his voice.

"Your guess is as good as mine, Dredd. No one's been able to track her down since she broke out of med-bay and boosted that Lawmaster."

"Wilco, Giant. I'm coming out of the elevator now. I'll do what I can down here, until your squads can make it down to meet up with me. You hear anything about Anderson, let me know. Dredd out."

He exited the elevator and marched along the corridor, the security doors obediently rumbling open in front of him. Sharkey McCann's three accomplice perps were exactly where he had left them and had cuffed themselves to the wall as ordered. They quaked visibly when they saw Dredd coming back towards them.

"That's the idea, creeps," he warned them as he strode past. "Just make sure you keep it like that."

Out in the stairwell, he could hear the snarling and moaning sounds echoing from the levels above. He recognised them from Judgement Day. Zombies, lots of them. And on the move, coming down the building towards where he was. He could hold this stairwell by himself, he knew, as long as his Lawgiver ammo lasted, but how many of the things were there, and how many other ways down were now standing unguarded?

Dealing with these creatures would take time, time he didn't have. Not with the Dark Judges on the loose somewhere out there in his city.

So where the drokk was Anderson?

Judge Anderson was almost in a trance as she piloted the Lawmaster at speed through the dark and mostly deserted streets of the city's dock-side areas. She had switched her radio off some time ago, finding the angry calls from Control demanding that she report her position imme-diately too much of a distraction while she concentrated her psychic abilities on finding the Church of Death's headquarters.

She was getting close now, she knew, homing in on the place she had seen in the mind of the vampire thing. She could sense how close she was – just as she could sense that something had gone terribly wrong at Nixon Pen, and that the Dark Judges were free once more.

She could feel them too, floating somewhere in the psychic ether over the city, sense their hunger and eagerness to begin their sick work again as they looked down at all the life spread out below them. Something was calling them, she could sense that too, a summoning spell of some kind, and she was now using her psi-powers to focus in on it, following it back to its source, just as the Dark Judges themselves were doing.

She sped on, entering the maze of warehouse-lined streets clustered around the old dockside district. Dredd hadn't been able to prevent the Dark Judges escaping from their prison. Now it was up to her to stop them taking on physical form again.

Inside Nixon Pen, the walking dead were on the move. Something was calling them too. Obeying some invisible summons, they left the places where they had died at the fangs of the vampires and flocked out into the corridors and cell-wing landings, crowding the stairwells, some even tumbling down the powerless grav-tubes, in search of a means out into the city beyond. Some were trapped and picked off by Giant and his men as they pushed down through the prison building, retaking it level by level. Others ran into the immovable obstacle of Dredd who had taken up station in one of the lower level stairwells, and was mowing them down by the dozen just as fast as he could reload his Lawgiver. But even he was just one man with just so many bullets, and, just as Dredd had already grimly surmised, there were other stairwells and other exits.

The zombies flooded out of the prison building in their hundreds, breaking through locked doors and barriers by sheer weight of numbers, passing unhindered through guard posts and security checkpoints left unmanned as more and more Judge-Wardens had been called away from their posts to deal with the rapidly spreading disaster that had enveloped the prison.

Most of them were still not even cold yet, raised from the dead before the heat could leave their bodies. Most wore the bright yellow uniforms of the iso-cube inmates, marked with prominent target symbols on their front and back, but there were the uniforms of Judge-Wardens amongst them too. Perp or guard, the vampires hadn't discriminated when it came to satisfying their blood-thirst.

All of them were splattered with gore and bore the marks of the circumstances of their own deaths: clawed-open throats, teeth-ripped jugulars, some even eviscerated or with their ribcages brutally pulled open and chest plates smashed through to expose the empty hole where blood-gorged hearts had hungrily been ripped out. The retrovirus was in their polluted bloodstreams, infecting their nervous systems and replicating within it, bringing them back to life again as these shambling, ravenously hungry creatures, connecting them to the vampire-things that had killed them and infected them with their bite, connecting them further to the figure who had created the vampires, and connecting them finally to the Dark Judge whom the vampire creator ultimately served.

The zombies poured out of the prison, heading towards the lights of the city beyond, eager to feast on human flesh and spread that infection even further.

Judge Ashman had graduated from the Academy to make full Street Judge status in 2018. She had still been a cadet when the zombie war known as Judgement Day had happened, and had missed the whole thing. Her class had been amongst those put on alert to join the battle on the West Wall perimeter, bringing desperately needed reinforcements to plug the gaps in the Justice Department defences as they struggled to fight off the massive zombie army encroaching in on the city from the Cursed Earth. In the event, the zombie war had been over before they could go into action, won not on the bloody battle lines along the West Wall borders or in the similar, desperate battles taking place at every other Mega-City on the planet, but in the tunnels beneath the mystic Radlands of Ji, where Dredd and a small, elite band of Judges from all across the world had destroyed the power of Sabbat the Necromancer and broken his psychic control over his deathless hordes.

Ashman had always wondered what it would have been like to be there on the West Wall in the darkest hours of Judgement Day, fighting off an enemy coming at you in countless numbers; an enemy that shrugged off wounds that would have killed any living human; an enemy that came on mindlessly and relentlessly, never tiring or despairing, its only motivation being the most basic animal impulse to kill and eat its prey.

Now she was about to find out. She and her partner Farrer were the first Judges to make it through the Death cultists' ambushes and roadblocks, and they were just pulling up on their Lawmasters in front of Nixon Pen when the horde of zombies started flooding through the iso-block's broken gates. Their Sector House Control was in radio communication with Giant and his squads within the prison, and so the two Judges had been warned what to expect when they arrived.

On the other hand, being confronted by a shambling, howling, flesh-hungry mob of the walking dead was a career first for both young Judges, and it took them some vital moments to adjust to the situation.

"Holy Jovus!" shouted Farrer, only a few months as a Street Judge after being promoted and transferred over from more sedate duties in the Justice Department's Traffic Division. "There must be hundreds of them! What do we do?"

"This," answered Ashman, dropping to one knee, taking aim with her Lawgiver and opening fire with calm, accurate precision at the first ranks of the approaching zombie horde. Farrer hesitated a moment, then followed suit.

Zombie after zombie fell to the ground, bullet holes drilled through their skulls. As each one fell, though, others instantly came forward to take its place, all of them pushing eagerly forward towards the two Judges.

"Code 99 Red!" Ashman shouted into her helmet mic, giving the Justice Department emergency code that signalled a Judge in trouble, designed to bring the nearest backup units scrambling to their assistance. "They're out in the open here at Nixon Pen. We need help down here now!"

She looked over at Farrer, relieved to see that he didn't seem to be showing any more signs of panic. "How you doing?" she shouted over to him, raising her voice to be heard over the sound of Lawgiver fire and the hungry moans of the zombies.

"Sure beats being back at Traffic and giving out parking tickets and speeding fines!" he shouted back, blowing the top of the head off a zombie dressed in the shredded remains of a Judge-Warden uniform.

"Reloading!" he called over to her again, as his Lawgiver gave a warning beep to signal that its magazine was empty.

"Covering you," confirmed Ashman, picking off a zombie from her side of the firing line and then rapidly switching her aim over to those on Farrer's front, shredding three of them with a single Hi-Ex shot. A few moments and six more destroyed zombies later, her own Lawgiver gave the same warning alert.

"Reloading!" she shouted, reaching down to her belt pouch for a fresh magazine. "Covered!" confirmed Farrer, bringing his aim round to return the favour. This time, however, the arrangement didn't quite go according to plan.

A zombie stumbled forward towards Ashman, taking advantage of the lull in fire from her position. Farrer saw it and nailed it with one shot, but his aim was slightly awry and he only blew off the lower half of its face. His second, hastily fired shot only winged it in the shoulder, while his next two shots, fired in growing panic, both missed it completely.

The dead thing came on at Ashman, growling hungrily, a mess of blood and juices dripping from the ruined remains of its face. She dropped her Lawgiver with a curse, snatched her daystick from the loop where it hung from her belt and swung it with every bit of strength she could muster. There was a sickening crunch as the blow struck the zombie and it fell lifeless to the ground, its brains dribbling out of its smashed-in skull. Ashman ducked down, trying to scoop her Lawgiver up from the ground, but the flailing hands of several more zombies reached out, trying to grab hers, and she snatched them back quickly, shocked by how close these others had got. She retreated back, abandoning the precious weapon to the advancing things.

Things were bad, but a glance over at Farrer's position told her they were about to get a lot worse.

In trying to cover her, Farrer had been forced to take his fire off the zombies advancing on him, and now they were upon him. He must have switched to Incendiaries as they closed in on him, because several of them were ablaze, something that didn't seem to trouble the mindless things too much as they clustered in on him, hungrily falling upon him.

"Farrer!" she shouted in anguish, hearing his screams as the zombies started to tear into him with their teeth. The flames covering the bodies of those struck by Farrer's Incendiary shots quickly spread to the others packed in close around them, and soon the whole pile of them would be ablaze. Not that this would be enough to deter them from eating Farrer alive as they all burned away to nothing together.

Farrer's Lawgiver lay teasingly nearby, knocked aside by a hungry zombie but, like any other Lawgiver, it was coded solely to its owner's palm-print, and Ashman knew it would be as dangerous to her as it would be to any other perp who foolishly tried to pick it up and fire it.

The zombies were closing in on her too. She turned and ran back towards her Lawmaster, popping a stumm gas grenade as she did so and throwing it behind her back into the midst of the pursuing zombies. Designed to incapacitate and render unconscious rioting citizens, the non-lethal gas would do nothing to walking, reanimated corpses that no longer even had the need to breathe, but Ashman hoped that the thick cloud of white gas that spewed out of the grenade would at least succeed in blinding or confusing them for a few vital moments.

Her bike! She had to get to her bike. Its twin-linked cannons would make short work of these things, and there was the scatter gun in the bike's saddle holster for more close-up action.

She made it onto the bike, was starting up its engine with one hand and pulling the scatter gun from its holster with the other, when the lead zombie grabbed her. She smashed an armoured elbow pad into its decaying face, knocking it away, but plenty more were already closing in. They grabbed for her, their fingers clawing at her body and the pieces of her uniform, the creatures mindlessly unable to distinguish one from the other as they tried to pull her apart. She was dragged off the bike, giving an involuntary wail of despair as she felt herself being pulled down, felt the first teeth bites starting to worry at her flesh. The scatter gun was still in her hand but it was useless, the arm holding it pinned to the ground by the weight of a zombie body.

She looked and saw the barrel of the gun pointing towards the underside of her bike's fuel tank. A Lawmaster's fuel tank was heavily armoured, but at this extreme close range, and firing into one of its more vulnerable and lesser armoured sections...

She felt something nuzzling roughly at her throat, and then felt the sharp pain of something biting excitedly into the flesh of her neck. After that, what came next was easy. A defiant curse on her lips, she pulled the trigger of her scatter gun.

The explosion immolated everything in a five-metre radius around the bike, killing Ashman and more than twenty zombies. The other remaining creatures took little interest in the charred and scattered remains of what only moments ago had been living prey.

Confused by the explosion and the sudden, disappointing lack of living flesh to consume, the zombie mob began to break up, individuals or groups of the creatures shambling off to begin their own search for more tasty prey. They would spread out into the sector around the prison with alarming speed, and the retrovirus-infected and partially consumed corpses of their victims would rise a few hours after death to join them. For days afterwards, the citizens of Sector 57 would hide behind their doors as the Judges and eager citizen squads of volunteer zombie-killers hunted the creatures down and destroyed them. After that, disappointed by the lack of further targets, some of the more over-enthusiastic volunteer groups of zombie-hunters would ignore the Justice Department's order to disband, preferring to turn their guns on any unfortunate citizen who in their opinion looked too suspiciously zombie-like. The last of these renegade zombie-hunter groups would be rounded up by the Judges after the notorious Oliver Street Soup Kitchen Massacre, when the vigilantes would learn that the line "Well, they kinda looked like zombies to us" was not a legitimate excuse for the murders of thirty-seven homeless street bums.

All this, however, was still to come. Right now, the only thing that mattered was the zombies and their growing hunger.

In life, Mikey "Swifthands" Liebling had been an expert pickpocket and thief. Known as a "dunk" in Mega-City criminal underworld slang, his favourite hunting grounds had been the city's many large and busy shoplexs and mega-malls. Cube-time was an occupational hazard of his chosen profession, and he had been about halfway through a five-year sentence when the attack on Nixon Penitentiary had happened and to his eternal surprise a vampire had torn through the door of his iso-cube and ripped his throat out. Now, in death, only the vaguest and most fragmentary memories of the circumstances of his life remained in the mind of the zombie-thing that he had become.

The thing that had been Mikey Liebling dimly remembered a place near the prison, a place where it had gone before, a place where it had found in plentiful abundance the things he had gone there looking for. As Mikey "Swifthands" Liebling, what it had been looking for back then were crowds of people and plenty of inattentive shoppers who wouldn't even notice that their wallets or cred-cards were gone until minutes after Mikey had struck. The needs of the thing that used to be Mikey Liebling were different, but something told it that it would still find what it was looking for now in that selfsame place.

Slowly, acting on the most dimly held trail of memory, he stumbled off on his own, not even noticing as first one and then another zombie mindlessly followed him. Many others wandered off in other directions, following their own random and unknowable impulses, but, by chance or instinct, the greater part of the horde shambled off after Mikey as he mindlessly led them to their night's feast.

* * *

Dredd exited the prison a few minutes later, taking in the situation at a glance. The pattern and number of zombie corpses and the remains of the two dead Judges told him the story of almost everything that had happened out here. Grimly, he bent down over the remains of one of the Judges, picking up the heat-fused badge lying there. The name on it was still barely legible: Ashman.

He had never known Judge Ashman, but she and her partner had both died bravely, fighting by themselves against overwhelming odds. Too many Judges had died already today as a result of the events at Nixon Pen. As a senior Judge, Dredd would see to it that these two, at least, would receive posthumous commendations for their courageous actions.

Going over to the Lawmaster that still remained intact, Dredd used his autokey to open its stowage pod, rummaging through it in search of the spare Lawgiver magazines that every Judge carried with their bike supplies. The battle in the iso-block had left him seriously short of ammunition, and he needed every spare mag he could find. It had been a busy night, and Dredd didn't have to be a Psi-Judge to realise there was probably a lot more to happen yet.

He clambered onto the Lawmaster, activating his helmet radio as he did so.

"Giant – Dredd. What's the situation?"

"Not good, but getting better, Dredd. We've retaken the top thirty levels, and we've probably already seen the worst of the opposition we're going to encounter. Besides, given a choice between us and those vampire creeps, most of the perps in here would prefer us any day. They know we're the only thing that's going to protect them from the vamps and they're surrendering to us whole levels at a time."

"Back-up?"

"On its way, thank Grud. They'll be here any minute to secure the lower levels and prevent any more of these creeps getting out."

"You'll have to manage with a couple of units less when they get here," Dredd told Giant. "I need them to deal with these zombie things."

"Understood, Dredd. Any idea where they went?"

"Working on it now. Dredd out."

Dredd rode off at a slow pace along the prison's approach road. He flicked on the bike's front-mounted powerful UV beamer, flooding the area in front of the bike with ultraviolet light. Since they were dead, the zombies would generate nothing in the way of body heat as their bodies eventually cooled to room temperature , but it had been less than an hour since most of them had died, and there were hundreds of them grouped together en masse, so Dredd figured they had to have left some kind of heat trace behind him.

He was right. The UV beam revealed the faint but discernible marks of hundreds of pairs of feet on the ground in front of him. They were heading in a disorganised pattern away from the prison and towards the more populated areas of the city, but at a point a hundred or so metres on, there was an abrupt break in the pattern. Some continued on towards the pinnacles of the city blocks in the distance, but the greater part of the zombie tracks broke away from the main skedway, taking a side-road instead. Dredd followed those ones, accelerating off in pursuit. Even before he saw the bright, gaudily coloured sign pointing the way ahead to the large and equally gaudily coloured building in the near distance, he already knew where the zombies were heading.

"Control – Dredd. Be advised: large group of zombies, estimated several hundred strong, on their way to the Winnie Ryder Mega-Mall. Am in pursuit."

TEN

Judge Anderson turned her stolen bike onto the dark, warehouse-lined street, recognising it immediately as being the same as the one she had seen in the mind of the vampire. The psychic summoning call that she had been following up to this point was overpoweringly strong this close to its source, and it was with a real mental effort that she finally managed to wrench her mind separate from it. She didn't need any psi-powers, just plain old Judge's instincts, and her first act was to switch on her bike radio to report in.

As soon as she did, the urgent-sounding voice of Control came flooding through to her. "...repeat, Control to Anderson, call in your location and situation immediately. This is a direct order from the Chief Judge. You must respond immediately, Anderson!"

Oh Grud, she thought to herself. Well, I knew I was going to get into trouble when I started out on this thing.

"Control – Anderson," she started, cutting off Control's immediate angry response. "Have located the Church of Death HQ. They're on Jack Kevorkian Street, down in the old Black Atlantic dockside district. Get everything you've got rolling and on its way here fast. My hunch is the Dark Judges are going to be putting in a surprise guest appearance down here any minute now."

"Understood, Anderson. Maintain position and wait until backup units are–"

"Jovus, didn't you here me, Control? I'm talking about the Dark Judges! They're going to be here any moment. This is the place where they'll get new bodies again, and if that happens then Grud help us all. No time to wait for backup – I'm going in now!"

She broke off radio contact again, cutting off Control's expected objections in mid-sentence.

Roaring along the street, she saw two figures on the road ahead of her. They were both wearing robes marking themselves as members of the

Church of Death, and both were armed: guards, posted to keep a look-out on the street outside.

"Well, so much for trying to sneak in the quiet way, Cass," she told herself as she saw them pointing in alarm towards her and unslinging their spit guns.

She didn't have her Lawgiver, and the scatter gun was too unreliable firing at this range from a moving Lawmaster.

"Bike cannons it is then," she decided, hitting the weapon's firing switch.

Thirty millimetre armour-piercing cannon shells chewed up the road surface, cutting a line directly towards one of the guards. The line reached him and suddenly he wasn't there any more, disappearing in a spray of blood and bullet-shredded clothing.

The other guard was running for her, opening fire with his gun. Anderson crouched low on her bike, as bullets whistled over her head. She'd been shot already today, and had no intention of having it happen to her again. Still, there was another problem to deal with. The street ended in a dead-end, which Anderson was now rapidly approaching on a speeding Lawmaster.

Time to kill two birds with one stone, she thought, wrenching the handlebars, hitting the brakes and throwing the big bike into a controlled braking skid. The Lawmaster hurtled sideways in a wide skid manoeuvre, slamming at speed into the gunman. He flew through the air, slamming into the wall at the end of the street some twenty metres away. By the time what was left of him had messily slid down the surface of the wall to land on the ground, Anderson had already dismounted from the now stationary bike and was sprinting towards the warehouse building that housed the cult's headquarters.

Another cultist emerged from the doorway, raising his gun to fire at her. Anderson didn't even bother with the scatter gun in her hands, and let fly at the creep with a powerful psi-blast right into the centre of his cerebral cortex. The gunman hit the ground as if he'd been pole-axed, lying there drooling, with a glazed and stunned expression on his face. In direct breach of Psi-Div regulations, Anderson hadn't even tried to regulate the strength of the blast she'd hit him with, and the after-effects of the attack would be unpredictable. The creep could wake up in a couple of hours with a raging migraine, he could wake up in a couple of days with the mental age of a small child or he could lapse into a persistent vegetative state and never wake up again at all. With so much at stake, with the Dark Judges on the loose again, Anderson frankly didn't care which way it went for the Death-worshipping freak.

Scatter gun at the ready, Anderson charged into the lair of the Church of Death. And her psi-senses screamed at her in warning, telling her the Dark Judges had arrived ahead of her.

DeMarco was still waiting for the right moment to make her move. A sick feeling of growing dread inside her kept on telling her that she'd probably already missed her chance.

Maybe she should have done the good cit thing after all, and just called the Judges much earlier on, before she'd slugged that guard and dragged his unconscious body into a nearby alleyway, stripping and cuffing him before putting on his Death cultist robes and just walking into the place wearing them, mingling unnoticed among the other Death worshipper freaks.

Or maybe she should have done something when the ceremony started and they'd brought out Joanna Caskey.

The ceremony was taking place in the central warehouse area. The windows of the large room had all been blacked out and the walls covered with black and red drapes, embellished in gold and silver with what DeMarco assumed were supposed to be arcane, magical symbols. The only real source of illumination in the place came from the numerous tall, black candles around the room, and most of these were clustered in what was obviously supposed to be an altar area on the elevated stage at the front of the room. So far, so run-of-the-mill hokey occult mumbo-jumbo, DeMarco decided; half the sectors in the city probably had hidden set-ups like this, bored cits looking for some kinky, illicit thrills by dressing up in these mad monk outfits and mumbling some cod-Latin gibberish before stripping off and getting down to the real point of the exercise.

However, it was when they dragged the girl out that things started to turn deadly serious.

They had drugged her with something, that much was plain to see, and she had lain down all too placidly on something that was clearly and gruesomely supposed to be a sacrificial altar. There were four other similar slabs there too, two of them on each side for the sacrificial altar, and with a stone column with more occult markings upon it standing at the head of the altar. There were four other shroud-covered figures lying upon the slabs beside the altar. From where she was standing amongst the Death worshippers at the rear of the congregation, DeMarco couldn't make out anything of the bodies under those shrouds, although she couldn't help but notice the reverence with which any cult members up there on the altar platform treated the four figures lying there whenever they came near them.

If DeMarco was having any thoughts about slipping quietly away and alerting the Justice Department to what was going on, these were swiftly ended when the doors to the place were sealed and two long lines of cloaked and hooded figures were marshalled into place on either side of the main congregation. DeMarco didn't much care for the sound of snarling and growling coming from beneath those hoods, and she liked it even less when the hoods came off and she saw the shockingly feral faces of the fanged, white-skinned things beneath them.

The vampires – DeMarco couldn't really think of any other term to describe them – hemmed the congregation in, leading them in the droning chant begun by the priest figure on the altar platform. The priest stood over the altar, a gleaming black, horned skull in one hand – the remains of some kind of Cursed Earth mutie specimen, DeMarco imagined – and a curved-bladed dagger in the other. DeMarco didn't like the look of that at all, and realised that she was going to have to do something about this.

She had been edging slowly forward for a while now, taking advantage of the darkness and the semi-trance state into which many of the congregation members seemed to have entered to slip forward surreptitiously, row by row, creeping towards the front. There were over a hundred of them and only one of her, and all she had was her pistol held inside her robes and her training as a Judge, but she had a job to do, and she wasn't going to stand by and watch these sick freaks kill an innocent girl.

Up until now, DeMarco still wasn't completely worried. If worse comes to worst, she told herself, she was going to use her first shot to save the girl from whatever they had planned for her, and then use the rest of the clip to kill as many of these creeps as she could. It was only when the four spirit-shapes started materialising in a greasy cloud of dripping, dark-coloured vapour in the air above the altar platform that she finally realised just how far out of her depth she was.

"Yes!" the four voices hissed in unison. "Complete the ceremony. Give us flesh once more!"

The air was charged with psychic power. The congregation's chanting was nearing its frenzied climax. The vampire things prowling round the sides of the room were filled with a terrifying anticipation and excitement. Unable to control itself any longer, one of them leapt upon a member of the congregation, hungrily tearing out his throat. Several more of the creatures rushed to join the feast, and their eager snarling and the scent of freshly spilled blood only added to the highly charged atmosphere inside the place.

The priest stepped forward, raising his dagger. DeMarco slipped her pistol out from her robes, mentally drawing a bead on him as she raised the weapon to fire. Two in the chest, one in the head, she decided, and then everything else for the creeps around her. The dagger in the priest's hand began to descend. DeMarco's finger began to tighten on the trigger.

There was a loud gunshot explosion from behind her – a scatter gun shot, DeMarco's Judge training instantly told her – and the doors crashed open. Two more scatter gun blasts sent the cultist guards flying through the air.

"Justice Department! Party's over, freaks!" shouted a commanding female voice.

"Andersssson!" the four things hovering in the air above the altar hissed as one, their voices full of hatred. And something else, DeMarco detected. There was fear there too.

"Kill her!" they ordered their followers. "Finish the ceremony. Give us flesh!"

The priest raised the dagger once more, getting ready to strike. DeMarco beat him to it, putting two slugs into his chest, as promised. The one intended for his head instead found its way into the big creep in front of her, who had turned and tried to grab her as she began firing.

There were more scatter gun blasts from behind her, together with the screams and howls of dying cultists and vampires. Whatever Anderson was doing back there, she was going about it the right way. DeMarco pushed forward through the throng of panicked cultists, trying to get to the figures on the altar platform. She pistol-whipped one cultist who tried to block her way and delivered a swift kick into the crotch of the next creep who came running at her with the same idea. The rest of the time she simply cleared a path through with her pistol, firing blindly into the bodies of any robed figures that stood before her.

Somewhere in the distance, above the sounds of the melee, she thought she could hear the sounds of Judge sirens. Lots of Judge sirens, in fact. Help was on its way and closing fast. DeMarco just hoped she could stay alive long enough for it to matter.

Incredibly, the priest creep was on his feet again, still holding the knife and staggering determinedly towards the girl on the altar. Ignoring for a few vital seconds everything else going on around her, DeMarco took careful aim again and put two more slugs into his back. Her gun clicked on empty the third time she pulled the trigger.

The creep was still staggering forward, but he had lost the knife now.

"Yes, serve us," the spirit-shapes commanded him. "Be our sacrifice. With your own life's blood, make us flesh again."

The priest pitched forward with the last of his strength, throwing himself forward against the stone column. As he touched it, smearing the blood from the bullet wounds in his chest across its surface, the spirits of the four Dark Judges gave a hellish shriek of triumph. The stone suddenly seemed to suck the life out of the figure clinging to it. Sorcerous energy crackled forth from it, touching first the disembodied spirits of the Dark Judges and then down into the four forms beneath the shroud covers. The spirits of Death and the others flowed with the energy stream, allowing them to take possession of the corpses their devoted followers had so carefully prepared in advance for them.

It all happened with surprising speed. One moment, Death and his super-creep pals were floating about in the air in spirit-form, and the next the four corpses on the slabs were rising up with preternatural speed and an awful, unnatural stillness. The shrouds of Death and Fear fell to the ground at their feet. The one covering Fire fell away in burning fragments. That covering Mortis simply rotted away into stinking, mildewed pieces in seconds.

There they stood, reborn: Death, Fear, Fire and Mortis. The four Dark Judges, who had expunged all life on their own world and had come to this one to do the same here.

One of the Death cultists clambered eagerly up onto the platform, throwing himself down to kneel, hands clasped in supplication, at the feet of Death. "Master!" he begged. "Grant me eternal existence. Let me join you there in the glorious realm beyond life and death!"

"With pleasure, sinner," cackled Death, sinking his hands seamlessly through the shell of the man's skull and squeezing its contents with his clawed fingers. The cultist fell dead at the monster's feet, the frozen expression of pain and horror on his face suggesting that the experience had been somewhat different from what he had hoped.

"Don't be shy, sinners. Who's next?" Death asked with an inviting leer, looking round, his cold, inhuman gaze finally settling on DeMarco. She wanted to reach for the spare ammo clip she had on her, load it into her pistol and empty it into the thing in front of her, but found she couldn't.

She couldn't do anything, in fact: move, scream, call for help or turn her gaze away. All she could do was stare back into that ghoulish caricature of the face of a Judge, as Death loomed up towards her.

"NO!"

It was Anderson's voice, and there was real power in it, enough to break whatever psychic spell Death could cast over his would-be victims.

With a shock, DeMarco realised that it hadn't been Death that had been moving, it had been herself, shuffling unwillingly and unconsciously towards him to receive his twisted sentence of judgement.

Death looked up, all interest in DeMarco forgotten as he saw his old nemesis running towards him. There were other Judges arriving on the scene too, crowding in through the door behind her, and DeMarco could hear the distinct heavy engine thrumming of at least one large H-wagon circling above the building. But the Dark Judges had sightless eyes for only one person.

"Anderssson," hissed Death. At his gestured command, one of the vampires hurled itself at her. She blew its head off in mid-air with a scatter gun blast and kept on moving.

"Anderssson," gloated Fear, throwing one of his vicious mantrap weapons into her path. Another scatter gun blast sent it flying out of harm's way, and still she kept on moving.

"Anderssson," blazed Fire in hatred and raised his burning trident weapon, sending out a blast of supernatural flame. Anderson twisted out of the way and the blast struck behind her, consuming several panicked Death cultists and reducing them to charred scarecrows in seconds.

Anderson strode forward, firing the scatter gun, and the weapon's high velocity shot load tore into the Dark Judges' bodies. Their Church of Death servants had done their work well, and each of the creatures was dressed in an exact replica of their familiar uniform, which themselves were grotesque, twisted parodies of the uniforms worn by Mega-City One Judges. DeMarco watched as Death slid one long, bony hand down to his version of a Judge's utility belt, reaching for the object attached there, reaching for what looked like a–

"Teleporter!" shouted Anderson in angry warning to the other Judges following in behind her. "For Grud's sake, shoot them. Stop them before they can teleport away!"

She opened fire again with the scatter gun, the roaring sound of the weapon joined seconds later by the crash of massed Lawgiver fire. A hail of Lawgiver fire, including Hi-Ex and Incendiary shells, struck out at the Dark Judges, but it was already too late. A dancing nimbus of energy surrounded the four figures on the altar platform, and the volley of gunfire passed harmlessly through their dematerialising forms as the activated devices teleported them away out of the Judges' reach.

"There is much work to be done, but we will meet again soon, Anderson," hissed Death as he shimmered into nothingness, his gloating gaze fixed on Anderson. A moment later, he was gone, his final words left echoing psychically in the minds of those left behind. "This time, we will not be stopped so easily."

Not wasting any more time, DeMarco scrambled forward up onto the altar platform, standing on the spot where the Dark Judges had been only moments ago. She heard the ominous clatter of a scatter gun being cocked directly behind her.

"Don't shoot! Family man!" she shouted, realising that in these robes she looked like any other Death cultist, and giving the traditional code phrase used by undercover Judges to identify themselves to other members of the Justice Department.

"Turn round. Slowly."

DeMarco did as ordered, seeing Anderson there, a hostile, suspicious look in her eyes, the scatter gun levelled straight at DeMarco's body. The look in the Psi-Judge's eyes intensified for a moment, and DeMarco felt cold psychic fingers picking through her mind, searching for the truth about her identity.

The fingers withdrew, the odd look left Anderson's eyes and the gun barrel was lowered.

"You're DeMarco?" asked Anderson, surprise evident in her voice. "The one that used to be Sector Chief in 303? The one that…"

Anderson's voice drifted off, but DeMarco knew what she had been about to say.

The one that's supposed to have tried to get Dredd into the sack with her? Yeah, that's me, ma'am. Guilty as charged.

"I guess that means I can lower my hands now without worrying that you're going to shoot me?" DeMarco said, continuing what she had been doing and going over to the prone figure of the girl on the altar slab.

"What are you doing here?" asked Anderson.

DeMarco laid a finger on the girl's neck, feeling for a pulse – and finding one. It was weak, but it was still there, thank Grud.

"Closing a case and saving a girl's life," she replied. "I guess you've got some important calls to make. Make sure one of them is for this girl. Grud knows what kind of drugs these freaks pumped into her. We need to get her into a med-unit fast."

Anderson nodded in understanding, and reached for her belt pouch radio.

"Control – Anderson. Things didn't go so well down here at Jack Kevorkian. Thanks to these cult creeps, the Dark Judges now have bodies and teleporters. They've escaped and are still on the loose. Wherever Dredd is, and whatever he's doing, tell him to drop it now. I need him to help track them down again before they start trying to wipe out the entire city."

ELEVEN

Fergus Munclie liked being a living mannequin. Sure, it wasn't the greatest job in the world, but it was still a job – and that was a damn sight more than most people in this city could ever say. He was the only guy on Level 271 of Jack Yeovil Block who even had a job, and the only other person in his extended family who had one was that dumb jerk of a brother-in-law of his, who had somehow managed to land a gig down at Resyk as a Part-Time Assistant Trainee Blockage Cleaner. Fergus had been down there once to see him, and hadn't been too impressed by what he saw. His brother-in-law worked in the sub-basement maintenance area directly below the main fat-rendering vats. The acidic fumes down there were pretty nasty, especially when the Resyk conveyor belts were running at full capacity, which was pretty much most of the time, and as far as Fergus could figure out, his brother-in-law's job mostly involved crawling about inside pipes and run-off troughs with the partially dissolved remains of recycled human organic matter dripping down on top of him.

No, Fergus was much happier where he was. Sure, he had to cross two sectors to get there, taking three zoom train interchanges and a hover-bus journey to do it, but any job was better than no job, he figured.

He had been employed as a living mannequin at the Ryder Mega-Mall for the past three years. Some people couldn't handle the job, having to stand still for eight hours a day, minus lunch-breaks, but Fergus adored it. It got him out and about amongst people, and he enjoyed being the centre of attention, as passing shoppers stopped to check out what he was wearing, and gangs of juves pulled faces and made gestures at him through the glass, trying to make him move or react. He was good at it too, able to come up with some truly novel and dynamic poses and hold them for hours at a time, able to look good in whatever they required him to model each day, and skilled at really selling the product, tailoring the intensity and excitement of his pose to whatever it was he was supposed to be modelling.

The mall management moved him around a lot, but most of the time he spent his work days in the window displays of shops like Kneepad-U-Like, Mosgrove & Thung and Ugly Kid Joe's; solid, respectable, middle-of-the-marketplace chains found in every mall and shoplex all over the city.

Of course, what he really dreamed of was a move up to the top tier: the prestige gigs working in the window displays of high-class retail outfits like Sump Couture, Khaki-a-Go-Go and Military Junta. All the mall's mannequins took home the same pay cheque at the end of the week, but the mannequins in those particular stores were still rated a cut above the rest. They got to put on the most daring, imaginative and outrageous poses – poses that the traditionalist management of family orientated stores like Mosgrove & Thung would never approve of – and in the staff canteen they always sat at a table of their own, never mixing with the other mannequins. All the other mannequins hated them, of course; all the others wanted to be where they were.

Fergus was pretty sure he was getting close to that dream . His posing work a few weeks ago in the "Give Me Victory, or Give Me Death" window display of Harv's Sports Gear & Armoury had been the talk of every mannequin in the place. Better still, while he had been standing there in the display, dressed in a Juggernaut strip and holding a copy of the Inter-Meg Smashball trophy aloft in one hand and the blood-dripping, severed head of one of his shop dummy opponents in the other, he had seen none other than the assistant display arranger from Sump Couture sidle past the outside of the shop, clearly sent to check out his work on the sly.

Yeah, Fergus was pretty sure that he was on his way up, and that soon enough it would be him there in the window displays of those places, modelling all the latest in high-Meg fashions.

Assuming, that was, that he didn't get eaten by rampaging hordes of zombies in the meantime.

They were everywhere in the mall. Where they came from, Fergus had no idea. What they wanted, though, was clear enough. Trapped there in the Cursed Earth safari-wear display outside Ronnie Radback's, he had watched as at least half a dozen people were eaten alive right there in front of him. He was wearing the latest in anti-rad fashion and had a machete in one hand, swinging it in frozen motion at the head of the giant fibreglass ant coming out of the ground in front of him, but the weapon was useless, as fake as the cardboard rad-counter in his other hand, so all he had to depend on to keep himself alive were his wits and his Grud-given abilities as a living mannequin.

On the plus side, he knew he could remain in this pose for hours yet. The zombies were everywhere, milling all around him, one or two of them even brushing against him, but as far as he could tell, they were simply too dumb to realise that he was flesh and blood, and not the inanimate object he appeared to be.

On the minus side, his display partner today was the new kid, the girl who had just started last week. Fergus hadn't been happy with being paired with her. Her stance ability was all wrong, she had no idea about dynamic posing, her muscle control was sadly lacking – and now, to top it all, she was probably going to get him killed and eaten.

She was playing his wife in this display, cringing in fear before the giant ant model while showing a very customer-pleasing amount of leg and cleavage, as Fergus, the intrepid Cursed Earth explorer, strode forward to defend her. She didn't have to fake that frozen look of terror on her face anymore, but she was visibly trembling in barely contained panic, and her skin glistened with a clammy fear-sweat. She couldn't take much more of this, and when she screamed, tried to run or even just moved, the zombies were going to realise that they were there amongst them.

They could hear screams from all around, echoing through the cavernous space of the multi-level mall, along with all the snarls and moans of the zombies as they fell upon the terrified shoppers in the place or fought amongst each other for some of the choicest scraps of meat. There were security droids hovering around the place, spraying the zombies with knock-out gas or zapping them with stunner shots, although as far as Fergus could see these attacks were as much use against the things as the stern cease-and-desist warnings issued by the droid units. The droids were designed to take legal, non-lethal action against shoplifters, pickpockets, juve troublemakers, loiterers, buskers and mimes, but apparently their programming didn't cover eventualities like zombies invading the place to eat the shoppers.

Incongruously, in amongst all the carnage, the mall's auto-ads kept on running, broadcasting their hard-sell messages to terrified shoppers and the roaming packs of zombies that were hunting those same shoppers.

"Important new Mega-Mall research by top scientists has proved that buying things may actually boost your immune system, clear your complexion, improve your eyesight and sex drive, and even significantly reduce cholesterol, so get those creds out, shoppers, and spend, spend, spend! Your continued health and well-being may depend on it!" boomed a tannoy announcement, as a gang of juves in the ground level vid-arcade pulled out their illegal las-blades, preparing to go down fighting against the zombies now crowding into the place.

"Grot Pot! When a snack's this cheap, delicious and easy to prepare, who gives a drokk about nutritional value?" suggested the Grot Pot dispenser machine at the entrance to the level one drop-tubes, unaware that most of its customers were being attacked and eaten by ravenous zombies.

"Take two bottles into the shower?" squealed a holo-ad projection of a near-naked female model in the main foyer, looking down blindly on a pack of zombies tearing apart a screaming family of Fatties. "Not me! With Otto Sump's new Sham-Poo, I just stink and go!"

"Tired? Stressed? Bored of a lifetime of endless unemployment and poor-quality leisure time?" asked a wandering hov-unit, trying to sell its ads to the corpses strewn along the main concourse. "Why not take a vacation in our new Cursed Earth holiday work-camps? We promise back-breaking hard labour, brutal overseers and the best protection from the surrounding hostile mutie tribes that money can buy!"

"Brit-Cit! Where outdated tradition, and useless pomp and ceremony still reign triumphant! And all of it just a quick trip away through the Black Atlantic tunnel!" boasted another hov-unit in a typically snooty Brit-cit accent, as it followed its rival in the holiday ad business along the same concourse.

The hov-units weren't going to be doing much business amongst the shoppers tonight, but they seemed to have attracted the attention of the zombies, and a group of the things were shambling along the concourse behind them, drawn in by the sound and movement generated by the devices. That meant, Fergus knew from long days watching them go round and round, that they were coming straight towards him and the girl.

The girl gave a whimper of fear and shifted slightly.

"Don't move! Just let them pass us by!" Fergus hissed urgently through gritted teeth, knowing it was probably not going to do any good. She was too far gone, and probably going to start panicking any second.

The hov-units were past them now, still blaring out their ad messages. The zombies were only a few metres behind them. The girl moved again, and gave a stifled scream. The slight sound or movement was enough to catch the attention of at least one of the creatures. It looked round towards the display, studying the two immobile figures with its dead, blank gaze. It took a step towards them, and then another one–

There was a loud, shocking report of a gunshot. The zombie fell one way, most of the contents of its skull went the other way, propelled out in a gory spray by the bullet that had just passed clean through its head.

More gunshots rang out, felling more of the creatures. Some of the shots lacked the fatal headshot accuracy of the first and instead hit the zombies' bodies, making the creatures dance and stagger under the impact of multiple hits. Fergus heard the pounding of heavy booted feet coming towards them along the concourse. Like any other citizen of Mega-City One, he recognised the sound immediately. Unlike many of those citizens, though, he thought it was the happiest sound he'd heard in his life.

Thank Grud, the Judges had got here at last.

Six of them came pounding along the concourse, gunning down zombies as they went. The bullet-riddled shape of one of the creatures picked itself back up off the ground and threw itself snarling at the lead Judge. Without breaking stride, and while gunning down another undead freak at the same time, the big Judge simply grabbed the zombie as it attacked him and hurled it over the side of the concourse, sending it crashing down onto the roof of the luxury Foord Falcon grav-speedster on the Mega-Mall prize giveaway promotional stand on the ground-floor concourse, three floors below.

The big Judge turned round, and Fergus recognised him from his voice even before he saw the name on the badge on the Judge's chest.

"Spread out," Dredd commanded the other Judges. "Two-man teams. Secure the exits on this level and check for any cits that might be hiding around the place. Remember, if it's moving but it hasn't got a pulse, shoot it in the head."

Dredd paused, glancing round at the two immobile mannequin figures. "And you two can quit playing possum. Danger's over now. Clear the area, citizens. That's an order."

With the mall's entrance and exits secured, and with the bulk of the surviving staff and shoppers who had been in the place when the zombie attacked now safely evacuated, the clean-up op could begin. No zombies could get out of the mall, and the only thing that was going to be coming in through its doors were more and more Judges, so Dredd didn't think there was much more of a problem here, and gladly relinquished command of the situation to a Tac Watch Commander from Sector House 57.

That the situation at the Ryder Mega-Mall was no more or less under control didn't exactly please Dredd. It had been nothing more than an annoying distraction from his main duty, and it wasn't even over yet. Reports were coming in of more zombie attacks in the area around the iso-block as the creatures spread further out into the sector, although it seemed as if the main concentration of the things had been trapped here at the Ryder Mall. Now all that was left to do was a tedious but necessary mopping-up operation throughout the rest of the sector to prevent the zombie contagion spreading any further.

Judges were flooding in from all the adjoining sectors, adding to the available manpower. By all accounts, there were almost as many Judges as surviving perps inside Nixon Penitentiary, and Giant reported that the situation there was well under control. The remainder of the vampires and any zombies that had remained in the building were now confined to just three levels in the prison's lower sections, and Justice Department heavy weapons teams armed with flamer units were already on their way to remove their polluting presence for good from the prison.

Two problems down, but what was by far the biggest issue was still unresolved. The Dark Judges were still out there somewhere and every minute they remained free, the danger to every living person in Mega-City One increased accordingly.

"Control – Dredd. Any update on the Dark Judges?"

"Negative, Dredd. We've got Anderson and half of Psi-Div scanning for them, and so far they've come up with zip. No reports of any sightings coming in either, and every slab jock in the Department is out there looking for them. If Death and his pals are out there, they're managing to keep a real low profile."

"Give 'em time, Control. Maybe they're planning something, but they'll turn up sooner or later. When that happens, all we can do is start following the trail of dead cits."

"Wilco, Dredd. Chief Judge says she wants you and Anderson together on this one. We're sending an H-wagon to pick you up."

Dredd considered the situation for a moment. He was no longer needed here, and he and Anderson together had proven themselves in the past to be the best weapon Mega-City had against the Dark Judges, but too many unanswered questions still remained.

Someone had created the retrovirus that had given birth to the vampire and zombie creatures.

Someone, possibly that same someone, had carefully planned the attack on Nixon Pen that had allowed the Dark Judges to escape.

The members of the Church of Death were no different from the fanatical kooks who filled the ranks of at least a dozen other similar illegal crank-cults, but someone had organised and funded those creeps and turned them into a weapon to be used against the Justice Department at the crucial moment of the Dark Judges' escape.

Someone was behind everything that had happened so far, and Dredd and the rest of the Justice Department didn't have a clue yet who that someone could be.

First things first, decided Dredd angrily. First we deal with Death and the others, then we find out who was responsible for this whole mess.

"Understood, Control. Awaiting H-wagon pick-up. Dredd out."

He was at the outside of the mall, supervising as meat wagons and med-wagons arrived to take away the dead and injured, and pat-wagons delivered more Judges to deal with the situation inside the mall. As he watched, a group of injured cits were brought out of the place. Six of them were stretcher cases, and the walking wounded were splattered with gore and nursed blood-soaked bandages showing where they had been clawed or bitten in zombie attacks. A Med-Judge accompanied them, saw Dredd and came running over to him.

"The wounded are starting to stack up, Dredd. We've got over two hundred injured cits, all the victims of zombie bites. What little we've got to go on with these things suggests that they were reanimated by a retrovirus passed on to them by bites from the things that attacked Nixon Pen. What do we do if the retrovirus affects living victims the same way?"

"Quarantine?" asked Dredd.

"That's what I'm thinking," nodded the Med-Judge, grimly. "If I've got a couple of hundred injured cits who are maybe going to turn into vamps or flesh-hungry zombies in an hour or two, then we need to do something to either cure them or contain them."

"Good point," agreed Dredd, activating his helmet radio again.

"It's an interesting question, Dredd," said Helsing, bending over the zombie specimen on the autopsy slab in front of him. Even with most of its cranium missing, destroyed by one of Helsing's own Lawgiver shots, they weren't taking any chances with the thing. It was secured to the table by metal restraints, and there were armed Judges standing by in the room to make sure that the zombie and the rest of its equally dead friends weren't going to pull any more surprise resurrection stunts. Helsing was glad of the guards' presence, and was fairly sure that if they had arrived a few moments later when he had first raised the alarm then he would probably be lying stretched out on one of his own autopsy slabs along with the rest of the dead meat on display here.

"As far as I can tell," he continued, talking via radio link to Dredd while he neatly sliced into the zombie's body with his trusty las-scalpel, "the virus changes structure when it jumps from the vampires and into the bloodstreams and nervous systems of their victims. It degenerates, becoming less effective, so that when the dead tissue is reanimated, virtually all the higher brain functions are lost, and all that remains are the most basic and animalistic urges such as hunger and aggression."

"But is it contagious?" asked Dredd, a clear note of impatience in his tone.

"To anyone non-fatally bitten by these things? I'm not sure, I'm afraid. I'll have to do tests on blood samples for the bite victims, but it's my hope that the more degenerative form of the virus only affects dead tissue. In fact, it was only when I saw it in its degenerated form that I realised where I had seen it before—"

"You've seen this virus before? Where?" The note of impatience in Dredd's voice had suddenly been replaced by one of alert interest.

"In molecular form, it's strikingly similar to the chemical formula recently patented by the EverPet Corporation."

"Pet Regen? The stuff that brings cits' dead pets back to life?" The disbelief in Dredd's voice was clear.

"Basically, yes," answered Helsing calmly. "It's very possibly an early test-form of the final product."

There was a pause on the radio link before Dredd answered: "Good work, Helsing. Keep me informed if you find anything else. Dredd out."

Helsing bent over the corpse again, wincing from the pain in his arm. He'd had the wound dressed and had allowed a Med-Judge to administer him some minor pain-killer tabs, but nothing that would interfere with his thought processes or cloud his judgement, and he had absolutely refused the Med-Judges' suggestions that he go into med-may for observation.

One of the zombies had got a little too close for comfort, and had taken a bite out of Helsing's left arm before the Judge had managed to jam his las-scalpel deep into its brainpan. Despite the worrying certainty that he, too, had the retrovirus coursing through his bloodstream, Helsing tried to look on the bright side, telling himself that having a personal stake in this case would give his work an added impetus.

After all, now he was in the same boat as the other injured citizens who had been bitten, and if the retrovirus was contagious in this fashion then it really was in his interest, just as much as theirs, that he find a cure as soon as possible.

Humming quietly to himself, he applied the las-scalpel to another part of the zombie's exposed innards, calmly continuing on with his work.

Someone had deliberately engineered the virus that had created the vampire and zombie creatures. Someone had organised and funded the Church of Death and had mounted a successful operation to free the Dark Judges from their prison – but now Dredd had a good idea just who that someone might be.

"Control – Dredd. Been a change of plan. I still need that H-wagon, but the rendezvous with Anderson will have to wait. If she needs backup, recommend Judge Giant for the job. Tell my pilot to pick me up and then plot a course at double-speed for the EverPet Corporation's HQ, and give me everything you've got from Central Records on the company."

After so long shut away in the darkness, disembodied and under constant guard, it was good to be free to kill once more. Their servants had done well – the teleporters were a good copy of the devices the Dark Judges had used on their own world – and now those devices had brought them to this fine place where there were so many sinners to be judged, and no interlopers with their guns to interrupt Death and his brethren in their sacred work.

Fire lashed out with his burning trident. More of the crude dwellings burst into flame. Screaming figures stumbled amidst the inferno, burning from head to foot. The others fled from where they had been cowering, flushed out from hiding by the flames, herded by further blasts from Fire's trident straight into the deadly embrace of the other three Dark Judges.

Death pushed a hand into the chest of one sinner, his fingers twisting amongst the arteries of his heart. With his other hand, he thrust into the back of another fleeing figure, withdrawing it again almost as quickly, leaving Death clutching his gory, dripping prize in triumph. The man kept on running for a few steps more, and then collapsed to the ground, an expression of utter and horrified disbelief fixed on his face. Death threw the still-beating heart into the spreading flames and then moved on to judge more of the sinners.

Mortis looked down at the begging, whimpering figure kneeling before him. There was decay in this one already, he could sense. Disease festered within him, his insides eaten away by the bottles of low-grade meths-brew he had been consuming for years. All it would take to bring it out to full bloom in the sinner's body was the merest touch from the Dark Judge.

Mortis's fingers stroked the man's face, leaving deep, pus-filled boils where they brushed the skin. Almost instantly, the man fell writhing to the ground, maggots boiling out of his rotting flesh as it slewed away wholesale from his bones. Mortis hissed in pleasure, and strode on to bestow his gifts on the next sinner in turn. Where he walked across the uneven, broken ground, where his feet made contact with the polluted soil there, maggots and other carrion insects sprang out of the earth in the wake of his passing.

Fear flowed out of the shadows of a heap of crumbling war ruins, seemingly appearing from nowhere to the rabble of sinners who had been fleeing the wall of flame behind them. The barred gate of his helmet visor gaped open, and the first few sinners in line caught a glimpse of what lay behind that visor, and fell lifeless to the ground, their hearts frozen solid like blocks of ice, fireworks exploding amongst the darkness of their dimming vision as their brains were wracked by a series of instantly fatal embolisms.

The others turned and fled, seeking escape amongst the ruins. Fear spread his cloak wide, revealing the living darkness that lay beneath the garment. Shadow-shapes, moving too swiftly to be properly seen, flew out of that darkness and flitted after the escaping sinners. As each shadow-shape found its target sinners fell to the ground screaming and writhing, their minds filled with images of the things they had previously glimpsed only on the furthest fringes of their worst nightmares. Fear stalked forward to find his prey and finish them off, his mystic senses guided by the screams in the darkness and by the delicious taste of the victims' terror.

Death stood upon a small mound of the corpses of his victims and exalted in being free once more. The place they had found – the place destiny and their teleporters had brought them to – was one of those places where the lost and dispossessed drank to blot out the worst details of those existences. Of all the inhabitants of this city, these were amongst the most wretched and miserable, with little or nothing left to live for, but still they had tried to run when the Dark Judges had appeared amongst them. As all foolish mortals did, they had tried to survive rather than surrender to the inevitable.

What was it about these sinners, Death wondered, that they wanted to compound their crimes by hanging onto the sin of life for as long as they could? With more co-operation, with more understanding of what it was he and his brethren were trying to achieve, their great work would be done all the sooner, and then first this city and then the rest of this world would know peace at last.

The giant towers of the city loomed up around this area of waste ground where the lost ones had made their home on the ruins of one of the city's past wars. So many wars these sinners fought amongst themselves, and still they had not succeeded in wiping themselves out. So disappointing. That was why their great work was so necessary, Death knew. If the sinners did not have the courage to end their own existences, then it was the task of the Dark Judges to do it for them.

The sound of H-wagon engines interrupted Death's contemplation. He saw the running lights and search-beams of the aerial vehicles coming closer across the darkness of the ruins, and realised that time was short.

He called his brothers to him. Some of the sinners still lived, fleeing in terror into the darkness and towards the city lights beyond, but it did not matter. Their escape was only temporary and they, like the rest of this doomed city, would be judged soon enough.

"They have found us," said Fire. "We must leave this place and continue our work elsewhere."

"There are only four of us, and many of them. They will be determined to stop us, just as they have stopped us before," said the dead, cold voice of Mortis.

"We are still weak from our long captivity," noted Fear, his whispering voice like a cold shiver running down the spine. "Perhaps we should return to Deadworld to gather our strength. We have more power there than we have here."

"Or perhaps Deadworld should come to us."

It was Death who spoke. The other three Dark Judges looked at their leader. With all their minds psychically linked, it took only a moment for them to realise the intent of his words. His plan was instantly met with a low chorus of approving hisses.

"I will gather the sacrifices and go to the Under-Place to prepare the way," whispered Fear. This too met with an approving chorus of hisses.

It was Death that spoke next. "They seek four of us together. If we are apart, they will be confused. Their forces will be spread thinly as they attempt to find us. The carnage we other three bring will distract them. They will not realise what it is we plan to do until it is too late to stop us."

Death looked at the other three Dark Judges. "Judge well, brothers. When next we meet, in the Under-Place, this city will finally be ours."

The H-wagon reached the spot less than thirty seconds later. Powerful search-beams played over the place, and Tek-Judges aboard the vehicle scrutinised monitor screens that displayed the entire area on spectrums far beyond the power of the naked eye, but there was nothing to find.

The Dark Judges were gone.

Icarus sat in the darkness of his laboratory, quietly satisfied with the way events were proceeding. The Dark Judges had been freed, and soon his own elevation to a higher state beyond life or death would begin. Of course, the Church of Death, which he had secretly set up and then funded, had been virtually wiped out by the night's events, but that didn't really matter, not in the grand scheme of things. Those fanatics had died happy in the knowledge that they had helped set free their precious masters and, more importantly, their role in Icarus's plans was over now anyway. After that, he really didn't care what happened to them. The only thing that mattered was what was going to happen to him tonight.

Rebirth.

Transcendence to a new and greater level of existence. That was why he had freed the Dark Judges, so that they could elevate him to the same status of everlasting life that they had achieved. The Dark Judges existed at a state beyond life and death, and so would Icarus.

"You cannot kill that which does not live," he murmured to himself, picking up the large syringe of fluid that lay on the desk before him. It contained the Regen retrovirus in its final, perfected state, and was far removed from the debased stuff that he had tested on the Death cult members to create his vampire creatures, or the even further adulterated muck that he had marketed as the EverPet product in order to fund his work.

No, the contents of that syringe represented his life's work. Everything he had strived for since the scales had been lifted from his eyes during the time of Necropolis was held within the dark, swirling liquid inside the syringe.

He picked it up, pushed the needle into his skin and pressed the injection switch. The liquid flooded into him, mixing with his bloodstream, the retrovirus molecules instantly attaching themselves to his blood cells, beginning the rapid process of reprogramming his DNA in preparation for what was to come.

The final stage would be death itself, the virus spreading to infect every cell in his body, going to work on his necrotised flesh. Icarus had a range of chemical substances that would bring on his own death quickly and painlessly. Many of them were the same Justice Department-approved compounds used in the city's chains of euthanasia clinics. Still, none of them seemed quite appropriate, Icarus felt. For his death, for rebirth and transcendence to the state of eternal undeath, something more dramatic than mixes of toxic chemicals was called for, surely?

As if on cue, the radio intercom on his desk buzzed.

"A Justice Department H-wagon landing outside. There's a Judge getting out of it."

"Just one?" asked Icarus, puzzled.

"Just one, answered the Death cultist in charge of security at the facility. "It looks like it might be Dredd."

Dredd! Icarus's mind thrilled at the news. How appropriate, he thought. Fate was obviously at work. Dredd was death incarnate. The biggest mass murderer on the planet, the man who had pressed the button on East Meg One and consigned hundreds of millions of people to nuclear oblivion, the man who had given the brutally necessary order that would condemn billions more people to death during Judgement Day.

Yes, how appropriate, Icarus decided. This was destiny, this was fate. This was clearly how things were meant to happen.

"Stop him," Icarus ordered over the radio, knowing that there was no way the defenders he had left would ever be able to stop Dredd, even if he was on his own. "Make sure he doesn't get to the lab."

Yes, Dredd would come here, and Icarus would allow Dredd to kill him and elevate him to his destiny.

And then, after that?

Icarus was distracted for a moment by another barrage of angry fists pounding on the thick vault doors behind him. He smiled, thinking of the creatures contained behind those doors. Vampires, newly created and still filled with the worst after-affects of the virus flowing through their veins.

So let Dredd come, Icarus smiled. After he had fulfilled his purpose and sent Icarus on the path to his destiny, he would find his supposed victory to be very short-lived indeed.

TWELVE

Dredd exited the H-wagon at a sprint. He'd been on duty for over twenty hours, which wasn't completely unusual for him, but in that time he'd fought a couple of dozen vampires, battled his way through the middle of a prison riot, missed preventing the escape of the Dark Judges by the skin of his teeth, single-handedly taken on a couple of hundred zombies and commanded the clean-up op at the Ryder Mall, saving the lives of hundreds of cits.

Even by his standards, it had been an eventful day – and it wasn't over yet.

Now, though, he could feel the exhaustion starting to build up in his body. He'd been a Judge for over forty years, and had pushed himself to the very limits of human endurance just about every day of every one of those years. His body was a machine, crafted from fifteen years of the toughest training on Earth at the Academy of Law and honed to near-perfection by four decades patrolling the streets of the biggest, most dangerous and crime-ridden city on the planet.

But even the best machines start to wear out after a while, Dredd knew. The Justice Department knew it too, and they'd already lined up his replacements, clones from the same precious bloodline as himself. The first of them was already on the streets. How long did Dredd have left, people secretly wondered within the Department? How long could he keep on pushing himself at the same rate that he had sustained for so many years?

For as long as necessary, Dredd told himself. For as long as his city still needed him.

He'd downed some standard-issue pep tabs in the H-wagon to fight off the worst of it, and from long experience he knew they'd keep him alert and on his feet for another six hours or so.

Long enough to stop the Dark Judges and save his city? Grud only knew, but Dredd hoped it would be enough.

Through the speakers in his helmet, Control fed information through to him straight from the files held in the giant MAC computer system at the Grand Hall of Justice.

"Icarus, Dick. Real name: Martins, Vernon. Born 2078, Betty Boothroyd Maternity Med. Graduated Meg U, class of 2101, first class honours in Biochemistry. Employed as biochemist at DaneTech Industries, 2102-2115. Specialist field of research: Longevity and age retardation."

Dredd was at the doors to the lab facility, using his override card to open the doors as the calm voice of the Justice Department's anti-crime super-computer continued to feed him information.

"Left to establish own company, 2115. EverPet Corporation. No criminal record. Admitted for psycho-cube observation, 2112-13, following death of wife and daughter in citywide Necropolis disaster of 2112."

A spell in the kook cubes. That caught Dredd's attention. Not that Martins, or Icarus, or whatever he wanted to call himself, was unique in that respect. Necropolis was like an open wound in the city's psyche; sixty million citizens had died, and tens of millions more had suffered severe mental trauma, filling the city's psycho-blocks to maximum capacity for years afterwards. Some had recovered sooner than others. Clearly, the psycho-cube docs had thought Martins/Icarus was one of them, but now Dredd knew different.

Using MAC's resources, he'd uncovered a lot on the H-wagon ride out here. All the information had been there all along, for anyone who wanted to go digging for it. Dredd knew that, with over four hundred million citizens to watch over, the Justice Department couldn't keep a close eye on all of them, but there were enough anomalies in the records to have maybe raised at least a few questions in someone's mind.

EverPet's financial records were a revelation. The Pet Regen product was a commercial success, but the company was still trading at an enormous loss. Their public accounts records showed huge amounts of money being ploughed into unspecified "research projects". Using MAC's high-powered analytical abilities, Dredd had quickly found out what that really meant.

Money had been transferred to overseas accounts and then shifted back into the city in the guise of charitable donations to various minor religious organisations, all of which, Dredd suspected, would quickly be revealed as mere fronts for the Church of Death. Other funds had been siphoned off to set up the facility Dredd was about to enter now, even though there was no official record of the place in the list of the company's property holdings.

A secret lab, hidden away from the prying eyes of the Justice Department. A biochemist with a history of mental disorder, connections to the Church of Death and whose research speciality was the reanimation of dead tissue.

Didn't need forty years on the streets to put this one together, Dredd figured.

Icarus, for whatever reasons of his own, had funded the Church of Death, created its vampire shock-troopers, freed the Dark Judges and caused the deaths of a lot of cits and Justice Department personnel. The mood he was in now, Dredd would be happy to just put a few Standard Execution rounds into the murdering creep at the first provocation, and let some of the big brains down at Justice Central figure out all the hows and whys of whatever it was Icarus was hoping to achieve from all this mayhem.

"Help you, sir? I'm afraid this facility is closed to the general public, but if you want a tour of the main EverPet labs, then our Citizens Relations office will be happy to arrange it. Their office hours are 0900 to 1700, and you can contact them on–"

Dredd silenced the security droid in the foyer with a single Armour Piercing shot, instantly transforming it into just so much expensive junk. Another shot silenced the alarm that had started shrieking as soon as his first gunshot rang out. His override card took care of the second and more serious set of security doors, and then he was through and into the lab complex proper.

The H-wagon Dredd had rode in on was a command model, with a fully equipped mobile armoury of Justice Department standard-issue weaponry. Dredd hadn't been shy about helping himself to whatever he thought he was going to need. When he exited the H-wagon, he had been carrying enough weaponry to fight a small block war all on his own.

Beyond the doors, a group of Death cultists were waiting for him. High on hate and eager for death, they charged down the corridor towards him, firing off indiscriminate volleys of bullets at him. Dredd raised his Lawgiver and introduced them to the gun's rapid fire setting, giving them an object lesson in what tight, accurate bursts of fire were all about.

Four of them hit the ground in as many seconds, Resyk-bound. Dredd popped a stumm grenade and let the rest of the survivors share its contents out amongst themselves. Respirator down, Dredd strode on through the midst of them. Choking and retching, completely incapacitated by the effects of the gas, Dredd knew none of these creeps were going anywhere in a hurry. One of them still managed to rise staggering to his feet. Dredd slammed him hard in the face with the butt of his Lawgiver. The creep ate floor, fast and sudden. Next stop for him would be a med-unit to fix his broken nose, busted teeth and severe concussion, before the Judge-Wardens threw his deranged butt into an iso-cube for the next twenty years or so.

Dredd strode on. A chorus of snarls and growls warned him what was waiting for him round the next corner. Dredd figured that Icarus's retrovirus didn't do much for IQ and common sense when it came to lying patiently in ambush. He also figured that, since they had been voluntarily infected with the virus, Icarus's vampire-things were, to all intents and purposes, legally dead. That being the case, they weren't entitled to the same legal rights as any ordinary, decent citizen that still had a pulse, and hence Dredd's next actions weren't governed by the regulations that normally applied in matters relating to the correct use of the proper and legal amount of force to be applied in carrying out his judicial duties.

Besides, he reminded himself, both the retrovirus and the Dark Judges were clear and present dangers to the lives of everyone in Mega-City One, meaning that any extra-judicial force he chose to employ was officially permitted under the terms of the Security of the City Act. Short version: no arrest, no warning shot, no shooting to wound. These creeps were going straight to Resyk.

Dredd reached for the first of the surprises he'd taken from the H-wagon armoury, popping the safety caps and timer fuses on them and throwing them almost casually round the corner. The explosions came just a second later, but Dredd had already moved into the cover of the near wall to avoid the dual waves of flame and shrapnel that came roaring round the corner.

A vampire, completely bathed head to foot in fire, came staggering round the corner. The phosphor chemicals from one of Dredd's grenades had already burned away its eyes and face, but somehow it could still sense his presence. It turned and came charging towards him, screaming in rage and pain. A moment later, anything that was left of it was decorating the walls, floor and roof of the corridor, liberally distributed there by the Hi-Ex shot Dredd had calmly snapped off.

Round the corner waited more evidence of the aftermath of the phosphor and fragmentation grenades that Dredd had just used. The shredded and burning remains of several more – Dredd estimated at least four – vampires littered the place. One of them, its lower body torn away by shrapnel, its remaining upper half charred and burning, still managed to summon up the strength to start crawling towards him, making a hideous mewling sound as it scrabbled at his Judge boots with its burning claws. Dredd put two Standard Execution rounds through the top of its head and carried on.

It was at the next corridor junction that he started to run into trouble. He was just finishing mopping up the combined group of vampires and cultists who had foolishly imagined they could lure him into some kind of crossfire ambush there. He'd picked off the first few of them with shots from his Lawgiver, demolishing one of the barricades they'd been sheltering behind with a double-blast of Hi-Ex. Heatseeker hotshots had flushed the remaining cultists out of hiding. The vamps, whose inhumanly low body temperature barely registered with the Heatseeker warheads' targeting systems, Dredd took care of with one of the other weapons he was carrying, hosing them down with a spread of rapid-fire explosive shell fire from the Colt M2000 Widowmaker.

The M2000, a replacement for the old Lawrod weapon in providing Judges with some additional heavier firepower for on-the-street use, had first come into widespread service during Judgement Day. It had proved highly effective then against zombies, so Dredd didn't see why vampire targets would prove any more resistant to its devastating effects.

He wasn't wrong. The vampires disintegrated bodily under the impact of the volleys of high-calibre shotgun shells. One of them, which had come at Dredd with an industrial las-burner, was blown clear across the corridor by the impact of the shells into its body, hitting the far wall with a sick, wet splat.

It was only after the roar of the weapon's fearsomely loud gunfire reports started to die away that Dredd heard the other sound coming from the corridor behind him: the loud, pounding tread of metallic feet, too heavy to be anything human, too regular and steady to be anything other than a droid. And not just any kind of droid.

War droids were supposed to be illegal in Mega-City One. Even before the Second Robot War, when crimelord Nero Narcos had used an army of war droids to try and overthrow the entire Judge system and install himself as the city's new ruler, the manufacture and ownership of any kind of combat-orientated robot unit was highly illegal. The Justice Department had its own war droid reserve resources, of course, although a scheme under the late Chief Judge McGruder's administration to make up the growing shortfall of patrol Judges by putting robot Judges onto the city streets had not met with success. Nevertheless, the private ownership of such droids was forbidden.

Such devices were still available elsewhere, of course. Asiatic mega cities such as Hondo Cit, Sino Cit and Nu-Taiwan did a roaring trade in war droid manufacture, and even in Mega-City there was always a thriving underground black market in war droid units still left over from previous conflicts, stretching all the way back to events as long ago as the early twenty-first century Volgan Wars. In fact, the ABC Warrior unit, dating from the mid-period Volgan Wars, was still highly prized for its combat abilities, even now more than a hundred years after its original construction, and there were those collectors and aficionados of such things who considered the ABC unit so durable and easily adaptable that they claimed they could still be in active service even thousands of years from now.

Dredd dived, rolling for cover, as the metal brute stomped up the corridor towards him, opening fire with its own inbuilt weaponry. Bullets ricocheted off walls and careened off the stone floor as the droid's weapons systems tracked Dredd, his speed and reflexes managing to keep him just that vital hairsbreadth ahead of its targeting sensors.

He dropped the M2000, knowing its high-calibre shotgun capabilities, although devastating against unarmoured human opponents, would be useless against a heavily armoured droid. The droid kept on coming, its thunderous footsteps cracking the stone of the floor. It was too big and heavy to be one of the sleek new Hondo-cit jobs that had been coming onto the market in the last few years, and superior targeting programs on the Nu-Taiwan models would most likely have found him and vaporised him by now, so Dredd's best guess was that it was probably an old Sov Blok unit, probably even pre-Apocalypse War. The details didn't worry him; if they wanted to, the Tek-Judges could try and identify it from whatever scrap metal was left when he had finished taking care of it.

He came out of the roll, Lawgiver in hand, firing as he went. Armour Piercing shells ricocheted off the droid's armoured carapace, barely even denting the thick armour there to protect its CPU core. A Hi-Ex shell took care of the heavy spit-blaster mounted on one of its shoulders. Dredd was just about to fire a second shot to destroy the mini missile launcher on the droid's other shoulder, when it hit him with the auxiliary electro-gens built into its chest unit. Crackling lightning bolts of electricity filled the corridor in front of it, leaping from metal wall to metal wall, striking Dredd multiple times. The heavily insulated material of his uniform's bodysuit saved him from the worst of it, but the blasts still threw him several metres back, slamming him painfully against the corridor wall. His Lawgiver flew from his nerveless grasp, landing far away from where he fell.

He slumped to the ground, hearing the stone-cracking impacts of the droid's footsteps as it stamped forward to finish him off, its servo-motors growling in what sounded almost like eager anticipation.

Muscles cramped with pain from the effects of the electricity blast refused to respond. Dredd's vision swam, the heavy, deadening weight of imminent oblivion pressing in on the edges of his consciousness.

Get up, old man, he told himself. You're not out for the count yet, not while your city's still in danger.

The reminder was like a shock to the system. He was moving even as the droid's giant metal fist jack-hammered down towards him, pile-driving into the area of the floor where only moments ago Dredd's head had been resting. He scrambled away from it, reaching out for the nearest weapon, which instinct and more than forty years of combat experience told him should still be lying right where its previous owner had dropped it.

The las-burner wasn't designed for combat use, and wasn't a particu-larly easy thing to operate, usually requiring a physically strong operator or even work-droid to wield properly. Its main purpose was to cut up dense materials like metal or reinforced plasteel. Perps had quickly found its uses when it came to slicing through inconvenient obstacles like vault doors and walls. It probably didn't say anything about it in the manufacturer's manual, but disabling maniac war-droids seemed to be another one of the multi-faceted tool's many useful applications.

In an impressive feat of strength, Dredd swung the heavy device one-handed, activating its power supply with a flick of his finger. The tool's las-beam instantly hissed into life, projecting several feet from its end, burning with a cold, clear light that made Dredd's eyes hurt, even through the polarised visor guard of his helmet.

The las-burner sheared through the armoured metal of the droid's right arm as if it was nothing more substantial than raw munce. The metal monster's hand fell to the ground with a loud clunk, twitching in distressed reflex, sparks and oily black hydraulic fluid spraying out from its severed end. The droid made a dull roaring sound that was either a mechanical expression of pain and anger or merely a change in the pitch of its servo-motor system as it shut down the flow of power and fluid to the damaged limb.

Dredd was moving again, rolling between the thick metal tree trunks of its legs as it swivelled round in search of him, trying to bring its remaining weaponry to bear on this one unexpectedly troublesome human target. Designed mainly for frontal assault, the droid was more vulnerable to attack in its more weakly armoured rear sections. Hefting the las-burner, Dredd quickly got to work on the backs of its legs, slash-ing into the joint-pistons and power cables there.

Hamstrung, with both legs disabled, and bellowing in impotent mechanical distress, the three and a half metre tall droid pitched forward onto its face, with a crash that reminded Dredd of the sound of a conapt building or small-sized city block being demolished.

It lay there, emitting strange mechanical growls as its servo-motors whined in protest, flailing its one still-functioning limb about the place in futile protest. A few more brief seconds' work with the las-burner put paid to even this much activity from it. Dredd walked away, leaving the now-deactivated weapon buried deep into the fused slag that had been the droid's CPU unit.

Icarus had been surprised how easy it had been to track Dredd's progress through the complex by the sound of the gunshots alone.

First had come the loud and intense sounds of several different guns firing at once, as Dredd encountered and dealt with the main groups of Icarus's security detail at the main entrance points to the lab. After that, the gunfire had become more sporadic as it crept closer to where Icarus was and Dredd penetrated further into the complex, encountering the occasional wandering vampire or small pocket of Death cultist resistance. Amidst these had come the odd explosion, the sounds of those also coming progressively closer as Dredd methodically destroyed lab after lab, wiping out years of Icarus's research into longevity and various possibilities for sustaining life after death. It didn't matter, Icarus knew. He already had everything he wanted from his research, and it was coursing through his veins, changing his mind and body in ways that puny, mortal intellects like Dredd's could never imagine.

The last explosion had come about half a minute ago, no doubt caused by Dredd laying waste to the lab just down the corridor, where the vampires' blood serum food supply was produced. If that was the case, then by Icarus's calculations he should be entering the...

Right on cue, the lab doors obediently opened in response to the Justice Department override device's command. Dredd walked in, his Lawgiver aimed at Icarus. Apart from the two of them, there wasn't another living soul in the lab.

"Dick Icarus? Fun-time's over, creep. You're under arrest."

"Really? On what charges?" Icarus's tone was casual and breezy, his voice deliberately raised to distract Dredd's attention away from the faint pounding sounds on the incubator vault door on the wall to the side of them.

"Don't get cute, punk. So far tonight, you've been responsible for the deaths of thousands. Grud knows how many more are going to die before we take care of the things you've unleashed on this city."

"Aren't you even going to ask me why?" asked Icarus, glancing down at the weapon he'd left on the desk top beside him. It was only an arm's reach away. All he had to do was–

"No need. You'll tell us everything we need to know soon enough, as soon as we get you into an interrogation cube," promised Dredd. "Why you did it, what you know of the Dark Judges' plans, any more little surprises you had planned for us. You won't hold anything back for too long. We've got interrogation techniques that'll make you tell us things you didn't even know you knew, and that's even before we bring in the Psi-Judges to go creeping around inside your mind."

"I did it because I want to live forever, and because the Dark Judges have the power to grant me that wish." Icarus was almost shouting, as much to drown out the sounds from behind the vault door as from the sense of rising excitement he felt within him. The moment was so close now, so close.

Dredd wasn't impressed. "So thousands have to die to feed your sick fantasy that the Dark Judges will give you eternal life? Grud alone knows how you managed to convince anyone to let you out of the kook cubes, Icarus. The only wish the Dark Judges are ever going to grant is a death wish. You'd have to be completely insane to ever think you could make a bargain with those things."

Dredd was walking across the room towards him, reaching into a belt pouch for the handcuffs to secure his prisoner. The noise from the vault door finally drew his attention. He paused, glancing suspiciously over at the door.

"What you got in there? More bloodsuckers?"

Icarus knew it was now or never. "Why don't you see for yourself," he screeched, making a grab for the weapon on the counter.

It was a good choice of weapon, he thought. A Flesh Disintegrator, instantly recognisable to someone like Dredd, and instantly lethal to anyone on the receiving end of its organic matter-destroying field. Icarus had had cause to use it several times before, in dealing with difficult-to-control lab specimens infected with some of the early versions of the retrovirus, and he could happily attest to its deadly capabilities.

He knew he wouldn't be able to grab the weapon, pick it up and fire it before Dredd could fire his own weapon. But then, as Icarus reminded himself, that was something he didn't have to worry about.

His hand was barely on the weapon's grip before the first Lawgiver shot punched into him, followed by two more in the space of a heartbeat, all three closely hitting in a tight cluster over his ribs. Icarus felt his heart explode, torn apart by the bullets' paths through his body. He had wondered many times what this moment would be like. His knowledge as a medical research scientist and his experiences from studying death in all its many forms over the last eight years suggested to him that it would all be quick and refreshingly pain-free. His knowledge and practical experiences had lied to him, he now knew; being shot dead hurt, and seemed to take much longer than you would reasonably expect.

A tremor passed through him. The formula coursing through his bloodstream seemed somehow to realise the fact of his imminent death, and was reacting accordingly. Icarus felt it release some of its strength into him, and he began to rise again to his feet, still clutching the disintegrator weapon, still bringing it up to bear on its target.

Dredd, caught by surprise by the fact of the nondescript-looking scientist's unexpected reliance, almost hesitated for a moment.

Almost.

Three more shots ripped into Icarus, hurling him backwards, knocking the gun from his hand. The scientist sank to his knees, blood pouring out of him. In spite of the pain from his torn-apart innards, he still managed to look up at Dredd and smile.

"Me, I know I'm coming back. For you, though, this is the end of the line."

He fell dead to the ground, Dredd at the same time spotting the small remote device held in Icarus's other hand. Icarus's hand had squeezed around it at the moment of death, activating it, and now the vault door on the far wall was sliding open. An alarm blared in warning, and over it Dredd could clearly hear the excited snarls and ravenous growls of the things behind that door.

They poured out of the vault: vampires, maybe a hundred or more of them, naked and newborn, hungry for blood, keen to start killing and spread their retrovirus further.

When they had joined the Church of Death and volunteered to undergo Icarus's retrovirus transformation process – a "rebirth into a glorious state beyond life and death", he had promised them – they had imagined that they would become natural-born predators, with nothing to fear and none strong or brave enough to stand against them. They were wrong.

Dredd's Lawgiver and M2000 roared together, their combined firepower blasting into the first few rows of vampires, picking them up and hurling their bullet-shredded bodies back into the ranks of those following on closely behind.

Dredd's marksmanship was almost as good with his left hand as it was with his right, and he kept up the punishing hail of fire with both weapons. The M2000 was difficult to control one-handed, but at this range, and with the weapon's devastating area of effect, all he really had to do was keep it trained on the general area of the open vault door, forcing anything that tried to come through that doorway to pass through the barrier of gunfire. His Lawgiver was in his left hand, picking off any vampires that managed to make it relatively unscathed through the curtain of Widowmaker fire. Vampire after vampire was knocked back, screaming and hissing, by the combined fire of both weapons, but there were still many more vampires in the vault than Dredd's guns had bullets for, and he was fast using up the magazines in both of them.

The M2000 was the first to run dry. With its final shot, it hit an enraged vampire that it had already hit at least once before, flaying its flesh even further and hurling it once more back into the vault with the others. Dredd dropped the weapon, knowing he didn't have the time to reload it. He emptied his Lawgiver of its remaining Incendiary shells, firing them into the mass of bodies in the vault's doorway, buying himself a few more seconds as the vampires retreated back, hissing and snarling, from the wall of flame that was now between him and them.

He reached for the weapons pack holding the last of the ordnance he had brought with him from the H-wagon. He activated it with a flick of a switch and threw it into the vault, throwing himself at the heavy vault door as he did so, slamming into it hard and using every bit of his strength and body weight to push it shut. Slowly, painfully, it swung shut. For one terrible moment, a mere hand's breadth before it sealed shut again, Dredd felt the weight of the vampires hurl against the other side of the door, threatening to push it back wide open in seconds, but a moment later the device he'd thrown into the vault went off, and all that remained after that was the terrible roaring sound from beyond the doors.

A second after that, Dredd pushed the door fully shut, the door's seals engaged and the vampires were trapped amidst the inferno raging inside.

Dredd had grabbed the thermal bomb as soon as he had seen it in the H-wagon armoury, intending to use it as a weapon of last resort in case Death and the other three super-creeps showed up at Icarus's labs. They hadn't dropped by to pay their respects to their liberator, but, as it turned out, the thermal bomb had still come in handy after all.

Detonating inside the thick-walled vault, it had immediately raised the temperature inside the place to well over three thousand degrees. The air beyond the reinforced doors would have ignited instantly, and everything combustible in there would be reduced to ash long before the oxygen supply had been burned up. Dredd could feel the heat radiating through the thick metal of the door, and knew that the clean-up crews would probably need to use las-burners to cut through into the vault afterwards, since the heat inside it would almost certainly have melted and fused the door workings.

He didn't care. The Teks and Meds could come and take what evidence they needed from the wreckage of the labs, but, as far as Dredd was concerned, Icarus and his vampires were one less problem to deal with tonight.

Satisfied the vampires were destroyed, he stepped away from the door, speaking into his helmet radio.

"Control – Dredd. Clean-up crews required at the Icarus labs. Tell Chief Judge Hershey the vampire outbreak has been cut off at source."

"Roger, Dredd. And Icarus?"

Dredd glanced at the corpse lying on the floor nearby. Was it his imagination, or had the corpse somehow changed in the last few minutes? It looked different somehow, larger and strangely swollen. Despite that, he was still clearly dead. Something else for the Teks and Meds to look into, Dredd supposed.

"As dead as Judge Cal," Dredd replied. "Make sure the clean-up crew gets him properly bagged and tagged. I want him delivered to Helsing at Justice Central Forensics for a full autopsy. Any word on Death and the other three creeps yet?"

"Plenty. They've hit random points across the city four times, but every time we got there they teleported away. They seem to have split up after the first attack and are operating solo, which is a new strategy, but the death count is already reaching block war levels. We've got a confirmed sighting of Mortis at Clooney Memorial – Giant's on his way there now – and Anderson's picked up a psi-flash hunch that something might be about to happen at the Churchill Smokatorium. She's heading there herself."

"And the other two? Death and Fear?"

"Nothing yet, Dredd. We've got every spare badge we've got out on the streets, and a citywide alert's been given. If they turn up anywhere, you'll know about it as soon as we do."

It was the overpowering psychic stink of pure evil that alerted every Psi-Judge in the Academy of Law to Fear's presence in the building as soon as he teleported in. And it was the sound of the cadets' frantic screaming, mere seconds later, that alerted everyone else.

Tutor Judges came running in response as word spread throughout the building that something terrible was happening in one of the dorms reserved for Psi-Judge cadets. They hammered uselessly on the door of the dorm, unable to break it down. Fear had sealed it using one of his mantrap weapons, and it would need more than brute strength to over-come the device's mysterious psychic properties.

Meanwhile, for several long and terrible minutes, the Dark Judge was able to run amok in the dorm, with thirty young and helpless Psi-Judge cadets trapped in there with him.

The sealed door finally succumbed to a fusillade of Lawgiver fire and the combined psychic efforts of three Psi-Judge Tutors. What they found when they charged in, Lawgivers at the ready, was something from their worst nightmares. Fear was gone, teleporting away again, but leaving behind him the slaughtered remnants of an entire class of Psi-cadets.

However, it would be several minutes later, after Judge Tutors had fin-ished the grim task of compiling a roll call of the dead, that the most terrible thing of all would be discovered. Four of the cadets were miss-ing. A search of the entire Academy was ordered, but it was already clear to all what had happened to them.

Fear, for whatever twisted reasons of his own, had taken them. The four cadets were in the clutches of the Dark Judges.

THIRTEEN

Anderson had almost to be restrained from jumping out of the hatch of the H-wagon while it was still in mid-air above the Smokatorium. Anxious and impatient, she forced herself to wait as it came into land, her feet hitting the ground only seconds after the tarmac had been heat-scorched by the after-blast from the H-wagon's underside thrusters.

There were Judges everywhere, cordoning off the Smokatorium building from the rest of the city.

"Rosen?" she asked the nearest officer. He pointed to a harassed-looking female Judge nearby, who was issuing orders on the radio from the back of a Pat-Wagon. Anderson strode over to her.

"I'm Anderson," she told her. "What's the situation?"

Rosen looked at her for a moment. Anderson didn't need to use her telepath abilities to know what she was thinking. Anderson's reputation – as a troublemaker, as a maverick, as the best Psi-Judge the Justice Department had, as the woman who had saved the city from the Dark Judges several times before – preceded her everywhere she went within the Department.

"He's inside," Rosen said. "Somewhere in the main Smokatorium hall levels. He ported in while we were still evacuating the place."

"Casualties?" Anderson asked.

Rosen grimly nodded her head. "Too Gruddamn many, cits and Judges. It would have been a lot worse, though, if your warning hadn't reached us. There's still some cits trapped in there, we think, but we got everyone else out." She paused, looking at Anderson. "We were ordered to wait for your arrival. You're here, so what do we do now?"

She's scared, thought Anderson. She probably hasn't been on the streets more than five years. She must be good to have made it to Tac Watch Commander this early in her career, but she's too young to have been with the Department during Necropolis. She's never met the Dark Judges before, all she knows about them are the bogey man stories she's probably heard at the Academy – and now she's scared about facing the reality behind those stories.

"Just secure the area while I go in and get him," Anderson told her.

"On your own?" Rosen asked, doubtfully.

Anderson knew exactly what Rosen was thinking. There were now several dozen Judges on the scene. Leaving aside those needed for crowd control duty, that still left more than enough to provide Anderson with all the backup she would ever need.

"If you give him the space to use that flame weapon of his, Fire's the most lethal of all the Dark Judges," Anderson told her. "He can kill fifty of us just as easily as one with that thing. No point losing any more people than we have to. Besides, I've handled all four of these creeps before. One of them on his own shouldn't be too much trouble."

The last comment was said with half a smile. Anderson looked around. "Now all I need to do is find a gun to use."

At Rosen's signal, a Tek-Judge handed her a Lawgiver. "Straight from Tek-Div central armoury, already programmed to your palm-print. It arrived just before you did."

Anderson smiled and took the weapon, testing its feel and weight. It gave a series of coded bleeps, its built-in micro-computer acknowledging her palm-print signature and signalling that it was in the hands of its rightful owner. She checked the ammo counter, seeing that it was already fully loaded. She had a feeling she was going to need every one of those shots, and all the other ones in the spare magazines she was now cramming into her belt pouches.

"You heard about what happened at the Academy of Law?" asked Rosen.

Anderson nodded. The news had reached her while she was still en route aboard the H-wagon. Four Dark Judges individually on the loose, and now four Psi-cadets taken, not to mention the massacre of the rest of their class. The problems just kept multiplying.

The snatching of the four cadets was a new and worrying tactic. The Dark Judges didn't take prisoners or hostages, not before now; the only thing they were interested in was spreading death to every living thing that came into contact with them. So what did they need the cadets for, and why specifically Psi-cadets?

With a heavy feeling of foreboding, Anderson guessed she would probably find out the answer soon enough. Assuming she survived the coming encounter with Fire.

She hefted her Lawgiver and looked at Rosen. "Okay, I'm ready."

People were always jealous that he had a real, honest-to-grud, genuine job, Ernesto Kopinski knew. He wasn't so sure, though. Of course, it was a real job, not some airy-fairy pretend kind of job like that dumb jerk of a brother-in-law of his had.

Standing around all day pretending to be a shop dummy, what kind of a job was that for a grown man? Ernesto's job was different. It required skill, application, dedication, not to mention several tedious days of introductory training. It served a useful purpose, to the city and his fellow citizens, and, most importantly of all, it couldn't be done just as well by an inanimate object, unlike the so-called job that dumb jerk of a brother-in-law of his had.

Which still didn't mean that it didn't suck.

He crawled forward through the low-roofed tubeway, his thick armoured boots splashing through the bubbling acidic gruel that swirled around his ankles. More of the same kind of gruesome organic gunge dripped from the leaking pipes overhead, splattering on the acid-proof material of his protective hood and overalls. The pressure tanks on his back hissed and gurgled, and he adjusted the pressure gauge on the barrel of his sprayer gun accordingly. His task was to crawl around down here all day, clearing blockages in the run-off pipes and sluiceways leading out from the main fat-rendering tanks overhead. Strictly speaking, it was really a job best performed by maintenance droids, but the dripping acids and metal-corroding fumes made that an expensive proposition and so, bearing in mind Mega-City unemployment was still running at over 87%, it was far cheaper and easier to use human workers.

The business of Resyk was death. Or, more specifically, the breaking down and recycling of human organic material as the corpses of dead cits were delivered to Resyk from all over the city. Once here, they were reduced to their most useful base constituents for later use in a bewilderingly large array of commercial products and substances. Resyk ran day and night, and only the very richest citizens who could afford interment in a private cemetery – or, for the truly rich and dying, a place in cryo-facilities such as Forever Towers – could avoid that final trip along the Resyk corpse disassembly conveyor belts. "We use everything except the soul!" was the proud boast of Resyk management, and there was a steady belief amongst Mega-citizens that the scientists in Resyk R&D were working on ways to remedy even that little oversight.

None of this, however, was at the forefront of Ernesto Kopinski's thoughts right at this moment. All he wanted to do was clear this new blockage, finish his shift and get the drokk out of here with the minimum of acid burns and without inhaling too many of the toxic fumes.

"Ray? Billy?" he called out, thinking he could see two forms in the drainage chamber ahead of him. Ray and Billy were supposed to be working this area on this shift, and the blockage they had been sent to clear was still there, causing an overflow that was threatening to back up all the way to the bile pumps.

Gruddamnit, if he found out that they had been slacking off again, sneaking off down to the illegal card games run by one of the conveyor belt's assistant foremen in the maintenance sub-bay next to the bone-grinders, then there was gonna be trouble.

He stepped into the drainage chamber, seeing the two figures lying there in the swirling, acidic chem-fluids. Working at Resyk, you got used to the sight of corpses real fast, and Ernesto had no hesitation in deciding that both Ray and Billy were as dead as you could get. They could only have been dead for a short while, though, otherwise they would already have started dissolving into the bubbling tox-brew they were lying in. Ernesto had seen a lot of corpses, but he had never seen two likes these, especially with what he could only describe as frozen looks of horror on their faces.

He was just reaching for his radio headset to report on what he had found, when he heard splashing sounds from the sluice-duct to his right and looked round to see the silhouette figure of a Judge coming towards him. Sure, it was a real thin-looking kind of Judge, wearing some kind of extra funky looking uniform, but Ernesto knew there were all kinds of Judges with all kinds of different uniforms, and so he didn't see anything to get worried about – not until the thing he had thought was a Judge stepped out into the dim light of the chamber and reached out towards him with something that was more like a ghoul-claw than a human hand.

"Greetingsss, sssinner," it hissed. "Rejoiccce. Judgement is here."

Dredd was still in the air, aboard his H-wagon, when the news broke.

"Dredd – Control. Got a query for you from the clean-up crew at the Icarus lab location. You sure about that call on the Icarus stiff? The meat wagon crews say there's no sign of the body."

"That's impossible, Control," Dredd snarled into the radio mic. "I put six Lawgiver slugs into him, every one a kill shot. The only place that creep was going was Resyk. Tell them to check again and–"

"Hold it, Dredd," the voice of Control abruptly cut in. "Something coming in over the radio net now. Reports coming in about a possible Death sighting... Wait, that's confirmed! We've got a positive lock on Death's position."

"Where?" Dredd's voice, instantly commanding.

"Only half a sector away from your current position, Dredd. He's at Resyk, and he's killing every living thing in the place."

The H-wagon pilot must have been monitoring the conversation, because the vehicle was already swerving round in an abrupt change of course, accelerating off towards Resyk.

"Wilco, Control. I'm on my way. Dredd out."

Being dead wasn't nearly as dramatic as one might have imagined, Icarus had decided. For a start, he still had consciousness, although he wasn't sure how much that was to do with the retrovirus, which was now steadily transforming his recently dead body. The seat of his consciousness was still tied to that body, and he was aware of his surroundings and what was happening around him, but the sights and sounds were oddly dimmed, almost as if he were experiencing them all in a strangely detached, fugue-like state. He knew he was still within his body, but he had no sense of physical existence, and any kind of sensation of pain or bodily awareness was completely absent. That was probably just as well, he decided, considering the six Lawgiver bullets that had torn his insides apart.

As far as he could tell, he was somewhere in the Undercity, carried there by the last few vampires that had remained in hiding in his lab during the confrontation with Dredd. He had no idea where they were taking him, or why. To be honest, he wished he could communicate with them in some way. On the other hand, even if he had been able to, he wasn't sure they would take any notice of his commands any longer. The way they were moving, the way they seemed to work together in perfect accord without speaking, he got the distinct impression they were acting under the direction of some outside force.

His creations were no longer his to command. For the first time since he had taken his first steps on the long road to this point, Icarus began to feel a vague unease about his presumed pact with the things he had set free from Nixon Pen.

Meanwhile, while he dwelled on what Dredd had told him about the wisdom of making deals with the Dark Judges, his former servants continued on their mysterious journey, carrying him deeper and deeper down into the darkness of the Undercity beneath Mega-City One.

Giant still woke up sometimes at night in his dorm cubicle at the Grand Hall of Justice, sweaty and panicked from nightmares about his first encounter with Judge Mortis. The experience had been a defining one for him. And almost a fatal one too, he grimly remembered. Mortis had kept right on coming at them, as he and the others had pumped round after round of Lawgiver fire into the Dark Judge's rotted, ossified body. Even after a decapitating Hi-Ex round, the Dark Judge had simply picked itself up again and reattached its head to its body before continuing the pursuit.

Mortis's touch was literally death, and Giant could still remember the putrefying stench that had filled the air as he watched the flesh rot away in mere seconds from the body of one of Mortis's victims. The memory, together with the fear of those hands ever bestowing the same deadly touch on his own flesh, had stayed with Giant a long time. He had been a cadet back then, of course, not one of the rising stars of the Justice Department and Dredd's chosen right-hand man, but some things you don't forget. Especially in your nightmares.

Now here he was, ten years later and about to confront the source of those nightmares again.

He was leading a squad of Judges down the corridors of Clooney Memorial Hospital. So far, it hadn't been difficult to work out which direction Mortis had taken. Like Dredd said, all you had to do with the Dark Judges was follow the trail of corpses.

Mortis hadn't been here long – it was less than twenty minutes since the alert had gone out and Giant had jumped aboard an H-wagon and maybe broken the Department's aerial speed record to get here – but, by Grud, Mortis had been busy in that short time. He had been going from one ward to another, slaughtering every living soul he found, and the rooms and corridors of the place were choked with corpses and filled with that same awful and familiar reek of decay. Not even the droids had been spared, because Mortis's touch affected more than just flesh. Giant had already passed the rusted and corrosion-pitted remains of several robo-docs.

They were in the isolation ward now, and there were screams coming from further up the corridor. Mortis had been busy here too, going from room to room dispensing his version of justice, the occasional locked or sealed door proving no barrier to his material-corrupting touch.

Grubb's Disease. Rad-sickness. Creeping Buboes. 2T(FRU)T. The oddities of twenty-second century life threw up a bewildering variety of new and dangerous diseases, and this was where the sufferers of such contagious ailments were treated. Of all the deadly contagions that had been loose in here, though, Mortis was by far the most lethal.

The corpse of a fattie wearing a hospital smock was blocking the corridor. This one was fresh, the flesh on it still in the process of accelerated rotting, its body looking like a deflating tent as the decaying bulk of its mountainous belly melted away, leaving bare the bones of its massively expanded ribcage. Giant vaulted over it, homing in on the continued sounds of screams from just up ahead. They were close now.

"No, please! I-I'm sick!" came a voice from up ahead. "I got Super-Duper Creeping Buboes, or something real bad like that. You... you don't wanna touch me or you'll catch it too, I guarantee!"

"Life itself is a sickness, sinner," snickered the unearthly voice of the Dark Judge. "Death is the only sure cure."

Giant rounded the corner, seeing a terrified cit in a patient's smock in Mortis's grip. The cit was screaming, Mortis's horrific decay touch already going to work on him. Too late to save this poor creep, thought Giant, bringing his Lawgiver up to bear.

"Rapid fire," he ordered his squad. "Blow that bony freak to pieces."

Mortis looked towards them, hissing in irritation, the screaming cit still caught in his lethal grasp. In one movement he turned and hurled the cit at them, using him as a human shield, throwing him into the full fury of the Judges' weapons fire.

If the cit wasn't dead already from the effects of Mortis's touch, then he surely was now, as the hail of Lawgiver bullets struck him, tearing apart his decay softened, putrefying body and spraying Giant and his squad with the leftovers.

If Giant had ever forgotten how deceptively fast the Dark Judges could move when they wanted to, he got a sudden reminder now. Mortis was in amongst them in the blink of an eye, cackling in malignant glee as he went about the business of bringing judgement to the Judges.

Furio, a ten-year veteran who had been Giant's second-in-command, was the first to die, collapsing in a rotted heap as one of Mortis's claws punched right through him. Willot, whom Giant had first met when he had been briefly posted to Sector House 301 to help Dredd in his mission to clean up the city's most crime-ridden sector, was next to go. Screaming in agony as tumours and lesions spread in seconds through his body, Willot tumbled backwards, thrashing and writhing, knocking Giant to the floor.

In the time it took Giant to kick Willot's disease-bloated corpse away from him and realise that he had lost his Lawgiver in the fall, Mortis had already killed Judges Powers, Hiassen and Goldman. That left only Giant to be judged.

Mortis loomed over him, reaching down towards him. Giant stared into the empty sockets of Mortis's skull head, feeling the tug of the powerful psychic spell the Dark Judges were capable of casting over their victims.

"Come, sinner, why try to resist? Fighting me is useless. You cannot escape your fate."

Mortis's hand descended towards Giant's face. The Judge's own hand snatched down, finding and drawing his boot knife in one smooth motion.

"Heard it before, freak. It might have had more effect ten years ago, when I was still a frightened kid – but not now."

Giant's hand came up to meet Mortis's, the knife he was holding stabbing hilt-deep through the centre of Mortis's outstretched palm, stopping the Dark Judge's taloned fingers just centimetres away from Giant's face.

Mortis hissed in anger. His powers of decay were already going to work on the blade piercing his unnatural flesh, and the metal of the knife blade was quickly starting to crack and erode away in rusted flakes. Giant had only delayed Mortis for a few seconds, but those few seconds were all the defiant Judge needed.

Giant brought his feet back and lashed out with both legs, catching Mortis square in the chest with two Judge boots, propelling him backwards. Mortis crashed into the wall opposite with a dry, bony rattling sound, but recovered almost immediately and pulled himself up again. Giant rolled, grabbing his fallen Lawgiver and aiming it at the Dark Judge as Mortis advanced upon him again.

"We've met before, freak," he reminded him. "Remember this?"

The Hi-Ex shell tore Mortis's head off. Whatever he was made of, however light and frail his leathery, mummified skin and wasted, brittle bones appeared to be, the Dark Judge was a lot tougher than he looked. Anything else would have been blown to shreds by the same shot.

As it was, it was still enough to stop him in his tracks as he bent to pick up the skull and reattach it to the snapped-off, bony stump of his neck. Giant had seen this trick before. What was new, though, was that he found out Mortis could still speak even with his head separated from his body.

"Foolish mortal," rasped the voice from the bodiless skull. "When will you learn? You cannot kill that which does not live."

"Tell it to someone who gives a drokk," replied Giant, firing a brace of Incendiaries into the body of Mortis.

Even as the hungry flames took hold of him, Mortis still took the time to wait for his head to reattach itself. Meanwhile, Giant had been acting on instinct, just trying to survive the encounter moment to moment. Seeing the open doorway to the place directly behind where Mortis was standing, he suddenly saw a way to bring this whole thing to an end.

He charged towards Mortis, even as the Dark Judge staggered towards him. The fiend was wreathed in flames, a fact that would soon force him to abandon his current body, but not before he took one last sinner with him, it seemed. Even after his body had been destroyed by the flames, Mortis's spirit would still survive, roaming the city until it found another host form to occupy and possess. If that happened, Mortis would rise again, free to continue the same kind of carnage that had occurred here and elsewhere.

Giant wasn't about to let that come to pass.

He shoulder-charged straight into Mortis, turning his face aside and holding his breath to avoid scorching his lungs with super-heated air from the flames that were all over Mortis. It was like charging into a pillar of solid granite. A pillar of solid granite that had been set blazing alight. A lancing shot of agony told Giant he had probably dislocated his shoulder and maybe cracked his collar bone into the bargain. Numerous points of growing pain told him he was on fire down most of that same side. Giant could already hear the sirens of the med-wagon that would probably soon be rushing him to the nearest sector house med-bay.

Even so, what he had intended to do still worked. Mortis reeled backwards and through the open doorway behind him. Giant slammed a fist into the door-seal switch, not stopping to beat out the flames that were eating into the material of his armour and bodysuit until he was sure the door had slid securely shut.

He stared through the transparent material of the door, watching Mortis burn. Most of the Dark Judge's clothing and unnatural flesh had burned away, leaving little more than a skeleton covered in flame. Still, he wasn't ready to die yet and staggered forward, pressing one burning, skeletal hand against the transparent wall of the room he was in. His rattling hiss of fury increased sharply in volume as the material of the wall stubbornly refused to yield to his decaying touch.

"Reinforced glasteel, freak. Supposed to be able to last for centuries, maybe even longer. Maybe if you tried long enough you could rot through it, but I don't think you've got the time to do that, have you?"

Mortis's body was already starting to collapse, too much of it eaten away by the flames to allow him to sustain it any longer. He abandoned it with a final, whistling shriek, his spirit flowing out of it as it crumpled to the ground to form a small pyre of burning bones.

Mortis's spirit-form prowled round the borders of the room, restlessly seeking a way out, hurling itself against various portions of the floor, ceiling and thick glasteel walls. Giant laughed at its growing fury.

"Oh yeah, and it's airtight too, didn't I tell you that? You're in a quarantine cube. They use them to keep suspected contagious disease cases in isolation until they know what they're dealing with. That's what you are, freak: a disease. And I've got you where you belong, in quarantine."

Watching the furious contortions the thing behind the glasteel walls was going through as it relentlessly and futilely sought an escape from its new prison, Giant reached for his radio.

"Control – Giant. I need a Psi-Judge squad to Clooney Memorial. I've got Mortis trapped here in spook form. Tell them there's no rush, I don't think he's going anywhere in a hurry."

One down, three to go, thought Giant. He wondered how Dredd and Anderson were doing with their own super-creep Dark Judge freaks.

As another blast of supernatural fire blazed out towards her, Anderson dived for cover. She hoped Dredd and Giant were doing better than her.

She rolled past the shrunken and flame-blacked corpses of another row of smokers and popped up out of cover to snap off another few Lawgiver shots at Fire. Not that it would do any good, she reminded herself.

Every time she encountered the Dark Judges, they always brought something new to deal with, some new, never-revealed-before ability or power they could use to counter the Judges' best efforts to track them down and destroy them. In the past, it had been teleporters, psychic possession, mind control, the ability to body-hop when their own bodies were destroyed and then to rise up again in the flesh of the next nearest corpse. This time, Fire had found a brand new trick of his own and, by Grud, was it a doozie.

He could use the unnatural heat of the supernatural flames that permanently surrounded him to vaporise bullets before they could strike him. Incendiaries were useless against this particular Dark Judge, of course. Falling back on what had worked against him before, Anderson had fired off several rounds of Hi-Ex shells as soon as she caught sight of him within the main Smokatorium hall – only to see them vaporised as they struck the shimmering heat barrier around him. Every Standard Execution round she had fired since had gone the same way, either vaporised instantly or ineffectually striking Fire in the form of little more than a thin spray of molten droplets. Now, as the Dark Judge hunted her through the smog-filled, corpse-strewn interior of the Smokatorium, Anderson began to suspect she was in serious trouble.

She had borrowed a helmet from one of the Judges outside. Its respirator and visor provided some protection from the poisonous, choking fumes of nicotine and tar that surrounded her, but her eyes still stung from the effects of the thick cigarette smoke that hung heavy in the air of the place. Anderson always knew she would probably die in the line of duty one day, most likely at the hands of a major-league perp like one of the Dark Judges. Except she had figured it would probably be Death that would do the honours, not Fire. And she had always imagined her death as taking place somewhere a lot more glamorous than a city Smokatorium.

There were several Smokatoriums in the city, being the only places in Mega-City One where citizens were legally allowed to smoke. Anderson could never see the attraction in the filthy habit; there were enough unpleasant and hazardous things that could happen to you in this city without deliberately poisoning your body with the after-effects of inhaling burning tobacco. The circumstances in a Smokatorium, where smokers sat in rows wearing protective suits and smoking tobacco products through filter mouthpieces fitted into the air-sealed helmets they wore, made the whole thing look even less attractive than it already was, but the Smokatoriums were still very popular. Dedicated and die-hard smokers still flocked to them to smoke everything from the finest, hand-rolled cigars from the Cuban Wastes to the cheapest brands of Brit-Cit cigarettes. Only in a Smokatorium was smoking legal, and the money generated in the hefty smoking taxes imposed on everyone using them was always a welcome addition to the city's financial coffers.

Now the lifeless smokers sat in rows where they had died. With visibility poor due to the thick, choking cigarette smoke that filled the place, and with all sound muffled by the head-enclosing helmets worn by all smokers, many of them had probably never even known what had hit them as Fire stalked from room to room, incinerating everyone he found in all of them with fiery blasts from his trident weapon.

Justice Department med-programs and health education vidverts always stressed that smoking killed. Now the proof of that was here in abundance in the Churchill.

"Good to see you again, Anderson," cackled Fire. "Looking for a light?"

Anderson dodged again, narrowly avoiding another fire blast that struck the wall behind her, setting it instantly ablaze.

There were now numerous blazes burning throughout the building, some of them spreading rapidly, all of them started by the Dark Judge's deadly trail of destruction through the place. Idly, Anderson wondered if that meant she was still going to burn to death even if she managed to defeat Fire, and then decided that she would probably be long dead by the time there was any danger of the building burning to the ground.

Even more idly, she wondered why the building's fire control systems hadn't kicked in by now. After all, Smokatoriums were just one big fire hazard, so surely there must be...

Fwooosh!

She barely moved in time, as the hungry tongues of supernatural fire licked out towards her. She rolled away from them, feeling the flames caressing her back and legs, imagining her skin start to blister even under the heat-retardant material of her uniform.

She sprang back up and ran, snapping off several Heatseekers at the Dark Judge, knowing that they would have no difficulty in locking on to him, just as she knew that they would probably be almost completely useless against him.

Fire laughed as the tiny, buzzing heat-seeking bullet missiles vaporised harmlessly in the heat-shimmering air in front of his flaming skull face. His laughter was dry and crackling, like the sound of hungry licks of flames.

"Anderson, always so fast and so fortunate. But how long can you stay that way? You have to remain fortunate all the time. I only have to get fortunate once."

He stalked forwards across the wide space towards her, swishing his trident impatiently in front of him, tracing patterns of fire in the air.

He's been toying with me, Anderson realised, but the game was coming to an end and Fire was clearly intent on closing in for the kill. Anderson instinctively backed away from him, realising with a sick feeling that she was being herded into a corner with no other means of escape.

Desperately, she looked around her, for a way up. All the exits were behind Fire, as was a window looking into a small control room. No way out that way, since the only way out of the control room was a locked door leading back into the Smokatorium hall.

And yet... there was something about that small room that drew Anderson's attention back to it.

A control room, but a control room for what?

Something – a hunch or intuition – told her to glimpse upwards towards the roof of the high-ceilinged chamber. As soon as she did, she knew she had found a way to defeat Fire, and she was moving even before she had consciously started to formulate the plan that was about to save her life and put paid to at least one of the Dark Judges.

Fire brandished his trident and a column of flame leapt from it, chasing after Anderson as she ran. Heat splashed against the wall behind her, melting the surface of the wall's material, leaving a burning map of the direction of Anderson's sprint as it chased after her along the wall, always lagging a few precious moments behind her.

Anderson fired off a series of shots. Fire laughed in malign satisfaction at what he thought was a sign of growing panic in the mind of the Psi-Judge, since none of the shots came anywhere near him. In fact, Anderson had hit absolutely everything she had been aiming at.

The first few shots shattered the viewing window of the control room, making things a lot easier for Anderson for the moment when she would hurl herself through it a few seconds later. The last shot – a Rubber

Ricochet – hit the tiny panel set into the wall on the far side of the chamber, shattering the glass over it and hitting the large red emergency switch beneath the glass.

Not bad shooting, Cass, Anderson congratulated herself as she leapt through the smashed control room window and tumbled across the console inside, hearing the Smokatorium's sprinkler mechanism finally kick in in response to her activation of the building's fire control systems.

Water gushed down, smothering the fires here and elsewhere throughout the building. Judge Fire walked through the downpour, giving off a cloud of hissing steam as the falling droplets of water noisily vaporised as soon as they came into contact with the flames of his body. The flames he produced did seem noticeably diminished by the effects of the sprinkler downpour, but they were supernatural in origin, and Anderson doubted that anything could completely douse them as long as Fire's spirit remained in possession of its host body.

Fire laughed as he stalked closer. "Foolish Anderson, did you really think this would have any effect at all?"

Anderson waited before replying, carefully measuring Fire's progress towards her. She was trapped inside the control room, with nowhere inside it to take cover. One blast from Fire's trident weapon would obliterate everything inside the small room. If Anderson had misjudged anything at all, she knew she probably only had a few seconds to live.

"No, creep," she answered, grabbing hold of the big lever handle on the control console in front of her. "I did it so you wouldn't guess that I was really planning to do this."

She hauled on the lever, her action instantly rewarded by the ominous sound from the chamber roof of something large and heavy powering up. Fire hesitated and then looked up. Anderson didn't know if Dark Judges could actually visibly express panic and alarm, but she supposed that this must be what she was seeing, as Fire saw what was happening up there in the chamber roof.

Each day after it closed, the Smokatorium underwent a rigorous cleaning process, a giant rotary fan in the ceiling of the main chamber sucking the nicotine-choked air out of the entire building and into a series of rooftop filters where it was cleansed and purified of all traces of tobacco taint before being safely expelled out into the general atmosphere of the city. That was what the huge fan-blades spinning with increasing speed up there in the chamber roof were usually used for. Now Anderson had them in mind for a completely different purpose.

As far as she could see, as the air began to swirl round the chamber in a rapidly growing vortex, Fire was going to immediately do one of two things. One of them still meant almost certain death for Anderson.

Instead, he did the other, reaching down to the teleporter device on his belt instead of aiming his trident and blasting Anderson to oblivion. His burning fingers reached out to activate the device, but Anderson was already firing her Lawgiver. She had flicked the shell selector to Armour Piercing, hoping that the solid, diamond-hard titanium bullet would have more chance of making it through the slightly diminished hazard of Fire's heat aura. It was a gamble, but a calculated one.

The bullet hit and shattered the teleporter device before the Dark Judge could activate it. His screaming hiss of anger was lost amidst the growing hurricane roar of the effects of the giant fan mechanism overhead. Fire vengefully raised his trident to send a scouring, fiery blast into the control room, but it was already too late. The weapon was pulled from his hand by the force of the wind vortex that now filled the chamber and went flying towards the spinning blades. A second or two later, Fire followed it, sucked up into the fan's hungry mouth along with all the other loose material in the chamber. Corpses, charred fragments of corpses, the litter of ash and hundreds of cigarette ends: all of it went tumbling upwards into the blades. The last Anderson heard of Judge Fire was his unholy shriek of rage as his body passed through the fan rotors and was dashed to pieces by the spinning blades.

Wedging herself beneath the console to prevent herself suffering a similar fate, she shouted into her helmet radio, praying that the Justice Department units waiting outside could hear her voice over the roar of the vortex blasting around the chamber.

"It's Anderson. I've destroyed Fire's body, but his spirit is still going to escape. It's going to be coming out of the air vents on the Smokatorium roof any second. If there's any H-wagons in the vicinity, get them there pronto. Tell the pilots to use their underside airlocks. Evacuate the air from the airlock then hover over the vents and pop the airlock hatch as soon as Fire comes out. The sudden vacuum should suck him right in. It worked before, during Necropolis. Let's see if it works again."

She crawled out from under the console, anchoring herself securely to it as she disengaged the fan rotor control. The tornado force wind died away almost instantly. A few seconds later, Anderson gratefully received the message she had been waiting for over her helmet radio.

"That's a roj, Anderson. Manta Tank Four reports it's got Fire in the bag. Word's just come through that Giant has got Mortis under containment too, over at Clooney Memorial.

Two down, two to go. Anderson found herself almost giving a silent prayer of thanks. Cruel and capricious, contrary and whimsical though they may be, the gods of Mega-City One were being relatively charitable today. As bad as the carnage had been so far, it could still have been a lot worse if all four Dark Judges remained on the loose.

"Any word yet on the other two?"

"Death's turned up at Resyk. Dredd's there now."

Resyk was five sectors away. Anderson knew that, even if she left now on a fast-travelling H-wagon, she would still get there too late to be of any help. Dredd would have to handle Death without her, but if anyone could deal with the most dangerous and unpredictable of the Dark Judges, it would be Joe Dredd.

"Copy. Any sign of Creep Number Four?"

"Judge Fear? Nothing so far, not since he hit the Academy of Law. Looks like he's gone completely to ground."

Indeed he had, quite literally.

Fear was down there in the darkness beneath the city, preparing the way for what was to come next. Through the psychic links that connected all four Dark Judges, he already knew of the defeat of at least two of his brethren, but it was only a temporary setback, at worst. Soon his work here would be complete. Then the power of the Dark Judges would be multiplied many times over, and they would at last be able to bring justice to this city and then the sinful, life-filled world beyond.

He had gathered others down here in the darkness to aid him. Some were their would-be servants from the city above, the humans and the transformed Hungry Ones, who all foolishly believed that they would be joining Fear and his brethren in the dark new world they would soon be creating. Others were the simple, debased things that lived down here in the Under-Place already. Fear had found their primitive minds surprisingly and pleasingly easy to control. Seized by terror, possessed by a mind-numbing dread of the Dark Judge, they made useful enough slaves for the moment, but, like all of the Dark Judges' other erstwhile servants, they would be judged along with all the others when the time came.

Fear watched as his servants and slaves hauled the final plinth into position, bringing it into carefully judged alignment with the others. Nearby, the Hungry Ones held the moaning, terrified figures of the four kidnapped Psi-cadets. The vampires growled softly to themselves in irritation, their blood thirst held in check only by the all-powerful command of the Dark Judge.

There was the other prize too, although Fear barely recognised it as being the same human who had served them so faithfully in engineering their escape from their prison. Fear almost cackled aloud to himself at the idea that this wretched thing had thought itself worthy of being elevated to the same status as he and his brethren. The foolish mortal's desire for life-beyond-death was motivated purely by a terror of dying. Yet how could dying be something to be avoided, when death was the natural state to which all living things should be despatched as quickly as possible?

Still, thought Fear, there were interesting possibilities in this new form their servant had created for himself. These human forms he and his brethren inhabited, even when strengthened by the power of the Dark Judges' psychic possession, had too often proven to be too fallible for the great work at hand.

Perhaps, he mused, they would find a use for the corpse when the portal was opened and the business of judging this world began in true earnest.

FOURTEEN

If the business of Resyk was death, as the facility's slogan proudly proclaimed, then it was certainly a claim that Judge Death had taken seriously. By Dredd's estimation, by the time he and the other Judges arrived, the undead creep had already slaughtered his way through most of the staff of the entire day shift, as well as the crews of several meatwagons making deliveries to the place, and also four separate and well-attended funeral parties there to see their loved ones off on their final journey along the Resyk conveyor belt.

Dredd and the others had burst in on the fourth of these funeral parties, a mass event for sixteen victims of the recent Minogue Sisters conflict, just as Death was consoling one grieving window in his own unique way.

"No need to thank me, sinner," he hissed, laughing as he thrust one skeletal hand into her chest and squeezed her heart dry. "You'll be with him again soon enough."

Dredd caught his old foe's attention with three Lawgiver rounds through the head and chest. His fourth shot shattered the teleporter device hanging from Death's belt, destroying it with just the same intent as Anderson's earlier ploy.

"Now you're going nowhere, creep, except back to the place you escaped from," Dredd told him.

Death hissed angrily, discarding the lifeless corpse still held firm in his grip. Anderson had already found out that the Dark Judges were again exhibiting some unnerving new abilities this time around. Now Death was about to prove that Anderson's experience with Fire was no fluke. At a single gesture from Death, the lids flew off the row of coffins against the far wall where the corpses would be loaded down onto the conveyor belt below, and the bullet-riddled bodies of the sixteen block war combatants climbed out to attack the nearest living things around them.

"Just a taste of what is in store soon enough for you all, sinners!" Death hissed as the reanimated corpses hungrily charged at the terrified mourners.

Dredd didn't know how far Death's newfound zombie-making abilities extended, but the tactic had already achieved its immediate purpose. While the attention of Dredd and the other Judges was on the zombies, Death had already made his escape from the room.

"Teague and Goddard – with me!" Dredd shouted to the two Judges nearest him. "The rest of you – take care of the situation here!"

Dredd was already running through the door, pursuing Death along the catwalk that ran along the length of the huge processing hall, following the conveyor belt below and the corpses stacked up on it on their progress towards the Resyk grinders. Teague and Goddard came running along behind Dredd, both of them good backup men whom Dredd knew he could depend on against a perp as dangerous as Death. All three Judges snapped off shots at Death. Lawgiver rounds punched into the Dark Judge's lifeless body, doing little to no real damage but keeping the pressure up on the fleeing figure.

Suddenly and without any warning, Death turned and went on the offensive. He reached out and, with one skeletal hand, snapped off a two-metre length of steel tubing from the guard rail of the walkway. The amount of force needed to do this was impressive, showing the super-natural strength hidden within the Dark Judge's deceptively emaciated and cadaverous frame. What Death did next was even more impressive.

He hurled the steel pole like a javelin, sending it hurtling towards his pursuers. Dredd ducked, barely avoiding the missile as it flew past him at near bullet-like speed. Judge Teague, following in close behind, wasn't so fortunate or agile. The pole struck him full in the chest, impaling itself through him, and he collapsed to the ground with almost a metre of blood-slicked metal jutting out of his back.

His partner Goddard grabbed at him before his body could slip under the guard rail and fall onto the conveyor belt below.

"Call for med-assistance and stay here with him until it arrives," Dredd ordered grimly, knowing that Death had further whittled down the odds against him, promising himself that Teague was going to be the very last of Death's victims today.

Time to bring this chase to an end, decided Dredd, firing off a brace of Hi-Ex shells at the fleeing figure in front of him. Death eluded all of them, as Dredd suspected he would, but the Dark Judge hadn't been his primary intended target.

The shells exploded into the grillwork of the walkway in front of Death, blowing it apart. Suddenly there was nothing supporting that end of this section of the walkway, and so, with a loud groan of rending metal, it collapsed beneath Death's feet.

The Dark Judge plummeted, spilling onto the Resyk conveyor belt. A second or two later, Dredd landed on the same belt, about twenty metres behind him, having jumped from the walkway to continue the chase.

Death rose to his feet, snarling: "Fool! You still think you can defeat me?"

"Willing to give it my best shot, creep," countered Dredd, raising his Lawgiver.

Before he could fire, he felt something scrabbling against the material of his Judge boot. Looking down, he saw one of the corpses there hungrily trying to gnaw its way through the toe of his boot. A Standard Execution round through the crown of the corpse's skull put paid to that idea, but more reanimated cadavers were rising up all around Dredd on the conveyor belt.

More proof of Death's newfound zombie-making ability. They came at Dredd, snarling and clawing, all of them hissing at him in an eerily familiar voice.

"Fool! You cannot stop me now!" gloated one of them, just before Dredd blew its head off with a burst of Lawgiver fire.

"Give up, you have already lost!" mocked another, as a kick from Dredd sent it flying off the conveyor belt and into the giant metal rollers that kept the whole mechanism churning along.

"Why struggle when the end is inevitable?" suggested another, shrugging off the blows that Dredd pounded into its dead face. "Soon Mega-City One will be judged. Equal justice for all, that is what we will bring."

The corpse collapsed, lifeless, back to the ground as Dredd delivered a blow powerful enough to drive its nose bone back into the decayed mush of its brain. For every zombie that fell, at least another one rose up to take its place. They threw themselves at Dredd remorselessly, clawing and biting at him, tearing away shreds of both his uniform and the skin underneath as they tried to drag the Judge down by sheer weight of numbers.

Dredd shot, punched and bludgeoned his way through all of them, showing the same indomitable, die-hard determination that had kept both him and his city alive so many times before.

Suddenly, there were no more zombies in front of him. Only Death himself awaited, and Dredd barely had time to react as the leader of the Dark Judges lunged at him. Dredd knocked aside the clawed hand that might otherwise have squeezed the life out of his heart. The important thing, he knew, was to keep Death's hands away from him, and for this he brought his daystick into play, weaving it in the air between him and his old foe, using its weighted tip to parry away any of Death's sudden, darting attacks.

Equally important, Dredd knew, was to keep Death distracted, so that he didn't realise what was happening behind him, and just how close they were getting to the end of the conveyor belt.

Dredd had rarely been this close to his ancient enemy, and the stench from Death's lifeless, decaying flesh was almost overpowering. The most dangerous of all the Dark Judges literally reeked of evil and death, souring the air around him, tainting everything that came into contact with him.

Death lunged forward again. Dredd hit him a daystick blow to the side of neck that would have killed anything living, but this time Death's attack was in deadly earnest, and he didn't retreat again. His long, thin fingers darted out, sinking through the armour of Dredd's shoulder pad to penetrate through into the flesh beneath. To Dredd, it felt like being stabbed by five burning icicles of frozen venom. His whole right arm blazed with pain and then went completely numb. His Lawgiver dropped from fingers suddenly rendered senseless and he fell to the ground, the numbness creeping slowly into the rest of his body.

Death bore down on him, his other hand poised to push into Dredd's chest to find and close on his heart.

"Hurts, doesn't it?" cackled the Dark Judge, flexing his fingers inside the meat of Dredd's shoulder, exploring the contours of the bones and muscles in there. If he was expecting any cries of pain from Dredd, he was to be disappointed. "Don't worry. Your pain and sin will soon be at an end."

Death's other hand hovered over Dredd's heart. He leered down at his old enemy, their faces only centimetres apart. "Any famous last words?"

"Yeah, creep – eat helmet!"

Dredd's head shot up, the armoured crown of his Judge's helmet smashing into Death's grinning visage. Bone shattered, teeth went flying. As viciously brutal head-butts went, it was a move worthy of Mean Machine Angel himself.

Death reeled back, spitting teeth and curses. If his claws hurt as they went into Dredd's flesh, it was little compared to how much they hurt as they were ripped back out again. The entire shoulder and arm and a good part of Dredd's chest were shot through with white-hot needles of pain. The lawman hauled himself to his feet, fighting off the wave of nausea that welled up inside him. He couldn't allow himself to succumb to it, not when Death was still a threat. His gun-hand was useless, so he scooped up his Lawgiver with his left hand instead.

Death came lurching straight back at him. Dredd's Hi-Ex shot caught him square in the chest, blowing him backwards and knocking him to the floor of the conveyor belt.

They were only a few metres from the end of the belt now. After that, there was nothing but the drop into the corpse-grinding machinery. Death was starting to draw himself up again, his chest blown open but the rest of his body otherwise intact. Dredd ran at him, not giving him a chance to decide how to react.

Dredd leapt upwards, grabbing the bottom rung of the overhanging maintenance ladder with his one good arm, swinging both legs out as he did so to catch Death full in the face with the soles of both Judge boots.

"How about it? Any famous last words for me?" asked Dredd, as Death flew backwards over the end of the conveyor belt. Any answer he might have come back with was lost in the whirring thunder of the machinery below, machinery that was designed to render the human form – even one possessed by the spirit of a Dark Judge – down into its most basic constituent elements.

Dredd hauled himself painfully up the ladder, not sure he was going to have the strength to make it to the top. From long experience, he knew he was going to be spending a lot of recuperation time in a speed-heal machine after this.

"Dredd!"

Goddard's voice. Dredd gratefully grabbed the hand wearing a Judge glove reaching down towards him. A few seconds later, he was being pulled back up to the safety of the overhead catwalk.

"Teague?" he asked.

"The Meds have got him. They say he should pull through. Where's Death?"

Dredd glanced down into the churning machinery below. "He got recycled."

He activated his helmet radio. "Anderson – Dredd. Scratch Death off the list, at least for the moment."

"Copy that, Dredd. I got a sudden psi-flash when he hit the grinders. Trust me, you really don't want to know what his last words actually were, but you can be sure they were about you."

Two Med-Judges came running up, concern written all over their faces. Dredd waved them away in annoyance. In forty years on the streets, he'd been shot, stabbed, beaten, blown up and burned to within a centimetre of his life almost more times than he could remember. Whatever his injuries were this time, they could wait.

"He's out there in spirit form again. Any idea where he's heading now?" Dredd asked Anderson.

"The Undercity," came the reply. "That's all I could pick up from him before I lost contact again. I think Fear's down there too, with the missing Psi-cadets. I'm picking up a trace of their psi-presence. I'm on my way to the Gate 38 Undercity entrance. How soon can you meet me there?"

Dredd thought of his injuries. Sensation was gradually returning to the shoulder where Death's fingers had penetrated his flesh. As sensations went, the lancing bolts of pain he was experiencing weren't exactly what you would call comforting. Clearly, the smart thing to do would be to get his injuries fully checked out in a Sector House med-bay before he did anything else.

"Meet you there in twenty," he told Anderson.

FIFTEEN

The Undercity. The ruins of Old New York, abandoned and forgotten. A festering blight that Mega-City One's original architects had dealt with by simply building over the top of it, burying the decaying streets in a vast rockcrete shell that served as part of the foundations of the shining future city they erected above it.

The Undercity may have been abandoned, but that did not mean it was uninhabited. Criminals often sought refuge in its sheltering darkness from the prying eyes of the Justice Department. As refuges go, though, the Undercity was one fraught with dangers all of its own, for its derelict buildings and eternally dark alleys were home to mutants, outlawed cults, tribes of troglodyte cannibals and sinister outcasts from the city above.

When Judges could no longer serve on the streets, many chose to take the Long Walk, bringing law to the lawless regions that bordered Mega-City One. It was often a matter of locker-room debate amongst Street Judges about whether the wild, mutie-inhabited rad-deserts of the Cursed Earth were any more dangerous and challenging as a Long Walk choice of destination than that dismal, sunless place directly beneath the streets they patrolled every day.

Dredd and Anderson had both been in the Undercity before, and its eerie ghost town streets and crumbling, derelict twentieth century buildings and remains of skyscrapers held little that they hadn't encountered before.

"More troggies in front of us," commented Anderson casually, registering the dim shapes moving in the gloom ahead of them, just beyond the furthest fringes of their flashlight beams.

"I see 'em," answered Dredd. "Nothing to get worried about. Light's usually enough to scare them off. If that doesn't work, the sight of a Lawgiver or a Judge badge will do the trick. They know better than to mess with us."

Anderson ducked sharply, barely avoiding the axe weapon that was hurled at her from out of the shadows in front of them.

"You were saying?" she asked, bringing her Lawgiver up to bear as the troggies rushed at the two Judges.

They were in the area known as Central Park, having followed what had once been Park Avenue north from where they had entered the Undercity at Gate 38. Anderson didn't know what Central Park had been like back in the days of Old New York, but now it was an overgrown, tangled maze of petrified, leafless trees and weird thorny vegetation that still somehow managed to thrive down here in the absence of natural light. It wasn't the kind of place you chose to enter unless it was strictly necessary. Anderson was tracking Death's trail, following his psychic spoor. The Dark Judge's disembodied spirit had passed this way, and recently too. That meant Dredd and Anderson had to follow him in there too.

Dredd levelled his M2000 Widowmaker. He was just about to fire – at this range, the gun would wreak carnage amongst the charging troggies – when Anderson suddenly knocked his gun barrel aside.

"Wait, there's another way!" she shouted, changing the shell selector switch on her Lawgiver and firing the gun up into the air.

The flare shell exploded in the darkness overhead, bathing the whole scene in eerie, brilliant luminescence. The troggies, the spectrum of their vision atrophied through generations of life in the lightless depths of the Undercity, screamed as one and turned and fled, their hands shielding their sensitive, light-damaged eyes.

Dredd lowered his gun and looked at Anderson. "Didn't know you had a soft spot for troggies, Anderson. My way would still have been better. At least then they wouldn't have had a chance to regroup and come back for another shot."

"It wasn't their fault, Dredd," explained Anderson. "They're just simple, scared creatures. You were right when you said that normally they would be too afraid of us to attack, but something made them. I sensed it just as they attacked, and it was almost as if they were possessed by their own terror. Their minds were filled with nothing but–"

"Fear?" said Dredd. "With a capital F?"

Anderson nodded gravely. "Looks like Death and Fire weren't the only ones to pick up a few new tricks this time around."

The troggies tactic hadn't worked, so next time the Dark Judges used their other remaining servants. A few minutes further on, as Dredd and Anderson cleared a thicket of petrified trees, they were attacked by what must surely have been the last of the vampires and Church of Death fanatics.

This time around, Anderson wasn't so concerned about preventing a bloodbath.

Volleys of Heatseekers from her and Dredd unerringly sought out and found the warmer human bodies of the cultists amongst the lines of vampires. After that, with the cultists taken care of, the two Judges could both go to town on the remaining undead.

Anderson switched Lawgiver mags, loading one filled with nothing but Hi-Ex and Incendiary shells. Lawgiver special rounds might be expensive, but Anderson didn't think that Accounts Division would be querying the cost of any excessive use of them in this particular fire-fight.

In the space of a few seconds, three vampires exploded apart under the impact of multiple Hi-Ex rounds, while the same number were transformed into stumbling, screaming mannequins of flame by Incendiary hits. Over on his side of the battle, Dredd was doing plenty to keep up his share of the kill tally. The M2000 kept up a steady rate of fire, obliterating anything that came within five metres of Dredd's position.

Despite the carnage that was being inflicted upon them, however, the bloodsucking freaks just kept throwing themselves forward. They were probably psychically controlled too, Anderson realised, but why were Fear and Death throwing their remaining followers at her and Dredd in such a reckless, suicidal fashion?

A glance at the torch-lit area beyond the scene of the battle quickly told her the answer. She didn't immediately recognise the standing stone structure erected there, but she recognised its purpose, and she could clearly sense the strong psychic vibrations emanating from the shimmering patch of darkness between the pillars of the central stone arch. Even as she watched, she saw a group of figures hurrying towards it. The disembodied spirit of Death was with them, her psi-senses told her, and so were four other distinctive psi-presences.

"Dredd!" she shouted in warning. "They've opened up a gateway to Deadworld! That's where they're taking the Psi-cadets!"

"Cover me!" Dredd shouted, running forward, blowing apart the first vampire trying to stop him. Anderson dropped to one knee, gripped her Lawgiver in two hands and began picking off targets, Hi-Ex blasting anything that looked likely to get close to her fellow Judge.

Dredd, still running, drew his Lawgiver. The M2000 was good enough for the kind of work it was designed for, but he was a Street Judge, and a Lawgiver was his stock in trade. Bullets spat out at him from amongst the standing stones; armed cultists left behind to guard the gateway. Dredd picked them off with ease; all the suicidal determination and crazed religious fanaticism in the world was no substitute for Academy of Law training, where a cadet's marksmanship training began at age five.

The last cultist fell to the ground, and Dredd was in amongst the stones. He was approaching the gateway when a shape amongst the surrounding darkness detached itself from the shadows and flowed towards him.

Alerted by her senses a scant split-second earlier, Anderson managed to shout out a warning. The shape hissed in anger and hurled something at her. Anderson cried out in pain, and fell to the ground as she felt the mantrap device's jagged metal teeth bite into her leg, penetrating right through to the bone. Dredd spun round, instinctively firing several shots into the shadow shape's central body mass, and then the most mysterious of the Dark Judges was upon him. For the second time in his life, Dredd found himself gazing into the face of Fear.

The first time had been almost twenty years ago. He had been a younger man then, of course, completely sure of himself and his abilities, afraid of nothing, free of any of the doubts and fears that came with age.

And now? What was he afraid of now, when he had once taken the Long Walk into the Cursed Earth after losing faith in the justice system he'd served all his life? When he knew that he was no longer irreplaceable, when he knew that the Justice Department had a whole new series of clones sharing the same bloodline as him coming through the Academy?

Death? No. Everyone died, and death had been an ever-constant factor through his life, for as long as he could remember. He did not fear death.

Failure. That was what Dredd was secretly afraid, and that was what he saw there in the terrible black void within Fear's open helm.

He saw his city defeated and destroyed in a thousand different ways. He saw its walls crumble, and the teeming millions of howling, vengeful muties pour through into the city beyond. He saw a city ruled by a hundred different versions of lawlessness, but in all these visions the end result was the same: its citizens, free to do what they wanted, falling upon each other in a murderous display of the very worst aspects of unfettered human nature. He saw times when the place where Mega-City One stood was nothing more than a vast smoking crater or a dead landscape of nuked-out ruins. He saw the city empty and abandoned, its giant towers slowly crumbling to dust, with no clue as to what happened to its vanished inhabitants. He saw his city under occupation by its enemies, its citizens brutalised and enslaved.

He saw all this, and in every vision he knew what he saw had happened because he hadn't been there to stop it. One day, death, old age or bad luck would catch up with him, and then Mega-City would fall.

Fear hissed in satisfied pleasure as he sensed Dredd's worst nightmares bubbling to the surface. At last, he had found something that this most stubborn of sinners was afraid of. It was all Fear needed to push the door open further into Dredd's mind and flood it with sensations of pure, unadulterated terror. In moments, the sinner would be lying dead at Fear's feet, his eyes stretched wide in final horror at the things the Dark Judge had unleashed into his mind, and then Fear's triumph would be complete.

"Yes," the cold, ghostly voice of Fear whispered. "Look deeper. Gaze into the face of Fear and know what true nightmare looks like."

Dredd looked, and for a moment stood on the edge of the precipice. Then he remembered three things, and the shadowy terrors waiting for him down there in that abyss retreated back into the shadows, snarling in cheated anger.

He was Joe Dredd, a Judge of Mega-City One, and he wasn't going to lie down and die as long as his city still needed him.

"Told you once before," growled Dredd, reaching down to his belt pouch. "Maybe you don't remember, so here's a quick reminder…

"Gaze into the fist of Dredd!"

Dredd's fist smashed into the empty helm that was Fear's head. The Dark Judge reeled back, hissing in outrage. A moment later, though, Fear was rising up again, damaged but still intact.

"The years have made you weak, sinner. Now you no longer have the strength to defeat me!"

"Don't bet on it, creep," Dredd told him. "Check your headspace. I left something for you in there."

Dredd hurled himself aside as the frag grenade he had left inside Fear's open helm exploded. The blasted remains of Fear crumbled to the ground, trails of black vapour already starting to seep out of it as Fear's spirit abandoned its destroyed host body.

Dredd didn't waste any time. The suction trap device was in his hand even before the Dark Judge's spirit had finished seeping out of its former body. He threw it, its small anti-grav generator and gyro-stabilisers activating immediately. It hovered above Fear's abandoned body, powerful motors kicking in to draw in everything in the air around it, including the gaseous stuff of Fear's escaping spirit. Fear gave one last hissing scream as his spirit-form was drawn inexorably into the device, and then the trap sealed itself shut again. It fell to the ground, its power used up, giving little hint of the malign monstrosity safely held inside it.

Dredd picked it up, and looked over to where Anderson was limping towards him. The mantrap, its jaws prised open, lay behind her, as did the corpses of the last few vampires who had foolishly thought she was trapped there helpless.

He tossed the suction trap over to her. "Souvenir of your trip to the Undercity, courtesy of the Psi-Div Teks."

She caught it, wincing in pain from her injury. Fear's mantrap had done a real number on her leg, Dredd saw.

"Three down–"

"And one to go," Anderson said, looking at the swirling darkness of the dimensional gateway. "Death's escaped back to Deadworld, and he's taken the Psi-cadets with him. Grud knows what he's planning to do with them."

"Nothing good," decided Dredd, reloading his Lawgiver before moving off towards the gateway entrance.

"Wait, Dredd! You can't go through that thing on your own! You need me there too!" Anderson started limping forward after the other Judge, but her injured leg suddenly gave way beneath her. Giving an involuntary cry of pain, she fell forward. Dredd caught her and lowered her gently to the ground.

"You'll be more of a liability than a help in Deadworld, with that leg," he told her. "Wait here for backup. Anything except me tries to come back through that gateway, use Hi-Ex to demolish the whole thing. Check your chronometer – I'll be back within an hour."

"And what if you're not?"

Dredd was already walking away towards the mouth of the portal.

"Then Hi-Ex it anyway. If I don't make it, then at least we haven't left the door open for Death to come back. Whatever he's planning, I'm going to make sure it ends on Deadworld."

And then he was gone, swallowed up by the swirling darkness of the gateway.

Dredd's boots crunched noisily on the carpet of bones at his feet. The bleached litter of human remains stretched out in all directions, for as far as the eye could see in the perpetual twilight gloom of Deadworld. How many were there, Dredd wondered. Hundreds of millions? Billions? However many, it could never be enough for the Dark Judges. They had exterminated all life on their own world, and now they wanted to export this same nightmare to Dredd's world.

Dredd had been on Deadworld before. The carpet of bones, the twisted buildings with giant, screaming faces emerging out of them, the eerie, eternal silence that hung in the air, the sinister gloom that cast a lifeless pall over everything – all of it was familiar to him, like the memory of a particularly bad dream.

This is what my city will look like one day, he reminded himself, if we fail to stop Death and the others.

They were just ahead of him, he could see, mounting the bone-scattered steps of what had probably been this world's version of the Grand Hall of Justice. There weren't many of them left, Dredd saw. Four vampires or cultists, each one carrying one of the Psi-cadets, and another group carrying something large and shroud-covered on a makeshift stretcher. Dredd couldn't see the disembodied spirit of Death, but he knew it would be here somewhere, hissing commands and sinister exhortations to its servants.

The bloodsucking freaks disappeared inside the vast, fortress-like building. Dredd picked up his pace, hoping to catch them before they could begin whatever it was they were planning. He got halfway to the entrance of the building before, with a dry rattle like someone expiring on a slab, the inhabitants of Deadworld began to come to life again.

Skeletal fingers reached up to claw against the soles of his Judge boots, trying to pull him down into the writhing bone carpet at his feet. Empty skulls shouted out hate-filled insults or defiant threats, all of them speaking in Death's own hissing, mocking tones. Dredd kept on going, in places actually wading through the layers of human remains as they rose up around him.

They came up in massed groups, the tangled mess of bones creating strange skeletal hybrids as the fragments of different bodies were freely used to form brand new composite forms. Roaring blasts from Dredd's M2000 blew them back into the bone-dust from where they came. He kept on firing, destroying group after group just as fast as they rose up to face him. Those few that survived the furious barrage succumbed easily enough to punches or blows from his weapon butt, collapsing back into the ground whenever they were struck with enough force. It was grim, tiring work, but Dredd was in little real danger from the waves of skeletal figures that threw themselves at him. The real point, he knew, was to keep him busy and delay him from reaching Death's lair.

He broke through at last, reaching the entrance to the fortress in a few paces and discarding the empty Widowmaker as he sprinted up the steps towards the open doorway. The skeletal things pursuing him collapsed as one, the bones of the closest ones tumbling rattling down the steps behind him.

After that, Dredd was through the doorway, which took the form of a giant screaming mouth, and into the lair of the Dark Judges.

It wasn't difficult to work out which way to go. The rising sound of the chanting echoed through the dead, empty corridors and chambers of the place. All Dredd had to do was follow the sound back to its source.

The Judge found Death and the others in a vast, high-ceilinged chamber deep inside the fortress complex.

The four psi-cadets were tied down on the top of crystal slabs, grouped around a structure that was like a more elaborate version of the gateway portal in the Undercity. Crackling bolts of psi-energy leapt from the cadets to the dark, stone-like material of the new portal that dominated one wall of the place. As each bolt struck, flickering power runes became visible, carved into the surfaces around the edge of the portal, and the glowing, swirling haze at the centre of the gateway seemed to grow slightly larger and more ominous every time.

Dredd strode forward, sheer instinct warning him of the waiting ambush vital moments before it came. The vampire that leapt at him got a Standard Execution round through its head for its troubles. At the same time, however, a cultist hurled a dagger at him from his other side. Unable to dodge the weapon in time, Dredd simply chose the most expedient course and used his free hand to block the blade, which would otherwise have found his heart. A brief grunt of pain was his only reaction as the spinning knife sank through the material of his Judge gauntlet, impaling him through his left hand.

Dredd had better things to do than react to the injury. The knife-throwing creep got two shots through the heart back in return, and so did his pal while he was still fumbling to aim his spit pistol. Half of what he had left in his Lawgiver's magazine took care of the rest of the Dark Judges' remaining servants. A few seconds later, the last of the gunshots faded away, the last of the cultists slid to the floor, and Dredd declared the Church of Death officially out of business.

He ran towards the nearest of the Psi-cadets, intending to free them. As far as he could see, he and the four cadets were the only things left alive in the chamber.

And as soon as he'd formed the thought, the... the thing appeared out of the shadows on the far side of the chamber.

"Hello, Joe," it cackled in a voice that was both horribly familiar, but still somehow different. "Surprised to see me back so soon?"

"Icarus!"

Dredd knew this wasn't really the deceased Dr Dick Icarus, aka Vernon Martins, that he faced, even as the surprised exclamation of the name escaped from his lips. For one thing, Icarus was dead. For another, the last time Dredd had seen him, he hadn't been three metres tall and covered in thick bony plates of armour that rose out of his mutated, virus-warped flesh.

"Not quite," growl-hissed the thing in a voice that was half Death's, and half something even stronger and yet more monstrous. "Our servant's spirit has left this flesh, but his sinful attempts to attain eternal life would seem to have had their uses. His serum flows in this body's veins, transforming its dead flesh. Now it is truly indestructible, a fitting new form to contain my spirit and a vessel with which to continue our great work."

As the thing spoke, Dredd could see Death's own ghastly visage emerging at moments from the pulsing mass of flesh that was its face. It was still changing, still transforming before Dredd's eyes.

"Indestructible?" sneered Dredd. "Fine in theory. Let's see how it works in practice."

His Hi-Ex shots caught the Death-thing square in the chest, blowing it backwards off its feet. It landed heavily and twitched for a moment, lying in a spreading pool of its own fluids and exploded flesh. It lay there for a moment, but then began to climb to its feet again.

Dredd watched, seeing its flesh knitting back together, layers of hard bone-shell pushing up through the surface of the skin to provide additional natural armour. In what seemed like seconds, the thing's body had regenerated itself. If anything, in fact, it actually looked slightly larger, more powerful and menacing than it had before he had shot it.

The Death-thing growled in pleasure, pleased at this test of its new body's abilities. Dredd didn't give up. Standard Execution rounds struck against its bony armour, to little effect. A Hi-Ex round to the head wiped the gloating smile from its face, but only for a moment. After that, the smile just grew back again, along with the rest of its face. Several Incendiary rounds burst against it, setting it ablaze. The phosphor-fed flames caught for a moment but died away again, unable to affect the stuff of the thing's unnatural body. What little flesh had been burned flaked away in blackened scales, to be instantly replaced by newly regenerated tissue.

Death was shambling towards him all this time, forcing Dredd to circle away from him, keeping the altars with the Psi-cadets on them between the Dark Judge and his prey. A moan escaped from the lips of the cadet nearest Dredd, as another current of rippling psi-energy leapt out from her towards the portal. Death gloated at the sound, as if it was the sweetest music.

"Yes, with the energy from these little ones, I can open the dimensional gateways to their full extent. The Sisters of Death will be found and returned to us. Deadworld and your own corrupt dimension will merge together as one. I will cross over again to free my brothers. In this body, with our two worlds merged into one, I will be invincible, and all will finally be judged!"

"Right. And what makes you think we're going to stand here and let that happen?"

It was Anderson's voice. Dredd turned to see the Psi-Judge standing at the entrance to the chamber. She looked seriously haggard, worn out by everything she'd been through in the last twenty-four hours. Then Dredd remembered his own experiences in the same period, and realised he probably looked just as bad.

"Anderson! Thought I told you to–"

"Stay and guard the gateway in the Undercity? Yeah, well, you know me, Dredd. I never was much good at following orders. So how do you want to handle this?"

"Free the cadets. I'll keep gruesome here busy while you do it," Dredd ordered, snapping off another series of shots at the foul thing containing Death.

The brute charged forward, knowing that it was now under serious threat. Dredd hit it with everything he had, and then some more, just for good measure. The Death-thing staggered under the crippling impact of multiple Hi-Ex shells. Rapid-fire bursts tore into it. Incendiaries set it ablaze. Armour-piercing shells drilled through the bony plates of its chest, futilely seeking out vital organs to puncture and burst.

The Death-thing absorbed it all, and just kept on coming. Dredd stood his ground, knowing that every bullet impact still delayed it for one crucial moment more, giving Anderson more time to free the cadets. He risked a glance back, seeing that she had freed the first of them. He had only looked away for the barest of moments – but when he looked back the Death-thing was right on top of him.

It lashed out at him with its claws. Dredd felt razor-sharp talons shred apart the armour of his eagle shoulder pad and then he was flying through the air. The bone-jarring collision with the wall only added to the damage Dredd had just suffered, but even as he fell to the floor, he was reloading his Lawgiver and taking aim at Death's monstrous new form as it bore down on him once more.

Three Hi-Ex rounds staggered it in its tracks. A raking blast of Standard Execution rounds blew out both of its eyes.

Two cadets freed now. Weak and confused though they were, they still ran to help Anderson free their remaining companions.

An Armour Piercing shot erupted through the back of the beast's head, unleashing a torrent of black, slimy matter from inside the Death-thing's skull. Double blasts of rapid-fire took away its knees. It stumbled for a few seconds as its body regenerated the damage, and then kept on coming.

Three cadets free now. They huddled together in fear as Anderson hurried to free the last of them.

Dredd protected them, standing there pumping round after round into the Death-thing's body as it remorselessly came on at him. With a hellish shriek, it lashed out with one hand, knocking the weapon from Dredd's grip, grasping him by his empty gun-hand as it hauled him up off his feet, dangling him in the air in front of its grinning face.

Death squeezed, enjoying the spreading grimace of pain on the face of his old enemy as every bone in Dredd's hand was crushed, the broken bones grinding together under the relentless pressure of Death's grip.

Dredd blacked out for a few moments. The Death-thing dropped him with a disappointed shrug, and then prodded at the groaning figure lying at its feet. "Wake up, sinner," it hissed. "Judgement time is here at last!"

"Got that right at least, freak," Anderson challenged, standing with the four psi-cadets clustered around her. "You wanted to use these kids' abilities for your own sick reasons. Let's see how you like getting some of it back in return."

She and the cadets linked hands, linking minds at the same moment.

Psi-blasting was only taught to Psi-cadets in their last two years at the Academy of Law, and the cadets had just begun their training in it. Anderson had, however, had more than a few years' practice. She focused their power through her own mind, amplifying and focusing it, adding her own considerable psychic strength to theirs.

What hit Death was the psychic equivalent of a close-range blast from a sawn-off scatter gun. His bestial form reeled back, screeching in psychic and physical pain. Injuries he had thought safely regenerated spontaneously opened up again. Wounds blossomed across his body, overwhelming this new form's ability to deal with them. Death screeched hideously again, feeling his control slipping over his host body, feeling its strange, unnatural flesh begin to rebel against him.

"Now, Dredd!" shrieked Anderson, bringing her own Lawgiver up to bear. Dredd rolled and grabbed his own fallen gun. His gun-hand was useless, and his other hand was still injured, but as long as he could hold a gun, Dredd was still to be considered completely lethal.

The two of them opened fire simultaneously, and Death's new body was destroyed utterly in a few furious seconds of combined Lawgiver fire. Death's spirit was already abandoning the thing, even before the burning, shattered fragments of it hit the ground.

"Uh-uh," warned Anderson, focusing her psi-powers again. "Your non-corporeal butt's going nowhere, except back with us."

With her mind still linked to those of the psi-cadets, she reeled Death's screaming, struggling spirit-form in with relative ease. At the last moment, she broke off all psychic contact with the others – cadets that young and inexperienced weren't up to having a super-creep like Judge Death crawling around inside their minds, Anderson wisely decided.

Death's spirit flowed unwillingly into her, held fast in the iron grip of her psi-power. It was inside her, and she felt the old, sickeningly familiar lurch of repugnance as everything he was reached out to taint her mind and soul. With a final, wrenching mental effort, she seized hold of him and pushed him down into the dark, buried place in her mind that she had prepared for him. His screams of psychic rage filled her mind as he was forced in there and she slammed shut the mental barriers that would hold him until she was ready to undergo the long and stressful process, assisted by a carefully chosen group of other experienced Psi-Judges, that would be necessary to extract the Dark Judge's spirit again and force it into another, more permanent prison.

Her strength gave way as soon as she knew she had Death under control. She stumbled and fell forwards, only to be caught by Dredd, who by rights should barely have been able to stand himself.

"I'm... I'm all right," she assured him, weakly. She could still feel Death inside her mind, squirming frantically against the barriers of his psychic prison. "But I can't hold him forever."

She gestured towards the now-deactivated portal, which showed only blank stone where minutes ago there had been the swirling darkness of the extra-dimensional void. "Whatever you've got left, use it to destroy that. Even if they ever get out again, this is one option that's not going to be available to them again. And then, after that..."

She looked at the four, still-traumatised cadets. One of them was quietly sobbing to herself. Under normal conditions, had this been a Hotdog Run or any other kind of live training mission, that would have earned a cadet a reprimand, or perhaps even have been grounds for failure and instant dismissal from the Academy. Under the circumstances, though, even Dredd wasn't going to comment.

"After that, we go home," Anderson promised.

SIXTEEN

"And the gateway in the Undercity?" asked Chief Judge Hershey.

"Destroyed also," Psi-Chief Shenker assured her.

Hershey sat back in her chair, digesting everything she had heard in the last few hours as the Council of Five had convened in special session to discuss the aftermath of the recent carnage caused by the Dark Judges' escape.

It could have been a lot worse, she reminded herself, looking at the death toll figures that scrolled across the screen of the small desk monitor in front of her. It still made for grim reading but yes, she told herself, it could have been a lot worse.

The Church of Death was officially no more, its members either dead or locked up for life in the cubes. EverPet had been shut down, and Icarus's secret research work seized by the Justice Department before anyone else could try to replicate it. Even before Justice Department med-scientists had started going through it in detail, Judge Helsing had been able to successfully replicate a cure for the effects of Icarus's retrovirus. There would be no more outbreaks of any plagues of undead in Mega-City One for the foreseeable future.

Harsh lessons had also been learned. A new prison to hold the Dark Judges had already been built. Death and his three brethren would be its only inmates, and the facility's location was a closely guarded secret, even within the ranks of the Justice Department. Security procedures at the facility would be ultra-rigorous, with several systems of fail-safes in place. There could hopefully never be a repeat of the events that happened at Nixon Pen.

"We've heard all the reports," Hershey announced to her assembled Division heads. "Does anyone have anything to add?"

Ramos cleared his throat noisily and shifted in his seat. Hershey looked expectantly towards her head of Street Division. She could already half-guess what he was going to say.

Ramos pointed to the thick stack of files on the table in front of him. "With respect, Chief Judge, we've had full reports on all the facets of this incident, from all the senior Judges involved. Giant. Helsing. Grud, even Anderson managed to file something–"

Hershey interrupted him. "If you're wondering about Dredd, I remind you that his preliminary report is there in front of you, along with all the others."

"Yes, his preliminary report," emphasised Ramos, who was infamous in the Justice Department for his strict belief in the importance of proper paperwork. "But when can we expect to see his complete report?"

Despite the gravity of the events they had been discussing at the Council meeting today, Hershey still had to fight to suppress a slight smile as she answered Ramos's query.

"The Meds tell me Dredd is still undergoing speedheal treatment. I'm sure, however, he'll be looking forward to catching up on his paperwork and submitting a full written report to the Council when he returns to active duty in a few days' time."

"But, Dredd, you can't leave the med-bay yet! You've got to give the speedheal time to take full effect, and the Chief Judge's office said that they were to be informed before–"

Dredd's only response was a trademark menacing glower as he hit the activate switch and the elevator doors slid shut in the face of the pan- icking young Med-Judge.

Riding the elevator down to the Sector House motor pool level, Dredd activated his helmet radio. He was immediately immersed in the non- stop flow of comms data that was the strangely comforting background buzz to the daily life of every Street Judge in the city.

"Item: suspected mob blitz reported, Tony Soprano Skedway…"

"Item: riot by Human League anti-droid agitators in progress, Robot of the Year Show. Riot squad in attendance, Judge Giant commanding…"

"Item: multiple vehicle pile-up, Mo Mowlam Megway. Extra meat and med wagons required urgently. Sounds like a real mess down there on Mowlam…"

"Item: Justice Central reminds all units that there's a full moon tonight. Expect an increase in futsie crimes and general psycho activity. Additional kook cube space has been allocated for tonight's quota of loon-related arrests…"

Dredd flexed the muscles of his gun-hand as he listened to the litany of item reports. The speedheal treatment had been a perfect success, reknitting the broken bones in the hand in almost record time, and the Meds had assured him there was no nerve damage, but the hand still felt slightly stiff and unresponsive to Dredd's own hyper-critical sense of self-judgement. What might seem more than good enough to anyone else was more often than not completely insufficient for the exacting standards Dredd set for himself.

What he needed, he decided, was something to give him a chance to test his combat responses and Lawgiver-handling skills under real combat conditions.

"Item: block war flaring up at the Minogue Conapts. Looks like Kylie and Dannii are renewing hostilities again. Units already at the scene requesting Senior Judge assistance."

The elevator doors opened, and Dredd walked out to where the vehicle pool Tek-chief had a fully fuelled and ammo-loaded Lawmaster already waiting for him.

"Control – Dredd. I'll take command at the Minogues. I'm on my way."

His brethren at times fought and raged against the even more restrictive confines of their new place of imprisonment, but Death remained still and silent, content for the time being to merely observe the conditions of the barriers and wards that held them in check, and study the minds of their human jailors.

Slowly, imperceptibly, the thinnest, most invisible tendrils of his psychic aura crept out to explore the limits of this new place and of the living minds that inhabited it. He was patient, never rash or greedy, and his slowly expanding knowledge of all that was happening around him passed beneath the psychic perceptions of the batteries of Psi-Judges who were there day and night to keep watch over him and his brothers.

There were possibilities even here, Death sensed. Dim and remote they may be, but Death was patient in a way that his still-living jailers were not, and after all he had all eternity to wait and plan, if need be.

"Patience, brothers," he consoled the others, whispering to them in a voice so quiet that it existed at a level never even suspected by the living. "One day we will be free again, I promise, and then our great work will begin again."

On the other side of the dimensional void, in the empty silence of Deadworld, something stirred amongst the jumbled litter of ancient bones that was all that remained of the original victims of the Dark Judges.

Death had been wrong when he had thought he had seized control of an empty vessel when his spirit had flowed in to take possession of Icarus's retrovirus-mutated corpse. Some vestige of the body's original owner had lingered, remaining trapped and helpless within the prison of its own dead flesh, powerless to intervene as the Dark Judge had claimed that same flesh for himself.

That same remote vestige had survived the destruction of its body, but in being freed from that dead flesh, it found it had merely exchanged one prison for another, larger one. It wandered the far reaches of its new prison, receiving no response to its increasingly frantic entreaties for help.

Dr Dick Icarus, aka Vernon Martins, had achieved his wish at last. Here in the empty, still spaces of Deadworld, he would live forever, lingering bodiless and alone for all eternity, with nothing but the dead bones to hear his whispered, begging pleas to be granted the oblivion he so desperately craved.

BAD MOON RISING
BY DAVID BISHOP

MEGA-CITY ONE, 2126

PROLOGUE
SEPTEMBER 12, 2126

"Pull over!"

Muriel Staines jumped in her seat, startled by the bellowing voice. Her maroon roadster swerved across John Colby Overzoom before resuming its position in the fast lane, crawling along at half the minimum speed limit for any road in Mega-City One. The ninety-nine year-old motorist squinted at her rear-view mirror, trying to work out who had startled her. It was bad enough having to drive across five sectors in twilight to visit her older sister Grizzelda, especially with the way youngsters tore about the place these days. She didn't need some ninny shouting at her as well.

"Pull over – now!"

The voice was shot through with steely resolve, a bass growl of equal parts rockcrete and suppressed rage. Miss Staines felt sure she had recognised the voice from somewhere but couldn't quite place it. While Muriel searched her memory, the roadster wandered across six eastbound lanes. Normally such a manoeuvre would have caused a horrific crash but this stretch of road was curiously free of traffic.

"Pull over or else I will shoot out your tyres!"

The elderly spinster was the kind of motorist who saw thousands of accidents but never had one herself. The reason was simple: Miss Staines caused accidents, her erratic driving a catastrophic catalyst for chaos and carnage. Muriel had puttered on to John Colby three onramps back, leaving a trail of devastation of which she was blissfully unaware.

"This is your final warning, citizen! Cease and desist driving, or suffer the consequences!"

The mist surrounding Miss Staines's memory cleared and the oldster remembered where she had heard the voice before. A Judge had come to her block and addressed the Neighbourhood Snooper Society: a collection of elderly busybodies and curtain twitchers Muriel had founded in 2112. The Judge had been a stern-faced fellow, short on patience and terse of phrase. Now what was his name again? Dredger? Drood?

No, it was Dredd – Judge Dredd!

Muriel bit her bottom lip nervously. Why should he be shouting at her? "Oh dear. I hope I haven't done something wrong," she muttered.

Sixty-seven seconds later Muriel was in cuffs, the maroon roadster a crumpled write-off on the overzoom's hard shoulder. Standing over her was Mega-City One's most famous law enforcer. Dredd's motorcycle helmet obscured most of his head and face, so only his surly mouth and jutting jaw line were clearly visible. But his dark mood was all too evident.

"Driving below the legal speed limit – six months," he snarled. "Driving too slowly in the fast lane – six months. Reckless endangerment of other motorists – five years. Careless use of a roadster causing death – twenty counts, each carrying a tariff of twelve years. Failing to observe the commands of a Judge – five years. Total sentence of two hundred and fifty-one years, to be served cumulatively."

A hover-wagon descended from the darkening sky as the overzoom's streetlights flickered into life. It would soon be night. Dredd peered down at his prisoner. "How old are you, citizen?"

Miss Staines was affronted at such impertinence. "A lady never–"

"How old?!"

The eldster sniffed haughtily. "Ninety-nine, if you must know."

The Judge nodded. "I'm disqualifying you from driving for life – just in case. I doubt medical science will keep you alive until your three hundred and fiftieth birthday, but I'm not taking any chances." He nodded to two Judge-Warders who had just emerged from the hover-wagon. "Get her out of here!"

Dredd activated the radio microphone in his helmet as Miss Staines was led away. "Dredd to Control. I've dealt with the perp responsible for the John Colby pile-up. If you haven't got anything else for me, I'm signing off."

A brief crackle of static in Dredd's ear signified his transmission had been heard by one of the operators in Justice Department's despatch division. Control was populated by hundreds of Judges who sat behind terminals watching the city all day and night. They directed street patrols to crime scenes and potential trouble spots. The Big Meg was home to four hundred million people, crowded into several hundred sectors. Unemployment was endemic and the vast majority of citizens survived on welfare, bored beyond belief. Every one of them was a potential criminal.

"Control to Dredd. Sorry but you're needed elsewhere."

The Judge scowled, his pugnacious frown souring further still. "Control, I've been on patrol for twenty-three hours non stop. I need twenty minutes in a sleep machine and a chance to eat. What's so urgent?"

"Sector 87 is severely short-handed and Psi-Division precogs are expecting trouble there tonight. You've been assigned to augment the street patrols in 87. Chief Judge Hershey personally selected you for this job. Report to Sector Chief Emily Caine – she's expecting you."

"Terrif," Dredd growled under his breath. "Anything else I should know?"

"Yes. You're due at roll call in nine minutes."

"It takes half an hour to reach Sector 87 from here."

"Deal with it. Control out." Another crackle of static indicated the conversation was at an end.

Dredd strode to his Lawmaster motorcycle and gunned the engine into life. The fat black tyres squealed in protest as he peeled away from the remains of Muriel Staines's roadster, the bike rapidly accelerating past one hundred and forty kilometres per hour. Dredd had never missed the start of a roll call in his long career as a Judge and he wasn't going to start now.

Misch wasn't like most children in Mega-City One. For a start, her skin was blue and she had mottled yellow spots around her eyes and across the backs of her arms. Misch was humanoid, but her alien physiognomy displayed distinct differences from other children. Instead of hair, fat tendrils of excess flesh sprouted from her scalp and hung down from the back of her head. Her eyes were perfectly circular, and they had a nictitating membrane that protected them from the harsh sunlight on this strange world. Her hands had three digits and her mouth was filled with row upon row of sharp incisors. But the alien child had a friendly smile on her face most of the time.

This was not one of those times. Her broodfather, Nyon, was arguing with the creature that lived in the con-apt next door. Misch could hear them shouting at each other outside the front door; the paper-thin walls of the building ensured everyone else could hear the argument too. There were no secrets in Robert Hatch Block. Little more than a hovel, the structure housed three hundred alien families in tiny con-apts originally designed as single person dwellings.

Robert Hatch had been erected to cope with an overflow of newcomers from Alien Town; it was the Big Meg's sector designated for housing extra-terrestrials. The block was made of the cheapest materials available, its components prefabricated elsewhere and then slotted together on site. Robert Hatch had only been designed as a temporary solution to a short-term problem, with a maximum lifespan of eighteen months before it should have been demolished. Eighteen years later, the alien ghetto was still standing, an eyesore in the middle of Sector 87's most prosperous area.

Damp climbed the walls inside and out. The turbolifts had long since ceased working and no repair crew would ever set foot inside the building. Unless the residents were able to fix things themselves, they stayed broken. Paint peeled off the walls, light fittings flickered fitfully and the air conditioning system had surrendered years before. Down some corridors the air had a greasy, noxious taint, while ceilings were stained a sickly green.

Misch listened as her broodfather's guttural voice became harsher and more insistent. He was using Allspeak, the universal language adopted by most aliens when they were talking to each other.

"We have just as much right as you to live here!" Nyon protested.

"Maybe. But can't you do something about the stench from your con-apt? How am I supposed to eat with the smell of rotting flesh infesting my home?"

Misch could not help smiling to herself. Their neighbour was Kehclow, a gaseous lifeform from the Bilal Cluster who best resembled a translucent blue cloud. Misch did not doubt he could smell, but the thought of him having a nose amused her. It would look very out of place on Kehclow, who was seen floating along the corridors tutting to himself most evenings. The alien girl opened the front door a fraction so she could peer out at her broodfather. He did not look happy.

"Kehclow, you know perfectly well that my species are carrion eaters. We can only ingest nutrients from the corpses of animals that have been dead for several weeks. If you can suggest another way we could feed ourselves, I'd be happy to hear it. Otherwise, stop bothering me and my family about things we cannot change!"

Nyon's face was turning purple, a sure sign his temper was fast running out. Misch wished her broodmother was here; she would calm him down with a quiet whisper or two. But she had gone out to the alien shoppera in search of ingredients for their evening meal.

"If the air conditioning system was repaired–" Kehclow began.

"This wouldn't be a problem," Nyon agreed. "If each species was housed separately instead of being intermingled, you wouldn't have to tolerate our ways and we wouldn't have to tolerate yours. If, if, if – you can say 'if' all you want, but it won't change anything! Good evening to you!"

Misch retreated back into the con-apt, not wanting her broodfather to know she had been watching him. But she had heard Kehclow's final comment as Nyon began opening the door. "Vucking vultures."

Nyon stopped and looked back at his gaseous neighbour. "What did you say?" Misch's broodfather hissed, cold fury in his voice.

"Nothing, nothing," Kehclow replied, hastily retreating down the corridor. "Good morrow to you!"

Nyon stepped into the con-apt and slammed the door behind him. He let slip a string of obscenities in the native tongue of R'qeen before noticing his daughter in the corner playing with her toys. "Misch! I didn't see you there." Nyon shuffled awkwardly. "Don't tell your broodmother what I said, will you?"

She smiled at him, one hand spinning a multi-coloured hover-globe in the air. "Don't worry. I only speak R'qeen here. She says I have to use Allspeak or the human's language when I go outside."

Nyon crouched beside his daughter, stroking the side of her face with one hand. "That's right. If we are going to stay here, we have to make an effort to assimilate some of the culture from this world. That doesn't mean we forget who we are or where we came from – we will always be R'qeen."

Misch smiled and nodded but something was troubling her: the word that had so angered her broodfather. She had heard it before while playing with offspring from other alien species in the block. "What is a vulture?"

Nyon frowned. "You heard what Kehclow said?"

"I've heard it before. What does it mean?"

He stood up. "It is a bad word. Centuries ago there was a species of animal on this world that fed on carrion, like us. It was called a vulture. The creature was reviled and hunted to extinction. The humans describe anyone who preys on others, especially the helpless, as being vultures. When someone calls you that, they are saying you are no better than an animal. But we are not animals, are we?"

Misch shook her head. Nyon sighed. "I know it is not easy for you, Misch, growing up in this place, apart from most of your family and friends. But things will get better – I promise you." He bent down and held out his arms. "Come."

Misch jumped into her broodfather's arms, burying herself in his warm embrace. It felt like home, even if this strange world did not.

"Who's been assigned to bolster tonight's graveyard shift?"

Sector Chief Emily Caine was sitting behind the desk in her uncluttered office, enjoying the spectacle of her assistant squirming. Behind Caine was a window offering a breathtaking panoramic view of Sector 87. The last glints of sunlight were still colouring the sky but already the buildings, skedways and overzooms were being lit up in a spectacular display of colour and illumination. But Caine had no wish to admire the view. She was having far more fun with her deputy.

Patrick Temple was a weak-willed man who had risen to the rank of deputy Sector Chief by being little use at anything else. Nearly fifty, he had lost most of his hair and years of worry were etched into his nervous face. A failure as a Street Judge, Temple had been shifted sideways to administration where he could do less damage. Successive promotions had nudged him up the chain of command, more by virtue of seniority than expertise.

Caine liked to think of Temple as resembling the scum that floated on the surface of her morning cup of synthi-caff. When the drink was consumed, the scum remained, clinging to the side of the cup. So it was with Temple. Successive Sector Chiefs had come and gone but the deputy remained, never considered good enough for the big chair. At first Caine had considered dispensing with Temple altogether, but he proved an amusing distraction and a useful buffer between herself and the division heads within the sector house. Right now her deputy was reporting on efforts to draft in assistance from outside 87 to fill the gaps in their complement of Street Judges.

"Well, I put in a request to Justice Central for two dozen helmets, ma'am," Temple explained. "But I was told they couldn't spare that many, even bearing in mind the precog prophecy for tonight..." He trailed off ineffectually.

Grud, what a waste of skin, Caine thought to herself. She smiled broadly at the deputy. "So, how many are we getting?"

"Err, one."

"One?"

"Yes, ma'am." Temple shifted uncomfortably under his superior's gaze. "But he's very good. I've never met the man myself, but I understand he's something of a hero within the department." The deputy consulted the screen of his palm unit for further details. "Numerous citations for bravery and dedication above and beyond the call of duty. Seems to have saved the city single-handedly from several significant threats–"

"And who is this over-achiever coming to join our humble ranks?"

"Dredd. Judge Joe Dredd."

That got Caine's attention. Why him? Of all the helmets they could send, why Dredd? "Really? Well, we are honoured. A living legend in our presence."

Temple nodded enthusiastically. "He's on his way here. Do you want to delay the start of roll call until he arrives?"

Caine snorted disdainfully. "If Dredd can't be bothered to report to a new assignment on time, I fail to see why we should wait for him. Call the graveyard shift together. Roll call begins on time at twenty hundred hours. Dismissed!"

Temple scuttled from the room, already tapping instructions into his palm unit for display on screens spread around each area of the sector house. Once he had gone, Caine went to the spotless bathroom adjacent to her office. Most Judges in the building had to share unisex accommodation and cleaning facilities. Being Sector Chief accorded few privileges but Caine felt having her own quarters was one of the most valuable.

She threw some cold water on her face before staring into a mirror. Caine wore the usual Judge's uniform but dispensed with the helmet unless she was going outside the sector house. Her hair was a close-cropped mass of black curls, framing a lean face with piercing, hazel eyes. As she gazed at her reflection, Caine's thoughts kept coming back to the same question – why send Dredd? Did Justice Central know something it wasn't telling her? Was there some detail of the prediction that had not been passed on?

A small speaker set into the wall of her bathroom crackled into life. Deputy Sector Chief Temple cleared his throat before beginning the announcement. "Roll call begins in one minute. Could all members of tonight's graveyard shift please report to roll call now? That is all."

Satisfied with her appearance, Caine pushed aside the doubts raised by Dredd's imminent arrival. She would make sure he was kept on his toes for the next twelve hours – living legend or not. The Sector Chief smiled.

"I'm going to enjoy this," she muttered to herself before striding away.

20:00

Judge Lynn Miller hurried into the briefing room just as Caine reached the podium. Dozens of other law enforcers were already gathered in the large chamber, formed into lines facing a raised platform. Miller slipped into position among the other Judges; there was a conspicuous gap to her left. Deputy Sector Chief Temple was still droning his way through calling the roll to see who was present and correct for the night's grave-yard shift. The full complement of Judges for a sector house was three hundred, but only two thirds of them were assigned to street patrol. The rest were ancillary and support staff. Tek-Division looked after all equipment, such as Lawmaster motorcycles and H-wagons. Med-Division kept the Judges alive and fit for duty, while also providing forensic back up for cracking cases. The Armourer and his staff were responsible for all judicial weaponry, from the standard issue Lawgiver handgun to stumm gas and riot foam. The sector house had its own computer department, Judge-Warders policed the holding cubes and senior staff oversaw each sub-division.

Sector 87 had been through an arduous few months, losing nearly a fifth of its Street Judges. A badge-killer had accounted for more than a dozen before dying in a hail of bullets. Terrorist attacks on the Bloom-ingmacy's Shoplex by anti-commerce activists had claimed several more lives. In the last hour, Miller's partner Shurlock had been fatally wounded in an antiques heist that had gone spectacularly awry. A dozen perps tried to steal a priceless collection of real paper books from the Jackie Collins Museum of Literature on the corner of Steiner and Waldron. When the heist went bad, the thieves tried to shoot their way out. Shurlock had died thirty minutes earlier in the med-bay. Miller had been changing her bloodstained uniform when the summons for roll call came.

She pushed her shock white hair out of her eyes and looked up at Caine on the podium. The Sector Chief asked Temple for the tally. "Seventy-seven present and correct, ma'am. Five more on life support. We just lost…" Temple paused to consult with his palm unit. "Shurluck."

"Shurlock," Miller muttered under her breath, "you simp."

Caine nodded to her deputy before addressing those assembled. "Seventy-seven Street Judges present from the standard graveyard shift complement of a hundred. Not ideal but there's not much we can do about that now. I personally put in a request to Justice Central for replacements and they are sending us one helmet. When he deigns to show his face, I will introduce him. In the meantime, I don't want to hear any grumbling about having to pull extra shifts to cover for the shortfall. Suck it up, people! You're all here to do a job, so that's what you'll do. Anybody wants to whine about it, they can see me after roll call. But they may find it difficult to ride a Lawmaster with my boot knife up their ass – is that clear?"

Misch was bored. Nyon had gone out to a meeting of the block residents' action group and her broodmother had still not returned. The alien Shoplex was two sectors away and it was a convoluted journey just to buy the simplest of ingredients from offworld.

The R'qeen child wiped her blue hand across the con-apt's single window, clearing away the condensation long enough to look down at the busy skedway below. The walls inside Robert Hatch were permanently damp since the air conditioning had given way. The alien girl knew her brood was luckier than most because they lived on the third floor. Her cousins Coya, Aldre and Selmak were stuck up on the twenty-seventh floor, where residents had been forced to smash most of the windows to provide ventilation.

Across the skedway Misch could see two humans skulking in a darkened doorway; they were looking up at her building. Sector 87 was among the city's more affluent areas but vandals had broken many of the streetlights around Robert Hatch; just another symptom of the humans' hatred for the alien residents. A pair of Judges rode past and the humans shrank back into the shadows, one of them clutching a carryall close to itself. What have they got in there, the R'qeen girl wondered? She concentrated hard and reached out with her mind, trying to focus on their thoughts. Misch had found she could sometimes sense what humans were thinking, as if she had a window to see what they felt and imagined. If she did it too often, her head hurt. But it was a useful talent and one that had kept her out of trouble on more than one occasion. She bit her bottom lip and pushed.

Drokking freakshow central!

'Sright. Creeps shouldn't be here!

We'll show them. See how they like a taste of this.
Yeah. Where're we putting that sweet baby?
Downstairs. Near the foundations.
When that goes – these freakin' scum gonna fry.
Hot fat on a stick, man.
You said it.
Let's go!

Misch staggered backwards. There was a searing pain behind her eyes. She tripped over one of her toys and fell to the floor, temporarily blinded by the intensity of the emotions she had experienced. Hatred, raw and vicious, coupled with a hunger for inflicting misery. Something else too – a yearning to see flames burning, red and yellow and white, hot and alive. The alien girl cried out, overwhelmed by these sensations. She knew something terrible was going to happen but she couldn't hold back the blackness any longer. She let it wash over her, chilling her to the bone.

Tek-Division Judge Terry Brady owed his life to Dredd. Ten years earlier the mechanic had been a juve thief for hire, specialising in boosting high performance motorcycles and hover-cars. It was Dredd who caught Brady hot-wiring a Justice Department H-wagon to get initiated into Sector 87's leading street gang, the Doug McClure Runners. By rights Brady should still be serving a thirty year stretch in the iso-cubes, but Dredd had offered him a second chance: to join Tek-Division. The department needed new blood and fresh ideas.

At first Brady's rebellious streak almost persuaded him to turn down the offer, until he remembered his time in the juve cubes and decided to get smart. After a lengthy probationary period he emerged as the star pupil of his training class, able to invent unique solutions to problems thanks to a supposedly wasted youth of petty crime. Graduating with honours, Terry had been given the uniform of a Tek-Judge and offered his chance of placement. It only took him moments to ask for a posting back to Sector 87. That was five years ago and he was rapidly rising through the ranks. But he never forgot the man who had given him a second chance. The Tek-Judge hoped to repay that debt one day.

Brady was just starting the graveyard shift in the sector house's cavernous garage when he heard the familiar roar of an approaching Lawmaster. The motorcycle tore into the building, tyres protesting as the brakes were slammed on, a thick black skid mark smearing across the floor. Terry ran towards the new arrival who was already dismounting.

"Hey! You shouldn't treat your ride like that! Who the hell do you think you are, anyway? Look after your motorcycle and it'll–"

The Judge turned round and let Brady see the five letter name emblazoned on his badge. "D-Dredd? Judge Dredd?" The abashed mechanic stopped, unprepared for the encounter.

"Roll call. Where do I find it?"

Brady pointed to the nearest turbolift. "One floor up, in the briefing room."

Dredd was already moving. "Thanks!" he shouted over his shoulder.

"You're welcome." The Tek-Judge remembered hearing an earlier announcement. "But roll call started ten minutes ago."

Caine almost smiled when she heard someone striding briskly towards the briefing room. Good. She would make an example of this latecomer.

"As you may have heard, Psi-Division precogs are predicting trouble for this sector tonight. Frankly, that doesn't require any psychic abilities. There's a full moon tonight and we all know how that brings out the crazies. Coupled with that is the fact we are fast approaching–"

Dredd strode into the room and stopped, ready to report for duty. A few of the other Street Judges acknowledged his presence but the Sector Chief chose to ignore him and carry on with her address.

"We are fast approaching Friday the Thirteenth. According to the superstition, this is a day bedevilled by bad luck. While Justice Department may officially give no credence to such antiquated notions, the reality is that many of our citizens do. As a result, we can expect all manner of madness and stupidity across the sector tonight. The lunatic fringe will be out in force. Case in point: the Mega-City Anti-Superstition Society, also known as M-CASS, is planning a demonstration to prove there is no such thing as bad luck. We've already received reports of thirteen black cats having been stolen from a reserve for endangered domestic animal species. We don't know if these psycho-cube candidates are planning one of their stunts for our sector but, since the society's founder lives here, it seems likely."

Caine stopped and turned to look at Dredd. "Well, it seems our reinforcement has finally arrived. So kind of you to join us."

Dredd saluted crisply. "Excuse my lateness, I was–"

The Sector Chief held up a hand to silence the newcomer. "Spare us the explanations. If you can't make it to roll call on time, at least don't hold us up any further with some weak excuse." Caine stepped down from the podium and strolled towards Dredd, continuing to address the other Judges already assembled. "If there's one thing I cannot tolerate, it is lateness. This indicates a lack of respect not just for my authority, but more importantly a lack of respect for your fellow Judges. I understand some within the department look up to this man as a symbol of justice. Indeed, his volumes on comportment are set texts at the Academy of Law. But that is no excuse for being tardy." She stopped in front of Dredd and sneered at him. "I don't care whether you're a legend or not. While you are assigned to my sector house, you answer to me. Is that clear?"

"Yes, ma'am!" Dredd snapped back.

"Very well. Report to me after roll call and we will discuss the nature of your reprimand. You may now join the ranks of your fellow Judges – that's if you don't consider yourself too good for them."

"No, ma'am!" Dredd moved to fill the empty space beside Miller. Caine walked between the ranks inspecting the Street Judges while continuing with her briefing.

"Now, where was I? Oh yes, the M-CASS. Well, as I was saying before I was interrupted, that is just one of the problems you will face tonight. Sump Industries is hosting the regional finals of its Miss Mega-City-1 Ugly Pageant at the Sid Harmor Hippodrome. So we can expect trouble from anti-ugly activists intent on disrupting the festivities. To add to your fun, Weather Control over this sector has collapsed again. Tek-Division says we can expect temperatures to approach a hundred degrees with humidity in excess of ninety per cent. So, expect a sultry night's work."

The Sector Chief returned to the podium. "Last, but definitely not least, there are reports of more trouble centred on the alien ghetto in Robert Hatch Block – in-fighting between the various species housed there and threats against the offworlders from xenophobic elements in surrounding blocks. Human residents have called a public meeting to voice their disapproval at having to live next door to families of R'qeen and other offworld species."

"Don't blame them," one of the Street Judges muttered under his breath. "Drokkin' freaks oughta be shipped back into space where they belong–"

"Who said that?" Caine demanded loudly.

After an awkward silence one of the Street Judges stepped forward; his skull was shaved cleaned while a luxurious brown moustache adorned his top lip. The Sector Chief sighed. "Stammers, I might have known. You've been given one formal warning for inciting xenophobic behaviour. That little remark just earned you another. I will not tolerate bigots in my sector house!"

Stammers stepped back into line, his face flushed red with anger.

"All of you listen up!" Caine snarled. "These creatures may not be human but they have just as much right to live in Mega-City One as anyone else. Until the rebuilding of Alien Town is complete, they will continue to live in this sector and so they deserve our protection just as much as any other citizen. Do I make myself clear?" She turned to her deputy, who was still hovering to one side of the podium. "Temple, I have decided that you will address the public meeting as my representative. Take two Judges along as your escort, in case things get out of hand." Carter glanced back at her troops. "Miller – step forward!"

Judge Miller moved out of line. "Yes, ma'am?"

"You were Shurlock's partner?"

"Yes, ma'am."

"Then you'll need a new one. You can have Dredd, show him the ropes. Once he's settled in, the pair of you will be Deputy Sector Chief Temple's escort for the public meeting."

Miller saluted briskly before stepping back into position. Meanwhile Caine handed the briefing over to Temple. "Hand out the rest of the assignments and fall them out," she said before striding from the room.

Once they had been dismissed, Miller turned to her new partner, offering to shake his hand. "Lynn Miller – we've ridden together before. Ten years back, hotdog run into the Cursed Earth."

The pair began filing out of the briefing room with the other Judges. Dredd stroked his chin thoughtfully. "Been on a few of those... Miller? I once recommended someone called Miller as potential Sector Chief material."

The female Judge nodded. "That was me. Didn't get it. 'Too young' was the official reason."

"And the unofficial reason?"

Miller grimaced. "An incident from my time at the Academy came back to haunt me." Her gaze wandered temporarily to Stammers and his partner before returning to Dredd. "Don't worry about Caine, her bark is worse than her bite. She's just putting you in your place." Miller noticed Dredd regarding her bloodstained uniform. "Look, I need to get changed before we go out."

Dredd nodded. "I'll meet you at the garage in ten."

A heavy fist knocked on the Sector Chief's office door.

"Enter!"

Dredd walked briskly into the room, closing the door behind him before standing to attention in front of Caine's desk. The Sector Chief was reading through reports on a screen in front of her, and ignored Dredd for the moment. Eventually he cleared his throat to get her attention. Caine held up a hand, finishing what she was studying before looking up.

"Yes?"

Dredd grimaced. "You ordered me to report here after roll call, so we could discuss the nature of my reprimand."

Caine smiled. "Of course I did. Just wanted to make sure we both knew where we stood."

"Permission to speak candidly, ma'am."

The Sector Chief arched an eyebrow. "Permission granted."

"I was assigned to your sector house only nine minutes before the beginning of roll call. At that time I was half an hour away by Lawmaster. It was physically impossible for me to–"

"Excuse me for interrupting," Caine said, "but perhaps you didn't hear me earlier. I have no interest in your excuses. And since we're speaking candidly, there's something else you should know. I don't want you here, Dredd."

"Is that a fact?"

"Yes, it is." The Sector Chief stood up and began to stroll around her office. "I put in a request to Justice Central for at least a dozen replacement Judges. Instead they send me one: you. What am I supposed to make of that, hmm?"

"Resources are stretched to the limit. Few Judges can be spared for reinforcing individual sector houses," Dredd replied. By now Caine was standing behind him.

"You may well be right. But I sense the hand of our Chief Judge at work here," she said. "Of all the Judges who could have been sent, why you?"

"I was available and–"

"At least a dozen other Judges were available. Why you?"

"I don't know," Dredd admitted.

"Really? I can't tell if you're being disingenuous or genuinely ignorant. Either way, it does you no credit." Caine returned to her seat. "I've just been looking through your personnel file. Some very interesting reading, particularly in the sealed section about you and ex-Judge Galen DeMarco."

"Sector Chiefs do not have authorisation to view such data."

Caine smiled. "Let's say I have a few friends in the Chief Judge's office, a fact you would do well to remember." She referred back to the screen on her desk. "According to one report, you had an un-judicial liaison with DeMarco."

"She developed an emotional attachment to me. She subsequently resigned, recognising her feelings were incompatible with being a Judge."

"Well, that's one interpretation." Caine shut down the files before leaning back in her chair, fingers forming a steeple in front of her face. "I've also spoken to a few other former Sector Chiefs who have had experience of your methods, Dredd. Don't think you'll be able to pull the same tricks here."

"What do you mean?"

Caine gestured to the thousands of buildings beyond her office window. "This is my territory, Dredd, and you won't take it away from me. I've heard all about how you turn up, start playing the big man, claiming you are just rooting out corruption whereas all the time you are usurping the authority of those above you in rank."

"I have no interest in usurping anyone," Dredd snarled. "I only care about upholding the Law and–"

"Yes, yes, we all know of your lifelong dedication to the Law. You've made no secret of having turned down the chance to become Chief Judge."

"I felt I could better serve the city–"

"By staying on the streets? Perhaps. But perhaps you prefer the role of kingmaker, choosing the new chief judge and pulling their strings from behind the scenes. It's no coincidence that Hershey's first experience of law enforcement was under you. How far under you, I wonder?"

Dredd slammed a fist on the Sector Chief's desk. "If you're suggesting–"

"I'm not suggesting anything but I seem to have hit a nerve!" Caine smiled triumphantly. "Now hear this, Dredd. I have no time for grandstanding Judges who only want glory. The sooner you're out of my sector, the better. Do I make myself clear?"

Dredd leaned forwards to confront the Sector Chief. "I don't care what kind of inferiority complex you're nurturing, Caine, or what paranoid delusions you seem to be suffering from. I'm just here to uphold and enforce the Law. But if you repeat any of these baseless allegations outside this office, I will personally ensure you suffer the consequences. Do I make myself clear?"

The Sector Chief stood up abruptly. "You have your orders. Now get out of my face and out of my office." Caine pointed at the door. "Dismissed!"

Miller had just stepped under the shower when two male Judges walked into the ablutions area. In the lead was Stammers, a heavy-set figure in his early forties. He paused to leer at Miller as she soaped herself down. She had an athletic physique toned by more than a decade as a Street Judge, but her generous breasts always attracted too much attention.

"Looking good there, Lynn."

"Keep your eyes to yourself, Eustace," she replied, making no attempt to shield herself from his gaze. Unisex showers and changing rooms were standard in sector houses. Since no Judge was permitted to have a sexual or romantic relationship, it had been decided gender segregation was an unnecessary luxury. The idea was fine in principle, but could still create problems with undisciplined officers like Stammers.

"Nobody calls me Eustace!" Stammers raged, his right hand balling into a fist. "You little slitch, I oughta–"

Miller squared up to him, ready to parry any blow and strike back. But Stammers's partner Riley stepped between the two adversaries, keeping them apart. He was the same age as Miller, with a youthful face. "Step back, Stammers! You've already got two formal warnings on your sheet. Start a fight with another Judge and Caine'll have to bounce you out of here!"

Stammers continued to push towards Miller for several seconds before his rage subsided. "I wouldn't waste my effort on the likes of you," he snarled at the naked woman. "Doubt you could handle a real man, anyway."

"If you meet any real men, send them round and I'll find out," Miller replied with a smile.

Riley shepherded his partner away. "Come on, Stammers. We're due on patrol. Now."

Miller blew them a kiss goodbye before returning to her shower. "Stomm for brains," she muttered when they had gone.

Lleccas came home to find her broodling unconscious on the floor. The R'qeen woman dropped her bag of groceries and rushed to the child's side. "Misch! Misch! Are you all right?"

The girl stirred in her broodmother's arms. "You're home early."

"Never mind about that. What happened to you?"

Misch frowned, her head still pounding. "I can't remember. I saw two men across the skedway. They seemed angry. I was trying to reach them–"

"Reach them? What do you mean, reach them?"

The alien child realised she had said too much. She sat up, one hand rubbing her temples where the throbbing pain felt worst. "Sometimes, if I concentrate, I can sense what other people are thinking or feeling."

Lleccas looked hard at her daughter. "Can you tell what I'm thinking?"

"That I'm in trouble?" Misch suggested, smiling weakly.

Lleccas rolled her eyes and gave the child a hug. "How long have you had this gift?" Misch shrugged. "It's called *metema*, the ability to look into the souls of others," Lleccas explained. "My broodmother possessed it, and her broodmother's broodmother had it too. Metema usually skips a generation but I was beginning to think you did not have it."

The child was unsure what to make of this news. "Is metema a good thing?"

"It can be but you must use it sparingly, especially now when you're still so young. Later, when you've grown, you may be able to persuade weaker minds into doing what you want. But this is a powerful gift and should never be used unwisely. Some R'qeen have died from pushing themselves too far. That's why you were unconscious when I came in. It's the body's way of protecting you."

Misch nodded. She thought she understood but it was a lot to take in. At least she wasn't in trouble. Then the alien child recalled what she had seen inside the minds of the two humans. "I think something terrible is going to happen," she whispered.

Dredd strode into the sector house garage to find Miller waiting for him astride her motorcycle. His own bike was nowhere to be seen. "Where's my Lawmaster?" he demanded.

"Just coming!" Tek-Judge Brady emerged from behind a crumpled H-wagon, pushing Dredd's motorcycle. "I've given it a new set of tyres, recharged the laser cannon and restocked the ammunition panniers. You're all set."

Dredd glared at the mechanic. "And you are?"

"Tek-Judge Terry Brady. Used to be a booster for the Doug McClure Runners, until you set me straight."

Dredd took the Lawmaster from Brady and mounted it. "Thanks for the assist. Good to know I've got a few friends in this place."

"Anything you need, just let me know," the Tek-Judge added eagerly.

Dredd nodded before turning to Miller. "Ready?"

She gunned her engine into life. "Let's go!" she replied and peeled out of the garage. Dredd followed, accelerating quickly to catch up with her. Once they were riding side by side she activated her helmet radio. "Looks like you've got a fan in the garage!"

"Unlike Sector Chief Caine," Dredd replied.

"She's twitchy," Miller said. "Rumours of a reorganisation have been floating around for weeks. Scuttlebutt is Caine's going to be shifted sideways into administration or become warden of a work camp in the Cursed Earth."

"Why? She's still in her forties, physically active..."

"That's the question everyone's asking. Caine's under pressure and she's been looking for someone to take it out on. You're it."

"Terrif." Dredd switched channels. "Dredd to Control. I am starting graveyard shift in Sector 87 with Judge Miller. Anything for us?"

"Control to Dredd. Nothing at this time. Begin street patrol."

Riff Maltin had always dreamed of seeing his name in lights. He wanted to be famous more than anything else, with the possible exception of being rich like those billionaires living on the exclusive Ridley Estate. If he had to choose between the two, Riff favoured being rich while he was alive and famous in death. Ideally, he wanted to be rich and famous simultaneously but figured one would tend to beget the other. He had opted for finding fame first and letting the credits roll in later. There was no need to be greedy, after all.

There was only one major problem stopping his quest for fame; Riff Maltin had few obvious talents. He couldn't sing, couldn't act, and was useless at popular spectator sports like skysurfing or shuggy. He couldn't write, couldn't dance, and didn't have any unique or even unusual physical characteristics that might help him stand out from the crowd.

Of course, you could buy a distinguishing feature. Everybody in the Big Meg remembered the case of Citizen Snork, a fame-hungry teenager who paid to have his nose enlarged to an enormous size. It led to all sorts of trouble and strife, but it did achieve Snork's goal of grabbing the headlines. Riff contemplated a similar route but quickly realised the impediment to such a path – he wasn't wealthy enough to finance such an endeavour. It was just another example of how riches and fame went hand in hand.

Riff was despairing of his quest for the immortality of fame when he saw something intriguing on the tri-D. He had just been watching the grand final of the house cleaning competition *Mop Idol* when a news-flash cut into the broadcast. It showed an on-the-spot report from a street journalist in an attempt to free alien superfiend Judge Death from captivity. Sadly for the journalist, she died live on air, having wandered into the crossfire between Judges and the Death cultists trying to free their figurehead.

Afterwards, the tri-D invited anyone willing to take up this dangerous occupation to audition for the job. There was no pay on offer, just the chance to make a name for yourself – if you survived long enough. Riff was already dialling the auditions number before the programming returned to the window cleaning eliminator section of *Mop Idol*. Finally, among the millions of channels offering an inane selection of trivia masquerading as entertainment, here was a chance for Riff to find the fame he so desperately wanted!

At the audition, Maltin's naked ambition and raw enthusiasm won him a tryout, despite his lack of experience or expertise. After thirty minutes of training he was sent to the stores department to collect all the essentials for life as a street reporter: a badge with the words NEWS MEDIA on it, a handheld microphone and a hovercam. This last item was a small silver globe fitted with a camera, a transmitter and a tiny hover-engine to keep it floating two metres off the ground. Riff asked what special privileges the NEWS MEDIA badge earned him.

"None," replied the bored droid handing over his equipment at Channel 27. "But it does contain a homing beacon."

"Great! So, if I should be kidnapped or get lost while on the streets, you'll be able to alert the Judges to where I am?"

"Yeah, right," the robot replied. "The homing beacon is so the hovercam always stays within five metres of the badge. If you get kidnapped or lost, we'll be able to get our equipment back. Trust me, the hovercam is worth a lot more to Channel 27 than you are."

This news had perturbed Riff temporarily, but he soon pushed such worries aside. He was ready for glory. The channel's news editor had heard a whisper about trouble being expected in Sector 87. Maltin got the first zoom available and positioned himself just a few blocks from the sector house. If something bad was going down, it would be the Judges who responded. Riff planned to follow them to the scene of the crime. Wherever that might be. Quite how he was going to keep up with them on foot was another matter, but the would-be journalist decided to worry about that later.

In the meantime he decided to grab some vox pops from the locals to assess the mood on the pedways and skedways. Riff had never heard the term until his audition for the street reporter job. "Vox pops – vox populi, you dolt!" the news editor had snarled. The blank look on Maltin's face had obviously shown he needed more of an explanation. "It's Latin. Means the voice of the people. Man on the street interviews. Ever seen one of them?"

Riff checked his reflection in the metal surface of his hovercam. His black hair was slicked down close to the scalp, his eyebrows were bushy and luxurious and pimples surrounded his thin-lipped mouth. Maltin looked like a simp and he knew it. But that will be my secret weapon, he told himself fervently, I'll be able to get the stories nobody else can, because I don't fit the glamorous image most citizens have of the news media. Satisfied with his rationalisation, he took a firm grip on the microphone and approached the nearest man on the street.

"Good evening, my name's Riff Maltin and you're live on–"

"Drokk off, spugface!" The burly citizen shoved Riff aside and kept walking. Maltin picked himself up and decided to try again. A grey-haired eldster was approaching on a Zimmer-Skimmer, her kindly face offering more hope.

"Excuse me, madam, but I'm a street–"

The handbag connected brutally against the side of Riff's head, sending him sprawling. "Keep away from me! I'm a granny with attitude and I ain't taking any stomm. You hear me, sonny?"

Maltin nodded weakly as she zoomed over him. Once she was gone he sat up. Never judge by appearances, he told himself. Getting back to his feet, he saw a middle-aged woman walking towards him. She was twitching and mumbling to herself. There was a line of drool hanging from her mouth. In normal circumstances Riff would have stepped aside and let her pass, or even crossed the skedway to avoid her. But after two rejections he was determined to get an interview, no matter what. The would-be journalist stepped into the woman's path and rested one hand gently on her shoulder.

"Excuse me, citizen. May I have a moment of your time?"

It was only then Riff noticed the kitchen laser she was clutching.

"Alot of construction underway in this sector," Dredd noted as he and Miller passed a building site. The half-formed tower was illuminated by massive arc lights suspended from industrial hover pods. A cluster of tall metal droids was slotting together the framework for a new citi-block. Each robot stood nearly twenty metres tall, equivalent to a six-storey building. Their human controllers were visible in glasseen domes positioned inside each droid's chest.

"Part of a sector-wide rebuilding programme," Miller told Dredd via their helmet radios. "We got hit pretty hard by a meteor shower last year, damaged more than a third of all structures. Construction company called Summerbee Industries picked up most of the contracts by underbidding their competitors. The deals were all sanctioned by Justice Central."

"They're using Heavy Metal Kids," Dredd noted, gesturing at the building droids. "I thought they had been superseded by more reliable models."

"That's how Summerbee undercut the opposition," his partner responded. Their exchange was cut short by a crackle of static.

"Control to all units, Sector 87. Report of a female futsie running amok near the corner of Merrison and Currie!"

"Miller to Control. Dredd and I'll take it, we're less than a minute away!"

* * *

"Look, lady, I just wanted a few quotes. Nothing complex. You don't need to overreact like this. Just say no and I'll go away." Riff swallowed hard, a task not made easier by the Q-Tel Kitchen Laser held at his throat. Try as he might, Maltin couldn't help recalling the tri-D advertising slogan for the product. Apparently it sliced, diced and julienned vegetables in seconds, whatever the drokk "julienning" was. Riff made a silent pledge to find out if he ever got away from this crazed citizen.

"Cut you up... It's the only way... Only way to be sure... This is tomorrow calling, see... Slice and dice, twice as nice... Meat, meat, dead meat... hanging from the branches of the petrified forest," the woman replied.

Riff felt the woman's drool running down the back of his neck. She had been sniffing at his scalp for more than a minute while swiping backwards and forwards just in front of his neck. "Fascinating, really quite fascinating. You could probably have a lucrative career as a writer coming up with bon mots like that. Have you ever thought of sending them to a publisher?"

The woman just gurgled, her spare hand creeping down inside Riff's u-fronts to clasp his testicles. Riff lost the power of speech momentarily, such was his surprise. He only regained the ability to talk when he saw the two Judges roaring towards him on Lawmasters. "Sweet drokking Jovus, thank you," the fledgeling reporter whispered.

"Praise be his name," the woman responded, squeezing tightly on Maltin's scrotum. He winced, tears of agony brimming in his eyes.

The two motorcycles stopped at a safe distance and both Judges dismounted. They had Lawgivers in their hands but were not yet taking aim. The male law enforcer took the lead, walking slowly towards Riff and the gibbering citizen. "Citizen! Drop that weapon and step away from the simp!"

"Hey! I'm not a simp!" Riff protested. "I'm a journalist!"

"Whatever," the Judge responded. "Do as I say and nobody gets hurt."

"Cuts and peels, but it never says hello... Cuts and peels, but it never says hello... See what it does to flesh..." The woman released Riff's testicles and flung out her arm. Burnt into her arm were the number four and the word REALITY. "Needs to cut more now... Needs to cut this one all up..."

Maltin could hear the female Judge calling in the case to Control. "Definite case of future shock. Woman seems to be obsessed with her kitchen laser. Futsie is holding another citizen hostage." After a few moments the Judge nodded and then joined her colleague. "Med-wagon's on the way. If it gets here in time, that'll take her to the psycho-cubes."

Riff didn't like the sound of that. If it gets here in time? What if the med-wagon *didn't* get here in time? What would happen to him? His first day on the job was not going well so far. His only compensation was that the hovercam had been capturing all of this and transmitting it back to Channel 27. If he did die in the next few minutes, the broadcast might still grant him a fleeting moment of fame in the day's news summary.

"Cuts and peels," the futsie muttered. "Juliennes too, they were right about that... Right about that... My husband, he didn't know what juliennes was. Tried to tell me it was a clear broth, the fool – so I showed him... Slice and dice, slice and dice... He's in shreds all over now..."

"You have ten seconds to drop the weapon and step away from the citizen," the male Judge commanded. Both law enforcers raised their handguns and took aim at what little they could see of the futsie. "Ten. Nine."

"All over the kitchen... Tasty little shreds... That showed him..." The crazed woman was pressing herself against Maltin's back, grinding her groin against his buttocks. On any other occasion he would have been flattered and all too willing to return her attentions. But the presence of the hot kitchen laser at his throat was hampering any sexual desires he might have felt.

"Eight," the Judge continued. "Seven." He stepped sideways to get a better shooting angle and Riff was able to read the name badge: DREDD. The reporter would have felt reassured but his attention was taken by something happening behind the two Judges. "Six."

A heavy vibration ran through the pedway, like an earth tremor. "Five." But it was followed by another, then another, each tremor greater in magnitude than the last. "Four." As the tremors grew closer, so did a thunderous sound, rockcrete protesting as tonnes of metal thudded into it. "Three."

It was the female Judge who turned first to see what was causing the cacophony. "Dredd!" she hissed to her partner.

"Not now, Miller. Two."

"Dredd, you better see this!"

"Stay where you are citizen," Dredd warned before glancing over his shoulder. One of the Heavy Metal Kid robots from the construction site was marching towards them, massive metal arms flailing in the night air as its mighty feet crunched into the pedway. In the glasseen dome the body of the controller was slumped forwards, either dead or unconscious. Either way, the construction droid was out of control. "Drokk!"

"Exactly," Miller agreed. "You stay here – I'll stop this!"

"No, wait–" Dredd began, but his partner was already running back to her Lawmaster. She gunned the engine into life and sent her motorcycle spinning round in a tight half-circle until it faced the rogue robot.

"Bike cannon!" Miller unleashed a fusillade of firepower that ripped apart the metal just below one of the mechanoid's knee joints. The Judge shouted a new command to her motorcycle's voice responsive computer control system. "Laser cutter!" A beam of red light sliced through the air, searing across the section made vulnerable by the previous attack. As the Heavy Metal Kid lurched forwards at Miller, its crippled leg tore apart, sending the droid tumbling sideways, arms still flailing. It crashed through a multistorey hover pod car park, howling impotently at the air.

Dredd turned back to the futsie and her captive. "One," the Judge announced and shot the distracted woman through the shoulder. Her arm went limp and the kitchen laser dropped to the pedway, turning itself off. Riff threw himself to safety, not wanting to be near the futsie for another moment. She staggered backwards and collapsed into a crumpled heap, still muttering strange phrases and threats. The Judge activated his helmet radio.

"Dredd to Control – futsie is down, but Med-Wagon still required. Citizen is unhurt."

"Control to Dredd – that's a roj."

"Miller is dealing with a rogue construction droid..." Dredd paused to watch his partner in action. She had cracked open the control dome of the fallen robot and was deactivating its remaining systems. "But she seems to have that under control. Better send a clean-up squad down here."

"Noted."

"And get in touch with the boss at Summerbee Industries. It was their droid that ran amok. Tell them they'll have to answer to me."

"Roj that. Control out."

Miller had finished with the Heavy Metal Kid and was strolling back to join Dredd. "Our metal friend is out of action. Controller's still groggy but said the systems just went haywire. Lie detector backs him up."

"Like I said – unreliable."

Miller admired Dredd's handiwork with the futsie. "How'd you–?"

"Waited until the rampaging robot distracted her," he explained.

"Worked out well then." She smiled before addressing the citizen still cowering on the ground. "What's your name?"

"Riff. Riff Maltin." The reporter stood up, trying to assume a more relaxed guise. "I'm a street journalist for Channel 27."

"Not a very good one," Dredd commented, pointing at the silver globe floating nearby. "You haven't taken the lens cap off your hovercam."

"Oh!" Riff checked his equipment and realised the lawman was right. Miller managed to suppress her laughter. "What were you doing here?"

"My news editor wanted some vox pops. You know, the voice of the—"

"We know," Dredd growled. "Next time I suggest you choose your interview subjects more carefully."

By now the Med-Wagon had arrived and the wounded futsie was being strapped on to a hover-stretcher before being taken away for treatment. The two Judges turned and began walking back to their motorcycles. Riff scampered after them.

"Err, your honours, I was wondering if–"

Dredd and Miller stopped, exchanged a glance and then turned back to face Maltin. "You were wondering what?" Miller asked tersely.

"If you'd be willing to help me recreate the incredible spectacle that just took place here. It would make for amazing tri-D viewing and I'm sure it wouldn't be too much trouble to just… to just…" The remorseless gaze of the law enforcers brought Riff's suggestion to a shuddering halt. "No, I guess not. How about an exclusive interview where you talk about what just happened?"

Dredd and Miller resumed striding to their Lawmasters. "We better get back to the sector house," the female Judge said. "We're supposed to be escorting Deputy Temple to this public meeting."

"Just a quick quote, perhaps?" Riff was jumping up and down, trying to pluck the lens cap off his hovercam. By the time he had finally succeeded, the Judges were already riding away into the distance. "I'll take that as a no, shall I?" Maltin's shoulders sagged.

Not a great start to my quest for fame, Riff thought bleakly. Then he remembered the carnage caused by the collapsing mechanoid and hurried towards the smoking remains of the car park. "Still, not a completely wasted opportunity."

21:00

The Leni Riefenstahl Assembly Rooms were only a few minutes' walk from Sector House 87 but Temple insisted on travelling by H-wagon, accompanied by Dredd and Miller.

"How would it look if I arrived at a public meeting on foot? Hardly the image the Justice Department wishes to project to our citizens, is it?" he explained fussily. Dredd scowled a little more than usual while Miller kept her own counsel. She had no wish to antagonise a senior officer, even one as inept as Temple. He was a disgrace to the uniform of a Street Judge: prissy and pedantic with an over-developed sense of his own importance. A weak chin, flabby cheeks and beady, little eyes did not improve his appearance. It was a wonder Temple had survived this long, Miller thought to herself.

They arrived just as the public meeting was starting. Rather than take an unobtrusive position at the back of the room, Temple insisted on striding up the centre aisle and sitting with the other dignitaries on the raised dais at the front. Dredd had been obliged to follow but whispered to Miller to stay out of sight. He pointed at the building's closed circuit security cameras. "Find out where those images go and route them through to the PSU for processing."

It had been a simple task for Miller to follow the wiring to a control room near the building's main entrance and arrange for the signal to be shared with the Public Surveillance Unit. Located inside the towering Statue of Judgement, the PSU maintained the Justice Department's vast network of security cameras and alarm systems across the Big Meg; both overt and covert. Hundreds of operators monitored the output from these to identify crimes in progress and anticipate future lawbreaking. Coupled with the efforts of Psi-Division's precogs, the PSU's bleeding edge technology gave the Judges a powerful head start towards keeping the city and its citizens under control.

Once the signal had been rerouted through PSU, Miller returned to the main assembly room to watch the public meeting for herself. It had been called by a self-appointed committee of concerned busybodies, the Sector 87 Citizens for Collective Responsibility. The leader of the group was a middle-aged woman with blue-rinsed hair, Carolla O'Hare. She was addressing the meeting, peering over her horn-rimmed glasses at the gathered throng.

"I have nothing personally against these extra-terrestrials being allowed to stay within Mega-City One, as long as they stay in their place. The Judges permitted them to have residences in the sector known as Alien Town; fine, so be it. But what I do object to is having these, these... creatures... living in the block next to my own. Property values in Sector 87 have dropped dramatically since Robert Hatch Block was given over to housing these creatures from outer space. What I want to know is when will these beings be leaving? Deputy Sector Chief Temple, perhaps you could answer that question for us?"

The matronly speaker invited Temple to take his turn at the microphone. While he went through an elaborate ritual of being coaxed forward, Miller scanned the gathered crowd. Most wore the usual assortment of synthetic clothing, a few of the more affluent flaunting their wealth with designer kneepads from outlets like Tommi Illfinger and the Gyp. But most noticeable was the high proportion of citizens wearing camouflage and Citi-Def insignia. Each citi-block had its own defence unit, a volunteer reserve called in to support the Judges against only the most dangerous threats, such as an invasion.

Citi-Def squads could be a useful resource at times, but in Miller's experience they tended to attract gun nuts and those with extremist tendencies. Getting such a militia force to stand down had often proved problematic and many questioned the wisdom of retaining this throwback to the days of global conflicts like the Apocalypse War. Others felt it was a useful diversion that kept the more right-wing elements within each citi-block occupied.

Miller surveyed the crowd more closely. Two particular Citi-Def squads were heavily represented; they were from Oswald Mosley and Enoch Powell Blocks. Both had caused trouble in the past with their xenophobic tendencies, mostly due to a personality clash between their respective leaders. It now seemed Oswald Mosley and Enoch Powell had found a common enemy – the residents of the alien ghetto at Robert Hatch. Miller's attention returned to the dais as Temple began to address the gathering.

"My fellow citizens," he began to murmurings of dissent. "First let me thank you for the invitation to speak here today. I offer apologies from Sector Chief Caine, who would have attended herself but for more urgent matters." Temple smiled weakly and continued. "I would like to reassure you that the problems surrounding Robert Hatch Block are among our highest priorities. The rebuilding of Alien Town continues apace and we are hopeful its residents will soon be returned to their own sector."

"When?" a woman shouted from the crowd.

"The exact timing of this remains uncertain. However–"

"When? When are you getting these bug-eyed monsters out of our sector?" The heckler stood up and pointed accusingly at the Sector Chief. She was a small woman with swarthy skin, thick black hair and fierce features. The insignia of Oswald Mosley Citi-Def was displayed proudly on her shoulder. "You've been giving us promises and false hope for years, Temple, but you never deliver. We want to know when you will!" Those around her nodded in agreement, and murmured their approval.

"Perhaps you could identify yourself?" Temple asked.

"You know me. You all do! My name is Conchita Maguire and my husband died fighting aliens to protect this city. Now those same scum live alongside us and you say we should all try to get along!"

Temple nodded at her. "Ahh, Ms Maguire, I should have recognised your voice. Your husband died after picking a fight with an alien who was legally visiting his family in this sector."

"He was protecting this city!" she screamed back at him. "Anyone who says otherwise is a liar!"

"Be that as it may, the residents of Robert Hatch have as much right–"

"Rights? Don't talk to us about rights, Temple!" Maguire snarled back. "You Judges are all too willing to step forward and protect these creatures' rights. What about ours? The right for our children to play freely without fear of being molested or worse by these freaks? The right to breathe air that hasn't already been breathed by these monsters? The right to live out our lives without continually fearing that these things will murder us all in our beds and claim this sector, this city, as their own?"

By now those around Maguire were up on their feet too, cheering her on. Temple did his best to calm them down but was unsuccessful. "Please, please, if you'll just listen to me," he pleaded in vain.

"We've listened enough," Maguire cried out. She picked up a small girl from the chair beside her and held the child in the air. The girl had an ugly bruise around her left eye. "This is my daughter, Kasey. She got this black eye when she fell over, running away after being scared by one of those freaks at the Shoplex. Should our children be put in danger like this?"

Miller's helmet radio crackled into life. "Dredd to Miller, you hear me?"

"Loud and clear. You going to step in?"

"Only if Temple can't get them back under control."

"I'm standing ready to back you up."

"Roj that – Dredd out."

Nyon returned home from his action group meeting to find Lleccas and Misch waiting for him. "What is it? What's wrong?" he asked, concerned by the look in their eyes. Lleccas told him about their broodling having metema. Nyon gave his daughter a hug, delighted for her. But he could sense something was still troubling Misch. "You should be happy – some of the greatest among the R'qeen have possessed this gift."

She nodded as tears welled in her sad, little eyes. Misch explained about what she had sensed in the minds of the two humans earlier. "They wanted to hurt us all," she said.

Nyon brushed the tears from his broodling's face. "They are afraid of us, because we are different. Beings of all kinds fear that which they do not know nor understand. Before I came to this world I feared humans. But there are many among them that are kind and generous. They may not understand our ways but they are willing to learn."

"But what about all I saw in their minds? They wanted to burn us!"

"Many beings have hate in their hearts. Some may even think about hurting us and those like us. But very few ever act upon such impulses," Nyon whispered soothingly. "You're safe here with your broodmother and me. We will always look after you. You believe that, don't you?"

Misch managed a weak smile and Nyon hugged her again, the proudest of broodfathers. "Everything will be all right," he said, rocking her gently.

But Nyon was wrong. Lleccas had walked to the doorway of their con-apt, sniffing at the air. "I smell something strange," she said quietly.

"Probably Kehclow boiling a Joshua cactus again," Nyon replied. "You know how he likes to inhale the fumes."

"No, it's something else," Lleccas said urgently. "It's smoke. Acrid, burning... I smell fire!"

Temple was still ineffectually trying to bring the meeting at the Leni Riefenstahl Assembly Rooms to order. "Please, you must understand that my hands are tied in this matter. The alien ghetto, sorry, the alien settlers in Robert Hatch Block are perfectly entitled to–"

The deputy Sector Chief's nasal, whining voice was cut short by a kneepad slapping against the side of his head. "Who threw that?" Temple demanded to know but mocking laughter was the surly crowd's only response. He blushed crimson with rage and embarrassment before storming off the dais. "I've never been so insulted in all my days as a Judge!"

Maguire was leading a chant, aided by her brothers in arms from the Oswald Mosley Citi-Def. She had taken to standing on her chair and shaking her fists in the air, exhorting those around her to join in. "Alien scum out, human beings in! Alien scum out, human beings in!"

A single gunshot echoed round the room, sending nearly everyone present diving for the floor. Dredd was standing on the dais. A wisp of smoke curled from the end of his Lawgiver. "You've all had your say – now it's my turn."

"Hey, what gives you the right to–" Maguire began to protest, climbing back to her feet. Dredd silenced her with a glare. The rest of the audience stayed silent as the lawman surveyed them.

"That's better," he said eventually. "First of all, you should know that we've been transmitting closed circuit camera footage of this meeting to PSU. Facial recognition software says forty of you have outstanding warrants against your names. There's an H-wagon waiting outside. Turn yourselves in quietly or suffer the consequences. That includes the individual who threw the kneepad at Deputy Sector Chief Temple. Secondly, we know the identity of each and every person present here. If any one of you gets involved in anti-alien violence or related crime, you will be severely punished. Thirdly, you will disperse quietly and return to your homes. Otherwise I will not hesitate to fill this room with riot foam and leave you all here overnight to cool down. Do I make myself clear?"

There were some murmurings and a shuffling of feet, but none of the citizens dared to contradict Dredd. At the back of the chamber Miller smiled despite herself. He might be getting on in years but Dredd possessed a real presence, a gravitas the likes of which Temple could never hope to have.

Just as Dredd was bringing the meeting to a close a juve ran past Miller and into the assembly room. "Fire!" the kid shouted. "There's a fire at Robert Hatch! The aliens are burning!"

The blaze had started in the basement, just as Misch had foreseen. It quickly spread, smoke and flames escaping into the ventilation shafts running the height of the building. Within minutes the fumes were choking the corridors on most floors, while tongues of fire licked at the walls and danced across ceilings. The defunct turbolift shaft was a breathing tube for the inferno, drawing air in from above to feed it.

All citi-blocks were required to have smoke alarms and thermostat warning systems to alert residents to danger. All citi-blocks were required to have more than sufficient fire escapes so everyone inside could get out in time. All citi-blocks were required to have sprinkler systems and flame retarding sprays to keep signs of fire in check.

Robert Hatch Block had all of these – but almost none of them were working. Years of neglect and anti-alien prejudice finally found their target.

Nyon made sure Lleccas and Misch got out before preparing to go back for others. He realised how lucky they were to be housed so close to ground level. Getting down the smoke-clogged stairs had been difficult enough for them – what must it be like for those ten or twenty storeys up? Just as fortunate was his sibling Keno and her brood. The family of four had been visiting friends in Alien Town when the blaze started. They returned to find Robert Hatch on fire and Nyon's brood huddled outside.

Nyon looked at the upper levels of the building. The fire was clearly visible against the night sky, smoke and flames billowing out of most windows. The R'qeen tore a strip of fabric from his tunic and tied it around his face as a filter mask. Where were the Judges? Why hadn't Weather Control responded to the fire, and doused the sector with rain to help slow the progress of the blaze?

Nyon hurried into the lobby of Robert Hatch and back up the stairs. If nothing else, he might be able to help his immediate neighbours to escape. Nyon touched a three-fingered hand to the front door of the con-apt nearest the stairwell. It was cold, so the R'qeen hammered on the surface, shouting in Allspeak. "Gruchar, can you hear me? It's Nyon. You have to get out, the block's on fire!"

No response. "Gruchar, are you there? It's Nyon! Can you reach the door?" Still no response. Nyon leaned back and kicked at the door. The weak lock collapsed inwards with little resistance.

Inside, the arthropod from Andromeda IV was slumped against a white-hot wall, gasping for breath. Steam was rising from Gruchar's back where the alien was being cooked by the heat behind it. Gagging on the stench of frying skin, Nyon dragged Gruchar out into the corridor. "Can you make it down the stairs?" The arthropod nodded and began dragging itself away. Nyon moved onto the next doorway and found it open, the tiny room beyond empty. Next was Kehclow's con-apt. The door was ajar but the room was filled with flames. The gaseous entity was trapped on the other side of the blaze, pinned into a corner.

"Kehclow, come out. We've got to go!" Nyon shouted.

"I can't pass through the flames!"

"Why not?"

"Beings from the Bilal Cluster are flammable..."

Nyon looked around desperately. "Can you get to the window?"

"I had it sealed to stop myself sleep-floating. It's welded shut."

"Not for long," the R'qeen vowed. He ran into his own con-apt and retrieved an Aurillian Hope Crystal the size of his fist. Nyon hurried back to Kehclow who was fast running out of air in which to hover. The R'qeen hurled the crystal at the only window in the room but it bounced off uselessly.

"I had them specially reinforced," Kehclow explained, "to keep out burglars. I didn't trust anyone else here." The cloud folded in on itself. "I should have trusted you. Goodbye, Nyon." Flames licked up into the air, engulfing the gaseous entity. Kehclow died screaming.

Nyon stumbled out of the con-apt. By now the fire had spread into the corridor and was crawling up the walls. If he wanted to get out alive, the R'qeen would have to run through flames.

Riff Maltin was basking in the glory of his "construction droid running amok" exclusive when he heard about the fire. Channel 27's news editor had called the fledgeling reporter and offered him a permanent job, communicating via the small replay monitor on the hovercam. "Good work, Maltin. Keep feeding us visuals like that and you'll be famous within a week."

Riff had glowed at this praise but it was short-lived. "What we really need," the news director continued, "are some good human interest stories. Tug at the heartstrings stuff, show us the face of tragedy and terror."

Maltin was about to respond when a crowd of citizens poured out of nearby Oswald Mosley Block and began running down the skedway. "What's the rush?" Riff shouted after them.

"Fire at Robert Hatch!" one of the citizens responded. "Get your mushmallows, we're going to watch those alien freaks burn!"

"Yeah! Anyone here like barbecued vulture?" another of them joked.

Maltin turned back to his boss. "Sorry, but it sounds like a story–"

"Go!" the news editor commanded.

By the time Dredd and Miller arrived, Robert Hatch was a charred and blackened husk, burnt out from the fifth floor upwards. The smell of burning flesh and charred rubble hung in the air. A cloud of smoke created a haze around the streetlights nearby that still worked. A few fires still illuminated the middle levels of the citi-block but everything above that was ominously dark and lifeless. H-wagons with water cannons had been brought in to extinguish the blaze but the response was too late to save most of the building's alien residents. A crowd of rubber-neckers had gathered around the smoking remains, held back by a Justice Department cordon. For those outside the barriers there was a carnival atmosphere, with plenty of laughing and anti-alien jokes doing the rounds.

"What do you call a vulture from Robert Hatch?" one of the bystanders shouted out.

"Well done!" replied another, to collective laughter.

Inside the cordon was another matter. H-wagons with red crosses on their sides were clustered around the building as Med-Judges tried to help those lucky enough to escape the blaze. Their job was made harder by the rich variety of alien species that had resided inside Robert Hatch. Treatments appropriate for human burn victims could hardly be applied to creatures with chitinous skins, a hundred legs or no corporeal existence.

A pair of Tek-Judges was emerging from the burnt out remains of the building. Dredd suggested Miller talk to the Judges manning the barriers to see if they had heard anyone bragging about involvement with the blaze, while he quizzed the two fire investigators. Dredd waited until the Tek-Judges had removed their breathing apparatus before approaching them. The elder of the pair went into a coughing fit, trying to gasp in the old night air.

"Dredd – I'm on assignment to 87 for this graveyard shift."

The other Tek-Judge was a young black woman. "Kendrick." She indicated her partner, a heavy-set man in his forties still coughing heartily. "This wheezing bag of blubber is Osman."

Dredd jerked a thumb towards the remains of Robert Hatch. "Where did it start?"

"Basement. Could have been electrical. Whole block was a deathtrap waiting to happen. All the fire safety systems were broken or disabled. We'll be pulling charred remains out of there for hours," Kendrick said grimly.

"Could be electrical, you said. Are you thinking there's another possibility?"

Osman had recovered enough breath to answer. He gestured at the jeering crowd beyond the perimeter. "The aliens in this ghetto weren't exactly the most popular residents in the sector. There is no shortage of people wanting to torch this place."

Dredd nodded. "You find anything to back that up?"

Kendrick shrugged. "No obvious accelerants. If it was arson, it'll be almost impossible to prove and harder to trace." Osman began coughing again. Flecks of blood stained his chin. "Right now I need to get my partner some clean air," she said. "So if you don't mind…"

Dredd stood aside. As he did so, the Judge noticed a cluster of alien survivors gathered around a tall, blue-skinned creature. It seemed to be the dominant presence. Perhaps it could help identify how and why the fire began.

Miller found Stammers and Riley together at the barricades, talking with some of the bystanders. Stammers shared a joke with those beyond the cordon. "You'd think the vultures would be happy about the fire. Now they don't have to bother cooking their next victims!" Stammers howled with laughter at his own jest, not bothering to hide his amusement, even when Miller made her presence known. "Well, well, if it isn't the luscious Lynn. How's life with Old Stony Face, Miller? Can he still get it up?" Stammers formed his thumb and forefinger into a circle before thrusting his daystick back and forth through the gap.

Don't rise to the bait, Miller told herself. Don't give this drokker the satisfaction. She turned to Riley instead, pulling him away from the cordon. Once they were out of Stammer's hearing, she took off her helmet and asked Riley if anyone in the crowd had tried to grab the credit for the fire.

"Not that I've heard, but Stammers talks enough for five people."

"All of it trash," Miller commented. "How can you stand having that jerk as your partner?"

"Somebody else turned me down, remember?" Riley looked at her intently. "That can still change, if you want it to."

She shook her head. "I left all that back at the Academy. It was a mistake, one that nearly cost me my badge."

"But that was different. We were–"

"No!" Miller realised she was shouting and dropped her voice before speaking again. "Look, keep your ears open, okay? Dredd thinks this could be arson, so anything you hear that's relevant, pass it on."

"Whatever. Far as I'm concerned, the ETs got what they deserved." Riley returned to his partner, leaving Miller silently fuming. Most of the time Riley was a good Judge, but his attitude to the city's alien residents sickened her to the stomach. She noticed Dredd approaching.

"Riley heard anything?"

"Nothing useful," she replied, surveying the crowd. "But if it was arson, I'm betting our firestarter is among the crowd. They'd want to see the show."

"Agreed." Dredd looked at the survivors again. "How's your Allspeak?"

"Why did the humans do this? What do they hope to gain from our misery?" Nyon asked.

Less than a hundred residents had made it out of Robert Hatch alive, from a total population of more than a thousand. A third of the survivors were still being tended to by the Med-Judges. The rest were gathered around the R'qeen male, huddled under blankets for warmth. A few of them clutched whatever possessions they had carried out of the burning building. Nyon had been the block representative for his species on the action group. Now he was emerging as a leader for all the survivors.

"Perhaps it was an accident?" Gruchar ventured. The arthropod always thought the best of everyone – a common trait among its kind.

Nyon's sibling Keno agreed with this. "We all knew about the problems with the turbolifts and the fire escapes," she said, hugging her three broodlings.

But Nyon shook his head, anger darkening his blue skin to indigo. "My broodling Misch has the gift of metema. She saw into the minds of those responsible for this atrocity."

"Misch has metema?" Keno asked Lleccas.

"We only discovered–" But the R'qeen female was interrupted by her pairling. Nyon was still convinced by his own theory about how the fire started.

"This was deliberate!" he thundered at the other survivors.

"What was deliberate?" Miller and Dredd strode towards the survivors, the female Judge fielded the question while her partner observed.

"This fire. You humans started it!" Nyon replied.

"You have proof of this?"

The R'qeen leader was going to respond but Lleccas stopped him, gently applying pressure to his arm. Nyon looked into her eyes and saw her concern. Then he turned to the Judge. "Nothing that you would believe."

"Try us."

Nyon shook his head. "We look after our own. We will see justice done."

Dredd stepped towards the R'qeen. "We cannot let you or anyone else take the Law into your own hands."

"If you believe you have been wronged," Miller said, "let us take up your case. While you live here, you are one of us and we look after our own too."

Nyon pointed at the charred, smoking citi-block. "Like you looked after everyone who lived inside this building? Where were your promises then? Hundreds of our kind burned alive while you humans watched, laughed and cheered!"

Lleccas spoke up for the first time. "Why do you humans attack us? We have done nothing wrong. All of us here are refugees. We may have different ways from yours but that is no reason to fear us. To hate us." ·

Miller hung her head, ashamed. "Not all humans are alike," she said.

Dredd looked around the rest of the survivors. "Unless you help us find those responsible for this crime, they may escape punishment. Is that what you want? You may not trust us, but we are your best hope."

Nyon picked up Misch and hugged her. "Then we have no hope."

Dredd stomped away from the survivors. Miller ran to catch up with him. "For the love of Grud, will nobody see sense?" he muttered darkly.

"You can't blame them for being suspicious," she said. "Humans haven't given them much reason to trust us."

Dredd nodded unhappily at the truth of the remark. "Until we get feedback from the PSU and the forensic team, there's not much we can do here. I'll call the sector House. No doubt Caine has a new assignment ready for us by now."

Miller noticed a silver hovercam floating at the edge of the cordon. She went over to investigate and found Riff Maltin leaning over a barricade for a better view. "What are you doing here?"

"Where the news is, I follow!" he replied. "Quite a blaze. I only caught the end of it but it was still good footage. Any hot tips you can give me? Cause of the fire, how many fatalities, that kind of thing?"

"Hundreds have just died in that building!"

"Yeah, what a break – and on my first day too!" Riff smiled happily. Miller clamped one hand over the lens of his hovercam, and at the same time her other hand grabbed him by the throat.

"Xenophobes call the R'qeen 'vultures' because they feed on rotting flesh, but stomm like you are the real vultures, feeding on pain and misery!" She threw Maltin to the ground. "Now get out of my sight, you little drokker, before I run you in!"

Riff protested to the bystanders around him. "Judicial brutality! You all saw that, you're all my witnesses. Judicial brutality!"

Miller glared at the crowd, which shrunk back. The citizens nervously hid their faces in the darkness. "Anybody here just see anything?" Miller demanded, but nobody spoke up. "Thought not." She sneered down at Maltin, and let the hovercam float free again. "I'd think twice before you shout judicial brutality, Maltin. The Justice Department does not look kindly upon citizens who make false accusations against its law enforcers."

"Miller!" Dredd was shouting to her from his Lawmaster. "We're needed elsewhere!" She nodded and strode back to her motorcycle.

"Where are we going?"

"You wouldn't believe me if I told you," Dredd scowled.

"Try me."

"It seems we're providing extra security for an ugly pageant at Sid Harmor Hippodrome."

Miller smiled despite herself. "Grud on a greenie – what next?"

22:00

Carla Prins would have been considered one of the world's greatest beauties if she had been born at any other time in any other city on the planet. She had the physique and stunning good looks that would reduce most men to gibbering wrecks and send bitter shards of envy and hatred through the soul of any woman she encountered. Carla was tall and slim, every part of her body in perfect proportion. The crowning glory was her face, with luscious lips, a cute upturned nose and eyes that hinted at pleasures beyond imagining. By rights Carla should have been celebrated and adored.

But Carla had been born in Mega-City One just three days after Otto Sump appeared on *Sob Story*. Sump was perhaps the ugliest man alive, with a face so hideous he had been fired from his job as rat scarer after protests by animal rights campaigners. Otto had then appeared on the tri-D hit show *Sob Story*, pleading his case before the Big Meg's viewers. The response was overwhelming and within days Sump became a billionaire thanks to all the donations he received. He was a cause célébre. He used this new-found wealth to launch a series of ever more bizarre business ventures, that cashed in on the citizens' mania for crazes.

In a metropolis where fewer than one in seven people had a job, boredom was a universal problem. The populace responded by embracing whatever outlandish concept caught its fancy. And millions of them joined in with every single fad. Sump Industries responded to that demand, most famously with its line of Get Ugly cosmetics. Such was the impact of Otto's first tri-D appearance that thousands of citizens wanted to replicate his appalling visage. Beautiful was out, ugly was in. The more pitiful your face, the more popular you were. Overnight the fashion industry was revolutionised: distorted noses, pus-riddled skin and unsightly facial hair became all the rage.

Otto had since died but his influence remained. Sump Industries continued his crusade to celebrate the foulest of features, smells and sights. The centrepiece of this campaign was the Miss Mega-City Ugly Pageant, an annual event staged at Sid Harmor Hippodrome to find the ugliest looking woman in the Big Meg. Unsightly juves from all sectors of the city competed against each other for the prestigious title and a lifetime supply of Sump Industries products like Pimple-On, Skank-Breath-U-Like and I Can't Believe It's Not Pus.

For Carla Prins, being one of the world's greatest beauties was of no use in such a city. Her incredible good looks and flawless skin had been the source of shame and humiliation all her life. At school, the other students had taunted Carla, calling her cruel nicknames like Spotless and Pretty. Each night she cried herself to sleep, praying for a pimple or cold sore to form on her face. But every morning the horror staring back at her in the mirror was the same; she was beautiful and there was nothing she could do about it. Too poor to afford any of the products that might artificially render her ugly, Carla retreated into herself and became ugly on the inside instead.

She made contact with other beautiful women and formed a pressure group – Pretty People Opposed to Ugly Stereotypes. PPOTUS developed its own constitution, registered as a political activist alliance and staged demonstrations. At first these were low-key affairs: they disrupted the ugly products department at Bloomingmacy's or painted the moustaches off billboard posters of ugly supermodels such as Caitlin Lichen and Sofia Dull.

But tonight PPOTUS was going for maximum exposure at the Miss Mega-City Ugly Pageant. Carla and three of her fellow activists had acquired media credentials for the event and had secreted themselves among the audience. The rest of the group was staging a rowdy protest outside. The plan was to storm the catwalk during the symphony of suppurating skin and wart-encrusted limbs that was the swimsuit competition. But the members of PPOTUS hadn't counted on Judges Dredd and Miller being assigned to provide extra security for the event.

"You can't do this to me! I have a legitimate right to display my feelings," she shouted. Carla and her trio of fellow protesters had stripped naked and charged on to the stage just as the result of the swimsuit final was being announced. The four women had handcuffed themselves to the winner, Prunella Fernandez, a jaundiced fattie from Sector 66 with a gloriously malformed chin and half her nose missing. Fernandez shrieked in horror at having such beautiful people standing beside her. Her pitiful cries alerted the two Judges.

"It's not displaying your feelings that's illegal," Dredd replied, pulling a small laser-cutter from one of the pouches on his utility belt. "It's the rest of you."

The angry crowd began shouting and screaming at the protesters, demanding that their perfectly formed features and immaculate bone structures be banished from the building. Miller took off her helmet and held it in front of Carla's flawless face, to shield it from the audience's gaze. "Say another word and I'll add inciting a riot to your list of crimes," Miller shouted at Carla, struggling to be heard above the howls of the audience.

"These contests demean women everywhere," Carla cried out. "We shouldn't be forced to conform to ugly stereotypes, and to debase ourselves for the benefit of companies like Sump Industries."

"And stripping naked in front of all these people isn't debasing yourself?" Dredd asked while slicing through the protesters' handcuffs.

"This is a legitimate act of outrage. All those who condone pro-ugly attitudes must be confronted by the truth!" one of Carla's fellow activists yelled.

A squad of backup Judges arrived to haul away the protesters from PPOTUS. Dredd jerked a thumb at the exit. "Get 'em out of here! I've seen enough of their truths for one night!"

Carla was still shouting at the contestants as she was dragged away. "Don't be stooges of the ugly industry! Embrace your inner beauty. Don't be defined by your pimples and imperfections!"

Miller shook her head as the last protester was removed. "You'd think they'd learn to cope with being beautiful. Why inflict their troubles on others?"

Dredd shrugged. "Misery loves company." The helmet radios of both Judges crackled into life. "Speaking of which..."

"Control to Dredd and Miller. You finished with the Ugly Pageant?"

"That's a roj."

"You better get back to Robert Hatch. Things are getting out of hand."

Dredd scowled. "Aren't there Judges already on site?"

"Stammers and Riley," Control replied. "They need backup. Control out."

Miller sighed. "I'm not surprised. Those two."

"Tell me on the way," Dredd said, already striding towards the exit.

Riff decided to stay close to the burnt-out shell of Robert Hatch. The fire might have been extinguished but he was hopeful of catching some good footage of charred remains being pulled from the building. His decision proved critical in what followed. Most of the bystanders had dispersed and gone back to their own blocks. With Weather Control offline, Sector 87 was sweltering in an unusual humidity. The ambient temperature had dropped since dusk but was still well above the norm for this time of year. All in all, it was a hot and sticky night.

As the crowd thinned out, Riff sidled across to Riley and Stammers. The two Judges were still maintaining a cordon but their attention was on the huddled survivors being treated at the scene. "Wasting good resources on offworlders again," Stammers sneered to his partner. "They should send them all back to where they came from, and get them out from under our feet."

Riley nodded his agreement. "My brother told me the vultures used to keep the dead in charnel pits before eating them. Now those freaks are living here, taking up homes that decent humans could be using." He spat on the ground. "Peace treaty or no peace treaty, they shouldn't be here. Danny'd still be alive…"

Riff introduced himself to the two Judges. "How'd the fire start?"

Riley shrugged. "We're still waiting on forensics from the Tek-Judges."

Stammers laughed. "It was arson and you know it! Somebody went in there and did a little fire starting. Know what I mean?"

"We don't have proof of that–"

"Give it time. Then they'll want us to find whoever started the fire and arrest them. If you ask me, I think we oughta give whoever did this a medal!"

"Well, that's definitely one point of view," Riff said noncommittally.

Riley pointed at the blackened front entrance to Robert Hatch. "Come on, Stammers. Let's see if the Tek-Judges are finished inside."

His partner followed Riley away from the cordon, still grumbling. "These freaks can bring out their own dead, that's what I say."

Riff waited until the two Judges had gone inside before slipping under the barricade. The reporter edged towards the survivors, his hovercam floating behind him. Riff was not fluent in Allspeak but knew enough to make himself understood. "Excuse me, I'm a reporter for Channel 27. Is there anyone here who can speak English?"

An R'qeen male stepped forward, replying in halting words of English. "I can, a little. My name is Nyon. What do you want of us?"

Maltin was taken aback by how tall and imposing the R'qeen was; Nyon towered over him. He had seen the species on tri-D before but never in the flesh. "I just need to ask you some questions, if that's all right?"

"Ask your questions, human."

"I've been told this fire was deliberately started, probably by some anti-alien faction here in Sector 87. How do you feel about that?"

Nyon's three-fingered hands began clenching into fists and unclench-ing again, his head leaning forward to hiss at Riff. "We will not stand by and see our kind butchered by those who would cast us out!"

"Are you saying you will retaliate?"

"We will lay our dead to rest – then we shall see."

Riff nodded. He could sense the alien's anger bubbling below the surface. It would be dangerous to provoke this creature further, but it might also make good viewing. "I've just recorded some comments by one of the Judges responsible for investigating this terrible fire. Perhaps I could show them to you, see if you have anything to add?"

Nyon agreed, so Riff grabbed his hovercam and scrolled backwards through its most recent recordings. After carefully selecting what to replay, the journalist turned the silver globe so Nyon could see the monitor screen.

"It was arson and you know it!" Stammers announced to the camera. "Somebody went in there and did a little fire starting, know what I mean?" Riff then pushed the sequence forward a few seconds to another comment by Stammers. "If you ask me, I think we oughta give whoever did this a medal!"

The other survivors had crowded forward to watch the playback. They reacted with horror and anger towards the Judge's comments. Nyon pushed the hovercam aside and grabbed Riff by the throat, lifting the reporter into the air. "Where are they? Where are the ones who said this?"

Riff shook his head weakly, gasping out an answer. "Inside... The Judges went inside."

Nyon threw the reporter aside and stormed towards the entrance of the block, followed by the other aliens. Riley and Stammers were just emerging from the smoke-stained lobby, brushing themselves down.

"Forget it," Stammers announced. "I ain't touching them. Hell, the vultures will probably want to eat what's left of their families anyway..." His voice trailed off as he registered the crowd of angry aliens surrounding the entrance.

Riley was first to call for backup. Stammers had already drawn his daystick and was pointing it at the survivors. "Just move away and nobody needs to get hurt," he commanded.

Nyon stepped forward to confront the Judge. "Many of our kind died inside that inferno," the R'qeen spat back. "Is that not enough hurt for you?"

"Now look, I didn't mean anything by it," Stammers began.

"Perhaps you were busy thinking about the medal you are going to award to whoever is responsible for this fire?"

"What medal? What are you talking about?"

Nyon pointed at Riff, who was still recovering on the ground nearby. "He showed us what you said. You want to see us all dead, don't you?"

"Now I never said that..." Stammers protested.

"How do we know you didn't start the fire?" Nyon demanded, sniffing at the law enforcer. "I can smell your fear, human. What are you afraid of?"

Stammers glanced back at his partner. "Where the hell is that backup?"

Dredd and Miller were speeding from the ugly pageant back towards Robert Hatch, but a traffic jam on the Arthur Hayes Underpass forced them into a detour. Dredd used his helmet radio to quiz his new partner about Stammers and Riley. "You weren't surprised they were in trouble. Why not?"

Miller didn't reply straight away.

"Well?"

"Riley and I were at the Academy together," she said. "He was Roll of Honor material but had a blind spot when it came to offworlders. His older brother died in the colony wars on R'qeen when we were out on our first hotdog run. Riley and his brother had been very close, so when he got news of what had happened..."

"He blames all aliens for what happened to his brother?"

"Especially the R'qeen. As for Stammers..." Her voice trailed off, but Dredd would not let the matter lie.

"I'm not SJS, Miller; I'm not conducting any covert investigations despite what Caine might believe. I'm just here for a graveyard shift."

She nodded. "I know, but talking about another Judge like this, it makes me uncomfortable."

"Then get over it. We're partners. What you tell me goes no further."

"All right," Miller said. "Stammers is bad news. Not corrupt as such, but extreme in his views and prone to using excessive force, especially where offworlders are involved. If you're on his side, there's nothing in the world he wouldn't do to protect you. If you're not, watch your back."

Dredd considered this. "And Stammers has taken Riley under his wing?"

Miller nodded. "Caine put them together, the worst possible combination. Riley's becoming more and more like his partner. Sometimes I still see traces of the friend I knew at the Academy, but..." The duo was back on a direct route to the alien ghetto. Miller switched frequencies on her helmet radio and called Control. "Dredd and I will be back at Robert Hatch within sixty seconds."

"Roj that – the sooner, the better!"

Miller acknowledged the message and activated her motorcycle's siren. The device was not often used but was a good way of driving off minor lawbreakers who preferred to avoid the Judges. Dredd followed her example and the duo rode down an off-ramp towards the smoking remains of the alien ghetto.

Who struck the first blow was never clear. Nyon had been looming over Stammers, intimidating the lawman with his superior height. But the Street Judge would not back down, his daystick drawn and ready for action. Riley had tried to persuade his partner to avoid the confrontation but Stammers refused to budge. "No bug-eyed monster is pushing me around," he hissed.

"What did you call me?" Nyon demanded, one arm ready to lash out.

"You're a no-good, blue-skinned, stomm-eating son of a Grud-alone-knows-what. The sooner you drokkers get off my planet the better!"

Within seconds the pair were sprawled on the ground. Stammers was clubbing the R'qeen repeatedly with his daystick. The alien tried to defend himself, pushing his long fingers inside the Judge's helmet, gouging at Stammers's eyes. Riley tried to pull the combatants apart but Nyon caught him a glancing blow with an elbow. Riley lashed out with the butt of his Lawgiver, pounding it against the side of the R'qeen's head. The rest of the aliens gathered round the brawl in a circle, urging their leader on against the two humans.

Riff skirted around the edges of the melee, content to send his hover-cam in to capture footage. The reporter transmitted a running commentary of the scrap. "Live and exclusive here on Channel 27, a grudge match between the aliens burnt out of their home at Robert Hatch Block and two Judges trying to bring peace to this troubled area of Sector 87. The leader of the aliens has accused the lawmen of starting the fire that gutted this once noble building, causing the deaths of hundreds of residents. The two Judges were outraged and now the conflict has escalated into this: a knockdown brawl in front of the still smoking structure!"

The sound of approaching sirens cut through the air. The alien spectators parted to reveal the combatants, so that all three fighters were clearly visible in the headlights of the two Lawmasters. Nyon and Stammers were too intent on throttling each other to notice the new arrivals. Riley hammered at the R'qeen's head with his Lawgiver.

"What the drokk is going on here?" Dredd demanded. The Judge climbed off his bike and strode through the gap in the spectators, followed by Miller.

Riley looked up and quickly holstered his handgun. "Dredd!" He stepped back from the tangle of limbs and anger on the ground. "This vulture accused us of starting the fire. When we tried to arrest him for slander, he resisted and we were forced to subdue him."

"Is that right?" Dredd snarled. Stammers and Nyon were still grappling with each other. "Miller, will you do the honours?"

She drew her Lawgiver and fired once into the air. The alien spectators drew further away, and the shot finally got the attention of Stammers and Nyon. They stopped fighting and rolled away from each other before getting to their feet. When questioned, Stammers repeated the same story as Riley. Nyon told a very different tale, recounting how the reporter from Channel 27 had shown him Stammers's xenophobic comments.

It was Miller who saw Riff trying to creep away. "Maltin!" she shouted, stopping the reporter in his tracks. "I might have known you'd be where there was trouble. Is your hovercam working now?"

Dredd and Miller reviewed the footage from Riff's camera before discussing what to do. "I'll deal with this," Dredd told his partner. "I'm only here for one night. You have to work alongside these two for months or even years to come. If they want to blame someone, better they blame me."

Miller reluctantly agreed. The pair returned to the main gathering. Stammers and Riley were sporting bruises and scrapes but Nyon looked much worse. The skin across his left cheek was split, the pupil of one eye appeared bloody and he was nursing his right arm. An R'qeen female and child helped tend his wounds as best they could.

"I've reviewed this incident and there is clear evidence of provocation by Judge Stammers," Dredd announced. "I will be recommending a reprimand be placed on this officer's permanent record. In view of the circumstances, I will let this R'qeen male go with a verbal warning. But if I see him fighting again, I will consider initiating deportation proceedings." Stammers was outraged. And the aliens were less than impressed; they abused Dredd in their native tongues.

"Last but not least, Riff Maltin." The reporter had been enjoying the show, but his face fell as he was included in Dredd's judgement. "I suspect you provoked this conflict just to create news for your broadcast. If I find you using similar tactics in future, you will be spending the next year in the cubes. Do I make myself clear?" Riff nodded hurriedly before making himself scarce, relieved to have escaped incarceration.

"You've got no authority to put a reprimand on our records," Stammers sneered. "I know Caine – she'll never let it stand. You're wasting your time."

"Maybe," Dredd agreed. "I can only recommend you get a reprimand. But I want that on record, even if Caine does choose to protect the likes of you."

"It sounds like I've arrived at just the right moment," a woman's voice interjected. The four Judges turned to see Sector Chief Caine walking towards them. "I heard someone called for backup and decided to visit the scene for myself. Now, who is protecting whom, exactly?"

Conchita Maguire switched off the tri-D in her cramped con-apt. Channel 27 had been broadcasting coverage of events at Robert Hatch, thanks to the presence of Riff Maltin and his hovercam. But after Dredd's intervention the channel switched its focus to the finale of the ugly pageant. Conchita felt no need to see some sow-faced juve showered with gifts and adulation.

After the public meeting at the Leni Riefenstahl Assembly Rooms had broken up, Conchita had brought her daughter home to Oswald Mosley Block. The single mother's heart sank every time she walked into this con-apt. How was a family of four meant to live in just three tiny rooms? Conchita was forced to share a bedroom with her eight-year-old daughter Kasey, while her two sons slept in the largest room, which also served as kitchen and dining area. The smallest room was the bathroom, a space barely large enough for the toilet and the tiniest of shower cubicles. If you wanted to dry yourself, you had to step outside into the hallway.

On the rare occasions Conchita lured a colleague from the Oswald Mosley Citi-Def back to her bed, she always turned the lights off so they couldn't see the dismal limitations of the con-apt for themselves. In the morning, the faces of her lovers reminded the single mother of just how shabby and hopeless her existence appeared to others. The Maguire family home was a dump, the taint of sweat and despair stained every surface.

Trapped on welfare and starved of adult company, Conchita had devoted herself to the block's Citi-Def squad. Membership was usually an all-male affair, but Conchita had proved herself the equal of any man in shooting, fighting and her utter hatred of all outsiders. She despised their rivals in Enoch Powell with a passion that frightened others. If you believed the rumours – and Conchita did little to dispel them – she had killed two men from Norman Tebbitt during the madness of Block Mania more than twenty years ago.

But her greatest hatred was for offworlders. They represented everything that was wrong with this city. How could the Big Meg provide a home for alien scum when decent citizens like her had to get by in this hovel? How could the Judges betray the valiant struggle of warriors like herself during the Apocalypse War, defending the city from Sov-Block invaders, only to allow freaks like the R'qeen and their kin to settle in

Sector 87? Conchita hated aliens with a passion that made her blood boil. She would happily die in a nuclear holocaust if she could take all the aliens with her to hell; it'd be worth it. Sometimes she seriously considered taking a machine gun from the Citi-Def armoury and running amok in Alien Town, taking out as many of the offworlders as possible before the Judges gunned her down.

There was one ray of hope that kept her sane. For the past month decorating droids had been refurbishing the top floor of Oswald Mosley Block. Half a dozen spacious new con-apts were being created and the Maguire family was at the top of the list for relocation. Moving day was coming soon and then everything would be different, Conchita promised herself. Maybe then she could learn to stop hating so much.

Conchita had rejoiced in the carnage at Robert Hatch but had not dared visit the scene of the blaze herself. Her anti-alien sentiments were well known and she would be a prime suspect unless she could prove otherwise. To make sure of her alibi, she had deliberately drawn attention to herself at the public meeting. Judge Dredd himself had seen her and Deputy Sector Chief Temple had singled her out from among those attending. Nobody could blame the fire on her.

"They'll be home soon, go back to bed," Conchita said brusquely.

"When's soon?"

"It doesn't matter! Go back to bed."

But the child ventured closer to her mother. "Why did you lie tonight?"

"What?"

"In that big room full of people. Why did you tell that man I fell over? That isn't how I hurt my face."

Conchita pulled back a hand, ready to slap her daughter. "I warned you, Kasey! We don't tell outsiders what happens inside these walls. Remember?"

The girl shrank back, shielding her face from fresh blows. "I remember," she whimpered.

Conchita closed her eyes. What has gotten into me, she wondered. Why am I so angry that I hit my own daughter? Conchita crouched beside Kasey and gave her a hug. "I'm sorry, my darling. I didn't mean to frighten you."

Kasey was sobbing quietly, sniffing and snivelling.

"For Grud's sake, Kasey, stop crying!"

But the girl kept on sobbing.

Conchita could feel anger growing inside her again. Why did the child always have to do this? Why did she have to antagonise her? "Did you hear me? I said stop crying!"

Kasey's hands began shaking in fear. A dribble of mucus hung from each of her nostrils; Urine soaking the front of her night-gown, dripping down on the floor. Conchita lost control of her temper shouting with frustration as she lashed out. It was only the return of Dermot and Ramone that stopped her raining blows down on Kasey's head and arms. The little girl ran into the bedroom as her mother began mopping the mess from the floor.

Dermot winced in disgust. "Jovus, don't tell me she's done it again! We've got to sleep in here!"

Ramone jabbed his twin brother in the ribs with an elbow. "Save it. We've got good news for you!"

Conchita smiled at her boys. "I know, it was on Channel 27. Did anyone see you go into the basement?"

Dermot shook his head. "No way. We planted that thing more than an hour ahead of time, then went to the Shoplex like you said. When the device went off, we were being cautioned for defacing a plastic tree."

"Yeah, it was sweet. Just like clockwork," Ramone agreed.

Caine listened while the Street Judges gave their differing accounts of what had taken place outside Robert Hatch. Dredd restated his belief Stammers should receive an official reprimand for conduct unbecoming of a Judge. Caine asked Miller for her opinion.

"Why me?"

The Sector Chief smiled. "With all due respect to Dredd, he has only been assigned to 87 for a few hours. You have been here much longer and have worked alongside Judges Stammers and Riley. Do you believe they should be reprimanded as Dredd suggests?"

Miller shifted uncomfortably under the accused officers' gaze. "Dredd believed only Stammers should be punished."

"But surely Riley is just as culpable. If he failed to report his partner's failure, is he not just as complicit?"

Miller nodded unhappily.

"Well," Caine demanded, "should Riley and Stammers be punished?"

"Yes," Miller replied, aware of the growing hatred etched on their faces.

The Sector Chief folded her arms. "I disagree. Stammers's comments were personal opinions obviously made in the heat of the moment, when he was unaware that the hovercam was recording him. While his attitude does him no credit, I shall not punish a Judge for having opinions. As long as Stammers continues to enforce the Law equally for all residents of this sector, I am prepared to overlook this lapse in judgement. The same applies to his partner. As for you, Miller, you would do well to think twice before accusing fellow Judges. I doubt such actions will encourage them to help you in future."

Dredd cleared his throat. "Permission to speak, ma'am."

"I was wondering when you were going to stick your helmet in," Caine said. "You've only been here since eight and already you are finding fault with my Judges. What exactly is your agenda here, Dredd?"

"I have no agenda. My first and only ambition is upholding the Law."

The Sector Chief laughed. "We both know that is far from being the truth."

"If you don't believe me, use a birdie." Dredd retrieved the palm-sized lie detector unit from his utility belt.

Caine shook her head. "Another of your grandstand gestures? I think not. Fooling a birdie might impress younger Judges but that doesn't convince me."

Miller pointed at Nyon and the other offworlders. "What do we do about these survivors?" she asked Caine. "They can't spend the night out here. It might be warm enough but Tek-Judges say the building will probably collapse before morning. The fire has left it structurally unsound."

The Sector Chief turned to Dredd. "You seem to be full of ideas for how to improve performance here. What do you suggest we do?"

"House them in temporary accommodation overnight. Some citiblocks in this sector have spare capacity. Displaced Persons can find new homes for these unfortunates in the morning."

"Finally, something we agree on!" Caine said, her voice heavy with sarcasm. "Stammers and Riley, since you have such a close relationship with the aliens, I suggest you help them into temporary accommodation. The refurbishment projects at Enoch Powell and Oswald Mosley are nearly complete. Take the aliens there for tonight." The two Street Judges saluted and bustled Nyon and the other survivors away.

Dredd stepped towards Caine. "Could I have a word with you in private?"

She smiled broadly. "Why in private, Dredd? I have no guilty secrets. Perhaps there is something you wish to conceal from your partner?"

"Of course not!"

"Then let us speak freely. I encourage a lively debate," Caine said.

"Very well. I believe you are making a grave error. From what I saw at the public meeting earlier, both Oswald Mosley and Enoch Powell are focal points for anti-alien activists, especially from within their Citi-Def squads. Moving these offworlders into those blocks is an act of folly, bound to provoke reprisals."

"Really?" The Sector Chief turned to Miller. "Do you agree with your partner's assessment?"

"I would suggest there are less volatile places the aliens can be sent."

Caine leaned closer to Miller. "Are you dancing to his tune already? That doesn't say much for your powers of judgement or your loyalty."

"You asked for my opinion, ma'am. I gave it to you," Miller replied. "This is not about loyalty, it is about commonsense."

"Indeed?" Caine turned back to Dredd. "Well done. It seems you have gained one ally for your little crusade. But remember this, it was you who suggested the aliens be shifted into citi-blocks temporarily. If this goes wrong, I will make sure the decision leads directly back to you."

"But–" Dredd began.

"Silence!" Caine snarled. "I have nothing further to say on the matter. Now get back on patrol. This graveyard shift is short-handed as it is. We need Judges visible on the skedways, not arguing with their superiors. Dismissed!"

23:00

Dredd and Miller accelerated away from Robert Hatch on their Law-masters, both remaining silent for several minutes. Miller had expected her partner to rant and rave about Caine's behaviour but he kept his own counsel. She was about to ask for his opinion when Control got in touch. "PSU has finished analysing the crowd from the meeting at Leni Riefenstahl. All civilians present were residents of Sector 87. More than twenty of them have convictions for crimes against aliens, mostly xeno-phobic abuse and threats. PSU has backtracked their movements to before the meeting and has monitored them since it ended. No one has been within sight of Robert Hatch for more than twenty-four hours," Control reported.

"Among those with convictions, how many have affiliations with their block's Citi-Def squad?" Dredd asked.

"Hold for that," was the reply. A few moments later the radio crack-led back into life. "More than half. In fact ten of those all belong to the same squad."

"Oswald Mosley?" Miller interjected.

"Yeah, how did you–"

"Call it an educated guess," she replied. "I made several of those arrests. A citizen named Conchita Maguire is the ringleader."

"That's a roj. But she was at the meeting," Control noted. "No way she could have been involved with the arson attack."

"Tek-Division is convinced it's arson then?" Dredd asked.

"Preliminary report lists the blaze as suspicious, yes. Tek-Judges Kendrick and Osman are analysing samples from the scene now. They estimate having a final report ready within an hour or two."

"Dredd to Control, standby for a moment." He switched channels so that only Miller could hear his transmission. "The presence of all those anti-alien activists at that public meeting when Robert Hatch caught fire – it's too much of a coincidence."

"You think they used it to establish their alibis?" she replied.

"That would be the smart move," Dredd agreed. He reactivated the link to Control. "I have another request for PSU. We need a list of all Sector 87 residents with convictions for crimes against aliens who weren't at the public meeting. How long will that take?"

"At least an hour," Control said.

"Also, we need a name and residential address for the boss of Summerbee Industries. Get back to us – Dredd out!"

Tarragon Rey did not believe in bad luck. He did not believe in good luck either, not any form of good fortune, happenstance or kismet. To him all such notions were the sort of superstitious nonsense that should have been left behind in the twenty-first century. For Grud's sake, this was 2126! Surely the human race should be beyond blaming its own errors and missed opportunities on the fates, the stars or any other random scapegoat.

Rey's view stemmed from the bizarre death of his mentor, the celebrated thinker and skysurfer, Osvaldo Carlos. Carlos liked to muse on the nature of human existence while soaring high above Mega-City One. He began to ponder the way so many people credited responsibility for their own flaws and foibles on random elements. After spending five days and nights atop his surfboard half a kilometre over the city, Carlos had a brainwave. All superstition was self-delusion and only those who foreswore such foolishness could hope to achieve true nirvana.

Carlos told another skysurfer of his vision and convinced them of the truth behind this belief. Soon word spread of a messiah in the sky, preaching a new gospel of accountability and modernist rationalism. Rey had only been seventeen years old at the time, an impressionable juve who fell under the spell of this charismatic speaker. But it was the manner of Carlos's freakish demise that convinced Rey this doctrine was worth demonstrating to all those still trapped on the ground, trapped with their witless beliefs and fears. Few men are killed by a number thirteen hoverbus carrying thirteen mirrors at 13:13 in the afternoon on Friday the Thirteenth. The fact that the hoverbus was operated by The Black Cat Pet Transportation Agency was just coincidence, nothing more.

So Tarragon Rey gave up skysurfing as a hobby and devoted the rest of his life to exploding the myths of superstition. His first step had been forming M-CASS, the Mega-City Anti-Superstition Society. For its emblem the group chose an image of Mama Cass, an obscure and obese singer from one hundred and fifty years before who had choked to death on a ham sandwich. Her passing had little to do with superstition, Rey once admitted, but her name fitted the initials perfectly.

For the past decade M-CASS had been staging events across the Big Meg to prove its case against the belief in luck of any kind. The society had always staged these extravaganzas on Friday the Thirteenth, the ultimate bad luck day in the minds of most people. If Rey and his fellow members could defuse any notion that this random date held any special terrors, then eliminating irrational worries about the breaking of mirrors or the spilling of salt would be easy.

The last series of events had not gone well. For a start, shouting the name "Macbeth!" at actors had proved to be rather limited as a visual spectacle. Driving a hover pod through thirteen large mirrors had seemed a good idea in principle, but the practicalities of it were rather painful. The driver and all the passengers had been cut to ribbons by the shards of glass and had only got as far as the eighth mirror before crashing to a halt. Channel 27 dubbed the fatalities as "Bad Luck Plagues Anti-Superstition Loons,", not exactly the publicity that M-CASS had been seeking.

But Rey believed this time was going to be different. This time everyone would see that luck, good or bad, was just a myth. Stealing thirteen black cats had proved easy; the home for endangered domestic animal species had little funding to spend on security. Getting the felines lined up on one side of Anton Diffring Overzoom was another matter. The cats insisted on doing whatever they wanted, and not what Rey desired. Whenever he had most of them together, two would immediately wander off, another would start licking its backside and the rest would just glare at him with withering contempt.

Finally, he resorted to stuffing them back into their carrying cages and lining these up along the side of the overzoom. Rey had planned to release the cats at midnight but a call from one of the society members posted on lookout back along the overzoom hastened his hand. "Pair of Judges on their way," the society's treasurer warned. "PSU cameras must have spotted you."

Rey dismissed this suggestion. "We chose this part of the overzoom because it isn't covered by a camera tower."

"Maybe a spy-in-the-sky hovercam?"

"No, I don't think so." Rey had tried to keep watch for the roving devices but coping with the cats had taken most of his attention. He glanced around but could see no sign of a silver globe floating nearby.

"Must just be bad luck then," the treasurer suggested. "Oh! Sorry!"

"Don't say bad luck," Rey fumed. "There's no such thing!"

"Well, that 'no such thing' will be beside you in less than a minute."

Rey looked at his watch – still more than half an hour until midnight. But the Judges would surely see him and intercede. It was now or never.

Rey ran along the line of cages, pulling up the flaps and tipping the cats out on to the edge of the overzoom. "Go, you so-called talismen of misfortune. Show the people of Mega-City One there is no such thing as badluck!"

"Control to all units, Sector 87! Major collision is taking place on the Anton Diffring Overzoom, between exits 13 and 13a. More than a dozen vehicles already involved with more impacting by the second!"

Dredd and Miller were passing exit 12 when they received the bulletin. "Dredd and Miller responding!"

Misch did not like the two humans herding them into the hoverbus. Lleccas was helping Nyon into a seat while Misch waited outside. The humans had hurt her broodfather. They wanted to hurt him again, given the chance. She didn't need metema to sense that, it was obvious. But she couldn't understand why they hated offworlders like herself so much. What was wrong with them? Without thinking about the consequences, Misch closed her eyes and reached into the mind of Judge Eustace Stammers.

The little boy heard his mother crying out. She was in pain, he had to help her. He pushed against the door but couldn't open it. He reached up and turned the handle, opening the door a fraction. Inside, he could see her on the bed, pinned underneath a monster. It had blue skin and yellow markings. It kept pushing against her, straining and sweating. Another monster was standing nearby, touching itself and muttering in words beyond understanding. The boy could see his mother's face contorted strangely. She was urging the monster on, telling it to go faster. She reached down between her legs and–

The boy screamed at them to stop, to leave his mother alone. She shouted at him to get out of the room. The monster standing up pushed the boy out and slammed the door shut. The boy hammered at the door with his tiny fists but got no response. He then collapsed to the floor, sobbing.

Later the monsters left, gurgling in satisfaction and leaving a handful of credits by the front door. The boy's mother came out and began beating him. She screamed at him never to interrupt her again when she had visitors. The little boy had never understood the words scrawled across the front door to their tiny con-apt before, but now he did: ALIEN WHORE.

Misch snapped back out of the trance to find Stammers standing over her, one hand clutching at his helmet. "You little slitch," he snarled. "I know what your kind can do. Stay out of my mind or else!" The Judge drew back a fist, ready to lash out at the R'qeen broodling until Riley intervened.

"Stammers! For Grud's sake, leave her alone. Haven't you gotten us into enough trouble for one night?"

"She was poking around in my head," Stammers protested. "I could feel it. She's got no right to–"

"She's just a kid," Riley replied. "Get her in the bus and let's go."

Stammers picked up the R'qeen broodling and held her in front of his face. She could smell his shame and anger and sense his frustration. "You tell anyone what you just saw," he hissed in Allspeak, "and I'll kill your parents. Then I'll do to you what your kind did to my mother. You understand me?"

Misch nodded, too afraid to speak.

Satisfied, the Judge pushed her into the hoverbus and slammed the door. "That's the last one. Get them moving!" he shouted to the robot driver, banging a fist against the side of the vehicle. "We'll follow you."

There were more than a hundred vehicles smashed into each other when Dredd and Miller reached the back of the impact zone. Control had shut down the section of the overzoom immediately behind them, rerouting traffic down off-ramps and emergency exits to other routes. The resulting traffic chaos was likely to bring much of the sector to a standstill for the rest of the night. Fortunately, "Judges-Only" bypasses would keep some paths open for 87's law enforcers, but everybody else was being advised to stay home and avoid making any unnecessary journeys.

The citizens caught up in the carnage on Anton Diffring Overzoom were not so fortunate. A handful of those in the first few pods and road-sters that collided had managed to stumble away from their vehicles to the safety of the hard shoulder. Meanwhile more and more travellers slammed into the back of the metal melee, most dying on impact. Within a minute of Tarragon Rey opening the cat cages, fifty-three people were dead or dying. Then things got worse.

Once all five lanes were blocked by the crash, drivers swerved on to the hard shoulder to avoid a collision. Those who had sought refuge there were run down, adding to the death toll. Vehicles that tried to avoid the pedestrians either thudded into the side of the impact zone or rebounded against the side railing and were flipped over the top, falling the equivalent of fifteen storeys to Soren Linsted Skedway and starting another pile-up.

By the time Dredd and Miller reached the scene the death toll was over a thousand on Anton Diffring and still rising. Judging by the sounds of metal crushing into metal and the screams drifting up from the skedway below, a similar number of deaths were occurring down below.

"Grud, what started this?" Miller wondered. She switched off the engine of her Lawmaster and dismounted, stepping into a dark, crimson stream of blood and oil that rolled from the pile-up. The sounds of the wounded punctuated the night air with cries of pain and fitful screams for help. A blur of black fur passed the Judges as a cat ran past them, away from the bloody carnage. A second feline followed it, then a third. "Cats? Why would cats–"

Dredd left his Lawmaster and joined her. "M-CASS. At roll call Caine said the anti-superstition society had abducted thirteen black cats."

"But what are they doing here?"

"We can worry about the cause of this later," Dredd replied. "Let's concentrate on the effects." He activated his helmet radio while still assessing the carnage. "Dredd to Control, am at the Anton Diffring crash site. Estimate hundreds dead, many more injured and/or trapped in the wreckage. Expect similar below us on Soren Linsted Skedway. We need a fleet of med-wagons and an H-wagon overhead loaded with fire-fighting capability. Better add some riot foam as well, in case things get out of hand."

Miller waited until Dredd signed off before asking about the riot foam. "I'd have thought that's the last thing we'll need – the survivors are in shock."

"Maybe. But if my suspicions are correct, things could get ugly and fast."

One by one, the survivors began to emerge from the wreckage. Most were bloodied, many badly injured, but all were glassy-eyed and shivering despite the humidity. "What happened? What could have caused this?" they asked the Judges.

Another cat crept out from a gap between two crushed roadsters, its black fur matted with blood. Dredd pointed at the animal. "I suspect someone released thirteen black cats into the path of the oncoming traffic."

"But why? What possible reason could they have for–"

"I did it!" a lone voice announced proudly. It came from the edge of the fast lane, where a man's arm protruded from beneath a jumble of twisted metal and glasseen. Miller held the growing crowd of survivors back while Dredd pulled back the ruptured remains of a roadster to reveal the instigator.

"Tarragon Rey," Dredd muttered. He grabbed the M-CASS leader and pulled him clear, paying little heed to Rey's protests about having a sprained ankle, cuts and bruises. Dredd dragged Rey to his feet and forced him to look at the pile-up. "See this? Hundreds dead, perhaps thousands by morning. Lives ruined, families torn apart, people left in pain and misery – and for what? What were you trying to achieve?"

The M-CASS leader shrugged. "I was just proving that having a black cat cross your path wasn't proof of good luck. I didn't mean for all of this–"

Dredd shook Rey as if he was a puppet, trying to rattle some sense into his brain. "Have you any conception of the human cost for this demonstration of yours?"

But Rey remained undeterred. "Sacrifices must be made if progress is to be achieved. Superstitions belong to centuries past. We must drag ourselves into the twenty-second century!"

Dredd looked over his shoulder at the crowd gathering behind Miller. "See all those people? They're the lucky ones: they survived. Right now they're looking for somebody to blame. What do you think would happen if I told them you caused all of this, just to prove some deluded belief?"

The M-CASS leader's face hardened. "You wouldn't explain it to them properly. The fact that you call the beliefs of the great Osvaldo Carlos 'deluded' proves my point. Let me speak to them."

Dredd almost smiled. "Perhaps you're right. You speak to them." He stepped behind Rey and pulled the culprit's wrists together before snapping a pair of handcuffs around them. "Are you sure you want to do this, Rey? They may not share your more enlightened viewpoint."

"I insist! Once I make them see the sense of this, they will thank me."

"Have it your way, creep," Dredd replied. He pushed the prisoner towards the survivors. "Listen up! This man has something he wants to tell you."

Rey cleared his throat and began shouting to the gathered crowd of bloodied and bruised motorists.

Dredd retreated to the side of the overzoom, taking Miller with him. "Dredd, what exactly are you doing?" she asked.

"He insisted on having the chance to explain his actions to the survivors."

"But they'll tear him apart once they find out."

"Don't worry, I've got riot foam standing by."

Now The crowd was becoming restive and angry, as it realised the implications of what Rey was saying. Fists began to clench and faces hardened into rage and murderous fury. Within thirty seconds Rey was sprinting away from the pile-up towards the nearest off-ramp, pursued by an angry mob. Miller called in the H-wagon with riot foam before turning back to her partner. "You wanted Rey to feel the same terror as those who died in this crash, didn't you?"

Dredd nodded. "Chances are he'll spend the rest of his life in either the iso-cubes or the psycho-cubes, depending on how Psi-Division judge his mental state at the time he caused the crash. Either way, it'll never bring back his victims. But at least he'll remember this moment of pure terror that will stay with him. It isn't justice, but it's a start."

Evan Yablonsky had been a news editor at Channel 27 for nine years, having fought his way up from cadet reporter. His ruthless advance on the ladder of promotion marked him out as a man willing to do almost anything to get ahead, a quality underlined by his determination to run the stories other tri-D news channels would never touch. It was Yablonsky who pioneered the audition process for prospective journalists, along with the "all aspects" waiver those auditioning had to sign. If they unearthed a scoop and survived their first night on the skedways and pedways of the Big Meg, they were offered a job. If they died or were incarcerated for going too far, Channel 27 retained culpable deniability and avoided any financial responsibility for the consequences.

The anonymous news hotline was another of Yablonsky's innovations. Citizens could call in with information about anything. The Dish-Dirt-Today line (known as DDT in the office) had proved a valuable source of leads. Everything from the neighbour that had let their goldfish licence lapse to the serial killer down the corridor was good news for Channel 27. It was most useful as a conduit for the city's criminal organisations if they wanted to stitch up their opposition. A call tipped off Channel 27, then Yablonsky passed this information to the Judges and claimed the reward for any wanted perps captured as a result. It was a sweet deal all round.

So when the DDT vidphone began ringing, the news editor did not hesitate to answer, even when it was an audio-only call. The voice was heavily distorted too, undoubtedly by some electronic means. Yablonsky set the auto-trace programme running more from habit than any expectation of it identifying where the call originated. Whoever was going to this much trouble to mask their identity was not going to give themselves away that easily.

"I have a hot tip for you," the caller said, the words sounding harsh and metallic. The news editor could not even determine the gender of the voice, so heavy was the distortion.

"Tell me more," Yablonsky drawled in his Texas City accent. He had grown up in the Lone Star city-state before moving to the Big Meg as a juve.

"The fire at the Robert Hatch. It was arson."

The news editor sighed. That was old news and he said so.

But the caller was not done yet. "The device used to start the fire, it could only have come from one of two sources – a Citi-Def squad or the Judges."

"Prove it."

"Tek-Division will find traces of a chemical compound called Lucir-74 near the seat of the fire. That compound is used exclusively for incendiary devices issued by the Justice Department to Citi-Def squads."

"Jovus drokk," Yablonsky gasped. "How do you know this?"

But the DDT line was already dead.

Yablonsky sat by the hotline for another thirty seconds, his mind still racing through the implications of what he had just heard. If it was accurate – and that was a big if right now – then there was a major scandal brewing. Could someone within the Justice Department have deliberately torched Robert Hatch and roasted most of the alien residents inside? Why would they do that? It was more likely the work of a rogue Citi-Def squad. Sector 87 had more than its fair share of those, several with strong anti-alien elements.

The news editor hurried back to his own desk, trying to decide who to call first. He needed at least one source to corroborate the story before running it. Channel 27 might be at the edge of what was acceptable for broadcast in Mega-City One but even he balked at accusing the Justice Department of using arson to commit mass murder without any evidence to back it up. It was time to call an old friend inside Tek-Division. But first Yablonsky needed to get his street journalists close into the action. He hit the transmit button on his communications system. "All Channel 27 reporters call in. I need to know your positions. Now!"

Miller and Dredd stayed beside the Anton Diffring pile-up until clean-up squads were able to cut a path through the carnage. As Med-Judges began the grisly job of removing corpses and severed body parts from the crushed metal, the pair rode through the gap on their Lawmasters. Once clear of the wreckage, Dredd called Control for progress on his previous enquiries.

"Kendrick says she's found the residue of an unusual chemical compound among the samples taken from the basement of Robert Hatch. Something called Lucir-74."

"I've heard of that," Miller said.

Dredd nodded his agreement. "What else, Control?"

"PSU has cross-checked all current Sector 87 residents with anti-alien convictions against all those who attended the public meeting at Leni

Riefenstahl. Only three such residents were not at the meeting out of more than two hundred."

"That's some turnout," Dredd noted. "Who are the three and what are their locations?"

"Roberto Conti, currently in traction at St Peter Root Hospital after losing a fight with an alien last week," Control replied. "Also out of the running is Huston Wark, resident at a hospice for those with terminal cases of Jigsaw Disease. The only other candidate is a juve called Benoit Roth. He was arrested six hours ago and is sitting in a holding cell at Sector House 87."

"I'm the one who arrested the little punk," Miller said. "He's too fond of wall-scrawling anti-alien slogans for his own good."

"What about the boss at Summerbee Industries?" Dredd asked Control. "Anything further on him?"

"That's a roj. Werner Summerbee resides at number fifteen, Ridley Estate, but lives most of the year in tax exile on the Moon. Returned to Mega-City One this morning, according to spaceport records, but is only here for another twenty-four hours."

"Thanks, Control. Dredd out."

A watch-post platform jutted from the side of the overzoom ahead of them. Dredd began to slow down as they approached it and motioned for Miller to join him. Once they were stationary Dredd switched off his engine and helmet radio, his partner following suit. From this high platform they could look out over the sector, at a million lights glowing in the darkness. The full moon was rising in the distance, appearing unusually large as it cleared the horizon. But both Judges had other things on their minds.

"Lucir-74. That's a compound in incendiary bullets, isn't it?" Miller asked.

Dredd nodded. "And in some explosives issued to Citi-Def squads."

"Backs up our alibi theory, but doesn't get us any closer to knowing who planted it," she commented. "The device used to start the fire could have been planted hours or even days earlier but–"

"But that would have made it more susceptible to discovery," Dredd said. "Much more likely to have been put in place within an hour or two of the fire starting, cutting down the risk of detection. So it probably wasn't anybody at the public meeting."

Miller scowled. "There's another possibility. It could have been a Judge."

"Perhaps, but we're hardly inconspicuous. Even the likes of Stammers isn't stupid enough to be seen planting such a device." Dredd stroked his chin. "No, I suspect someone else was used, a go-between, somebody whose name wouldn't show up as an obvious suspect with PSU."

"So we're back to square one?"

"For the moment." Dredd looked out at the city, deep in thought. "There's something else going on here, Miller. Something below the surface."

"Like what?"

"I don't know," he admitted. "Just a suspicion, nagging at me."

Miller smiled. "I thought you were double-zero rated, no discernible psychic abilities."

"Gut instinct has its uses too. The precogs were expecting trouble–"

"Haven't we had enough already?"

Dredd shook his head. "Nothing more than you'd expect with a full moon and Friday the Thirteenth starting in a few minutes. Precogs wouldn't issue a sector-wide warning without serious concerns. Whatever's coming, we've only seen the leading edge of it." His shoulders slumped momentarily, exhaustion evident on his features.

"When was the last time you got any rest?" Miller asked.

"More than twenty-seven hours ago."

"Then we should get back to the sector house. Control can spare you for ten minutes on a sleep machine." Miller reactivated her helmet radio. "What about Summerbee? Do you want me to see him about that rogue droid?"

"He can wait. Right now we–"

"Control to all units! There's a hundred members of a doomsday cult on the roof of Maurice Waldron Block. Can anyone respond?"

"That's just below the next off-ramp," Miller noted.

"Guess that sleep machine will have to wait for me," Dredd said before signalling Control they would take the call.

00:00
FRIDAY, SEPTEMBER 13, 2126

Sharona Moore was disappointed. For five years she had been leading a cult of eschatologists, watching for the signs and portents that indicated the end of the world. Her team of researchers had scoured all the ancient texts for clues: the Book of Revelations from the Bible, the prophecies of French visionary Nostradamus and the collected horoscopes of fabled Brit-Cit astrologer Russell Grant. From these diverse sources had emerged fragments of evidence, all of them pointing to this time and this place.

Revelations spoke of a full moon rising on the last night, while Nostradamus wrote of the apocalypse enveloping the city of the one Magi (Mega-City One was the accepted modern interpretation of this sixteenth century text). Russell Grant suggested Friday the Thirteenth would bring disaster for all those under the star sign of Libra. Grant also suggested there was a chance for new romance and the day's lucky colour would be blue, but the researchers dismissed these elements of the prophecy as droll fripperies inserted to satisfy the low brow culture prevalent back in the year 2004. Every member of Sharona's cult had been born under the star sign Libra, confirming the truth of the flamboyant soothsayer's vision. In fact, all members were the product of conceptions fuelled by festive season inebriation, but they preferred not to discuss this.

So it had come to pass that one day, one date and one time stood out from all the years of contemplation and interpretation – Friday, September thirteenth, 2126 AD. As this day began, a mighty calamity would decimate Mega-City One and the creator of all things would come down and rescue all those (and only those) who were ready to accept deliverance. At least, that was how Sharona saw it. If pressed, she was willing to admit the exact year was never stipulated and the presence of blue as a lucky colour still worried her. And how could there be a chance for new romance to blossom if the world was going to end?

But Sharona had put those doubts aside and gathered her followers. The cult was a hundred strong, mostly adults with a smattering of juves. Sharona had gathered them to herself with charismatic speeches, a litany of salvation for a select few and free memberships for anyone born between September twenty-fifth and October first. Setting up her own cult had proved surprisingly easy. The Justice Department favoured a policy of religious tolerance, so long as the religion frowned upon all forms of lawbreaking. Once the Sect of the Last Redemption was registered with the necessary authorities, Sharona was free to hold meetings, predict the end of the world and organise pre-apocalypse fund-raising sales of baked goods.

The cult members were now gathered atop Maurice Waldron Block, waiting for the end of the world. All were resplendent in their purple and gold robes, specially purchased for Judgement Day from the proceeds of baked goods sales. Everyone had said their goodbyes to the non-believers in their immediate family and friends. It wasn't easy to mentally prepare yourself for salvation, knowing so many were not to be spared the full horrors of the apocalypse, but Sharona counselled her followers not to fret. The creator might take pity on associate members and upgrade them to full redemption status.

So the one hundred waited, their hands linked together. They recited a fervent prayer over and over again as the moment of destiny approached. "Creator of all things, hallowed be thyself. Thy kingdom is nearly come, thy will be done, in the Big Meg as it is wherever you hang out. Give us this day our ticket off this stommhole and forgive us our hoverbus passes. Lead us not into a cul-de-sac but deliver us from bad stuff. For thine is the kingdom and the glory and stuff like that, now and forever and a day. All right?"

Sharona smiled – she was fond of the prayer, it struck just the right note of reverence and informality in her opinion. You could be too drokking pious, you know?

It was ten minutes after midnight when the prayers began to falter. Everyone still believed the end was nigh, but they were starting to get a little impatient. A half-hearted chorus of "Why are we waiting?" was stifled by a harsh glance from Sharona.

"Do not goad the Creator!" she shouted. "If, in his or her infinite wisdom, he or she chooses to be a little late, that does not mean we should be any less respectful of our saviour."

By quarter past it was obvious something had gone awry. Sharona did her best to conceal the disappointment from her followers. "Perhaps we have misinterpreted the signs and portents," she allowed.

"But you seemed so sure," her main disciple insisted. Gunther Beck had been the first to join the cult, admitting to Sharona his life was a barren, soulless existence since his mother died two years earlier. The fact he believed in her, had a small personal fortune and was also eager to pleasure her with oral sex had in no way influenced Sharona's decision to make Gunther a disciple. Well, the belief and the credits had perhaps played a small part in the decision, but the erotic encounters were just a bonus.

"Well, everybody makes mistakes," she admitted. The cultists groaned, some mumbling that they had been duped, others wondering about how they could get their old jobs back. Sharona realised events would spiral out of her control unless she exerted some authority.

"Everyone, listen to me. I am experiencing a vision!" She fell to her knees and pointed at the full moon overhead. "I can now clearly see what we must do. If the apocalypse will not come to us, then we must go to the apocalypse!"

"Err, Sharona, you're not making much sense," Gunther whispered.

"It's simple. The Creator will only save us if we deliver ourselves to him!"

"And how do we do that?"

"By killing ourselves, of course!"

Riff Maltin had been wondering where his next story would come from when the call came through from Channel 27's news editor. Yablonsky wanted all his correspondents to investigate anti-alien sentiment in the sector's Citi-Def squads. Riff had glowed inwardly with pride at being referred to as a correspondent. But there was no time to savour the moment. Yablonsky was already handing out assignments, sending his best reporters to those blocks with the most rabid Citi-Def squads. Riff knew he couldn't leave this to chance.

"I want Oswald Mosley!" he shouted when the news editor paused.

"Why?"

"Call it a hunch," Maltin replied.

"Fine, whatever. The new boy's going to Oswald Mosley. Next..."

Riff had more than a hunch backing his request. He had returned to Robert Hatch after Dredd left and witnessed the survivors being loaded into hoverbuses. Creeping closer, he had overheard Judge Stammers directing the driver droid to deliver its cargo of aliens to Oswald Mosley. Riff had already seen what strong feelings the offworlders aroused. The residents of Mosley had a reputation for being notoriously anti-alien. The arrival of their new neighbours was bound to cause more trouble and that meant news.

Riff caught the midnight zoom train across Sector 87, luckily avoiding the traffic caused by the Anton Diffring pile-up. As a result the roving reporter reached his destination ahead of the hoverbus. He approached Oswald Mosley with some trepidation. It was a typical citi-block, one hundred storeys of con-apts and support facilities providing homes to sixty thousand residents. Residents could be born, live their whole lives and die without ever leaving the building. It contained shops, recreation areas and a medical centre. None of that worried Riff. But the scrawl emblazoned across the entrance to the block: ALIEN SCUM STAY OUT! attracted his attention. If the Judges were planning to relocate survivors from Robert Hatch to here, there wouldn't just be trouble – there was going to be a riot.

Riff smiled. Why was he worrying? A riot was exactly what he wanted. Grud knows, it would make good viewing on tri-D. It wouldn't be long before the hoverbus arrived. Now was his chance to alert the residents to what was coming, and stir them up a little. Maltin remembered the lecture Yablonsky had given him at the audition. "You can't always break the news. Sometimes you have to manufacture it – by any means necessary."

The reporter hurried into the block's entrance, encountering a surly juve inside picking his nose. "Do you know who runs the Citi-Def squad here?"

Ramone Maguire peered at the stranger. "Why do you want to know?"

"My name's Riff Maltin, I'm a reporter for Channel 27." He gestured at the hovercam just above his right shoulder to prove his identity. "I've got news about a threat to the security of this block and its residents."

Ramone shrugged. "You want my mom: Conchita Maguire, con-apt 729. But she won't be happy about you waking her up at this time of night."

"She'll thank me when she hears what I know."

"Have it your way." The juve jerked his head towards a phone on the wall. "You can call her from there. But I'm telling you, she won't be happy."

Riff soon discovered the juve had not been exaggerating. It took several minutes of cursing and swearing before Conchita calmed down enough to hear what Maltin was trying to tell her. "Offworlders? Coming here?"

"Yes." Riff heard the telltale hiss of a hoverbus stopping outside the entrance. "I think their transportation has just arrived outside."

"Those freaks aren't coming into my block!" the fiery Maguire vowed and slammed down the phone.

Riff smiled, the reason he had been sent to Oswald Mosley long forgotten. He could smell trouble and it was coming at his command.

* * *

Dredd and Miller screeched to a halt outside Maurice Waldron Block. A crowd of bystanders had formed around the building, many of them pointing upwards and discussing previous suicide jumps they had witnessed. Up above, a line of people could be seen standing on the edge of the roof, their figures silhouetted against the full moon overhead.

"One of us will have to stay here on crowd control until backup arrives," Miller observed, frowning at the ghouls gathered on the ground. "If the cult members do decide to turn themselves into street pizza, we don't want them taking out the bystanders as well."

"Agreed," Dredd growled. "You stay here. I'll go up."

"Hey! Why do you get to go?"

"Trust me. I've dealt with more leapers than you. I'll get these punks down, one way or another."

"Have it your own way," Miller said. "I'll contact the block maintenance droid, make sure countermeasures are available if the worst happens."

"That's a roj." Dredd dismounted from his Lawmaster and strode into Maurice Waldron, checking he had a full clip of ammunition loaded.

Miller watched him go in before looking up into the air again. "Drokking full moon, always brings out the crazies," she muttered.

On the roof Sharona Moore had convinced her acolytes that suicide was definitely the way to nirvana. "Just before we reach the ground the Creator will reach down and scoop out our souls, preserving us for all eternity," she announced with a smile.

All one hundred of the cult members were standing in a line along the edge of the roof, gazing out across the city. To Sharona's left, Gunther was having second thoughts. "Are you sure you've got the prophecy right this time, my darling?" he whispered from the side of his mouth. "I don't mean to question your wisdom, but earlier you were saying the entire world was coming to an end. Now you think it's just us who have to die."

"Do you doubt me, Gunther?" Sharona asked.

"Well, frankly, yes."

"Can't say I blame you," a gruff voice interjected. Sharona and her disciples swung round to see Judge Dredd emerging from the rooftop access door. "Seen a lot of religious types in my time and few of them have got any proof to support their claims of divine guidance."

"Unbeliever!" Sharona shouted, pointing an accusing finger at Dredd. "You know nothing of what you speak!"

"Maybe, but it doesn't sound like you've got a hotline to Grud yourself, or whoever you believe in."

"We believe in the Creator of all things," Gunther said, trying to be helpful.

"Uh-huh. This creator says it's a good night to fall a hundred storeys before going face-first into a rockcrete grave, does he?"

"The Creator does not have a gender," Sharona snapped. "They are beyond such worldly concerns as gender and sex."

"I know the feeling," Dredd replied. "Well, off you go."

"Sorry?"

"Jump. I'm not stopping you."

Sharona was perplexed. "If you're not going to stop us, why did you come up here?"

"Justice Department requires I try to talk you out of it, but I can't be bothered tonight. I haven't eaten in fifteen hours, I haven't slept in nearly twice that time and I couldn't give a flying drokk whether you jump or not." Dredd put his Lawgiver back into its holster. "Makes no difference to me."

"Oh. Err, okay." Sharona turned back to her disciples. "Well, if everybody's ready, we'll go on a count of three. One–"

"There's just one thing," Dredd said.

Sharona sighed in exasperation. "And what's that?"

"I can't let you take all these people with you."

"Why not?"

"You want to kill yourself, be my guest – one less kook to put in the cubes. But taking all these citizens with you, now that's mass murder."

Sharona frowned. "You can't be serious."

"Try me," Dredd growled.

"These people have agreed to follow me wherever I go. If that means jumping to their deaths, they will do so."

"I'm not convinced."

"You're not convinced?"

"No," Dredd said, shaking his head. "The citizen on your right, for a start. He didn't seem too sure when I came up the stairs. Since he's standing next to you, I'm guessing he's probably one of your assistants. Now, if you can't convince your assistants that suicide is a bright idea, well…"

Sharona glared at Dredd malevolently. "Have you quite finished?"

The Judge nodded.

"Fine. Then I shall prove how wrong you are. I will step off this roof and fall to my death. And all my acolytes will follow me. Now, if you don't mind."

"Go right ahead. Turn yourself into street pizza. No skin off my chin."

Sharona rolled her eyes before readying herself. "On my mark. One. Two. Three!" She stepped off the roof and began falling.

It was then Dredd realised all the cultists were tied together. Once Sharona went over the side, the others followed, whether they wanted to or not. Dredd began running towards the edge of the roof but was too late to grab the last of the sect members before they were dragged over. Instead he dived off the roof after them.

By the time Stammers and Riley reached Oswald Mosley, more than a hundred residents had blocked the entrance to the building. The two Judges had been called off escort duty to help with the aftermath of the Anton Diffring pile-up. They were now faced with another angry mob – only this one hadn't been immobilised with a bombardment of riot foam. The protesters had surrounded the hoverbus filled with aliens and were trying to tip the vehicle over.

"Terrif," Stammers muttered darkly. "As if this night couldn't get any worse." He fired six shots into the air. Most of the crowd scattered, falling back to the block's entrance. But a hardcore of two dozen remained around the hoverbus, all wearing flak jackets and helmets marked with CITI-DEF insignia. At the front and in the centre of this group was a woman with a face like thunder. She marched towards the two Judges.

"How dare you fire upon us! These are decent, law-abiding citizens staging a non-violent protest!" the woman snarled with venomous fury.

"Trying to turn over a hoverbus? Not exactly a page from the passive resistance handbook, is it?" Stammers replied sarcastically. "Anyway, we didn't fire on you. Those were warning shoots. What's your name, citizen?"

"Conchita Maguire, leader of Oswald Mosley Citi-Def."

"Well, you're not setting much of an example," Riley observed. "You're supposed to welcome and protect new residents – not attack them."

"So it's true! You intend to bring these alien scum inside our building!"

Stammers decided to take a more placatory approach. "Look, lady, I ain't any happier than you about this. But the situation is just temporary. Tomorrow morning they'll probably be moved to another facility."

"Temporary – that's an interesting word," Conchita said. "I had a friend in Robert Hatch who was temporarily moved out to make way for the vultures and all the other freaks. How many years did that temporary measure last?"

"Citizen, you can bitch and moan all you like. That ain't changing the fact these aliens are being housed here for the night," Riley replied.

"Where?" Conchita demanded. "Every con-apt in this building is already full beyond capacity. Where do you intend to put these, these, things?" She spat on the ground between the two Judges to underline her hatred.

Stammers smiled. He'd tried being nice but that didn't get him anywhere. He was fast losing patience. Time to put an end to this. "I'm told the top floor refurbishment is nearly done. The aliens can spend the night up there. We'll move them out in the morning."

That was when Conchita lost it. She could see her one dream, her last hope disappearing before her eyes. If the aliens shifted into the new home meant for her family, would the monsters ever move out again? She would remain trapped in her con-apt for Grud knew how many more months or years! Even if they were relocated, she wasn't sure she could stand to live where the aliens had been. It would be like sharing her body with them.

The red mist descended and Maguire went into a frenzy, running towards the hoverbus and throwing herself at the doors. One fist smashed through the glasseen, tearing the skin off her knuckles in the process. "I'm gonna kill you! I'm gonna kill you all!" she kept screaming, over and over. The rest of the Citi-Def squad took up her chant, banging their fists against the side of the hoverbus. Inside, the alien passengers cowered back from the windows, huddling against each other, terror and anger in their eyes. Meanwhile the rest of the residents were cheering the Citi-Def squad on.

The two Judges exchanged a glance.

"Stumm gas?" Stammers asked his partner.

"Stumm gas," Riley replied, already reaching for a canister of the paralysing liquid attached to his utility belt. The Judges pulled the pins simultaneously and rolled the smoking tubes towards the hoverbus, before pulling down the respirators on their helmets.

Stammers stepped away from his motorcycle and drew out his daystick. "Let's bust some heads!"

Dredd dived headfirst from the roof of Maurice Waldron Block, streamlining his body shape so he fell faster than the cultists below him. Sharona Moore and her ninety-nine disciples were tumbling slowly through the air like a human charm bracelet, each member tied to another at the wrist. Maurice Waldron was a hundred storeys high, giving the leapers plenty of time to scream for help as they fell towards the pedway below. Dredd activated his helmet radio.

"Miller, can you hear me?"

"Yes. Dredd, the cult kooks have just jumped off the roof!"

"I know. I jumped after them."

"You did what?!"

"I jumped after them. Are the block safety measures fully functional?"

"Yes," Miller replied. "I can control them from the onboard computer on my Lawmaster. Do you want me to deploy them?"

"Not yet."

"Why the drokk not?"

"I want to arrest these creeps on the way down," Dredd said.

"Well, I estimate you've got another sixty storeys and half a minute left."

"Roj that. I'll keep this channel open!" By now Dredd had caught up with the last of the cult members, a gibbering woman. Being at the end of the human chain, only one of her wrists was tied to another disciple. Her purple and gold gown was flapping around her face, revealing that she was otherwise naked. "You're under arrest," Dredd announced, "Attempted suicide, disturbing the peace and gross indecency. Six months for each charge, eighteen months in all."

"Are you crazy?" the woman screamed. "We'll all be dead in a minute!"

"If that happens, I'll let you off the attempted suicide," Dredd replied, handcuffing himself to her free wrist. "But the other charges still stand."

"You are crazy!" his prisoner replied.

Dredd ignored her and shouted so the other leapers could hear him. "You're all under arrest for attempted suicide and disturbing the peace! Come along quietly or there will be trouble!"

Misch had watched as the two Judges attacked the protesters outside the hoverbus. She felt waves of hatred and anger surging from the crowd but this turned to terror when the stumm gas canisters began billowing clouds of paralysing smoke into the air. Some of the gas seeped into the hoverbus through a broken window. The arthropod Gruchar began spewing green bile into the air while a family from Wolfren were sent into a frenzy of howling and tears. Misch was grateful for the R'qeen respiratory bypass system. The gas made her a little dizzy but that was the limit of its effects.

Among those caught in the conflict was a human Misch could recall seeing outside their old home. He was followed everywhere by a floating silver globe that seemed to be watching what was happening. The human threw himself against the doors of the hoverbus, begging to be let inside. He was clubbed to the ground by one of the Judges. It was the man with the moustache whose mind she had reached into. He was grinning, enjoying every second of this carnage.

Once the gas had cleared, the broodling could see the battered and bleeding bodies of the protesters scattered around the entrance of the building. Most of the others had retreated inside and shut the doors. But the two Judges overrode the electronic locks and drove the residents back up the stairs or into the lifts. Only when a path had been cleared into Oswald Mosley did the aliens dare venture from the hoverbus.

Nyon was first out, leading his family into the block lobby. Lleccas had fashioned a sling for his shattered arm. Misch clung on to her broodmother's arm, not wanting to be separated. She had grown to know their old home but this one was new and strange. The R'qeen girl could feel a seething resentment all around them, as if the building itself was willing them to go. The others slowly emerged from the hoverbus and joined them inside the block. In all there were half a dozen families: four R'qeen, one from Wolfren and Gruchar. Keno and her brood were one of the other R'qeen families.

The Judges reappeared down the staircase. "Turbolifts are stuck on the seventy-second floor. Residents have jammed them." It was the human with the moustache again. He seemed grimly satisfied with the situation. "You'll have to go up the stairs."

"How far?" Nyon asked.

"You're on the top. A hundred storeys up."

"But some here have injuries from the fire. Others are still suffering the effects of your gas. You can't expect them to climb a hundred flights of stairs."

The Judge leaned close to Nyon's face. "I don't care if it takes you all night, vulture. Get moving!"

Misch could feel her broodfather struggling to control his anger, a great mass of red and black boiling inside him. Eventually he walked past the human towards the stairs.

"Wait!" the Judge commanded. "Riley, you better take the lead. We've dealt with the worst of the troublemakers but they might still be planning another protest. I'll cover the flank. Okay, let's move!"

On the ground Miller's hand hovered over her Lawmaster's on-board computer while she watched Dredd and the hundred cultists plunging towards her. "For the love of Grud, you're running out of time!" she shouted into her helmet radio. "When do you want me to engage the countermeasures?"

"They're all under arrest," Dredd responded. "Engage now!"

Miller slammed her fist down on the computer screen. Wall panels two storeys up from the ground slid backwards into the building and several giant nets spat outwards, forming themselves into huge hammocks on all four sides of the block. Less than a second later Sharona and the other cult members plunged into the suicide nets, their fall slowed and halted within moments. Dredd was last to hit the netting, landing astride the nearly naked woman, his crotch jamming into her face.

The deployment of the building's safety measures brought a groan of collective disappointment from the bystanders but they soon began applauding Dredd's daring manoeuvre. Underneath him the scantily clad woman was struggling to make herself heard. "I can't breathe," she gasped. Dredd uncuffed himself from her wrist and clambered off her face.

"My apologies, citizen."

"Are you all right?" Miller shouted up to her partner.

Dredd gave her the thumbs up before swinging himself over the side of the net and dropping to the ground below. "Dredd to Control. We need catch wagons outside Maurice Waldron to collect a hundred religious kooks; twelve months each in the psycho cubes."

"What about me?" the nearly naked woman asked from atop the pile of cult members.

"Correction, Control," Dredd said. "Ninety-nine kooks at twelve months each and one simp who wants an extra six months."

In the nets Sharona overheard the request. "You can't do that! You've denied us our religious right to worship as we see fit."

Miller jerked a thumb at the bystanders who were now drifting away. "Religious tolerance stops when you endanger the lives of others."

Gunther was squeezed next to his leader in the nets. "You know, the signs and portents may have been right about the date of the apocalypse. We may have simply interpreted the wrong year from the prophecies."

Sharona smiled at him. "You mean the end of the world might be happening at midnight between June twelfth and thirteenth next year?"

"Maybe."

"Maybe," Sharona agreed before calling down to Dredd. "Excuse me, Judge. How long did you say our sentence was?"

"Twelve months for everybody except the woman who was cuffed to me – eighteen months for her. Why?"

"It's just we might have miscounted the date for the apocalypse. Same time next year, what do you say?"

Conchita Maguire had been one of the lucky ones during the brawl outside Oswald Mosley. Her sons had pulled her away from the worst of the stumm gas and bundled her inside before the Judges laid into the others with daysticks. Conchita wanted to fight alongside her fellow squad members but Ramone and Dermot would not let her. "We'll get our chance," Ramone said. "But you choose the time and the place, not them."

He was smart, that boy, Conchita had to admit. She decided on a tactical retreat, leading her sons and those squad members that had escaped the gas up to the seventy-second floor. Once there they disabled all the turbolifts, knowing the Judges would have to bring the aliens up the stairs. Conchita returned to the family con-apt to get changed, her squad uniform splashed with blood from the melee.

Inside 729 she found Kasey snivelling by the bedroom door, a red cloth wrapped round her left foot. "Please don't be angry," the girl said.

"What have you done now?" Conchita demanded.

"I didn't mean to," Kasey stammered. "It just happened. You were gone so long and I got thirsty..."

Conchita went to the icebox. Broken glasseen was splintered across the floor. Bloody footprints led away from an orange stain of Gloomy-D synthi-juice. "You cut yourself?"

Kirsty nodded, heavy tears brimming in her frightened eyes. "I didn't mean to get blood on the floor..."

A fist hammered against the con-apt's front door. "Conchita! Paul called from twenty-two: they're on their way up now!"

"Get everyone gathered by the stairs. I'll be right there."

"Gotcha!"

Conchita glared at her daughter, the anger rising inside once more. "Why can't you be more like Ramone or Dermot? They're ready to defend this block from the aliens and all you can do is make another mess."

Kirsty's bottom lip began to wobble. "But I didn't–"

Conchita advanced on her daughter, one hand clenching into a fist. "You have to be punished. I warned you before – learn to clean up your own messes or suffer the consequences."

Kirsty closed her eyes, whimpering in terror.

Miller pushed the last of the cult members into the back of a catch wagon. Dredd shut the door, then banged his fist on it. "Okay, take 'em back to the sector house for processing." The vehicle rolled away from Maurice Waldron Block, leaving the two Judges behind.

"Want me to catch the paperwork on that lot?" Miller offered. "You look like you could do with that sleep machine session about now."

"You might be right," Dredd replied. "It's–"

Their helmet radios crackled into life. "Control to all units, east side of Sector 87. Garbled reports of a confront between Judges and the Oswald Mosley Citi-Def. Can anyone respond?"

Dredd was about to climb on his Lawmaster but Miller stopped him. "That's the other side of the sector. By the time we get there it will all be over. We're not the only ones on this graveyard shift, you know." Within seconds several Judges much nearer were responding to the incident. Sector Chief Caine called Control to announce she would lead the backup team. "See what I mean? Come on, let's get back to the sector house."

"All right," Dredd reluctantly agreed. "But you go on ahead. I've got to put in a call to an old friend – in private."

His partner smiled. "Got a guilty secret you're trying to hide?"

"I don't have any guilty secrets," Dredd responded humourlessly. "The less you know about what I'm going to do, the better your future in Sector 87."

"I can take a hint," Miller said, climbing on to her Lawmaster and gunning its powerful engine into life. "See you back at the sector house."

Once she was gone Dredd activated his helmet radio. "Control, put me through to Chief Judge Hershey's office. I need to speak with her – Urgently!"

At first, Riley thought the chanting must be from a resident's tri-D set, the noise drifting down the emergency stairwell in Oswald Mosley Block. That would be a code violation, section 56b of the noise pollution regs: minimum sentence of three months, with a month added for each decibel of noise above the legal limit. Judging by the cacophony, the perp responsible was facing three years in the cubes, maybe more. Street Judges had discretion when it came to sentencing, but mandatory minimums set the bench mark.

Riley enjoyed being a Judge, the feeling of making a difference. The lives of every human being in this sector were a little better because Riley was on the job. He didn't count offworlders as citizens. To him they were a mistake. Justice Central should never have granted these things the right to stay in the Big Meg. It was our city, not theirs. Good men and women had died to defeat alien species like the R'qeen; now vultures could become citizens! Well, they might be legal aliens, but they would always be scum to Riley.

Besides being able to help people, there was another aspect of the job Riley found even more satisfying – administering the firm spank of authority. He liked the power, liked knowing he could take charge of almost any situation, that he could determine the fate of other people's lives, even whether they lived or died. It was a trip and no mistake. But you had to be careful. All that power could be intoxicating. Riley had seen what happened to Judges who got addicted to the buzz, and got caught. Not me, he vowed.

When he reached the sixty-ninth floor, Riley realised the noise was not coming from one of the con-apts. Looking up he could see dozens of residents three storeys above, chanting the same phrases over and over. "One, two, three, four, kick the aliens out the door! Five, six, seven, eight, keep the scum from our top floor!" Riley drew his Lawgiver and called down to his partner via helmet radio.

"Stammers, we've got a problem up here. I think the residents are planning another protest against the aliens."

"Keep going. Control says backup is on its way."

"You sure?"

"Do it, Riley! If the residents want another taste of my daystick, I'm more than happy to administer it to them. Stammers out!"

Riley looked back at the aliens climbing the stairs below him. They looked exhausted, easy meat for any citizens carrying a grudge. Riley almost felt sorry for them, until he remembered what had happened to Danny. "Drokk 'em," he whispered and resumed his progress up the stairs.

Conchita Maguire and her sons were blocking the seventy-second floor landing, along with dozens of other residents. Dermot and Ramone had gone from door to door, rousing their neighbours and spreading news of the aliens taking up residence in the penthouse con-apts. It didn't take much provocation to draw citizens out of their beds.

Conchita stepped in front of Riley when the Judge reached the landing. The aliens were still climbing the stairs behind him. "They're not going any further," she said. "Send 'em back where they belong. Not here with decent citizens."

"Step aside or I'll arrest all of you for disturbing the peace," Riley warned.

"We're making a legitimate protest," Dermot replied. "Try to arrest one of us and you'll have a riot on your hands. Is that what you want?"

"I've been cracking skulls since before you were born, juve. You want a piece of me? Bring it on," Riley said.

Dermot began towards the Judge but Conchita stopped him. "No, that's exactly what he wants. Don't give him an excuse."

"What's the problem?" Stammers bellowed up the stairwell from the floor below. "What's happening?"

Riley was about to answer when he heard a familiar noise from beyond the crowd of residents. "Residents won't let us past. Looks like we've got a stand-off, but that's about to change."

Conchita smiled. "Why? You backing down?"

"No, you are!" a woman shouted from behind the residents. They swivelled round to see a dozen Judges emerging from the turbolifts, all heavily armed. Standing at the front of them was Sector Chief Caine, a small electronic key held in her left hand. "Judicial override. Nice work jamming the circuits but Tek-Judges soon found a way to bypass your efforts." Caine drew her Lawgiver and aimed it at the residents gathered on the landing. "Now, you've all got five seconds to stand aside or else we take you down. Permanently."

"What do we do?" Ramone asked his mother. The other residents were all looking to her for guidance, unsure how to react.

"Stand aside," she hissed, her voice shaking with anger.

"But we can't–"

"Stand aside!" Conchita screamed at her eldest son, shoving him against a wall. She glared at the other citizens. "You heard me!" They all moved away from the stairwell, creating a gap for the aliens.

Caine told Riley and Stammers to transport the newcomers the rest of the way up Oswald Mosley in turbolifts. "I think they've been through enough for one night, don't you?" The rest of the Judges began ushering residents back to their own con-apts, the confrontation defused for now.

The Sector Chief was about to talk with the protest ringleaders when her helmet radio crackled into life. "Control to Caine. Message for you from the Chief Judge's office."

"At this time of night?" she wondered outloud, before responding to the call. Caine listened intently, her face becoming a scowl. Once the call was finished she resumed her conversation with Control. "Where is Judge Dredd now?"

"En route to your position at Oswald Mosley. Should be outside soon."

Caine nodded grimly. "Good. Tell him to wait for me in the lobby. I'll see him once I've dealt with the situation here."

Dredd had despaired of getting a reply from the Chief Judge's office, so he decided to confront Caine instead. When he arrived at Oswald Mosley Block a clean-up squad and half a dozen Med-Judges were dealing with the aftermath from the earlier brawl. Dredd saw Maltin slumped against a pillar nursing a head wound, his hovercam dutifully shooting every moment of Riff's agony. "You were outside Robert Hatch," Dredd recalled. "I warned you to stay out of trouble."

The reporter shrugged. "Can I help it if trouble follows me around?" A Med-Judge began examining Riff's skull, pushing aside hair matted with blood to examine the wound. "Hey, careful!"

"Stop your griping, citizen," the physician retorted. After a cursory study of the contusion he handed Riff a rapi-heal patch. "Stick this on it. Should be good as new by morning." The Med-Judge was already moving to the next injury.

"What about the pain? Give me something for the pain," Riff pleaded.

"Get over it," the physician replied. "Feel better now?"

"Oh yeah. Just terrif!"

Dredd nudged Maltin with his boot. "What happened here?"

"Difficult to say," Riff admitted. "Residents tried to stop two Judges taking the aliens inside. Thirty seconds later the place was awash with stumm gas and one of your colleagues was trying to reshape my head with his daystick."

"Who was it?"

"I don't know, I was too busy bleeding to get a look at his badge. But he had a big moustache and a way with a beating, know what I mean?"

Dredd's helmet radio demanded his attention. "Control to Dredd. Sector Chief Caine requests that you wait for her in the lobby of Oswald Mosley. She should be with you presently."

"Roj that. Dredd out." He looked at Riff thoughtfully. "Stick around. I've got more questions for you."

01:00

Misch had only known about her gift for a few hours, but she was already beginning to think metema was as much a curse as a blessing. Being able to read the thoughts and feelings of others whenever you wanted was a good thing. But the emotions around her now were so strong, so overwhelming, it was all she could do to keep them out of her head. The woman who had been stopping them from going any further was the worst. Her anger and hatred was so palpable she appeared as a red blur on Misch's thoughts. Some of the others were almost as angry, but none with such power or conviction. Being the target of such hostility left the R'qeen child quivering with fear.

The Judges had begun moving the Robert Hatch Block survivors into the turbolifts, but there wasn't enough room for everyone to travel to the top floor at the same time. Nyon volunteered his family to stay behind and wait for the next turbolift. Misch wished her broodfather hadn't been so generous, but it was typical of him to put others first. That was his way and she loved him for that.

Misch had been holding on tightly to her broodmother's hand, not wanting to be left behind when their turn came. Then a fresh mind caught her attention. There was a girl nearby, not far from her in age. She was so sad, sadder than anyone Misch had ever met before. The R'qeen child let go of her broodmother's hand to look for this girl. Perhaps she could make her happy.

"Don't go far," Lleccas said. "The turbolift will be back for us soon."

Misch nodded dutifully to her broodmother before wandering away. She knew the sad girl was close by, but where? Misch closed her eyes and let the emotions draw her near. The unhappiness called to her, clearer than any voice. She felt her way round a corner and reached out with her mind.

Can you hear me?

The other girl was frightened by the thoughts suddenly appearing in her head. *Who are you? What do you want?*

Misch tried to think a smile of reassurance. *I don't want to hurt you,* she thought. *I just want to know why you are so unhappy.*

I–I can't–

The R'qeen child received a mental flash of a clenched fist. *Somebody hurts you? Hits you?*

How do you know that? Can you see that in my head?

Misch had stopped at a doorway. She was very close to the girl now. *I can sense what others think and feel. Don't be afraid. My name is Misch.*

The door opened a fraction and a small, frightened voice spoke from inside. "I'm Kasey," the girl said.

Misch opened her eyes. Through the gap in the doorway she could see a little of Kasey's face. It was mottled with black, purple and yellow, but Misch knew those were not the usual markings of a human child. "Hello Kasey." The R'qeen broodling was startled to realise she was speaking the human's language, despite never having learned it. This must be another aspect of metema. She would have to ask her broodmother about it later.

"Do you want to play?" Kasey asked, biting her bottom lip hopefully.

Misch smiled. "Yes please!"

Miller was delivering Sharona Moore and her disciples to the desk sergeant at Sector House 87 for processing when a thought occurred to her. What if the incendiary device that gutted Robert Hatch had come from within the Justice Department? She and Dredd had assumed it must have been taken from a Citi-Def squad's armoury, but these could not be easily accessed without judicial authority. The device might have been stolen from the sector house, or more likely from the panniers on a Judge's Lawmaster. It was a long shot, but still worth investigating. Miller took a turbolift down to the Armoury in the lowest sub-basement of the sector house. The storehouse of ammunition and weaponry appeared deserted until the night droid appeared from behind a crate of Lawgivers.

"Armourer not around?" Miller asked.

"At one in the morning? You jest," the robot replied impatiently. The mechanoid announced it was busy with the overnight stocktake. "Can I help you with anything?"

"There was a suspicious fire at Robert Hatch a few hours back. Tek-Division detected Lucir-74 among the chemical compounds left as a residue. I was wondering if any incendiary devices have been stolen or reported missing in the last, say, seventy-two hours?"

"Nope," the droid said without hesitation.

"How can you be so sure? You didn't check the computer."

"No need." The robot tapped the side of its head unit. "I have a direct link to the system in here. Plus I undertake a full and thorough stock-take of the armoury's entire inventory every night at this hour – assuming nobody disturbs me. Nothing comes in or out of here without my knowing about it."

Why did department droids always have to be officious, Miller wondered? Just once she'd like to encounter a robot that didn't consider itself a cut above its masters. "Well, it was just a hunch," she said, beginning to leave.

"The only recent change in our stocks of incendiary devices was last night when a colleague of yours collected one for a demonstration. It's due for return at dawn. Other than that, nothing to report."

"Right." Miller smiled and continued towards the door. She stopped on her way out, calling back to the droid. "Tell you what, give me the name of the Judge and I'll remind them about returning the device."

"It was Stammers. Judge Eustace Stammers."

Stammers was standing inside the turbolift, glaring at the two remaining aliens on the seventy-second floor of Oswald Mosley. "Are you coming or not?"

Lleccas shook her head. "It's our broodling. She's missing!"

Stammers sighed, not bothering to mask his exasperation. You'd think these vultures would have enough sense to keep a firm grip on the creepy little creatures they spawned. "Then find her, for Grud's sake! I ain't holding these doors open all night," he growled in Allspeak.

"Why don't you help us?" the male R'qeen asked, nursing one of its arms. "What if something has happened to Misch?"

"Just one less of you freaks for me to worry about," Stammers said with a cruel smile. "I'll give you two minutes to find her. After that you make your own way to the top of this dump." The R'qeen looked ready to attack Stammers but was dragged away by its mate. It was only after the aliens had gone Stammers realised the male was the same one he had fought outside Robert Hatch. Damn vultures all looked the same.

Sector Chief Caine was lecturing Conchita in front of the citizen's sons. "What sort of example are you setting for these juves? Children learn how to hate and who to hate from their parents."

"They don't have parents, they just have me. Their father was killed by a vulture years ago. It was Judges like you who let his murderer get away."

"Don't call them vultures!" Caine growled. "The R'qeen may be carrion eaters but they are also residents of this sector. They have as much right to live in this block as you do, citizen."

Conchita shook her head. "Those con-apts on the top floor, they were being refurbished for families like mine. Decent families, human families. Not the bug-eyed monsters you've put up there!"

"This is a temporary measure until–"

"Cut the stomm, lady!" Dermot said. "We know what's going on here!"

"Yeah," his brother added. "You want us out so you can fill the building with these freaks! Your kind makes me sick. Drokking vulture lover!"

Caine glared at both juves before regarding their mother. "Congratulations. I see you've done a good job teaching these two to hate."

Conchita pulled back a fist, ready to strike, but stopped herself. Instead she smiled at the Sector Chief. "Nice try." The smile drained from her face as two R'qeen approached. "What are those things still doing on this floor?"

"Excuse me," Nyon said, his English heavy with accent. "We are looking for our – how do you say – our child?"

"Your broodling?" Caine asked.

"Yes, our broodling, Misch. She has wandered off..."

The Sector Chief activated her helmet radio. "Caine to all units in Oswald Mosley. There is a..." She stopped, having noticed movement over Conchita's shoulder. "Cancel that. All units return to what you were doing. Caine out." She stepped past Conchita and pushed open the door of con-apt 729. Inside an R'qeen child was playing with a human girl. "Is that your broodling?"

Lleccas rushed forward and grabbed her daughter. "Misch, what were you doing?" she whispered in R'qeen. "We didn't know where you were. Your broodfather and I have been searching for you."

"This is Kasey. She was sad, she didn't have anyone to play with," Misch replied in her native tongue.

"That's all very well but you should have told us where you were going. We were so worried about you!"

"I'm sorry." Misch waved goodbye to Kasey, who shyly waved back.

Conchita watched with horror and then anger as the two R'qeen females walked out of her con-apt and down the corridor to the turbolifts with Nyon. "I'll deal with you soon," she hissed at her daughter before closing the con-apt door. "Was there anything else?" Conchita asked Caine.

"Yes. I notice your daughter has bruises on her face and arms."

"She's a very clumsy child, always hurting herself."

"I wonder if she would say the same thing – especially if tested against a lie detector?" Caine reached into a pouch on her utility belt and pulled out the palm-sized birdie unit.

"You come near my daughter with that thing and I'll show you the meaning of hate," Conchita warned.

"Is that a threat, citizen?"

"That's a promise!"

Caine held up the lie detector to show Conchita. The display was green. "It seems you're telling the truth – for once." By now the rest of the Judges had finished returning the other residents to their con-apts and were gathering in the corridor. "All units return to patrol. Nothing more to do here." Soon it was just Caine left facing the Maguires.

The Sector Chief stepped closer to Conchita. "I'll be keeping an eye on you. If there's any more trouble in Oswald Mosley tonight, I'll hold you personally responsible. That's a promise, by the way, not a threat."

"You brought the aliens here. When they step out of line – and their kind always do – you'll be the one responsible," Conchita replied before leading her sons into their con-apt.

Caine stood outside the door listening, but heard no sounds from inside. Satisfied, she went to the turbolifts. It was now time to deal with Dredd.

"She's gone," Dermot said, his right ear pressed against the con-apt's front door. Conchita nodded, one hand clamped over her daughter's mouth.

"Good. Take your brother down to the juve hall. Once the Judges have left the building, I want you to contact our friends. We'll need help if we're going to get rid of the scum on the top floor."

Once Dermot and Ramone had gone, Conchita released her daughter. Kasey tried to hide herself in a corner, but there was no escaping the disgust in her mother's eyes. "I can't believe what I just saw," Conchita began. "A child of mine communing with one of those... those creatures. What possessed you?"

"She seemed nice," Kasey whimpered.

"Do you know what their kind do? They kill other animals and let the flesh rot until it is putrid. Only then do they eat it. The vultures are carrion eaters, the lowest of the low. They carry diseases and bacteria everywhere. And you let one in here. We should burn everything that monster touched!"

"Misch isn't a monster!" Kasey protested. "She's my friend!"

Conchita slowly undid the belt from her waist. Clasping the buckle firmly, she looped the belt several times around her fist but left half the strap hanging free. "Scum like that will never be our friends, Kasey. I've told you that before but it seems you weren't listening. So now I'm going to beat that lesson into you."

Dredd had been waiting in the lobby of Oswald Mosley for nearly ten minutes before Caine stepped from the turbolift, carrying her helmet under her arm. "Good, you're here," she said. "I understand you wanted to see me–"

"What happened up there?" Dredd demanded.

Caine sighed. "Going to be like that, is it? Very well. There was a confrontation between the residents and the new arrivals. The conflict has been defused and all involved given a verbal warning. I doubt we will see any more trouble from Oswald Mosley tonight."

"Then you're living in a dream!" Dredd replied. "This place is an explosion waiting to happen. Putting the aliens here, even temporarily, was a colossal misjudgement. I guarantee this place will be in flames before dawn."

"Well, thank you for that outburst – I'll take it under advisement. Was there anything else?" the Sector Chief asked.

"That street reporter for Channel 27, Riff Maltin. His credentials should be withdrawn. He seems more interested in creating news by provoking anti-alien hatred than simply reporting what happens."

Caine shook her head. "I've seen no evidence to confirm such an allegation, Request denied. What else?"

"Have you suspended Stammers and Riley yet?"

"Why should I?"

Dredd jerked a thumb at the scene outside the lobby. "They caused that chaos. Those two are out of control, especially Stammers."

"Is that right?" Caine asked.

"Yes!"

She smiled. "For somebody who's just arrived at this sector, you seem very quick to pass judgement on your fellow law enforcers. I wonder what they would have to say about you?"

"What do you mean?"

"I wonder how they would feel about you calling the Chief Judge's office to complain about this sector's performance."

"I have requested an urgent meeting with the Chief Judge, but that is all. How do you know about that?"

"I told you before, Dredd, you're not the only one with friends in high places. Don't expect the Chief Judge to respond to your request anytime soon. By the way, it may be some hours before she receives it." The smile faded from Caine's features as she stepped closer to Dredd. "If you've got a problem with somebody under my command, you bring it to me first."

"What if you're the problem?"

"The procedure remains the same," Caine replied. "While you're under my command, you have to respect my authority and the chain of command."

Dredd shook his head. "This sector is a pressure cooker waiting to blow and you keep turning up the heat, Caine. Putting these aliens here is just the latest in a long line of bad calls you've made. No wonder Justice Central is getting ready to take you off active duty. You're a liability. The sooner they get you away from the streets, the better," he snarled.

"Keep this up and I'll be more than happy to have a formal warning put on your permanent record," Caine hissed back.

"Be my guest," Dredd replied. "What I want to know is how the likes of you got to be Sector Chief in the first place. Your record suggests you used to be a good Judge until your ego got the–"

"My ego?" Caine burst out laughing. "That's rich coming from the king of the grandstanders, the legendary Judge Dredd, who has to be the star of every incident he attends. Frankly, I'm amazed you deign to help us mere mortals!"

Dredd began striding to his Lawmaster, Caine following him. "Don't you dare walk away from me! I haven't dismissed you yet!"

Dredd stopped, turning back to face Caine. "Then dismiss me. I've got better things to do than be lectured by the likes of you."

"That's it! Now you've gone too far!" Caine pulled on her helmet and activated its radio. "Sector Chief Caine to Control, I wish to lodge a complaint against Judge Dredd. The charge is gross insubordination."

"Control to Caine, not sure we heard you right."

"I want a formal warning placed on Dredd's permanent record and a hearing held within twenty-four hours. Is that clear enough for you?"

"Roj that. Control out."

Caine smiled at Dredd. "Happy now?"

"Ecstatic."

Caine mounted her Lawmaster motorcycle. "Try to go over my head again and I'll have your badge for breakfast." She offered one final comment before accelerating away. "Now you're dismissed!"

Dredd looked around but Maltin was nowhere to be seen.

Miller completed her paperwork for the suicidal cult members while pondering what the armoury droid had told her. Stammers was an ultra-violent xenophobe but even he would stop short of committing arson, wouldn't he? She couldn't believe Riley would be a part to such an atrocity, even with his feelings about aliens. Yet there was no record of either Judge being involved with any incendiary device demonstration. Something didn't add up.

Where was Dredd, she wondered. He should have been back at the sector house by now. Miller considered calling him with the new information she had gleaned, but thought better of it. Any such call would be broadcast via Control and the content was bound to reach one of her two suspects. Better to leave him a message and investigate further on her own. Miller recorded a vid-message for Dredd and took it to the garage where Tek-Judge Brady was refuelling her Lawmaster.

"Could you give this to Dredd when he comes in next?"

The mechanic was bemused by the request. "Why not just–"

Miller laid a hand on Brady's shoulder. "Let's just say it's for his ears only and leave it at that."

"Okay, if you say so. Your bike will be ready in a minute."

Miller called Control. "Can you give me a current position for Judges Stammers and Riley?"

"That's a roj. Both are leaving Oswald Mosley now, en route for the Sector 87 dust zone. You want to be connected to them?"

"No thanks, it's nothing urgent. Miller out." The dust zone was one of several areas in the city devoted to industrial factories and warehouses. Many had been abandoned following the shift in production to cheaper labour markets like Indo-City. As a result dust zones were favourite haunts for fugitives and criminals. Perhaps Stammers and Riley planned to pick up some easy collars there, but Miller wasn't so sure. She collected her Lawmaster from Brady and rode out into the sultry night air.

"Miller to Control, am going off-radio to follow a lead."

"Roj that. Call back in when you're ready to receive messages again."

Lleccas was stunned when she saw her family's new accommodation. It was only supposed to be for one night, but already she was hoping they never had to leave. After the crumbling edifice that had been their old block, the top floor of Oswald Mosley was grander than any Lleccas had seen on this world. The emergency stairs curled up the centre of the circular building, surrounded by the turbolifts. Around these was a wide corridor, subtly lit with glass panels in the ceiling revealing the night sky overhead.

Doorways opened from the circular hallway on to six luxurious conapts, each set against the outer wall of the building. In the middle of each con-apt was a communal living area with plush, comfortable furniture and warm lighting. Instead of an external wall the room had glasseen picture windows from floor to ceiling, affording a dramatic view of the full moon hanging in the air over Sector 87. Further rooms ran off the main space, offering sleeping quarters for at least half a dozen residents along with cooking and cleaning facilities. A few rooms remained unfinished but the con-apt was still a palace compared to the damp, fetid, decaying hovel that had been Robert Hatch.

Lleccas was blinking back tears as she went from room to room. "All of this for us?" she stammered in amazement to Nyon.

Her pairling nodded sadly. "Yes, but this is just for tonight. No doubt we will be returned to our appointed place in the morning."

Lleccas knew he was right but she was still determined to enjoy this rare treat, no matter how brief it might be. "Misch, which room do you want?"

The R'qeen child emerged from one of the bedrooms, dragging a blanket and cushions out into the main space. "I want to sleep here, so I can watch the sun rise," she said. "Is that allowed?"

Nyon could not help smiling at his broodling's enthusiasm. "Yes, that's allowed. Now, let's get some rest. It's been a long night and we don't know when the Judges will come for us in the morning."

Misch was already settled into a well-padded chair facing the windows. "Goodnight," she said, wrapping blankets around herself.

Lleccas and Nyon kissed their broodling before retiring to the main bedroom and quietly closed the door behind them. Lleccas sighed as Nyon drew her into his embrace, careful not to brush against his injured limb. For the first time in too long, she felt safe again.

When Kasey regained consciousness all she felt was pain. The left side of her body throbbed. She had turned into the corner to keep the worst of the beating off her face and body, and had offered her left side to the belt her mother wielded. She was now paying the price for it: her left arm was all but useless, her left leg a mass of lumps, bruises already crowding both limbs. Angry red weals crisscrossed her skin where the fabric of her clothes did not reach.

Kasey did not know how long she had been in the darkness. A light still seeped from beneath the door of the bedroom she shared with her mother, but Kasey was not going back in there tonight. She had to get away. The little girl was not the brightest of children but none of the other children she knew in Oswald Mosley seemed to have marks like her. She never heard anyone else crying themselves to sleep at night. But where could she go?

Kasey, are you all right?

The voice in her head made the girl jump. She concentrated, trying to reply by only saying the words in her thoughts. *Misch, is that you?*

Yes. Are you hurting?

Kasey nodded before realising her friend could not see her. *Yes*, she thought. *My mom hit me with her belt. She said I had to be punished.*

Show me, Misch asked.

So Kasey recalled a little of the beating before the memory was too much to bear. *See?*

Why does she do that? My broodmother would never hurt me.

I think she hates me. She hates you too.

I know.

Kasey waited but no more words came into her head. *Misch? Are you still there?*

Yes, the R'qeen girl replied. *I was just thinking. Would you like to come up and stay with me? We have plenty of rooms...*

Could I?

Yes! It'll be an adventure!

Kasey shook her head. *No, you'll get in trouble. Your mom might get angry and punish you too.*

Not if we hide you.

All right, the human girl decided. *But how do I find you?*

Just concentrate on my voice. It will bring you to me.

Kasey stood and began walking slowly towards Misch's words.

Miller rode her Lawmaster into the dust zone, headlights turned off to avoid attracting too much attention. The full moon overhead might bring out the kooks but it also provided enough light to see where she was going. Even so, Miller kept to a low speed, not wanting to ride into a chem pool and find herself sinking into the acid-laced liquids. She activated the heat sensors on her Lawmaster's computer, scanning the surrounding area for movement. The hotter an object was, the brighter it appeared on screen.

Two dull red shapes were moving ahead of her from the east. A bright white shape was converging on them from the west. The computer identified it as a Lawmaster, the heat from its engine and exhaust emissions all too characteristic. Miller shut down her own motorcycle and continued ahead on foot, Lawgiver drawn. Perhaps Stammers and Riley had split up to hunt perps in the dust zone. That would explain why only one Lawmaster was evident; the other could be several klicks away, out of the computer's sensor range.

Another thought occurred to Miller, one that gave her hope for Riley's future. Perhaps only Stammers was involved with the arson attack? He could not have placed the incendiary device that torched Robert Hatch, but Stammers might have supplied it to someone else. A gruff voice in the distance brought Miller to a halt. She dropped to a crouch and moved sideways to take cover behind an abandoned roadster.

Ahead was a clearing illuminated by the moon; eerie blue light bathed the empty space. Two figures sauntered into view, their faces obscured by hooded clothing. Miller pulled tiny binoculars from her utility belt to get a better look at the pair. Despite keeping their faces hidden, both were obviously juves, neither of them eighteen yet. They looked around, seemingly expecting someone else to be present. "Hey, we're here! You can come out now!" one of the juves shouted. A Judge walked into the clearing from the opposite side.

"Keep your voices down," Stammers said, his gruff voice recognisable now Miller could hear him properly. "We don't need an audience."

The taller juve pulled back his hood and laughed. "It's gone midnight, lawman! There's nobody here but us." Miller didn't recognise his face.

"Even so," Stammers replied. "No need to take unnecessary chances. You did well at Robert Hatch."

"Yeah, and how did you repay us? By helping those bug-eyed freaks move into the top floor of our building!"

Miller smiled. That narrowed down the number of places where these juves lived considerably. Keep talking bigmouth, she thought.

"Sector Chief's orders. Nothing I could do about that," Stammers said.

"Well, we need your help to get them back out. Or else," the second juve said, pulling back his hood to reveal similar features to his partner in crime. Miller decided the pair must be brothers.

"Or else what?" Stammers sneered. He stepped towards the juves, Lawgiver held casually in one hand. "You boys shouldn't try making threats. You haven't had the practise to carry them off."

"Or else we tell your Sector Chief what you've been up to behind her back," the second juve said, trying not to be intimidated by the Judge. "Caine will rip you if she ever finds out."

"Then we'll have to make sure that never happens," Stammers said. "What can I do to help you?"

The two juves smiled at each other. "That's better, lawman," the taller one said. "Give us the codes to unlock the Citi-Def armoury in the basement of our block. We need those weapons to take on the vultures."

"Anything else?"

"Keep the rest of the Judges away from Oswald Mosley until dawn. It'll all be over by then," the other juve said cockily.

Stammers began laughing at them. "You two ought to be on tri-D."

"Why you laughing at us, lawman?" the elder juve demanded.

"Did you honestly think I'd kow-tow to punks like you?" Stammers's Lawgiver spat twice, death punching holes through the protesting juve's head. The Judge turned to the other juve, ready to shoot again. "Now it's your time, stomm for brains." Another shot and both juves were dead on the ground, their bodies still twitching.

Kasey closed the front door of the con-apt quietly behind her. She did not often venture outside during the day without Ramone, Dermot or her mother to accompany her. Sneaking out in the middle of the night would provoke severe punishment if she was caught.

Kasey, are you all right? Misch's voice was inside the human girl's head, guiding her forwards.

Yes, Kasey thought. *Now where do I go?*

Turn right and walk to the turbolifts.

Kasey followed Misch's instructions, her progress hampered by the severe contusions down her left side. Her leg was already stiffening up, making it difficult to walk. Kasey staggered sideways as she approached the turbolifts, her shoulder brushing against a doorbell pad outside a neighbour's con-apt. She hurried on as best she could but the door to 721 behind her opened before the turbolift arrived.

"What the drokk do you want at this hour? Haven't I had enough disturbances for one night?" Kurt Sivell glared up and down the corridor, one hand trying to rub the sleep from his eyes, a gown wrapped round his ample girth. An immigrant from Euro-Cit, Sivell had little time for the Citi-Def squad, calling them power-crazed tin-pot tyrants. He was surprised to see Kasey by the turbolifts.

"Was that you, juve?"

Kasey nodded. "Sorry, it was an accident."

"Well, don't do it again," he replied, wandering towards her. "Where are you going at this time of night?"

Misch, what do I say? Kasey asked in her mind.

Tell him you're going to see a friend, the R'qeen broodling suggested.

Sivell was unconvinced by this explanation. "Does you mother know about this? Perhaps I should call her—"

"It was her idea! She says the further I am away from those things on the top floor, the better," Kasey replied at Misch's prompting.

"Quite right too." Despite being an immigrant himself, Sivell wanted no truck with offworlders. Mankind had enough problems learning to get along with itself. There was no need to throw aliens into the mix as well, in his opinion. "Well, your turbolift is ready. Off you go."

Kasey smiled at her neighbour before stepping into the turbolift. Without thinking, she pressed the button for the top floor and the doors began to close. "Goodbye," she said and waved with her good hand.

Sivell returned the wave and waddled back towards his con-apt. Only when the doors had closed did he look back to see where the turbolift stopped next. To his surprise, it was going up instead of down. He must mention that to Conchita in the morning. Right now he needed sleep and no disturbances. A good dose of Double-Doze ought to do the trick.

Miller could not believe what she had witnessed. Shocked from the first shots, she was too late to stop the second juve being executed. She held back, watching to see what Stammers would do next. He holstered his Lawgiver and began dragging one of the corpses towards a chem pit. The body slid down into the acidic liquid, bubbles and acrid smoke rising from the surface as the juve dissolved. Stammers went back for the second body. Miller waited until he had his hands full before emerging from cover, Lawgiver ready to fire.

"Don't move or I shoot!" she commanded.

Stammers looked up and grimaced. "Ahh, stomm!"

Miller moved into the clearing but kept a safe distance from him. "Is that all you've got to say? I've just watched you gun down two juves in cold blood."

"They were responsible for the arson attack on Robert Hatch. They planted the incendiary device that killed thousands of aliens."

"And we both know how much you care about offworlders, right?" Miller sneered. "You gave them the incendiary device, you probably told them the best place to plant it. Those juves were no innocents, but you're just as guilty as them."

Stammers let go of the corpse and straightened up. "So what are you going to do about it, Miller? Send a good Judge to Titan just because a few vultures got overcooked?"

"You don't honestly think I can overlook this, do you?"

He shrugged. "I could make it worth your while."

"Adding bribery and corruption to your crimes won't help, Stammers."

"Maybe not, but I'd be more worried about my own future if I were you."

Miller frowned. "What do you mean by that?"

Something blunt and heavy smashed against the back of Miller's helmet, sending her sprawling. She narrowly avoided falling into the chem pit but her Lawgiver was not so fortunate: it disappeared into the bubbling liquid. Miller rolled over to see Riley looming above her, a Widowmaker rifle clutched in his hands. "Riley? Not you too."

"Sorry, Lynn," he said, reaching down to snap off the microphone from her helmet radio. "You shouldn't have come here."

Miller could feel the darkness overwhelming her. Concussion, possibly a fractured skull, she decided. Got to stay conscious.

She tried to focus on the moon overhead but it had disappeared behind clouds. In the distance she could hear a pathetic gurgling sound and realised it was her own voice, trying to form words. Something warm and metallic filled her mouth, salty to taste – her blood, no doubt. Miller's legs had gone numb and she felt cold, far too cold.

Going into shock now.

Stupid way to die, so stupid–

02:00

Dredd had searched in vain for Maltin, determined to learn more about what had happened earlier outside Oswald Mosley. But the reporter had gone to ground, ignoring Dredd's command to stay put. The Judge began travelling back to Sector House 87 on his Lawmaster, the route still requiring a lengthy diversion while the Anton Diffring Overzoom was cleared of debris. En route Dredd called Control for Miller's whereabouts.

"She went off-radio twenty minutes ago. Said she was following a lead."

"Did she specify further?"

"Negative."

Dredd pulled into the sector house garage to find Tek-Judge Brady waiting for him. "I was wondering when you'd come back here," the mechanic said, holding out a small silver disc. "I've got a vid-message for you from Miller. She told me to deliver it personally. You can use the tri-D screen in my office."

After closing the door to the office, Dredd slipped the disc into the tri-D player. A mechanical voice announced the message had previously been played zero times, then a holographic image of Miller appeared in the air. She spoke quickly, her voice just a whisper but her features full of concern.

"Hey, partner. Sorry I'm not there but something's come up I couldn't broadcast over the radio. Seems Stammers 'borrowed' an incendiary device from the Armoury matching the sort used to torch Robert Hatch. Stammers and Riley have gone to the local dust zone so I'm going off-radio to find them, see if this hunch plays out. To be honest, it could be something or nothing. I don't know if Stammers is behind the fire and, even if he is, I've got nothing linking Riley to it. If I haven't reported in by three, you'll know where to find me. Miller out."

The holograph turned to a blizzard of static before the tri-D player switched off, ejecting the disc. Brady knocked on the office door before entering.

"Anything interesting?" he asked.

"Time will tell," Dredd replied. "Thanks for the use of your office."

Conchita Maguire woke with a start. She had been dozing on her bed, with the lights still on. The last thing she remembered was hearing the front door opening and closing, and thinking it was Ramone and Dermot returning home. But she had heard nothing more since then, certainly not the usual late night jumble of noise she associated with her sons stumbling in. Conchita rolled over and realised Kasey was not in bed. Then she remembered the thrashing she had given her. Grud, that temper... She had better check Kasey was all right.

Conchita pulled on the khaki trousers and vest from her Citi-Def uniform before venturing out into the main room. She turned on the light but could see no sign of Kasey or the boys. Fighting back a rising wave of panic, Conchita hurriedly began checking the other rooms. But it was a tiny con-apt and there were only so many places the little girl could be. Conchita searched again and again without result. A chilling thought occurred. The noise of the front door earlier; maybe that had been Kasey going out, not the boys coming back in.

"Oh my Grud," Conchita whispered, the hairs on the back of her neck standing up. She pulled open the front door and peered out into the corridor, hoping and praying to see her daughter. But the hallway was empty. Only the erratic flicker of overhead lights provided any movement. Conchita went to the nearest con-apt and began pounding on the door, her spare hand pressing on the doorbell pad repeatedly. "Come on, open up! Please!"

Misch opened the front door of her family's new home and let Kasey inside. The R'qeen child was shocked by the new injuries Kasey had suffered since they first met. Why would anyone hurt their broodling like this? It didn't make any sense to Misch but there was much about the natives of this world she didn't understand. Metema might give you access to the thoughts and feelings of others, but it couldn't explain everything about them.

"Are you okay?" Misch whispered, keeping her voice quiet so she wouldn't wake her broodfather and broodmother.

Kasey smiled. "I am now." She looked around the interior of the main living space, amazed at how large it was. The con-apt's lights were off, but the room was still illuminated by the night-time cityscape beyond the floor-to-ceiling window. "You live here? Just the three of you?"

"Only for tonight. Tomorrow the Judges will take us away again."

"Mom says we're supposed to be shifting to the top floor when it's ready."

Misch took Kasey's hand and reached her thoughts into the human girl's mind. *Let's talk in our heads – that way nobody else can hear us.*

Kasey nodded happily. *It'll be our secret!*

Misch tugged on her hand. *Come on, I'll show you the rest of the con-apt. If you're going to live here, you'll want to choose the best room.*

Evan Yablonsky was not having a good night. Since getting the anonymous tip-off about the incendiary device, Channel 27's news editor had been harassing his correspondents out on the skedways and pedways for proof so they could broadcast the story. All of them had come up empty, with the exception of Riff Maltin. The first-timer had sent back some great footage of a riot from outside Oswald Mosley with two Judges brutalising a crowd of residents (at least, that was how the footage looked to most viewers), and some nice comedy moments of Maltin being treated in the aftermath. But Riff had disappeared soon afterwards, with Yablonsky getting no reply from the rogue reporter and no signal from the hovercam.

When Riff finally did call in, the news editor was overjoyed and enraged at the same time. "Where the hell have you been?" Yablonsky demanded. "You're supposed to be impressing me with your professionalism. Not disappearing for hours at a time when you feel like it!".

Maltin protested his innocence. "I've already been threatened by one Judge, beaten by another and Dredd wants to interrogate me. So you'll have to excuse me if I decide to lay low for a while!"

"All right, all right," his boss conceded. "What's new? What have you got?"

"Nothing. I've been laying low."

Yablonsky rolled his eyes. "For the love of Grud, get back to Oswald Mosley. I think your hunch was right. That place is a tragedy waiting to happen and I want you on the inside, broadcasting every moment. You got that?"

"Got it."

"Do this right and you'll be famous overnight," the news editor said.

"Now you're speaking my language," Riff replied.

Conchita had roused all the residents on the seventy-second floor of Oswald Mosley, along with those on the floors immediately above and below. Each level had a representative on the block's Citi-Def squad. Conchita had her colleagues from seventy-one and seventy-three coordinate the search for Kasey on those floors, while she forced her way into the con-apts on her own level. Despite disturbing most of her neighbours, she had been unable to locate her missing daughter. Her sons were also absent but Conchita believed they would return soon.

Eventually she conceded defeat and decided to contact the Justice Department. It hurt her pride to ask for assistance from the same people that had helped those freaks move into the building – into her new home, for that matter – but they were best equipped to search for Kasey. Conchita made the call from the vid-phone in her con-apt. She had to ask a neighbour what number to dial, having never contacted the Judges herself. But when she got through to the Justice Department Hotline, it took her several minutes just to navigate the tortuous automated system. Finally, she was speaking to a human operator. A bored female Judge appeared on screen, rubbing the sleep from her eyes.

"Justice Department Hotline. What crime do you wish to report?"

"My daughter is missing!"

"Uh-huh. What's your name?"

"Maguire, Conchita Maguire."

The Judge began entering these details into a computer terminal. "And where do you live?"

"Con-apt 729, Oswald Mosley Block."

"How many people live at that location?"

"What the drokk does that matter?" Conchita exclaimed. "My daughter is missing! I need your help to find her."

"Citizen, we have a procedure we have to follow. If you deviate from that procedure, you will only exacerbate matters."

"Fine, whatever! Four people live here: myself, my daughter Kasey, and my two sons, Dermot and Ramone."

"How old are your sons?"

"What does that matter?" Conchita demanded.

"I am assessing the background circumstances, to ascertain whether a crime has actually been committed."

"My sons are both seventeen. Happy now?"

The Judge looked at Conchita with exasperation. "Citizen, I must ask you to desist with this aggressive, sarcastic tone, otherwise I shall have to report you for making abusive vidphone calls."

"For the love of Grud, my daughter is missing! I don't care if you make me dance naked in front of the Halls of Justice, I just want my daughter back!"

"I must ask you to calm down or I will be forced to terminate this call."

Conchita fought back the urge to smash her fist through the vidphone screen. "I'm sorry, I'm sorry – I'm just worried about Kasey, that's all."

"That's perfectly understandable. How old is your daughter?"

Conchita's mind went blank. "Eight? Or nine? I'm sorry, I'm so stressed I can't remember right now. I think she had a birthday recently."

"Eight or nine, that's fine. I'll cross-check against our records. And how many days has she been missing?"

"Days? You think I'd wait days before reporting my own daughter missing? What kind of mother do you think I am?"

"Citizen, I must warn you again. Persist with that tone and I am required to recommend your arrest. Now, how many days has-"

"It's hours, she's been missing one or two hours."

The Judge sighed. "What about your sons, do you know where they are right now?"

"Not exactly," Conchita admitted. "They went out a few hours back. I'm expecting them home any time."

"But you haven't reported them missing?"

"Of course not! They're juves, they can look after themselves. Kasey is just a little girl."

"A girl who has been missing less than two hours." The Judge had stopped taking notes of what Conchita was saying. "I'm sorry but the Justice Department only investigates missing persons cases where the citizen has been absent for at least twenty-four hours."

"What?"

"Your daughter has been gone for less than two hours. For all you know, she may be with her brothers or her father."

"Her father is dead!"

"Nevertheless, the length of her absence is not sufficiently serious to warrant a response from the Justice Department at this time."

"Not sufficiently serious?" Conchita could not believe what she was hearing. "But she's gone and-"

The Judge was no longer listening to her. "In fact I would be within my rights to file a complaint against you for wasting our time with this call."

"No, you don't understand-"

"Bearing in mind the circumstances, I have decided not to do that."

"You've got to be drokking joking!"

"May I suggest contacting your daughter's friends to see if she has gone to visit them? Also, try getting in touch with any relatives nearby."

"We don't have any relatives in the city!" Conchita protested.

"Be that as it may, we cannot action your call until at least twenty-four hours have elapsed since you last saw your daughter. There are four hundred million citizens in the Big Meg. If we tried to investigate every person that had been missing for a few hours, we would never be doing anything else."

"But she could be dead by morning! Anything could have happened to her. It could be happening to her right now!"

"As I said, please wait–"

"No! I will not wait! If the high and mighty Justice Department is not willing to help one of its citizens, then I will have to help myself!"

"I must warn you against taking the Law into your own hands. The Department will not look kindly upon–"

"Drokk you and drokk your Department!" Conchita screamed, slamming her fist through the vid-phone screen. Sparks flew from the monitor and shards of glasseen embedded themselves in her raw knuckles but Conchita did not notice the blood dripping from her hand. She walked out of her con-apt to the corridor where the Citi-Def representatives from the levels directly above and below were waiting.

Kevin Amidou was from the seventy-third floor. A portly gun nut, he always dressed in camouflage with a black bandanna tied around his sweaty brow. "So what did they say?"

"Call back when she's been missing twenty-four hours," Conchita replied, her rage subsiding into a numb determination.

"But that's ridiculous! She could be anywhere by then."

Conchita nodded grimly. "We can't wait that long." She reached into the pocket of her trousers and pulled out a tiny red card encased in plastic. Conchita snapped the plastic in half, releasing the card from inside. "I'm mobilising the rest of the squad."

"Are you sure that's wise?" the other Citi-Def member asked. Mikell Fields was a cautious man in his fifties, pallid of skin and attitude. He wore old-fashioned metal glasses hooked over his prominent ears. "We're only supposed to be called out in the event of a city-wide emergency. After what happened outside the lobby–"

"I don't care about that!" Conchita hissed. "My daughter is missing and the Judges won't do a drokking thing to help. So we're going to find her ourselves."

She marched to a sign on the corridor wall marked CITI-DEF ALERT STATION. Beneath it was a slot in the wall just big enough to take the card in Conchita's hand. She rammed it inside and a red light began flashing overhead. "As leader of Oswald Mosley Citi-Def, I hereby summon the squad into action. We meet downstairs in ten minutes!"

The Med-Bay in Sector House 87 was at ground level, just below the check-in area where Judges brought perps for processing. Dredd was walking past the front desk on his way to the turbolift when a familiar

voice called out. "Dredd? I didn't know you were working out of here!"
He turned to see a black Judge entering the building, dragging an
unconscious perp. The new arrival's name was clearly visible on his
eagle badge: GIANT. The two Judges had known each other for more
than a decade. Giant often worked undercover for the Wally Squad but
tonight he was clad in a Street Judge's uniform.

"Pulling a graveyard shift," Dredd explained. "Who's your friend?"

Giant had reached the front desk and rested his perp against it. The
unconscious prisoner was a muscular woman clad in strips of PVC with
enough body piercings to set off every metal detector in the sector. Tattoos across the knuckles of her hands spelled the words BADD BLUD.
"Her name's Big Bad Bertha, small-time muscle angling for a place in
Jesus Bludd's crew."

"Not very talkative."

Giant smiled. "She popped a fistful of amp when I tried to arrest her.
Took three of us just to beat her unconscious. The other two are still
being treated at the scene by Med-Division."

"You getting anywhere infiltrating Bludd's crew?" Dredd asked.

"Nope. I've yet to find anyone who's even met Bludd, let alone someone who can tell us anything about him." The Big Meg's criminal
underworld had been going though one of its bloodier phases with different gangs trying to assert their authority. The fall of crime boss Nero
Narcos several years earlier had left a power vacuum and Jesus Bludd
was among those who had emerged with plans to take Narcos's place.
Unlike most of his competitors, Bludd was smart enough to keep a low
profile, letting his crimes do the talking while others preferred to culti-
vate a cult of personality. As a result, getting an undercover operative
close to Bludd was proving unusually difficult for the Judges.

"Stick with it," Dredd said. "Everyone makes mistakes. When Bludd
makes his, you want to be ready."

"Natch. Heard you've been having problems with the Sector Chief
here?"

Dredd grunted. "Word spreads fast."

"No secrets in this job," Giant replied with a smile. "Where you
headed?"

"The sleep machines in Med-Bay. Been a long night and I don't think
it's over yet. See you on the streets." Dredd strode towards the turbolifts, while Giant presented his captive to the Desk Judge.

"Let's make this snappy," Giant suggested. "You don't want my friend
here waking up before we get her inside a cube."

* * *

Kasey and Misch had chosen a room with a large picture window look-ing out over the city. The interior was still unfinished, with discarded materials from the rest of the con-apt piled against a wall. The two girls used these to build a lean-to by the window, their playhouse hidden from the door by the rest of the building supplies. Misch pulled a small globe from her pocket. She carefully placed her right hand's three fin-gers in a triangular shape on the side of the globe. It began to glow, gentle lights coming alive inside.

"That's beautiful," Kasey gasped.

"It's the only toy I saved from our old con-apt," the R'qeen girl explained. "Now watch this!" She whispered a few words in her native tongue and the globe began to float in the air, shooting beams of coloured light around them.

Kasey watched, entranced. "I wish I had a toy like that," she said wistfully.

"You can keep it, if you want."

"I'd like to," Kasey admitted, "but it's your only one. Anyway, my mom would never let me have anything like that." The human girl looked away, ashamed. "She doesn't like aliens."

"I know. She seems so angry."

Kasey shivered, remembering the earlier beating. "Let's talk about something else, okay?"

Misch nodded hurriedly. "Why don't we–"

A hammering at the front door silenced her. "Open up!" an angry voice shouted from outside.

"Who's that?" Kasey wondered.

The banging resumed, with more shouting. The two girls could hear movement and a voice from another room in the con-apt. "That's my broodfather," Misch said, standing up. "You better stay in here. I'll see what's going on." She went to the doorway and peered out into the main room.

Nyon was pulling a robe on as he walked to the front door, the bro-ken arm hampering his movements. After tying the robe together, Nyon opened the door. Three humans clad in Citi-Def uniforms pushed past him, storming into the con-apt. "What are you doing?" Nyon protested in Allspeak. "You have no right to come in here!"

One of the squad members, a wiry man clutching a laser-blade, pushed Nyon back against the door. "Shut your hole, ya alien freak! We got every right! My name's Billy-Bob Jolie and I'm the Citi-Def representative for the ninety-ninth floor of this block. Now you aliens may be too dumb to know any better, but Citi-Def members like us can go pretty much wherever we please. Ain't that right, boys?" The other two nodded their agreement. Satisfied, the leader sneered at the R'qeen patriarch. "Now, where is she? And speak English this time – none of your offworld mumbo-jumbo, blue boy!"

"Where is who?" Nyon asked in halting English, struggling to understand what the intruders were saying.

"Where's the girl? Not one of your vultures either. She's a human girl! Her name's Kasey Maguire and she was seen coming up here!"

"There are no human girls here," Nyon protested. "There is just myself, my pairling Lleccas and our broodling, Misch. Now, leave before I call the Judges!"

Billy-Bob punched Nyon in the midriff, winding the R'qeen. As he slumped to his knees, Lleccas emerged from the bedroom, still pulling on her clothes. "Nyon? What is happening here?"

"Lleccas! Go back inside!" Nyon shouted.

But one of the other humans had already grabbed the R'qeen woman and pushed her back into the bedroom. "Let's see what you've got hidden in here, you blue-skinned slitch!"

"Lleccas! No!" Nyon shouted. He tried moving towards the bedroom but Billy-Bob thrust the laser-knife under his throat.

"One more move and I'll take great pleasure in gutting you, boy!" Billy-Bob jerked his head at the remaining human in the main room. "Aaron, you check out the other rooms in this place."

Misch hurried back to the lean-to where Kasey was shivering with fear. "Three men. They're looking for you!"

The red-haired girl nodded. "Don't let them find me. If my mom knows I've been visiting you, she'll–"

"Shhh, it'll be okay," Misch said, giving Kasey a hug. "I'll send them away."

"How?"

The R'qeen child remembered what her broodmother had said before, about being able to push weaker minds. "I think I know a way."

Dredd was growing visibly frustrated. He had come to the Med-Bay for ten minutes on a sleep machine, but had spent fifteen minutes answering questions from a pedantic droid. It was now examining his medical records, having got his permission to download them from Justice Central. "Good, good," the mechanoid said as it studied the files. "Glad to see you haven't been overusing the sleep machines. Some Judges abuse the system. Just because a short stint is equivalent to a good night's bed rest, doesn't mean you should substitute one for the other. The human mind is a tricky creature, it needs to dream just as much as it needs rest. Take the case of–"

"Are we done with the preliminaries?" Dredd demanded.

"Well, yes, I suppose so," the droid replied petulantly. "But there's no need to snap. These procedures exist for a reason. You're new to this sector house, so I am obliged to go through the–"

"I said, are we done?"

"Yes, we're done. Machine six is waiting for you," the robot said, gesturing down the corridor. "Just place all non-essential items into the holder so they don't interfere with the–"

"I know the drill," Dredd growled, stomping away.

The droid sighed. "No pleasing some people!"

Dredd sat on the edge of the sleep machine, a long silver bench with a matching cover hanging in the air above it. He removed his utility belt, boot knife and Lawgiver, dropping them into a bin beside the machine. Finally, Dredd took off his helmet and rested it atop the other items. He swung his legs up on to the bench and then lay down full length, resting his head against a small pad. "I'm ready," Dredd called to the droid. "Activate the–"

"Control to Dredd!" The metallic voice issued from a speaker above the sleep machine. "Please respond immediately. Control to Dredd, please respond immediately!"

Grumbling beneath his breath, Dredd sat up again and pulled on his helmet. "Dredd to Control, go ahead."

"Reports coming in that the Oswald Mosley Citi-Def has illegally mobilised itself and is harassing some of the residents in that block."

"Acknowledged. Haven't you got any units nearer the scene that can respond? I was about to have a sleep machine session."

"Sector Chief Caine requested you attend personally, says you have a particular interest in this block."

Dredd's shoulders sagged. "Terrif!" He collected his belongings from the bin beside the sleep machine and stood up, wrapping the belt around his waist again. "Am responding now. Should be on the scene within fifteen. Dredd out!"

He marched past the droid on his way back out of the Med-Bay. "Excuse me, Judge, will you be back later to complete your session?" the robot asked. Dredd continued on his way, an angry snarl his only reply.

"I'll take that as a maybe," the droid decided.

Aaron Pressland was not the brightest member of Oswald Mosley Citi-Def by any recognised method of measurement. A mighty bear of a man, his vocabulary was limited, his general intelligence was even less and his ability to think sadly underdeveloped. But Pressland did have two key qualities that made him a valuable member of the squad – he was utterly loyal to the block, especially his neighbours on the ninety-eighth floor, and he was not afraid to kill.

During the dark days of the Apocalypse War back in 2102 he had murdered three Sov-Block soldiers single-handedly while defending the honour of Oswald Mosley. The Chief Judge had pinned a medal on Pressland's chest and pronounced him one of the bravest civilians in the Big Meg. The fact that he was also one of the dumbest was neither here nor there. So Pressland was not afraid when he found an R'qeen girl blocking the entrance to an unfinished bedroom in the penthouse con-apt. "Step aside, freak!" he bellowed at her.

The alien child did not flinch. Instead she smiled, revealing row upon row of teeth hiding inside her mouth. Creepy, Pressland thought, it looks just like... *It looks empty inside this room.* The Citi-Def member shook his head. He thought he could hear a voice inside his mind, talking to him. But it wasn't his own voice, it was somebody else's.

That's right, the voice replied. *I'm your guardian angel.*

"What the drokk?" Pressland said, banging a fist against the side of his head. "What are you talking about?"

You remember during the war? So many times you could have been killed. I was there to save you.

"Who are you?"

I'm your guardian angel. You believe me, don't you? Misch pushed with all her might, trying to convince the slow-witted human.

Pressland shrugged. "I guess so."

Good. Now, let's have a look in here.

Misch stood aside and let the squad member step into the unfinished room. Pressland began to wander about the space, peering into corners and lifting building materials aside for his search. He was getting closer and closer to the lean-to. Misch touched Pressland's hand, startling him.

"Hey, what are you–"

Don't worry, there's nothing to be afraid of.

"I'm not afraid!"

Of course you aren't. You're big and brave. You fought in a war.

"That's right!"

Now, when you look inside that lean-to, all you will see is an alien girl.

"An alien girl?"

That's right. Are you ready?

"I guess so."

Then have a look.

Pressland bent over and peered through a gap at the inside of the lean-to. Kasey pushed herself away from him, terrified at being discovered. Pressland found himself smiling at the girl before standing up again.

Now, what did you see?

"Just an alien girl, like you said."

Exactly. And that's what you'll tell the other men, yes?

"Yes," Pressland replied, turning to leave the room. He stopped at the door. "Will I always have a guardian angel like you?"

If you want.

"Good." The war hero left the room, smiling to himself. Misch listened as he reported back to his leader. "Nobody in there but an alien girl."

"All right," Billy-Bob replied sourly. "Seems these freaks were telling the truth. We better move on. Plenty of other places to search."

As the men were leaving, Misch told Kasey to stay where she was. "I've got to see if my broodfather and broodmother are all right. I'll come back and play with you soon."

The human girl pointed at her friend's face. "You're bleeding."

Misch wiped a trickle of blood from beneath her nostrils. "I'd better not try pushing anybody else for a while."

Lynn Miller regained consciousness when a rat ran across her hands. Her head was pounding fit to burst, like a Heavy Metal Kid was trying to hammer its way out through her forehead. There was a dull pain at the back of her skull, but other than that she felt only the usual aches and muscle strains that came with being a Street Judge in the Big Meg. She was aware of two different movements nearby: the footfalls of a person in heavy boots, and the rat as it scampered across uneven ground. Metal bit into her wrists behind her back, suggesting she had been handcuffed. The vermin began nibbling speculatively at her fingers with sharp incisors. Miller flicked the creature away, catching the ear of whoever was leaning close to her.

"You're a lucky girl," someone said near her face. Stammer's rank breath and deep voice were unmistakable. "I wanted to let you die but Riley insisted on putting a rapi-heal patch on your head wound." Stammers nudged her in the stomach with a boot. "Don't try and pretend you're still unconscious. Sit up."

Miller opened her eyes and shivered. It was a hot, sticky night but a cool breeze was wafting through the dust zone, chilling the sweat on her arms and chest. While she was out cold either Stammers or Riley had stripped away much of her uniform. Gone were the shoulder, elbow and knee pads. Also missing were her boots, gauntlets and utility belt, and she was without her Lawgiver and boot knife. Miller's bodysuit had been unzipped and rolled down to her waist, exposing the white sports bra underneath. She forced herself up into a sitting position, a task made difficult by the handcuffs restraining her.

"That's better. Let me take a good look at you." Stammers was standing in front of her, and the moonlight glinted off his shaved skull. His helmet was resting on the seat of a Lawmaster nearby. Miller's own helmet was a fractured shell on the ground, large cracks visible in its reinforced casing. Riley must have hit her with tremendous force. Stammers noticed where her gaze had wandered. "I know. You've got a skull like rockcrete to have survived that."

"My weapons?" she asked.

"Dissolving at the bottom of a chem pit. I wanted to throw you in too but my bleeding heart partner said he could persuade you not to talk."

Miller glanced around. "Where is Riley?"

"Dealing with your Lawmaster. That's the first thing PSU will look for when the search begins." Stammers sighed. "Well, Lynn... I can call you Lynn, can't I? Seems less formal than Miller."

"Be my guest," she replied sarcastically.

"Well, Lynn, how are we going to kill some time until Riley gets back?"

"Let's play twenty questions. Why did you kill those two juves?"

Stammers shrugged. "You heard them, they were trying to blackmail me. They were useful once but they were starting to overreach themselves."

"That doesn't justify murder."

"Those two were responsible for the deaths of hundreds in that fire. Killing the juves was a summary execution. I call it justice."

"You don't have the right to use that word," Miller spat at him. "I always thought you were a dirty badge, Stammers. I'm just sorry you've dragged Riley down to your level."

"Really? But it was Riley who first suggested torching Robert Hatch with all the aliens still inside."

"You're lying."

"Am I? You know how much my partner hates offworlders – especially the vultures. How far do you think he'd go to get revenge?"

"I don't believe you," Miller maintained.

Stammers chuckled. "Your words say one thing, but your face says another, Lynn, You're just not sure anymore, are you?"

"Drokk yourself sideways with a daystick."

"An interesting invitation, but I'm just as fond of using a blade as a bludgeon." Stammers bent over and extracted his boot knife from its sheath. "How about you and I get to know each other better? I've seen you naked often enough and I've always liked what I've seen."

"You're disgusting," Miller sneered.

Stammers dropped to one knee in front of Miller and flashed the blade through the air, neatly slicing through one of her bra straps. "I'd be careful what you say next, Lynn. You wouldn't want me to slip while I've got this knife in my hand, would you?" He rested the flat surface of the knife against her skin. The touch of cold metal made her jump. "Now, where was I? Oh yes, we are going to become friends. Good friends."

"Not if my life depended upon it," she said.

"We'll see about that," Stammers whispered. He drew the blade sideways and cut through the other bra strap. "I don't want to hurt you, Lynn. Not unless you ask me to."

Miller licked her lips and swallowed. "All right. What did you have in mind?"

"Well, you mentioned something about a daystick. It's surprising the uses I can find for one of those."

Miller arched an eyebrow and leaned closer to him. "Perhaps you'd like to surprise me," she whispered. Stammers grinned wolfishly and moved closer to her, one hand stretching out to touch her–

Miller lunged at Stammers, smashing her forehead into the bridge of his nose. He fell backwards, clutching at his face, blood gushing from his nostrils. His knife fell to one side. "You slitch! You drokking slitch!" Miller scrambled after him, one foot kicking the knife out of reach.

Stammers reached for the Lawgiver in his boot holster, but Miller was already on top of him. Stammers clawed at her with his hands, fingernails tearing into her flesh. "You fight like a girl, Stammers!" Miller shouted. "Let me show you how a real man is supposed to fight!" She lunged at him again with her head, smashing it against his broken nose. Stammers cried out in agony. She head-butted him in the face once more. A sick, wet sound echoed around the dust zone as bone fragments from Stammer's broken nose were forced backwards into his brain. He cried out, twitched once and then he was dead, blood oozing from the mashed pulp that had been his face.

Miller rolled away, struggling to wipe the crimson viscera from her face. She had to get these cuffs off before Riley came back. She twisted round so her back was to Stammers, enabling her hands to get at the pouches on his utility belt. The electronic key for the cuffs should be in–

"Move away from him please, Lynn." Riley stepped out of the shadows, his Lawgiver trained on her.

"Riley, I–"

"Move away!" Riley shouted.

Miller shuffled away, still on her knees. Once Stammers was out of her reach, Riley retrieved the electronic key for the cuffs. "Looking for this?"

She just nodded. "He was going to rape me."

"Maybe. But you'd say anything now to stay alive," Riley replied.

"It's the truth! Use your lie detector if you don't believe me."

Riley just stared at her for a while. "Grud, what a mess!" he sighed, staring at the corpse of his dead partner, the Lawgiver still aimed at Miller. "What are we going to do about this?"

The carnage on Anton Diffring Overzoom had finally been cleared away and traffic was moving smoothly through 87 once more. Dredd returned to Oswald Mosley, having raced across the sector. He strode inside, not noticing the furtive figure of Riff Maltin lurking in the shadows nearby. The street reporter sidled into the building after Dredd, followed by the hovercam.

Inside, the lobby was packed with disgruntled residents shouting at each other. Seeing a Judge arrive, they began directing their ire at him instead.

"One at a time, one at a time!" Dredd commanded, shouting to be heard above the babble of voices. An eldster emerged from the throng, his thinning white hair almost as frazzled as his expression.

"My name is John Pigott, con-apt 333. You've got to do something about those Citi-Def hooligans, Judge! They've been tearing this block apart searching for some missing child while decent citizens are trying to sleep. I thought there were regulations about how and when the Citi-Def could be mobilised!"

"There are," Dredd replied. "What about the rest of you? Can you back up what this eldster says?" Another babble of voices filled the air, confirming they shared similar complaints. "Enough!" Dredd shouted before going back to Pigott. "You! Where were these squad members last seen?"

"Heading for the basement, I think. They were mumbling about breaking open the armoury and issuing weapons. There ought to be a law against it!"

"There is," Dredd snarled before raising his voice again. "All of you – return to your homes immediately. Anyone still in this lobby when I return will spend the next six months in the cubes. Do I make myself clear?"

Maltin stepped into a turbolift headed for the upper floors, keeping the crowd of residents between himself and Dredd. The news editor was right – there were enough stories inside this one block to keep Channel 27 on air for a month, maybe longer. And all of them were going to be Riff Maltin exclusives.

* * *

In the basement, Conchita was pounding on the door of the Oswald
Mosley armoury. Every block had a cache of weapons in an underground bunker, for use by the Citi-Def in the event of a significant threat
to the Big Meg. But to prevent the armoury being raided by perps or
rogue squads, entry could only be gained with the proper access codes.
These were held at the local sector house and were only released with
the authorisation of the Chief Judge. The entrance to the armoury was
made up of six inches of reinforced steel and rockcrete, proof against
almost any force. The thinking behind this was simplicity itself – if you
had enough firepower to break into the armoury, you wouldn't need to
break in.

Two-dozen squad members were waiting their turn to attack the
door, while those who had already tried and failed were resting
against the walls of the basement. "Drokk you, open up!" Conchita
screamed at the doorway, her bloody fists flailing against its imper-
vious surface.

"You're wasting your time," a low, gravely voice boomed. Conchita
and the others looked at the staircase. Judge Dredd was walking down
the steps, his Lawgiver drawn and ready to fire. "You'll never be able to
open the Armoury."

"We need those weapons!" Billy-Bob Jolie shouted at the lawman.

"Why?"

"My daughter has been abducted," Conchita replied, "and your precious Justice Department won't lift a finger to help. So we're helping
ourselves."

"Do you have any evidence your daughter has been abducted?"

"I don't need evidence!" Conchita fumed. "She's gone and somebody
took her. That's all I need to know!"

Dredd moved through the squad members towards the leader. "I
checked the files on your family while travelling here. Several times
anonymous callers have accused you of beating your daughter. Perhaps
she ran away to escape the violence. Or perhaps you finally went too far
and beat her to death. So you panicked, disposed of the body and are
now staging all of this as an alibi."

"How dare you!" she raged. "You have no evidence for those allegations!"

Dredd almost smiled. "But you just said you don't need evidence to
know that your daughter has been abducted. Why should I need evidence to accuse you of beating or even killing her?"

"I'll kill you myself!" Conchita hissed, lunging at the Judge. Billy-Bob
and the other squad members held her back.

"Don't do it, Maguire. He's just trying to bait you!" Billy-Bob hissed.

"Threatening a Judge is a serious offence," Dredd noted. "I could arrest this citizen here and now."

"Do that and you'll have a riot on your hands," Conchita said. "You may be a Judge but you're just one man, surrounded by dozens of my squad members. The odds are too great, even for the great Judge Dredd!"

"Perhaps," he conceded. "But I'm the only one with a gun and that's the way it is going to stay. I want all of you to return to your con-apts and stay there until morning. Once the sun is up, I will personally lead a search for the missing child. But until then I don't want to hear another report of trouble from this block. If I do, I'll be back here to arrest each and every one of you. Consider this an informal curfew. Break it and I'll break you."

Dredd glared at the squad members, his face utterly implacable. No one spoke, no one challenged his authority.

"That's better," he said finally. "Now go back to your homes and your families. And remember what I said!"

The residents began filing out of the basement. Conchita stayed until all the others had gone. "This isn't over," she warned. "Not by a long way."

"Save it for your followers," Dredd snarled. "I'm not impressed."

Conchita walked out of the basement, followed by Dredd. As he returned to his Lawmaster a message came through from Control.

"Dredd, when did you last see Judge Lynn Miller?"

"In person? Outside Maurice Waldron Block, about two hours ago. Why?"

"She went off-radio more than an hour past and hasn't reported back in."

Dredd scowled. "Better list her as missing and alert all Judges in Sector 87 to be–" He stopped in mid-sentence.

"Control to Dredd, you still there?"

"Yeah. Just remembering something someone said to me. Forget what I was suggesting. Sector Chief Caine runs 87. Notify her that Miller has gone missing and let her decide what to do about it. I'm just a Street Judge here."

"That's a roj. Control out!"

Dredd activated his on-board computer. "Show me the quickest route from my present location to Sector 87's dust zone."

03:00

"You'll have to kill me," Miller said. "If you think logically about this, you'll know you have to kill me." She was sitting on one side of Stammers's corpse, her hands still cuffed behind her back. Opposite her Riley was perched on a rockcrete slab, his Lawgiver clasped in one hand. Overhead the moon was beginning to descend across the night sky; the light reflected from its surface threw strange shadows across the dust zone.

"Don't say that," Riley replied.

"It's the only logical course of action. I know Stammers supplied the incendiary device that torched Robert Hatch. You're his partner, you must have known about it. Stomm, he said it was your idea!"

"It wasn't."

"I know that," Miller said. "You might have looked the other way, but you never enjoyed killing like Stammers, never got the same thrill from it he did."

"I always told Eustace he'd go too far one day."

"And you were right. But you should have turned him in, told the SJS what he was doing while you had the chance – while your hands were still clean."

Riley slipped off his gauntlets and held up his hands. "These? They stopped being clean a long time ago, Lynn."

"Why? At the Academy you were Roll of Honor material–"

"That was before Danny died. Everything changed after that."

"I know," Miller said. "I was there, remember?"

Riley smiled. "You were my best friend for all those years while we were cadets. I loved you like the sister I never had. But then..."

"Then you heard about Danny." Miller could not help thinking back to that day. She and Riley had been out in the Cursed Earth, fifteen year-old cadets on their first Hot dog Run. A message pod reached them from the Big Meg about the death of Danny Riley during a battle on the R'qeen homeworld. Miller had watched her friend scream and sob, wanting to ease his suffering in any way possible. That night they were posted together on sentry duty. That was when it had happened; the incident that almost cost both of them their badges.

"You should never have kissed me," Riley said, staring at his partner's corpse. "I wouldn't have dared to kiss you."

"You were hurting. I wanted to make you feel better."

"You did – until Judge Hallvar found us."

Miller smiled. "The most embarrassing moment of my life..."

"I didn't mind getting sent back to the city in shame, or losing my place on the honours board or the black mark on my permanent record," Riley said. "What I couldn't stand was the way you were with me afterwards: distant, aloof, as if you didn't want to admit it had ever happened."

"That was how I felt."

"But you never asked how I felt, did you? You showed me a brief glimpse of what my life could be like – to be wanted, to be loved – and then you tore it away. You showed me I could break the rules, Lynn... and then nothing!"

"I'm sorry..." she stammered. "I never knew."

"No. And you never gave me the chance to tell you!"

"Grud, what a mess," Miller said to herself.

Riley stood up, still clutching his Lawgiver. "So I tried to forget it ever happened – but I couldn't. When I got transferred to Sector 87 I put in a request to become your partner but you refused. Do you have any idea how that made me feel? I had lost someone I loved, lost my best friend – and now you were rejecting me again. So Caine partnered me with Stammers, and look where that's led us! Congratulations, Lynn. You just wanted to make me feel better. How's that plan working out now?"

"I didn't know," she protested. "I couldn't have known..."

"Didn't know or just didn't want to know?" Riley raged. "Grud forbid anything should get in the way of your glorious career! I bet you've had to work twice as hard as everyone else to overcome that blemish on your record. So sorry that I've inconvenienced the rise and rise of Judge Lynn Miller!"

"Is that how you see me? Too ambitious to care about anybody but myself? Too driven to give a stomm what happens to you?" Miller struggled to her feet to confront Riley. "You've no idea, have you? How many times I've covered for you and your precious partner! How many times I've cleaned up the messes you two left behind! Just a few hours ago I was telling myself I could never believe you'd had any involvement in that fire. I came here, hoping against hope to find it was just Stammers, that you had nothing to do with it!"

"They killed my brother!" Riley bellowed. "The R'qeen gunned him down and then they took his body away and hung it on a hook for days and days and days. Finally, when the rotting flesh was hanging off his bones, they cut off one of his arms and they were eating it when the rescue squad found them. I saw the report from the Med-Judges identifying Danny's body – or what was left of him!"

Miller shook her head. "You could never have seen a report like that! Such findings are confidential, never revealed to any family members. Who showed that to you? Stammers?"

Riley ignored her question, too involved with his memories to hear it. "Afterwards, all I wanted to do was watch those monsters burn. They butchered my brother. I wanted them to suffer just a fraction of what he suffered!"

"So you arranged for hundreds of innocents to be burned alive? Is that justice? Is that what your brother would have wanted?"

Riley aimed the Lawgiver at Miller's head. "Don't you dare try to tell me what Danny would have wanted! You didn't know him, you never met him. You haven't got the right to talk about him! Just shut your drokking mouth before I do it for you, slitch!"

"That's Stammers talking, not you."

"You think so?" Riley moved his finger to the trigger. "Let's see."

Riff had been working his way up Oswald Mosley Block, trying to coax information from the residents about the latest incidents. Few would talk and those that did gave accounts so heavily laced with expletives that any attempt to broadcast them would be pointless once the Justice Department auto-censor had done its job. But the reporter was able to glean enough facts to know what questions to ask when he reached con-apt 721.

It took several minutes of insistent knocking and bell ringing before Riff heard movement from inside. Another two minutes had elapsed when the front door opened to reveal the scowling face of Kurt Sivell. "What the drokk do you want? Do you know what time it is?"

"Sorry to disturb you, sir," Riff began, "but I'm interviewing residents about the missing child. What do you think has happened to her?"

"To who? What missing child?"

"I understand her name is Kasey Maguire. She's from this floor, actually. Did you know her at all?"

"Did I know her?" Sivell was mystified by the questions. "Why are you using the past tense? Is she dead?"

Riff admitted he didn't know, but that was one theory he had heard. "You seem unaware of Kasey's tragic disappearance. I've been told the

Citi-Def squad had searched almost every con-apt in this building look-ing for her."

"When was this?"

"Just in the past few hours!"

Sivell ran a hand through his greasy, thinning hair. "The past few hours?" The resident shrugged. "Well, nobody searched my con-apt. But I've been out cold since I took those Double-Doze. I'm amazed you managed to wake me."

"Really? Well, that's fascinating." Riff was ready to move on, having had enough of this slow-witted, half-asleep simp. He almost missed out on the scoop of his fledgeling career – almost. But Sivell grabbed the reporter's shoulder, a look of revelation on his face.

"Did you say Kasey Maguire was missing?"

"Yes."

"But I saw her, just before I took the sleeping pills. She accidentally brushed against my doorbell and woke me up."

Now Riff was paying attention again. He activated the hovercam from its rest mode to record what Sivell was saying. "When was this? Can you remember when you saw Kasey Maguire, the missing girl?"

"Yes, it was just before two this morning. I recall the time because I looked at the clock when I was woken up. I was going to give whoever rang the doorbell a piece of my mind!"

"But it was Kasey who rang the bell–"

"By mistake, yes. She must have leant against it on her way to the tur-bolift."

"You saw her get into a turbolift?" Riff was excited now, he could sense something important was about to happen.

"Yes, yes. But before that I asked Kasey where she was headed at that time of the morning. She said she was going to stay with a friend on a lower floor," Sivell explained. "Then I saw Kasey get into the turbolift and the doors closed behind her. That was the last I saw of her."

"Are you sure about this, citizen? The girl's mother has made no men-tion of such an arrangement."

"Yes, quite sure. The reason it stuck in my mind was I looked back to see what floor Kasey was going to – just being nosy I suppose. The tur-bolift went up, not down."

Riff felt the hairs on the back of his neck rising. "Do you know what floor the turbolift went to?"

"Yes, of course. It was the top, the one hundredth floor – where the aliens are." Sivell frowned, unaware his next set of words would set in motion a tragic series of events. "You say Kasey is missing? I hope those vultures on the top floor haven't got her – they eat human flesh you know!"

Riff thanked the citizen for his time and apologised again for disturbing him. Once Sivell had gone back to bed, Riff contacted his news
editor. "Tell me you got all of that!"

"You better drokkin' believe it!" Yablonsky screamed into Riff's earpiece. "Give an intro to the hovercam and we'll cut it together here. You
have five minutes before it gets broadcast. Get up to the top floor now
and confront the aliens with what you know. We'll cut to you live when
you're ready!"

Riff smiled. Fame and fortune, here I come.

Dredd rode into the dust zone, scanning his surroundings for any sign
of Miller. A call to PSU had provided her point of entry but surveillance
beyond the perimeter was almost non-existent. That made the dust zone
a perfect rendezvous point for anyone wanting to meet in secret. Dredd
slowed his motorcycle to a crawl and activated the bike's on-board computer while calling Brady at Sector House 87. "Miller's gone missing and
I have reason to believe she's in the dust zone," Dredd said. "Is there
any other way of tracking her besides PSU's spy-in-the-sky cameras?"

"You could try her transponder," the Tek-Judge suggested. "Justice
Department vehicles have a transponder built into them. They transmit
a constant homing signal, unless they are destroyed or tampered with."

"I thought only H-wagons and flying vehicles had a transponder?"

"That was recently extended to Lawmasters and other ground-based
transportation," Brady explained. "We've been fitting them over the past
month. I put one into your bike when you arrived at the sector house."

"And Miller's Lawmaster also has one?"

"Yes. I've been recalling its data, in case anyone asked. Normally the
PSU cameras are enough to track anyone within the city, but…"

"Can you upload that data to my bike's computer?" Dredd asked.

"That'll take a few seconds, but I don't know how much help it will
be," Brady said. "Miller's transponder stopped an hour ago."

"Meaning?"

"Either her Lawmaster has been destroyed or the transponder was
sabotaged. Okay, your on-board computer should show Miller's last
recorded location and the route her Lawmaster took to get there."

A map of the dust zone appeared on Dredd's computer screen with a
red line leading into the area. The line stopped not far from Dredd's
position. "Thanks for that, Brady."

"Don't mention it. I just hope you find her alive."

"One last thing. Who else knows about these transponders?"

"Everyone in Tek-Division, some Street Judges, Sector Chiefs, plenty
of people at Justice Central. An announcement about them is due any

day. Oh, and the external company that supplied them – Summerbee Industries."

"Second time I've heard that name tonight. Dredd out." He switched off his motorcycle and dismounted. If Miller's ride had been sabotaged or destroyed nearby, those responsible might still be in the area. Advancing on foot could provide an element of surprise. Dredd crept forwards on foot.

Getting anyone on the top floor of Oswald Mosley to open their door proved even more difficult for Riff than further down the building. His report suggesting aliens were responsible for Kasey's disappearance was due for broadcast any minute. It was doubtful the new arrival on the hundredth floor would be watching Channel 27, but some human residents below might be. When that quote from Sivell went out, the trouble inside Oswald Mosley could only escalate. This was Riff's last chance to get the aliens' side of the story.

He had hammered on the doors of all the top floor con-apts without success. Either those inside did not hear him or they were refusing to answer. Eventually a fearsome R'qeen appeared. One of his arms was broken and his head badly bruised. The reporter recognised him as the offworlder who had fought the two Judges outside Robert Hatch. Could abducting the girl be some kind of revenge for that incident? Riff kept his speculations to himself and smiled broadly.

"My apologies for disturbing you at this time of the night."

"What are you doing here?" Nyon demanded in Allspeak.

The reporter hoped Channel 27 had access to auto-translators and asked his next question in halting Allspeak. "I understand there has been some commotion in Oswald Mosley Block tonight. Residents have complained about their con-apts being subjected to an unauthorised search by the building's Citi-Def squad."

"Are those the thugs who stormed in here and assaulted my pairling?"

"Yes, I believe so. I'm investigating this for Channel 27. Would you be willing to talk about what happened?"

Nyon smiled. "Yes! The truth about this must be told!"

"Perhaps I could come in?" Riff asked, smiling ingenuously.

The R'qeen stood aside, letting Maltin and the hovercam enter. Once they were inside Nyon began ranting and raving about the methods used by the Citi-Def. "One of them threatened our broodling Misch. We have only been in this building a few hours and already we are accused of a crime!"

"What crime was this?"

"The humans claimed we had taken one of their young. They searched this and all the other con-apts, but could not find her because she is not here. They probably thought we planned to kill her and then eat her!"

Riff nodded. "There is a lot of misunderstanding about R'qeen ways."

"We have endured enough. No more humans should be allowed to set foot on this floor. Those that try will learn exactly what R'qeen do to their enemies!"

Lleccas emerged from one of the side rooms. "Nyon!" she said in R'qeen. "What have you been saying to this human?"

To Riff her alien speech sounded harsh and frightening. Perhaps now was a good time to make his way back to safer territory. He had no urge to end his days as a rotting corpse in an R'qeen charnel pit. The reporter began backing towards the front door. "Thanks for your time and hospitality," he said in Allspeak. "Perhaps we shall meet again soon."

Nyon marched towards him and threw open the door. "Go now and tell the others. None may come here anymore. We have suffered enough at the hands of the humans. We will defend ourselves – by any means necessary!"

Riff ran for the turbolift, the hovercam hurrying after him.

Misch closed the door, having witnessed the encounter between her broodfather and the human. Bringing Kasey here had seemed like a good idea. But now events were beginning to spiral out of control. Misch did not know what to do next. If she sent her new friend back home, Kasey would probably suffer another beating. But if the human girl stayed here, Misch felt certain some greater tragedy lay ahead of them all.

The R'qeen child returned back to the hiding place beneath the lean-to. Kasey was fast asleep, her face happy and contented in contrast to the dark bruises on its surface.

I can't send her back, Misch decided. She's my friend. I have to protect her.

"For Grud's sake, Riley, put the Lawgiver down," Miller pleaded. "We both know you're not going to shoot me."

"Do we?" Riley asked.

"Maybe it's not too late for you. I could testify on your behalf, say Stammers had some hold over you. He was threatening to tell everyone about us, what we did on that hotdog run."

"One lie to solve another?"

"What are your alternatives?" she asked.

"Kill you and push your body in the same chem pit as your Lawmaster. Say Stammers attacked me when I discovered he was behind the fire at Robert Hatch and I killed him defending myself. I'll probably get a commendation."

"I wouldn't hold your breath," a voice growled from the shadows. Riley spun round to see Dredd walking towards him, with his Lawgiver ready to fire. "You might be able to get off a shot before I do. I'm getting old and some people think I'm slowing down. Maybe they're right and maybe they're wrong. But you better kill me with the first shot to be sure – you won't get a second chance."

Riley's glance flickered sideways to Miller. "How long have you known he was watching us?"

"Long enough," she said.

"So the offer to lie for me. That was another betrayal?"

"I had to keep you talking long enough for Dredd to get into a better position."

"Grud but you're a bitch, Miller!"

"No, I'm a Mega-City One Judge doing my job," she snarled, leaping at Riley. He tried to bring his Lawgiver round to fire but she was too fast. She knocked him to the ground and sent his helmet flying off. Dredd moved towards them, trying to get an angle for a clean shot, but the pair kept rolling over and over, the gun trapped between them. Then a single shot echoed around the dust zone.

"Miller! Are you all right?" Dredd shouted.

She rolled away from Riley, her chest covered in blood. "No, no..." she sobbed. But it was Riley who lay dying, a gaping wound underlining his fate.

Dredd crouched beside the body, straining to hear any last words. "Have you a final confession to make?"

Riley nodded, blood welling in his mouth then running down either side of his face. He coughed a red mist before speaking. "They-they used us... Used me... Showed me a file–"

"Who used you?" Dredd hissed.

"Summ-Summerbee..." Riley whispered. Then his eyes rolled back into his skull and he was gone. Dredd leaned forward and brushed one hand over the dead man's eyes, closing them.

"Rest in peace," he murmured.

Miller was still sobbing on the ground between the corpses of Stammers and Riley. Dredd waited until the worst of it had passed before speaking again. "Looks like you've been in the wars."

"Is that a joke?" she asked.

"Simply stating a fact. You should know by now, I don't make jokes."

"Jovus, do I look that bad?" Miller staggered to the nearest chem pit to look at her reflection. "Yes, I do. How'd you find us?"

"A tip from Brady got me to the remains of your Lawmaster. Riley's ranting and raving was loud enough to bring me here." Dredd pulled an electronic key from his utility belt and undid the handcuffs behind her back. Miller winced as she tried to rub some life back into her arms, the wrists red and raw from where the metal had cut into her flesh. Dredd helped pull her bodysuit back up into place.

"Stammers wanted to get up close and personal," she said. "I persuaded him it was a bad idea, Mean Machine style."

"That explains your black eyes."

"What did Riley say before he died?"

"That he'd been used. Someone showed him a file."

"Who?"

"Summerbee." Dredd studied the dead Judges. "Miller, do you know anything about this file he mentioned?"

She zipped up the front of her bodysuit. "Riley saw a sealed report on how his brother was killed and eaten by the R'qeen during the Colony Wars. That's why Riley was willing to see Robert Hatch burn. But how would Summerbee Industries have access to that file?"

"A good question," Dredd replied. "I think it's high time I paid a visit to Werner Summerbee, to find out if he has the answer."

"You want me to come along as backup?"

"I can handle anybody called Werner," Dredd said. "Besides, you need to have Med-Division check your injuries and get a fresh uniform. What's left of that one doesn't exactly meet regulations." He activated his helmet radio. "Dredd to Control: I've found Miller. Judges Stammers and Riley are dead – they were holding Miller prisoner in the Sector 87 dust zone and planned to execute her. Have you got a trace on my signal?"

"That's a roj," Control replied.

"Good. Send a meat wagon for the stiffs and an H-wagon to take Miller back to the sector house."

"SJS will want to interview both of you."

"Stammers and Riley will still be dead at the end of my shift. Tell the SJS they can interview me then. Dredd out!" He switched frequency on his helmet radio. "Bike to me!" Within seconds his riderless motorcycle had rolled into the clearing, responding to his summons. Dredd removed emergency flares and a first aid kit from the motorcycle and threw them to Miller before riding off, calling, "See you on the streets!"

* * *

Conchita felt as if she were losing her mind. Frustration, anger and worry all fought for control of her feelings. Not only was Kasey still missing, but Dermot and Ramone had not returned from their rendezvous with Stammers. The Judge had been the investigating officer when Conchita's husband died. Stammers wanted to have the off-worlder cubed for murder but was overruled by his superior officer, Judge Temple. Afterwards Stammers approached Conchita, expressing his dismay at how the case had gone. They had become lovers for a brief time but she broke off the relationship, not wanting to get Stammers into trouble with his superiors.

A week ago he had returned to her con-apt with a question – how would she like to get back at the alien who killed her husband? Conchita had been sceptical, fearing it was a Justice Department trap. But Stammers used his own lie detector to prove the offer was genuine. The R'qeen alien now lived in Robert Hatch Block. Stammers would supply an incendiary device to torch the building, something that couldn't easily be traced. He even suggested she organise the public meeting protesting about aliens in the sector as a way of creating an alibi for herself and other likely suspects. Conchita got Ramone and Dermot to plant the device while she was at the meeting.

The plan had worked perfectly – until Stammers and his partner arrived outside Oswald Mosley with a hoverbus full of aliens. To maintain the pretence of not knowing Stammers, Conchita had been obliged to start the brawl, leading her fellow Citi-Def squad members against the one person who had helped avenge her husband's death. All her children were now missing and aliens were living in the home her family was meant to be shifting into any day. Where had it all gone wrong?

Sick of pacing up and down inside her cramped con-apt, Conchita turned on the tri-D. At this time of the morning there would be nothing worth watching, but the programmes might bore her to sleep. She set the tri-D to scroll through the thousands of channels broadcast across the Big Meg. Hearing her daughter's name, Conchita stopped at Channel 27 and watched a report by Riff Maltin. The journalist was looking into the camera sternly, his face contorted in a parody of concern.

"Tonight, a mother fears for her missing daughter. In a city of four hundred million people, what is one life more or less? To the Maguire family of Oswald Mosley Block here in Sector 87, it means the world. Little Kasey Maguire has been missing for hours and the Justice Department refuses to help. When the building's Citi-Def squad instituted a search for the missing girl, they were told to stand down.

"But while the authorities stand idly by and leave a little girl to Grud knows what fate, I – Riff Maltin, roving reporter for Channel 27 – have found a vital clue to the whereabouts of this lost angel. Less than an hour ago I interviewed Kurt Sivell, a neighbour of the Maguire family on the seventy-second floor of Oswald Mosley. It seems he was the last person to see little Kasey alive, witnessing her getting into a turbolift. I asked him where that turbolift was going. Here, in a Channel 27 exclusive, is what he told me..."

The tri-D screen hissed static for a moment before cutting to footage of the citizen frowning in the doorway of his con-apt. "It was the top, the one hundredth floor, where the aliens are. I hope those vultures on the top floor haven't got her. They eat human flesh you know!"

The image cut back to Riff. "Just before Kasey went missing, the Judges moved six families of aliens into Oswald Mosley. Among those are several from R'qeen, an offworld species of carrion eaters, also known as vultures. The R'qeen kill their food, then let it rot before consuming it. After hearing what citizen Kurt Sivell had to say, I confronted the aliens, speaking to an R'qeen male. Here is what he had to say. Viewers not fluent in Allspeak or who do not wish to read subtitles should engage their auto-translators."

After another burst of static, Nyon appeared on screen, his face a terrifying visage. "The humans claimed we had taken one of their young. They searched but could not find her because she is not here. They probably thought we planned to kill her and then eat her!"

Riff reappeared, his face even more serious than before. "Chilling words there. This alien denies having any knowledge of little Kasey Maguire's location but is he telling the truth? I asked him what would happen if anyone tried to look for her on the top floor again..."

Nyon was back on screen, his features savage and severe. "We have had enough. Not one more human shall be allowed to set foot on this floor. Those that try will learn exactly what R'qeen do to their enemies!"

Channel 27 cut back to Riff for the last time. "After that I was forced to leave the top level of Oswald Mosley, the alien's threats still ringing in my ears. All of this leaves three vital questions to be answered: why have the Judges been so lax in investigating this case, a case that will horrify and frighten parents everywhere? Secondly, why are the aliens so unwilling to let anyone search their quarters on the top floor of Oswald Mosley – what do they have to hide? Thirdly, and most importantly, what has happened to little Kasey Maguire? Is she now in the possession of flesh-eating monsters from another world and who will save her? More on this story as we get it. This is Riff Maltin, handing you back to the studio!"

Conchita sank back into her seat, stunned at what she had just witnessed. Had her daughter fallen into the clutches of those monsters?

Then the doorbell rang.

Choking back tears of rage, Conchita ran to the door and pulled it open. "Kasey? Is that you?"

Standing outside was Riff, his hovercam filming them both from just behind the reporter's right shoulder. "Conchita Maguire? My name is Riff Maltin from Channel 27. I was wondering if you could spare me a few words."

04:00

Caine was waiting on the landing pad when the H-wagon arrived at Sector House 87. She helped Miller climb out of the vehicle before it flew back into the night sky. "How are you?" the Sector Chief asked, shouting to be heard over the H-wagon's engines as it ascended.

"I've been better," Miller replied. "You heard what happened?"

Caine nodded as they entered the sector house. "I've always had my suspicions about Stammers, but Riley as well? This incident is not going to be good for 87's reputation. Where's Dredd?"

"Gone to interview a suspect, Werner Summerbee."

The Sector Chief reacted with surprise. "Of Summerbee Industries?"

"Before he died Riley suggested Summerbee had some peripheral involvement with the fire at Robert Hatch. Dredd's gone to follow that lead." Miller staggered, exhaustion from the night's events catching up with her. Caine grabbed the Street Judge's arm to stop her collapsing.

"You'd better get to Med-Bay, have them check you over. I've already lost two Judges tonight," Caine said. "I don't want you joining them." Miller started towards the turbolift. Her Sector Chief had a final remark for her: "The SJS will be here soon. They'll want to interview you and Dredd about what's happened."

Dredd stopped his Lawmaster outside the entrance to Ridley Estate. This ultra-secure enclosed community was home to the richest of the rich in the Big Meg. The waiting list to buy a home here was decades-long, with prospective purchasers required to pay a deposit of several million credits just to be considered for inclusion. Outside the estate, a city of four hundred millions citizens struggled to survive, crowded into towering citi-blocks and eking out a meagre existence on welfare handouts. For the precious few who could afford it, living on the Ridley Estate was like having your own private utopia, far from the madding crowd. The residents were almost untouchable – almost.

The Judge approached the perimeter, where five fearsome security droids blocked the entrance. "State your business," the lead robot grated.

"Judge Dredd, here to see Werner Summerbee."

"Do you have an appointment?"

"At four in the morning? Of course not!"

"Unless you have an appointment, I must ask you to leave – now." The droids began charging their weapons systems.

"Unless you let me in I'll have to disarm you. Permanently."

The droid was not giving in that easily. "You have ten seconds to comply with our request or there will be... trouble."

Dredd sighed wearily. "Have it your own way. Dredd to Control!"

"Beginning countdown to pre-emptive action," the robot said. "Ten."

"Control to Dredd, go ahead."

"Nine."

"Am outside Ridley Estate. Some tin-pot guard droid refuses to let me in."

"Eight."

"Is that it counting down in the background?"

"Seven."

"That's a roj. Request security override for Ridley Estate."

"Six."

"Could take a few seconds, Dredd."

"Five."

"The sooner the better, Control."

"Four."

"Just coming..."

"Three." The droids began moving into attack positions around Dredd.

"Running out of time, Control!"

"Two." The robots obtained target lock on the lone motorcyclist.

"Here it comes..."

"One." The lead droid raised its weapon to fire. "Please accept our sincere apologies for your imminent death. All units, open fi... " At that the robot fell silent, its silver limbs frozen in place. The other mechanoids were also still, the hum of their systems slowly dying away.

Dredd relaxed, letting his breath out again. "Thanks, Control. Try not to cut it so fine in future."

"Roj that. Opening gates for you – now."

The entrance to Ridley Estate swung open and the Judge rode his Lawmaster in, swerving between the statuesque security robots. Once past the perimeter it was easy to see why this was the Big Meg's most exclusive address. A long driveway curled through acres of real grass and trees, not the usual synthetic plants. Ahead, a series of palatial bungalows sprawled across the grounds, each with its own private hoverpad. In a city where each cubic millimetre of room came at a premium, devoting so much to gardens and open spaces was evidence of vast, almost incalculable wealth.

Dredd rode on towards the luxurious lodgings, intent on locating number fifteen. No doubt the security droid had sent an alarm to Summerbee before the override took hold, warning about the arrival of a Judge. It would be interesting to see how the wealthy industrialist reacted.

Riff had to hand it to his interview subject, she could take up crying for the Mega-Olympic team. Conchita had been sobbing her heart out ever since the hovercam entered her con-apt. Yes, she had seen the report on Channel 27, just a few minutes before. No, she had not given her daughter permission to go out or to visit any friends. Conchita had forbidden Kasey from having any contact with the aliens, especially after the incident earlier.

"What incident was this?" Riff asked, looking back over his shoulder to smile at the hovercam. A winking red light on the side of the silver globe told him the interview was being broadcast direct to air. After this Channel 27 could not help but give him a permanent job.

"I staged a peaceful protest, here on the seventy-second floor, when the Judges were escorting the aliens up to the top of the building. While I was distracted one of those creatures lured my daughter away and was... doing things... to her."

Riff did his best to be soothing. "I know this is difficult and painful. But could you tell us what... things... this alien was doing to your little girl?"

Conchita's face contorted with disgust. "It was... touching her."

"And what did you do when you discovered this?"

"I dragged my daughter away. I thought I'd saved her. But now..."

Riff stroked his chin thoughtfully. "Which of the alien species was it that you saw with your daughter?"

"R'qeen," Conchita snarled. "One of those filthy vultures!" She collapsed into hysterics again, tears flooding down her face. "It was a vulture that killed my husband, that murdered Kasey's father!"

"This is shocking, Ms Maguire, absolutely shocking!" It's also great tri-D, Riff thought, but kept that to himself. The woman looked at him, a new horror of realisation creeping across her face.

"You don't think when the freak... touched Kasey earlier, that it put some sort of influence on her? I've heard some of these R'qeen have mental powers, like Psi-Judges, only much stronger."

"It's possible, I suppose," Riff agreed. "That might explain how the R'qeen were able to lure your daughter to the top floor – if that is what has happened to her. Right now, the details remain uncertain."

"They've got her, haven't they?" Conchita cried out. "Those offworld freaks have taken my daughter, put her under their spell. Kasey may already be dead and rotting in one of their charnel pits, just waiting to be eaten..." She was falling apart now, her words panted out between sobs. "Kasey, my poor, sweet, innocent Kasey. What are they doing to you? Those drokkers, those devious, murderous, alien drokkers."

Riff decided Conchita could take no more of this. He turned round to the camera and delivered a few closing remarks. "There you have it – the terrible torment of a mother who knows not where her child is. Has Kasey been abducted by carrion-eating creatures now living in the luxurious new con-apts atop this terrified block? Is this beloved child already dead and being subjected to some unknown horrors? Why have the Judges refused to step in and relieve the suffering of this poor woman? Only one thing is certain – the battle lines are being drawn between human and alien, and it seems nothing can stop this situation from descending into bloody and brutal conflict. This is Riff Maltin for Channel 27, handing you back to the studio with this final thought: do you know where your children are right now? Goodnight."

The red light on the hovercam blinked off, the transmission at an end.

"Is that it?" Conchita said between sobs.

"Yes, it's over now. Thank you so much, you were so brave," Riff said.

"Save the stomm for your viewers," she replied, wiping the tears from her face. All trace of hysteria was gone, hatred and grim determination the only emotions remaining. "I've got a fighting force to mobilise."

"But you were... you were..." Riff stammered.

"Falling apart before your eyes? Weeping my little heart out?"

"Well, yes–"

Conchita held open her hands to reveal two halves of a synthi-onion inside. "Rub these into your eyes and you'll weep your heart out too."

"Sweet Jovus! Then all of that was just an act," Riff realised.

"I want those scum out of Oswald Mosley, one way or another. Once everyone else sees that performance, they'll be ready to burn or butcher each and every one of those freaks on the top floor. And I'll be there to lead the mob!"

* * *

Deputy Sector Chief Temple was sorting reports on screen when Caine strolled into his office. "Ahh, Patrick. Glad to find you still here," she said.

"The sector never sleeps," Temple replied.

"Yes, I often feel the same." Caine leaned on the edge of her deputy's desk. "Look, I know we've had our differences in the past. You were probably expecting to be promoted to my position before I arrived and that didn't help matters. But if there's anything that's troubling you, I'm always available. You know that, don't you?"

"Yes, ma'am. Of course, ma'am."

"Good, good. Well, that was all I wanted to say. You've seemed a bit preoccupied lately, so I just thought…"

Temple smiled at her. "Everything's fine. There have been a lot of rumours flying around about the future of this sector house and its senior staff, but I've always had total confidence in you, ma'am. If there's ever anything I can do for you, just ask."

"Excellent! Well, I must be getting on," Caine said cheerfully, making her way out of the office.

She paused at the doorway. "I've just remembered, there was something else. Psi-Division precogs foresee more difficulties at Oswald Mosley. That place is like a magnet for trouble tonight. Perhaps you could take a few helmets down there and sort things out, once and for all?"

"Of course, ma'am. That shouldn't be a problem," Temple replied.

"Good, good. Well, carry on!"

With that she was gone, leaving her deputy trembling with fear at his desk. It was years since he'd seen active duty. He was now being volunteered to quell a potential riot! Temple held back the vomit just long enough to reach the nearest bathroom cubicle.

Miller emerged from the Med-Bay to find three SJS Judges waiting for her. She recognised their leader, a fearsome black woman called Jefferson. "Let me guess – the Special Judicial Squad wants to congratulate me on killing two dirty helmets and sparing your blushes for not having caught them in the act?"

"We need to see you," Jefferson replied, her face utterly emotionless. "Interrogation Room Eight, now!"

"Why do we need to go to an interrogation room? Are you three shy?" Miller's joke got no response from the trio. She looked down at the remains of her uniform. "Could I at least get changed first?"

"Interrogation Room Eight. Now."

"What can I say? You're really sweeping me off my feet. Tell you what, let's all go to Interrogation Room Eight and you can impress me further with this witty banter of yours." Miller began strolling towards the tur-bolift, the SJS trio following close behind her.

Werner Summerbee was an ugly man, both physically and emotionally. His face was pitted and scarred from a childhood infection of the deadly hybrid disease Rubellaria, his body left utterly hairless by the wasting illness. Few survived the contagion and Summerbee had spent long years quarantined until every trace of the disease was eradicated from his body. In that time he had only robots and books for company. His parents were mildly wealthy and were able to afford the exorbitant treatments necessary to save their son's life, but they believed lavishing presents upon him avoided the need of loving Werner.

By the age of ten he was recognised as having the intellect of a genius. What the tests did not quantify were his character flaws. Love and friendship meant nothing to him. He just wanted more. By twenty-five he had seized control of his parents' business in a hostile takeover. By thirty-five he diversified into a dozen different areas such as terraforming planets for colonisation, developing new technology for the Justice Department and helping revitalise derelict sectors of the Big Meg. Summerbee Construction became Summerbee Industries, one of the world's richest companies. Soon its leader's wealth was such that he had to live in tax exile on the Moon; accountants only let him visit Mega-City One for thirty-seven hours a year.

Now, at the age of forty-one, Werner Summerbee was all but untouchable. His actions affected the lives of millions and his opinion could make or break almost any venture. But what he wanted most of all was a challenge. Just how far could he go before getting caught? Were there any limits left to him? So Summerbee was quietly delighted when woken with news of Dredd's imminent arrival. He dressed in a robe of pure black silk and dabbed a few drops of exquisite scent behind his ears. Satisfied with the foppish effect, Summerbee sauntered into the lounge to meet Dredd.

The room was a sprawling, open plan space with a central area delineated by capacious sofas. The Judge was standing beside one of them, his back ramrod straight, a house droid keeping him company.

"Mr Summerbee," the robot said. "This gentleman insists on seeing you."

"Very well, Giles. You may go for now." Summerbee waited until his house droid had retired from the room before approaching the new arrival. "You must be the legendary Judge Dredd. I've heard so much about you!" Summerbee pulled a slim silver case from his robe pocket and flipped it open to reveal a row of cigarettes inside. "Smoke?"

"The consumption or burning of tobacco is illegal outside authorised smokatoria," Dredd snapped, "as you well know."

"Of course." Summerbee strolled to one of the sofas and flopped down upon it. "I just wanted to see how you would react. Please, take a seat."

"I prefer to stand."

"Have it your own way." The businessman smiled warmly. "Now, how can I help you at this time of the morning? I suppose this isn't a social call."

"Hardly. Werner Summerbee, I have reason to believe you are an accomplice to a serious crime."

"Goodness! Me, involved with a crime? This will be interesting."

"Less than an hour ago, Judge Riley from Sector House 87 died. Did you know him?" Dredd asked sternly.

"Can't say that I do, but then I meet so many people."

"You don't seem concerned that he's dead."

"In a city this large I'm sure tens of thousands, even hundreds of thousands must die every day. It's a shame this poor fellow has passed away, but these things happen – even to Judges."

"Is that a threat, Summerbee?"

"Merely an observation."

"Before dying, Riley named you as a co-conspirator in the arson attack on Robert Hatch Block, an attack that killed hundreds of residents."

Summerbee looked idly at the ceiling. "I do believe I may have seen something about that on tri-D before going to bed. But I certainly know no more about it than that. How can I possibly be a co-conspirator, as you so quaintly put it?"

"Riley said you used him."

"Could you be more specific, Dredd? I've 'used' many people in my time, but that doesn't make me an accomplice to mass murder."

"Riley said you had shown him a file, a confidential Justice Department report about the circumstances surrounding the death of Riley's brother during the colony wars."

"Really? Well, this is a fascinating story but it's all news to me."

"You deny showing Riley this file?"

"I've already told you, I never met this unfortunate so I certainly couldn't have shown him any file. Besides, you say this was a confidential Justice Department document. How could I have access to such data?"

"Your company was the driving force behind efforts to terraform the R'qeen moon, triggering the colony wars. It's not impossible for Summerbee Industries to have obtained such files through bribery and corruption."

The genial smile faded from Summerbee's face. "I would choose your next words very carefully, Dredd. I employ the best lawyers on this planet and a successful slander suit against you could bankrupt this city."

"Is it true one of your companies supplies the new transponders that are being installed on all Justice Department vehicles, including Lawmaster motorcycles?"

"It may well be. Summerbee Industries is an umbrella organisation for dozens of smaller companies. Frankly, I am only aware of a fraction of the business we do. Why do you ask?"

"Before he died Riley disabled the transponder on a Lawmaster with ease – despite the fact most Street Judges are unaware their motorcycles even have such devices fitted."

Summerbee shrugged. "I'm terribly sorry, but I still can't see what that has to do with me."

"Last night a construction droid operated by one of your companies ran amok at the corner of Merrison and Currie. Dozens, perhaps hundreds, of casualties were averted thanks to the quick action of my partner."

"Well, you must make sure they get a medal for that."

"Why does your company use notoriously unreliable Heavy Metal Kid robots when other construction droids are available?"

Summerbee stood up abruptly. "You'll have to ask the appropriate manager that question, Judge. Now I think I've been more than patient, especially considering the timing of this unannounced visit, but unless you plan to formally arrest me I must ask you to leave. I only have a few hours before my business here is concluded and I fly back to Luna-City."

"So you deny all involvement with the arson attack?"

"Absolutely. Use your birdie on me if you doubt my word."

Dredd grimaced and held up the lie detector concealed in his hand. "I already have. It confirms everything you have said. But that's no surprise, since the device is built and supplied to the department by Summerbee Industries. No doubt you have countermeasures fitted in this building to negate the effectiveness of my birdie."

"Less charitable minds might consider that to be a rather paranoid conclusion," Summerbee said. "Now I must insist you leave. So far I have been most tolerant but that time is past. You have made serious allegations based upon the slightest of circumstantial evidence." Werner smiled. "It must be unusual for you to find someone who cannot be easily intimidated or browbeaten into a confession. Most perps probably give up hope when they see the name on your badge. But I wonder what would happen if you encountered a criminal equal or superior to you?"

"Like you, Summerbee?"

"There you go again – another unfounded allegation! If you had any rockcrete evidence you would arrest me, instead of simply making snide remarks." The billionaire called to his house droid that bustled into the room. "Please escort our visitor to the front door. He is leaving now."

"I don't think so," Dredd replied, pulling handcuffs from his utility belt. "Werner Summerbee, I am arresting you on suspicion of conspiracy to commit murder."

"I'm sorry sir, but I cannot allow you to threaten my master," the droid announced. One of its mechanical hands fell away to reveal a gun barrel inside the arm. "Leave now or I will be forced to terminate you."

Keno had been watching the news broadcasts from Channel 27 with increasing trepidation. She had come to Oswald Mosley with her three broodlings, hoping for a fresh start like the other survivors from the fire. The violent welcome soon put paid to that hope. That fool Nyon seemed intent on stirring up more trouble. They were all stuck here on the top floor, and the only way out was by passing the human residents. Challenge enough people to a fight and some of them will oblige you, or so Keno had been taught by her broodmother. If only Nyon had listened to the same lesson.

It was Conchita's performance that convinced Keno it was time to get out while they still could. The human female seemed to be crying but she had madness and hate in her eyes. Keno went into the next room and roused her three broodlings, Coya, Aldre and Selmak. "Come on, wake up. We're going away on an adventure!" The young R'qeen grumbled about getting up so early but the eldest, Coya, soon took charge of his siblings.

Keno gathered what few belongings they had rescued from their old home at Robert Hatch and pushed these into a carryall. After making sure her offspring were warmly dressed, she opened the front door and led them out into the hall. The nearest turbolift was just round the corner but Nyon was already standing beside it, clamping an electronic pad over the doors.

"What are you doing?" Keno demanded.

"Sealing off the turbolift access," her sibling replied. "From now on nobody but us will be allowed up here. It's for our own safety."

"What happens if there's an emergency?"

"We use the stairs like everyone else." Nyon finished his task, only then noticing Keno and her brood were dressed to leave. "Where are you going?"

"I don't know," she admitted, "but anywhere else has to be safer than this place. The humans want blood and your outburst only provoked them further." Keno stretched out her long blue arms to hug her brood closer to her. "Come away with us, Nyon. Don't stay here."

But he shook his head, face set into a frown.

"Then let me take Lleccas and Misch somewhere safe," Keno pleaded. "You might be willing to die here but don't condemn the rest of your family to the same fate!"

"They stay with me. We stay together," Nyon insisted.

"Fine. Be stubborn, like you always are. At least reopen the turbolift so I can get my own brood out."

Nyon pressed a button on the pad he had clamped over the turbolift. The doors sealed themselves together, metal fusing with metal. "You'll have to take the stairs," he said, no hint of apology in his voice.

Keno sighed. "Nyon, when will you learn it's just as brave to walk away from a battle as it is to join one? To fight fools is to let them drag you down to their level." Her sibling did not reply, folding his arms. "Fine, on your own head be it," Keno snapped. "Coya, take Aldre and Selmak round to the emergency stairs. I'll be with you in a moment."

She watched as her eldest son led the other broodlings away before she turned to Nyon for the last time. "Farewell, Nyon. I hope I see you again." Keno kissed him on the cheek before hurrying away. Her brood were waiting at the top of the stairs, a hundred flights spiralling down through the centre of Oswald Mosley. "Coya, you lead the way. Aldre, hold on to Selmak's hand. I'll be right behind you." Keno and her family began the long descent.

"Let's go over your story again."

Jefferson loomed over Miller, who sat at a table inside the interrogation room. The other SJS Judges were standing either side of the locked door, their faces devoid of emotion.

"It isn't a story, it's the truth, and I've been through it three times already!" Miller protested. "If you don't believe me, go ask Dredd. He should be back from interviewing Summerbee by now."

"Summerbee?" The leader of the SJS trio glanced at her colleagues. "Werner Summerbee?"

"Yes. Dredd said Riley had named Summerbee just before dying."

"Stomm! Why didn't you mention this before?"

Miller rolled her eyes. "Evidence gained by hearsay isn't admissible as a defence against SJS investigation, you should know that by now. Or don't they teach you that at goon squad training school?"

Jefferson turned away, cursing under her breath. "Jefferson to Control, put me through to Dredd." After a few seconds she swore again.

"Well if you can't get him, contact SJS HQ. Tell them Operation Werner has been compromised. Send in the troops right away!"

"This is very interesting," Miller said with a smile. "So Summerbee is involved with judicial corruption? I think it's time you started talking yourself, Jefferson."

Billy-Bob was visiting the eighty-second floor for an impromptu meeting of the Citi-Def squad's upper levels representatives. As most con-apts in Oswald Mosley were cramped, it was impractical to gather all one hundred squad members in one place. Instead they divided into four teams of twenty-five. Billy-Bob was leader of the 76-100 team until a new representative from the top floor could be found. Being chosen to lead these two dozen men and women was a proud achievement for Billy-Bob, who had failed to excel in every other aspect of his life. Citi-Def had consumed him, driving away his wife and children; it had taken up every waking moment.

Billy-Bob had called the meeting after hearing about the broadcasts on Channel 27, gathering everyone outside the turbolifts on the eighty-second floor. "By now you've all seen the news about little Kasey Maguire being abducted by those alien freaks on the top floor," he began, to murmurs of assent from the others. "We don't know if she's still alive up there. If she is, I plan to rescue her personally and Grud help the alien who gets in my way. If she ain't alive, Grud help them all up there."

"Billy-Bob?" A lone voice spoke out from the others. Aaron shuffled forward, his right hand in the air.

"Aaron, I done told you there's no need to raise your hand. Just say what you want to say – we're listening." That brought a laugh from the others. Pressland might be the biggest among them physically, but he was not the brightest of men. Aaron smiled with them, not realising the joke was at his expense.

"Well, you and Sam and me all searched the top floor and we didn't find no humans up there. Plenty of those blue aliens and some other kinds, but no sign of this missing girl. And that was after she was supposed to have gone up there already. Where can she have been?"

"That's a good question," Billy-Bob conceded. "But those aliens, I've heard tell they can do fancy mind tricks, stranger than any Psi-Judge. So maybe they pulled a swift one on us, to make us think Kasey wasn't there when she was."

The others murmured in their agreement. Who knew what things those offworlders could do to you? "I say we go up there and search the top floor again," Billy-Bob announced, raising his voice over the hubbub. "I say we make those aliens surrender little Kasey Maguire. I say it's time we stopped talking and started fighting back. Are you with me?"

The squad members were nodding and clapping.

"I said, *are you with me?*" Billy-Bob demanded, raising his voice to a shout. The others shouted back their agreement. "All right, that's better!" their leader yelled. "Now, Aaron tells me those sneaky freaks have locked off turbolift access to the one hundredth floor, so we'll have to find another way up. I want half of you to go up the emergency stairs. The rest of us will go up to ninety-nine in turbolifts and meet you there. Let's do it!"

Keno and her brood had reached the eighty-fifth floor on their long trek down the emergency stairs when shouting voices began to drift up from below. "Sssh, listen!" Coya hissed, stopping his siblings' descent. The voices were calling out in the human language, the words strange but the violent emotions behind them all too evident. "They're coming up towards us," Coya realised.

Keno peered over the edge of the metal banister, down the circular stairwell. Below she could see human faces looking up, their features contorted with anger and hatred. One of them pointed at her and screamed to the others. The humans began running up the stairs, some clutching laser blades and other weapons. Keno shrank back, her worst fears confirmed.

"What do we do?" Coya asked, his face full of concern.

"We go back to the top floor. We'll be safe there," his broodmother decided. "Come, we must hurry!" She picked up Selmak and began carrying him up the stairs, Coya following with Aldre.

But they had only ascended two floors when more human voices could be heard echoing down the stairwell from above, getting ever closer. "We're too late," Keno gasped. "They're above us and below us. We can't get back to the top floor – we're trapped!"

Coya shook his head. "Not yet!" He opened the door to the eighty-seventh floor. "We can go in here and get the turbolift down. Come on!" The R'qeen boy grabbed his sibling and hurried through the doorway to the hallway beyond.

Keno shook her head in dismay. They should have walked down one flight of stairs and then taken the turbolift the rest of the way; she just hadn't thought of it. She prayed that mistake did not cost them dear. Still carrying Selmak, Keno followed her other broodlings. Coya was already running along the hallway. "The turbolifts are just down here!" he shouted.

* * *

Billy-Bob had taken the turbolift up to the ninety-ninth floor only to discover the aliens had also barricaded the emergency stairs leading up to the top level. But a shout from below soon erased that disappointment. "We got 'em!" Aaron shouted from below. "They're on the stairs above us!"

"Where are you?" Billy-Bob bellowed back.

"Just passing eighty-three!"

"Keep coming. Drive them up to us!" Billy-Bob sent the others down ahead of himself. He was about to follow when a thought occurred. What was to stop those freaks leaving the stairs and trying to escape by turbolift? He grinned as the answer came in a flash – he was going to stop them. Gripping his laser-blade tightly, Billy-Bob rushed back to the ninety-ninth floor. The Judges had deemed him too mentally unstable to see active duty in the colony wars. Well, this was his chance to prove them wrong.

Summerbee hurried back into the lounge, now dressed in a business suit and clasping a hastily packed suitcase. "So sorry to keep you waiting," he said to Dredd, "but I hadn't planned on leaving for the Moon until midday. Your intervention has forced my hand, bringing forward my departure from this city."

The Judge was still standing in the same place, but now he had his hands clasped behind his helmet. The house droid kept its weapon trained on him, ready to fire. "You won't get far," Dredd replied. "Control knows where I am. If I don't report in soon, backup will be despatched to this address."

"Not in time to save you."

"Werner Summerbee!" a voice shouted from outside. "Your residence is surrounded by Justice Department forces. Surrender now or suffer the consequences!"

"You were saying?" Dredd asked, resting his hands on his helmet.

His captor moved to the window and peered out. "Not regular Judges; those look like SJS insignia. How tiresome."

"Take their advice, creep. Give yourself up and you might live long enough to swap this place for an iso-cube."

"A tempting offer but one I must decline," Summerbee replied. "Droid, keep Dredd busy here while I take my leave."

The droid turned to acknowledge its master's command. "Yes, Mr–"

Dredd ripped the helmet from his head and threw it at the robot's gun arm in one smooth movement, but the droid was already firing back.

* * *

Keno found Coya jabbing the buttons beside the turbolift, still waiting for one to arrive. The other broodlings were frightened, too terrified to speak. Keno thought about knocking on a con-apt door to ask for help, but decided it was too risky. What little she had seen of the human residents told her they were on their own in this building. Nobody wanted them here.

"This one's coming!" Coya shouted, pointing at one of the turbolifts.

Keno set down her youngest broodling. "Coya, keep hold of Aldre and Selmak. We have to stay together. Do you understand?"

The eldest of her brood nodded.

"The same goes for you two," Keno said, her back to the turbolift. Behind her the doors began to open and she swung round to check if it was safe. Keno never saw the weapon that killed her.

The first shot punched through the top of Dredd's shoulder pad, narrowly missing his head. The second creased his side, slicing through the Kevlar-reinforced uniform and punching a hole just below his ribs before exiting his back. The third hit the flying helmet and ricocheted away.

Dredd was already diving sideways behind one of the sofas, drawing his Lawgiver from its holster. "Armour piercing!" he shouted, activating the handgun's ammunition selection and drawing the required round into the barrel. The Judge was firing before his body hit the floor, the shots piercing the sofa in front of him and thudding into the house droid. It fell backwards with a metallic squawk, still firing into the air. By the time Dredd hit the carpet the droid was permanently disabled, its systems shutting down.

The entire sequence took less than five heartbeats.

Billy-Bob found himself confronted by one of the freaks. Instinctively he lashed out with the laser blade, slicing the monster's head clean off in a single movement. As the creature collapsed to the floor three more of its kind began screaming, their strange alien noises scratching the inside of Billy-Bob's mind. "I got one!" he shouted delightedly. "I got me one of these freaks!"

Two of the aliens ran off down the corridor but one stood over the still twitching body. It shouted something at Billy-Bob. The words were unknown but the meaning was clear – this little freak wanted to fight.

"Now you're talking my language," Billy-Bob said, blue light from the laser blade illuminating his face. He stepped out of the turbolift and advanced on the alien child.

* * *

Dredd was crouching by Summerbee when the SJS Judges burst into the luxury bungalow. Subsequent forensic investigation would prove the shot that killed the billionaire had been fired by the house droid. The internal security cams showed Summerbee being more than a little surprised when hit by the shot that ricocheted off Dredd's flying helmet. He had fallen backwards over his case and collapsed in a heap on the floor, blood pooling out from beneath him and soaking into an antique sheepskin rug.

"Why?" Dredd hissed in the dying man's ear. "Why did you show Riley that report about his brother?"

"Needed him... to help Stammers... The incendiary..."

"But why torch those aliens? What did you hope to gain?"

"Not the aliens... The building..." Summerbee gasped, then lay still.

The SJS Judges swarmed into the building but their quarry had eluded them. "What did he say?" their leader demanded.

Dredd put his helmet back on before replying. "What's it to you?"

"Summerbee Industries has been worrying the Special Judicial Squad for some time," Jefferson told Miller in the interrogation room. "The many companies that make up the Summerbee empire have their tentacles into far too many areas of the Justice Department for our liking: weapons research and development, supplying crucial equipment, even taking over construction of new department buildings. We began to hear whispers about Summerbee's underlings using bribery and corruption to win contracts. After what happened with the Mark Elevens, we didn't want a rerun."

Crime boss Nero Narcos had begun supplying the department with a new model of Lawgiver, through a legitimate company. The Mark Eleven had been a big improvement on the old handgun and thousands were issued to Street Judges as their standard issue weapon. But Narcos had installed a modification of his own. When he decided to seize control of the Big Meg, the crime boss sent a signal that meant each Mark Eleven would explode when fired. The result temporarily crippled many Street Judges and made the new Lawgivers unusable. It was a masterstroke and one the department was keen to avoid happening again.

"So you launched an investigation into Summerbee Industries," Miller said. "But Dredd and I stumbled upon something you didn't know about."

"We knew Summerbee was close to winning the contract to build a new Grand Hall of Justice. That's why he came back to Earth. He was due to sign the deal today. The new site is being announced at midday. Our sources suggest it was going to be here, in Sector 87."

324   I Am The Law: The Judge Dredd Omnibus

"But that's not possible," Miller replied. "There's nowhere central enough that could be used for such a large..." Her voice trailed off as realisation dawned on her face. "Of course – Robert Hatch!"

Jefferson was one step behind her. "The alien ghetto that burned down?"

"That's what the fire was about. It had nothing to do with anti-alien xenophobia. It was to clear a site big enough for the new building!"

Jefferson nodded. "Yes, you're right. That must be it." The SJS Judge stopped, concentrating on a message being relayed to her helmet radio. "That's a roj – Jefferson out."

"What is it? Is Dredd all right?" Miller asked.

"Yes, just a flesh wound. Summerbee is dead." Jefferson took off her helmet and threw it against a wall in frustration. "Drokk it! Six months of investigative work down the drain!"

"But if Summerbee is dead, isn't the threat dead too?"

"Maybe," Jefferson told Miller. "But what about the corrupt Judges that were helping him? They're still hidden within the system!"

Aldre and Selmak were huddled against a door, trying not to listen to the screams of Coya dying. A jumble of humans burst into the corridor from the emergency stairs. One of them spotted the two R'qeen children and shouted to the others. They surrounded Aldre and Selmak, a selection of weapons in their hands. Aldre hugged Selmak to her chest so he couldn't see what was coming and then closed her own eyes for the last time.

05:00

Dredd was returning to Sector House 87 after agreeing to keep details of the SJS's investigation secret for now. He was travelling via the Anton Diffring Overzoom when a call came through from Control. "Request you divert to Oswald Mosley. Deputy Sector Chief Temple is taking a dozen Judges there to quell a new disturbance and Caine wants you there as backup."

"I've had about enough of this," Dredd said. "Control, put me through to Sector Chief Caine. It's time I had words with her." Dredd pulled into a Judges-only stop while waiting for the Sector Chief to call him back.

"Caine to Dredd – I understand you wish to speak with me?"

"That's a roj."

"Make it snappy. I haven't got all night to be dealing with the complaints of a single Street Judge."

"Fine by me," Dredd replied. "What I have to say won't take long. Tell me this – what the hell is going on, Caine?"

"Could you be more precise?"

"You've had me running from pillar to post since I set foot in this sector, traipsing back and forth to Oswald Mosley."

"Are you challenging my right to choose which Judges receive which assignments?"

"No, but I–"

"Perhaps you think the problems at Oswald Mosley are beneath you?"

"No, that isn't–"

"Then what the drokk is your problem, Dredd?" Caine snarled. "I said you'd be trouble and that's exactly what you are. You and Miller caused a riot on Anton Diffring, shutting that overzoom down for several hours."

"It had already been closed by a multi-vehicle pile-up–"

"You've flooded the holding cubes with a hundred religious kooks, all thanks to your grandstanding tactics!"

"I was not–"

"Rather than talk them down, you let them jump off Maurice Waldron and then you jumped off after them! If that isn't grandstanding, I don't know what is! You called the Chief Judge's office to lodge a complaint about me. When I asked you to defuse the situation at Oswald Mosley you bungled that too."

"The Citi-Def squad was forced to stand down. It was a final warning that the whole block would be placed under curfew if trouble started again," Dredd replied, finally getting to finish a sentence. "What more was I supposed to do?"

"Don't you try to deny your mistakes! We've got precogs saying there will be a riot in that block within an hour and a reporter called Riff Maltin's broadcasting inciteful footage from inside the building."

"I said Maltin should be–"

"Don't interrupt me either! I'm still your superior, despite your best efforts to steal my job! Last but by no means least I learn you've been involved in the killing of two of my Street Judges. Perhaps you'd care to explain that?"

"Stammers and Riley were dirty badges," Dredd snarled. "You should have known that and acted against them sooner! But you've let your own paranoia and insecurities blind you to what's been going on under your nose!"

"It's always somebody else's fault with you, isn't it, Dredd? Well, not anymore! I'm recommending the SJS launch a full investigation into your behaviour. I'm going to have them so far up your ass you'll need a teleporter to take a dump!"

"My conscience is clear," Dredd maintained.

"Really?" Caine said, laughing bitterly. "Well, since you helped Miller kill two of my best Street Judges, I suggest you go to Oswald Mosley and try to take their places. Unless that's beneath you?"

"No, but I–"

"No buts, Dredd. Just do what you're told for once! Caine out!"

Temple didn't know whether to be excited or terrified. It was years since he had seen active duty. A dozen Judges were now waiting for his order to move into Oswald Mosley. They had erected a cordon around the building so all the skedways and pedways nearby were empty – for now. Keeping bystanders out was easy at this time of the morning. When the sun rose and the city awoke it would get considerably more difficult.

Jumbled reports were emerging from inside the building, with residents on the eighty-fifth calling the department about a bloody incident in the hallway. At least three aliens were dead, apparently butchered by vigilantes. More worrying were the pictures being broadcast by Channel 27.

Reporter Riff Maltin had been chosen by the Oswald Mosley Citi-Def as its official war correspondent. Dressed in camouflage with his own flak jacket and helmet, Riff was now providing a running commentary on events within the block. While Tek-Division tried to jam the signal and prevent anti-alien violence from spreading to other parts of the city, Temple watched the live pictures in an H-wagon parked outside the building.

"Breaking news from inside strife-torn Oswald Mosley Block!" Riff announced. "The Citi-Def squad has accepted my credentials as a journalist and agreed to me being embedded with them. That means I will be able to provide live and exclusive coverage of this crisis as it unfolds. We already know the Justice Department has surrounded the building and is letting nobody in or out. I don't know how long these broadcasts can continue before they are jammed or censored, but everything that happens here will be recorded. Even if this signal is not escaping the building, my footage will be released at a later date exclusively on Channel 27! Now, back to the studio."

Temple switched off the tri-D and left the H-wagon. His squad gathered around him. "What do you want us to do?" a black female Judge called Washington asked. She had travelled to the scene on her Lawmaster after being diverted there from other duties. "It'll be dawn soon. Once residents in the surrounding blocks wake up and discover what's happening, the trouble will only spread."

"Tek-Division will soon have that signal jammed," Temple replied. He refused to countenance the use of immediate force. "If we could just gain access to the top floor and prove the missing girl isn't there; that would take the heat out of the situation."

"And how do you suggest we do that, sir?" Washington said. "The aliens have sealed off the emergency stairs and all turbolift access."

Temple realised the solution was just behind him. "Simple! I'll go up in the H-wagon and talk some sense into these offworlders. Once they see I mean them no harm, they're bound to let me in."

Washington shifted uneasily at this, glancing at some of the other Judges. "Are you sure about this, sir?"

Temple nodded happily. "Yes, definitely. If we can resolve this situation peacefully, it will be quite a feather in my cap!" He got back into the H-wagon, his uncertainties banished. "Washington, you'd best stay here and keep an eye on things from the ground. The rest of you are coming with me."

The other Judges reluctantly clambered in after Temple. Washington closed the side door of the vehicle once they were inside. "I've got a bad feeling about this," she muttered under her breath.

The H-wagon lifted into the air as Dredd arrived on his Lawmaster. "Where are they going?" he asked.

"On a fool's errand," Washington replied. "Temple thinks he can talk the aliens into surrendering."

Dredd used his helmet radio to call the deputy Sector Chief. "I've just arrived as backup. Where do you want me?"

"Stay where you are and take no action," Temple replied. "That's a direct order, Dredd. Caine's told me what you're like. Temple out!"

Riff was admiring himself in a mirror when the hunting party arrived with its trophy. The reporter decided he looked good in camouflage, and he adjusted his combat helmet to a jauntier angle. He was due back on air in a few minutes with an update. Yablonsky had been full of praise for Riff's work so far but reminded him that most viewers were still asleep. The big ratings would not kick in until after dawn when the slumbering citizens woke to what was happening at Oswald Mosley. Already the feed was that Channel 27 was being picked up on a dozen larger stations in other sectors. It was only a matter of time before the broadcast spread citywide. Riff smiled at that – only a matter of time.

"Where's that dang fool with the hovercam?" a gruff voice demanded outside the bathroom. Riff emerged to find Conchita's con-apt filled with Citi-Def squad members. The person speaking was a thin, wiry man clutching a heavy carryall. "There he is! My name's Jolie, Billy-Bob Jolie. I'm head of the 76-100 team. Boy, have we got a story for you! Do you like hunting at all?"

"Can't say I've ever–"

"Get your hovercam rolling and feast your eyes on this little beauty," Billy-Bob said, digging his hands into the carryall. He struggled to get the contents out, shaking the bag vigorously until it fell free. Billy-Bob proudly help up the severed head of an R'qeen female. "Cut it off myself, only took one swipe. Used a laser blade, so that it cauterised the wound and stopped the blood getting everywhere. What do think? Is this newsworthy or what?"

Riff could feel his insides pulsating. It had been hours since he last ate but what little remained in his stomach was in a sudden hurry to leave again. "Oh my Grud," he gurgled, clamping one hand over his mouth.

Billy-Bob jerked a thumb towards the door. "We got the rest of the body outside if you'd like to film that too. I'm thinking of getting this one stuffed and mounted when all this is over. You know any good taxidermists?"

Riff couldn't hold back any longer. He ran back into the bathroom, vomit already spilling out between his fingers. "Excuse me!" he shouted.

"That's all right, we can wait," Billy-Bob said. "I'd have shown you the three little alien critters we killed too, but the boys got over-excited and made a real mess of them. Not much left to see, if you know what I mean. Besides, they were so small we should have just thrown them back."

Riff wretched again and again.

Billy-Bob grabbed hold of the hovercam. "Say, this red light just came on. Does that mean I'm on the air?"

Nyon was leaning against the doorway to the emergency stairs, listening intently. He had sealed it like the turbolift doors but still feared the humans would find a way through. Most of the other aliens were asleep and unaware of what was happening. Nyon did not like to think what their reaction would be to his actions, but he would deal with them when the time came. For now he was more worried about the safety of Lleccas and Misch.

His pairling called from the doorway of their con-apt. "Come away from there, Nyon! You need to sleep – we all do."

She was right, of course. Nyon couldn't recall the last time he had rested or eaten. The fire at Robert Hatch seemed like a lifetime ago instead of just a few hours. He returned to the con-apt. The first glints of dawn had begun to lighten the skyline outside the floor-to-ceiling windows. But there was something else out there, a dark shape moving towards them.

"My name is Deputy Sector Chief Temple!" an amplified voice bellowed from beyond the window. A spotlight swung round to illuminate the interior of the con-apt from outside, dazzling Nyon and Lleccas. "I need to talk to you!" the voice continued in Allspeak. "Can you understand me?"

Nyon peered between gaps in his fingers, trying to see what was outside the window. He could just discern the shape of an H-wagon, hovering near the top of the building. The R'qeen leader went to the glasseen wall and opened one of the windows. "Get that light away from us!" he bellowed, raising his voice to be heard above the H-wagon's engines.

"Move that light!" the voice outside commanded. The dazzling spotlight shifted sideways, enabling Nyon to see who was speaking. A human in the uniform of a Judge was clinging to a walkway extended from the H-wagon.

"What do you want?" Nyon asked.

"We need access to the top floor of your building. A girl is missing and we need to prove to the other residents she is not in there with you."

Nyon almost laughed. "The humans have searched here already. Once was enough. No more!"

"I understand you have barricaded yourselves inside."

"That was for our own safety. Two humans set fire to Robert Hatch; my broodling saw it in their minds. Hundreds of our own kind died in that fire but no more will die this night."

"If you let us in, we can protect you," Temple offered.

Nyon heard Lleccas gasp behind him. She was watching the con-apt's tri-D set, a luxury their previous home had not afforded them. Nyon looked at the images being broadcast. The same human who had threatened him earlier was appearing on the tri-D now, proudly holding up the severed head of Keno.

Nyon flew into a rage, hurling objects at the tri-D until it exploded. Lleccas tried to comfort him but Nyon pushed her away. Instead he returned to the open window and screamed at the H-wagon about what he had just seen. "No human sets foot on this floor while we still have life!" Nyon vowed.

"You are being foolish!" Temple retorted. "What if there is another fire?"

"Then we will burn and it will be on your conscience, human!" Nyon pulled the window shut and locked it. He found Lleccas standing beside him, sadness and regret in her eyes. Neither of them noticed Misch watching them from the doorway of her room.

"They killed Keno, butchered her," Nyon snarled, his face risen with anger and sorrow. "What have those monsters done to her brood?"

Misch closed the door quietly and realised Kasey was standing nearby. "I thought you were asleep," the R'qeen girl whispered.

"Loud voices outside woke me. What did they say?"

"The humans want to search the top floor again." Her voice trailed off.

"For me?" Kasey asked. "Then I must go back."

"You can't."

"I know my mom will hit me again, but that's–"

"No, I mean you can't go back, even if you wanted to. My father has barricaded us all in on the top floor. We're stuck here."

"Oh," Kasey said.

Misch gave her a hug. They needed each other more than ever now.

Temple retreated into the belly of the H-wagon, unsure what to do next. They could try and storm the top floor, but that would not be easy. If the aliens were holding the girl hostage, she would certainly be dead before Judges could rescue her and that would turn the block into a war-zone. Anti-alien hysteria could spread and engulf the sector, perhaps the entire city. No, he would not be responsible for starting that. If the aliens would not budge, perhaps the human residents could be persuaded to take a step back.

The Deputy Sector Chief called Control on his helmet radio. "Get me in contact with the leader of Oswald Mosley Citi-Def. I don't care how you do it, but I need to talk to them right away!"

Conchita returned to her con-apt to find Billy-Bob and his cronies from the 76-100 team holding an impromptu news conference, using the hovercam to film each other. "What the drokk are you doing?" she demanded. "Where's Riff?"

"In your bathroom, puking his guts out," Billy-Bob said with a smile. "Where the hell have you been?"

"Working with the other team leaders to develop a strategy for reclaiming the top floor – a meeting you should have been at!"

He held up Keno's severed head. "Yeah? Well, while you were busy talking, we were taking action. Got us a count of four so far, including this one."

"Get that out of my sight," Conchita warned. "I lead the Citi-Def squad, not you, and I decide when we take action. Is that clear?"

Billy-Bob winked at his team members. "Well, I'm not so sure about that anymore. Seems to me that we've just–" His next words were cut off by a sharp intake of breath as Conchita grabbed his testicles in her right fist and began squeezing them together.

"Now, you were saying?" she asked, smiling sweetly.

"Nothing..." Billy-Bob gasped. "I wasn't saying nothing."

"That's better. Now, who's in charge of this Citi-Def squad?" She gave his testicles a violent twist, enticing a shriek of pain from him.

"Y–you are!"

"And don't you forget it, drokker!" she growled in his ear. Conchita abruptly released Billy-Bob and stepped clear as he collapsed to the floor, whimpering in pain. "Anybody else want to challenge my authority?" The rest of the 76-100 team quickly denied any such ambitions. "Good. Now get the drokk out of my con-apt and take this rat-weasel with you."

They were all gone when Riff emerged from the bathroom, still wiping his mouth clean. "Conchita, you're back – thank Grud! Those goons that were in here before..."

"I got rid of them," she replied. "I've been talking with the–"

The reporter pressed a hand to his earpiece. "Hold it, I'm getting a message from Channel 27. Have you got a vidphone here?"

Conchita grimaced. "No, I smashed it earlier, Why?"

"Seems the Justice Department want to talk to you. Also my news editor has a message for you from someone called Stummers?"

"Stammers?" she suggested.

"Could be. He's got something you want. After that, the message is just gibberish, a bunch of numbers and letters all jumbled together."

Conchita was perplexed. "Something I want?" she wondered, before her eyes widened. "The code. That must be the override code! What is it?"

Riff relayed the rest of the message to her. "What about the Justice Department? My news editor says a Judge called Temple still wants to talk."

"They can wait. I've got more important things to do right now." Conchita strode purposefully from her con-apt. Riff and his hovercam followed.

Dredd and Washington were still in position outside Oswald Mosley, looking up at the H-wagon. It had hung in the air for several minutes without changing position or taking any visible action. "For Grud's sake, what is Temple doing up there?" Dredd growled.

"He hasn't been out from behind a desk in years," Washington said. "I don't know why the chief sent him to sort this mess out. We should be inside now, rounding up the ring leaders and imposing discipline before the rest of the block wakes and things get out of hand."

They were interrupted by a high-pitched screeching from above, then the sound of Temple clearing his throat. "Testing, testing, one, two, testing."

"What the drokk is he doing?" Washington wondered. "He'll wake up the whole block if he uses the H-wagon's public address system!"

"I think that's the idea," Dredd replied, scowling with dismay.

"This is a message for all residents of Oswald Mosley Block. My name is Patrick Temple and I am Deputy Chief of Sector 87. As of now your block is being placed under curfew. No citizen may enter or leave the building without permission of the Justice Department. Furthermore, no resident may leave his or her con-apt without permission until the curfew is lifted. That is all!"

After another ear-piercing squeal of static the speakers shut down again. Washington and Dredd exchanged an unhappy look. "The precogs predicted there'd be a riot and Temple has just ensured that prophecy comes true," Washington said. "Now the stomm really hits the fan."

* * *

In the basement of Oswald Mosley, Conchita punched the code supplied by Stammers into a keypad. The reinforced steel and rockcrete door to the armoury swung open, revealing a vast array of weapons and ammunition stored inside. Conchita turned to the other Citi-Def squad members crowding the basement. "I want only six people in the armoury at a time. There's no need to fight each other for the best weapons, there's plenty for everybody. All of you take a gas mask. The Judges have already used stumm against us once tonight, they'll probably try it again."

Riff was standing near her, his hovercam capturing every moment. As the squad members began raiding the armoury's contents, he pulled Conchita aside for a quick interview. "Ms Maguire, you're the leader of Oswald Mosley Citi-Def. Why have you raided the block's cache of weapons, in clear breach of Justice Department guidelines?"

She stared directly into hovercam. "We no longer recognise the authority of the Justice Department. It was not willing to intervene and save my daughter from the alien scum on the top floor of our block. But one Judge, a true patriot, was ready to break the rules and give us the code for this armoury. Now, armed and ready, we will take the Law into our own hands!"

In the garage at Sector House 87, Brady was watching the live Channel 27 transmission from Oswald Mosley. What Judge would be foolish enough to give the armoury code to those trigger-happy kooks? His thoughts were interrupted by a call from outside the sector house. "Brady, I need your help again," Dredd said. "PSU has been monitoring a broadcast–"

"About Oswald Mosley Citi-Def getting the judicial code for the armoury? I was wondering when you'd call," the Tek-Judge replied. "I'll start a trace on all incoming calls and messages to that block."

"If a Judge did send that code to Maguire, it's doubtful they did it directly," Dredd suggested. "Try to identify any third parties who could have helped."

"I'll contact Channel 27, see if they have been passing on messages via their reporter inside," Brady offered. "But what if they refuse to help?"

"Remind them they live in Mega-City One, where freedom of the press is a privilege, not a right. They give you full cooperation or I'll extract it from them personally – with my daystick."

"That's a roj, Dredd. I'll get back to you."

* * *

Ken Amidou was the first Citi-Def squad member to emerge from the armoury. While his colleagues were selecting bat-glider suits and body armour, Amidou was content just to grab a gas mask and a shoulder-mounted rocket launcher. The portly citizen shoved three missiles into the belt of his camouflage trousers, hitching the elasticated waistband up above his ample belly. "Let's see how the Judges like a taste of their own medicine," he muttered.

A quick trip in the turbolift took Amidou back to his con-apt on the seventy-third floor. Once inside he ripped the seal off the rocket launcher and began reading the simple instructions printed on its side: PLACE MISSILE INSIDE LAUNCHER – TAKE AIM – PULL TRIGGER – BOOM! It all seemed simple enough. Amidou plucked one of the missiles from his belt and dropped it into the launcher's long barrel. It fit snugly inside, clicking into place.

The Citi-Def member carried the launcher to his living room window and looked out. Yes, the H-wagon was still hovering outside, but it had moved sideways. To get a better shot Amidou needed to fire from the bedroom. He marched into the next room and clambered over the bed, startling his obese wife, Gerta.

"Ken! Where are you going with that thing?"

"Just a little target practice, my beloved," Amidou replied soothingly. "You go back to sleep, nothing to be alarmed about."

"Nothing to be alarmed about? It's five in the morning!"

"Hush now, sweetness. I've got a job to do." He pushed open the window and pointed the rocket launcher out into the cool early morning air.

"Come back to bed," Gerta urged. "I'll give you a job to do."

"Not just now, dear." Amidou closed one eye and took aim, sighting down the barrel at the bulky profile of the H-wagon. He closed his finger around the trigger, ready to pull. "Be with you in a minute..." Amidou pulled the trigger. The missile flew out of the launcher and through the opposite wall of the bedroom. It continued through five more walls before exploding in a con-apt on the far side of the block, incinerating the residents of 737.

Amidou opened both his eyes again and looked out of the window. The H-wagon was still intact, no damage visible on it in the blue light of near dawn. "Strange. I followed all the instructions – that should have worked." A podgy finger tapped him on the shoulder. Amidou turned in time to see the fist his unhappy wife threw at him, but not soon enough to avoid it. He sunk to the floor, quite unconscious from the mighty blow.

Gerta picked up the rocket launcher and took one of the remaining missiles. "You want a job done properly, get a woman to do it," she said, slotting the rocket into place. Making sure she had the arrows labelled AIM THIS WAY facing out the window, Gerta got a bead on the H-wagon and closed her finger around the trigger.

"What do you mean, you don't know what caused that explosion?" Temple demanded. "A con-apt inside Oswald Mosley just got incinerated and I want to know why!" He was shouting at three Tek-Judges manning consoles inside the H-wagon, but his words were lost among many others on various channels.

"Temple, this is Dredd," a familiar voice shouted into helmet radios. "What the drokk are you doing? Did you just open fire on Oswald Mosley?"

"Dredd, this is Temple. No, we did not open fire! Now get off this line–"

"Sir, I think you ought to see this," one of the Tek-Judges interrupted.

"Will you be quiet?" the Deputy Sector Chief demanded. "I am trying to maintain discipline here and I will not be interrupted."

"But sir, there's a woman on the seventy-third floor. She seems to be–"

"I don't care what she seems to be doing. I only want to know what caused that explosion!" Temple replied.

"Looks like a missile went off inside one of the con-apts, origin unknown," another Tek-Judge shouted. "No heat trail leading into the building."

"Well, that's something," Temple said. "We don't want another block getting involved with this. We've got enough problems–"

"Sir, this woman: she's got a rocket launcher. She's about to fire at us!"

"What?" That got Temple's attention. "Why didn't you say so earlier? Control, this is Temple. We are under attack fr–"

But his next words were never uttered. The rocket punched a hole through one of the H-wagon's windows and exploded inside the cabin, killing everyone inside almost instantly. The fireball blew out the windows, spraying glasseen and other shrapnel across five blocks nearby. Its engines destroyed, the H-wagon began to fall from the sky.

Gerta smiled in satisfaction as the rocket penetrated the H-wagon. As she bent down to remonstrate with her husband, she missed the fireball blossoming outwards from the exploding vehicle towards their con-apt. "See? All you had to do was point this thing the right way and you–"

Her next words were lost as the flames scorched the skin from her flesh, then the flesh from her bones, and then Gerta Amidou and her husband were no more.

Dredd and Washington were right underneath the H-wagon when it was hit. Washington stared at the spectacle, mesmerised by the fireball exploding outwards from the vehicle overhead. "Sweet Jovus..."

Dredd gunned his Lawmaster into life. "Come on, Washington – we've got to move!" But the other Judge remained where she was, transfixed.

"But it's... it's impossible..." she whispered.

Dredd leaned across and activated the engine on Washington's bike before yelling at her. "We've got to move! Go!" He tore away, the tyres on his motorcycle squealing in protest. The noise finally jolted Washington into life and she accelerated after him, just clearing the deserted skedway before the burning remains rained down upon her.

A fresh explosion tore the H-wagon apart as it hit the ground, fragments flying out in all directions. A shard of metal sliced through the rear tyre of Washington's Lawmaster, sending the bike careering out from under her. The Judge skidded along the ground at high speed before slamming headfirst into a rockcrete wall with a sickening thud. Dredd slammed on his brakes and ran back to Washington with a med-kit, the scene lit brighter than day as the ammunition inside the crashed H-wagon exploded. But Washington's helmet had cracked open like an egg, a crimson pool forming beneath her.

"Dredd to Control, all hell's just broken loose at Oswald Mosley. We lost the H-wagon and everyone inside. Looked like it was hit by a rocket fired from inside the block. The vehicle has crashed in front of the building, killing another badge on the ground in the process. I'm the only Judge left alive on the scene! I need everything – Meds, Teks and backup – and I need it now!"

"Roj that, Dredd. Units already on their way!"

He looked at the carnage around him. "Send more," Dredd growled. "And tell Sector Chief Caine I'm assuming control of this crime scene. If she wants to argue with me about it, she'll have to come down here herself. Dredd out!"

The detonation on the seventy-third floor of Oswald Mosley had woken most people inside the building, as the shockwave had sent shudders throughout the structure. The explosion that incinerated the H-wagon woke up the rest of the residents. Those on the eastern side of the block hurried to their windows in time to see the Justice Department vehicle slowly tumble downwards, turning end over end as it fell to the deserted skedway below. Few who witnessed this terrible spectacle would forget the image of the burning H-wagon's descent.

On the top floor Misch and Kasey ran out into the central room of the con-apt, terrified by what they were witnessing. Lleccas embraced her broodling while Nyon stared in dismay at the human child. "Who is this?" he demanded.

"Kasey," Misch said. "I hid her when the men came."

Nyon sunk to the floor, his head in his hands. "Oh no..."

"She's my friend," Misch explained. "Her broodmother hurts her. I could feel how unhappy Kasey was, so I told her to come up here."

Lleccas put her broodling down. "Do you realise what you've done? We told the humans she was not here. Your broodfather has..." Her voice trailed off, as she realised the enormity of what they faced. "We cannot go back now. Even if we wanted to, we cannot send her back. And if we did, it would just prove the humans were right and we were liars."

Misch began crying, her unhappiness setting Kasey off too, even though the human girl had understood nothing of the R'qeen words. "I'm sorry, I didn't mean to..." Misch sobbed, her emotions over-whelming her words. "I'm sorry."

Lleccas embraced her daughter and then drew Kasey to her as well. "It's all right, it will be all right," the broodmother said soothingly.

Nyon looked up at her from the floor. "Will it?"

Riff was still in the basement with Conchita as the last weapons were removed from the armoury, so he didn't see the H-wagon get hit. A slight tremor ran through the building's superstructure as the vehicle exploded but it was little more than a twitch.

"What was–" Riff began, but his question was cut short by the scream of metal and rockcrete when the H-wagon crashed outside.

"Sweet Jovus, what's going on out there?" Conchita wondered. Mikell Fields ran down into the basement, pointing behind himself.

"Somebody just took out an H-wagon! It's crash-landed outside the lobby. No survivors!" he gibbered.

"Terrif," Conchita hissed as she strapped a flame-thrower to her back. "They couldn't maintain discipline, could they? Our fight is with the aliens, not the Judges! Now the whole department will come down on us."

Riff picked up a discarded gas mask and looped it over his head. "What are you going to do?" he asked the Citi-Def leader.

She noticed the hovercam was still watching her. "In every battle there are casualties. But our war with the aliens is just beginning. Let's go!" Conchita ran up the stairs, a gas mask in one hand and a heavily laden carryall in the other. Riff went after her, determined not to lose his place on the front line.

Miller was changing into a fresh uniform when the news about the H-wagon reached Sector House 87. She ran to the briefing room where all available Judges were being assembled at Caine's request. The Sector Chief was visibly shaken by what had happened but warned against retaliatory action. "As far as we know, the attack on the H-wagon was an isolated incident by a single individual from the Oswald Mosley Citi-Def. Make no mistake, they will be made to pay for what they have done. But our first priority is to restore law and order in that block. Punishments will be handed out after that is achieved, not before or during. Do I make myself clear?"

"Yes ma'am!" the gathered Judges yelled back at her.

Caine nodded her approval. "All right, now Dredd's the only helmet still alive on the scene. Others nearby are scrambling to his position. But we need a cohesive strategy to retake control of Oswald Mosley. Miller?"

"Yes ma'am?"

"I want you to form a strike team. Choose two dozen of your colleagues and get suited up. The Citi-Def members have obtained access to the block armoury, so they've got enough weaponry to start a small war. Your job is to stop them. Prepare for the worst. Got it?"

"Yes ma'am!"

"Everyone else, listen up. If this lawlessness spreads, we can kiss this sector goodbye. Miller and her squad will be fighting it at the source. Your job is making sure nobody else takes this incident as a sign that we're fair game or that the Law has forsaken 87. Crush all resistance, be utterly ruthless. At least a dozen Judges have already died tonight. Don't let those deaths be in vain. Show the people of this sector and this city who is in charge. Dismissed!"

Dredd emptied Washington's utility belt to replenish his own supplies of extra ammunition, stumm gas grenades and other equipment. Using a tool from his bike he disabled the palm recognition unit on her Lawgiver so anyone could fire it safely. He then added a fresh clip of ammunition. After switching his motorcycle to voice-activated remote control, Dredd lowered the respirator on his helmet. He rolled three canisters of stumm gas into the lobby of Oswald Mosley, the interior quickly filling with the noxious yellow gas. No doubt the Citi-Def members were wearing masks but the canisters' contents would still obscure the vision of those guarding the entrance.

"Dredd to bike," he snarled into his helmet radio, "Enter the lobby – now!"

The Lawmaster revved its engine and roared into the gas cloud. A hail of bullets blazed past the motorcycle, uselessly passing through the air where its rider should be. But their direction gave a good clue to the location of those inside. After letting his bike draw the enemy out, Dredd ran into lobby, both Lawgivers blazing. His remorseless advance was rewarded with the screams of men and women dying. Dredd was taking no prisoners.

Conchita and Riff had already reached the fiftieth floor when Dredd launched his attack on the lobby. The Citi-Def leader received a brief progress report from Fields, who was guarding the ground floor entrance with half a dozen others.

"Maguire, we're under attack! At least two Judges, maybe more. We can't hold them back, we–arghhhh!" The radio cut to static, then the sound of heavy boots approaching. Someone picked up Field's discarded radio.

"This is Judge Dredd. Who am I speaking to?"

"Conchita Maguire, leader of Oswald Mosley Citi-Def. We have taken control of this block and are ready–"

"Listen to me, Maguire. Stand down your teams or you will all suffer the consequences. A dozen Judges have just been murdered by a rocket attack launched from within this building. The penalty for killing a Judge is death. Surrender now, all of you, and I'll commute that sentence to life in the cubes. Otherwise I shoot to kill. What's your decision?"

"You're just one man, Dredd."

"But dozens of other Judges are on their way here now. You've got two minutes at most before Oswald Mosley is surrounded and your precious block becomes your tomb. I'm giving you one last chance. What do you say?"

Riff could hear Dredd's words, utterly implacable. The Judge would kill them all if necessary. Riff willed Conchita to listen to reason, but she was already shaking her head.

"This is our block now. The Justice Department refused to help rescue my daughter, so Oswald Mosley no longer recognises your authority!"

"Wrong answer," Dredd replied. "You just signed your death warrant."

The radio cut to static. Conchita switched frequencies. "Maguire to Citi-Def members. Judge Dredd has entered the building and is threatening to kill all of us. The solution is simple – kill him before he kills us. Maguire out!"

"Are you sure that's wise?" Riff asked.

Conchita drew a pistol and aimed it at Riff's head. "Are you questioning my judgement, Maltin?"

"No, no! I just–"

"Then you better take this." She threw the handgun to him. "You're going to need it to get out of here alive. Now come on: we're going to the one hundredth floor and nothing is going to stop us!"

Having cleared the lobby, Dredd broke open the Oswald Mosley environmental control box. Inside were all the building's failsafe systems, including secondary power, air conditioning and the anti-suicide nets.

"Dredd to Control, I need the judicial override invoked for air conditioning within Oswald Mosley."

"Roj that. Overriding system now."

"Got it. Dredd out." He was now able to vary the contents of the air being pumped into each con-apt and corridor. After the anarchy of Block Mania more than two decades before, the department had installed concussion gas cylinders in each citi-block. The contents could render every citizen inside a building unconscious for hours. Dredd began flooding each floor with the gas. Those Citi-Def members who kept on their masks would not be affected, but it should keep all the other residents out of the way while the block was subdued.

On the top floor of the building Nyon was arguing with the other alien families: two R'qeen, one from Wolfren and Gruchar the arthropod. The explosions had woken and frightened them all. But when they tried to leave they were dismayed to find themselves barricaded in, trapped on the one hundredth floor by Nyon's conflict with the human residents.

The argument had raged for many minutes and showed no signs of abating. It was only the gas seeping in from the ventilation shaft that stopped it. Gruchar was the first to react, his head lolling forward and his limbs sagging sleepily. Eventually the arthropod rolled over onto his back and stayed there, snoring loudly. Nyon realised what was going on.

"Something in the air!" he shouted. "The humans are trying to gas us all! Quickly, use your respiratory bypasses." All R'qeen had the ability to breathe by two distinct methods: taking air into their lungs like humans or by filtering air through the fat tendrils of flesh that hung from the back of their heads. The latter method required much more concentration and was only used in environments where the atmosphere was close to poisonous.

The family of creatures from Wolfren had no such capacity and quickly succumbed to the concussion gas seeping onto the top floor. Nyon returned to his con-apt to find Kasey also out cold, being nursed by Misch and Lleccas. They had realised what was happening and were breathing via their tendrils. "Who is doing all this?" Misch asked.

It was then that the first wave of bat-gliders began attacking the top floor.

06:00

Billy-Bob had volunteered to lead the bat-glider attack on the one hundredth floor, hoping to redeem himself after the incident in Conchita's con-apt. That slitch might believe he was a redneck who liked to kill first and think later, but he wanted to show the others he was the right person to take her place. Billy-Bob had his doubts Conchita was getting out of this mess alive, especially if he got the chance to take her out amidst all the confusion. Being leader of the 76-100 team wasn't enough anymore; he had higher ambitions.

Bat-gliders were cumbersome pieces of aerial equipment that looked much like they sounded, transforming the person inside the suit into a cross between a bat and a glider. Put one on, jump off a high building and extend your wings to fly – it was that simple in theory. In reality becoming proficient at bat-gliding required years of practice to learn how best to use the up-drifts and air currents around every citi-block. Prospective Citi-Def members were required to take a proficiency test with the equipment before being admitted to the squad.

Billy-Bob's second-in-command Aaron had passed the test with flying colours. The only problem was somebody else had snatched Aaron's specially enlarged bat-glider from the armoury before he arrived. The big man now found himself wedged inside a suit made for someone much smaller. It was all Aaron could do to keep the wings out level.

Once snug inside his own suit, Billy-Bob led the two dozen bat-gliders up to the ninetieth floor which had a special launching area built into a public balcony. The first wave of twelve flung themselves off the balcony, Billy-Bob at the front. They let the warm up-draft catch their wings and send them soaring towards the higher floors. The second wave was Aaron's responsibility but he fell like a stone after leaving the balcony, dropping twenty storeys until he got control of the under-sized suit.

"Aaron, what the hell are you doing?" Billy-Bob demanded. Each suit's flying helmet included a tiny receiver, transmitter and microphone for ease of communication.

"Just… coming," Aaron gasped, his breath stifled by the tortuously tight harness. He didn't have any children and Pressland doubted he would still be able to after this, such was the pressure applied by the crotch straps.

"I'm going in," Billy-Bob announced to the others. "First attack wave, follow me down!" He flipped one wing of his suit up and went into a steep dive, flinging himself towards the windows of the top floor con-apts. To the east the sun was just appearing over the horizon, light rising from beyond the Black Atlantic in the distance. Morning was breaking over Mega-City One.

In the lobby Dredd had used his judicial override to lock down Oswald Mosley's turbolifts, restricting the Citi-Def squad's movements. But solving one problem created another; how was he to gain access to the aliens on the top floor? Getting them out of the building would help defuse the situation, the sooner the better. "Dredd to Tek-Judge Brady, can you hear me?"

"Brady receiving. No answer yet about who supplied the armoury code."

"Acknowledged. I need a fast alternate route to the top of Oswald Mosley. Turbolifts are locked down and the stairs are perfect ambush territory."

"Hold on – I'll call up the building's blueprints." Seconds later Brady offered a solution. "Try the cleaning probe. It's a small platform that scuds up and down a tube at the side of the block, scouring the ventilation shaft. I'm sending a visual to your bike computer now."

Dredd strode to his Lawmaster, activating the small screen positioned behind the handlebars. It showed a tiny circle rising and falling just inside an exterior wall of Oswald Mosley. "Doesn't look very big," Dredd noted.

"It's not," Brady agreed. "Just over half a metre in diameter. You'll have to shed your shoulder pads, probably your elbow pads too to squeeze yourself in. When the probe reaches the top or bottom of the shaft, it pauses for six seconds before moving again. Makes the trip up and down once a minute, travelling at about ten metres a second."

"Sounds like being stuck inside a bullet," Dredd said.

"That's not a bad analogy. You wanted a fast alternate route – you never mentioned comfort."

"Roj that. Dredd to Control: where's my backup?"

"It'll be there soon," Control replied. "However Sector Chief Caine has imposed a no-fly zone around Oswald Mosley. Says she doesn't want to lose any more H-wagons to rocket attacks. So your backup is coming by road, not by air."

"Well, I can't wait any longer. Dredd out!"

Lleccas screamed when the first bat-glider thudded against the floor-to-ceiling window. Billy-Bob used the suction pads on his knees and elbow pads to cling to the exterior, his wings a frightening silhouette in the dawn's early light. With his hands free, Billy-Bob pulled a laser-drill from his belt and began slicing through the glasseen of the window. More and more of the bat-gliders landed beside him, swarming over the outside of the building.

The other R'qeen families ran into the con-apt, looking for Nyon. "You brought this upon us," one of the broodfathers said accusingly. "What do you suggest we do now?"

Nyon looked at his pairling who was still hugging Misch and the human child to herself. "We fight back!" he vowed. 'Lleccas, take all the broodlings into one room and keep them there. We will stop the humans as long as we can."

She nodded hurriedly and began ushering all the offspring away. Nyon followed her, pressing a laser-knife into her hand. "You saw what they did to Keno. If we can't keep them out…"

Lleccas took the laser-knife and kissed her pairling. "I understand."

Dredd pulled open an access hatch to the cleaning probe. Inside was a smooth circular shaft, cool air rushing outwards from it. Dredd leaned in to peer upwards but hastily withdrew his head. The probe was racing down the shaft towards him. It paused briefly in front of the Judge then shot back up again. Brady had been right, the interior was only just large enough to accommodate a human passenger. Dredd hastily began shedding the bulkier elements of his uniform, aware he only had one minute before the probe returned.

Fifty seconds later the air began whistling past Dredd again, indicating the probe was returning. He stepped back two paces and prepared to throw himself into the space. The probe arrived and Dredd flung himself at it, just pulling his arms and legs inside before he was shooting up the inside of the shaft, metal screaming past him in a blur.

Billy-Bob smashed in the section of window he had been cutting, the glasseen dropping into the con-apt's main room. The aliens had retreated to other parts of the top floor but they would soon be found, Billy-Bob was confident of that. He punched the clasp on his chest, letting the

wings of his now redundant bat-glider fall away. Billy-Bob drew a bulging
Deathbringer machine pistol from the holster at his waist and signalled
the others around him. "I'm going in. Follow me!" He lowered both his
legs inside the hole and dropped to the floor of the con-apt before scuttling across the main room like a beetle. More and more of the Citi-Def
bat-glider squad dropped in behind him.

A shape raced past the front door of the con-apt, a blue blur of movement. Billy-Bob began firing, his Deathbringer spraying the doorway
and the wall beyond it with bullets. Others joined in the shooting, happy
to have the chance of using their training for once.

"Cease firing!" Billy-Bob shouted. By now nearly a dozen of the Citi-
Def had joined him inside. Billy-Bob could see Aaron and the second
attack wave circling overhead, awaiting the order to come in.

"Aaron, you and your boys hang back for the minute. We don't know
how much resistance we're dealing with here."

"Affirmative," Aaron replied.

Billy-Bob sent half his men up one wall of the con-apt and the rest up
the other side. As they reached a doorway two of the Citi-Def would
burst in, guns blazing. But the con-apt had been evacuated, with no targets emerging so far. Billy-Bob stood up, relaxing his grip on the
Deathbringer. "All right, everybody knows the drill. We secure the floor
room by room, going two by two. Check all the corners and watch each
other's backs. I don't want any nasty surprises!"

Billy-Bob stopped as a long drip of mucus fell on the barrel of his
weapon. "What the drokk?" He looked up in time to see Nyon and the
other R'qeen clinging to the high ceiling of the con-apt, their three-
fingered hands adhering to the surface above them, razor-sharp talons
growing from each finger like knives. "Sweet baby Jovus..."

Nyon screamed an attack cry and the R'qeen dropped on their prey.

Dredd checked the clips in his two Lawgivers as the probe hurtled
upwards, the g-force pulling at his facial muscles. Then the air-piercing
noise began dropping pitch as the probe's upwards momentum
decreased. When it reached the top, there would be only seconds to get
out or die trying. Abruptly the probe stopped, throwing Dredd up into
the roof.

Five seconds. He slumped back down to the floor, still trying to get his
bearings. Four. Dredd kicked out with his boots, smashing away the
exterior access hatch. Three. The probe would slice him in two if he
wasn't all the way out when it began descending. Two. Dredd had one
leg and one shoulder out, but his twin Lawgivers were caught on the
side of the access hatch. One. Wrenching his weapons clear, the Judge

threw himself away from the probe. Zero. The probe flung itself downwards again, wind whistling past Dredd as he lay gasping for breath on the floor.

Once the probe was gone, he could hear screaming and gunfire nearby. The Citi-Def must have found its own way up to the top floor. Dredd was too late – the slaughter had already begun. Pulling himself to his feet, Dredd ran towards the sounds of death, both guns ready to fire.

Aaron watched in horror as the aliens attacked his friends, tearing at the Citi-Def members' protective clothing, slicing through metal and flesh. As the first gout of blood coloured the air, Billy-Bob's bellowed command almost overloaded Aaron's helmet radio.

"Get them!"

The 76-100 leader began firing randomly, his Deathbringer swinging through the air, bullets indiscriminately puncturing R'qeen and human. The others began shooting too, screams and gunfire filling air already crowded with cries of pain and death.

The other bat-gliders still in the air were also watching, unsure how to react. "What do we do, Aaron?" one of them asked.

The big man floated above the melee. He had never wanted this, never expected to see active duty. For him the Citi-Def was a way of making friends. "Stand down," he said. "We can't help them now."

"But you can't leave them!"

"Watch me," Aaron replied and let one wing dip. He glided away in a slow spiral, descending to the deserted skedway one hundred storeys below. A few stayed above the battle scene watching impotently, but the rest followed Aaron's example. They might not like having aliens in the block but it wasn't a cause worth dying for.

Billy-Bob had lost his Deathbringer and was now down to just a kitchen laser. He passed it back and forth between his hands as he retreated towards the glasseen window. The alien leader was closing in on him, its lips pulled back in a cruel mockery of a smile to reveal row upon row of teeth.

"Stay back!" Billy-Bob warned. "I know how to use this thing!"

"So do I," Nyon replied in halting English. "My brood shall feast on your remains for many weeks, human."

"Drokk you!" Billy-Bob screamed and threw himself at the alien.

When Dredd reached the con-apt the floor was soaked red with blood. The walls were studded with bullet holes and scorch marks, while the room was strewn with severed limbs and corpses. One of the R'qeen was still alive, just. It gestured to Dredd who approached, stepping carefully through the carnage. "Too... late..." Nyon gasped. "You're... too late... human..." Then he said no more.

The Judge activated his helmet radio. "Dredd to Control, I've reached the top floor of Oswald Mosley. Citi-Def got in here, looks like they came by bat-glider. There was a pitched battle – plenty of casualties on both sides. I'll investigate the rest of the rooms for survivors. Where's that backup?"

"Just arriving now."

Miller had the transporter stop just short of Oswald Mosley. "We go the rest of the way on foot," she told her strike team. They were all clad in a double-layer of body armour, with Widowmaker assault rifles at the ready. "No point giving these Citi-Def bozos any big targets to fire at. Spread out and move in."

The Judges jumped out of the vehicle and began advancing on their target. Miller had the three best long-range shots stay at the perimeter of the nearest building, Enoch Powell Block. "I want you scanning the windows for snipers. If you see anyone firing from inside, take them out. Shoot to kill." The trio nodded grimly and moved off to find the best vantage points. "The rest of you: keep it tight but don't get bunched up. I'll lead."

Miller emerged from cover and started running towards Oswald Mosley, zigzagging from side to side as she did. Shots began ringing out from the upper floors, but the snipers were soon eliminated by Miller's sharpshooters. She was across the open space in thirty seconds, the remainder of her strike team following. Within a minute all twenty-two Judges were in the lobby.

"Turbolifts are locked down so we take the stairs, two by two," their leader said. "This is going to get bloody but we're not taking any prisoners. If it moves, shoot it. Last one to the ninety-ninth floor has to help carry out the bodies. Let's move!"

Dredd found five unconscious aliens in the hundredth floor's central circular corridor. He recognised one of them as an arthropod, no doubt from Andromeda IV. The others were all from another species, their bodies covered in thick hair, prominent ridges running down the centre of their faces.

"Dredd to Control, I've located five alien survivors in Oswald Mosley. Looks like the concussion gas kept them out of the fighting. Am continuing my search of the top floor."

The Judge began moving cautiously onward when a gasp from nearby stopped him. Somebody else was alive up here.

Misch could feel the intruder getting closer. She was leaning against the door of the dark chamber. Behind her Lleccas, still clutching the laser-knife, was guarding the other broodlings and Kasey. Misch concentrated herself on the approaching human.

She had sensed her broodfather's death and the loss of so many others, both R'qeen and human. It was an ugly thing that had happened. Misch did not know if she would ever recover from the shock of what she had felt. But her gift was important, it could help keep the rest of them alive.

The human who was approaching was ready to kill, she could sense that, but there was something else clouding his thoughts. Unable to easily discern them, Misch reached out with her senses.

Too many dead already – wasted lives.

Need to find the others.

That sound – is the girl here after all?

Wait, something else – something in my head!

Get out! Get out of my mind!

Misch fell backwards, as if she had been punched. She cried out as her head hit the ground with a thump. No, no, she thought, I've given us away! The door was ripped open, and light flooded in, temporarily blinding those inside. Standing over them was an imposing figure, weapon drawn and ready to fire.

Lleccas stood up, brandishing the laser-knife. "You shall not take them," she screeched in R'qeen. "I will die killing you before that happens!"

The human took a step forwards to confront Lleccas.

"No, wait!" Misch cried out in Allspeak. Her broodmother and the human stopped. "He's here to help us, I can feel it!"

Dredd touched a hand to his helmet. "You were the one in my head."

The R'qeen girl approached him. "Yes. I had to know whether you wanted to hurt us." She took his hand in her own, the green gauntlet dwarfing her three small fingers. "Thank you for rescuing us."

Dredd looked around the room. "Are there any more elsewhere?"

"No," Lleccas replied in Allspeak. "We are the last." She rested a kindly hand on her broodling's head. "Misch told us what happened to my pairling Nyon and the others."

The Judge began to usher them out into the circular corridor. "We need to evacuate all of you, the sooner the better. The Citi-Def has already launched one attack on this floor and failed, their leader will be getting desperate. There's no telling what she'll try to do next." He reactivated his helmet radio. "Dredd to Control, I've located the last of the aliens. Immediate evac required!"

"No can do, Dredd. Caine is keeping the no-fly zone in place."

"Put me through to her!"

Conchita and Riff had reached the ninety-ninth floor, the reporter left breathless by the long climb. Conchita had gathered a dozen Citi-Def members on the way up, ordering the rest to defend the stairwell below. She was dismayed to discover the emergency access door to the top floor was still impassable.

"I had hoped Billy-Bob and his bat-gliders would take care of this for me," Conchita scowled. She tried to contact them but the aerial wing's radio channel remained silent. "Typical, have to do everything myself. Pass me that carryall." From inside the bag Conchita pulled out a rubbery grey brick and a fistful of wires. She clamped the brick to the side of the door near the hinges and began plunging wires into it.

"What's that?" Riff asked, aware his hovercam was still recording events, even if his earpiece had long since fallen silent.

"An incendiary device, not unlike the one my boys planted in Robert Hatch. Blow the door in and burn out the top floor of this block," Conchita said.

"But if your daughter is still alive up there, won't the fire kill her too?"

"She chose to be with the aliens instead of me," Conchita replied. "She has to face the consequences."

"But you told me she'd been abducted!" Riff protested. "That was the reason you mobilised the Citi-Def!"

"She chose to be with those alien freaks. She has to pay for that!"

"With her life? And what about all those from your Citi-Def squad who have sacrificed themselves for your crusade?" Riff turned to those gathered behind him. "How do you feel about this?"

"We didn't know," the nearest one admitted. "We thought this was a righteous cause, defending our block against–"

He was cut short by a bullet through the brain. Riff was sprayed with the dead man's blood. When he had wiped it away from his eyes, he found Conchita pointing her gun at him. "You're drokking insane!" he whispered.

"No, I'm a mother and I love my daughter. If she won't listen to me then she has to be punished," Conchita insisted. "Now, I suggest you all leave. This is between me and the aliens."

The remaining squad members were already retreating down the stairs but Riff stayed for one last question. "I've still got that pistol you gave me. What's to stop me shooting you?"

Conchita smiled. "It isn't loaded. If you're leaving, you better hurry. This is going to blow in the next few minutes."

"No, Control, I do not wish to speak with Dredd," Sector Chief Caine said. "I'm rather busy. Tell him to be patient. Caine out!" She returned to deleting files from her office computer system as someone knocked on her office door. "Come in." Brady opened the door and entered. "Close the door behind you, we don't want to be disturbed." Brady did as he was bid and then stood in front of Caine's desk.

"You sent for me, ma'am."

"That's right. I understand you've been giving Dredd a lot of help during this graveyard shift."

"Yes, ma'am. He helped me become a Tek-Judge instead of just another perp, so I wanted to repay a little of that debt."

"Commendable sentiments. However there is little room for sentiment within the department." Caine pulled open a drawer in her desk and reached inside it with both hands. "I notice you've been making particular enquiries about the armoury code for Oswald Mosley Block, trying to find out who leaked it to the Citi-Def. What progress have you made?"

"Well, it's proving to be something of a mystery. Channel 27 eventually admitted to acting as a conduit for the code's transmission into Oswald Mosley, but the news editor claimed he had been sent it by Judge Stammers."

"That fits Stammers's profile," Caine said. "Rabidly anti-alien and just stupid enough to do something like this. So where's the mystery?"

Brady's face lit up. "The message was sent to Channel 27 just after five this morning. But Stammers was reported dead two hours earlier!"

"So he recorded the message before he died and arranged for it to be transmitted later. I still don't see–"

"That's just it. Channel 27's system shows the message was sent as a live text-only message, not as a recording. And there's something else. It wasn't sent from any public vidphone booth, it came from inside this building! So someone here leaked the code to the Citi-Def squad. Whoever did that is culpable for the rocket attack on the H-wagon that killed Deputy Sector Chief Temple and eleven other Judges."

"This is shocking news," Caine said. "Have you told anybody else about this yet? I wouldn't want word leaking out. The culprit might hear and take flight."

"Nobody else knows except you and I," the Tek-Judge said.

"Let's keep it that way, shall we?" Caine pulled a Lawgiver from inside the drawer of her desk, a silencer fitted snugly over the end of the barrel.

She fired twice, both bullets thudding into Brady's chest. He tumbled backwards to the floor, still reacting with surprise. Caine stood up and walked round the desk to examine the dying Tek-Judge. "After all, we wouldn't want to create a panic. *Sector Chief Escalates Anti-Alien Conflict* doesn't make a very good headline for the department, does it?"

Brady coughed up blood, his hands feebly trying to staunch the bleeding from his wounds. "W–why?" he gasped.

"You and Dredd have forced my hand," Caine replied. "I had hoped to slip away quietly, with nobody else getting hurt. But your private investigation triggered the alarms I had built into the sector house comms systems. So you had to die. Sorry about that, but these things happen. Now, if you'll excuse me, I have one or two little chores to complete before I depart this sector. Goodbye, Brady." She snapped the microphone from his helmet radio and switched off the computer screen on her desk before leaving, locking the door on her way out.

Brady tried to drag himself across the floor towards the desk, but his strength was fading fast. A coughing fit gripped his body, blood spread outwards across the floor beneath him, and his spasming legs kicked splashes against the side of the desk. The Tek-Judge looked up at the picture window. The sun was over the horizon now, lighting up the cityscape once more. Despite the absence of Weather Control, it was going to be a glorious day. But Brady's eyes could no longer see the brilliance of the blue sky. Brady's eyes could no longer see anything.

Miller and her strike team had met surprisingly little resistance as they climbed the stairs inside Oswald Mosley. A cluster of hardcore Citi-Def members had attempted to lay an ambush at the twenty-seventh floor but it only required a mixture of ricochet and heatseeker bullets to kill the ringleaders. Those left alive quickly surrendered, grateful to have met someone other than Dredd. "He says he's gonna kill us all if he finds us," one squad member said, her face full of fear.

Miller shoved her Widowmaker assault rifle under the woman's chin. "Get on your frequency and tell the others. If they surrender now they might get out of here alive. If they don't, we'll let Dredd have them. It's their choice."

After that the charge up the stairs passed with little incident. Each new group of Citi-Def fighters they encountered were more than happy to lay down their weapons and surrender. Miller's biggest problem was having to assign two of her team to supervising the removal of each group of prisoners. Still, the concussion gas had done its job and kept the other residents sedated and out of danger. The remnants of Miller's team were passing the sixtieth floor when another cluster of Citi-Def members appeared, all with their hands behind their heads. "We surrender, we surrender!" the man nearest the front cried out.

"How many of you left?" Miller demanded.

"There's just Conchita Maguire. She's still up on the ninety-ninth floor," another voice replied. Riff Maltin appeared from among the squad members and approached the Judges, his hovercam just behind him as always. "She's got an incendiary device like the one used at Robert Hatch. She plans to burn out the aliens on the top floor."

"You're the one who's been inciting these idiots to riot!" Miller snarled at the reporter. Her first punch broke Riff's nose, sending blood gushing down his face. Her second punch broke his jaw, the bone smashing beneath her gauntlet's steel-capped knuckles. The reporter collapsed to the stairs, his hovercam moving in for a close-up of his injuries. "Without your inflammatory reports, the Citi-Def would have seen sense and backed down hours ago. But you kept turning up the heat, until Conchita and her cronies didn't dare lose face. I'll be holding you personally responsible for every death that's taken place here!"

She swung the hovercam round so it was filming her face. "The same goes for everyone at Channel 27 and anybody still watching this. Turn yourself in to the nearest sector house. This transmission ends right now!"

Miller smashed the hovercam against a rockcrete wall repeatedly until few fragments bigger than her fist remained. She assigned half of her remaining team to escort Riff and the other prisoners down the stairs, while she pressed on with three other Judges. There was just the ringleader left to subdue, but Conchita was always going to be the most difficult. It was her missing daughter that had been one of the catalysts for all of this. This wasn't just about hating aliens, this was personal.

Conchita finished wiring the incendiary device together and set the timer for sixty seconds. That would give her enough time to retreat a safe distance down the stairs and get her flame-thrower ready. Any aliens that survived the initial explosion were going to be burnt to a crisp, one way or another.

Caine emerged from the turbolift into the sector house's registration area, a smile playing about her lips. The Judge behind 87's check-in desk saw her and called out. Caine stopped, sighed and walked towards him. "Yes, what it is? I'm running late for an early meeting at Justice Central."

"It's just that Dredd's been trying to contact you for some time. Apparently he's very unhappy about something."

"Well, that's no great surprise. I've got a hover pod waiting for me outside. Tell Dredd I'll give him a call en route to my destination. Anything else?"

"No, ma'am, just that."

Caine smiled. "Very well. Oh, could you tell Tek-Division that Brady is fixing a fault in my office and is not to be disturbed under any circumstances. He tells me it may take several hours. Is that quite clear?"

"Yes, ma'am!"

"Excellent. Well, see you on the streets." She marched from the sector house, never to return. Once outside she stepped into a waiting hover pod. "The spaceport and make it snappy," Caine told the droid driver before activating her helmet radio. "Control, this is Caine. Patch me through to Dredd."

Dredd sealed off the air vents, stopping the flow of concussion gas into the top floor. It didn't take long for Gruchar or the Wolfren family to revive, no doubt thanks to their alien physiognomy. But the Judge was having less luck undoing the damage Nyon had wrought on the turbo-lift doors, which remained fused shut. He would have to find a way to reopen access to the emergency stairs, unless an H-wagon could be brought in to evacuate the aliens. A voice from his helmet radio offered new hope. "Miller to Dredd, can you hear me?"

"Loud and clear. What's been happening?"

"I brought in a strike team and we've cleared most of the hostiles. Just Conchita Maguire left."

"Do you know where she is?"

"According to the others she's about to detonate an incendiary device on the emergency access door to your floor. It could blow at any time and we're still forty storeys below you!"

Dredd shouted at Misch and the other aliens to start running. "Get as far from here as you can!" He pulled open a door and crouched behind it, using the metal rectangle as a shield.

"Caine to Dredd: you wanted to talk to me?"

"Not now! This place could–"

The explosion cut off his transmission.

Caine pulled off her helmet, the radio a frenzy of white noise. "How very rude."

The emergency access door exploded into the top floor of Oswald Mosley. It sliced neatly through three walls and out of a large glasseen window. It took nearly a minute for the crumpled and charred rectangle of metal to hit the ground below, burying itself into the deserted skedway.

The fireball from the explosion expanded into the circular corridor and split into halves, each flying out sideways. The door Dredd was crouching behind buckled and boiled, but the reinforced metal core held firm, protecting him from the flames. The twin fireballs scorched round the corridor, splaying sideways through any open doors and incinerating everything in its path. Fortunately Kasey, Misch and all the other aliens had retreated to the far side of Oswald Mosley, closing the doors behind them. By the time the fireball had reached the final barrier, the flames were burning themselves out.

Dredd stood up and looked along the corridor. The walls and floor were still burning but the immediate danger was past. But smoke inhalation or fire could still claim everyone alive on this level. The need to evacuate was now more urgent than ever.

"Where is she?" a woman's voice screeched. "Where's the little monster that caused all of this?" Conchita Maguire stepped through the now empty doorway to the emergency stairs, a lit flame-thrower clasped in her hands, twin fuel tanks mounted on her back.

"Are you talking about your daughter or yourself?" Dredd asked from behind the protection of his door.

Conchita whirled round, sending a fresh ball of flame at the wilting rectangle. "I'm talking about Kasey! My darling little Kasey, the waste of skin and bones that has shamed me from the moment she was born!"

"Not what I call motherly love," Dredd replied, his words goading Conchita still further. He was rewarded with another dose of flame.

"What would you know about it? Did you ever have a mother?"

"The Law is my family!" Dredd shouted. "Look what's happened to yours!"

"My family loves me!" Conchita screamed.

"Your daughter ran away, she'd rather be with aliens than with you."

"Not that little slitch! She was a mistake. I'm talking about my sons!"

"Ramone and Dermot?"

"That's them. Two of the finest boys a mother ever had."

Dredd was backing slowly away from Conchita, always keeping the door between himself and her. "If they're so fine, why haven't you heard from them?"

"How did you know that?"

"Because they died last night. Judge Stammers gunned them down in cold blood and pushed their bodies into a chem pit." He listened carefully to her reply, using it to determine her position and take aim.

"No, you're lying!" Conchita raged.

"You'll never know – I just wanted you to think about that as you died. Armour piercing!" Dredd fired six times in succession, each bullet piercing the door and travelling on through Conchita's body. As they spat out of her back the bullets punctured the tanks of the flame-thrower, releasing jets of flammable gas into the air. It mingled with the flames from the nozzle of her weapon. Conchita was toast.

Miller was running up the stairs past the ninety-fifth floor when the sec-ond fireball exploded. It flung itself out of the doorway five storeys up and surged down the stairwell, roasting everything in its path. "Take cover!" Miller screamed.

Dredd rolled over and over, trying to extinguish the flames that had engulfed him, but their grip on his uniform was too strong. He was being burned alive. It was the aliens that saved him; Lleccas and Gruchar dragged him out of the corridor and doused him with water. Misch and Kasey had closed the door behind them so now all the sur-vivors were trapped in one room.

Once the flames were extinguished, Dredd reactivated his helmet radio. "Miller, can you still hear me?"

"Just," came the coughing reply. "What was that second explosion?"

Dredd noticed Kasey, her face still showing the bruises and scars inflicted by her mother. "Conchita Maguire won't be hurting anyone anymore."

"Well, that's good news," Miller said. "The bad news is we can't get close to you. The fire has cut off all access from below. What's your sta-tus?"

"Not good. All the survivors are in one room with me, but we're cut off by the flames. There is no escape except the window. We need evac and now!" A burst of static indicated another voice cutting into the con-versation.

"Control to Dredd: Chief Judge Hershey has overruled the no-fly zone imposed by Sector Chief Caine. H-wagons should be with you any minute."

"Thank Grud for that. Dredd out!" He let himself slump against a wall, exhaustion catching up with him.

Misch whispered something in her broodmother's ear. Lleccas smiled and nodded. Then the R'qeen child ventured over to the Judge and cleared her throat. "Excuse me," she said in perfect English. "Would you like me to make you feel better?"

Dredd opened his eyes and looked down at the broodling. "Why? Have you got a med-kit stashed about here somewhere?"

"No, but I do have the gift of metema. It can ease away your weariness."

Kasey stood beside her friend. "She makes everyone feel better."

Dredd shrugged. "Give it a try, kid."

Misch rested her hand inside that of Dredd and closed her eyes, reaching out to drive away his fatigue. After a few moments she staggered and took her hand away, Kasey helping the R'qeen girl to stay upright. Dredd straightened. His muscles and joints were not as stiff as before, and his back was slowly unbending.

"What's your name?"

"Misch."

"Thank you, Misch. If there's ever anything I can do for you..."

She beckoned him to bend over and whispered something into his helmet.

Dredd frowned slightly, before nodding. "I'll see what I can arrange."

Then the H-wagon appeared out of the dawn sky, the sunlight glinting off its metal panels and glasseen windows.

07:00

Caine emerged from the spaceport restrooms a different woman. Gone was the close-cropped mass of black curls; a copper bob replaced them. Shed was the Sector Chief's uniform, supplanted by a stylish catsuit of black leathereen that gripped her in all the right places. She wore matching stiletto boots. Her eyes looked different: dark green contact lenses in place of the usual hazel pupils. Even her travel documents were a lie; she now assumed the fresh identity of galactic bounty hunter Dakota Biggs. The new persona helped explain the small but deadly weapon concealed in her hip pocket.

The flight to Luna-1 and then onwards to the Eden colony on Mars, had already being called. Caine presented her documents to the Judge on Customs, careful to keep her smile friendly while idly leaning forwards to give him an eyeful of her cleavage. Law enforcers might not be permitted sexual or romantic liaisons, but that didn't stop them looking, in her experience. Sure enough, he waved her through to the first class waiting room after admiring the view for a few moments longer than were strictly necessary.

The waiting room had been an agonising experience. Caine's eyes constantly darted to the doorway, expecting a Judge to burst in at any time looking for her. But the expectation went unmet. After several minutes the first class passengers were called through to take their seats on the flight. There were only three others joining her on this jaunt, all of them frequent flyers judging by their bored expressions.

Even while being strapped into a seat for lift-off, Caine found herself waiting for a gauntlet-clad hand to rest itself on her shoulder, a quiet word in her ear as a Lawgiver was pressed into her back. But the preflight procedures passed without incident and the engines were engaged. At last Caine let herself relax. She ordered a champagne cocktail from the robotic steward and closed her eyes. Now, this was the life! No more reports to read, no more bureaucracy to tangle with, no more responsibility. She was looking forward to being a rich, dangerous civ...

"Your champagne, ma'am," a voice growled.

Caine looked up to find Dredd standing over her, Lawgiver in one hand, a glass of bubbling liquid in the other. His uniform was a charred mess, his face blackened and burnt. Caine took the glass and sipped at the contents. "This is warm," she protested.

"So was the top floor of Oswald Mosley. Get over it."

"Fair point," Caine agreed and took another sip. "How did you find me?"

"The Desk Judge at the sector house got suspicious after you said 'See you on the streets' as you left. you'd never been that nice to him. They found Brady's body in your office. He had written CAINE = KILLER in his own blood. Seems the SJS have been watching you and Summerbee for months."

"I've had my suspicions of that," Caine conceded. "When you turned up, I was convinced Hershey had sent you in to find evidence against me."

"That's why you reacted so strongly to my arrival."

"It seemed the best strategy – keep you off-balance, moving from one end of the sector to the other and you wouldn't have time to investigate me. None of it would have been necessary if the Heavy Metal Kid had done its job properly."

"That was meant for me?"

"Just like you should have died inside Oswald Mosley. Grud knows, I put enough obstacles in your way." Caine finished her champagne. "Well, what's the plan now? Shoot me here or ship me to Titan for a long slow death there?"

"I'm asking the questions," Dredd snapped. "The fire at Robert Hatch; you used Stammers and Riley to torch the building so Summerbee could get the contract to construct the new Grand Halls of Justice there. What was your cut of the deal? Half? A quarter?"

"I don't know why you bother asking me questions if you're going to answer them yourself," Caine said, shoving her hands petulantly into her pockets. "Summerbee and I were going halves, my nest egg for retirement."

"Judges don't retire. They die in the line of duty or take the Long Walk."

"That's where you're wrong, Dredd. The department was about to retire me. Except they called it a sideways promotion. I was a rising star once, destined for big things. I thought I'd be heading up a division of my own by now, perhaps have a seat on the Council of Five, maybe even be Chief Judge one day. Instead I was to be shuffled sideways, pushed out for someone younger so Hershey can make her mark on the department! Well what about me? What about my contribution? Twenty years a Judge and what did I have to show for it? Nothing, except a synthetic lung and bionic eye implants. I was getting put out to pasture, past my prime, out of date. Well not this Judge!" Caine pulled her hands from her pockets, a tiny pistol in her grasp, one finger on the trigger.

"You can't escape," Dredd said wearily. "Every Judge between here and Pluto has your new identity by now. Fire that and you'll be dead in moments."

"How right you are," Caine replied, lifting the pistol up to her mouth. She pulled the trigger before Dredd could wrench the weapon from her grasp.

"She would have killed herself sooner or later," Miller said when Dredd walked out of the spaceship. "Least this way the department doesn't have to pay for her to be shipped to the judicial prison on Titan."

The two Judges strolled through the spaceport as a forensic team from Tek-Division moved in to clean up the mess. Overhead a robotic tannoy regretfully announced a delay in the departure of the morning flight to Luna-1 and Mars, due to "technical difficulties."

Miller smiled at the euphemism. "Technical difficulties must mean how hard it is to get fresh brains out of such plush upholstery."

Chief Judge Hershey was waiting for them outside. "I hear she's dead."

"Killed herself rather than go to Titan," Dredd said. "How long have you known about Caine?"

"Known? Only for the past hour or so. Suspected? More than a year. That's why I sent you in, Dredd. Thought it might make Caine show her hand."

"It did. You could have told me I was acting as bait for your trap."

"Better to keep you ignorant and Caine guessing at your motives," Hershey said.

"What about the plans to build a new Grand Hall of Justice in Sector 87? Was that just another lure for Caine and Summerbee?" Miller asked.

"Yes. It was the only way to draw out as big a fish as Summerbee. And it worked."

"Just a shame so many good people had to die to prove it," Dredd said.

Hershey nodded. "You know, with Caine and Temple dead, there's a vacancy for a new Sector Chief in 87…"

Dredd didn't want to know. "I did my time in the Pit. I like being out on the streets, not stuck behind some desk."

"Actually, I was making the offer to Judge Miller," the Chief Judge said.

"Oh." Dredd cleared his throat. "Good choice."

"That's what I thought," Hershey agreed. "Well, Lynn, how about it?"

"I didn't think I'd get a shot at the big chair, in view of my record."

"A dozen exemplary years on the streets, good leadership skills and a willingness to confront corruption in the force – even from old friends. I think that outweighs one youthful indiscretion," the Chief Judge said. "We've all made mistakes in our time, haven't we, Dredd?"

"Some more than others," he replied, prompting a smile from Hershey.

"It will still have to go before the Council of Five," she said. "But if you're willing to take the post it could be yours."

Miller nodded happily. "I'll do it!"

"Good. Well, if that's everything settled–"

Dredd held up a hand to interrupt the Chief Judge. "There's one other matter arising from the incidents at Oswald Mosley."

"I suspect Tek-Division will condemn the building. Those residents not going to the cubes for their part in the lawlessness will have to be rehoused until the block can be rebuilt."

"No, it was something else," Dredd said. "I have a request to pass on."

EPILOGUE
08:00

"You can open your eyes," Lleccas said. Kasey and Misch pulled their hands away from their faces and gasped. They were standing in the middle of a palatial bungalow, the open plan lounge sprawling out before them, large sofas and luxurious furnishings spread around the huge space.

"What is this place?" Misch asked.

"It used to belong to a rich man called Summerbee," Dredd said. "When he died he left all his residences to the city. The Chief Judge has said Summerbee's properties can be used to house all the alien families who lost their homes in the fire at Robert Hatch. Lleccas and Misch will be living here from now on, with several other R'qeen families."

"Oh," said Kasey sadly. "Where will I go?"

"That's up to you," Lleccas replied. "All your family are dead but the Judge says you can stay with us, if you want."

The human girl turned to Dredd, her face full of hope. "Can I? Really?"

"If you want. It may not be as easy as you think. Most of the R'qeen cannot speak English like Misch and many do not know Allspeak either."

"Misch will help me," Kasey announced.

The R'qeen broodling nodded. While Lleccas, Kasey and the others went off to explore the rest of their new home, Misch stayed behind with Dredd.

"I wanted to thank you, for making my wish happen," she said.

"Your broodfather is dead, you've been burnt out of two homes in twelve hours. Not what I'd call a happy ending."

Misch smiled. "It would have been worse, without you. Thanks."

Dredd nodded, watching the alien child run off to be with the others. The Judge walked back out of the luxurious home to his Lawmaster motorcycle. "Dredd to Control, you got anything for me?"

"Nothing at this time."

"In that case I'm done for this graveyard shift. Sign me off."

"Where will you be if needed?"

"On a sleep machine. I'll be back on call at nine. Dredd out!"

BLACK ATLANTIC

BY SIMON JOWET
AND PETER J. EVANS

MEGA-CITY ONE, 2130

1. DUST BUST

"Careful with that, you barely-sentient gimp!"

The woman's shout was so loud, so unexpected, that Arnold Crobetti almost dropped the canister a second time. He started, the mech-splint around his left leg whining and stiffening reflexively, and only just managed to pass the canister to the next man in line before it slid out of his fingers. Drokk it, the things were *heavy*!

Crobetti turned back to grab the next drum from the man behind, and saw the woman striding towards him, her long lab coat flapping. There was an expression on her sharp features that he didn't like the look of at all. "Aw c'mon," he whined. "I had my foot under it when it came down, honest. Barely scratched the paint..."

The woman stopped in front of him, glaring. "Listen to me, you throwback," she snapped, poking him in the chest. "Every one of these canisters is worth more than you are. More than your family, your friends, their friends and their pets put together!" One of the other men in the chain sniggered and the woman looked up and fixed him with that awful glare. The snigger trailed off into silence.

"That goes for all of you. Remember that your boss is paying for this. If the equipment gets damaged, so do you." And with that, she turned her back on the lot of them and stormed off.

Crobetti swallowed. "Man, is that any way for a professor to talk?" He took hold of the next drum – carefully – and handed it on.

Little Petey, the next man in the chain, lifted it out of his grasp without trying. "Doctor," he singsonged. "She's a doctor. I heard one of the tekkies call her doctor."

Oh brother. Crobetti's eyes went up. There were twenty guys in the chain, passing the heavy drums one to the next, all the way from the freezer wagon on the factory's loading ramp to the building itself. Twenty of Big Jimmy's finest, and he had to be next to Little Petey Steene.

Little Petey was a head taller than Crobetti, but there wasn't much inside that head to speak of. He could squash shell casings flat between his finger and thumb, but he had trouble counting past four and once he started talking it was difficult to get him to shut up. He'd just keep saying the same thing, over and over and over, with a grin on his face so wide it looked as though his jaw was about to fall off. Big Jimmy only kept him on as part of the MegEast Mob because he could pull people's noses off with his bare hands.

There was a small scar on Petey's left temple, and Crobetti wondered if maybe a bullet had gone in there one time and scrambled things up a little.

Not that Crobetti was exactly a stranger to bullets himself. The mech-splint holding his leg together was enough evidence of that. The wound he'd got from last month's rumble with those MegCentral sneckers hadn't healed yet, and the splint was old and needed tuning. It made him limp, and it had made him drop one of Doctor grud-face Hellermann's precious canisters.

"'Yes, Doctor Hellermann. Right away, Doctor Hellermann.' That's what he said," Petey was still chanting. Crobetti grimaced and hauled another drum around for him.

"Yeah, okay, Petey. Thanks for clearing that up. Now grab." Anything to stop him getting into a rhythm. Crobetti limped round to take another item of Hellermann's equipment – some kind of armoured crate, this time – and pass it on to Little Petey. He looked longingly at the pile of weapons he and the boys had brought with them from MegEast, expecting that the job would involve using them on members of the MegSouth mob. Not acting like a gang of baggage-bots at Grissom Spaceport.

"If I don't see another one of these things as long as I live, I'll be a happy man," Arnold muttered as he limped back to move yet another of the canisters down the line.

"I'm a happy man," Little Petey chimed in. "I've always been a happy man. Can't remember a time when I wasn't happy. Happy, happy, happy. That's Little Petey..."

Arnold Crobetti sighed. It was going to be a long night.

Tek-Judge Gleick was having a long night too. He had been watching MegEast mobsters haul drums about for far too long, and Little Petey's singsong ramblings were making the job almost intolerable. Still, annoying or not, these scum were certainly going to be a worthy catch for the ground team. Not only did most of them have a rap sheet as long as the proverbial Judge's arm, but the canisters they were manhandling from the truck were plastered with biohazard stickers – not something one would normally expect to find being driven about in a Sunshine Syn-thifoods freezer wagon.

But then, when Elize Hellermann was involved, nothing was normal.

Gleick was running a public surveillance workstation, situated in the Statue of Judgement in MegEast, not far from Big Jimmy's home turf. It was kilometres from the supposedly abandoned factory where Jimmy's boys were unloading, but the link between Gleick's workstation and the spy-in-the-sky camera he was controlling was close to perfect. He sent the insect-sized camera darting away from the chain of mobsters, past the wagon with its cheery logo of happy farm animals and up to a higher vantage point overlooking the factory.

Why farm animals? Cows, pigs, chickens – what kind of a futsie would enjoy the thought of eating extinct species? Gleich shrugged, and as the big mobster's voice faded he selected a reserved channel and opened it. "PSU 767 to Ground Team One, over."

"Receiving you, PSU." The answering voice was unmistakable, and Gleick couldn't help sitting up a little straighter in his seat. "Report."

"Loading is still in progress, Ground Team. Can also confirm that Hellermann is in the building. Repeat: Hellermann is in the building."

"Received and understood, PSU," came the rough sounding reply. "Maintain surveillance. Let us know when the last of the chemicals are off the truck."

"Acknowledged, Ground Team One. PSU out." Gleick tapped at the camera controls, guiding the spy back towards the loading bay. Petey's voice became louder in Gleick's earpiece.

"I don't know why I'm so happy. Poppa always said I smiled so hard it made him want to take his belt to me just to see my expression change..."

Gleick sighed. It looked as if listening to this drek was going to be the price he'd have to pay to be able to boast to his colleagues over breakfast that he had worked with a legend.

Elize Hellermann strode through the storage area on the far side of the loading bay doors. Yet more of Big Jimmy's men moved around her, stacking canisters from the freezer wagon for later use, or loading other containers and mixing vessels onto hover-pallets. Her own staff handled the ferrying, especially for the items that went through a set of automatic doors to the nursery.

Whatever machinery had once been housed in the factory had been removed decades earlier. She had chosen this location within the Dust Zone – sector after sector of automated industrial units grouped around the Power Tower at the centre of MegSouth – because so many of the units had been closed down during one of the sector's periodic economic collapses. Falls like that hit every sector of Mega-City One at some time or another; businesses that took their owners a lifetime to build up could be gone overnight due to anything from an alien invasion to a dip in the sales of Mockburgers. Any increase in the numbers of unemployed from such a collapse would be barely noticeable in a city of four hundred million, with an unemployment rate of ninety per cent and holding.

Hellermann couldn't have cared less. Over the years, the number of things she cared about had dwindled sharply. At present, the number stood at one.

This.

The nursery doors opened smoothly. Hellermann walked through, feeling the downdraft of the clean air curtain – the environmental control system was one of the first things she had installed.

It was warm in the nursery. The temperature was boosted by waste heat from the equipment packed around the walls and across the floor, and the air was permeated by a constant low hum from the portable generators, brought in to ensure that no one at Big Meg Power noticed a spike in demand where there should have been no demand at all.

The factory space had been retro-fitted to her specifications with equipment of her own design, bought with money loaned to her by Big Jimmy, the diminutive – some would say stunted – grudfather of MegEast. Of course, Jimmy hadn't the faintest idea what she was doing here. All he was interested in was the money she had promised it would make him. If she had mentioned the word "treason", even a mobster like Jimmy might have balked.

Treason, she thought sourly, walking between processing units, purifiers and regulators. A stupid, small-minded word made up by stupid, small-minded people. People like those who claimed to uphold the law, and yet had reduced her to this – bowing and scraping for mobster money so she could continue her life's work in a rusting, bug-infested factory in the middle of the Dust Zone.

Technicians made their reports as she passed them. Everything was proceeding smoothly; as well it should, given the success of the first decantation.

Hellermann moved to another section of the nursery, where large, ovoid growth tanks stood in ranks across the floor. Each had a viewport set into the armour, and Hellermann peered into the nearest, through cloudy fluid and soupy, filigreed membranes. Inside, something thrashed and convulsed, powerful muscles jerking as a direct neural link downloaded terabytes of information directly into its brain.

Hellermann had selected the data for download very carefully: medical files, survival tactics, a compressed database of mankind's entire accumulated wisdom on the subject of war and ninety-five separate and distinct ways to kill a human being.

Placing a hand against the transparent plastic of the viewport, Hellermann smiled as she watched the creature twitch in its nutrient fluid.

"Soon, my child," she whispered. "Soon."

"That the last of 'em?" Arnold Crobetti asked. A man ahead of him in the human chain nodded.

"Looks that way."

Crobetti stretched. His splint sensed the movement and kicked out, almost unbalancing him. The other mobsters in the loading bay pointed and laughed.

"That was funny, Arnold," laughed Little Petey. "You're a funny guy. That makes me happy."

"Yeah, yeah, very funny," Crobetti addressed his reply to everyone in the loading bay. An insect buzzed close to his ear, and he recoiled instinctively, waving it away with his hand. Damn bugs. "I don't remember seeing any of you mugs backing me up when I took a slug for Big Jimmy."

Getting his mech-splint back under control, he turned and made for the stacked weapons. The sooner he got back to MegEast, the better. If any MegSouth mobsters turned up now, he didn't trust his splint to get him out of the way of any more slugs.

"PSU to Ground Team One. The chemicals are off the truck. Repeat: the chemicals are off the truck. Perps are tooling up and preparing to leave. Repeat–"

"Acknowledged. Ground Team One, we move. Team Two stay alert; Hellermann might use the back door." The gravelly voice cut across Tek-Judge Gleick's by-the-book communication etiquette. Gleick figured that was okay, though, seeing as the Judge on the other end of the comm-link wrote the book.

As he made his report, Gleick remote-guided the spy-in-the-sky out of the loading bay and into the night. Activating the infrared system, he piloted the flying camera skywards, broadening its field of view. His headset filled with a network of feeder roads, alleys and the dark hulks of abandoned, ruined buildings. The Dust Zone.

There. Half a dozen multicoloured heat signatures, moving in two ranks of three down the main drag. Moving fast.

"You hear that?" Crobetti asked no one in particular. He'd been strapping on his gun harness when he'd noticed: the sound of powerful engines. At first he thought it might be heavy traffic on the nearby skedway, but then he realised it was growing louder.

Getting closer.

"Lights."

Six sets of infrared vision filters were disengaged and the beams from six sets of powerful sodium quartz headlamps arrowed through the darkness and turned the loading bay as bright as a minor sun. In the glare, figures scrambled blindly trying to find cover, shading their eyes and bringing weapons to bear.

"Break."

The Lawmasters to left and right swung out smoothly, hugging the road's shoulder as the first volley of gunfire, fired blind from the loading bay into the dazzling headlights, swept between them. A lucky round struck the front wheel housing of the lead bike, whining off the armour and into the night. The rider's only reply was to trigger his bike cannon.

The other Lawmasters followed suit. In the sudden hail of high-explosive shells, the loading bay began to fly apart.

The freezer wagon's auto-polarising windshield had adjusted its setting the moment the Lawmasters' headlamps flared into life. Sitting behind the truck's controls, Tony Soba had a clear, though slightly tinted view of six Mega-City Judges barrelling towards him at what seemed a suicidal rate.

Tony had been one of Big Jimmy's street soldiers long enough to know what would come next if those Judges were allowed into the factory – cube-time and lots of it. Tony had done time before when he was a young man. If he went inside now, he'd be a crock by the time he got out – if he got out at all.

"I ain't going back inside!" Tony roared, and slammed the wagon in gear. The truck leapt forward and howled down the drag to meet the oncoming Judges.

"I'll deal with the truck," snapped the lead rider. The other five Judges swung their machines wider and opened their throttles, surging past the freezer wagon and towards the loading bay. Behind them, the remaining Lawmaster's bike cannon hammered streams of fire into the darkness.

The front of the freezer wagon simply dissolved. The forward grille, the bodywork, the windshield and the driver behind it; everything turned to fragments as the cannon shells tore the truck apart. The onboard computer must have gone too, locking the brakes, because the truck's wheels immediately jammed. The tyres gave out a chorus of shrieks as the wagon's momentum continued to drive them forwards, laying long strips of synthi-tread on the plascrete road.

The truck fishtailed, its rear trying to overtake its ruined cab, its long bulk swinging round to block the skedway.

Seeing thirty tonnes of driverless wagon heading directly for him, Judge Dredd simply opened the Lawmaster's throttle, kicked the rear wheel round and laid his machine down.

"Code ninety-nine red! Repeat: Code ninety-nine red! Judge down! Grud, he went under the truck!"

From the spy-in-the-sky's airborne vantage point, Gleick watched in horror as the freezer wagon began to roll, digging chunks out of the road's plascrete surface. It was only a matter of time before...

There was a hydrogen fuel cell in the truck's cab and volatile chemicals in the freezer at the back. With a heavy, flat sound the wagon spat out a sheet of flame, then detonated in a fireball that lit up half the block.

"Oh, I like this!" Little Petey was shouting. Crobetti could hear him even over the sound of the Judges' bike cannon shells punching chunks out of the rockcrete walls all around him. "This makes me really happy-happy-happy!"

Pumping his double-barrelled stump gun in a mindless, grinning frenzy, Petey fired round after round into the oncoming lights. Impossibly, despite standing in the open in the middle of the loading bay's raised platform, he hadn't been touched, either by the high-calibre munitions that were flying all around him, or by the debris blown out from the walls. Crobetti couldn't believe the man was still alive.

"For grud's sake, Petey, get down!" Crobetti shouted from where he was sheltering behind a stack of packing cases. He had nowhere else to go as the loading bay doors had slammed down like a plasteel curtain as soon as the first bullets were fired. His wounded leg was jumping like crazy, as if his mech-splint had picked up on the wave of fear and adrenaline that was pounding around his body. This was definitely not how he had imagined the night would end.

For a heartbeat, he entertained the fantasy that if he stayed where he was and crouched down really low, making himself as small as possible, the Judges wouldn't notice him when they stormed the loading bay. Then a glancing hit from a Lawmaster cannon shell tore half the packing cases to splinters.

"Ah, what the sneck," he sighed. His face was bleeding from a dozen splinter wounds as he chambered a stub-shell and struggled round, his mech-splint still twitching, to get a good shot at the oncoming Judges.

And died, quite without pain, as a cannon shell turned his skull into little more than red mist.

"Dredd here. Cancel the code red. I'm fine. Tek-Judge Gleick, consider this your official reprimand for premature use of the distress code. There might be a Judge out there who really needs assistance."

Dredd hadn't been anywhere near the Lawmaster when the truck had gone up. He'd kicked away from it to avoid being crushed between the bike and the road. While the Lawmaster had skidded away at an acute angle, finally ploughing into the perimeter fence of the neighbouring factory lot, Dredd had slid right under the truck and out the other side, letting his uniform's armoured knee and shoulder pads take the punishment. As soon as he'd shed enough speed he was up on his feet and running, Lawgiver in his fist, heading for the loading bay. His controlled fall from the bike had taken him to within a hundred metres of the ramp.

The firefight in the bay was already over. One of the Judges – probably Marks, Dredd decided – had swung his Lawmaster around and gone up the ramp sideways, pinning several mobsters against the wall, while the others had dismounted and gone in with Lawgivers blazing, a standard Justice Department containment pattern. Dredd counted ten perps dead, three wounded.

Farrell, a young Judge not long out of his rookie's white helmet, was cuffing the three wounded mobsters as they huddled against what was left of the bay wall. Seeing Dredd step up onto the platform, he turned to greet him. "Glad to see you're still with us, sir."

"Eyes on your perps, Farrell," Dredd replied. He walked past the young Judge, who hastily returned his attention to the mobsters.

Marks ran his override card across the lock. The plain-looking slug was programmed to override any electronic locking mechanism in Mega-City One, but in this case it simply emitted a sad bleep of defeat.

"No go. They've shielded the lock." He grimaced, then noticed that Dredd now stood beside him. "Hi-Ex?"

Dredd nodded and Marks moved quickly to his Lawmaster, opening stowage pods built into the rear wheel housing. He took out three slabs of plasteen, Hi-Ex charges with integral detonators. Dredd looked at the charges, made a quick mental estimate of the strength of the doors, and decided that two would probably do it.

Still, nothing wrong with a little overkill. He brought his helmet mic down. "Dredd to Ground Team Two," he growled. "We're going to blow the loading bay doors. Prepare to move on my mark. Gleick?"

"Reporting, sir."

"What can you see?"

"I'm picking up a lot of activity inside; they're either destroying evidence, getting ready to bug out or both – Judge Dredd! Behind you!"

At Gleick's warning, Dredd whirled. One of the dead mobsters was getting up again.

Later, at debriefing, he would discover that the big man with the stub gun pointing at his face was "Little" Petey Steene, wanted for numerous counts including that of strangling his own father with a synthi-leather belt at the age of ten. At this moment the man's name was less than important: by the time the mobster had chambered his first shell Dredd had already fired two shots from his Lawgiver. The first round shattered Steene's gun and the hand that held it, and the second blew most of his head away. Little Petey died with a grin on his face, or what was left of it. The execution round had destroyed everything above his top teeth.

Dredd watched the corpse flop back down to the loading bay floor. "Watch your perps, Marks – even the dead ones." He glanced back to where Gleick's spy-in-the-sky was dropping down towards him. "Well spotted, Tek-Judge."

"Th-thank you, sir!"

"The reprimand still stands. Marks, where's that Hi-Ex? This raid has already taken longer than it should."

The shaped Hi-Ex charges blew a ragged hole in the plasteel door, roughly the shape of an inverted triangle. A white-coated tekkie must have been standing too close to the doors when they blew as Dredd had to step over his smoking corpse to get in.

"Nobody move!" he barked. Decades of street experience had given his voice a degree of authority that most citizens found themselves obeying before they realised what they were doing. "This is an illegal bio-tech operation and you are all under arrest!"

Two tekkies looked up from their terminals, stared at Dredd like frightened animals, then took off for a set of doors to one side of the main area.

"Ground Team Two, time to join the fun," Dredd snapped into his helmet mic as he brought down one of the running tekkies with a leg-shot. The second runner was reaching for the door controls when he was spun howling to the floor by a shoulder-shot from Marks, who had followed Dredd through the blast hole.

Some of the tech staff were armed. A small-calibre pistol cracked from an overhead gantry, its bullet kicking dust off the floor at Dredd's feet. In a single movement, Dredd picked off the gunman then returned his attention to his main target before the perp hit the ground. "You!" he bellowed. "Where's Hellermann? Give her up now and you might get out of the cubes while you're still young enough to walk out!"

The tech managed to get one hand away from the wound in her leg to point towards a set of big pressure doors on the far wall of the factory. "In there," she gasped.

"I knew you'd say that," Dredd sneered. He left the woman to either tend to her wound or bleed to death, and headed for the doors. Behind him, the other Judges in his team followed Marks through the door and spread out through the factory space. Shouts of command and the occasional gunshot began to echo among the equipment.

The doors slid aside and Dredd went through, feeling the pressure curtain brush at him. Beyond, rows of growth tanks stretched away, gleaming softly in the dim light. Cables and pipes littered the floor. Dredd tapped one with his boot and felt it thrumming through the kevlar sole.

He'd seen these tanks in the briefing vid, although those had borne the Justice Department eagle crest. These bore the logo of what Dredd guessed was a Hondo-Cit chop-shop, specialists in the reverse engineering and copying of virtually any piece of high technology. All Hellermann had to do was get the specs for the growth tanks to the chop-shop engineers and they could have turned out dozens of the tanks almost overnight, ready to be smuggled back to Mega-City One.

The woman would obviously stop at nothing. Dredd glared out into the gloom, making out a set of pressure-sealed doors in the end wall. According to the last set of building plans submitted to the MegSouth zoning board, those would have led to the works canteen. If Hellermann was there, she was heading right into the arms of Judge Mexter and the rest of Team Two.

But she was clever, he knew that. And there were plenty of places to hide right here.

"Hellermann," he called, stepping carefully over the cables. "You're under arrest. Make it easy on yourself."

As if in answer, one of the tanks shifted on its base.

Dredd heard it before he saw it; a heavy impact from within the plasteel and ceramic. He took a cautious step towards the nearest of the growth vessels. The lid was pale and opaque, with a viewport set into its curved surface. Inside, something moved spasmodically in gluey liquid.

The sound of the canteen doors blowing inwards caused Dredd to turn, Lawgiver unconsciously and immediately aimed. A loose, tangle-limbed figure in a singed and tattered lab coat flew out from the doorway and rolled to a messy halt on the floor. There were shouts and orders to freeze uttered by someone with Justice Department training, then screams and several secondary explosions. A squeal of feedback made the audio pick-ups in Dredd's helmet dull for a second to protect his hearing, then the lights throughout the facility dimmed as something short-circuited with spectacular finality and a last, loud explosion. The copper tang of burning circuitry wafted from the open doorway.

Elize Hellermann soon followed, cuffed, bleeding from a cut above her close-cropped hairline and pushed ahead of Judge Mexter and his team. One of the Judges had hold of another tekkie by the ragged collar of his lab whites. Cuffing him had been unnecessary as one arm and one leg were a mess of shrapnel wounds – he must have been standing far too close to whatever it was that had exploded in the canteen.

"Doctor Hellermann was bugging out just as we came in," Mexter greeted Dredd. "The canteen's been fitted out as a sterile operating theatre. Moment she saw us, she set the gruddamned robo-docs on us." He put a gloved hand up to a thin line of blood that ran the length of his jaw. "We hit them with a Hi-Ex each and they went to pieces. A couple of her assistants, too. But that was it for the power."

Dredd nodded. "I'll see Attempted Judge Homicide gets added to her charge sheet," he replied. "It's already an impressive–"

The lid of the growth tank next to him exploded outwards.

Dredd turned his face away as shards of razor-edged plastic spun into the air. A heartbeat later the entire lid of the tank whirled upwards in a shower of fluid, as something vast leapt out and hurled itself forwards.

In an instant Dredd was being battered against another tank. His Lawgiver had been slapped from his grip before he could react, and the thing had a massive hand around Dredd's throat, crushing his windpipe, and it was slamming him repeatedly against the growth unit behind him. If he hadn't been wearing a Justice Department helmet his skull would have been shattered.

The grip on this throat was incredible, stronger than a robot. His vision had already started to grey out; Dredd could hear the other Judges yelling and shots being fired.

"Hold your fire. You'll hit Dredd!"

His vision narrowed until all he could see was the thing's face, or what it had for a face. Pure hatred with teeth, and eyes that held far more intellect than such a monster should possess.

Enough, Judge Dredd decided, was enough. He sagged in the creature's grip and let his hand drop down to the top of his boot. When it swung up again, a broad, tempered blade protruded from his fist.

Dredd slammed his boot knife into the creature's chest, but the grip around his throat didn't weaken and now the grey fog was turning black. With the last of his strength, Dredd stabbed again, driving the blade between its ribs and twisting, probing for a vital organ.

With an involuntary squeal, the creature released its hold. Dredd hurled himself back. "Now!" he gasped, through a throat that felt as though he'd been eating glass. "Open fire!"

"No!" cried Hellermann, but her protest was drowned out by the sound of four Lawgivers firing in unison.

Dredd saw the creature's pale, unfinished skin explode in a dozen places. It reeled from the impact of the execution shells, then with a roar of fury it leaped towards Judge Mexter. A sabre of polished bone had already erupted from its forearm.

"Incendiary!" Dredd dived for his Lawgiver, snatched it up even as it was acknowledging his voice command, and pumped three shots into the monster's side.

Instantly it was ablaze – a bellowing, thrashing column of greasy flame. It staggered towards Mexter, but the flesh was already twisting off its bones. Within a metre it sagged onto its knees, and finally collapsed onto the factory floor.

It didn't stop trying to get to Mexter until several minutes later, when Dredd tired of its squealing and put an execution round through its skull.

"I'm just glad we caught them before they got shipped out," Mexter said later as Hellermann was being led away. "I can think of a dozen rogue states and twice that many crime bosses who'd pay good credits for just one of these killers. Imagine if they got their hands on an army of them."

"Um, Judge Mexter, Judge Dredd. About that." One of the Ground Team's Tek-Judges, Corben, had commandeered a workstation. He stood up from his seat as Dredd and Mexter came over.

"About what, Corben?" Dredd asked, aware that his voice sounded even more gravelly than usual. "Spit it out."

Corben nodded. "I've only just skimmed the surface of Hellermann's system," he began, "but there's something you should know. These tanks are holding the second and third batches Hellermann has produced. The first was decanted a week ago with a better than seventy per cent survival rate. Seems the duds were rendered down and used to augment the nutrients for the next batch." Corben looked down at his feet with a grimace. He was standing in a puddle of the solution that was leaking from the ruined growth tank.

"What happened to the first batch?"

"They were moved to one of Big Jimmy's safe houses out by the Kennedy Hoverport while a credit transfer was arranged," Corben continued, reading the information scrolling down the workstation's monitor. "A big credit transfer. I haven't been able to piece together the name of the buyer, but I can tell you that they went over the Atlantic Wall."

"When?"

"Yesterday."

"Dredd to PSU."

Tek-Judge Gleick started at the sound of Dredd's voice, almost spilling the cup of fresh synthi-caf he had ordered from the roving robo-dispenser. Since the raid on the factory ended, he had kept the spy-in-the-sky clear of the street Judges, and of Dredd in particular. One reprimand from the legend was more than enough for one night.

"Patch me through to the Chief Judge, Code Omega." Dredd was the only street Judge with the authority to demand a direct comm-link with Chief Judge Hershey. Gleick knew that Hershey and Dredd had a history – Dredd's recommendation had carried a lot of weight when it came time to elect a new Chief Judge, a little over two years ago.

"Yes sir," Gleick's hands flew over the comm-keys, bypassing the normal channels of communication which ran from street Judge to Sector House and on up the chain of command. "Chief Judge, I have Judge Dredd on the line."

Dredd spoke as soon as the channel opened. He didn't waste time with formalities. He didn't even wait for Gleick to get offline. "We're twenty-four hours too late," he growled. "Project Warchild is already in the air."

2. SPLASH

The Lindberg was flying low over the Black Atlantic, *really* low, and that made Taub nervous. To him, it seemed as though the cargo plane was barely skimming the tops of the highest waves.

It was an illusion, he knew. The cargo jet's autopilot was keeping a good forty metres between plane and water, but the slate-black surface of the ocean was so featureless, so vast, that it filled every part of the view from the cockpit. At times it looked as though the plane was barely moving, but then Taub would see a line of grey on the far horizon, and watch as it drew closer, speeding up, and resolving itself into a wavefront of scummy grey foam before it disappeared under the cockpit. The toxic surface of the Black Atlantic broke every now and then, but reluctantly.

Mostly it was just oily swell, and that got old really fast. Taub yawned, stretched, and said: "Want another caf?"

Hopkirk shook his head without looking up. The pilot had downloaded an e-zine to his dataslate the previous afternoon, and he'd been reading it continuously since switching the Lindberg to autopilot. Taub couldn't decide if Hopkirk was just a slow reader, or if he was just keeping his nose in the slate to avoid conversation. Neither explanation appealed to him very much, but who knew about these Brit-Cit types anyway? Stuck-up, at best. A serious stick up the rear at worst.

"Suit yourself." Taub got up, steadying himself against the back of his seat as the Lindberg rose slightly to avoid a swell, and made for the dispenser unit set in the cockpit's rear wall. While his drink was gurgling into a plastic cup, Taub surveyed the choices offered by the energy bar dispenser set next to the caf-machine. Five fruit flavours, all of which he knew from bitter experience would taste like damp cardboard. "What the drokk is a dongleberry anyway?"

"Sorry, a what?"

"Dongleberry. This bar dispenser's got a new flavour – Delicious Dongleberry."

"Yummy," said Hopkirk flatly. He still hadn't looked up from his slate. "It'll taste of cardboard."

Taub nodded to himself and took the plastic cup of lukewarm synthi-caf from the dispenser. "Yeah, I know. Just making conversation. Thought it might break up the boredom."

Hopkirk glanced up from his screen. "Bored?" He smiled thinly. "Well, if you want to break the monotony you could try working out whether we're still low enough to keep under Atlantic Division's radar, and high enough to avoid a megashark if one decides to jump up and take a bite out of the tail."

Taub blinked at him. "They don't do that, do they?"

In reply, Hopkirk just waved the data-pad lazily. "Should have down-loaded one, Taub. All the answers, right here."

"Ah, drokk you. You're just trying to freak me out." And it's working, thought Taub wildly. Brit-Cit snecker!

He ran his finger down the list of energy bars again, but decided against eating any more. It would have been the third one since taking off from Kennedy Hoverport and it wasn't as if he'd be expending a great deal of energy during this flight. Hopkirk had supervised the autopilot during take off, and would when they landed, too. The coffin-sized cryotanks in the hold were entirely self-regulating. He and Hopkirk were only on board to deal with the unexpected.

Taub went back to his seat and dropped into it, plucking an empty plastic cup from the drinks holder and inserting the fresh one. The empty went into the space between his seat and the curve of the fuse-lage. "Ah, don't mind me. I just get nervous, is all."

"Nothing wrong in that," said Hopkirk. "Keeps you on your toes. But as far as the Justice Department is concerned, we're just a perfectly ordi-nary private cargo flight to Brit-Cit. And since when did Atlantic Division have the manpower to check every flight?"

Taub thought about that and nodded, feeling a little better. All the paperwork for the flight had been in place before Eddie the Belly had even contacted him. Eddie was a good payer, for a Fattie, and had given Taub plenty of work in the past – he always seemed to need a pilot who wouldn't ask questions. The flight plan, the security tabs on the cargo bay doors and the customs clearance certificates had looked so good, Taub would have sworn they were genuine.

The Lindberg-CS13 was a nondescript plane, just heading towards obsolescence; no customs officer would give it a second glance. They would touch down in Brit-Cit long enough to refuel and change crews, probably handing over the flight to a couple of Euro-Citters for the next leg of the trip. By the time it took off, the plane would be flying under a new ident-number. To all intents and purposes, the plane now flying across the world's most polluted expanse of water would have vanished while sitting on the blacktop at Brit-Cit's main air terminal.

Taub didn't know the cargo's final destination, and he didn't care. He would take the zoom train home along the Trans-Atlantic Tunnel, running three thousand miles along the bed of the same polluted ocean he was currently flying over, and pick up his payment from Eddie. Simple.

Here's to "simple". Taub raised his cup of caf, took a gulp and almost choked. "Sneck! What the drokk do they put in this stuff?"

"Dongleberries," replied Hopkirk, waving the dataslate.

An hour later, Taub was almost relieved to hear the alarm chime. He had been staring vacantly at the sickly green flashes of a storm on the southern horizon, and there was a chance he might have nodded off for a moment or two. He wondered if he should have another caf, maybe an energy bar. Having Hopkirk report back that he had dozed off on the job would be a bad idea.

"What's up?" he asked, glancing across at Hopkirk. He was glad to see that, some time in the last hour, the Brit had put down his e-zine.

Hopkirk consulted his control board. "Proximity alert," he muttered, tapping at the screen. The chiming faded out. "Nothing serious. Whatever it is, it's on the surface and over a thousand kilometres away. It's big though. Very big indeed."

"Cityship, probably," Taub said. "They're nothing to worry about, so long as we don't get close enough for them to take a pop at us."

Hopkirk's eyebrows went up. "Do they do that?" Taub grinned at him. "What, not in your zine?" He sat back and stretched. "Yeah, it's been known. If they brought us down, their scavengers would tear the plane apart for salvage and feed us to the megasharks. Though we won't have to worry about them reporting anything to the Justice Department."

"Quite," Hopkirk replied. And picked up his slate again.

Taub returned his bored gaze to the southern horizon. The storm appeared to have blown itself out. The swirling funnel of dirty cloud that hovered over the ocean there had cleared, and all that remained was a curtain of greasy-looking mist, pierced here and there by shafts of sunlight breaking through the parting clouds. That didn't surprise Taub at all – the vast quantities of radwaste and industrial pollution that had drained into the ocean over the centuries had produced a virulent microclimate, capable of turning from placid to catastrophic in the blink of an eye.

Taub wondered what it must be like to be caught in a storm at sea level. He imagined the muties on their cityships closing hatches, shuttering windows and hiding in the dark, waiting for the storm to pass. He

imagined the violent rolling of the individual vessels that made up the
floating cities, the creak and snap of the cables, the moaning of the
welded joints that held the ancient craft together.

As he thought of the rolling ocean, his eyelids began to droop.

The next time Taub woke, it was to the sound of Hopkirk swearing.
Another alarm was sounding – not the chime of the proximity alarm,
but a more insistent, insect buzzing.

"What is it this time?" Every joint in his body felt stiff. He must have
been out for some time, and the seats weren't exactly built for restful
sleep. There was a cot in the back for that.

Hopkirk was stabbing at his control board, but each time one icon
blinked out another replaced it. "I'm not sure. Getting system warnings
– flaps and rudder are sluggish and the engines are losing efficiency.
Even the hydraulics are playing up."

That didn't sound good. Taub was instantly alert, checking his own
board. "You didn't see anything unusual?"

Hopkirk shook his head. "No, just this damn mist."

"Mist?" Taub looked up, out of the cockpit windshield. "*Mist*?"

Something was happening to the plexiglass. What had been clear and
transparent when he had closed his eyes had become frosted and semi-
opaque. Hundreds of tiny circles, like ripples on a pond, had scoured the
surface. "Oh grud. We're in an acid bank."

Acid banks were another of the random and deadly features of the
Black Atlantic's eco-system. Gases would bubble up from the ocean's
floor, emanating from any one of a dozen different sources: mutant life
forms, sunken toxic waste tankers, ruptured transit pipes and worse.
When the gas hit the air it would vaporise, turning into a wall of corrosive vapour that would hang above the ocean surface like a dirty
curtain. Acid banks were rare, but they did occur. And they were deadly.

"You dumb snecker, why the hell didn't you pull up?" Taub ran his
hands swiftly over the control board, disengaging the autopilot and taking over the stick from Hopkirk. "If this stuff gets into the engines we're
drokked!"

"I-I didn't see it."

"Didn't see it?" Taub was hauling back on the control stick with all
his strength, trying to bring the Lindberg's nose up before the acid
chewed clear through the fuselage. "You were asleep, weren't you? Or
you had your nose in that damn slate!"

"Blame me later," Hopkirk snapped. "Just climb!"

Taub didn't reply, he just kept dragging the stick back. The Lindberg
was groaning, wallowing, shuddering under him. The acid bank was

thick and heavy, not like air at all. It felt as though he was trying to fly the plane through soup.

Suddenly, the air cleared. The acid bank became a landscape of roiling vapour below them, dropping back out of sight. Taub eased the stick forwards, levelling the Lindberg out. "Made it!" he puffed, sweat rolling down his face. "Grud on a greenie."

Hopkirk looked white. "Is this going to screw up our flight schedule?"

Taub turned to him, slowly, giving himself time to think of something really foul to call the Brit-Citter. Finally, he fixed Hopkirk with a steely glare, opened his mouth, took a breath – and stayed with his mouth gaping wide open in horror as he saw what was happening to the port engine.

Smoke was vomiting from the sides of the pod, venting through holes and rips in the metal shell. As he stared, the smoke was joined by a belch of flame.

"Grud," he whispered. It would be the last word he ever spoke.

The engine blew up, the acid-etched fan blades giving in to the furious stress of their own rotation and whirling into fragments. The entire pod blasted apart, shattering into a ball of flame and shrapnel, tearing half the wing away. The Lindberg was instantly wrenched sideways and out of the air.

The impact killed Hopkirk instantly, tearing his pilot's throne free of the deck and slamming it with crushing force into the side of the cockpit. The plexiglass windshield, already weakened by the acid, exploded outwards. Taub felt the wind slam into him like a wall, battering him back into his own seat. The pressure was so great he couldn't even get his hands to the controls. He certainly couldn't scream even though the acid-laden air was already ripping into his skin.

His last vision was that of the gleaming Black Atlantic looming up to meet him.

The Lindberg hit the water like a missile, shearing off the remains of both wings. The shattered cockpit gaped even wider with the impact, swallowing tonnes of fluid in a second. The plane slowed in its forward motion and began to settle, dropping through the stew of toxins, radwaste and industrial pollutants that made the Black Atlantic one of the deadliest places on earth. By the time it hit the seabed it was almost unrecognisable, but not as unrecognisable as the corroded, rapidly decomposing body of co-pilot Taub.

The nose of the plane hit bottom first, and the acid-eaten fuselage gave way as it did so, splitting clear across. Debris drifted out into the murk. Most of it sank.

But ten self-contained cryotanks, their armoured support systems affected by neither the crash nor the poisoned Atlantic, did not sink. They were built to float. So they left the Lindberg to its fate and went spiralling slowly up through the black water like glossy bubbles, one by one, heading for light and air.

3. SCAVENGER HUNT

To the untrained eye, the scavenger ship *Golgotha* was as ugly as sin. Its hull was a bulbous, blunt-nosed mess, stained black by the Atlantic's toxic waters and patched with a thousand hastily welded plates. So many winches, booms, cranes and outriggers rose above the gunwales that the ship looked more like an upturned insect than a seagoing vessel, rolling drunkenly on its back and wiggling its legs in the air. And it was noisy – the creaking of the outriggers, sullen twanging of cables in the wind and the grind of heavy chain against pulleys was almost enough to drown out the chugging of the engine.

Golgotha wasn't pretty, but it was the closest thing to a home Gethsemane Bane had ever known.

She was up on the bridge, feet braced apart against the swell, standing at the helm with her hands white-knuckle tight on the controls. A storm had passed by this spot not long ago, and while the lashing acid rain and gale force winds were gone, they had left a roiling and disturbed sea in their wake. Bane was finding it hard to keep *Golgotha* on a level heading, and the thought that the storm might have roused a megashark – or something even bigger – kept flashing uncomfortably through her mind.

"I don't like it," she muttered, partly to herself. "Shouldn't we be able to see it by now?"

Most of the crew was out on the foredeck, clustered around the prow. The plexiglass of the windshield was so smeared and streaked that she could only make them out by the brilliant yellow of their protective slickers. She resolved to treat *Golgotha* to some new windows as soon as they got back to *Sargasso*, if they made money on this trip. It was a regular expense. Plexiglass didn't last long against Black Atlantic spray.

Dray was on the bridge with her, running the sensor station. He stood peering into the scope with his one good eye, the crocodile skin of his face painted over with the colours from the readout. "It's off the starboard bow, no more than fifty metres."

Bane triggered her headset mic. "Hear that, guys?" One of the yellow blobs waved in reply, and they all moved to starboard.

"I'll go help them," Dray said. "We're too close for this to be much use now." He turned from the sensor screen and reached for his slicker, which was hanging from a peg by the door.

Bane put her hand to his shoulder. "I'll go. You hold her steady. And get ready on the outriggers."

"Aye, aye, cap'n." Dray flashed her a reptilian grin. A mutant, like everyone on the scavenger ship, Dray had skin like leather and needle-point teeth. He had been on the *Golgotha* longer than anyone, Bane included, but he had been the first to start calling her 'captain'.

Bane grabbed her own slicker and shrugged into it, sealing it quickly before stepping into the wind and spray. The door whined closed behind her, and after waiting a moment to ride out another of *Golgotha*'s familiar rolling lurches, she headed along the companionway and down the stairs to the deck.

Everyone else was down there waiting for her, except for Orca. The big engineer was holed up in the drive room, as usual, tending his precious engines as though they were living things. Bane could have used his strength up at the prow, but she didn't feel it was right to disturb him. Besides, if the object was heavy, *Golgotha* might need an extra surge of power to the winches, and it would be Orca's job to provide it.

Bane had no idea what the object was. Or objects. Dray had been watching the signal it was giving out for more than eighteen hours, but he still couldn't tell her if there was one big source or lots of smaller ones close together.

One or many, it didn't matter. The object had power, components, and no one to take it home. That made it the personal property of Gethsemane Bane and the *Golgotha* crew.

As long as she could *find* the drokking thing!

She leaned over the bow rail, cupping a hand over her eyes to ward off the spray, and searched the sluggish, heaving surface for something other than polluted water and scum. Her eyes were good, but it was Angle, further along the rail, who saw it first.

"There!" he yelped, leaping up and down and pointing. "There it is!"

Angle's arms were too long, and looked as though they had been built with more than the usual number of elbows. But when he pointed at something, it stayed pointed at. Bane followed his arm and instantly saw what she'd been missing.

It was just under the surface, occasionally bobbing through and sleeting black water off its flanks. Something rounded and grey and artificial. "Good eyes, Angle! First round's on you!"

Angle grinned and punched the air. Bane could hear Dray chuckling in satisfaction, and Can-Rat was skittering from side to side in excitement. It had been a while since *Golgotha* had made a find like this. Once they got it back to *Sargasso*, it could make them a pretty cred or two.

"Dray?" She turned back to wave at the bridge, and saw Dray waving back through the grimy windshield. "It's not too big, and it floats. We'll need number four crane, but the outriggers can stay where they are. She won't tip."

"Got it," Dray replied, and instantly the medium starboard crane – number four – began to unfold itself from rest position.

"Hey, Angle." Bane moved over to where the slender mutant was still pointing and grinning. "You want to get out of buying that first round?"

"If Orca's drinking with us, yeah."

She snorted a laugh, hoping the engineer wasn't listening in. "Okay, if you can zap that thing with the magoon, I'll be buying. Deal?"

Angle let out a whoop and darted away. Damn, he moved so fast. Too fast for the deck of a ship, really, but he was young. Even younger than Bane, and she was only twenty-four. Young enough to get a real kick out of firing a magnetic harpoon at something, anyway.

She let him go and went over to join Can-Rat. "What do you think it is?"

"Coffin?" Can-Rat sniffed. "Looks like a coffin. Maybe some snecker's fancy idea of a burial at sea."

"With a tracer signal?"

Can-Rat blinked, small beady eyes bright and his muzzle wet from the sea. "Maybe he got lonely."

Angle appeared next to her, holding the magoon. The launcher was a metal tube as long as Bane was tall, with a pitted muzzle she could have put her head into. In contrast, the magnetic point of the harpoon itself looked surprisingly delicate. Like an origami teardrop.

"Maybe it's a treasure chest," said Angle, hauling the magoon up and snapping its mount over the bow rail. There was a loud metallic sound as it locked. "Fell off some rich eldster's pleasure cruiser."

"Pleasure?" Bane gave him a look. "Angle, if anyone's out here for pleasure, I don't wanna know what they keep in their treasure chests!" She paused. "What are you waiting for, kid? Zap the thing."

Angle rolled his head around on his thin neck, shrugged the kinks out of his shoulders, and then leaned down to aim the magoon. His long limbs and twitchy build gave him a combination of leverage and extraordinary delicacy of touch. When he squeezed the trigger, the magoon fizzed out of the launcher straight and true.

The point splayed in midair, faster than Bane could follow. One second it was a sharp point of overlaid metal plates, the next it was a wide dish slapping against the side of the object and grabbing on hard. The cable paid out behind it went taut, reeled back by the launcher's internal winch.

"Okay, Angle, hold it there." Bane slapped him on the shoulder in congratulation, and then gave Dray a signal. In response, the crane dipped low out over the water and released its grab.

"Something's wrong," Can-Rat said, very quietly, eyes fixed on the grab. "I don't like this. Something ain't right."

Bane felt the hairs on her arms and the back of her neck bristle. Can-Rat might not have been much of a sailor – he was too short and slender for the physical demands of life on the Black Atlantic, and seawater brought out his allergies – but, either due to some telepathic mutant ability or just keen senses, he always seemed to know when something bad was about to happen. Bane kept him on board as a kind of canary – if Can-Rat got nervous, so did she.

"Don't worry," she told him. "Almost there. We'll be gone soon."

The grab hesitated, waiting out a swell, then as *Golgotha* rolled back down it dropped, splashing heavily down onto the object. For a second Bane thought it was going to skate right off the slick surface, but Dray had been working the cranes for years. The grab scissored closed and came up in a single, soaring motion, showering the deck with grubby spray. Bane closed her eyes against it for just a moment, and when she opened them again the object was hanging a few metres above the deck. They had it.

It looked a lot like a coffin, actually. If the underside of the thing hadn't been a maze of sophisticated support pipework, she might have gotten nervous and dropped the thing right back over the side.

No, she told herself, no one was that stupid. Even a corpse could fetch a price if you sold it to the right people.

Dray was lowering the object onto the deck, and the others were moving towards it, eager to see what they'd picked up. Bane noticed that Orca had emerged from the drive room and was bouncing towards her. For such a huge man, he moved with surprising grace and lightness, as if he weighed almost nothing at all. Bane knew that wasn't true, but she also knew that his layers of protective blubber were thinly wrapped around enough muscle for three normal men. Orca's weight didn't slow him down because he had more than enough strength to carry it. A few people had found that out the hard way. As far as Bane knew one of them was still alive, but his family had to feed him through a straw.

Orca reached the object as it hit the deck and bent to study it. Bane joined him. "What do you think?" she asked, watching him running his fingers lightly over its glossy shell.

"Good quality," Orca muttered. "Mega-City workmanship, possibly, or a Hondo-Cit copy." His fingers moved across a flat panel at one of the shorter ends. "Maybe some kind of lock?"

"I'll get a wrench and a prybar," said Angle happily. Bane shook her head.

"Wait. We'll get more for this if we don't wreck it." She turned back to Orca, who was studying a fine, barely visible seal that ran completely around the object. "What would you put in a box like this?"

"In a hermetic cask? Something perishable. Something you want to keep fresh till you need it." He paused, stroking his cascade of chins. "Food, perhaps. Med-supplies more likely."

"Paydirt!" Angle whooped. "We'll get top cred for Mega-City meds on the *Sargasso*! Right, cap?"

"Right. We keep it sealed, make it fast and head for home." Bane couldn't help but smile. If Orca was right, the chest's contents would earn them good money in the dockside markets of the cityship. And the meds might even save some lives. Everybody wins.

Good news at last. Things had been tough for a while, with pickings so slim some trips had brought in barely enough to cover *Golgotha*'s mooring fees, and the little ship still needed fuel and spare parts, despite Orca's genius for repairs.

Abruptly, Bane glanced around. Can-Rat was back at the rail, staring out across the murky water. She trotted over to join him, and was startled to see that the furry mutant was shivering violently. "Grud, Canny, what's up?"

"I dunno." He turned to face her, his muzzle twitching with fear. "I think something's coming."

"Captain?"

"Dray? What is it?"

"Not sure. Something funny." She heard Dray tapping at a control. "The signal's stopped, cut out as soon as it hit the deck. But there's another one."

"Another signal?" Bane grabbed the rail and leaned over, scanning the inky water. "What, another coffin?" She was liking this less by the second. Can-Rat was spooked, more caskets were popping out of the Atlantic every second – what next?

"Hold on." Dray said, over her headset. "I've got another contact. It's weird. It only just appeared, even though the radar puts it nearby and closing fast."

"Another scavenger?" suggested Orca, next to her so suddenly that she jumped.

"Maybe." She was looking around wildly, trying to see what was coming, but the weather was closing in again. The oily spray was being joined by wisps of yellowish fog, and the swell was getting worse. A storm was coming.

"Can we get the other casket aboard before they arrive?"

"I don't know. Depends how close they are." She glanced back to the casket, still held firmly against the deck by the crane grab, and then went sprawling across the deck as Can-Rat barrelled into her from behind. She yelled in surprise and protest, but never heard her own shout. It had been drowned out by the explosion that blew a head-sized hole through the gunwale, just where she'd been standing.

The other ship was almost on top of them.

It loomed out of the rising fog, all flat panels and sharp edges. Stealth plates, she thought frantically, radar-absorbent ceramic. No telling how long the ship had been following them, guns trained, waiting for them to pick up something worthwhile.

Can-Rat had just saved her from being blown in half.

Dray was yelling in her ear, telling her to say something, let him know she was okay. *Golgotha*'s deck was up at a wild angle, so steep that she started to slide across it. Dray was hauling the ship around, trying to make a getaway before the stealth ship could fire again.

She saw the port gunwale coming up to meet her, but then Orca's massive hand closed around the hood of her slicker and hauled her back upright.

Bane scanned the deck, trying to see whether everyone was okay. Can-Rat was huddled behind the object, keeping its bulk between him and the other ship. She couldn't see Angle at all. "Where's the kid?"

"Stern," Orca shouted, raising his voice above the rising bellow of *Golgotha*'s engines. Dray was opening the throttles up, putting speed into the turn. "Said something about the guns."

Bane groaned. *Golgotha* had a pair of twin-linked spit guns mounted on a crude swivel behind the bridge. They would make a lovely noise, but the shells they fired were soft headed, designed for use against Black Atlantic wildlife, not stealth-armoured ships. If he opened up with those, the other vessel would shoot straight back at him. He was going to get himself blown to bits.

"Stay here," she yelled at Orca, gesturing at the casket. "Stay behind that thing and keep Can-Rat with you." With that she began scuttling towards the rear of the ship, keeping low to avoid drawing any more fire. The stealth vessel wasn't using up a lot of ammo. So far it had only fired the one shot.

There was an almighty noise and the light portside crane splintered in half, toppling drunkenly over the side. Two shots, Bane corrected herself, ducking under the splash. She wondered what kind of gun they had mounted in that thing. Whatever it was, it was big.

Not scavengers, then. Pirates. Tooled up and ready to make their profits the fast and bloody way.

The ship had completed its turn. Dray slammed the throttle open and it surged forwards. Bane, halfway along the portside companionway by that point, had to grab a rail and hang on as the deck reared up behind her and threatened to spill her into the stern.

Seconds later the spit guns opened up with a hellish racket.

She scrambled to a halt at the stern rail, trying vainly to cover her ears with one hand while hanging on for dear life with the other. Angle was hunkered down behind the guns, and as Bane watched he squeezed both triggers and sent another stream of shells thundering towards the pirate ship.

She saw figures on the deck scattering. Angle, to his credit, wasn't trying to damage the ship. He was aiming at softer targets. "Just keeping their heads down," he shouted, loosing off another volley. "If they're too busy ducking, maybe they can't spend so much time steering."

There was a dull sound from the pirate ship, and a puff of smoke. Part of the stern rail disappeared. Bane heard bits of it whining past her head.

"Okay, you drokkers!" Angle screamed. "You asked for it!"

The next time he opened fire, he was aiming lower. Bane almost told him not to bother, but then realised she had forgotten how accurate he had been with the magoon. Despite the wild pitching of *Golgotha*'s deck and the surging motion of the pirate ship, he put his next volley directly down the throat of the stealth vessel's big gun.

Bane didn't hear the explosion, but she saw it. A narrow slot between the stealth plates at the pirate's prow suddenly vomited smoke and fire. Seconds later, more smoke began to billow out from all the forward vents and view ports. The stealth vessel was swiftly engulfed in a greasy, flame-shot cloud.

"YES!" Angle stood up, leaning out over the guns. "Who's your daddy, eh boy? Who's your drokking daddy?!"

"Keep your head down, daddy." Bane hauled him back down. "They might send a thank you back with something smaller."

For a second Angle stayed where he was, shaking with fierce exhilaration. Then he sagged back. "Grud," he whispered. "Er, cap?"

"Mm-hm?"

"That was fun. Can we do that some more?"

The *Golgotha* powered due north until the pirate ship had been left on the far side of the stern horizon, when Dray throttled back to preserve fuel. Back on the bridge with him, Bane cranked the sensor net – another of Orca's jerry-rigged but remarkably sensitive creations – to full gain. The output screen filled with dots indicating inorganic debris on or near the ocean's surface. Solid gold to a scavenger under normal circumstances, but right now Bane was content to let it go.

There was an odd, flickering contact at the edge of the sensor net's range – the pirate vessel, its stealth shielding less efficient while it was on fire. It kept its position until it had left the scope. "Picking up the other casket?"

"Casket or caskets, yeah." Dray rubbed his chin, making a grinding sound against his scales. "Disappointed?"

"Nah. Something tells me one of these things is enough." She yawned and stretched. Night had fallen while *Golgotha* was fleeing the scene and the excitement had taken all the strength from her. "I'm going to turn in. Tell Can-Rat he's got the next watch."

"You sure you want to trust him up here on his own?"

"He'll be fine," Bane replied. "Just think of him as an extra early warning system."

Dray gave a half-amused, half-sceptical snort and went back to his instruments. Bane ducked through the aft hatch and found her way to the crew quarters. Hammocks swung lazily from the low ceiling and Bane dropped gratefully into the nearest.

Golgotha was running well, the bilges were empty and the decks were clear. Orca had taken the casket down into the forward hold, where he had locked it down firmly and covered it with tarpaulin. It would stay there until they docked with the cityship.

Not long now, Bane told herself. They had outrun the storm as well as the pirates. At this course and speed, they should be back in dock within a day and a half.

That thought was enough to comfort her, and the gentle rocking of the ship took her the rest of the way into sleep.

Down in the darkness of the forward hold, the casket lay and waited. Beneath its armoured carapace, machines tirelessly monitored the condition of its contents, logging their readings onto wafer thin data crystals. The support system continued to pump nutrient solutions around the inside of the shell; the temperature was kept constant and the final data downloads ran through their checksum routines.

And the timer, built into the lock that Orca had noticed on deck, kept counting down the seconds, just as it had been doing since the casket had been sealed.

As Gethsemane Bane fell asleep, the counter read just thirty-four hours, forty-nine minutes and a steadily decreasing handful of seconds.

A day and a half.

4. BREAKFAST TO GO

The best time for a crime swoop, Dredd had decided long ago, was dawn or even earlier. The worst excesses of the Graveyard Shift tended to fade out by four-thirty, and the day's hardcore perps wouldn't have roused themselves yet. This wasn't to say that Mega-City One in the early hours was a crime-free zone – that wasn't going to happen in Dredd's lifetime – but there was a dip in the graph before the sun came up.

Besides, a groggy citizen was a poor liar.

The doors on Les Dennis Block's eighty-seventh floor had been recently repainted; the last time Dredd had been here they were uniformly grey. Now they were uniformly green, which was as close to urban renewal as Les Dennis was likely to see in a while. Dredd strode up to number three-twenty, rapped on it hard, and waited. A few seconds later the door began to rattle: a full complement of latches, bolts and security chains were being unlocked behind the plasteen.

When the door finally opened, it only did so partway. Dredd saw a handspan of nervous, blinking citizen behind two more lengths of stout chain. "What–"

"Marcus Elizabeth Bropes? I'm here to search your apartment."

Bropes swallowed, nodded hard and eased the door back towards the frame so he could get the chains off. Dredd noticed how careful he was not to close it fully – that would get it kicked off its hinges in a heartbeat. The man had been swooped before.

Dredd pushed past Bropes and into the apartment as soon as the chains were down. Typical place: everything made from extruded plasteen, from the walls and the furniture to the half-dozen tacky souvenirs on top of the Tri-D. A table with one chair, facing the screen. Bropes had been in the middle of a bowl of Synthi-Flakes and a beaker of juice.

"You're up early, citizen."

"Uh, I have a job, Judge." Bropes was still in his night things, skinny white limbs emerging from T-shirt and shorts, red hair mussed and flattened from sleep. "I'm a pointer, down at Brendy's Pad-Mart."

"Pointer?"

Bropes nodded. "I point at things. Things in the Mart. Like pads, and stuff." He demonstrated, aiming a long finger at the beaker. "Draws people's attention to the products, makes them want to buy more."

"A laudable career, citizen. Committed any crimes recently? I'll know if you're lying."

"No Judge, no crimes. I couldn't be a pointer if I had a record."

The swoop took less than ten minutes. Bropes stood quietly to one side as Dredd went though his possessions. He didn't have that much: his clothes, souvenirs from various sightseeing tours, a collection of kneepads, all from the Pad-Mart where he worked. "Staff discount".

The apartment was clean. Dredd checked a couple of the kneepads against Justice Department records, but the sales were on file, and Bropes even had the receipts. Against all the odds, it looked as though he'd stumbled across a model citizen.

Still, he had to ask. "What's up with the middle name, Bropes?"

The man looked downcast. "The bot at the registration office had a malfunction. Pa always said he could see it sparking, but Ma wouldn't let him reregister me. Said she wanted a girl…"

"I see." Dredd got a feeling he was going to be regaled with Bropes's life story if he stayed any longer, and he needed to be back on the street. He headed for the door. "Thank you for your time, citizen. Enjoy your breakfast."

He was halfway out the door when it hit him. *Breakfast.*

He spun on his heel and was back at the table in two long strides. "Mind if I try a Synthi-Flake, Bropes? Hear they're pretty good."

Bropes was gaping. "I—"

Dredd took a single flake from the bowl, sniffed it, put it in his mouth. And spat it back again. "Wondered what you were spending your wages on, Bropes. Give it up."

Bropes sagged, like a puppet without its strings. He raised his bony arm and pointed at one of the souvenirs on the Tri-D. "Power Tower Tours," he whispered.

The flimsy plasteen tower came apart easily in Dredd's gloved hands, and a tiny amount of white powder flowed out into his palm as he tipped the remains. He didn't even need to taste it. "Life not sweet enough for you, citizen?" He crushed the replica Power Tower in one fist. "Code twenty, section two. Possession of an illegal substance with intent to use: two years."

"Two *years*? For *sugar*?"

"And compulsory rehab. Marcus Elizabeth Bropes, you've pointed at your last kneepad."

How could he have missed the sugar?

Dredd tooled his Lawmaster along Mandelson Overpass, disgusted with himself. He'd almost been out of the hab, and there was a bowlful of sugary Synthi-Flakes sitting right there on the table the whole time. The souvenirs should have been the first thing he looked at, crushing every one searching for contraband. Instead, he'd almost made a mistake.

Almost let a guilty man go free.

Dredd pulled the Lawmaster over to the side of the overzoom and gazed out over the city. He couldn't afford to make mistakes. No street Judge could. What was wrong with him?

Was he getting old?

No, he wasn't ready for the Long Walk just yet. He didn't like to admit it, but the plain fact of the matter was, there was something on his mind.

Project Warchild.

Depending on who you asked, Elize Hellermann was either a scientific visionary on a par with Newton and Einstein, or a borderline psychotic with no morals or scruples whatsoever. Everyone who worked with her could agree on one thing, however – her brilliance.

She was persuasive, too. Despite only being a member of Tek Division's civilian scientific staff, she had managed to convince at least one Chief Judge that research into intelligent bioweapons was a justifiable use of resources. And once she had funding, she had spent the next fifteen years working on a modification – some might say perversion – of Justice Department's cloning procedures.

Cloning was an integral part of the Justice Department, used in the selection and shaping of suitable Judge candidates. But Hellermann wanted to take it in a new direction. She wanted to build soldiers, warriors, programmable monsters that could be dropped into the most violent, crime-ridden areas to pacify them without human loss.

The project had been codenamed Warchild.

More bioweapon than biological organism, the Warchild would be able to operate in open battle or undercover, the offensive systems beneath its skin undetectable by normal scanning. Implanted neurocircuitry would render it entirely controllable. It was stronger, faster and infinitely more lethal than the Judges Hellermann intended to replace.

The proposal split Tek Division. Some saw the promise of her plan, others were troubled by the ethics of the whole operation. While they

debated, Hellermann set the project in motion without official sanction.
By the time it was decided to suspend the programme pending further
investigation and debate, Hellermann had proved her genius: Project
Warchild was on the verge of creating its first fully functioning
bioweapon.

When the full implications of the project were finally revealed,
Warchild was closed down in a day. The embryonic monsters were
destroyed and the staff who worked on them forcibly reassigned. Hellermann never turned up for her new assignment and dropped out of sight.
It wasn't until a year later her name resurfaced, when a routine crime
swoop in the MegEast docks turned up an illegal consignment of certain
chemicals. The chemicals were DNA recombinants and potent muta-
gens, with molecular triggers that matched those used in Justice
Department cloning.

The subsequent investigation eventually led Dredd and his team to a
derelict sector in the Dust Zone, and to Elize Hellermann.

The woman was finally in the cubes where she could do no harm. A
consignment of prototype bioweapons had been completed, but they
were out of the city, somewhere across the Black Atlantic. As far as
Dredd should have been concerned, the case was closed.

Dredd rubbed his throat idly, still feeling the Warchild's talons crushing his windpipe. One second after birth and the creature had almost
taken him down. It hadn't even been properly programmed – Hellermann had triggered its early emergence as she had escaped through the
nursery, trying for a diversion.

The creatures in the factory had already been disposed of but there
were ten more of them out there. Fully grown, fully programmed, utterly
lethal.

The case was closed. And it shouldn't have been personal.

But to Joe Dredd, Project Warchild felt like unfinished business.

5. SARGASSO

It was Angle who saw the cityship first. He was on watch, prowling *Golgotha*'s deck and scanning the moonlit horizon for any sign of salvage or trouble. He had just started shouting when it appeared on Dray's sensor board, and the proximity alarms were what woke Gethsemane Bane. They weren't loud, but some steady, unsleeping part of her brain had been listening out for them.

Golgotha and her crew were more than twenty-four hours away from their encounter with the stealth ship, and most of that time had been spent arguing about what was in the casket and which grudforsaken hulk the pirates called home. Bane had stayed out of the chatter to a large extent. Her near-death experience had taken more out of her than she was prepared to admit, and she had spent most of the journey back helping Orca fix the gunwales. He wasn't concerned about what was in the box or where the pirates had come from: he had his engines to think about, bullet holes in the upper hull and a missing crane.

It had been a long trip and Bane was dog-tired. So when the alarms went off and Angle started yelling "Land ahoy," she was up and out of the hammock in moments, hungry for the sight of home.

Dray was up on the bridge as usual, working both the helm and the sensors. He stepped aside when Bane bounded in. "There it is," he grinned, nodding at a speck on the horizon. "At drokking last…"

"Aw, don't say you haven't enjoyed this one, Dray!" Bane hunted around for her binocs and found them on a hook under her slicker. "I was thinking of swinging around and heading back out for another week."

"Wouldn't advise it."

She winked at him and raised the binocs to her eyes. For a moment all she saw was the darkness of nighttime on the Black Atlantic, with just a slivery gleam of moonlight to pick out the horizon. She then saw a dull smear of light directly ahead, and the binocs changed their focus a fraction to bring the cityship *Sargasso* into view.

From here, *Sargasso* looked less like a vessel and more like an island, a great dark slab of metal rising from the black waters in an insane sprawl of decks and towers and support cables. It was studded with thousands upon thousands of lights: searchlights, running lights and cooking fires. A warm light shone from untold numbers of portholes, and spots of sickly green phosphorescence lit up from the churning ranks of drive screws at the stern.

Home. Gethsemane Bane had never been more glad to see it. She stayed on the bridge for the next four hours, watching it grow in her vision, never taking the binocs from her eyes until she didn't need them any more.

It was impossible to say which ships had first joined together to become *Sargasso*'s original core. There were more than five hundred vessels in the structure, everything from pleasure cruisers to fishing boats, chemical tankers to factory vessels. It was even rumoured that an old twentieth century attack sub was bolted somewhere under the waterline. Some smaller ships hadn't actually touched the water for decades; their deck space was more important than their hull volume, so they had been hauled up level with their taller companions and fixed in place.

Safety came in numbers, nowhere more so than on the poisoned waters of the Black Atlantic. Maybe it was a desire for such safety that drove the *Sargasso*'s first component vessels to sail together. Maybe it was a need to hold formation among myriad ships of differing engine power that prompted their crews to begin lashing them together. And over the years, the crews had been joined by refugees from the ABC Wars, economic migrants and mutants driven out of the Mega-Cities because of their damaged DNA. As *Sargasso*'s bulk increased, so did its population. It stopped being a ship and had become a city.

Sargasso wasn't the only cityship afloat, but it was the largest at three kilometres from multiple bows to multiple sterns, with a wake that could swamp a battle cruiser and a million people calling it home.

Dray took the helm when it was time for *Golgotha* to dock. He always did. Only someone who knew every last detail about how the little vessel rode in the water would be able to manage it.

He began to alter course a few kilometres out, angling to port and *Sargasso*'s stern. The cityship's vast collection of hulls set up a web of chaotic crosscurrents and undertows that could tear a smaller vessel in half. The only safe way to approach *Sargasso* was from the stern, and even that took a master helmsman to get right.

Golgotha bucked and wallowed as it crested the outermost limit of the cityship's bow wave. Playing the helm like a musician, Dray brought the vessel in close enough to catch the wave and ride its rear slope back along *Sargasso*'s length. Then, after dropping back more than five hundred metres past the portside stern, he opened the throttles and began to catch up.

Sargasso wasn't a single, solid structure. Nothing so vast could survive on a moving sea if it couldn't flex and shift with the waves. According to its heading, *Sargasso* could gain or lose almost a hundred metres in length at any one time, and half that in width. It could open to let an especially destructive wave pass through, or narrow to let obstructions go by on either side. It had even sailed though an old Sov-Block minefield once, each ship in the structure moving apart just enough to avoid the floating thermonuclear weapons. It had almost worked. One of the mines had been sent on a new heading by the cityship's wake, and struck a trailing ship. Bane could still remember the citywide gasp as it had hit, and the cheering a few seconds later when it failed to detonate.

That fluid structure, essential as it was for the cityship's survival, also made it the devil to dock with. Bane looked across at Dray as he worked the helm, not daring to speak. Dray was sweating, his lips working, one good eye blinking rapidly as he calculated and recalculated *Golgotha*'s course. *Sargasso* had two main docks set on either side of the propeller fields, but the docks were moving and the props were thundering and the water behind *Sargasso* was a thousand tonnes of leaping, hissing foam in its wake. A computer autopilot would have had them crushed between a couple of hulls on the way in, or dragged down to a close encounter with a drive screw. Gethsemane Bane, who had captained *Golgotha* all her life – or at least, the only part of it that mattered – couldn't have done it. She was in Dray's scaly hands now. They all were, and they all knew it.

Bane returned her attention to the view out of the windshield. In front of her, the harbour entrance was already rearing up.

The doorway was twice as tall as the *Golgotha*'s topmast and four times as wide as its hull. There were huge doors inside made up of great slabs of formed and welded plasteen cut from the hulls of scavenged supertankers. In the event of an attack, the doors could be swung and locked closed, using power geared-up from the main engines. *Sargasso* hadn't gone to war in Bane's lifetime, but she knew there was always a danger. Not all pirate vessels were as small as the one that had taken off Orca's precious crane.

Dray was guiding the ship along the narrow safe channel between the propeller eddies, closing the last few metres of distance from home.

Bane saw the shadow of the harbour scan towards her along the deck, then it was over the bridge and she could feel the sudden coolness of it on the skin of her arms.

They were inside. They were home.

A cacophony of shouts and catcalls from the maintenance crews were greeting them from twenty metres up. They hung from cradles, greasing the huge rods and gears of the door mechanisms with rendered down megashark blubber. Angle and Can-Rat, who were up at the bow rail, returned the calls with some obscenities of their own, making Bane blush and grin.

Golgotha trundled along the harbour pool, hunting for a berth. Dray had the throttles back now they were in calm water and Bane could hear the familiar noises of the dockside over the throb of the engines: more shouts and greetings, engines and drive units rumbling, sirens, and loudest of all the hubbub of the dockside market that spread across the entire forward end of the harbour.

Sargasso had a complement of twenty scavenger vessels. The portside harbour was big enough to house them all, with plenty of space for visitors.

Bane couldn't keep the smile off her face. This should have been the busy time, the time when the ship had to be unloaded and refuelled and maintained. There were deals to set up, fees to pay, spares to buy and creditors to dodge. Gethsemane Bane, as captain and master of the scavenger ship *Golgotha*, was in for a harder time in the next few hours than she would be at sea. But despite that, she was grinning like a loon.

She was back. Everything was going to be all right.

Somehow, Bane always ended up thinking of Jester when the *Golgotha* berthed.

During the first years of her life, she probably didn't think at all. Those times were just a blur of hunger and violence. She had no memory of her mother or father, assuming she had either and wasn't just expelled from the guts of a slick eel dredged up out of the *Sargasso*'s bilges. She had a vague memory of someone telling her that was where she came from. And hurting her.

One day, she had been big enough to hurt him back. Very badly. Luckily, she had no real memory of that either.

The thing she could remember, far more clearly than she would have preferred, was hunger. It was an empty belly that had first taken her down to the harbour, driven her to creep along the dockside and dip a fist into the tank of bilge-filth fresh out of *Golgotha*'s pump to take that first slimy lump of decaying mutant fish, chew it and force it down.

She would have kept on eating the dripping waste until it killed her too, she was that hungry. Luckily for her, she was being watched, and before she had taken another bite she was lifted in one giant hand and hauled, kicking and screeching, onto *Golgotha*'s deck.

She had expected a beating. After all, that's what such digressions had always earned her before. Instead, she got soup.

Suspicious and terrified, she would have hurled the bowl away and bolted off the ship and into the water, had she not been so close to starvation. But the smell of the soup had a direct effect on her central nervous system, forcing her to sit and gulp it down, all the time avoiding the eyes of the big, shark-grinned man who had brought it to her.

Then she ran. But she was back the next day, and once again there was soup.

It got to be a habit.

Why Jester Bane, one of the most experienced scavenger captains on the *Sargasso*, should have considered the foul-smelling, suspicious and occasionally downright destructive child a suitable candidate for adoption, she still had no idea. But then again, he always did have an eye for a valuable piece of salvage. Maybe he could see the worth in that damaged child. That was how a good scavenger worked: sort through the garbage, ignore most of it, but take on board the pieces that will make a profit.

Jester Bane had never made a profit from little Gethsemane. But over the years, he did make a captain out of her.

"Remembering Jester, huh?"

Dray's question brought her back to the present with a jolt. She looked down at the deck and saw that it was clear; Can-Rat and Angle must have already gone down to the crew quarters, getting their things together for shore leave.

Golgotha's crew didn't spend a lot of time together when they were docked. Dray had family waiting for him and Angle would go and try his luck with anything female whose body temperature approached normal, while Can-Rat often just seemed to wander off, then wander back a while later. Either that or he would remain aboard and watch Orca, his intense gaze making the big engineer nervous.

"How could you tell?"

"The way you were smiling," Dray replied. "It reminded me of him. Without the teeth, of course."

Bane laughed quietly. "Did he ever..." Slightly embarrassed, she trailed off.

"Ever what?"

"Say why he gave her to me?"

"*Golgotha*?" Dray shrugged. "He knew you'd look after her. Us, too."

Bane thought about that for a moment or two. Then she shook her head and ran her fingers back through her short, cropped hair. "Ahh, since when did I get to be the mothering type? Get off the boat."

"You sure?"

"You've got a woman waiting for you, Dray. Go on!" She shooed Dray away and backed him towards the hatch down to the bunk-hold. "I'm going to see the Old Man, but I don't want to see you back here till you're too exhausted to stand up, understood?"

"Aye, aye, captain," Dray replied with a smile, and ducked quickly through the hatch.

Orca, to no one's great surprise, was down in the engine room.

He had been working on *Golgotha*'s drives for hours; running tests, making small adjustments, sometimes just sitting back on his vast haunches and staring off into space. It was during these periods of trance-like thought that he would often get his best ideas: new ways of tweaking the engines, filtering the fuel, modifying yet another wrench or electro-spanner out of all recognition.

The only disadvantage to these unfocused moments was that Can-Rat would be watching him the whole time. Orca would return to reality, full of new ideas, and get a jolt when he saw that hunched body and narrow, intense gaze aimed right at him.

Orca had been working when the others left the ship and he had continued working as night fell. And Can-Rat had been watching him the whole time. His small, jet black eyes had followed Orca incessantly around the engine room, and he had been scuttling about in swift, darting movements to get a better view of whatever the bigger man was working on.

Orca had long ago given up on being annoyed by this. Once, he had cornered Can-Rat and asked him if he wanted to learn about engines. Can-Rat had simply replied that he *was* learning.

The little mutant's mind simply didn't work the way that most peoples did, Orca had decided. Can-Rat was a bit like him in that respect, able to analyse the structure of a mechanism and thereby discern its purpose and operation, just by external study. It made Orca a great engineer, but what it made Can-Rat he wasn't prepared to say. He got the strange feeling that the furry little man wasn't just studying the engines; he was seeing the entire boat as one single, interconnected system.

And that included the crew.

However, for this night, study time was over. He had done all to the quiescent drive system that he could reasonably do. Time for other things.

He stood, wiping his hands, and backed away from the transmission unit's complex mesh of gears. The cover locked as he pulled it down, sealing the gears away. Later, he would open a lube-valve and fill the unit with oil.

Orca took the equipment he had been using back to his tool chest, stowing them carefully in their labelled drawers and niches. Then he waddled past Can-Rat and squeezed out through the engine room hatch. His curiosity, usually so easy to suppress, was getting the better of him. He sighed, and gave in to it.

Time to look at things other than engines.

Can-Rat watched Orca leave. He stayed where he was for a few moments, perched on top of Orca's workbench, then he hopped down and scampered after the engineer.

He knew Orca didn't like him much. None of the crew did, except Captain Bane, but that didn't matter. Can-Rat didn't see things the way other people seemed to. To everyone else, all the parts of the ship were separate; a vast collection of components that only worked when fitted together in a certain way. But to Can-Rat, the engines weren't distinct from the rest of *Golgotha*, any more than *Golgotha* was distinct from *Sargasso*. Even when the ship was out at sea, it was still connected, still part of the whole picture. The crew, too. On one level, they were individual people, but that level was the least interesting one to him. Without them, *Golgotha* was just dead metal. Without *Golgotha*, the crew would come apart, be homeless and hungry and miserable. Engines wouldn't work without a ship, and the ship wouldn't work without engines.

Why didn't people see that? It was so obvious.

That was why he enjoyed watching Orca at work, in as much as Can-Rat could enjoy anything. The big man often found that the engines worked better when certain parts of them were arranged in a slightly different way. Can-Rat had learned from watching Orca that there were hundreds, maybe thousands of ways that the engine parts could be arranged to work. And infinitely more ways that they could be made to stop working.

He couldn't have explained it to Orca even if he had wanted to. In the same way that he couldn't have explained how he sensed things that were about to happen before they did, because he could feel their connections shifting about. It would be like trying to describe what Synthi-Caf tasted like to a man born without a tongue.

Orca was heading along the spine of the ship, towards the forward hold. Can-Rat knew where he was going and found himself hanging back.

The casket.

It lay at the heart of a web of connections, darker and more tangled than he had ever seen. It made his head hurt just being around it. The others thought he had sensed the pirate vessel closing in on them before the sensors had picked it up, but he hadn't. It was the casket that had been bothering him.

Death lay within that thing, like a statue lies within stone, waiting to be freed by the sculptor's art.

And Orca was walking right towards it.

Can-Rat stopped where he was. The engines were part of *Golgotha*. They were part of Orca, too. If Orca ceased to function the engines would, and then the ship would. Gethsemane Bane was part of *Golgotha*. If Orca died, the engines would die, the ship would die, and Bane would... Die!

He didn't want that.

"Wait!" he called, his voice sounding reedy and thin as it bounced from the hull's metal walls. "Orca, wait up!"

Orca hauled himself along the length of the *Golgotha*, squeezing through hatches and passages and moving more easily through the ship's holds. The holds contained nothing but spare parts and provisions. The only salvaged booty lay in the forward hold.

He almost filled the narrow passage that led to the forward hold. Spinning the locking wheel in the centre of the door, he pushed the heavy metal panel inwards without even feeling its weight. Orca wore a layer of dense fat like a suit made for a giant, but he wasn't a weakling. It took powerful muscles to move his bulk, as more than one dockside loudmouth had discovered to their cost.

He turned sideways as he stepped over the hatch sill and eased himself through. The forward hold was in darkness. Orca heard Can-Rat saying something a few bulkheads behind him, but he chose to ignore it. The little man had bothered him enough for one day.

Light from the passage cut across the hold, drawing a bright line across the deck and up the far bulkhead. Orca reached out to the bulkhead by the hatch and turned the switch he knew would be there. Above him, blue-green fluorescent tubes fluttered into life.

The casket was open.

The cables holding it down to the deck had been broken, their frayed ends glittering in the light. The lid of the shell had flipped open and was now lying on the deck next to the body of the casket. Fluid, translucent and greasy-looking, had spilled out of it in considerable quantity and now lay in steaming puddles on the deck.

Orca hesitated, unsure of whether to step back into the corridor and slam the hatch, or try to find whatever had been released from the casket. Something organic had been sealed inside, he could see that from the exposed systems. There were data leads in the casket, drug injectors, a gas-transfer system. The lock had opened by itself. A timing mechanism?

Just as he thought that, Orca saw part of the far wall *shimmer*.

One second it was just shadowy, stained bulkhead metal, the next it was fluid, mobile, casting shadows that were all wrong as it separated from the wall.

And hurled itself towards him.

Orca didn't even have time to move before it struck.

Back in the passageway, Can-Rat saw Orca jerk suddenly, horribly. The web of connections that linked him to the rest of the world were already unravelling around him.

Can-Rat skittered to a halt. Orca was still on his feet, but he was sagging, as if his vast weight had finally caught up with him after all these years. There was the sound of something wet and heavy hitting the floor.

"Orca?"

The engineer must have heard his voice. He turned, awkwardly, his great shoulders rolling around first until he almost lost his balance, then his foot came up and moved back, slamming back down to the deck. He ended up facing Can-Rat.

There was an expression on Orca's face that was almost infinitely sad. He opened his mouth, but all that came out was blood, because there was a wound in his body that ran from his groin up to his throat. He had his hands across it, as though trying to hold himself together, but he was too late. His massive torso had already emptied itself over the deck.

Can-Rat screamed in horror and took an involuntary step backwards. Orca raised a foot and stepped forwards too, as though trying to get away from the hold, but before he could move again a long, shining blade, white and glistening like wet bone, exploded out of his throat.

Orca went down like a loose sack, sliding off the blade to crash onto the passageway floor. Blood, sent flying by the impact of his body, went halfway up the walls and painted Can-Rat from head to toe.

He felt the warmth of it, the sudden, acrid taste of it in his mouth, and he shrieked. At the sound of his voice, what he had thought was a shadow in the hatchway shimmered and flowed and then stepped out into the light.

Its skin was blue-lit metal and rust-stained wall, and then it was pale and slick and unfinished, like something unborn. Can-Rat saw it for a split second before the terror took him and sent him scrambling for his life back along the passageway. He had seen the half-made armour growing through it in patches, the blades, the nightmare it had for a face. He saw the way it was looking at him. Then he ran.

The cold intelligence in that awful stare was something that would stay with him until he died.

6. PROPHESY

"Central Dispatch, all Judges in sector twenty-one, please respond."

Dredd finished cuffing the unconscious perp to a holding post, shook a few gobbets of blood and hair from his daystick and shoved it back into its belt loop. "Responding."

"All points request for backup, Fresh Start Displaced Persons Habplex, off Weaver Skedway."

Dredd's Lawmaster was parked a few metres from the holding post, near the entrance to Hackin' Henry's Smokatorium. That was where the perp had been when Dredd pulled up: kicking the door and demanding to be let in. The Smokatorium staff had locked the doors from the inside, and little wonder, since the man had been wearing nothing except a small pouch of pipe tobacco. And that had been slung around his neck.

Dredd knew that tobacco addiction could do strange things to a citizen. Still, this had been an eye-opener. Even more surprising had been when the man had rounded on Dredd and tried to set him on fire with a cigarette lighter.

Dredd climbed quickly back onto the Lawmaster and gunned the engines. The big bike leaped forward with a throaty whine. "Acknowledged, Dispatch. What's the situation?"

"Attempted mass breakout, with associated damage to municipal property."

"On my way." Dredd took the Lawmaster left onto the intersked that would lead him onto Weaver. By his reckoning, Fresh Start had been due to pop for the past two weeks. He was quite surprised it had taken this long.

There were hundreds of Habplexes all over the city, unwelcome left-overs from the Apocalypse War. Areas that had been reduced to rubble during the conflict had been bulldozed flat, levelled out and used as the foundations for sprawling, fenced-in camps. Inside the fences, temporary hab-domes provided shelter for the unfortunate citizens made homeless during the war. Often they ended up camping on ground once occupied by the blocks they had lived in previously.

The Habplexes hadn't been intended as permanent accommodation, but as the years went by and disasters like the Necropolis Event and the Second Robot War had continued to stretch the city's housing budget, plans to close the camps down had been pushed back further and further until they were basically out of sight.

Every month or so, someone from the Habplex would get lucky and be rehoused; that was usually the trigger for the remaining ten thousand inhabitants to begin ripping the place apart. The fact that they were destroying their own homes in the process always seemed to escape them.

The intersked sloped up sharply, taking the road over part of the Meg-Way. The rise afforded Dredd an early view of the camp – a wide gap in the Mega-City skyline, maybe five kilometres away, and a distant smear of yellow security lights. There was smoke, too, lit crimson from within. Fresh Starters often tried to burn their way through the perimeter fence.

Dredd tooled his Lawmaster diagonally across the sked and into the exclusive Judges' Lane. He could move faster there. As he did so, his helmet comms hissed into life again. "Central Dispatch."

"Already have that Fresh Start call, Dispatch. I'll be there in three."

"Negative, Judge Dredd," the dispatcher told him. "Message is direct from Chief Judge Hershey, your request to be appraised of developments in the Warchild case."

That, Dredd thought to himself, was fast. Hershey must have been taking a special interest. "Go ahead," he replied. "But make it quick."

"The SJS got nothing out of Hellermann."

Dredd hadn't expected to hear that. The Special Judicial Squad – the Judges who judged the Judges – were masters at interrogation in all its forms. Truth drugs, psychic techniques, dream machines; they had all the tricks and showed no mercy in using them. Dredd knew Hellermann was tough, but SJS should have cracked her like a synth-egg.

"She's had herself modified," the dispatcher reported. "Artificial glands grafted into the brainstem. They release anti-serums that neutralise truth drugs. Looks like she'd been undergoing deep hypnosis, too. She has auto-suggestive blocks set up to stop her breaking under psychological duress."

"She knew what to expect if she got caught and prepared for it," Dredd muttered, guiding his Lawmaster onto a slipzoom. Already he could hear the dull roar of the riot, punctuated by the whiplash cracking of gunfire. Things, it seemed, were getting ugly.

"That was SJS's assessment, too," said the dispatcher. "Judge Buell has ordered that Hellermann be handed over to Psi-Division for deep psyche interrogation."

"Let the Chief Judge know I won't be holding my breath."

Ahead of him was the broad, flat expanse of waste ground on which the Habplex had been set up. Bathed in the nicotine glow of the security lights, rioting camp-dwellers moved through the area in destructive waves. At least half of the hab-domes were ablaze and most of the others were in ruins. From the look of them, many had been torn apart to provide weapons for the rioters.

A group of Fresh Starters had built a bonfire against the electromesh fence, hot enough to melt the wire and short out that section. Tearing the burning debris away from the blackened wire, they had succeeded in ripping a hole in the mesh. Dredd angled his bike towards the opening and thumbed its siren into life.

"Thank the Chief Judge and tell her I'll be in touch. Now get me Weather Control."

The journey from the harbour barge to the Old Man's chambers took Bane almost an hour, although part of that was spent in the dockside market looking for a suitable offering. Row after row of stalls were arranged around the forward edge of the harbour pool, covered against the constant rain of rusty condensation dripping from the metal roof. All the stalls had battery lamps and bioluminescent tubes strung from their frames, so that shoppers could see what they were buying in the cavernous gloom of the harbour barge. Some even had their own portable generators running noisy neon signs and matrix displays. Bane tended to steer clear of those stalls – if the owners had that much credit to burn, they certainly didn't need any of her hard-earned notes. There were plenty in the dockside market who did.

She settled on a bottle of potent brown spirits, no doubt brewed up from fruit mash and fish innards in some bottom deck bilge-still. It would probably taste ghastly, but the Old Man wouldn't mind and Bane had liked the little charms strung around the neck of the bottle on baling wire: sea creatures cut from scraps of thin metal, megasharks and octopi and long, looping serpents. They chimed against the glass and caught the light. Bane had thanked the toothless old woman behind the stall and handed over enough notes to pay for the bottle and a little more besides. An extravagance, she knew, but what was the point of making a good catch if she couldn't spread it around?

The market was packed – it usually was – and Bane had to duck and weave to get past the shoppers and back onto open dockside. From there she took the starboard ladder up five decks until she reached a hatchway in the barge hull. That led her out onto a narrow, hanging

mesh bridge that swung uneasily in the wind. That bridge – quite terrifying to cross, with the cables groaning and the black water rushing past
far below – had been the beginning of Bane's trek through the cityship,
across eighteen decks, up and down numerous levels, through tunnels
and up towers and down grimy, corroding ladders. She passed through
three more markets, a wedding, two brawls, an open air drinking competition and a minor fire until she reached the chem-tanker *Hyperion*,
only six hulls from *Sargasso*'s centre line.

By the time she got there she was cold, soaked from spray and very,
very tired. Her limbs ached from all the climbing and carrying the bottle around hadn't helped, either. Next time, Bane promised herself, she
would take the old fool a sandwich. At least she could stuff that into her
coat pocket and have both hands free.

She went into *Hyperion* through the deck where hatches had been cut
in the thick metal. Stairs led down through the levels until she was at a
point that must have been midway between the deck and the waterline.
There, a series of gangways opened out into multiple compartments, set
into what had once been the tanker's vast chemical storage tanks. Now
they were factories, homes, brothels, a hospital, and the chambers of the
Old Man.

A chem-tanker was as big as a small town, although it was still only
a tiny fragment of *Sargasso*'s total bulk.

Bane had been to see the Old Man so many times she could have
made the trip blindfolded. She had to go down two more levels and
through a narrow plasteen tunnel to get to his chambers and when she
finally arrived she found the way blocked.

Two huge guards crouched at the chamber entrance, their heads
almost touching the high ceiling. Everyone on board *Sargasso* was
mutated to some degree – the Black Atlantic did that to everyone after
a while – but this pair were extreme by anyone's standards. They had
biceps Bane could have curled up and hidden in, and one was carrying
a plasteen H-girder in one mighty hand, slapping it against the other
palm like a jetball bat.

The Old Man's guards were legendary on board *Sargasso*. One of them
was rumoured to be female, but Bane had no idea which.

"Hey," said the one without the girder as she stopped. Its voice was
surprisingly soft and high, almost childlike, like that of a singer. "Bane.
Good hunting?"

"Pretty good," she smiled. "Is he–"

"Expecting you? Yeah." The other guard stopped slapping its palm
with the girder and rested its end against the deck. Bane felt the mesh
sag slightly under its weight. "He's been asking for you."

"Right…" Suddenly, Bane felt unaccountably nervous. She swallowed hard, tugged her long coat a little tighter around her shoulders and stepped between the guards, the bottle a comforting weight in her fist.

It was time to meet the oldest man in the world.

The quayside under Angle's feet seemed to be pitching and rolling like the *Golgotha* in a heavy swell, which was just how he wanted it. After spending as much on grog as he had in the past couple of hours, he would have demanded his money back if he hadn't been at least partially drunk. As it was, he reckoned he was at least three quarters there, which he considered a pretty good deal.

Even though he was barely out of his teens and the youngest of *Golgotha*'s crew by far, Angle was already an experienced drinker. Luckily, the mutation that had given him his extra joints had also blessed him with a surprising capacity to metabolise alcohol, even the vicious algae-based grog they brewed on *Sargasso*. Within an hour or two he would be as sober as a Judge, which was a good thing. He was meeting Kerryanne, the barmaid from the Leaping Eel, after her shift was done.

There was a breeze coming in through the harbour doors, cool and tangy with the battery-acid smell of Black Atlantic seawater. It sent the quayside lanterns swinging on their cables and sent sprays of condensation drizzling down from the roof braces. Angle walked unsteadily between the moving cones of yellow light, feeling cold, rusty rain hit his shoulders and the top of his head as he headed for the *Golgotha*. If he was going to impress Kerryanne, he needed a shower and a change of clothes.

Behind him shone the lights of the three taverns in which he had spent his evening: the Dancing Norm, Lannigan's, and, of course, the Leaping Eel. The places had been jammed with all manner of revellers, from market traders and entertainers to cleaning crews and maintenance gangers down off the gantries. And, of course, the other scavengers. Angle had enjoyed the evening immensely, drinking the hardest of the gangers – a red-haired shift leader called Big Molly – clear off her chair, and swapping tall stories with the crews of every other ship in the harbour. But, as drunk as he was, he'd kept the secret of what lay in *Golgotha*'s hold to himself. The other scavs would find out about the casket on the day of the auction and not before.

The grog was warm in Angle's gut, the hour was late, and he was as relaxed as he had been for a while. So much so in fact, that he almost tripped over the corpse before he saw it.

It was in the middle of the quayside, in the shadows between two lanterns, and he had to stop himself stumbling into it. At first he thought it was a pile of old cargo nets, dropped carelessly in his path, but then he noticed something pale emerging from the bundle, splayed in a pool of lantern light. It was a hand.

Three of its fingers were missing.

Angle let out an involuntary yelp of shock and took a step backwards, his heart suddenly bouncing and hammering behind his ribs. There must have been an accident, he thought giddily. The crane operator, or one of the maintenance gangers, someone operating dockside machinery. Maybe the poor bastich had fallen into his own equipment.

Gingerly, he took a step forwards and rolled the body over. It flopped onto its back far too easily. Corpses tend to be heavier when their internal organs are still internal, not left lying on the quay and slithering greasily into the harbour pool.

"Oh, drokk!" Angle backed away, the alcohol-induced warmth vanishing in an instant. The expression on the corpse's face was terrible, a rictus of pure terror, and worse because it was a face Angle recognised. They'd been drinking together, not long ago; an hour, maybe less.

Ifrana Rokes, of the *Melchior*. She'd left the Dancing Norm to check on the moorings, and hadn't come back. Angle had figured that he'd been tactfully dumped and had switched his attentions to the Leaping Eel and Kerryanne instead.

And all the while poor Ifrana had been lying here. Murdered. Even in the bad light, Angle could see that this was no accident. Someone had opened the woman up in the same way as they might gut a fish.

He quickly looked up and down the quayside, his head spinning, but there was no one about. No one but him and the opened, stone dead woman at his feet. And possibly the murderer, he thought, feeling his spine turn to ice. Waiting in the shadows with a gutting knife the size of an anchor.

Angle realised that this was not a good place to be.

Golgotha was close by, bobbing listlessly in the water. Angle decided that if he had to make a stand anywhere, it would be there, where he could get the spit guns into play. He skirted around Ifrana's body, trying not to see the way her emptied torso was slowly collapsing in on itself, and climbed quickly up *Golgotha*'s gangplank.

The ship rocked slightly as he stepped aboard. Angle winced at the sudden movement and paused, holding his breath and listening intently. He heard the slow, even creaking of boat hulls in still water, the patter of condensation-rain on decks, the distant murmur of late trade in the market.

And a low moan from somewhere astern.

The noise was between him and the guns, he guessed with a mental curse. But then the moan sounded again and he realised it was Can-Rat.

"Canny? Stomm, what's going on?" Angle scrambled over to where his crewmate lay wedged between the gunwales and a winch drum. The little mutant appeared to have folded his body in half lengthways in order to fit into the gap, making himself almost invisible among the shadows.

"Angle, that you?"

"Yeah, it's me." Angle reached down, his multi-jointed arm moving easily into the awkward space. "Let me help you up."

Can-Rat shook his head. "I'm okay," he muttered, and unfolded himself from the bolt-hole with an oddly fluid grace, marred only by a sharp intake of breath and a gasp of pain when he was halfway upright. He sagged away from Angle's grasp and leaned heavily against the stern rail. "He got Orca," he said quietly.

"What?" Angle gaped. "No way."

Can-Rat nodded. "Down in the hold. Cut him up without trying. Then he came after me..." He tried to straighten, but the pain was obviously too much. "Grud, that hurts... I thought I'd be safe out here, but he's fast, and he can see in the dark. He hit me... Had a blade..." Can-Rat was beginning to lose consciousness. Pain and shock were dragging him down. Angle grabbed his thin shoulders.

"C'mon, you furry drokker, stay with me! What happened?"

Can-Rat swallowed, and shook himself. "Don't know. I heard screams. Maybe he got distracted."

Ifrana, Angle thought ruefully.

"I tried to get up, but I think my ribs are busted."

"Yeah, looks that way," nodded Angle. "Did you see who it was? How'd he get aboard – from the quayside or out of the water?"

"He didn't come aboard," said Can-Rat, wincing as he pressed a tentative hand to his damaged ribs. "He's been here the whole time."

The Old Man's chambers were welded deep into the inside of the chemtanker *Hyperion*. Originally it had been a vessel in its own right, a high-speed pleasure skimmer. The Old Man himself had sailed the Atlantic in that nimble little ship, back when the seas were still blue. He had been very old, even then, and very rich.

The cabins and decks of his skimmer were now black with age and the smoke of a thousand candles. Gethsemane Bane had to walk gingerly into the main cabin to avoid knocking over the hundreds of bottles and jugs that covered the filthy wood – offerings from those who had come to the Old Man over the years to hear his weird and ancient wisdom.

People from all over *Sargasso* would make the journey down into the bowels of the *Hyperion* bearing gifts. It seemed everyone had a question

that only he, in his strange trances and riddled speech, could answer –
who to let a daughter marry, where to hunt for the best salvage, how to
make a charm to ward off disease or turn the blade of an enemy. As long
as Bane could remember, he had never done anything else.

Bane had been coming to see the Old Man since she was a child, just
after Jester had first adopted her, but not for advice or readings. Despite
the Old Man's reputation as the *Sargasso*'s resident shaman, Bane simply came to see him because she liked him.

He was sitting in the middle of the cabin, surrounded by his candles
and bottles. His thin legs were crossed, his head bent so that the curve
of his naked back showed his spine and ribs in perfect detail under the
dark leather of his skin.

Bane crept towards him, very carefully, and sat down opposite. The
Old Man was naked except for a pair of baggy shorts. His skin was as
dark as mahogany, and his hair, cropped close to his skull, was pure
white. To Bane, he looked small and heartbreakingly frail.

"Hey, eldster," she whispered, in case he was asleep. "Brought you
some booze."

At the sound of her voice, the Old Man gave a reedy cry and threw
back his head. "Devil child," he spat, his eyes rolling wildly. "Evil you
are, evil I see! Terror you bring in your right hand, fire in your left!" He
raised a skeletal arm, finger outstretched. "Get thee gone! Sinner, harri-
dan, harlot!"

Bane was on her feet, shocked by the outburst. She felt something
against her boot and heard a bottle clatter onto the deck. "Hey, what–"

"How dare you bring foulness before me!" he yelled, shaking with
rage. The corners of his mouth were starting to quirk up. "Tempter,
destroyer! Er, scavenger..."

"Scavenger?"

The Old Man was trying hard to keep a straight face. Eventually he
gave up. "Ah, what do you expect, child?" He grinned, showing a wide
sickle of very white teeth. "When all you bring me is this rancidness?"

Bane lifted the bottle and shook it at him, making the charms rattle.
"You old phoney! You really had me going there!"

He shrugged. "It's my job. Hey, sit down, sit down." He waited until
Bane, now trying very hard to keep an angry look on her face, had settled back onto the deck. "I've got to keep in practise, haven't I? The
punters expect so much and I'm not as young as I was."

That, Bane knew, was an understatement. The Old Man hadn't been
young since before the ships that made up *Sargasso* were built. He had
seen the building of the Mega-Cities, the turning of the dry land into the
rad-desert known as the Cursed Earth. He had seen the Atlantic go black.

Something in his DNA had twisted, long ago, shutting down the processes of natural ageing. He had once told her that he had self-replicating telomeres, whatever they were. Then again, he had told her lots of things as she was growing up. Except his real name – no one knew that.

Bane glared at him. "Fraud."

"You and I both know," said the Old Man, "that isn't true." He presented Bane with his open hand. "Give, give…"

"Sure you want it? Rancid and all?"

He nodded vigorously. "Booze, child, is like sex and pizza. It's all good." He took the bottle from her and turned to place it among a dozen identical ones just off to his left. "You've been hunting."

"It's my job." She gave him a fond smile. "It's good to see you."

He nodded gently. It was all she needed. Embarrassed, she let her gaze drop to the deck, and changed the subject. "Look, I wanted to ask about–"

"Can-Rat," he interrupted. He often did that. Knowing what people were going to say before they said it was one of his talents. If he wasn't a natural psionic, he was something very like one.

"Mm." She looked up. "Is he one of yours?"

"Of mine?"

Bane nodded. "He sees things before they happen, I think. We were attacked out at sea, and he saw it coming." She grimaced, trying to put what she felt into words. "I was wondering if he saw things the way you do."

The Old Man fixed her with a steady gaze. "I've never met the man."

"That's never stopped you."

He shrugged. "Can-Rat sees connections. You've said before that he's odd and seems distant sometimes?"

"That's one way of putting it."

"He's like that because of the way he sees you. He's more interested in the links that bind you to everything around you, rather than you yourself. Gethsemane Bane as a wave function in the quantum network; a holistic entity, not a discrete equation."

Bane thought about this for a few moments then shook her head. "I don't have the slightest idea what you're talking about," she said. "But as long as he can keep knocking me over before bullets hit me, I guess he's okay."

"I think," the Old Man began, and then stopped. A strange expression crossed his face. "He's in danger."

"What?" Bane frowned. "What, now?"

"Yes, now!" the Old Man leapt to his feet, sending bottles flying. He hauled Bane to her feet with an astounding strength in those thin arms.

"Grud, child, what did you bring aboard?"

Bane had never seen him like this before, and it frightened her. "I don't understand! Can-Rat's in danger because of what we found?" No sense trying to hide anything from the Old Man. "Because of the casket?"

The Old Man suddenly reached out and grabbed her by the forearms, holding her still. "Listen to me, Gethsemane Bane," he hissed. "No tricks now. No trances, no riddles. Whatever is in that box is death, pure and simple."

"What–"

"I don't know!" he snarled. "There's no mind, no thought. Action, but no intent. A plan, but no purpose. Just death! And your people are in its way!"

He shoved her back. She stumbled, almost tripping over the bottles. Dozens of them scattered across the deck as she fought for balance.

"Go," the Old Man was shouting. "Go, before what you've brought here kills us all!"

7. THE SKIPPER

It was Erik, the younger and slightly brighter of the Tusk Brothers, who spotted the figure. It was gone almost before his eyes could track it, but it left an after-image in his brain: a tall, slender man, stooped, darting across the street and into the shadows of a nearby alley.

Erik might have been mistaken, but he could have sworn the man was naked.

"Hey." He used the back of his hand to slap Igor on the upper arm, drawing his attention. His brother was more drunk than him, and in a fouler mood. Hardly surprising, since it was Igor who had just been thrown bodily out of the Black Whale tavern. Erik had followed as a matter of course. The Tusk Brothers were rarely apart.

"Whassup?" Igor scowled. Erik put a finger to his lips, indicating silence. It took Igor's grog-addled mind a second or two to catch up, but when he did his big lower jaw closed with an audible snap.

Erik leaned close. "Just saw some guy, end of the street. Lurking around like maybe he doesn't want anyone to see him."

A slow smile spread over Igor's ruin of a face. "Yeah," he nodded, slowly. Igor did most things slowly, except drink. "Yeah. Right. So–"

"So," said Erik, finishing up for him, "maybe he won't shout so loud if we tap him, yeah?"

It was late; late enough for most of *Sargasso*'s honest citizens to be away in their beds. On most streets, especially in working spaces like the harbour, the only real foot traffic was security patrols by the skipper's men. The Tusk Brothers were on legitimate business, as much as they ever were – staggering home after being thrown out of a tavern wasn't illegal. But anyone darting naked into the shadows on a darkened street was obviously as eager to avoid the patrols as Erik and Igor.

The street was actually a metal companionway, slung out over two tiers of the dock district and, ten metres below, the quayside itself. The hull-side of the street was lined with stall fronts and kiosks, every one shuttered and locked for the night. Five minutes back towards the bow end was the Black Whale, its windows and open door throwing strips of warm yellow light across the mesh.

The alley was a dead end. Erik reached around to the small of his back, under his long fishskin coat, and drew the pair of narrow, double-edged daggers he kept there. Igor slipped a heavy billy club from his belt and tapped it experimentally against his palm. He grinned and nodded to himself, happy at the prospect of a little amusement.

Erik began to increase his pace, his coat – long ago acquired from an unlucky night-time pedestrian – billowing behind him. He wanted to catch the lurker before the man realised he was heading into a dead end and returned to the street. He winced as he heard Igor's heavy tread, keeping up. Igor wasn't the most subtle of men.

In fact, the brothers were not very much alike at all. Erik was small, lean and dark, while Igor was pale of skin and big in the bone. Erik was dextrous and could flip a knife more than twenty metres, hitting whatever he chose. Igor favoured a more direct approach and could shatter a man's spine in a single blow. Both had long, wicked tusks jutting up from their heavy lower jaws, but that was all they really had in common.

Apart from a mutual aptitude for relieving others of their possessions, of course.

They went around the corner together, shoulder to shoulder, blocking the alleyway. There wasn't much light to see by, just a couple of biolume strips throwing a dim, blue-green glow down the walls, but what Erik did see stopped him in his tracks.

The figure was naked, but it wasn't a man.

It had its back to the brothers; a hunched, ridged back that gleamed corpse-grey in the biolume light. There was something about the figure that looked raw, incomplete, like a statue half-made and then abandoned before all the rough edges had been chipped away. Its long, stick-thin arms were up, doing something to the service panel at the end of the alleyway.

As Erik watched, his oversized jaw dropping, the figure reached up and tore the panel free of the wall.

The screech of tearing metal as the fixing bolts ripped clear through the frame somehow launched Igor into action. Maybe the sound hurt his hangover – Erik would never find out.

Igor gave a roar and began barrelling up the alleyway, his billy club raised high and his boots crashing on the mesh.

The figure before them half-turned and made a strange, flipping motion with its hand, almost as though waving them away. The gesture seemed weird, almost effeminate, and Erik barked out a laugh of surprise. But as he did so, Igor tripped over his own feet and went sprawling to the metal floor.

Erik had seen Igor fall over drunk before but he usually got back up again. This time he stayed where he was, face down on the mesh. A shiver went through him and Erik heard him make a sound – a long, whistling groan, as though all the air was being squeezed out of his lungs. And then he was still.

When Erik looked away from his brother to see where the naked figure was, it had gone.

Something was horribly wrong here. There was simply nowhere for the figure to go unless it had climbed over the damaged panel and into the duct. But there hadn't been enough time for that. Igor had gone down almost instantly.

Erik trotted forwards, blades ready, searching the shadows but seeing no one. He reached Igor in a few paces and crouched down beside him.

Igor Tusk wasn't breathing. His face was turned to one side, his eyes wide and still. His pupils had contracted to tiny points.

There were three small needles, like tiny spikes made of plastic or bone, embedded in the skin of his face.

Erik had seen poison at work before, although nothing so fast or powerful. He shouted a curse and jumped up, and as he did so something tiny whipped past him, whining off the mesh a few metres back towards the street. Terrified, he stared up the alleyway, trying to see where the flying thing had come from.

Part of the wall moved. The rust-bubbled paintwork shifted fluidly, and just for a second Erik saw the outline the movement made: a man-shape, stooped and thin as sticks.

The figure had never gone away. It was there… with him.

Erik screamed, long and loud, and then he was running down the alley and onto the street.

It was Erik Tusk's screams that woke Dray from a very pleasant sleep.

He lay still for a moment, eyes closed, trying to identify the noise that had roused him. It had sounded like screaming, but who would be making such a deafening noise at this time of night? Maybe one of the kids was having a nightmare.

He sat up, making his wife stir and roll away from him, drawing the covers up over her head without waking. Dray smiled in the darkness and swung his legs out of bed, getting up carefully so as not to disturb her further, then padded across the room to the door.

He heard another scream just before he got there, and shouting. It seemed to be coming from below him.

Dray and his family lived in one of the dozens of habs on the upper level of the harbour barge; most of the scavenger crews resided there so they could be close to their vessels.

Dray didn't like being away from *Golgotha* for long, and since he had moved into the hab he had enjoyed being able to lean over the street railing outside his door and look straight down onto *Golgotha*'s deck, twenty metres below.

It got noisy sometimes, what with the stalls and the taverns on the next street down, but he was used to that. The Black Whale had once closed for a week while roof braces were being re-welded. Dray hadn't been able to sleep a wink.

Now, however, something far worse than the usual drunken row was taking place a level below his feet.

He leaned over to see what was going on. The patrons of the Black Whale were all out on the street, surrounding a man in a coat. It was the man who was screaming, something about his brother.

About a killer.

Dray didn't like the sound of this at all. He went back into the hab and dressed quickly, making sure he had a couple of good knives in his belt. Then, with his wife still asleep under the covers, he went out, taking care to lock the door after him.

A set of metal stairs took him down to the Black Whale, but most of the patrons had gone. He'd heard them yelling and whooping into the distance as he was getting his shirt on. There were just a handful left, talking excitedly by the door.

Dray recognised a barrel-chested docker called Tome and trotted over. "What's going on?"

Tome gave him a nod of greeting. "Looks like someone's gone kill crazy. Murdered Igor Tusk."

"You're kidding!"

"I wish. Erik came in screaming the place down, then someone caught sight of the killer and they all went after him. Gruddamn lynch mob. We've sent someone off to find a skipper's man."

"Nice to see someone's still thinking." Dray puffed out a long breath. People died on *Sargasso* all the time, he knew. The Skipper and his patrols did the best they could, but there were just too many people to keep track of, too many places to hide. Still, a murder practically on his doorstep... That wasn't a nice thing to think about, not with his wife and children asleep just a level above his head.

And the *Golgotha* below.

He rubbed his chin, nervously. "Look, Tome. I'm gonna check the ship. Kelli and the kids are still at home. You couldn't...?"

Tome grinned and slapped him powerfully on the shoulder. "I'll be right here."

Mako Quint didn't sleep much. Lucky for him he didn't need to, because the skipper of a cityship didn't get time to waste sleeping. When the telephone rang he was still at his desk, gulping at a mug of caf the size of his own head and working on his notes for the next day's council meeting.

The phone was his personal property; an antique, at least a hundred years old and held together with glue and silver tape. He lifted the hand-set from its cradle and spoke into the cracked plastic mouthpiece. "It's two AM!"

"Trouble at the docks, sir." It was Philo Jennig, his deputy. "Looks like three dead."

Quint closed his eyes for a second. "Where?"

"Two down on the docks, portside harbour. One near the Black Whale tavern. By the sound of it, we've got ourselves a lynch mob, too."

"Wonderful." Quint stretched, feeling the kinks in his neck and back crackle as he straightened. The harbour and the surrounding areas always had been a magnet for trouble. When people spent a long time out at sea things were bound to pop every now and then when they got home. One of his first acts as skipper was to double the number of patrols in those areas, especially at night. "Get a patrol on the tail of the lynch mob – we don't need any more deaths. I'll head down to the docks."

"The council?" Jennig asked.

"None of them will thank us for waking them at this hour," Quint replied. "Wait until we have something conclusive to tell them. I'll call you from one of the quayside boxes for an update. And, as this is a man-hunt, turn on the harbour lights."

The harbour was bathed in light by the time Bane got back. She'd made good time on the journey from the Old Man's chamber. All the way she'd been trying to calm herself down, to stop her heart yammering in her chest and her stomach flopping like a landed fish. He wasn't always right, she told herself a hundred times. He'd got things wrong before. He might have been drinking some of the offering booze, or maybe he was just stringing her along. Telling her a tale, trying to scare her.

No one was in danger from the casket. Everything was going to be all right.

428   I Am The Law: The Judge Dredd Omnibus

She almost convinced herself. But all her comfortable lies disappeared when she opened the hatch and saw the harbour lights were on.

The massive banks of halogens weren't cheap to run, and they were never turned on at night unless something bad was occurring. The last time it had happened was when Bane had been eleven and a megashark had come in through the harbour doors. It had taken two hours to drive it off.

There was no shark thrashing between the ranked vessels this time. Just skipper's men on the quayside and *Golgotha*'s deck, and thousands of people leaning over the railings on all the levels of streets above straining for a better view.

There were more of Quint's men guarding the hatch. One of them had told her that no one was being allowed in or out of the harbour, but then the other had asked which ship she was from, and when she told them they looked at each other and let her through. That was when she knew for certain something terrible had happened.

There was a mounded shape on *Golgotha*'s deck, covered with a tarpaulin.

As soon as she saw it, her stride faltered. She wanted, *needed*, to see what was lying there, but somehow her legs didn't want to move any more. She heard somebody make a choked, sobbing sound, and realised with no small surprise that it was her.

By the time she got to the gangplank all the strength was gone from her. She stopped at the foot of it, unable to take another step.

She heard footsteps and turned to see Dray and Angle coming towards her. They must have been talking to the skipper's men when she arrived, further along the Quay. Angle's face was whiter than usual. Dray's scales didn't show a colour change, but his expression was enough to confirm her worst fears. "Can-Rat?" she whispered.

Angle looked momentarily confused. "He's okay... Well, he's got a bunch of busted ribs, but otherwise he's all right."

Bane shook her head. "But the Old Man. I mean, up there..."

"It's Orca," said a quiet voice behind her.

She turned. Mako Quint was standing behind her, flanked by deputies and armed guards. Bane didn't think she'd ever seen the man this close.

"I'm sorry, Captain Bane. I truly am." He glanced at the covered body up the gangplank. "I know you were friends."

Bane's head felt as if it was going to come off her shoulders. The Old Man had seen Can-Rat in danger: why hadn't he seen this? "What happened?"

"Looks like he disturbed the killer," Quint replied. "Can-Rat too, but Orca got the worst of it."

"I need to see him."

Quint shook his head. "Trust me, girl, you really don't. Besides, it didn't end here."

Dray had stepped forwards. "Remember Ifrana Rokes, off the *Melchior*? He got her, too. And then Igor Tusk, up near the Black Whale."

"Oh my grud..." Bane stepped away, her mind spinning. "I don't get it. How could somebody kill Orca? He was–"

"He was a big man," Quint muttered, finishing the sentence for her. "I knew him. Not well, but we've worked together. Whoever killed him must be..." He shook his head. "I don't know. But this isn't over, captain. We've got a lynch-mob roaming the upper levels with Erik Tusk in charge. The harbour's locked down until my men find them, the killer or both. But that's not what I'm most interested in right now.

"I want you to tell me all about what's in your forward hold."

Quint had just finished questioning Captain Bane when one of the quayside boxes rang. When one of his deputies answered it there was a short conversation, some cursing, and then the phone was handed to him. "Quint," he barked.

"Jennig, sir. We, er, I mean..." He heard the man swallowing hard. There were other noises, too. It sounded as though someone was vomiting.

"Come on, Philo! Spit it out. Where are you?"

Perhaps "spit it out" hadn't been the best phrase he could have used. It took Jennig a few seconds to regain his composure after that. He cleared his throat. "Up on fourth, near the starboard vent ducts. Sir, you'd better get up here."

"Have you found the killer?"

"No. We found the lynch mob."

Three hours later, Mako Quint stood on *Sargasso*'s central bridge, watching the rising sun paint a sick yellow line across the horizon. He stood ramrod straight, hands clasped behind his back, his chin out, gazing through the wraparound windows with his customary cool, steady glare. The bridge crew expected nothing less of him. He was skipper of the biggest cityship afloat and he had a job to do.

Nevertheless, he was glad that he could keep his hands locked together like that. It stopped them shaking.

He had never seen anything like this in his entire life.

Jennig had found the mob near one of the harbour's huge ventilation ducts. The ducts were big enough to drive a ground car through, sealed with armoured plasteen grilles to protect the giant fan blades inside. The killer had torn one of the grills open and smashed a fan blade to get through, which meant he had easy access to the rest of the harbour barge's giant air-system and, if he wanted, the open deck. Despite all Quint's efforts, there was a multiple murderer loose on the *Sargasso*.

Before he had escaped, however, he had turned on the lynch mob.

At first, Quint thought the bodies must have been caught in the fan and then thrown back out by the airflow, but there was no blood inside the grille. It was everywhere else, though, spattered against walls and metal. The killer had gone through the mob like a mincing machine.

Later analysis of the bodies would reveal that, far from dying in a frenzied attack, the mob had fallen prey to an assault of almost unimaginable precision. Each corpse had sustained only a single wound, although those wounds were horrific beyond belief. Torsos had been sliced open, heads severed, throats and arteries cut. Erik Tusk had died when a blade had taken off the top of his head, from the eyebrows upwards. Another man had been sliced in half at the waist.

A couple of the Black Whale's patrons had tried to escape, but were put down with the poisoned needles that had claimed Igor Tusk. And with that, the killer was gone. People living close by reported hearing a disturbance that only lasted about half a minute.

In the hours that remained before dawn, four-man patrols of skipper's men had begun to move through the cityship, reporting back constantly to the central bridge. Meanwhile, Quint had interviewed Can-Rat, whose ribs had been tightly bandaged, then Angle and Dray, and spoke to Gethsemane Bane for a second time. What they told him had confirmed his worst fears.

There had been more than one casket"

The "man down" call came shortly after his second interview with Captain Bane. A patrol had come under attack as they moved through a hydroponics farm on board the bulk carrier *Castiglione*. Their attacker had shot one man and maimed a second, reportedly with a blade that was part of his arm, then made off in the direction of the *Mirabelle*, the *Castiglione*'s immediate neighbour. *Mirabelle* was another ancient tanker, but its hold space had been fitted with hab-units made from stacked and racked cargo containers. Almost twenty thousand people lived there. Fearing a bloodbath, Quint directed his men on the neighbouring ships to converge on the *Mirabelle*. The moment he gave the order, he found himself wondering how many of his people he had just sent to their deaths.

The dawn's yellow line had become a purple bruise across the sky. An hour ago the city council had been woken and called to an emergency session. The session was still in progress, but Quint wasn't chairing it for the moment. He had something more important to do.

There was a very good comms set on the bridge and Quint's radio offi-cer had already set it to the emergency frequency used by scavenger ships at sea. That frequency was on at all times, by *Sargasso* law. Every scavenger still out there would hear him.

The coiled wire stretched as Quint raised the microphone to his mouth and thumbed the "talk" button.

"*Sargasso* to all scavengers," he began. "This is a warning. Repeat: this is a warning. An unmarked watertight casket was salvaged and returned to the *Sargasso* in the last two days. Its contents are lethal. Repeat: lethal. We have at least twenty dead.

"If you have picked up a similar artefact, dump it immediately. Under no circumstances should it be brought aboard the city; anyone who does so will be shot on sight. Details of salvage coordinates to follow."

Quint paused. The sun's bloated bronze disk was rising above the horizon. The black ocean seemed to burn. He took a breath and began again.

"Repeat: *Sargasso* to all scavengers, this is a warning..."

8. DROPZONE

The floors of the Grand Hall of Justice were synthetic marble, polished to a near-mirror finish, and Dredd's footsteps echoed as he approached the office doors. On any other surface in the city the soles of his boots would have made no sound at all, but the builders of the Grand Hall had been very particular about such things. Dredd could have worn boots made of spiderweb and his footsteps would still have echoed loudly as he walked up the corridor. There were electronics involved.

The acoustics of the place had been specifically calculated to inspire awe. And to let the Chief Judge know who was walking up to her doors, of course.

The doors in question, Dredd was pleased to note, had been rein-forced again since he had last been here. Extra layers of bonded plasteen armour had been added to the outer panels, making the doors capable of withstanding assault by anything up to and including battlefield lasers.

Dredd approved of that. He took the safety of the Chief Judge very seriously indeed.

The doors opened as he approached them, smooth and whisper quiet. Dredd went right through across the wide floor and stopped in front of the Chief Judge's desk, rigidly at attention.

"At ease, Dredd," said Hershey quietly. She waved to an empty chair set to one side of the desk. "Take a seat."

"Thank you, Chief Judge. I prefer to stand." Out on the streets, Dredd didn't give two drokks about anyone's ideas of protocol or petty eti-quette. But here at the home of the Law, it was always going to be different for him. Here he could be nothing but the model of propriety.

Besides, one of the other chairs was occupied by someone Dredd pre-ferred not to sit with, however persuasive Judge Hershey was.

Judge Buell was the head of the SJS – the Special Judicial Squad. He was slender and sharp-featured, with the look of the now extinct hawk to him. The personality, too, Dredd knew from bitter experience. Predatory, he was.

Carnivorous. And more than willing to use the Law as a tool to further his own ends. Quite frankly, Dredd would have rather taken his rest next to an active Warchild. At least you knew where the attack would come from.

Across from Buell were Judges Duffy and McTighe. Duffy was head of the Atlantic Division; his remit was everything from the Mega-City Docks out as far as the territorial limit, two thousand kilometres offshore. McTighe was the Tek Division Chief. He and Dredd had crossed swords before, normally about McTighe's constant desire to redesign every piece of Justice Department hardware he could get his hands on. Personally, Dredd liked his daystick the shape it was.

"Duffy, McTighe," he nodded to the two men, and without turning back: "Buell."

Hershey raised an eyebrow at him. "Hmm. Anyway, now that the pleasantries are over and done with... I assume you've guessed what this is about?"

"The Warchild," Dredd replied. "Either you've located the first shipment, or Hellermann's cracked."

"The latter's proving difficult," Hershey muttered, sitting back in her chair. "You'll notice Psi-Chief Shenker hasn't joined us; Psi-Division's still working on Hellerman, but not having much luck. Her psyche's got more dead ends than a Mazny estate."

Buell sniffed. "Give her to me. She'll crack, given enough time."

"Time, Judge Buell, isn't on our side." Hershey touched a control on her desk, and a circular section in the centre of her desk fell away. The silvery disc of a Tri-D projector popped up to take its place. "Judge Duffy?"

Duffy leaned forwards, and set a small data slug into the projector's base. A globe of hazy light sprang up, filling the air above the desk. Justice Department eagle logos scrolled around its equator. "This is an electronic intercept, picked up by one of our listening posts along the territorial margin." In response to his words, the Tri-D globe unfolded into a map, showing the coast and most of the Black Atlantic. The margin lit up as a jagged line of bright dots. "It's audio only, I'm afraid, and not of the best quality."

"Let's hear it," Dredd snapped.

The map showed crosshairs and zoomed in to a point marked "Transmission Source." Dredd noticed its position was at least four thousand kilometres into the Black Atlantic, and then the air was filled with the raw scratching of static. And a man's voice, rich and commanding, with a hint of Euro-City in his accent.

"*Sargasso* to all scavengers," the man began. "This is a warning..."

* * *

The message ended. No one spoke. The map disappeared and the image returned as a spinning globe.

"Any thoughts?" asked Hershey after a few seconds.

Dredd folded his arms. "Sounds like they found a Warchild."

Hershey nodded. "Not much doubt about that. Dredd, what do you know about cityships?"

"Not a lot. Think I flew over one, once – a hundred or so surface vessels chained together into a kind of raft. It shot at us."

"No surprise there," sneered Buell. "Probably trying to knock you down for salvage. It's how those... " he paused, hunting for the right word, "*people* live."

Hershey shot him a glare, then turned her attention back to Dredd. "*Sargasso* is the biggest cityship afloat with over five hundred vessels. Last estimate put the population at almost a million."

"A million?" whispered Duffy. "Dear grud. If one of those things has gotten loose in there, the casualties–"

"Are nothing we need concern ourselves over," Buell interrupted. "Chief Judge, the cityships are out of Mega-City jurisdiction. And full of mutants, I might add."

"What do you suggest, Buell?" Dredd snapped, still without looking at the man. "Sit back with a long lens and count how many it eats?"

"Something like that."

"Gentlemen!" Hershey was on her feet. "Bickering is not going to help us here!"

"I concur," said Buell mildly. "Perhaps Judge Dredd would prefer to offer his own take on the matter."

"I would," Dredd answered immediately. "The Warchild is the product of criminal activity. It's evidence and it belongs in Justice Department hands."

"Thank you, Dredd. My thoughts exactly." She cast a dark glance in Buell's direction. "Not to mention certain ethical considerations. And there is one more factor to be taken into account: Hellermann claims she can control it."

"Really," Dredd grated. "Psi-Div finally get something out of her?"

Hershey shook her head. "Unfortunately not. The woman's as smug as they come. Believe me, I'd like nothing better than to see her snap. But whatever Psi Division came up with, it was bad enough to make her offer a deal."

"A deal? Chief Judge–"

"I know, Dredd! I know!" Hershey raised her hand. "Your feelings on these matters are on record. But we've verified with Tek Division that each Warchild has a control code, a word that will shut it down. Hellermann says she'll know which word when she sees the Warchild."

Dredd didn't like the way this was going. "And what does she want in return?" he asked.

"An end to the interrogations and transfer to a low security cube," Hershey replied. "I share your misgivings, Dredd. But as you say, the Warchild is our business and it belongs here. Not running wild on a ship full of civilians."

"Or possibly falling into the hands of our enemies," said McTighe, quietly.

"If Hellermann is able to do what she claims, I judge it to be a reasonable trade," Hershey continued. "Dredd, I want you to assemble a team. Get Hellermann close enough to the Warchild and let her shut it down. The Sargassans may not be pleased to see you, but I can't see them complaining if you can get rid of their problem."

"And if the word doesn't work?"

Hershey gave a small shrug. "Then I guess it'll eat her."

Dredd squared his shoulders. "A win-win situation. I like it."

"You'll need to come in fast and high," McTighe told him, as they walked through the Tek Division prototype lab. Dredd had followed McTighe there after the briefing had broken up. Buell had skulked off somewhere on his own and Duffy had gone to prepare margin clearances for the mission, plus any extra intelligence he could find on the cityships. He had warned Dredd that there might not be much – the titanic vessels tended to keep themselves fanatically to themselves.

McTighe was confirming that fact right now. "If they see a plane coming in low they'll shoot it down. Probably think it's an attack, plus they'd want the salvage. So we'll take you up to a safe altitude and drop you from there."

Dredd thought about parachuting on to the moving deck of a ship full of angry mutants and decided there was no harm in exploring other options. "Grav-belts won't do the job?"

"Not from the altitude you'll need," McTighe told him, as they walked past benches covered in components and various items of hardware. "You'd reach terminal velocity before they got low enough to activate. Never slow down in time."

Better to land on the deck than plough straight through it, Dredd had to agree. "So what are you thinking?"

McTighe had stopped near a rack of grey, rubbery-looking bodysuits. "The PFE Shrike. High-altitude, pressurised flight envelopes; radar invisible, with integral life-support." He reached into a nearby locker and pulled out a slim, streamlined casing fitted with heavy straps and covered in the same slate-coloured material as the suits.

"There are lift-generating surfaces built into the suits, under the arms. Equipment storage in the backpacks, along with nano-composite parafoils. You'll free-fall most of the way, then activate the foils and come in so fast they'll never be able to draw a bead on you."

Lift-generating surfaces, thought Dredd. Wings, in other words. They were going to jump out of an aircraft halfway out of the atmosphere and sail down into a combat zone wearing something a bat burglar would laugh himself sick at.

"Great," he muttered. "Reckon I'll need to assemble a team who can flap hard."

It took two hours to get the team in place. Dredd knew three street Judges with para-drop training, not including himself, but one was on secondment to Brit-Cit and couldn't be brought over in time. That left Larson and Adams, neither of whom Dredd had worked with before. Still, they had jumped out of aircraft at high altitudes and survived, which made them as qualified for the mission as anyone.

McTighe had insisted that a Tek-Judge be part of the team too and Dredd had to concur. Some scientific know-how could be invaluable when there was unknown technology involved, and Hershey had reminded Dredd that the Warchild wasn't the only X-factor he would be facing. The entire cityship was, at present, a virtual unknown.

The man McTighe had supplied would not have been Dredd's first choice. Tek-Judge Peyton seemed to be someone far more at home in front of a lab bench than out on the field, and he was less than happy about the para-drop. In his favour, however, was the fact that he had worked on the original Warchild Project.

Somehow, Buell had managed to get one of his people involved. When Dredd had arrived at Kennedy Launch Strip, SJS-Judge Vix had been waiting there for him.

Dredd had met Vix once, and not in the best of circumstances. He regarded the woman as acid in a uniform, a worthy student of Judge Buell and all his teachings. Buell's excuse for Vix's presence was that she was qualified in airborne operations and para-drops. She was also, Dredd knew, spying for the SJS. Dredd would make sure he didn't keep his back to her for any length of time.

Which, of course, left Elize Hellermann. She had arrived at the strip last in a pat-wagon. The look she gave Dredd when she saw him could have burned holes in plasteen.

So Dredd's team, at take off, consisted of himself, two Judges he didn't know, one he didn't trust, one who was scared witless and a mad scientist who would probably feed them to her pet monster at the earliest opportunity.

The day was just getting better and better.

They sat, three facing three, in the cramped body of the strat-dart as it arrowed across the Atlantic. The dart performed best in high, thin air, and the pilots had taken it up to forty kilometres as soon as they had left the launch strip. It had been a long climb, during which the occupants of the drop bay could do nothing except sit on the hard benches, review their mission data and think about what was to come.

There was little in the way of conversation. Dredd wasn't surprised, given the make-up of the team, and found it something to be thankful for. There was work to be done and he could do without the idle chatter.

The dart had been flying level for almost two hours when Dredd got a signal from the cockpit. He unstrapped, stood as upright as he could in the low-ceilinged bay, and went forward.

The pilot had activated a monitor screen between himself and his copilot. The screen must have been for Dredd's benefit since both fliers were wearing head-up display helmets. Everything they needed to see would be right in front of them.

There were no windows in the cockpit.

The pilot gestured at the screen. Concentric circles were scanning outwards from a bright point, partway across a stylised map of the Atlantic. "We've got your target."

"Can they see us?"

"Not yet. We're picking up passive scans from a spy-sat, so we're as good as invisible."

"That's about to change," Dredd replied. "Take us below the cloud layer and stand by to broadcast."

"Commencing descent to drop altitude." Dredd watched the pilot ease the control collective forwards and felt the angle of the deck beneath his boots begin to change. On the screen, the map disappeared and was replaced by an external view. Dredd saw an endless landscape, white and billowing, rising like a tide. It swallowed the view and the screen went blank.

"We'll be through the cloud layer in a few seconds," the pilot told him. He flipped down part of his control board, revealing the comms panel, and pressed several buttons. "Okay, Judge Dredd. Give the word and I'll slave this into your personal comms channel."

"We don't know what kind of equipment the cityship might be using," the copilot told him, "so we'll be sending across a wide frequency spectrum. I'll record as you speak and put it on a continuous loop until touchdown."

"Sounds good. Patch me in."

The monitor screen turned from white to black. One second it was blank and in the next the view had turned to that of a vast, oily sheet, glittering with tiny ripples of sunlight.

"Calling whoever is in authority onboard the cityship *Sargasso*," Dredd began. "I am Judge Dredd. I represent the law in Mega-City One. A piece of our technology has been taken aboard your city and I am leading a team that will remove it. Your assistance is not required, but your cooperation and that of your citizens would expedite our mission.

"My team will arrive by air. This is not an attack. Repeat: this is not an attack. But be advised, we will defend ourselves if fired upon. This message will now repeat. Dredd out."

The copilot pressed a key on the comms board. "We'll keep broadcasting until we hear you're down safely," he said.

"We're now at drop altitude," the pilot cut in. "Five minutes to marker. You ought to get back and buckle up."

Dredd turned awkwardly in the confined space and squeezed back through the hatch and into the drop bay. He was already wearing most of McTighe's Shrike suit: the radar-baffling grey fabric was a tight fit over his uniform and didn't allow for any great freedom of movement while walking. The lift surfaces under his arms flapped uncomfortably and he could barely turn his head. But already Dredd could see how it would turn a man into a missile in the air.

The rest of the suit was waiting for him in the bay. Adams helped him into the backpack which strapped on securely with reinforced webbing across his chest. The top of the pack – which contained not only the parafoil but also the bulkier sections of his uniform – looked oddly truncated, until he put on the flight helmet and locked it down. The helmet was designed to fit over a Judge's helm and turned his entire torso into a nearly rigid and highly aerodynamic capsule.

The others were already suited up. As soon as the dart had reached drop altitude the lights in the bay had changed from white to amber, giving them the signal to suit up and lock down. Dredd saw the inside of the flight helmet light up with icons and guide indicators, a full HUD that would tell him everything he needed to know on the way down.

He turned to Peyton. "How are you doing?"

"I'm, ah, okay, sir." Peyton was a faceless teardrop with arms and legs just like the rest of them, but his body language was all nerves. "My suit's slaved to Larson's flight controls, so I guess I'll be okay."

Larson slapped him on the shoulder. "Don't worry, tekkie. I won't put you down too hard!"

"See that you don't, Larson," growled Dredd. "If Hellermann doesn't come up trumps, Tek-Judge Peyton could be our last line of defence."

"So it's true." That was Hellermann. Her Shrike was covering up prison greys, and was slaved to Vix's. More for reasons of security than to give her an easy ride. "You were part of my operation."

Peyton's suit bobbed. Probably nodding in the helmet. "I was lead analyst on the resequencing team."

"No wonder it failed."

"Button it, Hellermann." Dredd moved down the line to stand at the bay doors. "There's only one word any of us wants to hear from you."

The lights in the bay went red and an armoured pressure door slid across the cockpit hatch.

"We're nearing the drop zone. Helmets on; make your final checks. Larson, make sure Peyton's harness is good to go."

They came out of the strat-dart in a long line, Dredd jumping first.

For a few seconds the slipstream tore at him. He tumbled, his view a spinning mess of black water and white sky, and then the Shrike took control. The lift surfaces between his arms and torso were filled with a complex array of hollow, flexible spines. The suit's onboard computer worked these effortlessly, filling some with air and emptying others, modifying the flight characteristics of Dredd's body until he was sailing through the air straight and true.

The strat-dart was a triangle of black shadow, already peeling out of Dredd's view and back into the clouds.

Dredd kept his body straight, his arms back and level with his torso splayed at forty-five degrees to give the lift surfaces their best angle of attack. He was moving forwards as fast and far as he was falling downwards.

Ahead of him, the cityship was a ragged island of metal, trailing a hundred kilometre wake.

"There's the target," Dredd reported. "Drop team, sound off."

"Adams here."

"Larson, all okay."

"Vix."

"Grud," gasped Peyton. "Grud! This is fantastic!"

"Don't get too fond of the experience, Peyton. We'll be down in sixty. Hellermann?"

There was a pause, then: "I hear you."

The cityship was growing like a stain. Dredd could see that every square metre of its upper surface was covered in buildings, everything from the original superstructure of *Sargasso*'s component vessels to sky-scrapers made from upended chemical tanks and great stacks of cargo containers. Everything was linked to everything else. Great spans of gantry and support cable and haphazardly swinging bridges glittered in the sunlight, looking from this altitude like the work of a deranged and hyperactive spider. There wasn't a flat spot anywhere.

"Drokk," muttered Larson. "We'll be in trouble if we can't find a land-ing strip."

Alarms began to go off in Dredd's helmet HUD. "Foil altitude!" he barked. "Drop team, deploy parafoils!" As he spoke, he keyed a control in the palm of his flight glove.

He felt the backpack shudder as it unfolded, and then he felt a mas-sive impact against his chest and shoulders – the parafoil had deployed. Instantly his flight-wings went limp and disengaged from his torso, leav-ing his arms free. He reached up and grabbed the foil's control handles, swinging himself around towards the port side of the cityship.

It was rushing up to meet him, filling his field of view, becoming more insanely complex with every metre he dropped towards it. There was detail everywhere: the stepped superstructures of luxury liners and the blocky conning towers of supertankers and anti-pol ships. Bridges and walkways were slung between individual vessels, while elsewhere the hulls of several ships appeared to have been welded tightly together. And, on every level, untold numbers of dots that grew and resolved themselves into figures.

Dredd watched as one of the dots looked up and stabbed a pointing finger skywards. There must have been shouts of surprise or alarm as other dots followed the first figure's lead, looking up and pointing. Some ran for the nearest doorway or hatch. News was spreading.

"There!" called Vix. "That Sov-ship in the middle, near the conning tower!"

Dredd scanned the cityship for the distinctive lines of a Sov-Blok vessel. He quickly saw that Vix was right; almost at the centre of the *Sargasso* was a gigantic mass of grey metal that looked like a Putin-class assault carrier. While most of the deck was taken up with hastily-constructed residential areas there was a large, uncluttered space just ahead of the superstructure. From what Dredd remembered about the Putin-class, that's where the primary weapons mounts would have been.

"Drop team, follow my lead. We're setting down." Dredd tugged at the control handles, spilling air from one edge of the parafoil and angling towards the open space. Whatever passed for city defence on board the cityship would almost certainly have realised where they were headed and, if they were anything like City-Def back in Mega-City One, they would be itching for some target practice. The presence of the Warchild would only make them more trigger-happy than usual.

"Get down and ready as fast as you can," he told the others. "If we're going to be sitting ducks, I'd sooner have my feet on the ground."

Seconds later, the deck came up and hit the soles of Dredd's boots – hard.

Instantly he slapped the foil-release on his chest webbing. There was the dull thump of explosive latches and the parafoil whipped up and away from him, skating across the deck. Around him, the rest of the team came down with varying degrees of success: Adams, Larson and Vix made good landings, but Hellermann seemed to crumple as her boots hit, and she went down heavily onto one knee. Peyton made a textbook landing but missed the release pad – the wind against his parafoil had him over – and for a few seconds he went slithering across the deck. Larson had to trigger his release by remote control.

Dredd hauled off his flight helmet and dropped it, undoing his webbing with his other hand. The backpack slid off his shoulders and he pulled it round and slapped a panel on the side. The pack popped open along a pressure seal and dropped a Lawgiver into his palm.

The rest of his uniform could wait. He checked the weapon over, made sure it was set to deliver standard execution rounds. By the time he had done that the rest of the team was assembling around him. Vix was helping Hellermann along – it looked as though the woman had damaged her knee on descent.

Peyton was last to join them, dragging his helmet off as he did so. "No welcoming party yet," he puffed, obviously unused to the effort. "Maybe Dredd's message worked."

"Judge Dredd – diplomatic attaché to a ship full of mutant scum," Hellermann sneered. "That has a nice ring to it."

"So does 'life without parole,'" Dredd growled. "I'd bear that in mind." He looked up at the long window of the *Putin*'s conning tower and saw faces pressed against it. They were unashamedly looking back at him.

"Defensive formation," he ordered. "Cover the angles and watch the shadows. Move slowly. We don't want to spook the locals."

Dredd could see movement all around: figures darting from cover to cover, heads peering over rails and out of windows. Weapons were no doubt being passed around. He needed to connect his sudden arrival with the message he had broadcast earlier.

He dropped his helmet mic and turned on the internal amplifier. "I am Judge Dredd!" he roared.

"And I'm Mako Quint." The voice was as commanding as his own, and very nearly as loud. Dredd turned to find its source and saw that a hatch had opened halfway up the conning tower. A man stood on a platform there, flanked by armed mutants, although he was a head taller than any of them.

At the same time, more mutants popped up from their hiding places. A lot of them. Dredd found himself, not for the first time in his life, standing in the crosshairs of several hundred weapons.

"This is my city, Judge Dredd," snarled Mako Quint. "And you are not welcome here."

9. POWER TO THE PEOPLE

Luckily for the mutants, none of them tried to take Dredd's Lawgiver away.

The drop team had been led into the *Putin*'s conning tower by a squad of armed men and women who appeared to be under Mako Quint's direct command. Some were obviously mutated, although many seemed human. Dredd guessed that everyone on the cityship must have been mutated to some degree but he also knew that DNA tended to start kinking on prolonged exposure to Black Atlantic water.

Quint had met them at the base of the conning tower, looked them over, and then turned away and walked inside without a word. He was a big man, physically larger than Dredd, and he carried his bulk easily. Under his clothes – dark shirt and trousers, fishskin jacket, heavy utility boots – he was all muscle. Dredd noted that if he and Quint came to blows, the other man would definitely have the advantage in strength. And Dredd couldn't rely on being too much faster, either.

Life on the Atlantic not only made people into mutants, it also made them tough. It would be a mistake, Dredd knew, to underestimate any of them.

Once inside the tower, they were taken by elevator to what had been the fire control deck. According to what Dredd knew about this class of warship, the *Putin*'s deck would have been ringed with weapons boards, sensor stations and comms equipment when it was operational. All that was long gone and in its place were blank walls painted a grim brown, biolume strips around the ceiling, and three rows of bench seats against the far wall. The seats were set at different levels with the highest at the back. To Dredd, who had spent a lot of time in the Cursed Earth, it was a familiar enough arrangement.

"Mutants," he growled, mainly to himself, "sure do love a council."

Quint had gone in ahead of them and his guards had stationed themselves around the rear wall of the chamber. The benches were already occupied – Dredd counted thirteen mutants there, none of whom could have been mistaken for human, even in the worst light.

Out in the rad-deserts and wastelands that surrounded Mega-City One, every second town or settlement Dredd had ridden through had some kind of council, quorum or elected body making life difficult. He didn't know why and didn't much care. They just seemed to like it. Maybe it made them feel important, worthwhile.

Human.

Dredd looked across at Quint. "I got the impression you were in charge here."

"Skipper Quint," said a mutant on the lowest bench, "is responsible for maintaining the rule of law on board the *Sargasso*." The mutant's voice was rich and fluid; strangely so, given that he seemed to consist of a head and very little else. The fleshy tentacle making up the rest of his body was curled up and strapped into a padded chair that was studded with interface jacks; presumably it could be bolted into a robot prosthesis to give the man mobility.

Dredd hadn't taken his eyes off Quint. "Then we have at least that in common."

"However," the mutant continued, "matters that concern the safety of the entire cityship come before us. My name is Jubal Haab, and we are–"

"The ruling council," Dredd cut in. "Or some variation on the theme." He stepped forward.

"Listen to me, councillor. You're wasting time. You know who I am and why I'm here – if you hadn't got my message we'd be shooting our way in to see you right about now."

"You wouldn't be getting far," rumbled Quint.

The limbless mutant gave Quint a dark look, then turned his attention back to Dredd. "I've no doubt you would have tried, lawman. And it would have been Quint's duty to stop you. We selected him for the post of skipper, just as we were elected to the council by the people of *Sargasso*. And we are very good indeed at choosing the right man for the job."

"Oh, terrific," snapped Vix. "A democracy. We could be here for a week."

At the SJS-Judge's words, the temperature in the room seemed to drop by several degrees. Dredd kept his gaze firmly on the wormlike mutant, but in his peripheral vision he could see Larson and Adams tensing up, shifting their body positions to allow for a quick draw from their temporary holsters.

He could also see that, while the guards still weren't aiming directly at him, their guns weren't exactly pointed anywhere else, either. This was bad. If push came to shove, the drop team was badly outnumbered, and they hadn't had a chance to take their Shrike suits off. Dredd didn't relish the idea of trying to shoot his way out of this place with ten kilos of McTighe's radar-eating rubber spoiling his aim.

"Perfect," he heard Peyton mutter. "I survive the drop and then get fragged because she doesn't like their politics."

Dredd pointed a gloved finger at Haab. "You can vote all you like," he grated. "Fact is, you've got a killing machine making synthi-mince of your population. All you have to work out is what's less welcome – us, or it."

"It's thanks to people like you that it's here in the first place!" hissed out the councillor to Haab's left. This one had three eyes staring out of a blank sac of a head and his reedy, outraged voice whistled from an opening at the base of his throat.

"Grafton's right," said a woman whose arms were as boneless and ceaselessly mobile as a squid's. "I say put them over the side and we'll kill this evil toy of theirs ourselves!"

At that, everyone on the bench was yelling. Thirteen councillors, thirteen opinions, thirteen voices raised above those of their neighbours in an attempt to get their messages across. Instant chaos. Fights broke out. Pieces of paper flew up into the air. Jubal Haab was howling for silence and Dredd saw that Quint was standing with his eyes closed, his head shaking slowly from side to side.

"Wonderful sight," said Dredd quietly. "Democracy in action."

"This *toy*," snapped Hellermann, stepping past Dredd and right up to the first bench, "is the most sophisticated biological weapons platform ever produced!"

The hubbub gradually died down. Within a few seconds, every one of the mutant councillors were looking at Hellermann, the sharp-featured, crop-headed woman with the bulky grey bodysuit and the voice that could cut through hull plating.

Hellermann folded her arms and glared up at the council with utter disdain. "What do you think this is, some B-Vid monster? Wandering about with its arms outstretched, picking off the odd screaming victim until the hero catches it off guard and pushes it off a cliff?"

She shook her head as if amazed by their stupidity. "The Warchild project took fifteen years and over two billion credits of research to develop. It's designed to operate independently for an indefinite period under the harshest battlefield conditions. It has internal weaponry, stealth skin and bullet proof armour. It can be programmed with any number of specific mission profiles, or left to its default settings – and believe me, even under default settings this thing is your worst nightmare!"

Hellermann stepped back, knowing she had the whole council's attention and obviously loving it. "Trust me; no matter how many people you send after this thing there's only one way you'll know if they find it. They won't come back.

"There's only one person on this cityship who can stop it. Me."

There was a long pause. Then Jubal Haab twisted in his support harness. "Is this true?" he demanded, staring directly at Dredd.

"That's what she says," Dredd replied. "She's the closest thing it's got to a mother."

Again, the council members began to talk at once. Haab called for silence and this time the noise ceased almost immediately.

"We should consider this carefully," Haab said. "In private."

Two council members – the one with the neck-mouth and a woman who had vestigial hands sprouting from either side of her neck – picked up Haab's seat and carried it out of the room. "Make yourselves comfortable," Haab told Dredd as he was carried towards the door. "Uninvited you may be, but you are our guests."

"I can't believe they thought we brought it here on purpose!"

Gethsemane Bane stopped pacing as Angle spoke. It was the first time in a long while that anyone in the cell had said anything, and sitting in silence had been driving her slowly insane. She often paced about on *Golgotha*'s decks, when the seas had been empty and the way home long and slow.

Of course, there wasn't as much room here.

There were five decks under the conning tower in the brig. The *Putin*'s superstructure housed the council chamber, Quint's office and the central bridge; all the machinery of law and order on *Sargasso*, in fact. So it was quite appropriate that anyone who transgressed those laws should be kept on the same vessel.

"They don't," Dray replied. He was sitting on the cell's one, narrow bunk, his eye closed and his back against the wall. "They're just drokked off with us."

"We'll still be punished, though." Can-Rat was next to him, curled up around the pain of his bandaged ribs. "Maybe they're trying to figure out what to do with us."

Angle, who had found a corner of the cell as soon as he had been thrown into it and had stayed there the whole time, punched the wall in frustration. "Should be a short debate," he spat. "I mean, what would you do to the dumb sneckers that brought a box-wrapped killing machine home to Mama?"

Can-Rat realised what Angle was talking about. "They wouldn't. Would they?"

"Exile?" Angle said, then shrugged. "Sneck. I would."

Bane closed her eyes. Exile was something she hadn't been letting herself think about.

Even for a scavenger whose life was measured by long periods on the open sea, the idea of exile was a nightmare. Those sentenced to it would be cast adrift in a small vessel, sometimes with a little food and water, sometimes without. The lucky ones would find themselves prey to Black Atlantic wildlife; megasharks, most usually, but there were bigger and nastier things under those inky waters. The less fortunate wouldn't be eaten at all. They would die slowly from hunger and thirst and the slow, insidiously corrosive effects of the ocean itself.

If you were strong and they gave you some water, you might last a fortnight.

Exile was the worst punishment available to the cityships – worse than execution, by far. When you were exiled, you had time to regret what you'd done.

"They wouldn't exile you," Bane whispered. "They wouldn't do that. *Golgotha*'s mine, I'm responsible. I won't let them punish you." She started pacing again, head down so they couldn't see the fear in her eyes.

"How, cap'n?" Angle was glaring up at her. "Sorry and all, but it doesn't look like you've got a whole lot of leverage from here!"

Dray opened his eye and gave him a look. "Calm down, kid."

"The sneck I will!" Angle leapt to his feet. Dray was up too, in an instant.

"I told you to calm the sneck down!"

"That's enough!" Philo Jennig had appeared at the cell door. As the crew fell silent, he gave a nod to the skipper's man who had been posted outside.

The guard unlocked the door and slid the bars aside.

"Jennig." Bane stepped quickly towards the deputy. The guard began to raise his rifle but Jennig shook his head.

Bane took a deep breath. The way things were going for her right now, she reckoned she had one chance at this, and one only. "Listen," she said, "I've told Quint and now I'm telling you. My people had nothing to do with this. If anyone should be punished, it's me."

Jennig cocked his head to one side. "You sure you know what you're saying?"

"Yeah. Tell them I'll accept exile." Behind her, Dray gasped, but she ignored him. "Drokk, I'll jump over the side myself if that's what it takes. Anything they want, as long as my crew goes free."

A grin spread over Jennig's face. "Captain Bane, I believe you just said the magic words."

For the drop team, comfortable meant being rid of the Shrike suits.

By the time the councillors began to file back in, Dredd was in full uniform again. His shoulder and knee pads were strapped on, his Law-giver and daystick were at his belt, and his badge of office was chained onto his uniform.

He was ready for work.

After the councillors had settled themselves, Mako Quint strode back into the chamber. This time, someone was with him; a tall, slender woman with short dark hair. She wore heavy trousers with pockets sewn onto every spare centimetre of fabric, a vest and heavy boots. She wasn't armed.

Her skin, under the glow of the biolumes, had a strange sheen.

"We have discussed the situation," began Jubal Haab, speaking as soon as his padded seat had been set onto the bench. "And your claim that you can solve it."

"And how many of your people have been slaughtered while you've been 'discussing?'" Vix spat.

Dredd raised a hand. "That's enough, Vix."

Haab fixed Dredd with a liquid stare. "You can take your weapon," he said. "Hunt it down, make it safe and take it back to your Mega-City. You will be escorted to the location of its last kill. From there, Gethse-mane Bane will guide you." With a jerk of the head Haab indicated the new arrival. "She captained the ship that brought your monster here."

Dredd gave the woman a sideways look. "Bad luck."

"No drek," he heard her whisper.

"You will receive no more help from us," Haab continued. "Find the rogue weapon and you are welcome to it. Die and we will find another way to deal with it."

"Sounds fair," Dredd replied. "Let's get to it."

10. THE HUNTER

They began at the vent. There was something at the site of that blood-bath Dredd needed to see.

The bodies had been taken away but the stains had not. No one had wanted to stay near the vent long enough to clean the deck – simply moving the corpses had been done with unseemly haste. Bane found herself treading carefully between the grisly evidence of what had occurred a few hours before: broad, ragged-edged puddles where men's lives had poured out onto the deck, wide triangles that spoke of arterial spray and tracks where hands and feet had skidded in blood.

There were round spots, too, where droplets had flicked through the air. In their thousands.

Most of the blood had dried in the warm wind from the vent, gone from bright crimson to a dark, rusty brown, but some of the puddles were too deep. Distressingly, those were often the ones that contained fragments of what Bane could only allow herself to think of as "material".

Others had walked here without as much care. Bloody footprints criss-crossed the deck.

Just being here was making Bane feel shivery and ill. Before this, she had only been told of what the Warchild was capable of – she hadn't even been allowed to see Orca's body. But now, although the corpses themselves were gone, the tale of their final moments was told in painful detail.

And the Warchild, as these intruders from dry land called it, could be anywhere. It could be watching her right now.

Bane drew her coat tight around her thin shoulders and stuffed her hands deep into the pockets. She allowed herself a quick, surreptitious glance at the intruders to see if they were as frightened as she was.

Apart from the woman that called herself Hellermann, the rest of them wore glossy armoured helmets that covered most of their faces. What little she could see showed different reactions: Dredd, the leader, seemed completely unaffected by the carnage, as did the female Judge with the skull on her helmet. Larson and Adams had gone a little pale, and the small chubby one, Peyton, looked positively sick.

Dredd had noticed that too. "Pull yourself together, Peyton," he growled. "Gonna get worse than this."

Vix, the skull-headed one, was crouching next to the vent. Bane watched her, trying to work out what she was doing; the way she was tipping her head this way and that seemed odd, until she spoke. "How many do you make it, Dredd?"

"Fifteen."

"That's what I got." Vix stood up. She must have been down there to get a different angle on the bloodstains, Bane realised. And from this mess they were able to tell how many had died?

Despite herself, she was impressed.

"Doesn't tally," said Peyton. "I asked that Jennig guy, the one with the head? He told me there had been fourteen bodies pulled out of here." He put his hand to his mouth and coughed weakly. "Well, he said it had come to fourteen when they put them back together."

"So we're missing one." Dredd rubbed his chin, thoughtfully. "Maybe he got away."

"I doubt it," Hellerman cut in. "It's not built that way."

Vix walked over to Hellermann and put herself right in the scientist's face. "Enlighten us, *doctor*," she sneered.

There was a long silence as the two women stared each other down. Vix, behind her grisly-looking helmet, had the advantage. Eventually Hellermann shrugged. "It doesn't leave witnesses," she said.

Vix snorted and walked away. As she went past Dredd, Bane heard him say: "Feel better?"

"Much."

I'm doomed, Bane thought wildly. These people were supposed to find Orca's killer, track it down through the kilometres of steel maze that made up the cityship's interior, and make it safe. Instead, they seemed more interested in scoring points off each other.

Anyway, Hellermann was wrong. "Can-Rat's alive," she said.

Suddenly, everyone was looking at her. "Say again," Dredd told her.

"Can-Rat. He's one of my crew. He was there when the, er, Warchild killed Orca, and it hit him, but then it got distracted and ran away."

"Which means?" Dredd was looking at Hellermann. The woman seemed momentarily confused.

"Another situation must have overridden its default program. It thought it was in more immediate danger from another source."

"Did you build it that way?" asked Larson.

Hellermann shook her head. "Not exactly."

"Great," muttered Adams. "It's malfunctioning."

"Which makes it even more dangerous." Dredd turned to Bane. "Okay, captain. This is where you come in."

Bane's eyebrows went up. "Me?"

"You're supposed to guide us, right?" He leaned close and pointed his gloved finger at her nose. "So get guiding. Or we'll throw you back to the council and make our own way."

He turned and stalked away, back to the vent. Behind him, Bane sagged.

An invisible killing machine in front of her and a troupe of bickering, trigger-happy fascists behind? Gethsemane Bane was beginning to think that exile would have been the easy option.

Unlike the Warchild, neither Bane nor the intruders had the strength to simply stop the fan and climb past the shattered blade. Dredd favoured putting a bullet through the motor but Peyton saved him the ammunition by tracking down the main power supply and shorting out the connections.

The fan whined slowly to a halt, rattling on its damaged bearings as the missing blade threw it off-balance. Dredd caught it once it was slow enough and hauled it to a stop. Thankfully, he didn't make Bane go through first.

He made her go second. "All clear," she heard from inside the duct. "Send the mutant through."

She climbed in gingerly, aware that the missing fan blade had left razor-sharp shards of metal sticking out from the hub. The rest of it, she saw once she was through, lay in dozens of scattered fragments all over the duct floor. Some of them had embedded themselves in the walls.

The rest of the team followed her in. The duct was big enough to stand up in and was constructed from heavy gauge steel. It still rang like a gong as soon as anyone took a step, and echoed horribly. "Say good-bye to a stealthy approach," said Larson ruefully.

"You won't be creeping up on it anyway, mister," Hellermann said from just inside the grille. Bane had noticed that the Judges were always careful never to let her get behind everyone else. As if they thought she might make a break for it. "It's got hearing that would shame a bat."

"You're proud of it," said Bane, in spite of herself. Hellerman gave her a withering glare.

"At least I have something to be proud of, *mutant*."

"Screw you." Bane turned her back on the woman and walked ahead a few metres. "Are you guys coming, or are you just going to stand there arguing about who's got the biggest helmet?"

454   I Am The Law: The Judge Dredd Omnibus

"Hey. Hey!" Vix was striding up behind her. Bane felt a gloved hand come down on her shoulder. "Don't get mouthy with us, girl. We're the ones who're going to save this cesspool of a city!"

"Oh yeah?" Maybe Vix was used to browbeating rookies or juves off the street, but Gethsemane Bane, for all her lack of years, was a captain of a Black Atlantic scavenger, and she got tired of her attitude very quickly. She threw the hand off and spun on her heel.

"Okay, skull-head," she snarled. "Riddle me this – two corners away down this vent shaft are three exits. They slope down at a real sharp angle, and they all look the same. One of them leads to the service ladder, the others don't. Which one are you going down?"

The outburst seemed to bring Vix up short. "Ah, the middle one?"

Bane made a buzzing noise in her throat. "Is the wrong answer! You're in the water, skull-head. And that's gonna burn that uniform off your ass pretty drokking quick."

She noticed that Dredd was suddenly next to them, not saying anything, just standing there with his arms folded. She hadn't even heard his approach.

Up close, he was big. Quint was bigger, but even the skipper didn't have the aura of raw command this man had. So far, she realised, he'd just chosen not to use it.

"Finished?" he said.

Bane nodded. Vix lowered her gaze and stepped back.

"Good." His voice level and even. "Defensive formation, Hellermann and Peyton in the centre. Bane, you and I are on point. Larson and Adams, watch our backs. Anyone tries getting into a pissing contest again and you'll have me to answer to when we get back to the Meg." He pointed to Bane. "Except for you. You'll answer to me right here. Now let's move!"

To get to all the areas of the harbour barge, the vent had been built in a series of sloping corners and wide loops. The team had been moving through the duct for about five minutes when Bane rounded a corner and saw something that stopped her dead in her tracks.

In the centre of the duct was a seething puddle of fur. Rats; dozens of them, as big as her forearm. They were feeding.

She could hear the steady crunching of teeth on bone.

Dredd had pulled his gun – a bulky, blunt-nosed automatic with a rotary indicator above the trigger. Bane had just enough time to get her hands over her ears before he pulled the trigger.

The gun thumped heavily in his fist and one of the rats flew apart. Bane felt the noise of the shot slam into her eardrums, even past her clasped hands. The rest of the rats were already gone, a scuttling, screeching mass whirling away down the duct.

Dredd walked up to the object they had been feasting on. "Looks like number fifteen didn't get away after all."

For a moment Bane couldn't grasp what she was seeing. Dredd was talking as though it was a body, but it couldn't be, could it? It was far too small and the wrong shape. Then her brain made sense of the image and her stomach flipped.

It wasn't an entire body. Everything below a ragged line diagonally across the torso, taking off one arm, was missing. What was left had been chewed to ruin by the rats.

"Peyton!" Dredd barked. "Hold onto your lunch and take a look at this."

Warily, the shorter Judge joined Dredd. "Grud," he whispered, just once. Then he knelt down by the carcass.

"Bite marks," he said, pointing at the torso. Bane, hanging back, didn't want to see in detail. "Big ones, not the rats. He's been chewed through here, here and here. This is a straight cut."

"So what are you saying?" asked Adams, obviously horrified. "It's eating people now?"

Dredd crouched by the corpse and reached down to the torn neck. He tugged something free and brought it up to the light.

It was a slender needle, as long as a finger, and carved from pale bone. "Toxin dart," Dredd muttered. "Shot this one and brought him along as a packed lunch."

Peyton nodded. "It needed to feed. But it waited until it was safe then ate what it could and left the rest."

"Which tells you what?"

"It's planning a lot of... activity" Peyton bit his lip.

Vix nudged the corpse with her boot. "At least we know we're going the right way."

"From here," Bane said, "there's only one way we can go. It's when we get on deck we have to start thinking."

She led them through the duct, luckily without further incident. By the time they got out of the harbour barge, night had fallen and a storm wind was whipping at the deck.

Bane came up first, climbing the service ladder she'd quizzed Vix about. Dredd was next to her in a second, scanning the deck with a flashlight clipped to his gun. Within a few moments the whole team was up, moving smoothly into a spread pattern, everyone covering everyone else's back.

The Judges' guns had integral viewfinders at the rear, above the grip. Bane caught a flash of Dredd's as he swung the weapon about and saw an instant of brilliant blues and greens. Thermal imaging. "Will it show up on that?"

"Probably not. Everyone else will, though."

Bane had to plant her feet apart against the wind. It was rising to a gale, whipping her coat about. "We're not all against you, Judge! The word will have gone out by now – news travels fast here."

"Forgive me if I'm still not expecting open arms. Which way?"

She pointed. "You can't get to the ship ahead directly from this one. No bridge." She turned her head to the side as spray blew at her. "We'll have to go starboard, to the *Castiglione*. From there to the *Mirabelle*, that's starboard too. But that's the last anyone saw of it. I don't understand why we didn't start there."

"You don't need to. After the *Mirabelle*, where then?"

Bane shrugged. "You tell me where you want to go, Judge, and I'll get you there. But tracking this thing is your job."

"That's right. It is. Which is why I needed to start back at the vent."

There were eight bridges from the harbour barge to the *Castiglione*, but most were too slender and unstable to use in the storm. Bane led the team downwards, using the mesh stairways that zigzagged down the side of the barge, until she reached the Bridge of Calm. Some weird pattern in the air-currents around the cityship caused a dead spot there. No matter how hard the wind blew, the Bridge of Calm was always rock steady.

As such, it was a common romantic spot for courting couples. But there were no lovers on the bridge tonight, just nervous skipper's men. Bane led the team quickly across and into the *Castiglione*.

A giant hydroponics farm took up most of the *Castiglione*'s internal space and they were able to move through that vessel quickly. But the *Mirabelle*, into which the Warchild had disappeared, was a different matter.

"It's a residential ship," Bane explained, as they moved through the short tunnel installed between the inner and outer hulls. "The habs are mostly cargo containers, shipped down there and welded together. I used to live there a long time ago."

"Where do you live now?" asked Larson.

"On the *Golgotha*. Well, I used to. Right now, I don't know."

"It depends on the outcome of our mission," Dredd told her. "If we succeed, you get your ship back. If we don't, it doesn't matter."

"I hadn't thought of it like that," said Bane. Her voice sounded very small.

The tunnel opened onto the lower deck of the *Mirabelle*. Bane stepped out of the hatchway and into open, smoky air. Behind her, she heard one of the Judges – Peyton, she was sure – give a low whistle.

She had to admit the *Mirabelle* was impressive in a certain way.

The chamber they now stood in was forty metres high, from the mesh deck to the roof braces. It stretched away in every direction for a much larger distance, but it was impossible to see how far – thousands of cooking fires had turned the air into a thick, pungent smog.

Stacked from floor to ceiling were the habs: ten metre cargo containers, bolted one on top of the other and side by side, in some places ten or more high. Open mesh walkways ringed every level of every stack, connected by an insane spider web of ladders and stairs. Washing lines were strung between the walkways, dripping processions of laundry hanging from them like limp flags. The walkways were strewn with potted plants, bicycles, children's toys, and garbage of every description – the accumulated detritus of human existence, poured into a big metal box and left to rot.

Great halogen lamps strung from the ceiling cast a sickly glow at street level, but most of the light came from windows. Rough cut squares glowed in every hab, far too many to count. Most of them also showed the silhouettes of watching figures.

Five thousand people lived in this compartment, and *Mirabelle* had four compartments. Even so, there was no one about on the streets or up on the walkways. Bane had never seen the vessel so empty.

She turned to the Judges. "Okay," she began, "now listen to me. This is a low cost residential area. I'm sure you have them in your city too. If you do, you'll know that there are places you go, and places you only go in pairs, right? Same here. I'll lead you through the safest way, but we go quickly, we go quietly, and we don't make any trouble."

"No argument," said Dredd. "If the Warchild came through here, it didn't stop. We'd know about it by now."

They began to move into the stacks. Bane knew that the biggest spaces between the habs would be the safest, as more light filtered down to the deck on the widest streets. She led them quickly around several corners, skirting an area she knew contained six dead ends and four taverns, and another where the lights were constantly being knocked out by juves on the top hab roofs.

Bane was heading for the Main Drag, a wide street that carved almost clear through the centre of the hold. She took the team along a row of small shop-fronts to get there, but when she turned the next corner it was blocked.

Someone had piled scrap metal into the space between two habs. There was tonnes of it, mainly rusted H-girders, but the gaps were filled with a lot of broken sheet steel and plasteen. Metre-long spikes of grimy metal stuck out from the girders at every angle. Climbing over the blockage would be impossible without getting impaled, or crushed as the whole unstable lot of it collapsed.

Bane didn't find either choice attractive. "They're barricading themselves in," she told Dredd. "They're terrified of the Warchild."

"No surprise there," the Judge replied. "Find us another way, fast."

She lead them back the way they had come, then took a different turning. Around the next corner she found the same result.

On the third roadblock she gave in. "No way through, not without getting ourselves torn up. We'll have to back onto the upper deck, see where we can get from there."

"And if the Warchild is in the middle of that lot?" asked Vix.

"As Dredd pointed out, I think we'd know about it by now." She walked past the group and back towards the tunnel. "Come on."

"Wait," called Vix. "Dredd, there may be another way. A couple of Hi-Exes should bring one of these barricades down, then we could go where we pleased."

Bane looked back and saw Dredd pondering the nearest roadblock. "Civilian casualties?"

"Probably minimal."

Then the air shifted.

Gethsemane Bane had been born with certain mutations and had developed others during her life on the Atlantic. Her tough skin, with its blue-steel sheen, had been with her since childhood. Another was a certain sensitivity to air vibrations and weather patterns.

It made her an exceptional sailor. Right now, it also told her that something terrible was about to happen.

She leapt at Dredd, yelling. She was fast, too, always had been. Certainly faster and stronger than he and his Judges had considered. He had barely turned towards the sound of her shout when she barrelled into him.

He went off-balance, but instantly corrected, only being driven back a metre or so. Vix went further because as Bane hit Dredd she'd also kicked back at the same time, catching the skull-head Judge below the ribs. All the breath went out of Vix in one go and she crashed backwards into a hab.

There was a massive, ringing pain across Bane's skull. Dredd had backhanded her away, slamming her across the deck and before she'd even hit the mesh his gun was centred on her heart.

Behind him, the first girder shrieked into the deck where he had been standing.

Another one came down next to it, huge and crudely sharpened. It punched into the mesh with a deafening howl of torn metal, tilted sideways, and was smashed flat by the next five girders that came down after it.

Bane was sitting on the deck, her head whirling from Dredd's blow. He'd hit her very hard indeed, she realised, and before she knew it the floor was tilting up behind her and hitting her in the back of the head.

Metal was still falling from the sky. Instead of girders, it looked like about two tonnes of nuts and bolts in a chain net.

Coming down right on top of her.

Far away, on another ship entirely, the Old Man woke from his slumber.

He had been asleep for a long time, since just after Gethsemane Bane had left. Reaching out through the multiple hulls and decks of *Sargasso* to find Can-Rat had been difficult enough. Worse still had been the waves of pain and fear that had come back up the connection to hit him.

He'd managed to hide the worst of their effects from Bane, but after she'd gone it was all he could do to make it back to his bed and collapse on it. He was sure that several bottles of offering spirit had been broken on that stumbling journey, a loss he would mourn later.

He blinked in the darkness. Hours must have passed. His guards had turned the lights out.

There was something ticking away at the back of his mind. Something that hadn't been there when he had gone to sleep.

A presence...

He reached out. A new mind had arrived on *Sargasso*, several new minds. Only one was of any interest to the Old Man, however.

"Dredd? Judge Dredd?"

It wasn't possible. The Old Man sat up, shaking off the last of his fatigue. He reached out again and found a mind made of steel.

The Old Man was no telepath. He had never read a thought in his life. But minds made ripples in the stranger surfaces of his world, like stones thrown into sump oil. Dredd's mind was like cold metal; utterly unyielding, totally hard. Unbreakable. To a psyker who sought out minds directly, the lawman would have been a blank as he was immune to such effects. But the Old Man's powers were far more subtle. He saw the oil, not the stone.

The Old Man felt a wide, predatory grin spread across his face. "Judge Dredd," he chortled. "This is a turn-up for the books, and no mistake."

He reached down and fumbled in the dark until his fingers brushed a bottle. Metal charms chimed against his knuckles as he lifted the bottle and twisted the lid off. It was the bottle Bane had brought him. He lifted it in salute.

"To Judge Joe Dredd," he laughed quietly. "Who I never thought I'd see again."

11. FALL OF THE GODS

"We shouldn't be out here," grumbled Sanny Fane. "They should give us guns if we're going to be out here."

Sanny was griping because he'd lost three rounds of rock-scissors-paper and thus was going down the access stairs first. Voley, who'd only lost two, was at the rear, and she could see Sanny's head turning left and right like a scanner dish, trying to see everywhere at once.

Personally, Voley thought that the stairway was probably the safest place to be because it was right out in the centre of the *Royale Bisley*'s main deck. Suspended from the ceiling girders, it took workers all the way from distribution on the upper hull to the maintenance level fifty metres below in one huge, narrow flight of open mesh steps.

No place for anyone suffering from vertigo, but it gave the only uninterrupted view of the *Bisley*'s interior.

Lox was going down second. He was three metres tall and there wasn't a single part of his body, head included, that Voley couldn't have circled with two hands. His ear-defenders had to be modified specially. "Guns wouldn't help," he said, ducking under a support brace. "Thirty guys from the Black Whale went after it with harpoon rifles and it took them all down."

"I heard that," nodded Sanny. "Reckon the thing's the size of a hab."

Lox leaned right down to him. "Long Sally from B-shift? Her sister goes with one of the skipper's men, and he said that they found the Tusk Brothers snapped clean in two!"

"Yeah," grinned Della Satori. "But anyone on the ship could snap you in two, Lox." She shook her head and turned back to give Voley a wink. "Grud, you guys are so full of it."

"Drokk you, Della," snapped Sanny. "If we're full of it, why did Quint call Mega-City One for a platoon of Judges, eh?"

"Guys?" Voley didn't talk much, so when she did the others tended to stop and listen. Sanny, in fact, stopped so suddenly that Lox almost tripped over him.

"Look, maybe this thing's as big as a hab, or maybe it's one futsie with a blade. But let's walk this shift together, okay?"

"That'll take four times as long," said Lox, gently.

Voley's long tail twitched. "Not if we go four times as fast."

Back in the day, *Royale Bisley* had been an anti-pollution ship. A century ago it had trawled the waters of the United States coastline, one of a vast fleet attempting to stem the tide of industrial waste seeping into the Atlantic. They had failed, of course. No fleet would have been large enough to deal with that amount of liquid garbage.

Now the vessel served a far more effective purpose. The huge pumps mounted in its blunt prow still dragged in thousands of litres of seawater a second, but certain other elements had been reversed in their function. Instead of housing the pollution and releasing clean water back into the sea, *Royale Bisley* and its sister vessels now did exactly the opposite. Together, the four ships provided clean drinking water for the entire cityship.

The system was largely automated, but it was also vital. Lack of water could wipe out *Sargasso* in a week. So every thirty minutes, the maintenance shift walked the length and breadth of the plant, checking the readouts on every filter, pump and boiler. And when that was done, they started all over again.

Whether there was a monster loose in the city or not.

Standard shift pattern was to start at the bow and work back. There were four pumps in *Bisley's* nose, and four sets of initial filters – gleaming steel cylinders as big as scavenger ships set on their ends. Each pump sent water back through three separate filters, only merging the flow when the water was clear enough to go into the big central boiler. And that was only halfway through the system.

There was a lot to check.

D-shift usually took a pump each, but not today. They ran through the system in a tight group, ear-defenders clamped on hard to protect their hearing, soaked with sweat almost instantly. The filtration plant was ancient, and as a result, it was big and hot and deafeningly loud. The shift had become adept at communicating in sign language.

It was Voley who first noticed something was wrong. She had been on D-shift for almost six years and she knew the pressure tolerances on the filter cylinders like she knew her own heartbeat. As soon as she looked at the reading on C-3, she knew something was amiss.

Voley skittered to a halt and went back to the cylinder readout. There was a big, easy-to-read display, and a smaller, more detailed version next to it. Voley had to climb a short ladder to get to that as she was very small at only a metre high.

The rest of the shift had stopped as soon as they realised she wasn't with them. They clustered around the base of the ladder. Lox didn't have to climb anything, of course. "Grud," he yelled, over the hammering din of the pumps. "Ten per cent down!"

Voley leaned back on the ladder, craning her neck to see the top of the cylinder. It stretched up above her, gleaming damply in the *Bisley's* dim internal lighting. She couldn't see anything amiss and was about to climb back down and call a supervisor when a fat drop of water hit her between the eyes.

It hit quite hard, slapping her back a little. She blinked, feeling the water running down her face, then scampered quickly up the ladder.

Heights didn't worry Voley, which was a good thing, since she didn't see anything of interest until she was at least twenty metres above the maintenance deck. At that height, the cylinder had already begun to curve inwards at the side, forming a blunt dome. It was here, where the metal skin of the filter could no longer be seen from the deck, that Voley found a hole.

She had been expecting corrosion, or maybe a split seam. Both had happened in the past. This, however, could only have been an act of deliberate sabotage. Something massively sharp had been simply punched through the metal, clear through both the outer and inner skins, plus the solid insulation between. Warm and frothy water from the filtration spinner was spitting fitfully through the opening.

Voley suddenly realised she was awfully exposed up there on the cylinder. She began to climb downwards, carefully, making sure she didn't lose her grip on the wet rungs. She might not have been worried about heights, but slamming into the deck from twenty metres wouldn't have done her any good at all.

When she got within a metre of the bottom she hopped off, ready to tell the others what she had seen. Driven by such tiny lungs, her voice wasn't loud and she was hoping they'd be able to hear her, as she wasn't sure what kind of signs she could use to tell them that someone had punched a spike through the cylinder cap.

There was no one at the base of the filter.

Voley stood where she was for a few seconds, trying to listen over the roar of the system, looking about for any evidence of her friends. After a time she called out, but there was no answer. Perhaps they hadn't heard her. Or maybe they had gone to some other readout, expecting her to be longer up the ladder.

If the shift was operating under normal circumstances, Lox would finish with filter C-3 and start tracing the pipes back to the boiler. The plan today had been to go back towards the prow after the C-line, and start on the D-filters in turn. Voley decided to go to cylinder D-1, closest to the bow pump. The others would be there, waiting for her.

She began trotting down the line of filters, peering around each one before she ran across the gap. She got all the way back to D-1 without seeing a soul.

By this time, Voley's heart was bouncing in her chest, and not from the heat. She resolved to head back to the boiler, and if they weren't there she would go back up the stairway and get help.

There was no one at the boiler, either.

Voley sprinted for the bottom of the ladder just behind the boiler and its bulky power units. She was most of the way along the port side when she ran through something slippery. Her boots went out from under her and she fell.

The boiler often leaked. Voley got up, cursing her own clumsiness, and then saw that her hands had blood on them. She must have come down harder than she thought.

There was blood on the floor, too. She walked back to where she had fallen and realised that she had slipped in a wide, crimson pool, collecting near the boiler's massive base.

The blood on her hands was not her own.

There was movement above her. She looked up, and saw something sticking out over the edge of the boiler. It was a long, thin arm, emerging from the sleeve of a maintenance worker's coveralls. There was most of a hand at the end of it.

Below the arm, blood was pouring down the side of the boiler, smoking from the heat within.

Voley gave an involuntary cry of pure horror. And as she did so, a face appeared at the edge of the boiler, near Lox's ruined hand, and peered down at her.

That was when Voley began screaming. It was a very long time before she stopped.

"Remind me of the penalty for assaulting a Judge," groaned Vix, wiping her mouth. The Bane woman had hit her in the guts so hard she'd thrown up.

"Code two, section one," Dredd replied. "Ten years. And you shouldn't need reminding, Judge Vix. Your ignorance of the Law will go on record to Judge Buell."

"Oh, give it a rest," Bane groaned wearily. "We're outside the territorial margin." Her face was badly bruised from where Dredd had backhanded her, and she was nursing any number of other contusions. They all were.

Dredd had seen the second half of the booby trap – the bundle of bolts pushed off the top of the hab stack – and had blasted it with Hi-Ex before it was halfway to the deck. That had separated the solid, lethal bundle into about four thousand separate components, but it hadn't altered their downward velocity. A hard rain had fallen on *Mirabelle*, and they had all been caught in the storm.

Bane was sitting with her back to the wall, near the access tunnel, and Judge Peyton was spraying the side of her face with something from a small surgical kit. Dredd stood over her. "You could have yelled."

"You could have been squished by a girder."

Peyton stopped spraying and Bane stood up a little shakily. The spray would have taken most of the pain away, but she wouldn't be able to see out of that eye for a while.

"Maybe. But you wouldn't have broken the Law."

Bane waved him away and walked back through the tunnel. The team had retreated there after the attack, safe from any more falling debris. Dredd let her go.

"We oughta get in there and bust the whole block," Larson was snarling. His uniform was cut in several places from the bolts and the skin beneath was lividly bruised. "They tried to wipe us out."

"They were trying to protect themselves," Bane told him. "They thought the Warchild was trying to break through. They have children in those habs, you know. Old people. What else could they do?"

"They should be letting us deal with it," said Larson. "Not dropping half a scrap heap on our heads."

Dredd was about to tell the pair of them to can the chatter when he heard footsteps pounding along the walkway from *Castiglione*. He pulled Bane to one side. Impetuous or not, the woman was valuable here. "Got company!"

Seconds later a skipper's man skidded to a halt just inside the tunnel and came face to face with the muzzles of five Lawgivers. Yelping in shock, he froze.

Dredd stepped forwards, the muzzle of his Lawgiver centred unerringly on the man's forehead. "What's the hurry, citizen?"

The man swallowed hard. "Judge Dredd?"

"What do you think?"

"Sir, I have a message for you from Deputy Jennig. He says there's been another attack."

It had taken Bane less than fifteen minutes to get Dredd and his team to the site of the attack. According to the shift supervisors on the upper deck of the *Royale Bisley*, D-shift had been observed no longer than ten minutes before the alarm was raised.

The Warchild was no more then twenty-five minutes away. Maybe less.

Dredd's first action had been to spread his team out, leaving Hellermann with the skipper's men while he searched the area. It didn't take him long to realise that the Warchild was no longer in the immediate vicinity, at which point he had sent Peyton up to check the bodies. Then he had taken Bane to see the survivor.

The woman was an obvious mutant, little more than a metre tall and with a long, naked tail poking out from under her orange work coat. Dredd had let Bane do the talking, but even her kinship with the mutant proved useless. The mouse-like woman was terrified beyond the capacity for rational thought. A doctor brought by the skipper's men had been forced to sedate her just to stop her shrieking.

Eventually Dredd gave up and pulled Bane aside. "We're wasting time. She's no use to us."

Bane nodded agreement. "Maybe later. Right now she needs to rest."

"Not my concern." Dredd stalked away. They were close to the Warchild; he could feel it. But there was a piece missing from the puzzle. He needed more information. For a moment he thought about retrieving Hellermann and grilling her, but the woman was too good a liar. He wanted to be sure about what he was hearing.

He went to the boiler, a massive cube of welded metal in the centre of the deck. The noise of the pumps was greater here and he was glad he could talk to the other Judges via helmet comms. "Peyton?"

The Tek-Judge was halfway down the ladder when Dredd arrived. "Here, sir." He jumped down the last few rungs. "Three bodies," he reported. "Two received fatal wounds from an edged weapon, one from toxin darts. Looks like the Warchild killed them on the deck then dragged them up out of sight." He lifted his helmet briefly to wipe his face with his hand. "Sorry, sir. I'll request more time in the Sector House gym when we get back."

"See that you do. Anything else?"

"No sign of, ah, ingestion. It must have eaten its fill back in the vent."

Dredd nodded. "What's its next move, Judge Peyton? Speculate."

Peyton appeared surprised. He must have known what Dredd usually thought of speculative thinking while on a case. Still, these were hardly usual times.

"You must understand, sir, I was only on the sequencing team. All the downloads, the important neural stuff, that was Dr Hellermann's field.

She designed its brain." Peyton took a deep breath. "But from what I know, I don't think it's following the default program."

"Explain."

Peyton gave a little nod as though he were getting things straight in his mind before he said them. "Okay," he began. "The Warchild is built to follow certain mission profiles; I'm not sure how many, but I think it's about fifteen. Stuff like all-out combat, single-target assassination, terror tactics, that kind of thing. Those programs are all hardwired into its brain before it comes out of the tank. If it doesn't get a mission program, it will follow a default program and then go dormant until it gets one. That's what Dr Hellermann was talking about in the council chamber." He spread his hands. "Sir, you should really be asking her about this."

"I would if I trusted her further than I could throw a Lawmaster," Dredd growled. "What's your best guess?"

"I think the Warchild units were programmed before they left Mega-City One. I think whoever bought them wanted them to perform in a certain way in a hurry, and the Warchild here is following that program. Otherwise it would have gone to ground."

"So it thinks it's in a war zone." Dredd rubbed his chin thoughtfully. "That's why we've got survivors – creep's mission is more important than not leaving witnesses."

"Judge Dredd!"

That was Adams, over the comm. "What have you got, Adams?"

"A lead, sir!"

Adams's lead was a scrap of human tissue that Peyton identified as part of a finger. It was lying near one of a row of service panels, where it had snagged on a sharp edge of metal. The service panels were all intact, not ripped open like the vent or the panel in the harbour barge, but when Dredd began tugging at those nearest the finger fragment one of them came away without effort.

Peyton inspected the other side of it while Dredd leaned carefully into the space behind the panel, Lawgiver ready and throwing out a steady cone of light from its clip-on flash. "Well?"

"The locks have been severed," said Peyton. "It pulled one corner open, used an integral blade to cut the locks then straightened the panel out and put it back. Stomm, do you know what that means?"

"Creep's getting smart," Dredd muttered. "Get the civvies. We're going hunting."

The team followed the same formation as in the vent: Dredd and Bane in front, Adams and Larson bringing up the rear. Vix kept an eye on

Hellermann who, along with Peyton, was in the centre of the group for protection.

The machinery behind the service panel had been ripped away and a hole was torn in the wall behind it. The Warchild had escaped into the space between the inner and outer hulls of the *Royale Bisley*.

It was a strange place; an echoing plasteen corridor only a couple of metres wide but dozens high. Girders crossed it at every level, strewn with pipe work and cables, and walkways had been set into the hull material at irregular intervals. The entire space stank of rust – oil and ancient metal.

There were places where the Black Atlantic had obviously eaten clear through the outer hull, and the plasteen had been patched on the outside with welded metal.

The constant racket of the filtration plant was muted here, but there was another noise that Dredd had trouble identifying for a moment. It was a rushing, thrumming sound, rising and falling and creating weird echoes that boomed and rattled between the hulls. Dredd had to listen for several seconds before he realised that the noise was that of the sea, moving past him just a few millimetres of plasteen away.

He tapped Bane on the shoulder. "You've got some pretty fancy mutant senses there, captain."

"Er, thanks. I think."

"Just keep 'em sharp. This is a great place for an ambush."

They moved on, heading towards the bow. "It'll open up, not far from here," Bane told him. "The power chambers are on either side of the boiler and the hull space connects directly to them. There should be a hatch."

Dredd nodded. "Let me know if you see it."

As he spoke, something scuttled past his head.

He snapped a hand out and brought it back with the scuttling thing clamped between finger and thumb. It was a pale, fleshy spider, with a body that seemed to consist entirely of one spherical eye. Dredd turned it over, his lip wrinkling in disgust.

The spider reminded him of something but he couldn't tell what. "Anyone else seen anything like this?"

There was a chorus of negatives. "Just some kind of mutant bug," said Larson. "Place is probably crawling with 'em."

Dredd showed the thing to Bane. "These common around here?"

She shook her head. "I've not seen one before," she said levelly. "But like Judge Larson says, we mutants live in such filthy conditions it's a wonder we're not knee deep in them."

The spider's eye was rotating wildly, looking at everything. Dredd squeezed his thumb and forefinger together until the creature burst wetly and died. He was wasting time. "We need that hatch, Bane."

"It's just up here." She ran forwards and stopped next to a doorway on the inner wall. Dredd hadn't seen it, even with the clip-on flashlight. The mutant's night vision must have been phenomenally good.

Dredd's wasn't bad. Better since he'd been given his new eyes.

Bane was smart enough not to try opening the door. Dredd got on one side of it and Vix took up position on the other. Dredd counted down from three on his fingers and then put his boot to the door. It crashed inwards, pieces of lock skating away across the deck.

He dived inside and came up with his Lawgiver aimed and steady. Vix was right behind him.

The room was empty. Blue-green biolume light shone off dozens of pipes and ducts, lining the walls from top to bottom in a maze of tubes. There were more pipes on the ceiling, too – it was like standing inside a giant junction box.

There was another hatch ahead of him, but that one was already open.

Dredd stalked forwards, his boots silent, his gaze flicking from the view straight in front of him to that through the viewfinder of his Lawgiver. He heard Bane and Hellermann come in behind the Judges.

There was movement at the hatchway. Another spider appeared around the frame, regarding him steadily with its great, liquid eye. It looked at him for a few seconds then darted away.

"Dredd," hissed Bane. "Wait."

"Spit it out, captain."

"It feels wrong here. I think–"

Something next to Dredd's left shoulder exploded with a deafening roar.

The blast threw him into Vix, knocking her off her feet. Dredd just managed to keep his balance, whipping the Lawgiver up around to find the source of the explosion. As he did, his gaze caught the edge of his shoulder pad. The armoured foam had been peppered with shrapnel and there were three pale, bonelike needles sticking out of it.

"It's a trap!" he roared. Ahead of him, pallid, fleshy pustules were oozing from between the pipes, swelling visibly as he watched.

"Behind us," called Larson. "They're everywhere!"

Dredd picked a pustule at the far end of the next chamber and put an execution round through it. It popped messily, vomiting white pus down the wall. "Standard rounds," he yelled, blasting another two. "Take them out before they arm. And watch for needles!"

The chamber became a flashing, booming nightmare of gunfire and bursting pustules. Dredd took out the nearest, with Vix using her SJS marksmanship training to rid the far chamber of dozens more. A couple had grown too quickly and exploded before she had the chance to shoot them. Poisoned needles whistled through the air, one bouncing off Vix's helmet.

Behind Dredd, the gunfire was joined by the sound of another explosion. He heard Adams give a choked cry, Peyton yelling that he was hit. "Judge down!" Larson screamed. "Judge down!"

"Fall back!" bellowed Dredd, hauling Vix up and throwing her bodily back towards the hatch. "Get the wounded outside, now!" Within seconds, all the Judges were out of the chamber. Dredd paused at the opening, grabbed the hatch with his free hand and brought his Lawgiver up. "Incendiary," he grated.

He had the hatch closed before the incendiary shell hit the furthest wall. There was a familiar thumping impact as it hit, and then the chamber walls were hammering as the inferno set off the remaining pustules. In a few moments, the hull space was silent.

Except for the sounds of Judge Adams trying to breathe.

The man was on his back on the walkway, every muscle rigid. Peyton was kneeling next to him, helmet discarded, bleeding from a dozen wounds of his own but completely ignoring them as he busily hunted through his surgical kit for a syringe. Captain Bane had both hands crossed over Adams's straining chest, pushing rhythmically, trying to keep his heart beating.

Dredd watched Peyton slam a pressure syringe to the fallen Judge's neck, take it away to adjust the dose, and then administer it again. It had no effect. A few seconds later, Adams gave an agonised, rattling groan, and died.

Bane sat back, her soot-streaked face running with tears. Peyton gave a snarl of fury and took her place, thumping Adams's chest five times, dropping his ear to the man's sternum to listen, then back up and thumping again.

"Let it go," Dredd said quietly. "He's gone."

At those words, Peyton sagged back against the hull. "There was too much toxin," he whispered. "He only took one needle, but there was too much..."

Abruptly, Vix leapt to her feet. "Drokk!" she yelled. "Where's Hellermann?"

While Dredd had been watching Judge Adams die, Elize Hellermann had escaped.

As soon as Hellermann had seen the spider, she knew that she was close to the Warchild's base of operations.

The bug that Dredd had so carelessly crushed was actually a miracle of biotechnology. Grown from spores hidden within the Warchild's body, it matured in hours into a tiny mobile surveillance unit, equipped with an organic radio link between itself and its one-time host. Mineral deposits in the legs formed an antenna array, capable of sending back pictures from the eye over a distance of almost a hundred metres.

The booby trap bombs were spore-grown, too. Once the Warchild had started eating its victims, she realised that it was planning to mature some of its on board weapons store.

She was close now. If the Warchild had been watching them, it couldn't have been too far away.

Hellermann had slipped away as Dredd ordered his retreat. She had seen Adams go down – a needle in his neck – and guessed that they would spend time trying to revive him. Fruitless, of course – the Warchild's toxins were based on those of the most lethal Black Atlantic shellfish. The man's nervous system had been pulp within moments. But it had given her a chance to escape.

She ran as fast as she dared down the space between the hulls. Ever since Justice Department had taken her project from her, she had frequented far worse places than this. A little grime meant nothing to her if it got her back within range of her creation.

Hellermann found the service panel where they had come in and squeezed back out onto the maintenance deck of the *Bisley*. The whole journey into the hull space had been a set-up, including planting the tissue fragment to lure the Judges inside. Thinking about that, Hellermann couldn't suppress a grim smile of satisfaction.

Constant self-improvement and evolution had been part of the Warchild's design from the beginning. It was, however, far exceeding her expectations.

Her offspring was doing better than she could possibly have hoped.

Hellermann paused a few metres from the service panel. The Warchild would have to stay within a hundred metres of the spiders to receive their signals. There wasn't anywhere within that distance it could hide, unless...

Royale Bisley was only about eighty metres across.

Hellermann belted across the deck, under the huge pipe that led from the boiler to the desalination filter, and towards the opposite side of the ship. There was a power chamber there, too, just like the one Dredd had just incinerated.

She wondered how long it would be before the fire shorted out some vital wiring and shut down the whole filtration plant.

Hellermann reached the power chamber in a few moments and searched until she found the hatch. It looked locked from the outside; even the display panel next to it said that it was. But she had taught her creation better than that. She looked quickly around to make sure she had not been followed and then pushed her way in.

The Warchild was waiting for her. There must have been spiders watching her approach.

She saw it for less than a second before it shimmered to near-invisibility, its mimetic skin perfectly matching the wall behind it. But that second was all Hellermann needed. "Götterdämmerung!" she snapped.

The Warchild froze. As she watched, it bleached back into visibility.

Hellermann let out a long, relieved breath. She hadn't been entirely sure the code word would still work.

She had been lying to Dredd all along, of course. Although each Warchild did have its own abort code, there was another code that would shut any one of them down. Dredd himself could have used it. That, however, would not have left Elize Hellermann out of Justice Department's clutches, on neutral territory and with the Warchild completely in her control.

Once she had demonstrated to the mutant council that she herself had rid them of their problem, she couldn't see any reason why they wouldn't grant her asylum.

The Warchild remained in front of her, swaying slightly. It's skin had faded back to a blank, pale grey, dry and leathery now it had been out of the tank for so long. The creature still looked rough and unfinished, but that was an illusion. It had matured perfectly.

Blades had emerged from each of its forearms, long and lethally sharp. They had hinged forwards, ahead of the slender, three-fingered hands.

"Well," Hellermann whispered. "Here we are. Together at last."

The Warchild stayed frozen, arms limp at its sides. Drool glittered below its toothy, lipless mouth. Only its eyes moved, following her as she moved.

Hellermann smiled at it, warmly. "You need a name," she told it. "After all, you're all grown-up now. Calling you child is... insulting."

She took a step back to admire her work. "I shall call you Freedom," she said. A movement on the ceiling caught her eye. There was a spider above the Warchild, watching her with its one limpid eye.

As she watched, another joined it. And another. They stood, upside down, in perfect formation.

"Wait," she whispered. "They shouldn't be able to do that. Not on their own."

There were spiders all over the ceiling now. "But if they aren't acting on their own, that means you must be–"

The Warchild snapped forward, faster than she could think.

12. QUIS CUSTODIET
IPSOS COSTODIES

On the cityship *Sargasso*, very little was ever used for its original purpose. It was something you got used to after a while; the fact that everything was made out of something else, or rebuilt to do a different job, or stapled to the deck and used as a family home. When a city's economy was based on fishing and scavenging, in roughly equal measure, recycling became a fact of life.

The same was true of Mako Quint's office. Correction: the skipper's office. Quint had to remind himself of that on a regular basis. Although he had been re-elected as skipper four times, and had held the post for seven years, he could be stripped of that title at any moment. Then he would have to pack his things and move back to his old hab in the *Middleton*, while someone else got to sit at the desk and read reports.

He had been in the office for so long, it was easy to forget that he didn't own it.

Perhaps the captain of the assault carrier had felt the same way, in the days when the ship was a potent and independent vessel. There was no way he could have known, back when the Atlantic was still partly blue, that one day his ship would form the governmental centre of a mobile city-state with almost a million inhabitants, and that his quarters would house the man whose word, in that state, was law.

Right now, Mako Quint didn't feel much like the law. He felt less in control of events with every report that dropped onto his desk.

Shift-workers killed on the *Royale Bisley*. Hab-dwellers on the *Mirabelle* setting traps for the Warchild and almost flattening Dredd's entire team. The Old Man had gone missing.

And now this.

In addition to being deselected by the council, the position of skipper would also pass on if Quint was dead, or too severely injured to carry on. With everything he was hearing about the progress of Judge Dredd and his team, that possibility seemed more and more likely.

The telephone jangled abruptly, jarring him out of his morbid thoughts. Time to be the skipper again. He lifted the receiver.

"Quint."

"Jennig here, skipper. You wanted me?"

That hadn't taken long. Quint had put the word out that he needed to speak to his deputy just ten minutes previously. He'd told one messenger, who had then told every skipper's man he could find. Each of the men he told then did the same thing, and before long Jennig knew he had to report in.

It was an efficient system, and vital since there was no centralised communications system on the *Sargasso*. Unless you included gossip.

"That business in the *Royale Bisley*," he said into the mouthpiece. "Heard it got messy."

"Wasn't pretty, skipper, no."

"Philo... Look, I hate to ask this, but did you get everything cleared away? I mean, no, er, body parts missing?"

"Grud, skipper, what do mean?"

Quint sighed. "Sorry to ask. But I'm getting reports about the water coming out of the *Bisley*. People are saying it tastes bad. Just wanted to make sure there wasn't a body in the boiler."

Jennig made a disgusted sound. "Charming thought. I'll get right on it, have a crew check the tanks. If we can't see anything obvious we might have to shut *Bisley* down and steam out the whole system."

"Thanks, Philo. Let me know what you find."

Quint replaced the handset and sat back. Four separate reports had come in about foul water being pumped out of the *Royale Bisley*. On a closed system like a cityship, that kind of situation could get out of hand, very badly and very quickly.

The last thing Mako Quint needed right now was a water riot.

They found most of Elize Hellermann outside the power chamber. The rest of her, the steaming mass that had spilled from her opened belly after the Warchild's attack, was still inside the hatchway. Hellermann had managed to crawl out of the chamber without it.

The expression frozen on her face was one of confusion rather than pain.

Bane gave a whimpered curse and stumbled away at the sight. Dredd let her go. She'd seen more horror on this trip than any civilian out of wartime, and none of the other bodies had been nearly so fresh. Heat from Hellermann's ruined corpse was still in the air, along with the coppery, faecal stench of death. Dredd saw Bane hit the chamber wall with her back and slide down it, her head in her hands, and – mutant or not – couldn't bring himself to despise her for it.

"Vix, Larson – you're with me. Peyton, see if you can work out what went wrong. Looks like Hellermann's word didn't work. I want to know why."

As Peyton trotted back to the power chamber, Dredd began to run a sweep of the surrounding area, with Vix and Larson watching his back. He knew in his bones that the Warchild had escaped them again; it never stayed around once it had made a kill. But procedure, not to mention plain common sense, dictated that he had to be sure.

He also wanted to get Larson and Vix back on track. Larson was taking Adams's death hard, and Vix was beating herself up for not keeping an eye on Hellermann. In normal circumstance Dredd wouldn't have hesitated in hauling Vix over the coals for it, but they were already a Judge down. He needed everyone frosty and aiming true.

The sweep took five minutes. Dredd had planned to order Vix and Larson back to the chamber and continue alone for a while, get a better feel for the place. But Vix cut in before he could speak.

"Judge Larson, we've already lost one scientist today. Go back to the chamber and assist Judge Peyton."

Larson frowned. "Ah, I'm not sure–"

"You're questioning my orders, Judge?" snapped Vix. "Consider how that would look on your SJS dossier."

Larson cocked his head slightly towards Dredd, looking for confirmation. Dredd knew that Vix was up to something – SJS Judges always were – but he wanted to know what. He gave Larson the nod and the other Judge walked quickly away.

When he was gone, Vix sidled closer to Dredd. "This is a disaster."

Her voice was quiet, despite the noise from the filtration plant. She was using its hammering to mask her words, even while speaking over a private comms channel. Typical SJS procedure.

"Like to tell me something I don't know, Judge Vix?"

"Dredd, I'm serious. We're really in the drek now, worse than you can imagine." She glanced over her shoulder. "Your mutant looks like she's lost the plot. With Adams down we're a gun short, and now Hellermann's toast. No way we can bring the Warchild to heel without her."

"Hate to break this to you, Vix, but Hellermann struck out. We'd have been no better off if she'd stayed." He fixed the SJS Judge with a steely glare. "You can take that back to Buell right now."

"My report to Judge Buell will be..." She trailed off. Dredd could see that, oddly, she was unsure of herself. Perhaps losing Hellermann had hit her harder than he'd thought.

"Judge Buell and I don't agree on everything," she said finally.

"Not what I heard."

"For grud's sake, Dredd! If you're watching anyone it should be Peyton!" She spun away from him and stood with her arms folded tightly. She's said too much, Dredd thought. And she knows it.

He didn't have the time or inclination to do this the slow way. "Judge Vix! If you've got information pertaining to this case, I suggest you give it up. Withholding evidence will get you ten to fifteen!"

She gave him a wry smile. "If I was afraid of cube time I'd never have joined the SJS." Still, she made that quick, almost unconscious look left and right before she spoke again.

"I didn't say this, Dredd. But the SJS is investigating McTighe's people. We've got good evidence that Tek Division didn't dispose of all the Warchild units like they were ordered to."

Dredd shook his head. "Impossible. McTighe's a tinkerer of the worst order, but he's not insane."

"No, but some of his people might be. Remember, when Project Warchild was broken up, Hellermann's staff were sent all over. Some of them ended up back in Tek-Div." Vix tilted her helmet back towards the power chamber. "Like Peyton. Not too hard to believe one or two might still be devoted to the dream."

Dream? More like a nightmare. The idea that Tek Division could be corrupted from within, that some of Hellermann's acolytes were still active and trying to bring the Warchild project to fruition was a disturbing one.

"My job was to keep Hellermann alive until she got a chance to use the word," Vix continued. "And to come back with it. So we could control the Warchild units if there were any still in the Meg."

"Hellermann said there was one word per Warchild. She had to see it to know which one."

Vix threw her arms up. "Oh, sure! If she got to read the barcode on the back of its neck!" She strode up to the nearest piece of machinery and kicked it, hard. "We've got the Psi Division reports. That's the only way she could work out which Warchild was which, and you know how fast they move. What was she going to do, offer it a haircut?

"There had to be one word for all of them. She got us to bring her out here on the pretext of a unique word, but there had to be a master key. Drokk!"

Vix sighed. "My guess is she was going to bring the Warchild down, then escape into *Sargasso*. Maybe even claim asylum."

"But it got away from her." Dredd turned and began to walk back to the power chamber. Vix followed him.

"Keep this to yourself," he told her. "Maybe Peyton's bad, and maybe he isn't. But right now, he's the best chance we've got."

When they reached the power chamber, Bane was draping a piece of tarpaulin over Hellermann's body. She'd already used a smaller piece to cover what lay in the chamber.

Peyton was waiting for them, his helmet off and dangling from his belt. "I found this," he said simply, and held out his hand.

One of the spider-like creatures lay there, half its legs smashed. It twitched and pulsed feebly. "There was another one, but I've already dissected that."

"People are dying here, Peyton," Vix hissed. "And you waste your time cutting up bugs?"

"Bugs," he replied, "is right in more ways than one. Look." He had a scalpel in his other hand, and he used this to lift and prod one of the spider's shattered limbs.

Dredd saw metal gleam among the ruins. "Wires?"

Peyton nodded. "Connected to a kind of organic transmitter behind the eye. The Warchild's remote sensors."

"Surveillance devices?" Vix leaned in closer. Trust the SJS to be fascinated by anything to do with spying. "What's the range?"

"A hundred metres, I'd guess."

Dredd lifted the spider out of Peyton's gloved palm and dangled it by one leg. "So if we see one of these things giving us the eye, that means the Warchild won't be far away." He dropped the creature and trod on it, felt it burst messily under his sole. "Good work, Peyton. Anything else?"

"Just speculation."

Vix folded her arms. "Spit it out."

"The Warchild's getting smarter. You said it yourself, Judge Dredd. It's covering its tracks, setting traps for us. Acting more like an enemy agent than a predatory animal."

"You think it got smart enough to ignore Hellermann's word?" Dredd saw the answer in Peyton's eyes.

"Grud," he snarled, turning away. "It's gone rogue."

As soon as Philo Jennig had finished his call to Quint, he had gathered a patrol of skipper's men and headed for the *Royale Bisley*.

He knew how serious a problem with the water supply could be, just as well as anyone. *Sargasso* relied on the four filtration ships like he relied on the four chambers of his heart. Out here, on the open ocean, there was simply no other source of water. A man can live for a fortnight without food, but without water he'd be dead inside two days.

If he tried to drink Black Atlantic seawater, make that two minutes.

Jennig had seen a cityship burning, once. It was on fire from bow to stern, so hot that the air above it caught alight and the pollution in the sea below solidified, turning to ragged strips of plastic that floated there to this day. The city had been small, with only a hundred thousand people aboard. But every single one of them had died.

The fires had started during a water riot. The city had only one filtration ship, and that had failed when a slick-eel had been dragged into one of the pumps. The way Jennig heard it, no one checked the grilles over the inlets.

Bits of the eel had gone into the boiler, contaminating the water supply. The cityship had run out of drinkable water before anyone could reach it and the population had torn it apart.

Sargasso was ten times as big. A riot could spread ten times as fast.

Jennig had been on the *Camberley* when he had made the call, using the telephone on its bridge. Once he had his patrol, he had taken them across *Camberley*'s deck and into the *Pride of Macao*, a residential vessel three ships starboard of the *Mirabelle*. It was during the journey through the *Macao*'s hab-stacks that he saw the first sick people.

Someone had recognised him as he led the patrol through the vessel's main street and begged him to help his children. Jennig, who had kids of his own, found it hard to refuse; besides, the man's hab wasn't far out of his way.

The man told him that the children had fallen ill very quickly, in less than an hour. Jennig peered into the hab doorway, saw the state of the sick kids, and backed out fast, promising to call a doctor as soon as he reached a phone point.

By the time Jennig was out of the *Macao*, he had seen nearly forty people with the same affliction. As soon as he was off the ship he found a phone point, connected his personal handset and called Quint.

"Philo, that was fast. You at the *Bisley* already?"

"Not yet. Skipper? I think we've got another problem." And, making sure that none of the skipper's men in his patrol could hear him, he told Quint what he had seen.

There was a plague on the *Pride of Macao*.

13. THE CORE DRIVE

When the telephone rang next, the voice on the other end of the line was not that of Philo Jennig. "Quint, this is Dredd."

The skipper's eyebrows went up into his hairline. "Dredd? How did you–"

"Trust me, Quint. It's not difficult."

Quint cursed silently. The phone points were for the exclusive use of the skipper and his men, not these gun-happy intruders from the Mega-City. He would have to increase security around them, or maybe invest in some kind of line encryption.

If Dredd could patch in to his office, anyone could. He'd never get a moment's peace. "The council's already given you all the help you're getting, Dredd. What do you want?"

"Two things. First off, I need your people to collect the bodies of Judge Adams and Dr Elize Hellermann. They're in the *Royale Bisley* starboard hull-space and portside power chamber respectively."

"Grud," Quint groaned, putting a hand to his head. "You lost Hellermann?"

"Let's say she lost herself. Secondly, I want you to put the word out for me. There's a new kind of bug loose in your city."

Quint almost spoke, then snapped his mouth closed. Did Dredd know about the disease? And if he did, just how far and how fast had the news spread?

He decided to play it cool and try to find out more. "What do you mean?"

"It looks like a white spider," Dredd replied. Quint let out a silent sigh of relief. "As big as your hand – okay, my hand. Body's just a big eye. They're the Warchild's pets, and if your men see any of these things around it means the creep's close by."

"Okay, Dredd, I'll spread the word. Anyone sees big bugs, we'll let you know."

He put the phone down. Let Dredd chase his pet monster. Right now, Mako Quint had other things on his mind.

Down among the hab-stacks of the *Pride of Macao*, the plague was racing out of control.

Bane had recovered a lot of her composure by the time Dredd had returned with the skull-headed Judge. She hadn't wanted to lose control in front of everyone like that, but the sight of Hellermann's carcass, sliced open so bloodily, had been one horror too many.

Orca had died like that. She wondered if he'd tried to crawl away, too.

The remaining team was heading up out of the filtration plant, using the long maintenance stairway. The respite from the plant's noise was welcome, but it's heat increased as they climbed higher and the stairway seemed terrifyingly narrow and flimsy. If she looked down, she could see the deck through the open mesh, tens of metres below her boots. She did that once, and after that made sure she didn't look down again.

It was a relief to get out of the wet, yammering heat of the plant and onto a solid deck. Bane led them through the distribution section, where bottles were filled with water pumped up from the final filters, and shipped out in their thousands to this quarter of the cityship. Once past that, they were in the open air again.

The storm seemed to have eased down since they were last on the cityship's upper surface. They were also shielded by some of the bigger structures – the *Bisley* was closer to the centre of *Sargasso*, and more habs and towers had been built around it. Bane took them into a street between two vast racks of storage drums. The drums had once held oil and noxious chemicals but now they were bolted together amidst great sheets of gantry and kilometres of support cable. Ladders were welded to every stack and windows sawn out of each circular end. The drums were big enough for one person to sleep in if they weren't too tall and slept curled up.

"Cheapest kind of housing," she told Dredd.

He seemed unsurprised. "Stackers," he said. "Got the same thing back in the Meg."

"Why are we here, Bane?" Vix asked, her voice as sneering and acidic as ever. "Maybe you need a place for the night, but personally I wasn't intending to stay that long."

Bane gave her the sour eye. "Keep your skull on. This is just the best place to get to anywhere else. Like an intersection."

"And what do we do now?"

"Well," Bane said carefully, cocking her head to the side. "Either we can run around all over the cityship like idiots, or we can wait."

They waited.

The Judges used the time to check and reload their Lawgivers, running checks on the voice-select systems and making sure the magazines were full, with spares in easy reach. Bane just paced.

She guessed that they probably wouldn't have to stand around in the drum stacks for very long. Once the word went out on *Sargasso* it tended to spread at an exponential rate. Every Sargassan was part of the communication chain – everyone would simply pass a message along to anyone they met, and even with most people hiding in their habs, terrified of being disembowelled by a rampaging killer, there would still be enough links in the chain to get the word from one end of *Sargasso* to the other in minutes.

She wondered if it was like that back in Dredd's city. No, she thought, looking at the reinforced knuckles on his gloves and the size of the gun he was reloading. It probably wasn't.

As it turned out, she was right about not waiting for long. Within a few minutes, a skipper's man came to find them.

The man was Loper, one of the more extreme mutants in Quint's employ. His short torso was balanced on a pair of supernaturally long legs, bent backwards at the knee and partially armoured to support their own weight. He looked like a human grasshopper. He was also the fastest man in the cityship, which made him invaluable as a message runner.

Bane knew that as long as *Sargasso* remained without a proper system of integrated communications, Loper would never be out of work.

The man bounded across the deck towards them, actually stepping over a couple of low-lying habs on his way to the drum stacks. "Judge Dredd," he called out, skidding to a halt and folding himself down to a more human level. When he did, his knees came up to the back of his head.

"Skipper Quint sends his regards," he quoted. "And he says that spiders have been reported in the *Kraken*."

Dredd threw a glance at Bane. "Know it?"

"*Kraken*'s one of the core drives, back at the stern. Dredd, there's only one way into a core drive. If we can trap it there..."

"Maybe it's thinking the same thing," said Peyton warily.

"Either way, that's where we're headed." Dredd gave Loper a nod of acknowledgement. "Give the skipper our thanks, and tell him to pull everyone back from the *Kraken*. We'll make a stand there."

"Hop along, now," Vix smirked. Loper raised an eyebrow at her.

"If there's any justice at all," he told her quietly, "you'll end this day knowing what your own guts look like." With that he stretched way up over their heads and stepped away. In a few strides he was out of sight.

Bane gave Vix a look. "You really do have a way with people, skull-head."

Vix shrugged. "If you find any 'people' on board this wreck, do let me know."

Bane put her face very close to the glossy front of Vix's helmet, smiled politely, and blinked at her. All three sets of eyelids. The Judge flinched involuntarily.

"Sure I will, " Bane said cheerily. "If you're still alive."

Bane ran next to Dredd as they belted across the deck towards the stern. "There are six core drives," she was telling him. "They're just floating engines: chem-tankers emptied out and fitted with the propulsion systems from old nuke subs. They give *Sargasso* most of its power."

"Motive or electrical?"

"Both. Left here." She pointed to the turning they needed to take, between two outlet funnels. "Most of the other ships run their engines on fossil fuels, and we can distil that straight out of seawater."

"Wondered how you kept running."

There was something she needed to make him understand, something she'd only thought of as they had begun running. "Listen, Dredd. Just because the drives are nuclear, doesn't mean they're clean. There's this stuff we call darkwater – mixture of coolant, lube oil, old fuel and concentrated Black Atlantic. The core drives get full of it, and it's not nice."

The lawman might have been big, but he certainly wasn't stupid. He caught on to what she was saying before she said it. "Flammable?"

"Sometimes yes, sometimes no. Look, I'm not saying don't use your guns. Just keep the incendiaries to a minimum, okay?"

Bane hadn't been exaggerating when she'd said *Kraken* was nothing more than a floating engine. The days when it could have been anything else had ended decades ago, when *Sargasso*'s work crews had sliced off the entire upper deck and stripped the inside of the hull bare. They had left the propulsion screws, but nothing more. Even the engines themselves had gone, lifted out on cranes and broken down for spare parts. In their place was a Sov-built nuclear power plant, the great armoured globe of the fusion core taking up the entire forward end of the ship.

The work crews had left the *Kraken* a vast, blunt-nosed slab of a vessel, covered in enormous welds. It didn't even have a superstructure any more, save the massive braces that connected it to the rest of the city-ship. The core drives were the only vessels in *Sargasso* that weren't covered in buildings, partly because of their function, but mostly due to the lingering, if irrational, fear of radioactive contamination.

The only raised structure on *Kraken*'s upper surface was a small blockhouse, two-thirds of the way towards the stern. When Bane and the Judges reached it, a wide half-circle of skipper's men was waiting for them, weapons centred on the blockhouse hatch. Spotlights from the nearest vessels had been trained on the *Kraken*, and in their harsh glare Bane noticed the shattered remnants of several eye-spiders.

"Skipper's men," called Dredd as he strode into the centre of the deck. "Stand down. We'll take it from here."

None of them budged, although at the sound of Dredd's voice a few lowered their weapons on reflex. One of the men gave Dredd a snappy salute. "Sorry, sir, but Skipper Quint's orders are to keep that hatchway covered, even after you've gone in. If it tries to go past you, it'll run into us."

Dredd seemed to mull this over for a second. "Agreed," he said. "But in that case, move your people back a few more metres. This thing's quicker than you can imagine."

With the warnings given, there was no reason for Bane not to open the hatch and go inside. Except that she didn't want to. Suddenly, on this wide open deck with the spotlights and the weapons all aimed at the small of her back, and the Warchild almost certainly waiting for her below and sharpening its knives, Gethsemane Bane found she had some difficulty getting her legs to move. From the neck up she was fine: determined, alert, anxious to find the creature and see it destroyed for what it had done to Orca and Judge Adams and all the others. But the rest of her body was a different matter. Her guts had turned to ice water and her boots were welded to the deck.

"Drokk it!" she growled angrily to herself. "I'm gonna take up fishing."

The hatch swung open as Dredd pushed it inwards. He had the flash-light clipped to his gun again, but there was no need for it as the interior of the blockhouse was as well lit as anywhere on *Sargasso*. The crews who provided maintenance for nuclear reactors liked a lot of light to work by, and the *Kraken* had power to spare.

Dredd ducked inside. Bane followed, trying to look everywhere at once. The blockhouse had no floor and the steps down into *Kraken*'s belly started right at the hatch. Dredd was already moving down, Law-giver held near his shoulder with the muzzle vertical, ready to drop down and fire in an instant. Watching him, Bane was struck by the fact that Dredd moved like a cat. He was encumbered by his shoulder armour, a helmet that couldn't have done anything for his field of vision, kneepads, bulky boots and gloves, but he went down the stairs in perfect silence. Not a single part of his uniform even brushed a wall.

Bane, who barely came up to Dredd's chin if she stood on her toes, could only wish for such grace.

The stairs went down for three flights before they reached a walkway. When Bane got to the bottom she moved past Dredd as carefully as she could, in order to spread out and let the others down. The stairs finished in the centre of the vessel, on a circular platform of open mesh. Bane looked down through the gridwork under her boots. Ten metres below her was a metal grille, just covering a long pool of evil-smelling black fluid.

She pointed. "Darkwater," she mouthed. Dredd gave a brief nod.

The interior of the *Kraken* was mainly one single, huge chamber. To the stern a bulkhead sealed off the drive shafts, and far away towards the bow was another lead-lined bulkhead that protected the work crews from the fusion core. Or possibly the other way around. The remaining space was filled with massive pieces of networked pipes and gantries. Bane saw rows of control boards with walkways between them, huge cylinders of coolant, and pipework everywhere.

A thousand places for the Warchild to hide, especially if it had chameleon skin.

The *Kraken* made surprisingly little noise, given that it was partially responsible for pushing the impossible bulk of *Sargasso* across the Black Atlantic. Instead of the deafening hammer of the *Bisley's* filtration plant, this was more of a constant, almost subsonic drone. If Bane put her teeth together, she could feel them vibrating.

The whole team was on the platform now. Walkways connected the disc fore and aft to bridges stretching clear across the width of the hull, and they in turn led to more platforms with railings ranged around the chamber's outer edge. Occasionally, ladders ran down to the lowest deck. Bane hoped she'd be able to stay on the walkways. The idea of being level with a sumpful of darkwater didn't appeal to her in the slightest.

Dredd was gesturing at the bow. He probably wanted to start a sweep there and flush the Warchild out towards the stairs. All the better, Bane thought to herself. If they drove it out of the blockhouse it would run into multiple weapons fire from the skipper's men.

She was just wondering how, if they didn't find the creature, they could get up the stairs and out without being shot themselves, when she saw the Warchild.

She froze, trying desperately not to scream. The others hadn't seen it.

Instantly she realised why. It was still camouflaged, its skin perfectly mimicking the clean grey walls of the *Kraken*'s interior. It was only because her eyes were different from theirs that she could see it at all, and then it was only an outline.

It was crouching on one of the bridges, near the control boards. Its posture was loose, relaxed; hunched on the mesh with one hand on the railing, the other arm dangling. She couldn't see any details – no eyes, or teeth, or whatever it used to open people up so efficiently – but its head was slightly to one side.

The Warchild was watching them. And Dredd was walking right towards it.

Bane knew that it could hear her. By now, it was probably smart enough to understand what she said, and if she just screamed and pointed it would be on them, or away, before they could do anything about it.

"I spy," she whispered, "with my little mutant eye, something beginning with Hellermann..."

To his credit, Dredd didn't alter his pace or make any physical sign he'd heard her. "Where?" he hissed.

"Two bridges forward, near the centre." Bane forced herself to look somewhere else entirely. "Watching us, real close."

"You're sure?" Vix said. "I don't see it."

"Advantage of being a filthy mutant, skull-head."

"Stow it," Dredd replied. "We've only got one chance at this. Hi-ex. On my mark, cover the bridge."

There was the soft, metallic sound of four Lawgivers having their ammo loads manually reconfigured. Bane knew the guns could understand voices, but if the creature could too...

The Warchild was on its feet. Dredd brought his Lawgiver up and said: "Mark."

The bridge flew apart in a cloud of fire and whirling metal.

The racket of the Lawgivers going off was hellish. Bane was crouching, hands over her ears, feeling hot shell casings hit her in the back. For a moment she thought the Warchild was gone, that it must have been shredded in the multiple blasts, but then the closest bridge to her shuddered under a sudden weight.

The Warchild had jumped out of the explosion and landed on the bridge, only metres away.

Bane saw it for a fraction of a second before it leapt again, too brief an instant to react to but enough to form a picture in her mind that would stay there forever. The Warchild, standing, its camouflage bleaching out into bone-white skin, lipless mouth frozen into a razor-sharp snarl. One of its arms had grown a long blade, extending a metre forward of its hand. The other was a shattered twist of flesh and broken armour.

Before she could even draw breath it had jumped again. It came down on the walkway between her and Dredd.

And it *moved*. Later, Bane would realise that the Warchild wasn't impossibly fast, even though it was quicker than she could ever hope to be. But it moved so fluidly, almost ballet-like in motion, as though unfettered by mass or gravity. Every separate part of it seemed to be doing something different at once, even the smashed arm, as though it had already adapted to the loss. It was like a master swordsman and an expert dancer rolled into one.

The remaining arm-blade sang out in a wide arc, taking Larson's head off without trying. At the same moment Dredd's Lawgiver had been kicked from his hand and another foot had slammed into the small of his back. The blade whipped around on the backswing to find Vix's belly, but Bane had moved too, launching herself up and back, powering into the woman at waist level. The blade corrected in mid-flight and carved a track across Vix's ribcage.

The broken arm belted Bane across the face, exactly where Dredd had struck her. Pain erupted through her skull and she tumbled back onto the mesh. Vaguely, she heard Peyton yelling that he couldn't get a clear shot.

The Warchild snapped round, its sword-arm poised to skewer her, and took Dredd's fist right in the teeth.

Its head rocked back under a blow that would have sheared the vertebrae of any human. Bane heard the impact and kicked blindly out at the Warchild's legs, and must have actually connected by pure luck. Unbalanced, the creature found itself being hammered by the reinforced knuckles of Mega-City One's finest fist.

Behind it, Judge Larson's body dropped to its knees. The fountain of blood from its severed neck hadn't even had a chance to slow. His heart didn't realise it was dead yet.

The Warchild darted away and Dredd's next blow hissed past. The blade came up, but the creature must have been affected by the punches, because it left Dredd enough time to leap forward and grab the bioweapon's remaining arm.

Bane scrabbled away from them, beyond all terror now, seeing the bone-white sword whipping left and right in Dredd's grip. The lawman's other hand was wrapped around its throat, trying to crush the life out of it.

Bane watched incredulously. Dredd was actually gaining the upper hand. The Warchild, for all its insect grace and speed and impossible strength, couldn't break his grip.

The sword twisted down and up, scooping out a half-metre of railing. Bane saw the piece of metal bar spin away, and in a moment of awful clarity realised what the creature was going to do. "Dredd!" she howled. "It's trying to take you down!"

It was already too late. The Warchild had bent back and to the right with inhuman flexibility, its torso curving almost completely around on itself. Before Dredd could react the creature's right leg folded, sending the pair of them tumbling through the gap in the railing.

Dredd couldn't let go of the Warchild's arm or throat. He went over without a sound.

There was a second of silence and then the ghastly cracking of two bodies, one human and one not nearly so, colliding with the metal grille over the sump.

Her head pounding, Bane rolled over and looked down through the mesh. Dredd couldn't have survived a fall like that. She wondered if the Warchild had.

Her vision was blurry from pain. She blinked rapidly, her extra eyelids sweeping away tears and blood, and when her eyes cleared she saw that neither Dredd nor the Warchild was lying dead on the grille.

The metal had given way when they had struck it. They were in the sump.

14. QUIVERS

Mako Quint's office was full of people, more full than it had been for years. From his position behind the desk, all the skipper could see was faces. Some of them were angry. All of them were frightened.

The faces belonged to local councillors, minor officials who ran the affairs of small areas of *Sargasso* – sometimes four or five ships, sometimes just one. Usually they kept themselves to themselves, but in times of need they would report back to Quint, or even the ruling council.

There were twenty of them packed into the office, which represented about a quarter of the entire city.

"I've never seen anything spread so fast," Lorton Umax was telling him. Umax was councillor for a small group of vessels that included the *Pride of Macao*, and he'd been down in the underdeck habs not long before. The rest of the councillors were trying to give him a lot of personal space.

"I'm not sure what the vector is," Umax went on. "In a place like the *Macao* it could be anything. Skin contact, droplet… Grud, it could even be airborne."

A woman next to him – Quint recognised her as councillor for the *Elektra Maru* – practically jumped. "Airborne? Skipper, we need to shut down their ventilation. What if plague germs come out and blow across the deck?" She glared at Umax. "Everything windward and astern of the *Macao* could take them in!"

"If you shut down the ventilation, the *Macao* will be dead in a day!"

"Better that than the whole city!"

"Calm down, Borla." Quint raised his hands in an attempt to soothe the woman of her fears. "No one's shutting down any vents. And I've never met a bug yet that could survive Black Atlantic air."

"It's not just that," said Umax. "Some of the skipper's men won't come down on patrol. They say they're being diverted away from normal duties, something to do with this Warbeast."

"War*child*."

"Whatever. We've got a crime increase down there, a big one. If it carries on like this we'll have a riot and people really *will* die."

Quint had taken more than enough of this. He got up, his hands flat on the desk, using his massive height to lean over them. "Councillors, I hear your concerns. And I understand that the situation on board the *Macao* is serious." He raised his hand again to stem a rising babble of voices. "Please! I'll double patrols in the *Macao* to keep order and help where they can. I've got Philo Jennig calling me every ten minutes, regardless, and I've stepped up the delivery of reports. I'll know what happens, when it happens."

"But skipper–"

Quint raised a finger at Borla, halting her in mid-sentence. "This disease is not fatal, but it is infectious. We need time for the doctors to determine the best treatment for those who are ill, and they need space in which to work. So I've sent skipper's men to the *Venturer*. They're moving the occupants away and setting it up as a hospital.

"We've been through this before," he continued. "We came through it then, and we will today. But I need your help. Stay calm, keep your people calm, try to carry on as normally as possible."

He straightened, raising himself to his full height. "Oh, and councillors? One more thing. If I hear anyone, and I mean *anyone*, use the word 'plague' outside this office, they'll find themselves changing blankets in the *Macao* in damn short order. Clear?"

As they filed out, Quint sank back into his chair. He moved a file on his desk, one that had been covering up the last two reports to come in. He couldn't let any of the councillors see what he had just read.

The first report had told him of the plague's first fatality. An old woman, in her nineties, had slipped into a coma and died not half an hour before. The eldsters were always the first to go, Quint reflected. Then the children would begin to die. When adults started to succumb, the first victims would be the parents of the dead children and the relatives of the eldsters.

The second report was worse. Far worse. Four victims had just been confirmed on the *Horizon Hope*, two ships to port.

The disease was already off the *Pride of Macao*.

The Warchild was gone.

Dredd had kept his grip on the bioweapon all the way down. As he felt himself toppling off the walkway he'd made a snap decision, not trusting the fall alone to kill it. He could have freed a hand in time to grab the walkway and hang on, but he'd gambled that he could do more damage to the Warchild by making sure it hit the deck just before he did.

He hadn't gambled on the sump grille giving way under him.

The darkwater Bane had told him about was hot and foul, thick as phlegm on the surface but watery beneath. When the Warchild hit, the impact had been so great Dredd had almost lost consciousness; and for a second, when the blackness swooped up to envelop him, he thought that he had. But it only took a second to realise he'd gone through the grille and into the sump. The darkwater had blinded him.

The thick surface layer hid something else about the sump. It had a current.

There must have been a pump forcing the stuff back towards the stern, probably to be filtered and recycled. As soon as they had gone under, the Warchild was torn from his grasp, ripped away by the under-tow. His hands abruptly free, Dredd had managed to grab something and hold on, his legs trailing in the vicious current. With his other hand he reached up to the front of his helmet and slid his respirator down over his nose and mouth.

The respirator wouldn't let him breathe under water, or under dark-water, for that matter. It was purely an air filter. But in the absence of air it formed a perfect seal over his nose and mouth, keeping the toxic stuff from getting into his lungs. Dredd could hold his breath for a long time and the respirator would give him a vital few minutes.

He couldn't tell where he was in the sump.

He wasn't even sure which way was up. The hot liquid was rushing past him so fast that it was robbing him of all sense of gravity. He wasn't sure if the object he had grabbed was a dangling part of a grille, and thus near the sump's surface, or whether it was something sticking out of the side. He was sure he hadn't gone down as far as the bottom of the sump, but no matter how he moved his free arm he couldn't feel the surface. And, bionic eyes or not, he couldn't see a thing in the darkwater.

It was getting hard to think. He hadn't been able to take a full breath before he'd gone under the surface. How long had he been down here? The stench of the darkwater was getting through the respirator, a sick-ening chemical reek.

The situation was getting desperate. He reached down to his belt to see if there was something there he could use. Perhaps if he dropped a grenade into the current it would destroy whatever pump was trying to tear him away. But did he have any grenades? He was no longer sure, and the darkwater was starting to burn his skin.

Something grabbed at his collar.

He twisted away and tried to reach down for his boot knife. The Warchild must have beaten the current and come back for him. But before he could get his hand down as far as his ankle he was wrenched free of the handhold. And pulled up through the gluey black surface of the darkwater.

He shook his head violently, feeling the slimy liquid drooling off his face and away from his eyes. When he opened them he saw Gethsemane Bane in the sump with him, her hair plastered to her scalp, skin black with darkwater residue. She had a hold of his collar in one hand and part of the broken grille in the other.

Dredd grabbed the grille and held on, then used his other hand to push his respirator back up and out of the way. He dragged in a breath.

His thoughts cleared. "Nice work," he told Bane. "You can see under that drek?"

"A bit." She blinked, three sets of eyelids clearing the muck from her eyes. "Where is it?"

"Gone. Current took it."

"Think it's dead?"

Dredd's lip twisted. "Not a chance." He got a good grip on the grille and hauled himself up, then reached down to pull Bane out of the stuff too.

"Thanks." She fell back onto the deck and stayed sitting there for a moment. "Larson's dead."

"I saw. Vix too."

She shook her head. "Skull-head's still alive. Cut up, but I think she'll live. Peyton's spraying stuff on her."

By the time Dredd had climbed back up the ladder and retrieved his Lawgiver from the walkway, Peyton had finished spraying and started bandaging. Vix was slumped against the walkway railing, her helmet on the mesh next to her. There was a deep cut in her torso, starting from her left armpit and stretching diagonally down to just under her sternum. Blood had soaked her uniform and Dredd caught a glimpse of white bone in the wound before Peyton covered it with a compression bandage.

She was, however, alive. Her eyes opened as she heard him approach and rolled towards him. "Sorry," she croaked.

"Save your strength," he told her. "You'll need it to get back up those stairs."

She gave a tiny, pained nod. Her face was paper white and her sandy hair was glued into rough spikes by sweat and grime. Dredd realised he'd never seen her without the helmet. She was a lot younger than he'd thought.

He couldn't resist one dig. "Looks like you owe Bane twice."

A weak smile spread over Vix's face and she chuckled, wincing. "Looks like I do."

Dredd moved past her to where Judge Larson had fallen. His body was sprawled over the mesh, the metal around it dripping crimson. His helmet lay a few metres away with his head still in it.

"Another street Judge down," Dredd grated.

"He died doing his job," Bane said quietly. "Doesn't that mean something?"

"Not enough." He walked back to the circular platform, and pointed down to the sump. "There's a current down there – some kind of pumping system. Know where it leads?"

"Not really. Sternwards, something to do with the coolant. There might be a vent out to open sea, but I'm guessing." She moved closer. "Dredd, we have to go back. Vix is badly hurt and there's no way we can search for the Warchild down in the sump, even if it is still there. It might be at the bottom of the Atlantic by now."

"You said you could see down there."

"See, yes. Survive, no." She spread her hands. "Dredd, we've got to fall back. At least talk to someone who knows the layout of the sump system, and get Vix to a medic."

Dredd didn't like it, but she was right. Hellermann's creation had slipped out of his grasp again, in more ways than one. Still, it was injured now. Dredd didn't know how fast it would heal, but even if it was able to self-repair at high speed, nothing could just regrow an arm.

That gave him an advantage. For a while. He just needed to know where it would end up.

Bane went up the stairs first, shouting a brief conversation with the skipper's men still on deck. When she'd convinced them that she wasn't actually the Warchild in disguise she helped Peyton carry Vix out.

Dredd didn't like having to leave Larson's body on the walkway, but that was part of the job. A fallen Judge was always treated with respect, but not at the cost of the case in hand. And Dredd had a monster to catch.

Monster. In a way that was the right word because the Warchild did things that were monstrous. But to call it that was to underestimate it. Dredd had tracked killers before, more than he could count. Seldom had he been on the trail of one so resourceful, so adaptable and dedicated.

Hellermann had wanted an army of these things doing Judges' work. If Vix was right, certain elements of Tek Division still wanted the same thing.

Dredd decided that he would be watching Judge Peyton very carefully from now on.

* * *

Bane thought the best place to go and regroup was the central bridge. The skipper would be there, and he would know whatever there was to know about the *Kraken*'s outlets.

They began to make their way back across the decks. Bane took them on a different route this time, further towards the stern. It wasn't the quickest way, but it was easier, since the height of the above deck structures lessened towards the cityship's edges. With her torso strapped up tightly by Peyton's compression bandages, Vix could walk, but not climb.

The SJS-Judge had asked Dredd to leave her and go on ahead, but he refused. "I don't want this team broken up any further. You're still capable of watching our backs, Vix."

They were about halfway there, moving down a long ramp between two rows of storage drums, when Bane stopped them. "Dredd, do you hear something?"

He listened hard. There was the sound of the sea, the rushing slap of waves against multiple hulls, but he'd become so used to that he almost didn't hear it any more. Behind him, at the stern, the core drives and other engines were still churning the ocean into froth. But there was something else, borne towards him on the dawn breeze from somewhere ahead. A familiar murmuring, shot through with higher cries and shouts of rage and fear.

Things breaking.

"Drokk! Citizen riot!"

"Here?" Peyton moved out from under Vix's arm – he'd been supporting her every now and then – and moved up level with Dredd. "Grud, I hear it too. What's going on?"

"Only one way to find out." He turned to the others. "Get to the bridge. I'll meet you there when I've suppressed this."

"Suppressed? Dredd, you're insane!" Bane was looking at him incredulously. "What about the Warchild?"

"Could be a direct result, especially if it's gotten into a hab deck." He put a hand up, stopping her protests. "No arguments. Get to the bridge and find out about the *Kraken* anyway. I could be wrong." With that, he turned and sprinted down the ramp.

The sound was coming from two or three ships ahead. Dredd was becoming used to the layout of *Sargasso* now, in as much as the place had a layout. Most of it hadn't been planned so much as evolved, as though structures had been dropped randomly from a great height and then bolted to the deck where they hit.

He skirted around a pyramid of containers and headed across a rigid walkway to the next hull. The sound of the riot was much louder, now.

Unmistakable. Pity he couldn't rely on Weather Control to quell it with a few well-aimed downpours, like he had at the Displaced Persons Habplex. No Lawmaster, either.

Ahead of him, a cordon of skipper's men had formed around the blocky superstructure of a bulk hauler. People were packing the balconies of the structure, crowding at the portholes, yelling and raging. Chunks of debris were being ripped away from the vessel and hurled down at the skipper's men on the deck.

Dredd could see groups of Sargassans sitting on the deck, apparently under guard. He ran up to the nearest skipper's man. "What's happening here?"

The man glanced around and almost recoiled in shock. "Judge Dredd!"

"Right first time."

"Ah, minor disturbance, sir. Nothing to be concerned about." As he spoke, a porthole in the hauler's upper structure shattered, vomiting shards of glass. Someone inside had put a prybar through it. Seconds later a bottle fizzed out of the broken port, trailing flame and shattering into a wide puddle of fire when it struck the deck. There was cheering from the balconies.

This was getting out of hand. "Minor disturbance? Sounds like somebody wants out."

The skipper's man turned to glare at Dredd. "Sir! This doesn't concern you. Go about your business!"

Two more bottles whirled trails of fire through the air. One bounced harmlessly across the deck, but the other hit a railing on the way down and exploded, showering the deck with flames. Several of the skipper's men fell back, howling, batting at their clothes where the burning liquid had struck them. A few droplets came down on Dredd's shoulder eagle.

He watched them fizzle out. "It concerns me now," he grated, and raised the Lawgiver. "Ricochet."

He aimed high and put the bullet through the broken porthole. The wasplike keening of the ricochet slug was drowned by a sudden chorus of screams as the bullet bounced wildly around the confined space. With its hard, rubberised tip, the ricochet slug was less likely to kill than an execution round, as it didn't spread out upon impact. It just barrelled on through and went on to hit someone else. But it was capable of taking a large number of perps out of action, very quickly indeed.

Dredd followed the bullet in, putting his boot into the hatchway so hard that the man crouching behind it was knocked senseless. Dredd could hear skipper's men yelling at him from outside, but he ignored them. Like any riot, this needed putting down fast and hard.

He dropped his helmet mic, setting the amplifier to maximum volume. "Attention citizens!" he roared, his voice hammering around the inside of the superstructure like thunder. "This ship is under arrest!"

He was in a short corridor at the port side of the structure, leading to a hatch forward and a set of stairs aft. Dredd made for the stairs, going up two at a time. The skipper's men could handle anyone trying to get through the hatch. The stairs opened out into a wide room, possibly the ship's bridge. Bottles of raw, reeking fuel were lined up against one wall. Two men had been filling them from a small plastic drum, using a funnel. As Dredd burst in they looked up and one reached for the knife at his belt.

Dredd put a stun shot into the first man, letting the residual power of the energy burst take the second down too. They rolled to the deck, twitching feebly. Dredd would have put an execution round through them in a second, but he hadn't wanted to set the fuel alight. The wrong bullet in the wrong place here could turn the structure into an inferno.

There was one more stairway. The bottles had been thrown from the level above. Dredd took these stairs more carefully but he needn't have worried. When he got to the top he saw that the ricochet slug had done his work for him.

One man was sprawled on the deck, a prybar in one hand and his left eye a bloody mess. The slug had gone in there and out of the back of his head. A woman was slumped in the corner with a shoulder wound and one more man was cowering against the far wall. Dredd wondered why, seeing no wounds on him, but then realised that the slug had gone through the bottle he had been holding. The man was soaked in raw fuel.

Dredd walked towards him. "Code thirteen, section two. Rioting: five years. Code seven, section two. Setting fires with intent to damage property: thirty years. I don't know what you people have instead of iso-cubes, citizen, but you're going to be spending a long time in them."

The man sank to his knees. "Dredd, please–"

"No appeals, creep. I've heard it all."

"I'm not making an appeal." The man wiped fuel from his face with one hand. "I'll go to the brig if that's what it takes. But please, tell them to let our people out."

Dredd frowned. "From where?"

"From this ship!" He pointed downwards. "We live here – the *Pride of Macao*. Some people aboard are sick, and the skipper's men have sealed us in. They're trying to shut down the ventilation system!"

* * *

The man's name was Viddington. After making sure his female accomplice wasn't going to bleed out, Dredd followed Viddington down through the superstructure and into the *Pride of Macao*.

It looked a lot like the inside of the *Mirabelle*, with stacks of cargo container habs filling a large internal space. The *Macao* was smaller, but it still housed a lot of people.

A lot of them were sick. From what Dredd could see, many were dying.

He was shown children, listless and semi-conscious, wracked with shivers, their dead white skin covered in tiny red sores. It wasn't just children, either; there were eldsters in the habs with the same symptoms, and younger adults, too. The whole ship seemed to be silent except for the ragged breathing and sobbing of the afflicted.

"There haven't been skipper's men down here in days," Viddington told him. "Some of the sick have been taken away, but they won't tell us where. People started saying they were being thrown over the side."

"Is that why you rioted?"

Viddington hung his head. "It didn't start out like that. We wanted to send a delegation to the skipper, to voice our concerns and get help for our people. But the deputies wouldn't let us out. They said *Pride of Macao* was under quarantine and we weren't allowed to leave." His voice turned abruptly hard. "Then we found someone trying to shut down the vents."

Dredd remembered the groups of Sargassans under guard on the deck. Could they have been responsible? But if the citizens of one ship were turning against those of another...

Sargasso could be on the verge of tearing itself apart.

"I'm going back on deck, Viddington. Hand yourself over to the skipper's men for sentencing under your laws. Maybe they'll be more lenient with you than me."

"I doubt that," Viddington sighed. "But will you help us?"

"I'm on my way to see Skipper Quint right now," Dredd told him. "He's got some explaining to do."

The Old Man was on the move.

Years had passed since he had last set foot out of his chambers. It had been a way of life he had come to enjoy, the lack of change. He liked the feeling of permanence and the knowledge that tomorrow, if it brought anything at all, would bring just what today had done. He had seen far too much change in his life, and very little of it had been for the better.

Besides, it helped him block out the screams.

Over the past few hours he had come to realise that changes happened anyway, whether a man cocooned himself away in a decommissioned pleasure skimmer or not. He also knew that it wasn't escape he had been trying to find. It was atonement.

All these years – wandering through the Cursed Earth, finding his way to the *Sargasso*, setting up home in the skimmer he had owned before the deaths – it had been one long pilgrimage. He had dispensed his drunken wisdom, blearily telling simple sea folk about the things he saw in his head, and their thanks had been a kind of forgiveness.

But not enough. People had died because of him. A lot of people. He had paid for it, but he could never stop paying.

It was hard to find peace with dead people constantly screaming in your head.

But now Judge Dredd was aboard the *Sargasso*. The circle was completing itself and maybe that would afford the Old Man an opportunity to find the peace he craved.

The Warchild was still in the cityship. He knew that it had been damaged, although he had no idea how. All he felt were the changes in the patterns it made, the subtle ripples and vibrations in the background medium of thought and life. The Warchild moved through the medium like a shark's fin through black water; utterly without mind but filled with driving intent. It was a weapon – a simple weapon, like a bullet or an arrow. It had been fired and forgotten. While those who had launched it looked away, the weapon would find its target.

Now the weapon had sustained damage and the ripples it made were ragged and chaotic. Somewhere, the Warchild was hiding, setting all its energies to making itself the way it was before.

If the Old Man knew anything at all, it was that Judge Dredd must have had something to do with the Warchild's wounding.

He had never thought to see the lawman again, not after all this time. Now that seemed unavoidable. His own patterns, those of Dredd, those of the Warchild and Bane and so many others, they were all merging, rippling across each other like still water in rain.

It was quite possible, the Old Man knew, that Dredd could still fail in his task. The Warchild could kill them all. If the full might of the Law wasn't enough to stop it, maybe something else was.

Him.

15. ABRAXIS

When Dredd got to the central bridge, Mako Quint was waiting for him. And he was spitting mad.

"Dredd," he bellowed. "What in grud's name did you think you were doing?"

"Putting down a riot," Dredd replied. "Stopping your men from being incinerated. Quint, what's going on down there?"

Quint turned away, obviously trying to keep a lid on his anger. Dredd noticed the rest of the bridge operatives studiously keeping their heads down. Bane and Vix were sitting over at the far wall.

"More than you know," Quint grated.

"Care to fill me in?"

"This isn't your concern, Dredd."

Dredd snorted. "Second time I've been told that today. From what I can see, I'd say it was everyone's concern. Your city's diseased, Quint."

"I know that." The skipper hadn't moved. He was still gazing out of the long front windows, over the city. The towers and gantries of *Sargasso* were beginning to gleam in the rising dawn. "There's an outbreak on the *Pride of Macao*. You know, you were there. We are doing everything we can to contain it."

"Somebody thinks you're not doing enough. Your men have arrested some citizens for trying to shut down *Macao*'s vent system."

Bane leapt to her feet. "What?"

"Is that why they went on the rampage?" asked Quint. Dredd shook his head.

"They rioted because some of them tried to see you and your men wouldn't let them off the ship. Because their sick relatives are being taken away to grud knows where. And yeah, because someone – and they think it was you – was trying to close off their air supply."

"Is that what they told you?" Quint looked over his shoulder at Dredd. "The sick have been taken to the *Venturer* – it used to be a

501

502   I Am The Law: The Judge Dredd Omnibus

pleasure liner and it still has plenty of facilities. We've converted it into a hospital for now."

"There are still sick on the *Macao*."

"I know," said Quint, very quietly. "The *Venturer*'s full."

Bane gave a shocked gasp and stepped back, covering her mouth.

"As for the ventilation incident," Quint went on, "some hot-heads from the *Elektra Maru* tried to do that. *Elektra*'s sternwards of the *Macao* and they've already voiced concerns about germs being blown back into their ship."

"Are their concerns genuine?" asked Vix. Her voice was still weak, but she seemed alert.

Bane shook her head. "I shouldn't think so. Black Atlantic air is pretty lethal to germs because of all the toxins in the water."

"Try telling that to a ship full of frightened citizens," muttered Dredd. He knew all too well how irrational fears, let loose among a close-packed community, could spiral out of control.

The plain fact of the matter was that in any given population, most people simply weren't very bright. It was one of the prime reasons that the Mega-Cities had given up on the idea of democracy decades ago; important decisions should be made by people smart enough to make them, Dredd had always believed. Leaving things to the citizens was a charter for catastrophe. They simply weren't bright enough to make the right choices.

It was also a truism that the more people there were in any given area, the stupider they seemed to get. On a cityship, with a million people packed onto cargo containers and set drifting off across a poisonous ocean, they could be very stupid indeed.

And stupid people could be dangerous.

"Dredd!" Vix called. She was getting up, leaning heavily on the back of her seat. "There's something else. Peyton's gone."

Bane gnawed her lip. "Once he heard about the disease, he said that there was something he needed to do. He left about ten minutes ago."

As soon as Judge Bryan Peyton heard about the disease outbreak, a nasty suspicion had entered his mind. He hoped he was wrong; after all, cityships had suffered plagues in the past. *Sargasso* itself had been the site of an outbreak of Spike Fever just nine years before.

But it was something that he had to check out and it couldn't wait. Dredd might have taken some time at the citizen riot, so Peyton had taken his own initiative and ventured out into the cityship alone.

He was, he thought as he sprinted across the deck, going to suffer one of two possible outcomes from his action. One: the Warchild would find him and kill him. Or, two: Judge Dredd would find him and kill him.

Peyton regarded both outcomes as equally likely. After all, in the vids the chubby guy always went off on his own and got eaten by the monster. As for disobeying Dredd's direct orders and leaving the team, well...

He'd sooner face the Warchild.

But it felt good to be away from Judge Vix, if nothing else. The woman was as nasty and spiteful as any Judge he'd met. That must have been a prerequisite for SJS personnel, but she really took it to extremes. Peyton wondered if the injury she had suffered was likely to mellow her at all while she was forced to stand down and recuperate. On reflection, he doubted it.

He got three-quarters of the way to the *Royale Bisley* before he had to stop. His lungs felt as though they were being sandblasted from the inside, and there was a stitch above his left hip that felt like someone had put the boot in. Tek Division Judges rarely went out on field missions and Peyton had fully expected to spend his entire career in a lab. While the Justice Department provided full fitness training for all its personnel, no matter how sedentary, Peyton had always been able to find other things to do.

"Not any more," he gasped out loud, holding his side and bending forwards to ease the pain. In the unlikely event that he should survive this mission, he swore he'd be in the gym every shift-end, and would only eat synthi-salad for lunch. If he never set foot outside the lab again, he'd be the buffest Tek-Judge there.

He reached the *Bisley* at a slow trot. There was heavy security around its superstructure and had been ever since the Warchild had attacked D-shift. Peyton waved to the skipper's men guarding the place and they let him in without a word.

Once inside, he went straight along to see the shift foreman, a reptilian-looking mutant called Teague. He'd interviewed Teague when the dead shift-workers had first been found, and although the man hadn't been able to tell him much, he'd been pleasant and helpful.

Teague's office was at the *Bisley*'s stern, past the bottling and distribution plant. But when he got there, the place was empty. A worker directed him down to the filtration plant.

"Great," Peyton muttered darkly. "Down the drokking stairway again..."

He met Teague down by the boiler. The mess from the Warchild's attack had been cleaned up and maintenance crews were once again moving between the filters and pipes, checking the readings. They were walking in pairs now, he noticed.

A sudden vision of Judge Larson's head spinning away from his shoulders filled his mind. He shook it away and decided not to tell the shift workers that it didn't matter if they were in pairs or not.

"Foreman Teague?" He had to shout the man's name as he walked up to the boiler. The filtration plant was as loud as ever.

Teague heard the shout and turned. "Ah, Tek-Judge Peyton. Back again?"

"Just briefly, foreman. I need you to tell me something. Since the, ah, incident, have there been any breaches in the system? Something that maybe caused a loss of pressure?"

Teague's scaly face creased in surprise. "Why yes. Once poor Voley Sparxx had recovered somewhat, she told me that she'd been investigating a pressure drop in cylinder C-3." Teague's voice was rich and booming and Peyton had no difficulty hearing it. "That's what she was doing when she was separated from the rest of her shift."

"Did you check it out?"

"We did. There's a split in the cylinder, up at the end cap. Not big, but enough to drop ten per cent of filtration pressure. We're hoping that's what is causing the bad taste in the water."

"Bad taste in the…" Peyton's heart flip-flopped behind his ribs. "Tell me you haven't sealed it yet."

"We're about to. We have a man working on it right now."

Peyton turned and ran, haring towards the cylinders. "Stop him!" he yelled. "For grud's sake, stop him!"

Peyton was in time. He was up the cylinder ladder, staring down at the hole Voley Sparxx had seen, when the call came in from Judge Dredd.

"Peyton, you obviously like the idea of a permanent posting to the Undercity."

"Sir, I'm sorry about leaving the team. But what I'm doing is extremely relevant to our investigation."

"Explain."

"Give me a few minutes, Judge Dredd. I'll give you all the explanation you need."

What Peyton needed was light. He took the flashlight from his belt pouch and instead of clipping it to his Lawgiver, he snapped it into a concealed port in the right side of his helmet. He wanted both hands free for this.

The beam from the flashlight speared down into the hole. Peyton could see where the two skins of the cylinder had been punched through, and then the hole deliberately widened. Inside the cylinder the water was dark and churning, frothy with heat and the constant rotation of the filter heads.

There was something in the water that should not have been there. Hoping his arms were roughly as long as the Warchild's, Peyton leaned in and thrust his hand into the scalding water.

* * *

"It was attached to the inside of the cylinder," he told Dredd later. "The Warchild ripped a hole in the top of the filter and just stuck it there."

The object was the size of his fist, a swollen mushroom covered in the same pallid, leathery skin they had seen on the eye-spiders and the exploding pustules in the power chamber. Peyton had sealed it in a clear jar of water and taken it back to the central bridge. Now he, Dredd, Quint and Bane were clustered around it, watching as it pulsed softly.

Quint had activated a table-map. The table had bright biolumes under the surface, for illuminating maps and charts from below. It also did a very good job of illuminating the thing in the jar.

"Every few minutes," Peyton continued, "it... Hold on, here goes."

As they watched, the mushroom drew back into itself, then gave a stronger pulse. Holes in its wider end dilated, allowing black dust to spill out into the water.

There was already a coating of similar dust on the bottom of the jar.

"Spores," said Peyton, straightening up. "Microscopic and tougher than Justice Department boots. It's been releasing them into the water supply since before D-shift was attacked."

"But the filters," Quint began. "Why didn't they–"

"If it had just put germs in the water, the filters would have killed them. The boiler would have made them safe before they got to distribution. But spores, some of them, can survive almost anything: trips through interstellar space, being cooked in volcanoes, and worse."

Bane looked puzzled. "So the spores get into the water, and into the bottles. People drink the water and get sick. But why?"

"Area denial," said Peyton simply. At Dredd's questioning glance, he continued. "Remember I said that the Warchild units had a number of mission profiles? I reckon this batch was set for area denial. Get into enemy territory and make it uninhabitable. It killed enough people to hide its intentions, ate enough of them to provide itself with biomass for the booby traps and the spiders and this, and then waited for the population to start dying off." He stepped back and folded his arms. "The plague and the Warchild are one and the same problem."

"Drokk," Quint snarled. "Unless we can cure this spore-plague, your monster has killed us all."

"I wish Hellermann was here," Peyton said, then noticed that the others were looking at him very hard. "No, what I mean is, we need her expertise. She'd know how this thing works."

"Wouldn't tell us, though, would she?" Vix was still slumped in her chair on the other side of the bridge. "She'd rather watch us all die."

Peyton had to admit that was true. He turned to Dredd. "Sir? I'd like to request a change of assignment."

"Wouldn't we all?" said Vix. Peyton narrowed his eyes in her direction then turned back to Dredd. "I'm no street Judge, sir, and face to face with the Warchild I'd be worse than useless. But this might be something I can help with. Request transfer to the *Venturer* so I can work on a cure."

"Peyton," whispered Bane. "That's suicide. It's obviously gone beyond something you catch from bad water. You'd get it too."

"Maybe. But hell, there's nothing like a tight deadline to sharpen the mind, is there?"

Dredd didn't like losing Peyton, but the man was right. There was far more he could do for the case on the *Venturer* than chasing after the Warchild.

Bane had helped him collect as much equipment as he could from the Judges' medikits, leaving just enough painkillers and bandages for Vix. There would be other equipment on the *Venturer*, Quint had told him. As *Sargasso*'s newest hospital it had already been fitted out with the best the cityship had to offer.

Dredd watched him go from the long windows, with Bane guiding him. Quint was studying a control board next to him. "Looks like you're on your own, Dredd."

"I work best that way." He waited for Vix to make a snide comment, but when he glanced over at her, she'd fallen asleep. "What can you tell me about the *Kraken*'s sump outlets?"

Quint was still studying his board. "Wait a moment, Dredd." The skipper walked to another board, one that looked like a comms set. He lifted a microphone on the end of a coiled cable. "Stern lookout, what have you got bearing one-seven-five?"

There was a hiss of static. "Ah, hard to tell, skipper. Lot of gunk in that direction. The screws are kicking up some real drek."

Quint made a face. "Keep looking."

Dredd watched him walk back to the board he had been working before. "What's the problem?"

"I'm not sure. Take a look at this and tell me what you see."

Dredd studied the monitor screen set into the control board. It looked like a broad-scan sensor array: feeds from deep sonar, surface radar, and even high-intensity laser-return sets all patched into one integrated system.

The monitor screen was largely blank, save for a few motes scattered around. But there was a hazy line dogging the lower edge. "Looks like a laser return."

"That's what I thought." Quint tapped commands into the board, cycling the screen through a number of different modes. Only one showed the ghostly line. "Yeah, laser all right. But why aren't we getting a return from anything else?"

"Stealth?" suggested Dredd. As he said it, Quint's eye went wide.

He raced back to the comms set. "Stern lookout, bearing one-seven-five! Switch off all electronic assist and use your eyes! What do you see?"

The silence was longer this time. "We have a sighting, skipper, mark one-seven-five. Another cityship at extreme visual range. It must be stealth-clad along the bow, that's why we didn't catch it."

"Stealth-clad? Grud…" Quint turned to stare out of the bridge's rear ports then went to a side door and shoved it open. Dredd saw him step out onto an observation deck and followed.

"What now, Quint?"

In answer, Quint stretched out a massive arm and pointed. "There. See it?"

On the stern horizon, past the fountains of spray kicked up by the drive screws, was a low, flat cloud of dark vapour. "Another city?"

"Another city. One with stealth plating, heading right for us."

Not all cityships, Bane told Dredd later, made their living by salvage and fishing. Some preferred quicker, riskier profits. Among the twenty or so cityships that plied the Black Atlantic, at least two were known pirates.

Instead of scavenger vessels, they had fleets of attack ships. Usually they would concentrate their efforts on single vessels, using suites of sophisticated sensors to detect them at long range, then creep in masked by stealth plates. The attack ships had such plates too. Bane knew this from bitter experience. She had almost lost the Warchild casket to a stealth-clad pirate. "Wish I had now," she sighed.

"You and me both," said Dredd. They were on one of the upper balconies, using Bane's binocs to watch the other cityship's approach. "How often do they attack another city?"

"Not once in my lifetime. But they're coming in fast. Quint says they'll be on us in about ten hours."

The other cityship had been identified as the *Abraxis*. It was smaller than *Sargasso*, but significantly faster. Quint had ordered the harbour barges to close their doors, and skipper's men had been stationed at the city's edges, ready to repel boarders. Heavy weapons were being prepared, but such things were rare on the open ocean. *Sargasso* had access to a few dozen twin-linked spit guns, a few ship-to-ship missiles, maybe even a torpedo or two. But nothing that could even dent an entire cityship.

"Dredd?" Vix had appeared at the balcony hatch. She was still pale and hanging onto the wall for support, but there was a familiar set to her jaw and she had her helmet back on. Despite being almost eviscerated only a short time ago, she was back on the case. Buell would have been proud. "You better come and listen to this."

Dredd and Bane followed her back onto the bridge. Vix had taken over one of the sensor workstations, and she led them there before dropping heavily back into its seat.

"The Sargassans have been trying to hail the *Abraxis* for an hour," she said, gloved fingers tapping at the workstation's keyboard. "No reply, of course. They're persistent, I'll give them that, but to be quite honest they couldn't run a listening post to save their lives."

"And you could?" Bane muttered. Vix grinned.

"It's my job. Now this is the interesting part. *Sargasso* did get a reply, but no one heard it. Before anyone saw the *Abraxis*, we got this."

She tapped a final key, and a long, wavering squawk of static erupted from the speakers. Dredd saw Bane wincing.

The static finished. "Well," Dredd growled. "Very enlightening."

Vix tapped more keys. "Okay, maybe I'm more used to this kind of thing. This is all the filters I have here – try now."

This time, there was a voice embedded in the static. It said one word. "*Everyone.*"

Another hour went by, during which time Dredd learned that the *Kraken*'s sump outlets could have deposited the Warchild in any one of fifteen different spots, all of them in easy reach of either the open sea or a way back to the cityship. Once again, he was reduced to waiting for someone to see spiders. In the meantime, the *Abraxis* drew ever closer, but neither modified its course nor sent any further transmissions.

Eventually, Vix took Dredd aside. "Sir, I've got a very bad feeling about this."

"When have you ever had a good one?"

"Captain Bane told me that there was at least one more casket out at sea when she picked her one up. We know that Hellermann's first batch consisted of ten Warchild units. What if the stealth ship that attacked Bane picked one up or more than one? They might all be on the same timer and they'd all have the same programming."

"So why aim *Abraxis* right at *Sargasso* and put their foot down?"

She shook her head. "I don't know. But maybe the *Abraxis* is unable to alter course. If they can't, maybe we should."

"They have. Quint slammed the *Sargasso* hard to port as soon as the *Abraxis* was confirmed. But with something this size, it's gonna be twenty hours before it even starts to turn away."

Vix sagged. "Twenty hours... Grud. What can we do?"

"I'm working on that," Dredd told her. "And in spite of my better judgement, I'll need your help."

16. ALWAYS AND EVERYONE

Peyton had been given a little office on board the *Venturer*. He had turned it as quickly as possible into a disease control laboratory, equipped with everything Quint had been able to find for him. He had microscopes, a spectrogram, bio-scanners and bacterial growth chambers. He had a small hot zone box, pressure sealed and with two heavy rubberised gloves poking into it from the front face. He had a computer. He had several competent, dedicated nurses, even if a couple of them did have more eyes than usual.

What he didn't have was a clue. People were dying around him and right now he didn't have the faintest notion of what to do about it.

Peyton put his notepad aside and rubbed his eyes. He'd only been working on the *Venturer* for a few hours, but he was already exhausted. There were six hundred patients aboard – the full capacity. When he had arrived there had been six hundred, then twenty minutes later there had been four hundred and seventy, plus one hundred and thirty corpses. Now there were six hundred again.

He could imagine this process continuing until there was no one left on *Sargasso* at all.

The disease killed everyone it touched. It was one of the very few infections with a one hundred per cent kill-rate.

There was a tap on the door. As he lifted his head, the door opened and one of the nurses looked in. "Judge Peyton? There's been another wave."

"How many this time?"

"Ninety-six," she said quietly, and drew the door closed behind her. Peyton groaned. The time between the waves of deaths seemed impossible to predict. They might come an hour apart, or a minute. But no one on the *Venturer* died alone.

In a while, skipper's men wearing breath masks would come in and take the bodies away, while more would bring the new arrivals. It was like a murderous production line. Bring out the dead, take in the living, and wait for them to die.

Judge Peyton sat back and wondered if was going to be any more use here than he would be facing an angry Warchild.

The hardest part was not going out into the ship to help the sick. That had been his first reaction upon reaching the *Venturer*, to don a mask and gown and help the nurses treat the fevers and the pains. Peyton had joined the Justice Department out of a desire to serve the people of Mega-City One, to help those in need, protect those who could not protect themselves. Here, on this great floating city-state, he was surrounded by people he couldn't help. He was watching them die right in front of him.

Victims of the disease rapidly became horribly lethargic, barely able to move. They were breathless, suffered terrible muscle pains and shivered constantly. Their skin, especially over the major blood vessels, became a sprawl of angry red rashes. They were feverish, coughing and terrified.

Then, very suddenly, they died.

And he didn't know why.

The stern lookout was set high above the deck. Unusually for the *Sargasso* it had been purpose-built – a tall, cantilevered tower topped by a plastiglass dome the size of a pat-wagon.

Dredd was able to get Vix into the lookout by means of a walkway leading from the central bridge. The walkway was narrow and flimsy, shuddering in the breeze and floored in the same open mesh that the Sargassans used whenever they had to build a platform over a long drop. Still, she never would have made it into the lookout by its other accessway; that was a ladder with more than two hundred rungs.

Quint had told the lookout operator to stand down while Vix was in the pod on Dredd's recommendation. Not that Vix needed to be alone to do her job, but if she were up there with anyone from the *Sargasso*'s crew she would probably end up provoking him into a fist fight.

Dredd watched as Vix settled herself into the lookout seat. The seat was on a rail that ran across the pod, port to starboard. She slid herself back and forward a few times, experimentally, making sure she was in easy reach of the various telescopes, binocs and scanners that were set into the pod's sternward side.

"Whee," she said flatly.

"This isn't a game, Vix," Dredd said. "You're supposed to be the big surveillance expert, so start surveying."

Vix rolled along to the big telescope in the centre of the pod. There was a video camera attached to the eyepiece, with a feed cable running back to a monitor screen. Vix tried to focus it for about four seconds before losing patience and tearing the camera away. The monitor screen showed a momentary whirl of colour, then the olive-green top of Dredd's boot.

"That's better," muttered Vix, peering directly into the eyepiece. "No resolution on that piece of drek worth mentioning."

"Never mind that. What do you see?"

Vix was silent for a long moment. "I've got the *Abraxis*," she murmured after a time. "Bridge, upper deck, top structures. A lot of armour. Stealth plates over almost everything. No crew, though."

"They hiding?"

"A hundred thousand people?" Vix frowned, increasing the magnification. "Maybe they're all concealed, but it would be quite a... Hold on, I've got someone. Ah."

"Is 'ah' an SJS term I'm not yet aware of?"

In reply, Vix rolled the chair away and gestured at the eyepiece. Dredd leaned down and peered through it.

Vix had focused the telescope on the bridge of the *Abraxis*. The scope was extremely powerful; all Dredd could see of the pirate cityship was a section of front window. There was someone sitting behind the window, looking out, headphones covering his ears. Probably a comms operator of some kind, thought Dredd.

Then he noticed that the man's face was paper white, scattered with dull scarlet rashes. The jaw hung slackly open and the eyes were rolled back, staring up at nothing.

"*Everyone*," hissed Dredd. "What, everyone's dead?"

"Dead, dying, what's the difference?" Vix sat back in disgust. "There's no one there to attack *Sargasso*. The place is a floating ghost town."

"No one to alter course, either...." Dredd knew what he had to do. If *Sargasso* couldn't move out of the way, then *Abraxis* would have to change course instead. Quint had told Dredd that *Sargasso* would take twenty hours to make any noticeable course change, but *Abraxis* was only one-tenth the size and built for speed.

It could work. But he'd need a boat and someone to watch his back.

"Vix. How would you like to stay up here for a while?"

The boat Quint found for him was called *Seawasp*, and it was the fastest vessel *Sargasso* had to offer. It looked like a rich man's plaything; little more than a slender, powder-blue polycarbonate hull five metres long, with a needle-sharp prow and a blunt, flared stern housing twin aquajet drives. A shallow windshield angled back towards a single bucket seat and a control board that seemed to consist entirely of throttles.

The whole thing looked flimsy and feathery, as though a good kick in the right place would send it to the bottom.

Bane was there to send him off. She'd taken him down to the harbour where *Seawasp* bobbed lightly among the scavengers and fishing smacks. "It's only used for observation, normally," she told him. "Scooting around the hulls, making sure everything's okay. Not much good for anything else."

"Will it get me to *Abraxis*?" Dredd was settling into the bucket seat and testing the controls. "Don't want to get halfway there and run out of juice."

"You've got plenty." She gave the hull a farewell slap. "Just try not to hit anything. The hull would shatter."

"Comforting." He thumbed the start key and heard the drives growl throatily behind him. Quint had already opened one of the harbour doors partway.

With Dredd's gloved hands on the throttles, the *Seawasp* nosed carefully around the massive door and out into the open sea. The sun was well up now and glinting off the sluggish, oily surface of the Atlantic. Ahead of him, Dredd could see the angular grey bulk of the *Abraxis*. It looked like a dark island, studded with sensor masts and weapons mounts. Even from this distance he could see that the pirate city had its harbours facing forwards, so that the attack vessels could go straight into action.

Like *Sargasso*, *Abraxis* was surrounded by a cloud of spray churned up by its titan engines.

Dredd eased the throttles forward. *Seawasp* slowly built up speed, nosing easily through the water. Then, quite without warning, the vessel leapt forwards.

Dredd found himself howling through the water at close to Lawmaster speeds. The rich idiot who had designed the vessel must have set a point on the throttle tracks that kicked in some kind of overdrive; no doubt to impress other rich idiots who might be watching. Dredd gripped the twin throttle bars hard, playing one against the other to keep *Seawasp* on track. Every wave on the ocean made the boat skip violently to one side or the other.

He dropped his helmet mic. "Dredd to Vix."

"I've got you, Dredd. Nice boat."

"Cut the chatter and keep watching, Vix. I'll need your eyes on me all the way." If Dredd's gut feeling about the *Abraxis* proved right, he'd need eyes in the back of his head for this trip. Vix, sitting up there in the stern lookout with her telescopes aimed right at him, would be those eyes.

He could have taken someone with him – Bane, maybe – but if he was walking into the lion's den he'd rather do it alone. Better to put himself voluntarily under SJS surveillance than to chaperone a civilian around. It was going to be tough enough guarding his own skin.

He pushed the throttles as far forward as they could go and aimed *Seawasp* at the *Abraxis*, piloting the little boat by feel as a mountain of grey steel grew beyond the prow.

While Dredd was skimming the black waves towards *Abraxis*, Judge Peyton was, against all the odds, making progress. Through a series of tests, biopsies and lucky guesses he now had a breakdown of how the disease functioned. He should have done autopsies, he knew, but there was no way he could bring himself to open up a corpse. The biopsies were hard enough. Peyton's training was in DNA resequencing and the largest part of a human being he usually handled was a fragment of genome. His knowledge of medicine was rudimentary, to say the least.

This, he'd decided, had to be the most radical cross-training programme in Justice Department history.

He had made his breakthroughs by ignoring the physiology of the victims, about which he knew very little, and instead concentrating on the spores that caused it. The DNA they contained was quite simple and easy to sequence. It was also encrypted, but since Peyton himself had worked on the encryption algorithms on the Warchild project, he could take that apart as easily as he could strip a Lawgiver.

His first clue had been the way the patients died in waves.

He had seen it with his own eyes. The nurses had been tending a small girl with silvery hair and two forearms emerging from each elbow. He had just taken a blood sample from the girl and been watching the nurses when the girl had suddenly convulsed on the bed and died. There was no hope for her: no heroic battle to keep her organs free from oxygen starvation, no electrical restarting of the heart. She was instantly, utterly dead.

Her nervous system, he later found out, had chemically broken down.

When the nurses had turned to check on the girl's brother and sister who were brought in at the same time, they were dead too.

His second clue was the noise they made when they died. A long, airy groan, as though their tiny lungs were being squeezed empty. He had heard that noise before when Judge Adams had died.

After that, it really hadn't taken him long to chart the processes of the disease. And what he had been able to discover both impressed and appalled him. It seemed that the Warchild plague, as he couldn't help but call it, was the kind of disease that could never have evolved on its own. It was too ordered, to specific to be natural. Only a human being could be so perverse as to create such a thing.

It began with the spores.

Infinitesimal and almost indestructible, the spores remained dormant in the water supply until ingested. The only evidence that a bottle of water contained the spores was a faint, but noticeable, aftertaste, probably caused by a chemical released by the tiny motes as they began to self-activate.

Their catalyst was human saliva. Peyton surmised that any mutant on the ship whose body chemistry was sufficiently modified might escape becoming a disease carrier, since the chemicals sought by the spores were quite specific. But that wasn't the end of the story, not by a long way.

The spores were not in themselves, even dangerous.

However, each one was a tiny factory. Once a spore had encountered the saliva-borne chemical triggers, it would open like a flower, attaching itself to whatever tissue it could find. Many would be washed through the host's system, but a few would lodge. They would then begin producing bacteria.

Once loose in the bloodstream, the bacteria would swarm and multiply at a ferocious rate. The human immune system did not affect them in the slightest – they had been designed very specifically to deal with it. Once in the bloodstream, they caused an allergic reaction, hence the rashes of red dots following infested blood vessels. They were also adept at spreading to new hosts, finding their way into the lungs and moving to new victims through droplet contact. A single sneeze could release a hundred million of them into the atmosphere.

The bacteria would spread through the victim's bloodstream until it had almost reached saturation point, making it difficult for the host to take up oxygen, and causing listlessness and shivering. Then, after a certain level of bacterial infection had occurred, they simply died. Every bacterium committed cellular suicide in a sudden, catastrophic cascade.

When they died, their last act was to release a tiny amount of toxin, very much like that in the Warchild's poisoned needles. The victim didn't have a chance. In seconds, the myelin sheath surrounding every nerve cell in their bodies would suffer total and complete breakdown.

So Peyton knew how the disease worked. But he still didn't have the faintest idea of how to cure it. The spores were difficult to harm and they would begin releasing their bacterial load after being in the host's system for only a few minutes.

He had to target the bacteria. But if he found a cure, something that killed the bacteria themselves, their deaths would also release the neurotoxin, crippling or killing the host.

"As a wise man once said," he muttered to himself, "you don't dare kill it."

He was still in the office, every microscope in use and the computer humming. He had stopped the growth chamber as he didn't need any more bacteria. Every time he had started to grow some they had multiplied at insane speeds, then broken down into a puddle of lethal poison.

It was getting hot in the office. Peyton turned to set the aircon a little higher, and then stopped. As he had reached for the control the sleeve of his uniform had ridden up a little.

Peyton swallowed hard, then pulled his sleeve up. The arm beneath was white with a scattering of crimson dots.

His deadline had just become a lot tighter.

Dredd took *Seawasp* around to the starboard side of *Abraxis*, skimming around the pirate city's perimeter with the throttles wide open the boat heeled over at a massive angle, almost on its side. He had to fight the controls as he went through the enormous wake at the stern – the city-ship's huge engines were ripping the water into a frenzy; creating a thundering grey storm of spray and lethal undercurrents.

Vix immediately told him he was out of sight, which was exactly what he didn't want to hear. He needed the SJS-Judge to be watching him constantly.

After he was out of the other side, he slowed *Seawasp* down and began to look for a way to board. The harbours, he had noticed on the way in, all had their doors closed. No way in there, and besides, it would make the journey to the bridge longer.

Here, close to the cityship's massive hulls, *Seawasp* had another advantage over larger vessels. The little vessel could skate right over currents that would drag a scavenger clear under the surface.

He tooled *Seawasp* around the port side of the city, hunting for a way to get on board. After a minute or two he saw it – a long service ladder stretching down to a tiny, sea level platform. He nosed *Seawasp* in and triggered the mooring clamps.

Cables hissed from the vessel's starboard flank, each tipped with a magnetic projectile. The clamps slapped onto the pirate city's hull, locking tightly, and then the cable drums in *Seawasp*'s shell began to reel in. In a few seconds, the little craft was securely moored next to the platform.

The hull next to him was a grey cliff of steel, stretching up out of sight.

Dredd clambered up onto the mesh and began to climb the ladder. "Vix, I'm aboard. Have you still got me?"

"I have. Climbing up an extremely tall ladder. You look like a bug on a drekhouse wall."

"Vix…"

"I'm checking the top of the ladder. There's a platform over the gun-wales. You'll have to step up onto that, then down onto the deck. No one about, as before."

"Acknowledged." Dredd took the last few rungs of the ladder more slowly, unholstering his Lawgiver as he reached the top. As Vix had reported there was no one in sight. Dredd leapt up onto the platform and then dropped to the deck, standing in a narrow area between the gunwales and an angled wall of stealth-plates.

The cityship was silent, save the distant bellow of the engines. Then Dredd heard another sound – a weird, directionless droning that he couldn't immediately identify. Other than that, nothing. He moved away from the gunwale and onto the open deck.

As he rounded one of the protective stealth-plates, he discovered what the droning sound was.

"Dredd?" Vix's voice was hissing in his helmet comm. "Dredd, I can't quite see you, but I can see smoke coming up. What is that?"

"It's not smoke," Dredd told her. "It's flies."

Abraxis was swarming with untold millions of flies. Clouds of them hung over the deck, swirling in great sheets and swarms around the hab-stacks and towers. Gantrywork that Dredd had taken to be painted black became abruptly metallic again as he approached, as the insects covering them leapt away. They were blocking out the sun.

"Looks like they got their Warchild casket open early," he muttered. "These people have been dead a while."

There were corpses everywhere, lying where they had fallen and coated in a thick, living blanket of voracious insects. Most of the population of *Abraxis* must have stayed below decks to die, but Dredd could still see a couple of thousand, just from where he was standing.

He was accomplishing nothing here. The bridge he had seen through Vix's telescope was a few hundred metres ahead and to his right. He began to make his way through the reeking corpses towards it. As he walked, flies billowed into the air whenever he put his boot down. The cityship was a nightmare.

Vix was silent for a while. Watching Dredd through the telescope, she must have been able to see the carnage too. Dredd was doubly glad he hadn't taken Bane along – she couldn't have handled this.

Finally, as Dredd was reaching the outer levels of the bridge, Vix spoke. "What do you think, were they trying to find help? They set course for *Sargasso* hoping someone there could help them?"

"Reckon." Dredd skirted around a pile of bodies and found an open hatchway into the bridge tower. "I'm going in."

"Get to the main command area as fast as you can. I'll be able to see you from there."

There was a stairway up the centre of the tower. Dredd climbed it quickly, ignoring the rooms full of twisted bodies to either side, and found his way to the main bridge.

The dead comms operator was still there. There weren't nearly as many flies inside the bridge as there were on deck, but a few still buzzed out of the man's mouth as Dredd approached. "I'm here. So is our friend."

"I've got you."

The entire forward edge of the bridge was a massive bank of control boards. Dredd walked from left to right, quickly scanning the boards and memorising their positions. Within seconds he'd worked out which ones were for weapons control, which for sensors and communications.

"I've got navigation." A large, complex board towards the right of the bridge housed the directional controls. Much of it was taken up with a single monitor screen, showing the pirate city's course in a series of animated maps and charts.

He was hoping there would be a single control, something that he could operate easily and then be away. But nothing was ever that simple. The navigation board looked as though it was mainly a signalling device, issuing orders to secondary computers in the core drives and the other sternward ships.

He began tapping at the keyboard, trying to open up a command chain. A window appeared on the monitor, overlaid over the maps. Standard enough for an antique.

Dredd typed fast, setting up a linked chain of navigation commands. He'd have liked to slam *Abraxis* to starboard and watch the cityship come apart at the seams, but the navigation computer was too clever for that. It knew exactly how much lateral stress the huge, fluid structure of the cityship could take, and wouldn't allow Dredd to go outside those boundaries.

He had to settle for a more gentle path, easing away to starboard in a wide, hundred kilometre curve. *Abraxis* would get awfully close to *Sargasso*, but as long as the bigger cityship maintained its speed there would be no collision.

He keyed the execution command. The window closed and the monitor showed a new map.

"Damned antiquated systems," he growled. It would have been far easier with a modern ship where he could have just called up the central computer and told it where to go.

"Dredd?" That was Vix.

"I'm done here. On my way."

"Dredd, don't go out through the port door. I just saw part of the wall move."

Dredd brought his Lawgiver up. The Warchild that had killed all on *Abraxis* was less than ten metres away from him. "Keep it in sight."

He began edging towards the starboard exit. Like *Sargasso*, *Abraxis* had a bridge that was roughly symmetrical, so there was another door on the opposite side. Dredd backed towards it, keeping his Lawgiver trained on the port door.

The hatch was just behind him now. He turned smoothly, kicked it open and a blade of white bone whickered down through the air towards his head.

Dredd moved aside, feeling an impact as the blade took a few centimetres off his shoulder armour. The Warchild's other blade whipped around at gut level, but Dredd was already wise to that trick, snapping himself out of the way and countering with a solid kick to the Warchild's side.

The bioweapon went over, correcting in midair and leaping up onto the nearest control board. Its camouflage shimmered.

"Dredd! Six o'clock!"

At Vix's alarm, Dredd whipped about and put a three-shot burst of execution rounds into another Warchild's chest. He heard it shriek and saw it go down, its camouflage flashing crazily. Then the first one was on him again, blades whirling. One went diagonally through the dead comms operator's skull, shearing most of his head off. Another sliced into a control board, sending up a spray of brilliant sparks.

Dredd hurled himself away. There was no way to block those blades – from the way they went through metal and bone with such ease, they must have been edged with monomolecular fibres. He heard a blade sing through the air again and the comms operator's chair fell away in two pieces. The corpse did too.

"The one you blasted, Dredd. It's getting up!"

"Drokk!" He brought the Lawgiver around and the injured Warchild's blade took it in half, clear through the magazine. Shell casings scattered across the deck.

Dredd flung the rest of the weapon aside. One of these creeps he could have handled, but two was pushing it. Time to bug out.

He slid his daystick from its belt loop and dived at the wounded Warchild. It flailed at him, but the heart shots, while not killing it, had damaged its balance. He added to its woes by slamming the daystick into the back of its opened skull as he went past.

The control boards were in front of him. He jumped, his hand coming down hard on the nearest board, propelling him up and sideways. The soles of his boots hit the big front window together.

The window – decades-old plastiglass scored through by years of Black Atlantic spray, shattered out of its frame. Dredd sailed on through, turning in midair to come down feet first. He heard Vix scream his name.

It was fifteen metres from the bridge to the deck.

Dredd had aimed his jump perfectly, coming down in a pile of *Abraxis* corpses. He felt bones shattering under his boots, insect-chewed flesh tearing away, and he instantly was surrounded by a droning, blinding cloud of flies. But the rotting bodies had given him enough of a cushion to survive the fall without his thighbones being driven up through his pelvis.

He slid down the stack of carcasses, rolled, and then jumped to his feet, batting the last of the flies away. He ran.

Behind him, up on the bridge, he could hear the Warchild units screaming.

"Vix!" he snapped, leaping another pile of corpses. "Update!"

"They're not following! Grud, Dredd, I can't believe you did that!"

"Sometimes we must call on the citizens to help us, Judge Vix." He reached the stealth-plates and ducked back around them, hunting for the ladder.

"Even if they're dead."

17. ELEKTRA DESCENDING

Councillor Atia Borla had worn a breath mask ever since the meeting in Quint's office. Every time she went up onto the bridge of her ship, she could see the boxy superstructure of the *Pride of Macao* just a few hulls forward. The constant breeze caused by *Sargasso*'s passage through the ocean must have been blowing gouts of infection clear back into the *Elektra Maru*.

The *Elektra* was a big vessel, a factory ship two hundred metres from bow to stern. In its day it had sailed the Atlantic's coastal waters, the robots in its multiple decks turning out cheap goods by the thousand. The goods might not have been very well made and the robots poorly maintained, but that didn't matter. The captain of the *Elektra* had been careful to shut down construction every time he strayed into anyone's territorial waters.

Now the robots were gone and the factory units broken up for scrap. *Elektra* had gone out of business when Mega-City One extended its territorial margin; the journey from the dockside markets out to the legal limit was now no longer cost-effective, and that was the end of the *Elektra Maru*'s trading days. Her captain – Borla's father – had died a broken man.

Now his dream, his home, was about to be wiped out by plague, all because Mako Quint didn't have the guts to deal with it.

Borla stood on the bridge of the *Elektra* and glared out across the deck. Last night a few of her people had gone across to the *Macao* and tried to close the vents off. They hadn't gone under her orders, or even with her blessing. But she hadn't exactly told them not to do it, either.

Quint's men had put paid to that plan, however. Now most of her security details were in the brig and Borla had a shipful of angry, frightened citizens to deal with. *Elektra* was one of the food production units in *Sargasso*, her empty factories now dedicated to the gutting of fish and the growing of algae. The workers who produced the food lived on board, in container-habs on deck and converted staterooms below.

Elektra Maru had a population of over five thousand and, like many vessels in *Sargasso*, was almost a self-contained community.

Not, in Borla's opinion, quite self-contained enough.

There was a knock at the bridge hatch. Borla had made it clear she didn't want to be disturbed, but it opened anyway. Fennet, one of the security men who hadn't been arrested, put his bullet-shaped head around. "Councillor?"

"What is it, Fennet?" She motioned him to come in, and noticed that as he did so he was careful to look outside, both ways, and close the door behind him.

"Councillor, we got a problem." Fennet was keeping his voice low. "I was talking with, well, a guy I know from *The Samarkand*. He knows someone who sends the skipper's reports up to centre bridge."

"Let me guess," Borla interrupted. "Some of the reports happen to fall open before they get onto Quint's desk."

"Gravity's a funny thing."

Borla gave him a grim half-smile, but then remembered he wouldn't be able to see it through the breath mask. "Okay, what did your friend have to tell you?"

Fennet reached into his coat pocket and tugged out a folded sheet of paper. "This didn't come cheap," he warned her. "But it makes good reading."

Borla took the paper and unfolded it, flattening the creases with the heel of her hand. The text on the page was quite dense and the copy not very good. But it only took Borla a minute or two to realise what it meant.

"Dear grud," she whispered. "It's already off. He lied to us."

Fennet nodded. "When you were in there, he already had this on his desk."

Borla took a deep breath. "Right," she said, after a few seconds. "The decision's been made for us. Break out the demolition charges and let me know when they've been distributed."

"You're going ahead?" Fennet, for all his bull-headedness and thuggish reputation, was starting to look worried. "What about the skipper?"

"He'll never know until it's a done deal." Borla reached out and slapped him on the shoulder. "Hey, don't fall apart on me now! If we do this right, all our problems will be over in a couple of hours."

Fennet left, shaking his head. Borla wondered if he was really the right man for the job in such troubled times, but she didn't really have that much of a choice. Still, he could always be replaced once the deed was done.

She turned back to the view from the window and began to contemplate blasting a ship clear out of the city.

Bane was on the bridge with Quint when Judge Vix came back across the walkway. They watched her approach, walking carefully on the swaying mesh and supporting herself with both hands on the railings.

Bane opened the hatch for her. "How are you feeling, skull-head?" she asked.

"Enriched," Vix replied, her voice a disinterested monotone. "I find life at sea so invigorating."

Bane threw Quint a knowing glance and turned back to the long window.

"Dredd's done the job," Vix continued. "He's on his way back and should be here in a few minutes. He's taken *Abraxis* on a starboard tack. It'll be close, but they should skate right past if we continue as we are."

"Well," said Quint, "some good news at last."

"Not for the *Abraxis*." Vix moved across the bridge, found a chair and eased down into it, wincing. "He said you'll need to stock up on bug spray."

Bane remembered the explosive shell knocking a splintered hole through *Golgotha*'s gunwales and found it difficult to feel sorry for the pirate city. *Abraxis* had been responsible for many atrocities in the past; when they attacked a vessel, the crew were normally killed in the battle or put over the side. Occasionally they set them adrift in lifeboats. On *Sargasso*, that was called exile, and was the worst punishment that could be meted out. On the *Abraxis*, it was called mercy.

"That's what you get for stealing my salvage, drokkers," she whispered.

"Which just leaves us the Warchild problem," Vix said quietly. She was looking out of one of the side ports. "And the plague."

"Peyton's working on that," said Quint. "Can't say I've much faith in Mega-City Judges, but that one seems all right. He may come up with something."

To Bane's surprise, Vix didn't offer any disparaging comments about that at all. "And the Warchild?" she said.

Quint was checking the navigation board, watching the operator key in the pirate city's projected course change. "I thought that was your job."

Vix gave a bitter laugh. "My job was to keep Hellermann alive, to learn what she knew about the Warchild so we could protect ourselves if there were any more." She shifted uncomfortably in the chair, still gazing out of the porthole. "Which I completely failed to do."

"What'll happen when you get back?" asked Bane, wondering why she was interested.

"If," said Vix, her voice still flat and dead. "*If* I get back. Well, maybe my boss won't have me accidentally assassinated. But I doubt it. Lot of activity on that ship, Quint."

Quint didn't look up. "Which ship?"

"*Elektra Maru.*"

Curious, Bane walked across and joined Vix at the porthole. The *Elektra Maru* was portside of the bridge, and a few hulls sternwards. As Bane looked down on it, she could see figures scurrying about the deck, moving from structure to structure.

"They're up to something," muttered Vix. She straightened a little; this had caught her interest, Bane could see. "You can tell by the way they're moving."

"Skipper?" Bane beckoned Quint over. "She's right, sir. You should have a look at this."

Quint's size meant that he couldn't use the same porthole as the two women, so he went to the next one along. He watched for about half a minute then turned and went quickly back to the comms board.

Bane saw him pull the microphone from the board so violently it almost came off. "Councillor Borla!" he roared.

There was a pause, and a hiss of static. Finally a woman's voice, hard and clipped, sounded over the speakers.

"Don't try to stop us, Quint. We're capable of defending ourselves!"

"Borla, this is insanity!"

"Don't lecture me on insanity, skipper!" the voice snarled. "You kept the facts from us! The plague was already off the *Macao* when we were in your office, and you've done nothing to stop it."

"That's not true and you know it. We've got people working on a cure right now, but this is not the answer! Borla, you know what will happen!"

"What will happen is that we won't be around to watch you die of plague, Skipper Quint!"

The line went dead. Quint stayed where he was for a moment, breathing hard. Then he turned to his comms officer.

"Get me Dredd."

Dredd was only a few minutes away from the *Sargasso* when the call came in. After the cityship's customary hiss of interference – the ancient comms system tracking down his frequency, he had learned – Quint's booming voice emerged over his helmet speakers. "Dredd, we've got a situation."

"Now there's a switch."

"One of the sternward vessels is trying to blast free by blowing her links and backing out of the city."

"Let me guess: they reckon they'll be better off on their own." Dredd had heard that story before, too. Religious maniacs leading their followers into the Cursed Earth for a "better life." Whole blocks trying to declare independence. It always ended in disaster, no matter how it was played.

"They're more likely to tear the city apart. Dredd, I've got Jennig and all the skipper's men I can muster on their way, but I'd like you there as well."

"Voice of authority?"

"Element of surprise."

Dredd could think of worse things to be. "I'm on my way. Quint, I need to speak with Vix."

There was a moment's pause. "Sir, this isn't our fight."

"It will be if those idiots break *Sargasso* in half. Do you have access to Larson's Lawgiver?"

"I can get it."

"Disable the SD charge and send it down with Bane to meet me at the harbour. Mine suffered a failure."

As *Seawasp* jetted back into *Sargasso*'s harbour, alert sirens began to howl out across the cityship. Dredd took the little boat in fast, flipped it around and slammed it against the side of the dock.

Bane was waiting for him, carrying something heavy wrapped in a piece of tarpaulin. "Special delivery."

Dredd took it from her and unwrapped the package. Larson's Lawgiver nestled inside, indicators already glowing on the ammo select. "I'd stand back," Dredd grated. "Wouldn't put it entirely beyond Vix to not disable the SD as much as she could…"

Thankfully, the SJS-Judge had followed his orders properly – the gun didn't blow his hand off. He wouldn't be able to use the voice-select until he had properly reset the on-board computer. To be honest, he didn't like using another Judge's gun, but he figured the *Elektra Maru* situation might be slightly beyond a boot knife and a daystick.

Bane showed him the quickest way up. Once he was on the deck it was easy to find his way to the *Elektra Maru*. He just followed the sound of the gunfire.

The crew of the rogue ship had obviously stashed some weapons away and was using them to keep the skipper's men back while they planted their charges. Dredd was interested to see that most of the gunfire was being aimed high, as if those firing were trying to keep casualties to a minimum. It was a laudable sentiment, and one encountered all too seldom back in the Meg, but it would mean nothing if the *Elektra* tore free and left *Sargasso* in tatters behind it.

Philo Jennig was on the *Mystere*, the vessel directly starboard of the *Elektra*. Dredd spotted him taking cover behind a vent funnel, and slid to a halt next to him. "Skipper said you might need some backup."

Jennig shook his head. "No offence, Dredd, but this is beyond backup. We haven't got the men."

"Maybe I can appeal to their better judgement."

Dredd broke cover and sprinted towards the edge of the deck. There was a group of the *Elektra*'s crew there, mostly wearing the blue coveralls of food workers. They were planting demolition charges around a structure there – one of the giant linking braces that held their ship to the next. Dredd could see other groups doing the same, working around the bridges and walkways. Some of the upper level ramps and walkways had already been severed.

This had gone far enough. He dropped his helmet mic and set the volume to maximum.

"*Elektra Maru*," he bellowed.

All activity aboard the food ship ceased, as Dredd's amplified tones blasted out across the deck.

"*Elektra Maru*, I am the Law! Drop those demo charges and step away. If you do not comply, there will be trouble!"

For a moment, it almost looked as if it would work. Several of the blue-clad workers did exactly as they were told, setting their charges down and moving back.

Others among them, however, were not so sensible. Dredd saw one man raise a half-empty bottle of spirit and fling it over the deck at him. "You can't shoot us all, Judge!"

Dredd snapped a round through the man's kneecap and watched him sprawl, howling. "Want a bet?"

But the spell had already been broken. A low murmur of anger was already rippling along the vessel. And out of the corner of his eye, Dredd saw something raised towards him.

He tried to bring the Lawgiver around, but it was already too late.

There was a snapping explosion and a hiss of cable. He saw the missile for a split second before it hit, just enough time to twist out of the way, but it had opened at the tip into a wide dish. It took him in the right arm, knocked him back with massive force and slammed him into a hab wall. It stuck.

The missile was a magnetic harpoon, a larger version of the docking projectiles on *Seawasp*. Dredd's arm was crushed against the hab wall as the magoon tried to reach the metal. His armoured elbow-pad had saved his bones from being shattered, but he was trapped and he couldn't get his Lawgiver around.

The magoon hummed with power. Its batteries could keep him there for a week.

Dredd dropped his free hand down to his boot and pulled the knife free. The broad, serrated edge slipped into a seam between two panels on the magoon's shaft, and with a savage twist Dredd had the thing open. He raised the knife and stabbed it down into a maze of exposed wiring.

There was a fizzing whine and the magoon fell away. Dredd whipped the Lawgiver around and put a bullet through a man who was aiming a second one at him, then headshot another who was arming a charge. "Jennig!" he roared, racing towards the *Elektra*. "Open fire! Drive them away from those charges!"

Elektra Maru's deck began to come apart, kicking up in clouds of splinters as spit gun fire raked across it. Blue-clad workers fell back, dead or injured or blinded by splinters, it no longer mattered.

He had to keep those charges from being set off.

Up on the *Elektra*'s bridge, Atia Borla could see the Mega-City Judge belting across the *Mystere* towards her ship. Dredd jumped, leaping the gap between the two vessels, landing easily on the deck. Her workers were already scattering.

If she didn't act now, everything would be ruined. She'd be in the brig when the plague came for her.

Before having the demo charges handed out, she'd switched them all to remote control. She hoped to set them all off when they were all in place and everyone was under cover, but that wasn't to be. She hoped history would forgive her for the sacrifices she was about to make.

The remote had a cover protecting the single button. She flipped the cover up and pressed the key.

Brilliant flashes erupted around the *Elektra Maru*.

A couple went off on the deck, where her people had dropped the explosives, and sent great clouds of splinters into the air. The rest detonated where they had been set, making bridges fly apart and the great braces near the prow shatter and collapse in on themselves. In a single second, nearly every link between the *Elektra Maru* and her neighbour ships turned to fire and whirling shrapnel.

One of the braces hadn't had its charges set properly. Dredd had shot the men there.

The deck was covered in dead and injured mutants, those shot by the skippers men and the many, many more who had been too close to the exploding demo charges. But the ship was free.

"Back us out," she told her helmsman. "Nudge the sternward vessels aside. If they've any wits at all they'll let us go."

With a grumble of long unused engines, the *Elektra Maru* began to rip its way out of the cityship.

Dredd had been close to a charge when it had gone off. The blast had rolled him across the deck and slammed him into the gunwales. His head felt as though someone had hammered it flat and his right arm would need some work when he got back to the Meg. He hoped the Speed-Heal machines were up and running.

He struggled up and opened his right hand, letting the Lawgiver drop into his left. Most of his targets were already down. The deck of the *Elektra Maru* was on fire in a dozen places, the ancient wood burning through and churning black smoke into the air.

The ship was moving.

Dredd could feel it dragging backwards, tearing the last of its links free. A mesh bridge snapped like stretched rubber only a few metres from him, and went whistling back to slam into *Mystere*. The engines were thundering, kicking spray high over the deck, and the whole vessel was beginning to shudder under his boots.

There was an awful sound from near the bow, a deafening shriek of stressed metal. He spun to see that one of the braces hadn't been blown apart and was gradually ripping its way free of the *Maru's* hull. It was twisting backwards on its huge bolts, the girders bending with long, agonised metallic moans.

Deck timbers shattered and spun across the deck.

Dredd started to head towards the bridge. There was a chance he could stop this if he could bring these lethal idiots to heel.

Borla watched Dredd running towards her. "Lock the bridge doors!"

The helmsman was cursing steadily, working the ships throttles. The days when the bridge merely signalled the speed commands to the engine room had been long gone before *Elektra*'s keel had been laid down, but even with sail-by-wire, the ship was massively slow to react.

The remaining brace was still holding. It was forcing *Elektra* over at an angle.

"Helmsman!" Borla yelled. "Full power, or we'll never break away!"

"She'll go into the ships sternward! They'll never move in time!"

She ran over to him and shoved the throttle back herself. "Full reverse!"

Behind Dredd, the last brace exploded.

The entire ship seemed to shift sideways. He looked back and saw the brace twisting apart, the great square base slamming up out of its mounts. The whole assembly seemed to teeter in the air for a long second, and then it crumpled down through *Elektra*'s gunwales and into the space between the ships.

Seconds later, *Elektra Maru*'s hull ground sickeningly against that of the *Waterloo Sunset*, on the portside. The deck tilted violently, sending Dredd sprawling towards the gunwales again.

The *Elektra Maru* was heeling over between the two ships. The helmsman was hauling on the throttles and manhandling the rudders for all he was worth, but it wasn't doing any good. "Cross-current!" he screamed. "It's got the prow!"

Borla was hanging onto a control throne to avoid being slung clear across the bridge. She could feel the ship sliding out from under her. The huge, complex shape of the cityship had always set up lethal currents for kilometres around, but as long as it stayed as one, the relatively fluid structure of its multiple hulls settled into a stable system.

But the *Elektra* was breaking that system.

Without warning, the current changed direction. The ship tilted massively to starboard and the bow tore into *Mystere*'s flank.

The current was shaking *Elektra Maru* from side to side like a dog shaking a rat. As soon as Dredd felt the ringing impact against the *Mystere* die away, the *Elektra*'s bow was already heading towards the *Waterloo Sunset*.

He got back onto his feet and hung onto the gunwale. The ship was tilted over at almost forty-five degrees. It had moved back out of formation by nearly a quarter of its length, and that was bringing it into contact with the ships behind. Its stern was hammering into their bows.

The ship was lost. Dredd was no sailor, but he could feel it through his boots. *Elektra Maru* was coming apart and there wasn't a gruddamned thing he could do about it.

Borla was on the deck of the bridge. The last impact had flung her from the seat and against the wall.

The bridge was in chaos. Half the crew were still at their boards, trying everything they could to slow the vessel's destruction, the other half were screaming and banging at the locked doors. The helmsman had slumped across the throttles; the last impact had been enough to fling his head fatally against the controls.

Borla got to her feet. She felt the ship swaying, wallowing, but suddenly the violent side-to-side rocking had ceased.

Maybe the *Elektra* was clear, she thought wildly. Then a groan echoed throughout the vessel, from prow to stern, almost as if the ship knew it was dying.

The bow had been destroyed by the repeated slamming against the nearest ships and seawater was rushing into the forward compartments. Hundreds of people must have already drowned, if they hadn't been crushed by the impacts.

The *Elektra Maru* groaned again, and dipped forwards.

That was when the two ships at the back hit it square in the stern, and drove underneath her.

When the ships collided, Dredd was already on the *Mystere*. He'd jumped across and only just been able to grab a railing on the other ship. It was Philo Jennig who'd pulled him up.

The noise of the collision was incredible, awful. Jennig was staring at the *Elektra Maru* in utter horror. Even Dredd heard himself cursing in shock.

The *Elektra Maru* was going up on her bow.

The two ships behind had slammed into its stern with crushing force, but they had been lower in the deck than the *Elektra*. Their forward momentum had driven them clear under the stricken vessel's stern.

Elektra's shattered bow had gone completely into the Black Atlantic, and stopped almost dead. Dredd watched as the whole vast length of the ship, shedding crewmen and debris and tonnes of noisome black water, went tilting up over his head.

He saw the propellers still spinning as the ship reached vertical. Then the superstructure ripped free and began to fall, tearing a path down through the deck.

The ship twisted in place, propellers still whirling, sheets of flame billowing from the drives. Then it began to tilt over the rest of the way.

It went over like a felled tree, gaining momentum as it did, thousands of tonnes of steel and wood and screaming, dying mutants soaring sideways and slamming, with ear-splitting force, into the deck of the *Mystere*.

18. FALLOUT

Peyton was still on the *Venturer* when the *Elektra Maru* came down. He wasn't in the office any more, as there was nothing more he could do there. He'd moved himself into the small cot room that adjoined the office and taken up residence on the bunk.

He was running out of time.

The disease had progressed swiftly in his system. Already he was a mass of rashes and he felt as though he were choking, as though the life were already being squeezed out of his lungs.

Eight minutes previously he had injected himself with the contents of a gas pressure syringe. The drug was the product of a short, extremely hasty burst of work in a completely new direction. Peyton would have preferred to work for longer on it, but he wasn't sure how much longer he had. Anyway, the lack of oxygen to his brain was affecting his thought processes.

He lay on his back, shivering violently, feeling waves of pain wash down him from the top of his head to the soles of his feet. He was hoping that the nurse wouldn't come in before the bacteria went into cascade suicide. He simply didn't have the strength to explain to anyone what he'd done.

As he lay there, he felt a strange sensation. At first he wondered if it was something to do with the disease, but he quickly realised that there was something physical going on. A vibration had run through the *Venturer*'s hull as though it had been shoved, hard.

There was another. Peyton tried to sit up, to call for someone to tell him what was going on, but he was too weak. There was too much bacteria in his system.

More thumps, faster. And a noise, distant through the *Venturer*'s walls. Screaming. The other patients were screaming.

Something terrible was happening to the cityship. Peyton knew that with a sudden, terrified clarity, just as the neurotoxin washed into his bloodstream, swallowing him in a flare of agonised darkness.

* * *

The Old Man was close to the *Elektra Maru* when it fell. He was on the same side of the cityship, and maybe three-quarters of the way along its length. He couldn't have said which ship he was on at the time, and he didn't really care. It was the people on them that mattered, not the words etched into pieces of their hull plating.

He had been making a final pilgrimage through the city. Like Peyton, he would have liked to have spent more time doing it, but simply didn't know how much time he had. That was always the way with the most important things, he told himself. They always got left until last. But if they got done first, they wouldn't have been important. It was a puzzle he no longer had time to solve.

The people he'd met along the way had been glad to see him. Many had offered him gifts, and asked him to sit with them and tell them what was going to happen. Most had just shaken his bony hands and wept, and told him that they were glad they had seen him, this one last time.

A lot of people aboard *Sargasso* believed they were going to die.

He had not taken the gifts, and anyone expecting his usual cryptic answers had been disappointed too. He had tried to reassure people wherever he went, and he believed that, quite often, it had worked.

While most of *Sargasso*'s component vessels were very densely populated, there would always be parts of it that were not. The Old Man sometimes walked through ships with no one on them at all, or with just a few work crews who would wave at him and carry on. Very rarely he was challenged, but only because the places he was about to go were not safe. It had never been difficult to simply take another route.

It had been on one of these seemingly random detours that he had found the Warchild.

That, of course, had been the other reason for his pilgrimage. He had been following the ripples left by the Warchild in the background of his mind.

The weapon hadn't moved for a long time, since just after it had been damaged. The Old Man hadn't known exactly where it was, or when he'd find it. He just knew he would. Sometimes, things came to him that way.

He had stopped to drink some water as it ran down the pipes in the hull-space of a giant chem-tanker. The water had been sweet and cool, and as the Old Man let his heavy head fall back to swallow it, he had seen the Warchild crouching in the gantry above him.

"Aha," he whispered. "There you are. I've been looking for you."

The Warchild didn't move. It was still badly damaged, with its arm wrecked and what looked like a catalogue of other injuries. It looked to the Old Man as if the weapon had fallen from somewhere very high. Its eyes were open, but it saw nothing. It simply didn't have any eyelids.

The Old Man didn't move either, He stood, looking up at the nightmare of exposed bone and white-leather flesh above him, and just watched. In his mind, his odd, mutant mind, the patterns it formed gradually fell away, layer by layer. It was as if the Warchild became a blueprint in his brain, a diagram. A complex artefact whose secrets were as open to him as a road map.

It took a long time.

Finally, the Old Man blinked and allowed a smile to creep over his face. "Well," he thought. "Somebody really did the number on you, didn't they?"

He had discovered something very interesting about the Warchild.

That was when the *Elektra Maru* fell over.

He had felt the impacts of the ship slamming against its neighbours, but only vaguely, like the grumbles of a distant storm. But when the *Elektra* twisted on her broken bow and toppled over into the *Mystere*, a great wave had crashed outwards from the collision. It hammered into the ship the Old Man and the Warchild were on, and sent it banging hard into the next vessel along.

The hull-space rang like a titanic gong, and suddenly the Old Man was being showered with kilos of ancient rust. He had to steady himself against the wall to avoid being shaken off his feet, and the rust-storm made him duck his head and close his eyes to avoid being blinded.

When he opened them again, the Warchild was standing in front of him.

It hadn't attacked and hadn't tried to camouflage itself, although the mimetic cells in its skin were sending subtle patterns across its body in a self-test routine. Its rough ball of a head tilted this way and that, as if slowly shaking itself awake. As the Old Man watched, its remaining arm-blade extended, hinging out and forwards until it extended a metre in front of its hand, almost touching the floor.

Without warning, it erupted into motion. The arm whipped out, too fast to follow.

The Old Man stepped aside and the tip of the blade whined past his face.

The cityship was still shaking. Noises filtered through the metal of the ship's hull.

The Warchild had taken a few steps back, confused. Its thoughts – no, its algorithms and programs – were still in turmoil. It simply couldn't understand why the target in front of it had not been subdued. It tried again, its blade darting out, but finding nothing but air.

Unluckily for the Old Man, the third attack coincided with the explosion caused by the *Elektra Maru*, now a twisted and broken wreck, slamming back through the two smaller ships behind it and crashing into the *Kraken*.

The wave this caused slammed into the ship on which the Warchild and the Old Man fought. The Warchild skidded forwards and the Old Man, knocked off his footing by the impact, spread his arms to catch it. It was a kind of reflex.

For a moment, they embraced like wounded brothers. Then the Warchild withdrew its blade from the Old Man's chest.

"Oh," he said, watching as it scrambled away. "That wasn't exactly what I'd planned..."

Gethsemane Bane was on the central bridge when the *Elektra Maru* took out the *Kraken*. She was there with Quint and Judge Vix, watching in utter horror as the destruction played out below her.

The fall of the food ship onto the *Mystere* had been enough to fling them all off their feet. Bane had seen it come down, had stayed with her eyes fixed on it as the superstructure had torn free of its mountings and ripped its way down the vertical deck. She had resolved not to see it strike the *Mystere*, to look away as the ships connected so she wouldn't have the image of their destruction embedded permanently in her mind. But when the moment came, she couldn't turn away. Couldn't even close her eyes. So she saw it all: the food ship slamming into the *Mystere* with such force that a great sheet of deck simply folded up around it, crushing dozens of habs and sending others spinning and whirling into the air, trailing pieces of gantry, bits of deck and occupants. Hundreds must have died in that second.

Then the wave hit. The massive wave had been sent skating through the hulls by the death of the *Elektra*. It had sent the *Putin* sideways about ten metres and tilted it over several degrees. That didn't make too much of a difference on deck, but on the bridge everyone who wasn't strapped down hit the floor and rolled.

Quint was on his feet first, already hauling himself back to the comms board as the ship tilted back the other way in the swell. He was yelling commands into the microphone, trying desperately to minimise the damage. Judge Vix had hit the deck and stayed there, on her back, breathing hard. Bane looked across at her and saw fresh blood soaking into her bandages.

She reached up to the rim of the porthole and pulled herself upright. Outside, the wreckage of the *Elektra* was being dragged back along the deck of the *Mystere* by the current, scouring it clean of structure. Bane could see tiny figures running like insects in every direction, and watched in horror as hundreds of them were caught by the *Elektra* and swept away.

Judge Dredd must have been one of those figures, if he had even lived that long.

The deck was shuddering under her feet, convulsions rippling through the *Sargasso*'s structure as the waves punched outwards from the collision point. She had to hold on tight to the rim of the port so as not to be thrown aside.

Finally, the *Elektra* came away from the *Mystere*. The part of it that had been in the water finally succumbed to drag and current, and pulled the rest away down into the Atlantic. Bane saw it topple sideways, taking a tangle of structures with it from the *Mystere*, and thump down into the water. A fountain of grey spume erupted upwards as it hit and went under.

"It's gone," she whispered. "It went under the water. It's gone."

"Ow," said Vix, very quietly.

Bane couldn't turn away from the porthole. Something hadn't happened yet, but her shocked brain couldn't work out what it was. When something goes into the water, she thought wildly, it sinks. If it's got air in it, it floats. But if it's heavy and it's got air in it, first it sinks, then it–

The *Elektra* came up again.

Like a drowning man reaching up into life and air one last time, the *Elektra Maru* roared backup to the surface. Its shattered bow speared upwards between the two ships that had battered its stern, as if in revenge, and then it was flung over again by the current. It tore a ragged gap between the two smaller vessels, sending their habs sprawling into the sea and finally, just before the ocean took it forever, it crunched into the nose of the *Kraken*.

The *Kraken* held a fusion torus. Bane was looking right at it when the magnetic containment field, holding a ring of sun-hot plasma in check, failed.

Judge Dredd was not on the *Mystere* when the *Elektra Maru* shattered its deck. Neither was Philo Jennig.

Both men had their own particular insight into what was about to happen when the food ship started to rise over their heads. Jennig had been a sailor all his life, he told Dredd later, and had never set foot on dry land. He had seen ships sink before and knew the way they died. He had known that this disaster, while doubtless the biggest he had ever witnessed, was going to play out in the same manner.

Judge Dredd, on the other hand, was not a sailor. But he had seen enough things come apart in his time.

As the *Elektra* began to tilt both men had been in full retreat, sprinting across the *Mystere*'s deck and yelling at anyone who would listen to do the same. A lot of Sargassans followed suit on reflex – had they seen these two men, the respected skipper's man and the feared lawman from the Mega-City, making a stand on the *Mystere*, they would have done the same and died with them. By knowing when to back out, Dredd and Jennig saved countless lives.

Dredd had his back to the *Kraken* when the fusion torus failed, which probably spared his bionic eyes some maintenance. Fusion reactors that suffer catastrophic failure do not explode. The plasma reaction they sustain is so volatile that as soon as the magnetic field begins to waver it simply breaks down. That breakdown could sometimes be lethal. When the *Kraken*'s reactor was struck by the *Elektra Maru*, its shattered magnets released, for an instant of time too small to measure, a horizontal tongue of plasma as hot as the surface of a star. It flashed out to port, impossibly bright, carving a glowing track ten metres high through the *Kraken*'s hull from bow to stern. The flash melted the hull of the next ship along, too, and dozens of mutants were rendered blind by the flare.

Sargasso got off lightly. Had the plasma lashed out into the water – if the *Kraken* had been heeled over, say – the steam explosion would have been enough to take the entire city out of the water.

As soon as they saw the flash and heard the screams, Dredd and the deputy realised just what had happened. At that time, though, it was only Jennig who realised the full implications.

Councillor Atia Borla, far from taking her people to safety across the sea, had instead doomed the cityship *Sargasso* to collide with *Abraxis*.

The immediate destruction had ended by the time Judge Peyton had woken up.

He lay still for a time, wondering what had happened to him. Realisation only came slowly, along with sensation. It was a minute or two before he could even see.

After a time he was able to sit up. He could still hear screams and shouting from outside the office, but he couldn't face that yet. He felt as though he'd been run over by a Mo-Pad.

He was, however, alive. Against all the odds.

The gas-syringe was still lying on the floor where he'd dropped it. He hadn't remembered that, but when he looked at it he knew that by the time he'd injected himself, he was so weak with the infection that he hadn't even been able to put it back on the desk.

He rolled up his sleeve. His skin was still corpse-white, but the rashes were fading. With the bacteria dead in his bloodstream the allergic reaction to their presence was dying too.

"Grud," he whispered, "I'm gonna get stuff named after me..."

He hauled himself up, staggered to the door and called for a nurse.

When Dredd got to the central bridge the place was in complete mayhem. Skipper Quint was running up and down the line of control boards, roaring orders as he went. Vix was lying in the corner with her bandages soaked in blood. It looked as though every operator was doing at least three things at once. Luckily, several of them had enough arms for it.

Bane had been darting about with a fire extinguisher, putting out small fires in the bridge's wiring. As Dredd stepped through the hatch she almost dropped it in surprise.

"Drokk! Where did you spring from?" She set the extinguisher down and ran over to him. "Are you okay?"

"Arm's broken," he snapped. "But it'll keep. What's the situation?"

"Not good." Quint stopped by a nearby control board and stabbed at several keys. The response he saw on the monitor made him growl under his breath. "We're having to shut down the rest of the core drives."

Dredd gave Bane a questioning glance. "*Sargasso*'s too fluid to survive the stress," she told him. "If the other drives keep going, *Kraken* will start to fall back. That'll have the whole quadrant pulling backwards on the rest of *Sargasso* and eventually we'll come apart."

"Got to be a phased shutdown," said Quint. "Take everything in stages, compensate for the currents and the damage. It'll take a while."

Dredd nodded. "How's Vix?"

"Unconscious," said Bane. "She fell really hard when the wave hit us. Dredd?"

"Hm?"

"I know you did everything you could."

Dredd scowled. "Not enough. Quint, how's this mess going to alter our course?"

Quint had obviously reached a point in the process where he had to stop and wait for a while. "If it was just an engine shutdown, we wouldn't have a problem. Under regular circumstances it takes a day to even start slowing down."

He gestured out of the long window. "But all this? We've got new crosscurrents, pieces of debris still attached and dragging us back, hulls taking on water and slowing the whole system. We're even losing hulls from the outer edges. We've had to send out scavenger ships to pick up survivors. It's chaotic." The skipper folded his arms and turned to Dredd. "Our best guess? *Abraxis* will hit us in about three hours."

"Then we haven't got long," Dredd replied. "Quint, start getting your best crews together. I'll need you and anyone relevant down in the council chamber in thirty minutes. That means keep the council out."

"What are you going to do?" Bane asked, her eyes wide. "Abandon ship?"

He shook his head. "We're going to sink the *Abraxis*."

19. THE RETURN OF METHUSALAH

The council chamber filled up quickly. By the time Mako Quint had brought in all the captains and skipper's men he needed, there was barely anywhere to sit.

Dredd preferred to stand. He took a position in front of the benches and waited for everyone to settle. Although time was short, he needed them all with him on this. Going in hard would accomplish nothing.

He'd taken a moment to splint up his broken arm. It was a temporary repair, but it would get him through the day.

It was Quint who spoke first. "I'll get straight to the point. Since the *Elektra Maru* went down we've had to initiate a phased shutdown of all engines, just to avoid *Sargasso* being torn to pieces. We've got a handle on that now, and given enough time we'll start off again with a redistributed drive load." He looked across at Dredd.

"Problem is, you don't have that time," Dredd grated. "*Abraxis* is on a new heading, but you know how long it takes these crates to turn around. It'll hit you in three hours."

Unlike Dredd's previous time in the council chamber, there were no immediate outbursts from the men and women on the benches – a few sharp intakes of breath, but little more. This, Dredd reflected, was the correct way to run a community. People capable of making the decisions, making them for those who weren't.

"We have a choice," said Quint. "We can break the *Sargasso*, take everyone we can to the outermost hulls and blow their links. We could get maybe thirty per cent of the population away on those vessels, and then move the others to the forward hulls. There's a chance *Abraxis* would be slowed enough by the first impacts to not drive straight through."

Bane, who had a place on the benches with the other captains, raised a hand. "Aren't there more Warchild units on the *Abraxis*?"

"Two," Dredd agreed. "At least. So the second choice is to sink the *Abraxis*."

That did ellicit more of a response. There were shouts of disbelief, and worse. The idea of sinking a cityship, even a pirate vessel full of corpses, was anathema to men and women who had spent their whole lives trying to keep one afloat.

"What about the Warchild on *Sargasso*?" one man yelled above the din. "And the plague?" Dredd fixed him with a glare.

"The *Abraxis* will kill you a lot faster than the plague will," he snarled. "As for the Warchild, leave it to me. That creep's going down, and I'm taking it there."

"I've seen your Warchild," said a voice behind him.

He turned. There, standing by the hatchway, was a very Old Man. His skin was dark, like ancient oak, and his hair was pure white. He wore a dingy pair of safari shorts and a fish-skin shirt, and dozens of totems were strung around his scrawny neck. He was so old, he looked like a skeleton draped in brown leather.

Everyone in the room, barring Dredd himself, gasped.

Gethsemane Bane jumped down from her place at the bench and ran across the room. She threw her arms around the new arrival. "Old Man! They said you were missing!"

"Guess I've been found," he smiled.

Bane smiled at Dredd. "This is our Old Man," she said. "He's our, well... He tells us things. He's like a teacher."

"More like a shaman," said Quint. "Although sometimes I think he's the only one with any wits on this city."

"We've met," said Judge Dredd.

Bane blinked at him. "Excuse me?"

"We certainly have," the old man grinned. "How long has it been, Dredd? Since you picked me up by the scruff of the neck and threw me out of your city?"

Suddenly, the council chamber was very silent.

"Twenty-two years," replied Dredd. "I never forget a case."

"A case?" Bane was aghast. "You *judged* him?"

"His name," Dredd told her, "is Meredith Caine, aka Methuselah. A mutant noted for his extreme persistence in staying alive. And certain empathic abilities."

"That's not exactly true–"

"Whatever you call them, Caine, you used them to con a lot of people out of a lot of money." He turned to Bane. "Your shaman was at the centre of a citywide cult. It took us three months to shut him down. Psi Division couldn't prove his psionic powers, but his mutant DNA was enough to convict him."

The Old Man drew himself up. "You sentenced me to exile!"

"You were judged according to the Law!" thundered Dredd. "There were thirteen suicides among your cult followers. People leaping off city blocks because they thought your magic would bring them eternal life!"

Caine lowered his head. "I know," he said. "I did those things, and I'm sorry. I heard the screams of those thirteen people, even from outside the city walls. They've stayed with me forever."

"And this is where you've been hiding out?"

"Dredd!" Bane rounded on him, still staying protectively near the Old Man. "Whatever he did in the past, that's nothing to do with us now. The Old Man's been the heart of this cityship for over twenty years. He's been more like blood to me than any real relative."

"Speaking of blood," Dredd pointed at Caine's shirt. "Cut yourself?"

"I said I'd seen your Warchild," the Old Man replied. "Trouble is, it saw me at the same time." He lifted his shirt. A rough bandage had been tied around his chest, and blood was soaking through it. "We had a little 'disagreement'."

Instantly the Old Man was surrounded. Bane grabbed a spare chair from the side of the room and eased the Old Man down into it. Someone else was keeping pressure on the wound, yet another man shouted for a medikit.

Caine seemed quite irritated by the attention. "For grud's sake," he snapped, brushing their hands away, "don't you have more important things to be doing?"

Quint gritted his teeth. "I have to agree," he said. "Despite our feelings for this–" he threw Dredd a vicious glance, "*man* – we have to decide."

"No!" Caine shouted. "No! Gethsemane Bane, you said yourself – what's in the past is in the past. None of that matters now. What matters is that Dredd's plan has to succeed!"

"But–"

"Follow him!" The Old Man's skinny finger was pointed at Dredd. "Follow the lawman, if you want *Sargasso* to survive. Don't fret about the plague, that's already been dealt with. Just get in your ships and go!"

For the next hour, *Sargasso*'s harbours thundered with activity. Every serviceable vessel, barring those that were out picking up survivors of the *Elektra Maru* disaster, was being loaded with demolition charges.

According to Bane, the charges were normally used for blasting massive pieces of salvage to a more manageable size. Dredd could only hope that they would be enough to fatally damage the *Abraxis*. In the plan's favour, it had only taken one rogue ship to threaten the entire survival of *Sargasso*. Big enough holes in all the right places should put paid to the pirate city, too.

Just in case, Dredd had convinced Quint to prepare a surprise. But he still didn't know if it would work.

There would have been no profit in telling Captain Bane that, however. She was with him on the quayside, helping her crew load demo charges onto the *Golgotha*. Dredd was putting as many as feasible onto *Seawasp*.

"I still can't believe you judged him," she growled.

"He committed a crime. While his acolytes were leaping from tween-block plazas, he was buying himself a pleasure skimmer."

"He's not like that now."

"Nothing's to say a perp can't be reformed, Bane. I just don't have much faith in the process." He picked up another case of charges and set it onto *Seawasp*'s floor. The vessel sank a little lower into the water. "Looks like that's about it. Are you done?"

"Almost." Bane handed another case to one of her crew, a young red-headed man with far too many elbows in each arm. She leaned on the gunwale and looked down at him. "Is this really going to work?"

"We have a chance."

She looked away and hugged herself. "A chance. What's your stake in this, Dredd? Why are you even here? *Sargasso*'s not your city."

"No," he said. "But the mess it's in came from mine. That makes it my job to clear it up."

Seawasp was out of the harbour first, going not much faster than a scavenger with all the demo charges weighing it down. Dredd took the little vessel out and then waited while the flotilla began to form up behind him. Up ahead, partially enveloped in a vast cloud of spray and flies, *Abraxis* looked like a mountain of grimy metal sliding across the sea towards him.

He opened his helmet comms and patched into *Sargasso*'s central bridge. "Quint, we're forming up. Should be under way in ten."

"That doesn't give you long to do the job, Dredd."

"Never mind that. Have you got the present ready?"

"All set to be unwrapped. By the way, I've someone here who needs a word."

Dredd felt his teeth grinding together. "Put her on."

"Vix here, Dredd. Going fishing?"

"Yeah, real pleasure cruise," he snapped. "How are you doing?"

"I'll live. It doesn't hurt as long as I don't breathe."

He couldn't help but shrug. "So don't breathe."

"Ha," she said flatly. "My report to Judge Buell is going to be a real doozy, you know that? Anyway, I've just got confirmation from Judge Peyton. He beat the plague, just like your Old Man said."

"I'm impressed."

"I hate to admit it, but so am I. Seems the disease's final stage kills with a dose of neurotoxin. Same stuff as in the needles. Peyton came up with an antitoxin, not a cure as such. The disease cures itself, but the antitoxin stops you dying before the bacteria do."

Behind him, the scavengers were in formation. He looked to starboard and saw Bane wave at him from the bridge of the *Golgotha*. "Guess that means the SJS gets something useful out of this after all. A defence against the Warchild poison."

"Dredd? If I hadn't seen your Psi-Division reports, I'd say you were reading my mind. Vix out."

Dredd let the mic snap backup out of sight and raised his right hand high. In response, the sirens on every vessel behind him – over forty little ships, from scavengers and fishing smacks to repair platforms with spare aquajets bolted to their blunt sterns – ripped out across the water. It was a mournful noise, but edged with anger, in the way some of the captains were hammering the controls. A stuttering, vengeful howl.

It was time to go and sink a city.

20. AREA DENIAL

The flotilla moved out on Dredd's command.

Bane was at the helm of the *Golgotha*, and it felt good to be back. Dray was handling the navigation board, while Angle and Can-Rat – his ribs still tightly bound – were down on deck, readying the demo charges.

The only empty station was down in the engine room. *Golgotha* would be able to make the party without Orca's tinkering, but it would miss him. Bane missed him already. There was, however, an unspoken rule already being enforced aboard the scavenger, and that was not to mention the loss.

"Grud," Dray whispered. "D'you hear that?"

Bane frowned. "I don't hear anything." In reply, Dray just nodded and gestured to stern.

Of course, Bane thought. The *Sargasso*'s engines weren't running. Every other time she'd left the harbour the noise of the core drives had been a roar, almost deafening. Spray had soaked the decks, and made the windshield run with grubby, foamy water. Now there was nothing past the sound of *Golgotha*'s engines and those of the other ships around it. Just a sluggish wake of rolling swells, tipping them back and forth as they left *Sargasso* behind.

There were two formations, one from each harbour. As it turned out, most of the port formation were scavenger vessels, because they tended to congregate in the port barge. The starboard crowd were more varied, with a lot of fishing vessels, maintenance sleds, and repair barges. And Judge Dredd, wallowing along in front in his little powder-blue speedboat. Bane hoped that, far above her head, some kind of spy satellite was looking down on them all and taking picture after picture. Because the world deserved to see this. It was a sight not to be missed.

Out past Dredd, the *Abraxis* loomed out of a cloud of oily spray; a dead thing, but still moving, bringing its corpses and its flies and its ravening monsters to crush her home. Bane found her hands tightening on the controls.

"Not on my watch, you bastich," she whispered, and eased the throttles forward, just a little.

It was going to be tough, she knew that. The currents around a city-ship's hulls were something to be feared, the reason every vessel coming in to dock at *Sargasso*'s harbours went in wide. Bane was hoping that *Abraxis* would throw out less of a swell, but if she'd had the slightest doubt that what they were going to do wasn't lethally dangerous she would have been fooling herself.

The two formations were closing up, stretching into long lines of vessels and closing in towards the *Abraxis* like the claws of a spit-crab. Up on *Golgotha*'s deck, Can-Rat was helping Angle strap himself to one of the starboard cranes.

Bane glanced across at Dray. "Can you take her for a second? I'll be back before the swell hits."

She darted out of the hatch, not even bothering to throw on her slicker, and clattered down the steps. When she reached the crane Angle gave her a lazy mock salute. "Captain on deck!"

"Yeah, yeah." She slipped behind him and helped Can-Rat tighten the straps until Angle wheezed. "Hey, a guy's got to breathe!"

"Breathe yes, fall off the damn crane, no." She looked ahead. *Abraxis* filled half the horizon. "This is it. Remember, throw them on – the magnets will be enough to hold them. If we start rolling towards *Abraxis* we'll swing the crane back out of the way. Get ready for a rough ride."

He grinned. "The rougher the better, captain. You know that."

"Ah, you wish." She waved him away. "Canny, you okay with this?"

Can-Rat, sensibly, had also lashed himself to the crane with a long cable. He'd be able to get all over the deck if he needed to, but a freak wave wouldn't be able to wash him overboard. "Yes, captain. Well, I've no choice, have I?"

She almost slapped his shoulder, then remembered his broken ribs and held back. "That's the spirit," she grinned then paused. "You don't, kind of, feel anything's going to, you know…"

Can-Rat shook his head. "Maybe if I was less terrified."

Bane couldn't ask for more than that. "Don't throw too hard," she yelled at Angle, then turned and ran back to the bridge.

Dray was waiting to hand the controls over. "Here we go."

Dredd's boat was level with the first hull in *Abraxis*.

He was ignoring it, powering on past. Amazing how he could operate the throttles with a broken ulna, but she'd always heard Mega-City Judges were built tough. Peyton had tested cures on himself while he was dying of Warchild plague. Vix had taken a monomolecular sword across the ribs and still had the energy to be suspicious, sarcastic and unpleasant.

Golgotha was fourth in line now the formation had closed up. Bane was watching the ships in front, seeing how they reacted to the swells and crosscurrents. Dredd's boat wasn't worth watching, it was too light, but the *Valentino* was next along and that had almost the same tonnage as *Golgotha*.

"Okay Dray, get him up." At Bane's command, Dray began to work the crane's controls. Can-Rat had already switched them from deck operation to the bridge. Bane watched as Angle was hoisted up and out over the side. He had a demo charge in his hand and two more of the head-sized devices dangling from his belt.

She saw him swing his arms up and hurl the charge forward. It hit the nearest hull-side and attached itself there. "Yes! First blood!"

Golgotha was trying to get away from her. Bane was watching the *Valentino*, trying to keep her eyes off what Angle was doing. The other scavenger was heeling violently to port, and then abruptly it swung around and to starboard. The captain brought it swiftly back to heel, and when *Golgotha* passed over the same spot Bane was ready for the change.

Angle had thrown all three charges he had with him. Dray brought him back to the deck for a reload.

Behind her, a fishing smack was taken too far by a crosscurrent. Bane heard the screams first then looked back to see the ship sliding sideways along the hull line. Seconds later it went over, shattering as she watched. The next scavenger in line rode right over it and only just avoided having the bottom of its hull torn open.

Bane felt the ship slide horribly sideways, quite without warning. She cursed her lack of attention and hauled on the controls, dragging *Golgotha* back on course. On the deck, Can-Rat sprawled as the vessel went over at forty degrees, but scampered back to his feet and went back to handing charges to Angle.

Suddenly, in a moment of awful clarity, she realised the plan wasn't going to work.

All the charges were going onto the outer vessels of the pirate city. When they went off, *Abraxis* would shed those hulls like a slick-eel's old skin. But there still wouldn't be enough drag to stop the cityship before it collided with *Sargasso*. If anything, they were going to make *Abraxis* faster. Sleeker.

She opened the comm. "Dredd!"

"I'm busy, Bane."

"Dredd, this isn't going to fly! We're just going to take the outer hulls off!"

"I was beginning to think that myself. Okay, Bane, change of plan. We're going for the core drives."

Bane felt herself go cold. "We're *what*?"

Dredd's plan was simplicity itself. If you wanted a simple way of getting killed.

Send as many ships as possible into the *Abraxis*, into the narrow channels between the hulls. Negotiate those channels until they reached the core drives. Plaster the noses of the drives with as many charges as possible, in order to knock out the fusion cores. At worst, if any ship got that far, it could stop the main engines of *Abraxis* and give the *Sargasso* maybe enough breathing room to get out of the way. At best, they might even cause a steam explosion.

But that meant steering bulky, wallowing scavenger vessels between linked hulls hundreds of metres long, each one sailing only a few metres apart and riding on cross-currents that were stable only when compared to the nightmare undertows at the outer hulls.

It was suicide.

And it was their only chance.

Most of the vessels would never get between the pirate city's hulls in the first place. Those that could assembled along the port side. *Golgotha*, as long as all the cranes were retracted, could just about make it.

Bane's stomach had turned into a small, hard knot the size of her fist. She couldn't even swallow properly. "C'mon, Dredd," she croaked. "Let's get it over with."

Almost as if he'd heard her, Dredd stood up in *Seawasp* and raised his hand.

"Here we go," said Dray quietly. "Nice working with you."

Bane didn't answer, just eased *Golgotha* forwards. Dredd was still alongside *Abraxis*, powering towards the stern. Suddenly, in a sheet of spray, he slung the little boat to starboard, disappearing between two enormous hulls.

The *Valentino* tried to go the same way, but its captain had judged the crossing a moment too late.

The scavenger almost made it. Then the starboard gunwales clipped the huge angular bow of the next hull in line. The impact caught the *Valentino* and battered it around, robbing it of speed. Suddenly, it couldn't get out of the way in time.

The pirate hull rode it down as if it wasn't there. Splinters of wood and plasteen spun across the space between the hulls. As Bane watched, bits of the *Valentino* began to surface alongside the *Abraxis* – a mast, half the bridge, part of the helmsman.

She looked away then took a deep breath, focusing every mutant sense she had, and slammed the *Golgotha* forwards. The next gap along leapt towards her and she hauled *Golgotha* over as it came past. Walls of metal raced past on either side and abruptly she was in darkness. The pirate city's deck was above her.

The second hull slammed into *Golgotha*'s stern and slung it around. Bane fought the throttles until the engines howled and brought the scavenger back into line.

Abraxis was still moving past her, but this time on either side and above. She turned all the searchlights on.

Bane let out a deep breath and waited. Another gap was coming up. Dredd wasn't in sight – he must have either gone further in or been ridden down by the cityship. Bane rolled her head around on her neck, trying to get the tension kinks out of her shoulders, then slammed the rudders over again.

This time she made it without even touching the sides.

"There!" Dray was pointing through the windshield. Several hulls ahead, something vast and round-nosed could be seen. Daylight, hazy in the spray, shone beyond it. If she wasn't looking right at a core drive, Bane would never see anything that looked more like one.

There was another massive impact on *Golgotha*'s stern. Bane couldn't help looking around just as a brilliant explosion lit up the underside of *Abraxis*'s hulls in every direction. Bane winced, remembering the pain of seeing the *Kraken*'s fusion torus go up. Only her extra eyelids had saved her from permanent blindness.

Out of the cloud of flame, the entire forward end of the *Melchior* spun out into the channel. The water shuddered and leapt under *Golgotha*. Bane had to drag hard on the rudders to avoid being slapped against the nearest hull by the shockwave.

Melchior had been struck by a hull and one of the demo charges on board had gone off.

Bane opened a general comms channel. "*Golgotha* to all vessels. Don't anyone else try to get in – we've got a core-drive in sight. If taking out one doesn't do the job, nothing will."

Dray was staring at her. "Cap'n, do you really think–"

"If this all goes to hell, maybe some of them can make it to shore." That was all she had to say on the matter. Her next action was to throttle *Golgotha* forwards.

When they got to the core drive, Dredd was already there. He was throwing demo charges up as high as he could, but they were heavy, and he was working with a broken arm. Bane told Dray to take Angle up as high as the crane would go.

She watched the lad going up, keeping *Golgotha* as steady as she could. The swell was awful and she was having to sail backwards to keep up with *Abraxis*. She wondered how far they were from *Sargasso*.

Angle had his arms full of charges. With his long, flexible limbs wrapped around as many as he could carry, he was still able to flick them underarm towards the core drive, even though the crane was swinging in every direction. *Golgotha* was wallowing badly and the motion was being transferred up the crane and being amplified by the height. With every swell, Angle was being sent ten metres forward and back.

He was throwing the charges when he was closest to the hull, and readying another on the backswing.

Bane saw him throw the last charge and wave wildly to be brought back down. She opened her mouth to ask Dray to do it when she saw part of the sky move oddly, high up between the pirate city's decks.

In happier times, she would have told herself that it was a drop of water running down the windshield, nothing more. Now, she knew exactly what it was. "Dredd! Warchild!"

As she yelled, it dropped down onto the deck.

Its camouflage shivered out, leaving it a white nightmare of armour and extended arm-blades. It saw Can-Rat and darted towards him. Bane heard herself scream.

Maybe Can-Rat's legendary ability to see trouble coming had returned, or maybe he was just lucky. Whatever the reason, he ducked once under the Warchild's blade and then, as it was whipping back for another blow, hurled himself over the gunwales.

Bane saw the cable go taut. She also saw a hands-length of Can-Rat's tail flopping on the deck.

Momentarily robbed of its target, the Warchild paused. Bane looked about wildly, trying to find Dredd. *Seawasp* had disappeared.

There was a heavy thump at the stern. Bane yelped. Hadn't Dredd told her that at least two Warchild units were loose on *Abraxis*? She turned to look, trying to see out of the stern ports, and then the windshield shattered.

The Warchild on the deck had put a blade clear through it.

Bane shrieked and dropped to the deck. The blade was slicing left and right, trying to decapitate her from outside. Dray cursed and fell aside, blood welling up from a thin line across his face. He'd taken the tip of the blade from jawline to nose.

Abruptly, the Warchild fell away. Something came down after it, something big and black and carrying a Lawgiver in its left hand.

Dredd had been on the roof.

Bane scrambled up and saw him fire at the Warchild – instead of a single bullet, the Lawgiver fired out about half a dozen, three of which caught the bioweapon across the chest. It staggered back, its skin flashing a wild pattern, its blades flailing.

Can-Rat was clambering back onto the deck.

The Warchild saw him and launched itself forwards. Dredd's gun flashed out another bullet, this time one that sizzled as it left a trail of fire through the air. It hit the Warchild in the head.

The bioweapon erupted into flames. The incendiary shell had turned it into a column of fire, lighting up the front of the core drive like a signal flare. The Warchild whirled away, howling. Dredd followed it and kicked it unceremoniously off the deck.

Bane snarled a wordless cry of fury and slammed the throttles open. *Golgotha* surged forwards over the stricken bioweapon and into the channel alongside the core drive. She felt a scrabbling as the Warchild went under the hull, still trying to rip its way in, then the propellers lurched and slowed. A second later, they spun backup.

Bane looked astern for just a moment and saw pieces of Warchild, still on fire, bobbing to the surface. Then the core drive was past them and they were into its wake.

The churning water took the scavenger and hurled it around, full circle, then sent it skating across a wild series of eddies. Bane whipped the rudders hard left, then hard right. She felt one of them come off. The ship went up on its stern, and then crashed back down in a blinding fountain of spray. With the windshield gone, Bane caught most of it in the face. Then they were clear.

Bane spat out foul Black Atlantic water, blinking it out of her eyes. *Golgotha* was still rotating slowly, but it was clear of the cityship's wake by a hundred metres or more.

By some miracle, they were free. Bane steadied the ship, stopping the rotation with the remaining rudder. As the vessel settled back to a straight course, the bridge hatch opened and Dredd ducked through. "Nice driving."

"Nice shooting." She had *Golgotha* on a wide course around the cityship. She could already see that it was frighteningly close to *Sargasso*. Dredd saw it too. Bane saw a tiny microphone drop down from his helmet.

"Dredd to all vessels. Get clear, we're blowing the charges in sixty seconds."

The ship was level with the multiple bows of *Abraxis*, drawing gradually past. Dredd gave the other vessels a time check on thirty, and then changed comm channel. "Quint?"

"I'm here. Glad to see some of you made it."

Bane wondered how many had, but she didn't ask.

"It's time," Dredd snarled. "Hit the button."

The charges went off.

Bane was looking back at *Abraxis* when the hulls blew. Everyone was. She saw a line of flickers race around the outer hull, each one sending out a great spray of metal and fire. *Abraxis* seemed to shiver from end to end. The deck turned hazy black as every feasting fly darted into the air.

Then the core drive blew, sending a brilliant flash of light erupting from the stern. Most of it was blocked by the cityship's vast bulk, but beams of it, for a tiny fraction of a second, strobed out from between the hulls like searchlights.

The outer hulls were starting to take on water. Great jagged holes had been torn into them. Many were on fire and smoke began to twist into the air. Bane saw one of the vessels begin to slide over sideways, ripping free of the deck above in a shower of debris and corpses.

A billowing cloud of flame spurted up from behind the cityship's bridge, surrounded by a wavefront of fragmented metal. There had been no steam explosion, but the dying fusion reaction must have caught a fuel store. In seconds, the whole rear section of *Abraxis* was ablaze.

It still wasn't going to be enough.

Dredd saw it too and cursed under his breath. He opened the comms again. "Quint? Time to deliver the present."

"Present?" asked Bane. "What present? Who's getting a–"

Something lashed out from *Sargasso*'s stern. Bane saw it carve a track through the water, impossibly fast, past the *Golgotha* and into the centre forward hull of *Abraxis*.

The hull lifted out of the water. When it came back down, the entire forward half of it was tumbling back in pieces. A shattering roar rippled out across the water, a disc of shockwave, and Bane felt it roll *Golgotha* hard as it struck.

The destroyed hull was digging down into the water. Its stern was up, like the *Elektra*'s had been, tearing upwards through the deck. Behind it, stealth-clad towers of habs were tumbling over like toys.

Abraxis was dying.

They'd done it.

21. GRUDSPEED

It would take hours for *Abraxis* to die. The cityship, small though it was compared with a leviathan like *Sargasso*, was still far too vast to go down all in one go. Bane estimated that it would be a day, maybe more, before it would finally slip beneath the surface.

By the time they got back to the harbour, the rest of the flotilla was already in. Out of more than forty ships, only eighteen returned. *Golgotha* was now one of only seven scavengers. Any real feelings of triumph were torn from her by the sight of all those empty berths in the port harbour.

Quint was on the quayside waiting for them to come in. He looked stricken. The loss of all those ships, all those crews, had taken its toll on him.

Skipper of a cityship had never been an easy job, but this was more than anyone should bear.

Bane helped Can-Rat and Angle down the gangplank first. Can-Rat had rebroken a number of his ribs on the way over *Golgotha*'s side, and the end of his tail was lost forever. Angle, after being whipped about on the end of a crane for the whole trip, had finally succumbed to the worst bout of seasickness Bane had ever seen strike anyone.

She had bandaged Dray's face on the way in. She sent him down next: as captain, she should be last off.

Dredd was waiting for her on deck. "Pretty fancy sailing," he said.

"Thanks." She knew it was as close to a compliment as she was ever going to get from the man. "But it's not over, is it? The Warchild's still aboard, and we don't know where."

"Caine knows where."

It took her a few moments to realise that he was talking about the Old Man.

After the ships were all docked, Dredd went to find Mako Quint.

The skipper was on the bridge. Dredd found him standing at the long forward window, looking out over the undamaged portions of the cityship. He looked old.

As Dredd approached, the man glanced around. "We killed a city," he said, his voice flat and dead. "No one's ever killed a cityship before."

"It happens." Dredd folded his arms. "Better them than you."

"I've been doing this job too long. You know something? Back when I started as skipper, I would have looked at *Abraxis* and thought, wow, that's going to keep us in salvage forever. Now I can't even bring myself to look at it."

"That's command, Quint. You're in charge of people, and people die. That's the job." Dredd nodded sternwards. "Think on this: if you hadn't salvaged a hellfire torpedo all those years back, you wouldn't be standing here."

Quint was silent for a long time before he gave a bitter chuckle. "Well, if those Sovs will keep leaving bits of submarine lying about…"

"You came up with the goods, Quint. No one on this city will say you didn't."

"And you, Judge Dredd? For a Mega-City man, you're not a half-bad sailor."

"I'll keep the day job, thanks. In the meantime, I need a word with your shaman."

The Old Man was up high, on top of one of the hab stacks. Dredd had to climb three ladders to get to him.

He was sitting cross-legged on the top hab, looking out at the *Abraxis*. The cityship was halfway gone, with several hulls almost vertical in the water, tearing their way gradually free and sinking below the oily waves. The process would continue for a while yet, but all the time it did the two cityships would be moving further apart.

"Judge Dredd," said Caine, not looking round. "Come to say hello?"

"I've come to find out where you saw the Warchild, Old Man." Dredd stood next to him, his boots planted firmly on the hab roof. A tangy and acidic breeze whipped up at him. "Which ship?"

"I don't know." Caine pointed vaguely forwards. "Somewhere over there. But it's not important."

"I'll be the judge of that."

The Old Man looked up at him, squinting into the daylight. "You know how I work, Dredd? How I do what I do?"

"Some mutant ability, that's all I need to know. More than that, I couldn't care less."

Caine ignored him. "Patterns, Dredd. That's what it's all about. Everything makes patterns: you, me, the Warchild, this city, your city… Look deep enough, and you'll see the signs. You can find out anything about anything, if you can read the patterns right."

"And you can fool a lot of people out of their money if you get the mumbo-jumbo right, eh, Methuselah?"

Caine roared with laughter. "Yes, that too. But I found out something about your Warchild when we met. Something quite important."

"Okay, I'll bite." Dredd leaned close to Caine's face. "Impress me."

"It's dying."

There was a pause. "Go on."

The Old Man shrugged. "What more can I say? It has massive internal injuries, shrapnel wounds. Only one arm. From what I could see, it looked as though someone had dropped it from a great height. Or dropped something heavy on it." He sniffed. "Possibly both."

"I wonder." Dredd straightened, looking out over the city. "It can self-repair. We know that from Hellermann."

"Grud rest her damaged little soul. Only to a limited degree, and if it can ingest enough biomass. But past a certain point, the energy levels required for it to regenerate its structure are greater than it can gain, no matter how much it eats." The Old Man smiled a secret smile. "Hellermann would have told you that, I think."

"So it's dying. How long will it take?"

Caine gave a shrug. "Longer than I will."

"You look all right to me."

"Well," Caine shifted a little on the deck. "A man's heart should beat, don't you think? Mine hasn't since the Warchild put his claw through me. I rather miss the sound of it."

"Are you telling me you've been walking around for half a day without a heartbeat?"

The man nodded. "Ask your Judge Peyton, he seems rather good." Then he stretched and sighed. "No, there's no time. It's goodbye, I'm afraid."

Dredd was suddenly unsure of what he was seeing here. "Caine–"

"Do something for me, Judge. Tell Gethsemane Bane that one day, she'll skipper this city." Then he gave Dredd a mischievous sideways grin. "On second thoughts, don't. Better to find out that kind of thing on your own, hmm?"

And he closed his eyes.

There were a lot of bodies to bury on *Sargasso*, and not much time to do it. Lying in state wasn't a good idea when there were Black Atlantic insects around, hungry for a meal and a place to start a family. Most of the dead would be weighted and dropped into the water en masse.

But the Old Man was different. As Bane had once told Judge Dredd, in his way he had been the heart of the city.

The funeral took place in the harbour, and was simple enough. Bane herself had wrapped the tiny, frail body in tarpaulin, and weighted it with chain. Then six skipper's men, Philo Jennig among them, had brought out a long crate. Bane lifted the body into it.

Before they closed the lid, they put some bottles of liquor in there with him, the ones with the charms around the neck. Just in case.

Gethsemane Bane was rather surprised to find herself still dry-eyed. She had thought when the Old Man finally passed on, that she would cry an ocean. Effectively he was her last remaining family. But after hearing about his past she realised that she couldn't shed him any tears. Not because of any evil he might have done in the past – that had been over almost before she was born. No, it was because she knew that he had finally got what he wanted after all this time.

He had peace. And a few good bottles of booze.

They took the body to the quayside. The harbour pool was open to the sea and away from the worst of the stern wake by necessity. Anything dropped there would be under the waves before the turbulence touched it, and heading for bottom by the quickest, smoothest route there was.

Oddly, the Mega-City Judges were there, but standing a respectful distance away. Bane couldn't quite work out why and she wasn't about to ask. But she had a feeling that for them, if they were there when one fallen Sargassan was sent on his final journey, it would be as if they had watched them all go.

Land-folk. Bane shook her head, silently. She could never understand them.

The crate containing the Old Man was heavy with all that chain. Bane helped the skipper's men lift it to the edge of the quay and slide it forward. It disappeared beneath the surface without fuss and was swallowed by the inky water.

Bane watched it go and raised her head. Something had moved, up above the harbour doors.

It took her a second to see it. "Oh, drokk!"

The Warchild had found them.

It was crouching in the door mechanisms, up on the huge horizontal shaft that connected the two drive motors. Its camouflage pulsed feebly and Bane could see that its damaged arm was still a shrivelled, opened wreck.

The quayside was suddenly a mass of screams and people running for cover. Bane scampered back to where the Judges had spread out, aiming their Lawgivers: Dredd left-handed, Peyton clutching his tightly in both fists, Vix with her free hand across her middle. Bane got behind Dredd, as it was probably the safest place to be.

The Warchild seemed to notice the Judge. It cocked its head slightly to one side and jumped. It hit the quayside, hard, with both feet, then raised itself to full height. It stood, swaying. Its arm-blade was already extended.

Dredd stepped forwards, Lawgiver centred on the creature's forehead. "Your move, creep," he snarled.

The Warchild slowly raised its blade past attack position until it was vertical – almost in salute.

And then it leapt.

Dredd's Lawgiver thumped once. The shot took the Warchild in the face.

The creature slowed, and stumbled to a halt. It seemed to look at Dredd hard, one last time. Then it stepped off the quay.

Roughly seven thousand people had died when the *Elektra Maru* tore itself free of *Sargasso*. The exact number was impossible to know since so many had been washed overboard, smashed to atoms by the falling food ship and incinerated by the *Kraken*'s plasma flare. Their bodies would never be found. It would be months before all the missing were listed. If they ever were.

The plague had taken more than twelve hundred. The Warchild had killed at least twenty-one, not counting Hellermann and the dead Judges. Out of a population of nearly a million, the numbers were perhaps quite small. But they would remain part of *Sargasso*'s history for as long as the cityship roamed the Black Atlantic.

Bane never saw the Warchild again. Later, on the deck of the *Putin*, she told Dredd that there was no way it could have survived. "You shot it through the face, Dredd. It had no brains left. Besides, it went under so fast."

Dredd's lip twisted. "Your Old Man walked around for half a day without his heart beating. On this ship, anything's possible."

Ahead of them a great, lumpy-looking machine was resting on the deck, just ahead of the bridge. There were big eagles painted onto it – Justice Department symbols. It had extended a ramp several minutes earlier, and the bodies of Hellermann, Larson and Adams had been loaded on board.

The three remaining Judges had been there to watch it land and had waited for the bodies to go on. Once that was done, there was no longer a reason for them to stay.

Dredd turned to her. "That's my ride."

"I'd guessed that. Dredd?"

"Hmm?"

"You gonna make that assault charge stick?"

"I'll think about it. Given that it was Vix you hit hardest." With that, he strode away, up the ramp and into the machine. Peyton gave her a rueful grin.

"That's kinda like 'Thanks' in Dredd-speak," he told her. "Take care, captain."

Vix was looking at her. She could tell, even though the skull-emblazoned helmet hid most of the woman's face. "What?"

The SJS Judge shook her head. "Nothing," she replied quietly. "Stay out of trouble, mu–"

She stopped. "Bane," she said finally, and followed the other two up the ramp.

Bane watched her go. Suddenly, she found herself grinning. She leapt up and down, waving madly. "Bye, Vix!" she called. "Hope your boss doesn't have you killed!"

Vix paused for a second at the top of the ramp. She didn't turn around, but she did wince visibly, almost as if imagining a blade in the back of her neck. Then she strode forward and was gone.

The machine turned on its drives, heavy turbines whining into life and sending spray whipping up off the deck. Massive landing struts folded back into its base. The machine drifted up, closing its ramp as it went, and then it tipped to one side and hurtled away.

In seconds it was a dot. Bane watched it for a long time.

Then she walked away, back across the teeming decks of the *Sargasso*, towards the harbour. There was fuel to be bought and paid for, damage to the gunwales and the cranes, and a windshield to be fixed.

Salvage didn't just scoop itself out of the water.

Gethsemane Bane had a lot to do. She grinned, and increased her pace, arms swinging as she headed back to her ship.

EPILOGUE

Gosnold Seamount – one week later.

As he strapped himself into the cockpit of the seeker pod and locked down the hatch, Zheng Zhijian knew the honour of the *Chaoyang* rode entirely on his shoulders.

Captain Shao himself had come down from the bridge to see him off. It was a mark of great respect to Zheng to even see the captain face to face, let alone for the man to shake his hand. Zheng had only realised the true nature of the honour when Shao had leaned close to him during the handshake and whispered in his ear that, should he fail in his mission this time, he may as well try to point the seeker pod at Mega-City One and just keep going, because the bay door of the *Chaoyang* would not open for him again.

In other words, if the *Abraxis* wreck site did not turn up an intact bioweapon, Zheng was a dead man. The seeker pod was fantastically resilient, built to withstand the crushing pressures of the deepest ocean trenches, but the Black Atlantic had already begun to eat its way through the hull.

The bay sealed itself around him and filled rapidly with water. Zheng began to take the seeker pod through its pre-launch checks, tapping at the band of touchpads that ringed the observation dome. The little submarine seemed to be performing well, despite what the Atlantic had done to its outer casing.

The seeker pod was very small and Zheng had to pilot it lying on his belly. His head and hands were completely inside the synthetic-diamond dome at its prow, which gave him a superb view of his surroundings. It also helped offset the claustrophobia caused by being wrapped in a coffin-sized cylinder of metal at the bottom of the ocean, in pressures that would crush a man to a pulp in a second.

Zheng put such things out of his mind and keyed the release signal. He had work to do.

Below him, the bay door hinged open from the stern, forming a long ramp down into darkness. Zheng felt the pod drop and lurch as the holding clamps let it go, then he opened the twin throttles and sent the machine scooting down the ramp. For a second the flattened, manta-like bulk of *Chaoyang*'s belly scanned above him, then he was in open water.

According to Sino-Cit intelligence reports, the wreckage of the cityship *Abraxis* had come to rest across the Gosnold Seamount, an underwater mountain that rose to almost fifteen hundred metres below the surface. This was easily within the seeker pod's capabilities, but the *Chaoyang* could not go nearly so deep. Zheng had to take the pod down in a steep dive for the first hour of his mission.

Although all Atlantic water was acidic and poisonous, the pollutants that turned it black tended to congregate at the surface. At two hundred metres down the *Chaoyang* had been drifting in water that was relatively clear. As Zheng dived deeper still, the water around him grew more and more transparent. There was no light, of course – he had to activate his flood lamps as soon as he had left the bay – but their cones seemed to stretch out forever in front of him.

At twelve hundred metres his sonar began to pick up the top of the Seamount. He keyed his comms unit. "Seeker One to *Chaoyang*. Come in"

"Base here, Zheng. Don't tell me you've found something."

Zheng made a face. "Don't get impatient, Li. I'm just reaching the peaks."

"Okay, Zheng. Next time I need to find a mountain, I'll send you to look for it."

Chaoyang had already tracked down the four Warchild caskets, all those that had not been picked up by scavengers. It hadn't been easy. Their broadcast frequencies had been supplied by Dr Hellermann before she had been arrested, but the Black Atlantic was a difficult place to search. On their second day out, they'd had to torpedo a megashark, and things hadn't got much better after that.

The first two cryopods had been on the surface, but by the time the *Chaoyang* had tracked down the other two the Atlantic's corrosive waters had broken through their seals, sending them to the bottom. The caskets and their contents had been designed to withstand a lot, but not the hammering weight of three thousand metres of acidic seawater. The caskets had been crumpled wrecks when Zheng had brought them aboard with the seeker pod, and their contents were so pulped that not even their DNA could be usefully extracted.

The pods on the surface were useless, too. Their countdown timers had reached zero and without other instructions they had simply opened, dumping their newborn contents into the sea. The area was known to be the feeding grounds of slick-eels and a particularly large variety of hellsquid, and so the retrieval of the bioweapons had been classed as "unlikely".

As pilot of the *Chaoyang*'s primary seeker pod, it had been Zheng who had brought each ruined, opened pod aboard in the machine's robot grabs. Thus, the dishonour of failure was his, four times over.

At sixteen hundred metres the pod's sensors began to pick up large amounts of metal. Zheng levelled the sub out and began to drift down horizontally, turning the machine on its axis as he did so.

Suddenly, a wall of metal scanned passed the dome.

Zheng yelped and hit the stops. When the pod was still he twisted the controls, turning the machine very slowly around. He brought it to rest with the flood lamps making twin discs of light on the hull of a chem-tanker.

The vast ship was resting almost vertically, its bow buried in the surface of the Seamount. Zheng brought the pod around until he was alongside the deck, then began to move down very slightly sideways, keeping the pools of light from his flood lamps steady on the side of the hull.

The further down he went, the more the wreckage of *Abraxis* rose up around him.

Within minutes he was surrounded by a forest of metal. He slowed his descent, letting the pod's sensors build up a model of the ruin around him. The cityship had come apart on its way to the seabed, the links between its component ships shearing and tearing free as the holed sections dragged their intact neighbours beneath the waves. By the time *Abraxis* hit the seamount, it had ceased to be a single, cohesive unit and had become a broad field of shattered metal ten kilometres across.

This, Zheng decided, was going to take a lot of searching.

Forty minutes later, one of his sensor readouts began to chime. He almost ignored it, as he was concentrating his attention on the pattern-recognition and DNA tracer systems. Zheng had gone down to the seamount hoping to find the body of one of the Warchild units lying intact, so it could be retrieved and dissected back in Sino-Cit. The motion sensor wasn't his primary concern.

Zheng frowned and studied the readout more closely. There was movement down here, that was certain. Not fast, and not coming towards him, which was a bonus. But the sensor had been programmed to screen out things like waving fronds of seaweed or objects drifting in the current. If the sensor was chiming, it meant that there was some-thing alive on the Gosnold Seamount.

"Seeker One to *Chaoyang*. I'm getting movement down here. Going weapons-hot."

"Acknowledged, Zheng. Try not to blow yourself up."

Zheng made an obscene hand gesture towards the comm but kept his silence. If he'd activated his weapons array without informing the base ship he would have been in even more trouble.

It was probably just a slick-eel anyway, feeding on the corpses that had come down with *Abraxis*. And there were a lot of those. Zheng angled the seeker pod towards the source of movement, and throttled very gently forwards.

A hundred metres ahead of him, around a pile of fallen container-habs, lay the broken hull of a mid-sized freighter. The ship had twisted on the way down, its own weight breaking its back as it hit the Seamount, and the entire superstructure had torn free and was lying a short distance away. Zheng eased the pod towards the ragged, open base of the ship's tower.

His pattern and DNA sensors lit up with a triumphant buzzing.

Zheng found himself gaping. It took him a moment to get his jaw closed so he could talk coherently to the *Chaoyang*. "Li? I've found something."

"You're kidding. A dead Warchild?"

"Not exactly…"

The superstructure was on its side, its lower edge half-buried in sand and debris. The starboard wall was now a roof to an open chamber, and from this roof – in surprisingly neat rows – were dozens of translucent sacs.

Each sac was bigger than a crouching man, roughly egg-shaped and covered in leathery, transparent flesh. Each was sending out the distinctive DNA signature of the Warchild.

Zheng brought the pod close to one of the sacs. As his lights hit it, something within twitched fitfully. He saw limbs through the translucent wall, and teeth. "They reproduced," he gasped. "They laid eggs. I didn't think they could–"

There was a massive impact, and the pod crashed sideways.

Zheng screamed. The pod had been struck by something very powerful. For a second he thought he had been torpedoed, but then he heard noises through the hull: a terrible scraping, scratching noise, as if something was clawing the machine apart.

Zheng slammed the pod into full reverse, taking it clear out of the chamber and into open water. The scratching was still horribly loud. Suddenly, Zheng saw something slap down onto the dome.

It was a hand.

It was corpse-grey, with three long, clawed fingers and armoured joints. It began to tear at the dome. Impossibly, the talons started to leave score marks in the synthetic diamond.

Zheng gripped the controls and spun the pod on its axis, hard, but the hand wouldn't come free. Instead there was a series of blows to the pod's stern and the controls went abruptly dead.

The seabed, rocky and strewn with acid-eaten corpses, came up and hit the dome, blocking out the light.

On the *Chaoyang*'s bridge, Captain Shao listened to the screams for about half a minute. Then he opened up a small panel on the command board and pressed the button it concealed.

The screams ceased at once. The button, protected by a panel that would only open to Shao's fingerprints, had detonated a micro-fusion charge set just behind the seeker pod's pressure cabin. The explosion would have reduced Zheng and his machine to thumb-sized fragments instantaneously. His attacker too, but Shao didn't need that any more.

"Pilot Zheng Zhijian has bravely sacrificed himself for the good of *Chaoyang* and Sino-Cit," he announced. "Let his name forever be spoken with reverence and honour."

He turned to his first officer. "Mr Yun," he smiled. "Now that whining little failure is history, please prepare the cryotanks and send out the secondary pod to harvest those egg-sacs."

Yun saluted and left the bridge. Captain Shao went back to the monitor screen. It had been showing a view from the seeker pod's forward cameras, but since Shao had pressed the button, all it showed was static.

He rewound the playback, and froze the picture at the best frame of the sacs, lined up along the inside of a sunken freighter.

"Perfect," he whispered. "Perfect."

These new bioweapons would be even better than the consignment Sino-Cit had bought from Dr Hellerman. Tempered in the fires of combat and the lethal waters of the Black Atlantic, they would be tougher, faster, and more adaptable than before.

And they had evolved a new capability – they could reproduce. Before long, Sino-Cit would have a new army.

And when it did, the world would fear.

ECLIPSE
BY JAMES SWALLOW

LUNA-1, 2126

1. MOON FALL

Calvin Spinker hated the Moon. Hated it. Hated, hated, mother-drokking, spugging, snecking hated the big airless ball of dirt with every fibre of his being. He hated the way that you'd bounce like a low-rent Boing freak if you forgot to wear gravity boots or stepped clear of a street with g plates. He hated the stupid mock seasons they had inside the Luna-1 domes, with synthi-snow, sprinkler rains and holographic rainbows. He hated how every damn thing imported from Earthside cost ten per cent more than the drab local produce, and some days he swore he'd wreck the next servo-bot that offered him a "Moon Pie" at the Eat-O-Mat.

But above all, the thing Calvin Spinker hated the most about the Moon was the air.

It had this sickly smell to it, see, this kinda plastic tang that reminded him a little bit of burning insulation or melting plasteen. It was every-where. He couldn't take a breath without the stink being right there in his nostrils. He'd tried nose filters, strong cologne, even breathing through his mouth for weeks on end, but nothing could make the smell go away. If Calvin thought hard enough about it, he would start to feel sick. He knew that out there in the airless wilderness of the lunar plains there were domes half-buried in moondust where the stale, used breath from millions of Luna-cit lungs was being sucked in and reprocessed. Then they pumped it back out, used it to supplement the raw oxygen that was flown in by astro-tankers, and channelled it back down to where Calvin could breathe it again. Back down to here, to Kepler Dome on the outer rim of Luna-1's conurbation. The top-level domes, places like Kennedy, Armstrong and Lovell, of course they would get the pure new air straight away. Not the reused gases he was breathing – no sir, those rich fat cats with their thick stacks of credits, they got the fresh air. Spinker hated them too, now that he considered it.

Sometimes Calvin would get giddy thinking about how many times the breath he was taking in right now had been recycled, scrubbed and sent around the system. How many lungs had it already gone through? What sort of people had tainted it before he got it? How the hell was anyone going to stay sane when all they had to live on was second-hand air?

For what must have been the millionth time in his life, Calvin thought about going home, getting back to Earth and starting over somewhere where you didn't have to pay to breathe in and out. Okay, maybe the air wouldn't be that clean, but at least it would be free. You see, he hadn't chosen to live in Kepler. He'd been on the Moon reluctantly clearing up a divorce settlement with his stupid ex-wife when Judgement Day had happened. Spinker had been trapped here, stuck without a place to stay or anywhere to go. He didn't know the ins and outs of it, but Calvin understood in his vaguely moronic way that back on Earth, some weirdo from the future – this guy called Sabbat or something – this dingus had made the dead rise from their graves and start tearing up stuff. He still remembered the day he walked into the Luna-1 starport only to be told that all flights to Earth had been cancelled "due to zombie infestation". When he asked the robo-clerk when the next shuttle to Mega-City Two would be leaving, the machine told him simply: "That destination no longer exists."

It wasn't until a day later he found out what that actually meant. Mega-City Two, his home, a massive city-state that covered most of North America's Western Seaboard, was gone, nuked out, vaporised. Overnight, he was a refugee. So Calvin was forced to stay in Luna-1 and eventually the city council found him a one-pod hab in Kepler. And there he sat, day after day, nursing his hatred and breathing in this repellent, germ-laden air.

But today, Spinker looked up from his cup of cold synthi-caff and something like confusion crossed his greasy knot of a face. Confusion, because he couldn't detect the stinky stale smell any more. Confusion, because the oxymeter in the ceiling of his hab that rattled around the clock had gone silent. Calvin stood on a chair and held his hand underneath the air vent, feeling for the telltale trickle of cool breathing gas that forever cycled through it.

Nothing. Not a single breath.

Then Calvin Spinker started to panic, and as his vision started to fog as carbon dioxide filled the cramped little bedsitting room, he found himself desperately wishing, praying, pleading for just one more lungful of that hated, loathsome air.

While Calvin and his neighbours choked to death, a different kind of panic was rising in a frenzied tide on the streets outside the apartment block. Ernesto Diaz did his best to hide beneath the counter in his corner café and not wet his pants.

The morning had begun like any other. Ernesto had climbed down from his Komfy-Koffin capsule bed in the roof space and rolled open the shutters to declare Diaz's Hotties open for business. He'd had the usual thin crowd of early risers and a few grey-faced workers on their way to the zoom terminal that would take them into the city proper, off to toil in the mines or the oxy cracking yards. By mid-morning, he had the mock-meat sausages on the grill sizzling up a treat, and he was filling the dispensers with synthi-mustard and thinking about the lunchtime rush; it started then. He happened to look out of the window, noting with studied disinterest a lone Judge outside the vacant store near the pawn shop – she'd rousted a couple of go-gangers and had them cuffed to a holding post. Ernesto frowned. He didn't like those punks, but he had to admit they'd done him a big favour by setting fire to the local branch of Luney Lunch.

Across the street from Diaz's store was a holographic billboard that was forever on the fritz. This week it had been running a recruitment advertisement for one of the ice mining concerns down in Clavius, but the braying voice of the announcer choked off in mid-sentence and the screen disintegrated into a storm of flickering pixels. Ernesto caught it out of the corner of his eye and looked up. A new image appeared on the billboard screen, a computer-generated cartoon character with a stylised moon for a head. It winked – right at him, so it seemed – and spoke in a chatty, conspiratorial manner. Every word the 'toon spoke was repeated in a ticker-tape stream along the bottom of the screen.

"Hey friend," it began, and now Diaz was sure it was talking to him. "Where do U go if U want 2 know what's up, up, up? Lemme tell U. Right here! Right now! Listen up, up, up! Moon-U has all U need to know, no matter what the Big Helmets say!" The little figure now sported a T-shirt with the words "Moon-U" emblazoned on it, and he struck a comic pose as a bumbling parody of a Luna City Judge ambled on screen. For a second, Ernesto looked around and saw that everyone on the street had stopped what they were doing to watch the billboard. From his vantage point at the café counter, he could see the Moon-U cartoon appearing on another public screen up at the Sagan Street crosswalk, and repeated here and there in the windows of the discount electrical store and on the back of some juve's telly-jacket.

"Shuddup!" drawled the caricature Judge in a thick Texas City accent, listing back and forth as if he was drunk. "Ya little runt! I ain't lettin' you flap yo lips–"

Moon-U gave Diaz a broad wink and out of nowhere produced a massive hammer that had the words "ten tons" written on it. Unbidden, hysterical laughter bubbled up out of Ernesto as the moon-faced figure used it to flatten the comic Judge into a bloody pulp. Someone chortled. "Yeah! Right on! Smash those Judges!"

Diaz saw the female Judge on the street corner speaking urgently into her belt mic.

"Quick! I gotta tell U before they get me!" Moon-U hissed urgently. "The Judges never did a thing for U, did they? And now they're gonna cut off the air!"

A ripple of anger and fear spread through the audience, and Diaz felt his heart tighten. Suddenly, strident voices were shouting.

"They can't do that! Stinkin' Judges!"

"They never liked Kepler, just 'cos we ain't a rich dome–"

"If those sneckers come down here, we'll bust 'em in the head–"

"They always pick on us! We gotta show them!"

"Ooh no!" cried Moon-U, and he pointed up at the dome ceiling hundreds of metres above them. "Look out!"

Like everyone else on the street, Diaz had looked up, and there he had seen something that made his blood run cold. At the very crest of the transparent glasseen dome, just as there was in every Luna conurb, a disc-shaped oxygen processor managed the airflow for Kepler, a train of green indicator lights forever marching around its base to signify its safe operation. The green lights winked out one by one and turned red. A muffled klaxon hooted: the air-warning siren.

Ernesto suddenly felt sick with fear. He stumbled back into the café, the mustard jar falling forgotten from his nerveless fingers. His mind was racing, caught in a whirl of emotions. Just seconds ago, he'd been laughing inanely at the cartoon without a care, but now he felt as'if his world was coming to an end. His head swam with nausea and anxiety.

He gripped one of the counter stools for support and dared to take another look out into the street.

Ernesto had a ringside view.

A cluster of citizens had surrounded the Judge. They were jeering at her and waving their fists; even one of the cuffed punks on the holding pole dared to lash out at her with a swift kick. Diaz couldn't make out what they were saying, but the meaning was clear. The Judge drew her daystick in a single fluid movement and brandished it in a wide arc, stabbing at the air with her free hand. Whatever she said appeared to have no effect; some of the people grabbed pieces of garbage and threw them.

The Judge blurred; Ernesto heard the high-pitched crack of the stick as it broke bone, and one of the citizens spun away trailing blood, hands pressed to a ruined face.

"Gee, that was a nasty thing 2 do," said the billboard.

With a roar, the crowd surged forward and the blue-black of the Judge's uniform vanished under a dozen kicking, punching, yelling bodies. Ernesto had to choke back bile when he saw something ragged and bloody – a limb, maybe? – go arcing up into the air to land on the pedway.

The screen began to show pictures, images from street cameras in different parts of Kepler, places that Diaz recognised like the zoom terminal, the Shoplex on Clarke Avenue, and the free clinic. There were people brawling everywhere, not just picking on Judges, but each other, fights breaking out all over as buried rivalries and petty disputes were given sudden, bloody purpose. He watched as the guy from the used droid place on the corner strangled some ugly kid with his bare hands, slamming the boy's face into the road over and over even after it was clear he was dead. Ernesto threw up and stumbled behind the counter to conceal himself, trying not to choke on the sickly cooked smell of the frying hotties.

He lost track of time; all he could hear was the rolling murmur of the mob outside, incoherent shouts and snarls melding into a landscape of violent noise. Glass broke and people screamed. Once, a brick shot over his head and smashed the bio-lume sign over the counter, showering him with flecks of plastic. Then there was a new sound that joined the rioting: the staccato popping of gunfire.

Diaz knew that sound all too well. He'd grown up in Banana City where the law of the spit gun had been the only law there was, but he had got out, gone to the Moon and found a life that, while not exactly better, was just a little less lethal. But now that sound brought it all flooding back to him, and Ernesto's gut knotted.

He took a careful look over the top of the counter and saw someone brandishing a pistol, cracking off shots at random, shooting out what windows were still intact or putting rounds into fleeing figures. The street, which before had been a decrepit permacrete avenue lined with dull little shops and limp moon-palm trees, was now a war zone. Cars were burning, sending palls of sooty smoke up to cluster in a thick disc at the apex of the dome, consuming vital draughts of oxygen. Plasteen lay in drifts around the yawning shop fronts and here and there dead bodies were lying like knots of discarded rags.

Ernesto flicked a glance up at the billboard, where images of the rioting continued to cycle, over and over. The only constant was the Moon-U logo, a laughing lunar face, in the bottom right corner. The man with the gun paused and fiddled with the weapon, and Diaz felt a sneer forming on his face. The half-witted idiot couldn't even work a snecking spit gun! What kind of moron was he? Without realising it, Ernesto drew up from behind the counter and moved to the door of the café to get a better view. The acrid smoke from the flaming cars tickled his nostrils with the scent of burning battery chemicals. His jaw hardened and a new bloom of hatred blossomed in his chest, hot and fierce. Clearly this jerk-o with the gun had no idea how stupid he was! Firing a gun inside a sealed dome, how idiotic was that? Sure, it would be a million to one chance that a bullet might penetrate a weak spot and cause a blow-out, but who would be Munce-brained enough to risk it?

Diaz's fear melted away and in its place was anger, pure and simple. His hands closed around the hilt of the knife he used for chopping up the hotties and he strode out into the street, spitting in fury. "Hey! Stupido! You wanna get us all killed?"

The gunman glanced up at him. "Get lost," he snarled back, and then he noticed the name of Ernesto's café on the cook's apron. "Diaz's Hotties? You're Diaz?"

"Yeah!" Ernesto brandished the knife, feeling potent and deadly. "What you gonna do about it, pendejo? I'm gonna cut you up and cook you!"

The other guy laughed nastily. "You know what? Your hotties suck, man. I liked Luney Lunch much better."

The gunman's comments made Diaz see red and he launched himself at him, swearing and stabbing. The cook plunged the knife into the other man's chest, his face splitting with a savage grin as blood spurted. All that Ernesto wanted now was to tear this fool apart and paint the street with his innards.

There was a crack of sound and Diaz reeled away and fell on his backside. It felt like a robo-horse had kicked him, and his right shoulder sang with burning hot pain.

The cook looked down to see a crimson patch growing around a blackened entry wound.

The gunman took a shaky step towards him, one hand clutching at the hottie knife still in his ribs, the other holding the smoking gun. "Y-you... You types. You think you're better than me, just 'cos you got a job." Blood trickled from his lips. "You ain't gonna look down on me no more. Not now I got me this." He nodded at the spit gun.

Ernesto tried to get to his feet. The flat of his hand fell on something angular and metallic – a pistol. Without hesitation, Diaz gripped the weapon and brought it up, pointing it at the gunman in a shaky, inaccurate grip.

"You dumb spug!" spat the gunman. "Lookit what you got there.

That's a Judge's rod. You can't fire that!"

The cook never took his eyes off his target, but he could see the bulky shape of the weapon in the periphery of his vision. The gun must have been tossed aside when the mob was busy taking that lady Judge to pieces. A small flicker of memory tickled at the back of Ernesto's mind, something important, something about a Judge's gun, but he shook it away. Angry thoughts crawled around the inside of his brain like a troop of ants, scratching for a way out, blanking out everything else. "Shut it! You can't tell me what to do, jerk-o!"

The gunman grimaced and pulled the trigger. The spit gun's hammer fell on an empty chamber with a hollow click. "Ah, sneck–"

Ernesto growled, teeth flaring in a feral grin, and fired as well. In the instant his finger tightened on the electronic trigger mechanism, his mind threw up the thing that had been nagging at him. All Judges' guns had a key characteristic in common: a tiny computer-scanner combination that checked the palm print of any person attempting to fire it. If someone other than the designated Judge pulled the trigger, a counter-measure was activated. In some models, this was a simple safety catch or an electro-stunner, but like the pistols used by Mega-City Judges, firearms issued by the Luna-1 Justice Department had a self-destruct charge fitted to them, equivalent in power to a hand grenade. The gun's detonation killed both men instantly, leaving two more shredded corpses to litter Kepler Dome's streets.

On the electronic billboard overhead, Moon-U broadcast a replay of the moment across the whole complex, repeating it on any screen that the pirate signal could infiltrate.

Judge Spring cursed inwardly as the low battery buzzer sounded on his sonic rifle, just as a smoke-blackened rioter vaulted over the plastiform barricade. Without wasting a moment to swap out the power pack, Spring flipped the weapon over and used the heavy butt to crack the lawbreaker across the face. "Get back, meathead!" he snapped and the rioter fell away, unconscious.

Spring reloaded by touch alone, scanning the open plaza in front of the Kepler precinct house for any sign of a new rush towards the barriers – but no, the citizens seemed happy enough to continue tearing into one another or smashing up property. The Brit-Cit Judge frowned. This wasn't like any typical confront or Block War, there was just no direction to it. It was nothing but wanton destruction; violence for the sake of violence.

He spotted movement close to the flickering panels of a cracked wallscreen and called out to his deputy on the line, a female Judge from the

Sydney-Melbourne Conurb. "Kenzy! Watch for any group movement."

She nodded. "On it. Where's that electro-cordon?"

He opened his mouth to answer, but a new voice interrupted him. "Spring! Where are you?" The Brit-Judge stepped back from the barricade as Senior Judge Koenig approached, emerging from drifts of grey smoke with a group of men in riot gear. Koenig was Sector Chief for Kepler Dome and Spring's direct superior. Spring had grown to respect the elder Luna-City officer during his secondment to the Moon and knew him well enough to read the grim set of his chin.

"Judge Koenig. Glad to see you brought reinforcements, sir. I hope they're not all you've got."

"Save it, Spring," Koenig snapped irritably. "What are you still doing here? We can't just hold the plaza, we need to move in and pacify."

"With respect, sir, we're spread too thin. Ten patrol Judges dead or incapacitated out in the field, a dozen more in medbay. The citizens outnumber the rest of us fifteen-to-one and we can't chance using riot foam or stumm gas until the oxygen supply is reactivated. I put in a call for cordons and Mantas from the main dome, but–"

"But they're not going to get here for another four hours, at least," Koenig broke in, seeing the Brit-Judge's jaw drop. "I've just come from the zoom terminal. Rioters sabotaged the track, the train has blocked the tunnel and we've had a blow-out in the zipstrip to Luna-1. We're on our own."

"Grud," mumbled Kenzy.

"We need to crush this, before it gets out of control," Koenig added.

Spring felt his annoyance flare. "Look around!" he grated. "It already is out of control!" He took a step closer to the senior Judge. "We've got the lowest manpower and hardware capability of any outer dome on Luna and we're coming apart just holding these crazies in place!"

"Then maybe you should have been aware of that before it even happened! You're my sector deputy! Where are your street skills?"

"Maybe if you got out of your office once in a whi–"

Kenzy shouted, her voice mingling with the sound of a high-powered spit carbine: "Sniper!"

With a keening ricochet, a bullet deflected off the crown of Koenig's helmet and the elder Judge cursed. "Drokk!" In a swift movement, Koenig's pulse gun was in his hand and he cracked off a trio of well-aimed shots. On the far side of the plaza, a man clutching a rifle fell out of a tree and lay still. Koenig looked back at Spring, the sudden anger that had been building between them dissipated for the moment. "Where are they getting these weapons from? This doesn't make sense. I'd expect panic from an oxygen outage, but not a full-blown street war."

"Surveillance has had absolutely no indicators of any serious tensions for the past three weeks. It's as if someone just pushed a button and got a riot, sir."

Koenig paused for a moment, considering. "All right, Spring, we'll do it your way. Bottle them up and let it burn itself out."

"Incoming!" called another Judge from further up the barricade.

"How many?" said Spring.

"Uh... All of them."

Koenig and Spring turned together to see a wall of figures boiling out of the entryways and into the plaza. Spring raised the sonic rifle and took careful aim, searching for obvious ringleaders.

"Form up!" Koenig shouted, his voice carrying over the line. "Set your STUP-guns to maximum stun. Knock them down!" The Judge flicked a glance down at his own pulse pistol and checked the charge. "Hold the line!"

Chief Judge-Marshal Tex flicked off the comm-screen with a grimace and pushed back the hat on his head, rubbing the furrows on his brow. From his office at the pinnacle of the Luna-1 Hall of Justice, the entirety of the Moon's largest city-dome was visible as a vast network of lights. Thousands of towers, bridges and sub-spheres all clustered beneath a huge silver-grey roof. From this height, Luna-1 looked like some intricately worked piece of jewellery, set in a cratered stone landscape. Kepler Dome was just barely visible, to the south west beyond the Armstrong Monument and the sky-scrapers of Von Braun Territory. From such a vantage point it was hard to imagine that Kepler's streets were alive with violence and flame.

"We could consider a Class One contingency," Tex's second-in-command, Judge-Marshal Che spoke quietly, his soft Mexican accent carrying across the room.

Tex removed his hat and shook his head. "A domewide lockdown? I reckon that'd be a death sentence for anyone still in Kepler."

"We have to keep it contained, Chief Judge," Che insisted. "This is the worst incident yet. If word spreads that we can't keep a lid on our own citizens–"

"What?!" Tex snapped. "You think the Triumvirate will come in here and fire us? Send us to Titan?" He shook his head wearily. "The day we took these badges we swore an oath to protect this colony." Tex tapped the star-and-crescent-moon shield on his chest. "I'm not gonna put myself before that. Not ever."

"So what do you propose?"

"We're fallin' apart up here and we know it, Che. We need help to get to the heart of this and I know just the man to ask."

Che's eyes widened. "With all due respect, sir, I must protest–"

"Protest all you want, amigo. But just get me a secured line to Chief Judge Hershey at the Mega-City One Grand Hall o'Justice."

2. THE DAY SHIFT

The deck of cards unfolded into a fan before the young woman's face and she found her attention fixed on their glittering, shiny surfaces.

"Watch and be amazed!" intoned the magician, his eyes flashing darkly from under his top hat. "Choose a card, my dear, but don't show it to me."

The woman did as she was asked, ignoring the sneer on the face of her boyfriend. She took a careful look at the card. "Okay!" she chirped.

She was a little excited to be getting involved with the street performer's act. It was nice to be the centre of attention for a change, as all the other people gathered around stopped to watch what was happening. Foot traffic across the Barry Waffle Plaza was slowing as more and more citizens drifted over. With nearly ninety per cent unemployment among the four hundred million-strong population of Mega-City One, anything that broke up the boredom was a big draw – even something as simple as a person doing card tricks.

The magician made a deep murmur in his chest and extended a hand towards the concealed card. "You chose... the three of diamonds."

"Ohmygosh! Yes! Yes, I did!" She held up the card and showed it to the audience, who clapped and smiled. All of them except her boyfriend.

"Is that it?" he griped. "That's the best you can do?"

The magician fixed him with a practiced glare. There was always one who wanted to make trouble. "Would you like to see something else then, sir? Another demonstration of the incredible powers *of the mind*?" He gave the last words an echoed emphasis, thanks to the hidden subdermal resonator taped to his larynx. "So be it."

That gave the guy pause, but he quickly overcame it and snatched the deck of cards from the magician's hand and shuffled them. Picking three at random from different parts of the pack, he held them away. "Okay, smart guy. You tell me what I got here, eh?"

The magician had to fight to hold off a smile. "You doubt me? Then perhaps you'd like to place a little wager on my abilities? Say, twenty credits?"

"Sure!" the man snapped, fishing a banknote out of his pocket. "You ain't no psyker, and I'll prove it!" A couple of other folks in the crowd waved money as well, eager to test his skills.

"We shall see." The performer gave a broad wink to the rest of the audience, who chuckled. I've got these mugs eating out the palm of my hand, he told himself. The magician concentrated again and closed his eyes. A collective gasp arose from the watchers as he slowly began to rise off the pedway until his feet were just barely touching the perma-crete pavement.

He fixed the boyfriend with a hard look and spoke in a deep, sepulchral voice. "You have in your hand the queen of spades, ten of hearts and..." he gave a wry smile, "the joker."

To the man's irritation, the magician was completely right. The money was gone from his fingers in a flash and the performer nodded to himself. Where none of the marks could see it, a small optical imager was fixed to the inside of his hat, using a low-power laser to project a readout into his eye. Micro-thin circuits inside the cards transmitted their location to the hat and the imager relayed that to the magician; he didn't even have to look at him to know exactly what the guy was holding. "And now, I will stagger your imaginations with a new illusion that will confound your very reason itself!" Surreptitiously, he touched a control disguised as a cufflink that powered up the short-range teleporter built into his kneepad; next, he'd do the pull-a-card-out-of-thin-air trick, maybe by 'porting it into the girl's blouse.

He looked back at the audience and saw that all of them, even the boyfriend, were silent and awe-struck before him. This is gonna be sweet, he told himself, I'm gonna milk these fools dry!

"Watch, as I exhibit powers that no mortal man could ever hope to achieve!"

And then from behind him, a voice all gravel and hard edges said, "I'll be the judge of that."

The magician's feet hit the ground and he whirled around. Too late, he realised that his audience hadn't been cowed by him. They were looking at a two-metre tall sentinel clad in midnight blue and adorned with gold armour pads. Colour drained from the performer's face and he felt his bladder loosen as he caught sight of the name on the Judge's badge: *Dredd*.

"Uh... uh," he managed.

Dredd extended his gloved hand. "Street performance licence?"

The magician looked dumbly at him.

"He conned me outta twenty creds, Judge!" said the boyfriend. "Bet me he could read my mind!"

Dredd gave the mark a brief look. "Betting is illegal, citizen. You're under arrest, one year in the cubes." He tossed a cuff-clip at the guy and waited. The boyfriend showed uncommonly good sense, meekly put on the restraints and stared at the ground. "As for you," Dredd took a step towards the performer. "I'm guessing you don't have a licence."

The magician suddenly found his voice again and raised his hands in defiance. "You cannot hope to, uh, defeat me! I have uncanny powers of the mind!"

"I don't think so," Dredd retorted flatly. Unknown to this loser, a pair of real Psi-Division operatives were working a block away on a murder case and the presence of any real, unlicensed telepath would have registered with them like a flare on a dark night. "Fraud, unauthorised street performance, gambling... Anything else to add before I take you and that chump there downtown?"

In reply, the magician jumped into the air, rising up and away, gaining height with every passing second. Dredd's hand darted forward to grab the hem of his overcoat, but the material ripped and fell away, revealing a small grav-pack on the performer's back; the kind that kids used for aeroball games.

"He wasn't levitating at all!" cried the woman.

Dredd watched the flyer wobble his way across the plaza. The grav-pack wasn't designed to hold an adult's weight and the motor was straining. It would be a simple shot for the veteran Judge, a single standard execution round from his Lawgiver pistol and the perp would come crashing to earth – but instead he just watched and waited.

When the magician was about seven metres high, the grav-pack belched smoke and spat out a nasty cloud of smoke. The performer gave a strangled yelp and dropped like a stone, tumbling head over heels to land in an ornamental fountain. Dredd hauled the magician's dripping form out of the water and slapped a pair of plastiform handcuffs around his wrists. "Read my mind," he said.

"Uh, I'm... under arrest?"

"Six years. You can practice your card games in the cubes."

Lacking a convenient holding post, Dredd tethered the two men to a bench in the plaza, where the local catch wagon would scoop them up on its next pass through the area.

His helmet radio crackled into life. "Control to Dredd. What's your location?"

"Waffle Plaza, east exit."

"Investigate reports of armed robbery with violence in progress, Mobi-Cred Autobank, heading west on Dave Fincher Overzoom."

"ARV, copy. I'm on my way." The Judge mounted his Lawmaster bike, sparing a glance up at the wide highway that passed over the top of the plaza at the twelve-storey level. There, on the city's high-velocity traffic lanes, massive computer-controlled transporters and mobile homes – mo-pads – roared along at speeds of over three hundred kilometres per hour. A large proportion of Mega-City One's population lived on the roads, never settling in a single place, constantly circling the metropolis in a vast, unceasing migration. Where there were people, there were also schools, shops, leisure facilities and even banks, built into mobile platforms following the course of the massive twenty-lane megways that formed the transport arteries of the city. But, like the static buildings they flashed past every day, they were just as prone to crime.

The Mobi-Cred resembled a big, fat bug on eight clusters of wheels, low to the highway and broad enough to take up two lanes. A docking plat-form to the right allowed foot traffic to step off another moving vehicle and board, while a small slip-ramp enabled groundcar drivers to use a drive-thru terminal. Right now the mobile bank was cruising much too fast for anyone to disembark, thanks to a hasty reprogramming job at the hands of one of the Dexter gang. Up to now, that had been the only thing that was going right about the robbery.

In the bank proper, it was hard to see clearly. A low fog gathered around the knees of Big Dave Dexter and his men, making their legs cold and forcing the bank staff and customers to huddle together to keep warm where they sat on the floor. It was still raining inside, thanks to the small cluster of storm clouds that floated near the ceiling. Big Dave made a face and gave his cousin Larry a blunt look.

"How much longer?"

"Couple o' minutes, I reckon." Larry hefted the large, complex-looking rifle in his hand and patted it with a smile. "I set this to 'Sunshine' and burned off the vault locks."

"First thing that snecking piece of junk did right so far." Dave grum-bled. "Why we couldn't just have used a plasma torch–"

"This is better!" Larry broke in. "What, you wanna be known as 'the plasma torch gang'? What kinda name is that? I told you, we got to have ourselves an identity. A gimmick, else we're just plain old bank rob-bers."

"Plain old, cold bank robbers," Royd, Dave's younger brother chimed in. "Plain old cold and *wet* bank robbers."

Larry was getting irritated. "You little spug! I didn't quit my job at Weather Control to listen to you whining! You're gonna be singing a different tune when we're all over the vid-news! Think about it, 'Judges Fail to Capture Weather Gun Gang'. It'll be great!"

"Uh-huh," said Royd, who then sneezed.

Dave's attention wandered to the drive-thru window and what he saw made his eyes widen. "Hey, you guys! We got company!"

Larry followed Dave's outstretched hand and saw the distinctive shape of a Lawmaster weaving between the trailing traffic, closing on the Autobank. "Crem! We ain't ready to go yet!"

"Royd, get Joe outta the vault," snapped Dave. "We'll take what we got and scram."

"No way!" said Larry, twisting the control setting on the weather gun to "Chill." "I'll deal with this. We take it all, right? I mean, we don't want to look like amateurs when they show us on *Mega-City-1's Most Wanted*."

"Dredd to dispatch, am approaching with caution. Get traffic control to set up a roadblock at the Bleeker off-ramp. I'll deal with this."

"Control here, that's a roj."

Gunning the Lawmaster's engine, Dredd brought the bike in line with the drive-thru ramp and hesitated, calculating the angles of approach. Movement at the rear of the mobile bank caught his eye and a figure emerged from cover, the bulky shape of a weapon in his hand. Without conscious thought, Dredd's training took over and he veered the bike out of the firing line, just as Larry depressed the firing stud.

An actinic flash of blue light leapt from the muzzle of the weather gun and struck the road with a crackling discharge of energy. Where it hit, rimes of ice instantly blossomed into existence, spreading over the asphalt in a broad fan. Super-cooled air buffeted the Judge as sleet and snow formed around him. Dredd gripped the handlebars grimly and worked the bike with his knees and arms, turning into a fierce skid as the Lawmaster's Firerock tyres lost purchase on the road. Dredd was dimly aware of wheels screeching behind him as mo-pads and robo-trucks spun out on the ice field. Larry hosed the weather gun across the road, painting white swathes of frost along Dredd's path. Any second now, the Lawmaster would flip over and send its rider tumbling along the highway at hundreds of kilometres per hour; it was a chance the Judge refused to take.

Dredd revved the Notron 4000 engine and aimed the bike squarely at the Autobank's rear. Spitting wet slush and chips of ice, the Law-master rocketed forward, even as inertia dragged it down. Dredd coiled his muscles and pushed off the saddle, arms outstretched. For one agonising instant, he seemed to be suspended in mid-air, and the next, his gloves caught on to a maintenance ladder and held. The Judge hauled himself up to safety, turning in time to see his bike vanish beneath the wheels of a massive roadliner. Pausing to draw his pistol, Dredd considered the Lawmaster; how many of them had he lost in the line of duty since his first days on the street? Fifty, sixty? It would mean more paperwork to complete when he returned to the Sector House at the shift's end – but for now he had more important concerns.

Working his way over the vehicle's hull, Dredd dropped down on to the drive-thru ramp. A wrecked robot lay in a sizzling heap, torn out from one of the teller's stations and in a corner, the Judge found an injured man, his face and hands lobster-red from what appeared to be sunburn. "How many in there?" Dredd asked.

"Fuh-four, Judge. One of 'em got me with a huh-heat ray."

"Stay put. Help is on the way."

Dredd crouched and made his way towards the bank entrance. Parked on the exit ramp was a sleek Korvette Slabster on auto, doors open, the engine idling. Taking aim with the Lawgiver, Dredd selected an incendiary round from the magazine.

"I lost him!" Larry shouted. "He went around the back!"

"I saw the bike go. He's gotta be dead," Big Dave added, as Joe and Royd emerged from the vault. Joe had two large carryalls in each hand, the zippers straining to hold in the wads of currency and Dave forgot all about the Judge when he saw them.

Joe Dexter's face was split in a grin. "First thing I'm going to get me is one of those luxy-apts in Central. Then a face change, make me look like Conrad Conn..."

"You won't be getting nothing if that Judge is still around!" spat Royd. "Where's the getaway car?"

Big Dave opened his mouth to answer but the words he spoke were lost in the sudden report of an explosion from the vehicle ramp. Larry's jaw dropped as he caught sight of the car vanishing in a puff of orange flames. Joe clutched the moneybags like long-lost children and Royd swore. None of the Dexter gang were looking the right way when Judge Dredd came through the doors at a run, picking out his targets.

He gave a mandatory challenge. "Weapons down, creeps! I won't ask again!"

"Take him out!" Dave shouted, firing off a round from his shot-blaster.

Dredd ducked and rolled, coming up behind a display screen and fired on the move. "Leg shot!" The standard execution round cut a supersonic course across the bank and shattered Big Dave's left kneecap, exiting the other side in a puff of blood. The eldest Dexter crumpled, screaming.

Royd fired wildly, his autopistol chattering, bullet discharges chewing through plasteen wall panels and blasting apart desks. Some of the citizens and bank staff cried or whimpered, trying to lose themselves in the thin mist.

Dredd shot back at Royd, but the perp was quicker, dodging behind a pillar. The Judge watched as the gunman he'd encountered earlier ducked out of hiding to grab at the bags of cash.

"Spug off!" Joe hissed. "We go together or not at all, Larry!"

Larry Dexter made a pained face and reset the weather gun to "Gale". "Fine. We'll blow this helmet-head out of the door!" He pulled the trigger and a concentrated blast of air boomed from the rifle, blowing a hole in the glasseen roof.

Dredd was ready when Larry's head popped up from cover and he fired; the bullet creased Dexter's cheek and embedded itself in the delicate electronics of his weapon. Larry tensed as the weather gun arced and vibrated. Without any intervention on his part, the gun's control switched over to "Hurricane" setting and hummed into life once more.

The weather gun coughed out a cone of force that tore across the inside of the bank, scattering papers and anything else that wasn't tied down into a vortex of racing wind. Larry held on to the weapon as the discharge slammed him back into Joe and sent the carryalls flying. The bags tore open and a storm of credit notes rippled into the air.

"Grud, no! The money!" Royd yelled, his gun falling away as he desperately tried to grab at armfuls of fluttering cash.

Larry struggled to deactivate the weather gun, but the weapon's gravity-energy coils were red-hot with overload and it continued to spit out a whirlwind inside the confines of the bank. Dredd wedged himself behind a stanchion and held on as the gale tore at him. Outside, a trail of debris spewed out into the Autobank's wake, thousands upon thousands of credits streaming into the air.

Royd hugged a million or so to his chest and grinned, but only for a moment. The edge of the continuous blast from the weather gun caught his legs and threw him upward. Dredd watched the perp go tumbling past him in a mess of flailing limbs, up and out of the hole in the roof. The Judge's jaw hardened; the next victim could be an innocent.

Summoning all his strength, Dredd braced himself against the wall and aimed his pistol at Larry Dexter. It took just one shot.

"Armour piercing," Dredd shouted over the wind and the audio-selector in the Lawgiver obeyed, chambering the round. The bullet struck home, cutting through the weather gun's power core and into Dexter's chest. Like a switch being flipped, the miniature hurricane died away and drifts of paper and banknotes settled to the floor.

Joe Dexter swore and held up his hands in surrender. Beside him, Larry was coughing up blood but was still alive. "Joe! Joe!" he choked, his voice urgent.

"It's okay, cuz. You'll be fine," Joe said wearily, as Dredd cuffed him.

"Who cares about that?" Larry managed. "We got busted by Judge Dredd! That means we'll get on *MegCrimeWatch* for sure!"

The Mobi-Cred came to a halt at the Bleeker Street roadblock and Dredd found an H-wagon waiting on the megway. The traffic control supervisor, Judge Evans, nodded at the blocky aircraft. "Got a call from Justice Central while you were busy in there. Chief Judge Hershey wants you in her office. Expedite immediate."

"I'm the arresting Judge. I need to stay on site until the situation's locked down."

"Negative, Dredd. I've been told to take over here. That H-wagon will get you to the Grand Hall."

Dredd grimaced; he didn't like leaving a job half-finished, but orders from the Chief Judge were not to be ignored.

"Look on the bright side," Evans continued in a dour voice. "At least you won't have to do the paperwork. You won't have to be there when accounts division hears you let a few million credits blow over the whole of Sector 40. That honour's going to be mine."

Dredd shrugged and made his way over to the flyer. "It's an ill wind..."

Hershey steepled her fingers and gave Judge Chapman a level gaze. "This situation..." she said carefully, "has all the makings of a political nightmare."

Chapman nodded, stroking the thin stubble on his chin. "Agreed, Chief Judge, but I don't see that we have a choice. The request was made. We can't ignore it."

"No. But let's face it, Dredd's last trip to the Moon wasn't exactly a roaring success. A dead Psi-Judge from Casablanca. A viral outbreak."

"Oh yes, that zombie doppelganger business," Chapman grimaced. "But that was seven years ago. Things have changed a lot since then, what with the expansion of the Triumvirate council and the global partnership treaty–" His sentence was interrupted as Hershey's intercom beeped.

"Judge Dredd to see you, Chief Judge."

"Send him in."

Chapman stood as Dredd entered, as a mark of respect for the senior officer. Dredd gave him a cursory sideways glance and nodded to Hershey. "Reporting as ordered."

"Take a seat, Joe." Hershey indicated a chair. "Sorry to pull you off duty in the middle of a watch, but we've got something that requires your specific attention." The Chief Judge ran a hand through her hair, brushing the dark strands out of her eyes. She seemed fatigued, Dredd noticed. The pressures of the high office were no doubt taking their toll on her – the woman who had accompanied Dredd on the quest to find the Judge Child was long gone now and in her place was a seasoned veteran, older and wiser but still showing the same iron-hard resolve. "This is Chapman, Space Division. He's here to provide some additional background."

"What's the situation?"

Chapman touched a control on Hershey's desk and the lights dimmed as a holo-projector in the ceiling came to life. "Space-Div has been monitoring increases in incidents of large-scale armed violence across the Luna-1 colony over the last few months, but we haven't been in a position to get involved, not without stepping on the toes of a dozen other city-states around the world."

Dredd watched as a hologram of the Moon formed, with markers pinpointing confronts all over the lunar territories. "So, what has changed?"

"This morning, Justice Three intercepted comm traffic from an outlying complex, Kepler Dome," said Hershey. "The place was in flames. Then an emergency call was placed via encrypted channels to Earth from Luna-1's Judge-Marshal Tex."

"Tex…" It had been more than twenty years since Dredd had served his time as Luna-1's Judge-Marshal and on his recommendation it was Tex who had been installed as the colony's permanent Chief Judge. So many things had happened on Earth in the meantime – the Apocalypse War, Necropolis, Judgement Day – and through it all, the proud Texan lawman had retained his post as governor of the lunar city with a reputation for fairness and strength. "If he's calling us for help, the situation must be grim," Dredd said.

"Actually, he's calling *you* for help," Hershey noted. "Marshal Tex contacted the Triumvirate council and specifically requested the assembly of a Judicial task force under your direct command, to assist the Luna Justice Department with the current crisis."

"Because Luna-1 is an international zone, the team will be drawn from five of the signatories to the partnership treaty." Chapman worked the projector controls and the image of the Moon was replaced by a map of the world, with the cities that were party to the treaty picked out in green. "East-Meg Two have selected a Judge from their Kosmonaut Directorate and the Pan-Andes Conurb has sent a man as well. You'll be joined by representatives from Brit-Cit and Simba City when you reach the Moon."

Hershey held out a datapad. "I've made arrangements for your caseload to be transferred, Dredd. Your briefing is in here. Get your gear and report to Kennedy Starport. You've got a seat booked on the next NEO-Clipper to Union Station."

"Why me?" Dredd asked. "Last time I set foot up there, the Luna Special Judicial Service tried to finger me for murder. I doubt they'll be happy to see my face again."

"You gave Tex his job, Dredd. He respects you and, more importantly, he trusts you."

"But there's more to it than that, isn't there?"

Chapman frowned. "Space-Div's intelligence unit has heard rumours that there are cracks forming in the global treaty. There's a chance that elements inside the international community are working to destabilise Luna-1. I don't have to tell you how valuable lunar territory is now, especially with the discovery of those new titanium deposits. If the Triumvirate... If *Tex* can't hold it together up there, things could get real ugly real quick."

"He wants you, Joe, because he knows you'll put the law above politics," added Hershey.

Dredd got to his feet. "When do I leave?"

3. UNION STATION

Dredd felt the familiar sensation of artificial gravity as he stepped down from the airlock and into the dock terminal. The floor curved away from him in a low slope in both directions, disappearing into the roof – or so it appeared – from his perspective. Like a lot of the larger Near-Earth-Orbit platforms, Union Station was a spin habitat, turning along its axis to provide gravitation for the transient population that passed through its halls. The Judge was familiar with the transfer procedure and made his way to baggage reclaim, snagging the heavy armourplas diplomatic case that contained the majority of his equipment, including his Lawgiver.

On a Freeport orbital like Union, Dredd had little jurisdiction to speak of, and in accordance with international space law the use of any projectile weapon he might carry was forbidden. The penalty for discharging a ballistic firearm on an orbital was quite severe, as he recalled – if convicted, the guilty party would be placed in an airlock and vented to space. Death by Lethal Ejection, they called it. Dredd approved: in an environment where one stray bullet could lead to the deaths of thousands from explosive decompression, the law had to be an effective deterrent.

The passport control droid scanned his ident card with a ruby laser beam, the thread of light flicking across his face and his badge. It paused as it examined the holo-pic on the card. "This doesn't show your face. Could you take your helmet off, please?"

"No." The force put into that single syllable made it clear Dredd would not tolerate an argument.

"Oh." The droid considered this, then decided not to press the point. "Business or pleasure?"

This time Dredd didn't even bother to reply.

"Business it is, then." The robot handed back the card. "Enjoy your stay."

Beyond the terminal, the station opened up into a vast, hollow cylinder, walls rising up to meet in an arched "ceiling". For the most part,

Union Station was a waypoint; a place that people stopped at on their way to somewhere else and the interior reflected this. Much of the habitat was given over to eateries, capsule hotels and arcades full of stores. The scents of cooking, human sweat and other, less identifiable smells, mingled in the air.

The station had a slightly shabby look to it. Developments in single-stage-to-orbit rockets and trans-shuttles in recent years had meant that the higher-paying passengers going interstellar didn't need to use NEO transfer stations any more, but there were still droves of ordinary citizens who took suborbitals from EasyMek or SpaceTrain, heading out to the Moon or leisure stations like Bacchus at the LaGrange points. People from dozens of nationalities swarmed back and forth in broad rivers of bodies, breaking apart like frightened shoals of fish to filter into food bars or down the entryways into the departure lounges. A troupe of Sino-Cit eldsters back from the spas on Ceres filed past a delegation of Uqquan traders from planet Qu, while a rowdy group of Oz skysurfers traded lewd stories with a party of dustboarders bound for the Martian sand-seas.

Dredd surveyed the crowd with a practiced lawman's eye. A place like this would be paradise for a tap gang or a pickpocket, but as he watched he saw little that set off his internal radar. Overhead, small oval watch-drones flitted about looking for troublemakers and, now and then, Dredd caught sight of a Duritz Securi-Bot ambling through the concourse. Dredd had little time for robot law enforcers – his encounters with the Justice Department's troublesome Mechanismo units had seen to that – but perhaps in an environment like this, machines were the best solution. He watched the droid as it clanked past him, a stun pulser at the ready in its grippers.

The chronometer overhead chimed the hour and Dredd took a moment to purchase a cup of synthi-caff in the waiting area; the dry, recycled air in the clipper had left his throat parched. Sipping the drink, he saw a flash of movement in the periphery of his vision.

A woman yelled something in Hindi that sounded midway between a curse and a sob, as two shapes vaulted away from her in opposite directions. A pair of juves, both with the wiry gait of orbit-born spacers, had grabbed her bags and bolted. They clearly knew the patrol schedule for the Securi-Bots – the area was clear of them – and they were sprinting for the drop tubes to the lower levels. Without putting down the caff, Dredd gave his case a swift kick and sent the container sliding across the plastic floor towards the closest thief. The juve ran straight into it and went flying, the lower gravity of the station granting him a graceful arc through the air just moments before he collided with a waste bin and crumpled into a heap.

Dredd finished his drink and strode over, recovering his case as he passed it. The thief was out cold. Dredd scanned the area to see if he could locate his partner, in time to see a figure in a helmet and a red rad-cape come from out of nowhere and drop-kick the second perp. The other thief took the hit hard, but didn't go down. Instead, he produced a wicked-looking knife from a wrist holster and made a savage swipe at his attacker. Spacers liked to fight with blades and melee weapons; there was no chance of a blow-out with a knife, a sword or a tonfa. The caped figure dodged the blade and stepped into the perp, planting a hard left cross to his cheek. The thief thrust the knife forward in a stab, but the other person drew the blade into the folds of the cape and twisted it, disarming him in one single action. Good technique, Dredd noted.

The caped figure gave the thief no pause and brought up a knee to strike him squarely in the crotch. Winded, the second perp dropped to the floor in a whimpering heap. Dredd took a handful of his thief's jacket and dragged him back to the victim, returning her bag. The caped figure did the same and only when they were closer did he recognise the outfit. The red and black cape was fastened securely at the throat with a bronze shield that bore a cluster of Cyrillic letters and the face beneath the bullet-shaped helmet reflected Dredd's own impassive gaze. It was probably the first time in Dredd's career he could ever recall sharing an arrest with a Sov-Judge.

The East-Meg officer gave him a nod – acknowledging a moment of shared purpose beyond national boundaries – and Dredd returned it, turning the criminals over to a brace of Securi-Bots that had belatedly arrived on the scene. He noted the small symbol of a stylised rocket on the Sov-Judge's uniform, the sigil of the Kosmonaut Directorate.

"Kontarsky?"

"Judge Nikita Kontarsky," she began, removing her helmet. "It is an honour to meet you, Judge Dredd." Her bright green eyes gave him a challenging look from a face framed with ice-blonde hair.

Dredd returned her appraising gaze. Justice Central's files had only had the vaguest details about the officer who would serve as his deputy on the task force, thanks to the typical East-Meg penchant for utter secrecy. Kontarsky was a high-flier in the Sov's space program and an expert in interplanetary law. But what the file had failed to mention was how young she was. The Sovs had sent a rookie. Looks like they're not serious about assisting Tex, he thought.

"I was approaching you when I noticed the crime unfolding," she continued smoothly. "I considered you would excuse a delay in our meeting in order for me to deal with it."

"Where's our third man, Rodriguez?"

Kontarsky pointed to the far side of the terminal plaza, where a dingy bar was situated. "There. He arrived just before you did." She paused. "May I speak freely, Judge Dredd?"

"There's little point in you being part of my team if you don't," Dredd answered as they walked.

"I believe that Judge Rodriguez may be unsuitable for this taskforce."

"Oh?" Dredd said. "What is the reasoning behind your assessment, Kontarsky?"

"His attitude is not... I feel he may not be a dedicated enough officer."

Dredd gave a cynical snort. "'Dedicated' is not a word you'll often hear applied to a SouthAm Judge."

Kontarsky chewed her lip as they entered the bar. Dredd spotted the Judge from the Pan-Andes Conurb at once, in close conversation with a female in a spacer's jumpsuit.

"Real big shot, chica, you understand?" he drawled, unaware of Dredd's approach. "It's a tough job, but when my brother cops on Luna called me, I had to come to their aid, you see? I, Judge Miguel Juan Olivera Montoya Rodriguez, am in charge of a special Judge squad and we're going to–"

"Do what?" Dredd grated.

Rodriguez turned a casual smile on the Mega-City Judge. "Hey, Dredd. Amigo. What a pleasant surprise." He held out a hand. "I heard a lot about you, man. It's a pleasure to be working with you."

Dredd ignored the offered handshake and eyed the glass on the bar. "Don't tell me you're drinking on duty, Rodriguez."

"What, we barely say hola and already you're busting my cojones? Don't forget, this is a Freeport, man. I don't have to follow your Mega-City rules."

Dredd nudged the half-full glass towards him. "Drink up, then. Go ahead, give me a reason to send you back down the well."

The SouthAm Judge's bluster faded as he realised Dredd meant every word and he gave a sheepish shrug. "Hey, well, it's just an eye-opener, you know? Those stratoflights, they really take it out of you. Look, Dredd, no need to kick me out before we even get Moonside, eh?" He gave the spacer girl a look, but she had clearly lost interest in him and stepped away. "Hey, chica, where you going?"

"You see my point now, Judge Dredd?" Kontarsky said.

Rodriguez sized up the female Judge with a leer. "Oh, hey. Maybe I can forget all about her and talk to you instead, eh? You look a little young for that uniform, though."

Kontarsky's eyes narrowed. "I am a fully qualified law officer of the glorious East-Meg State and a graduate of the Soviet Kosmonaut Academy," she growled, "and my age has no bearing on that fact!"

"Right," Rodriguez smiled. "So how many times you been into space, then?"

She bit out a reply. "This is my first assignment off-world."

Dredd frowned. Terrif. A wet behind-the ears Sov and a Banana City chancer. This team was shaping up to be a real set of aces. "I don't have time for this. Both of you, listen to me carefully, because it's the one and only time I'm going to say it. I'm in charge of this task force and I expect everyone in it to behave like a professional. If I see anything that looks like inexperience or disregard for protocol, you're on the next shuttle home. Am I clear?"

"Sí, amigo. It's no skin off my churro."

"Da."

"Then let's get to work. We have a transport to catch."

The spy kept watch on the bar until the trio of Judges had left, then he tracked them with care to the lunar departure terminal. He was very careful not to draw attention to himself, giving out the impression of a bored tourist wandering around as he waited for a connecting shuttle flight. Someone would have had to stand extremely close to him to have noticed the small holo-camera clipped to his air-cooled fan-hat; they would have to have looked very carefully to see the micro-miniature imaging lens as it recorded the movements and conversation of the two men and the young woman. Of course, if someone had been unlucky enough to have witnessed and understood what the spy was doing, soon afterwards they would have suffered from some sort of terrible and unexpected misfortune. One that left absolutely no doubt they had died completely by accident.

He went as far as he could go, up to the gates to the terminal and watched Dredd, Kontarsky and Rodriguez disappear into the airlock. Then, still mindful to make his passage as insignificant and unnoticeable as possible, the spy stepped into a nearby vu-phone booth and dialled a number in Antarctic City. An automated relay in a vacant apartment there scrambled his call and bounced it off two hundred other randomly selected relays before finally broadcasting it to a target receiver a few hundred thousand kilometres away.

"Yes?" The voice at the other end of the line was indistinct, electronically masked into mechanical flatness.

"He's on his way. The girl and the South American too. Maiden Galactic, flight six-six."

"I will inform the rest of the cabal. Do you have the holo-scan?"

The spy connected a thin optic cable from the camera to the vu-phone's data port. "Transmitting now."

"Excellent. Dredd will never see his precious Mega-City One again. The Moon will be his grave."

Much to Dredd's irritation, Rodriguez seemed intent on talking all the way to Luna-1 and as their shuttle's countdown edged closer to zero, he continued to bait the young Sov-Judge.

"So you must be pretty special, chica, if you got shipped up here to help out with us big dogs, eh?"

"I was top of my class in space law and colonial legal statutes, Rodriguez. I am more than qualified to be part of this task force." She gave him a hard stare that all but rolled off the casual Judge's manner. "Tell me, why are you here?"

"Why are any of us here?" he replied airily. "The universe, she is a mysterious thing. I merely go where she tells me."

Dredd gave him a sideways look. "Kontarsky's got a point. Your file was real short on explanations about that."

After a moment of awkward silence, Rodriguez made a face. "Look, you wanna know why I got sent on this assignment? It's not some big secret, Dredd. I grew up in Luna-1's Puerto Luminia enclave, so the Moon, I know her pretty well." He paused. "That and also I was suspended for, uh, a liaison with another Judge."

Kontarsky gave a derisive snort. "As I understand it, those sorts of 'liaisons' are commonplace among the undisciplined law officers of the Pan-Andes. They are tolerated and ignored. Why would yours be any different?"

An insouciant smile crossed Rodriguez's face. "Mine just happened to be with the lover of the sector chief." He glanced at the Mega-City Judge. "So what about you, Dredd? This your first time up on la Luna?"

"Not quite."

"He was Judge-Marshal here for six months from 2099 to 2100," Kontarsky began, as if she were giving a lecture. "During his tenure, Judge Dredd cleaned up a lot of the criminal elements inside Luna-1 and the surrounding Badlands. Among these, he was responsible for the arrest and prosecution of CW Moonie, the exploitative capitalist crimelord who persecuted the hard-working lunar colonists."

"No kidding?" said Rodriguez. "I remember Moonie from when I was a boy. My papa worked for him."

"Almost everyone worked for Moonie back then," Dredd noted. "He had his fingers in every part of the Luna-1 economy."

"Exactly," Kontarsky said. "He was a parasite feasting on the lifeblood of the workers."

"Something like that," added Dredd.

A two-tone signal sounded from the shuttle's public address system. "Your attention please. Trans-lunar injection will commence in two minutes. Please ensure your seat backs and tray tables are in an upright, locked position and please keep all hands, pseudopodia and tentacles out of the aisles until we have switched off the seatbelt sign. Thank you!"

"How come you know so much about Dredd?" Rodriguez pressed. "You a fan or something?"

"East-Meg Two's Judicial Directorate has very detailed files. It was deemed important to retain information on a man who was responsible for the total destruction of a Sov city."

"That was war," Dredd grated. "I took no pleasure in it. And let's not forget, it was East-Meg One that fired the first shots in that conflict. I did what was necessary to ensure the survival of my city."

"I do not disagree, Judge Dredd," Kontarsky said levelly. "Had the circumstances been reversed, I would have made the same choice. Just as you did once more during the madman Sabbat's assault."

"Madre de dios," said Rodriguez. "Now that was a dark day..."

"But the so-called Apocalypse War was not your first engagement with Sov forces, was it?" Kontarsky gave Dredd a piercing look. "You also fought them on the Moon, did you not?"

Dredd's jaw hardened. "Do you have a point, Kontarsky, or are you just going to keep listing my greatest hits? Yeah, I took part in a limited war. We used the old team-based system instead of all-out conflict. We won there, as well!"

A rumble began to build in the rear of the shuttle as the engines throttled up to full power and Dredd's voice rose along with it. "What else do you have to say? Come on, let's hear it."

"I was merely answering Judge Rodriguez's question," she snapped, her icy manner starting to slip. "I believe you returned to Luna-1 in 2118, where you were involved in a murder investigation. You were accused of a series of cannibalistic attacks, if my memory serves correctly."

"Did... did you say cannibal?" Rodriguez paled, edging away from Dredd as far as he could.

Dredd made an off-hand gesture. "I wasn't the perp. The killer was a zombie version of my future self from a parallel alternate timeline."

"Oh," said Rodriguez, in the same tone someone might use if they were speaking to an escaped lunatic. "Well, that explains everything."

"And now you're going back," Kontarsky noted, the roar of the rocket motors drowning out her voice. "I wonder, what history will you make this time?"

Dredd said nothing and let the G-force press him into his seat, as the shuttle powered away towards the grey disc of the Moon.

There were four men in the Silent Room. Two of them were subordinates, lackeys of the other pair, whose job it was to expedite the wishes of their masters. These servant men had servants and agents of their own and a degree of limited autonomy and command, but in all truth, theirs was a short leash. Neither man could move more than a little without the orders of his superior and although both of them were as different as two men could be, their polar opposite beliefs had come together for this one endeavour, in service for their masters.

The two men in charge faced one another across a table cut from black lunar basalt. The surface was so smooth, so finely polished, that it acted like a mirror, reflecting the sullen, watchful cast of their faces and the shimmering holographic display tank that filled the far corner of the room.

In actuality, the Silent Room wasn't silent at all, with the often heated discussions that had taken place between the two men in charge. It had the name only because it would appear silent from the outside. Millions of credits had been spent on just this one space, in order to render it utterly inert to any form of eavesdropping. Sensor baffles that could block radar, lidar, maser scans and tunnelling neutrino beams were embedded in the walls. Sound dampening panels in the structure meant that a nuclear bomb could be detonated inside it and the only thing a listener outside would hear would be the sound of their own breathing. The Silent Room had even been proofed against the more ethereal, less tangible forms of spying, blocking the probing psi-senses of telepaths with an array of cloned human brain tissue that broadcast the mental equivalent of white noise.

It was the ultimate sanctum from which to plot and scheme, an unbreachable preserve for these men, this cabal, to meet and to conspire against the Moon.

"I have the Justice Department report from the Kepler Dome uprising," said the thin man, the subordinate of the man who sat in the hoverchair. "Copies are on your panels, if you'd like to look at them."

The tall man, the opposite number to the man who sat in the hoverchair, smiled coldly. "I see your network of corruption still operates."

The man in the hoverchair gave a husky laugh. He was quite old and somewhat frail, but still potent enough to be dangerous. "There's always someone who wants a little more. Like you, my friend."

The tall man let the gibe pass unremarked, scanning the document. "This bodes well for us. The cause and effect still elude them and they are no closer to determining where the weapons came from. Perfect. We will soon be entering the endgame."

"You see?" the frail man said, sipping at a squeeze-bulb of water. "You had your concerns about mounting a full-scale test, but you understand now why I insisted on it. Kepler Dome was our last dry run. We're ready to begin."

The tall man's balding assistant smirked. "A 'dry run'? That's an interesting choice of words considering that the streets in Kepler ran with blood. I must admit I have my concerns that we may ignite a powder keg we won't be able to contain."

The tall man gave his servant a derisive look. "That is why you fail to move up in rank while I remain your superior. You lack the killer instinct."

"And killer instinct is what you need to survive in a place where nature herself is trying to murder you!" The frail man spat the words with vehemence.

The thin man interrupted with a polite cough. "At any rate, the process has proven itself to be a success. The only detail to be decided now is the date."

"If I may be so bold," the tall man said, "I have the very day in mind." When he told them, there was a chorus of grim laughter around the black stone table.

"Very theatrical," said the old man in the hoverchair. "That amuses me. Yes, yes, we'll proceed as you suggest. As the day dawns, we'll take the Moon for ourselves."

"There is another matter," said the bald man. "The secondary objective has been brought into play."

"Dredd." The old man spoke the name like a curse.

"Judge Dredd, yes. As we predicted, Judge-Marshal Tex requested his assignment and he will arrive within a day. Our operative on Union Station secured these images of Dredd and two of the task force sent to assist him." The bald man touched a control on his chair and the shimmering holo-projector began playing a loop of footage from the spy's camera.

"Who are these others?" said the thin man. "A woman and a Hispanic male?"

"They are known to us," replied the tall man. "They are of no concern. Plans have already been drawn up to deal with them. Dredd is where our energies should be focused."

The tall man shook his head. "I've said it before and I'll say it again. Why not simply use the contingency we set up for the Judge-Marshal and use it to deal with Dredd?"

"Oh, do shut up!" the old man growled. "I'll do everything in my power to ensure that Judge Joseph Dredd dies slowly and painfully. All of this," he waved a crooked hand at the holograms and the panels on the table, "none of it will be enough until I see Dredd on his knees, begging me for his life!"

"You'll have what you want, my friend," said the tall man. "We both will." He gave a nod to the bald man. "Let us extend a warm welcome to our guests from Earth. Send some of our associates to meet Dredd's party. I'm sure it will amuse us all to test their mettle."

4. THE EAGLE HAS LANDED

Kontarsky did her best not to show her excitement as she trailed Dredd and Rodriguez out of the shuttle gate and into the tunnel that led towards the starport. Outwardly, she was all business, her jaw thrust forward, helmet down over her face, the very model of a cool and composed East-Meg citizen; inside, she was bubbling with sensation, thrilling at her circumstances in a manner more befitting a child. Nikita tried to smother the butterflies in her stomach and failed – to be honest, some part of her actually liked the feeling. She was here, in space. At last.

They stepped on to the slidewalk to the port dome. As they passed underneath the world-famous Lunar Arch, a massive stone arc cut from porous moonrock, she couldn't help but read the words chiselled there and smile a little. *One Small Step for Man. One Giant Leap for Mankind.* It wasn't important that an American had said those words; the promise of a future in the stars they held was all that mattered. Kontarsky hadn't felt so alive since the day she had succeeded in making the grade for cosmonaut training, while still a Justice Academy trainee. They had praised her then, told her that she was a prodigy, a credit to the Motherland and she'd seen her own face on the cover of *Neo-Pravda* as yet another example of Sov superiority.

But it did not last. Young Judge-Kadet Kontarsky was just a momentary distraction for the East-Meg people, a propaganda subject one day, a forgotten footnote the next. It mattered little that she passed through space training with flying colours in the company of other kadets three or four years her senior. The State had chosen to give her a time in the spotlight and now it was over. She returned to her studies and excelled, but her teachers never made good on their promises of sending her to the stars. It would not be equitable to graduate you early, her mentors had told her. The State cannot give you special treatment. It seemed to Nikita that she had spent her entire life in training, in her orphanarium, at the Academy, at the

Baikonur KosmoDome out in the Russian rad-lands, but now it had
come to an end.

She would embrace this assignment and perform it flawlessly, she told
herself. It mattered little that she would be forced to work alongside cap-
italists and opportunistic nyekulturni like Dredd and Rodriguez. These
things were simply tests of her skill and her dedication. Sov-Judge
Nikita Kontarsky would be a shining beacon to the people of East-Meg
Two once again. Devoted. Strong. Indefatigable.

The SouthAm Judge made a weak joke and patted Dredd on the
shoulder, his breezy demeanour rebounding ineffectually off the Mega-
City lawman's hard gaze. Although Dredd was technically classified as
an Enemy of the Sov Nation, Kontarsky had to admit that she harboured
a sneaking admiration for him. It was something she would never dare
to speak of in earshot of any other East-Meg citizen, but in poring over
Dredd's files in preparation for the mission, she had learnt much more
about him than the typical State-sanctioned portrayal of a heartless
killer. Since childhood, Nikita had been in love with the thought of travelling into space, but that passion was twinned with another devotion:
to justice. Despite the yawning gulfs of creed and nationality between
them, Kontarsky saw that Dredd, too, held the law in the highest possible regard.

She halted this train of thought with a shake of her head. It would not
do for her to consider Dredd as anything more than what he was – a
grudging ally. Her briefing from Kommisar Ivanov, the East-Meg Diktatorat's lunar representative, had been quite forthright on that subject.
Kontarsky was to fulfil her function as Dredd's deputy and monitor him
for any signs of subterfuge or conspiracy against the Sov peoples. Any
other motivations were not to be considered.

"Moon-U?" Rodriguez said suddenly, pointing to pieces of graffiti on
the terminal wall. "What are they, some sort of new go-ganger crew or
Free Luna activists?"

"There's a lot of these pro-independence kooks up here," rumbled
Dredd. "They started making noise about 'liberation' a few years ago."

Despite herself, Kontarsky bristled. "Kooks, Dredd? You should not be
so quick to dismiss those with a revolutionary fervour and desire for
change. Was it not your own country that once sought independence
from the nations that had colonised it?"

Rodriguez rolled his eyes. "Ay, Dredd, you've started her off again.
Here we go, another political diatribe from the little red book, eh?"

Dredd did not reply, momentarily scanning a cleaning crew of four
men who were working to erase more wall-scrawls further along the
dome's inner perimeter.

"I was merely making an observation," Kontarsky retorted. "I make no apologies for my beliefs. The ordinary citizens of Luna-1 should be free to decide the path of their own future without the controls of a cap-italistic–"

"Fine, fine, lovely chica, but listen. Keep it to yourself, eh? Dredd and me, we got more important things on our minds." He glanced at the other lawman, who seemed fixated on the work crew. "Say, Dredd, right?"

Kontarsky saw the subtle stiffening of the Mega-City Judge's shoulders and instantly caught the same sense of threat in the air. Something was wrong.

"The cleaners…" Dredd muttered. "No droids…"

Although Luna-1 had a far lower unemployment level than Mega-City One, it was still a common sight to see robotic street tenders at work on building maintenance instead of humans. Most people, even up here, preferred to find jobs that were less demeaning than scrubbing stonework. One of the men produced a remote control unit and stabbed at a key with his finger. A hundred metres away, something inside the slidewalk control box fizzed and melted.

As they passed the clean-up crew, the slidewalk suddenly slammed to a halt and the tourists and travellers it carried fell like dominoes. Completely oblivious, Rodriguez took a nasty spill, collapsing over a portly woman and swearing in furious Spanish. Only Dredd and Kontarsky remained standing, both snatching at the guide rail for support.

The four men turned in unison, each of them brandishing a backpack-mounted splurge gun. Designed to remove even the hardiest paints from a surface, the sud-throwers projected streams of concentrated, heated detergent – and they could strip bare flesh to bone with a foamy deluge.

"Hit 'em!" yelled the leader, training his sud-gun on the slidewalk. "Moon-U! Moon-U! Lunar liberty!"

The other men took up the chant and fired. Streams of bubbling liquid gushed across the terminal plaza in thick white streams, hosing the Judges.

"Kontarsky, cover!" Dredd took the brunt of the discharge as he shouldered the Sov-Judge aside, flattening her against a support pillar. Acidic liquid hissed and spat as it ate into his shoulder pad and badge. Kontarsky's nostrils stung as she smelt the harsh zest of chemicals and the sickly scent of seared flesh.

The splurge-gunners continued to project the foam into the crowd, striking anything that moved without concern for who they targeted. People died with gargling, wet shrieks.

"We're pinned down!" Rodriguez yelled. "They're gonna bathe us to death!"

Kontarsky resisted the urge to make a flippant comment about the SouthAm Judge's need for personal hygiene and gasped in a breath. She hesitated. This was different from the two perps up on Union Station; the only goal of these criminals was to murder them all.

Inwardly, Dredd cursed his lack of a weapon and pulled at his ruined badge, snapping off the gold shield where it connected to his chain of office. "We need to take them together," he told the other two Judges. "I'll get the leader. Rodriguez, find a weapon! Kontarsky, you think you can handle this?"

The Sov-Judge's face reddened. "I am more than capable."

"Time to prove it, then, kid. On three! One…"

Rodriguez gave the obese lady a toothy smile and snatched up her plasti-cane. "Mind if I borrow this?"

"Two…"

"Moon-U! Moon-U!" chorused the shooters, spraying jets of hot foam over the pedway.

"Three!" Dredd sprang out from behind the pillar like a bullet from a gun, springing off the slidewalk guardrail at a shallow angle. He was ready for the lower lunar gravity and let it take him up and over the sud-gunman at the front. At the zenith of his jump, Dredd threw his badge like a shuriken and sent the plasteen shield streaking at the leader's bare throat. The badge struck his windpipe, embedding itself in the soft flesh and choking off his rabble-rousing chant in mid-flow.

At the same instant, Rodriguez popped up from behind the slidewalk and used the cane to swipe at the closest gunman. He struck the rifle-shaped weapon underneath the barrel and deflected it aside to aim at another one of the attackers, like a fencer parrying a sabre. Caught off-guard, the criminal inadvertently hosed his cohort with a point-blank blast of detergent, smothering him with boiling soap.

Rodriguez used the crown of his crested helmet to deliver a crippling head-butt to his target and sent him sprawling, blood spurting from his nose, to the ground.

Dredd came down hard on his shoulder and rolled, feeling the pain from the earlier chemical burn. Bad landing. I'm out of practice with this low-g stuff, he thought to himself.

The fourth man was waiting for him, splurge gun at the ready. "Moon-U!" he chanted, wild-eyed and snarling. "Mooooon-Uuuuu!" The sud-thrower barrel yawned before Dredd's face.

"Moon this!" Kontarsky's clipped voice snapped and Dredd caught the coughing report of a needler pistol. The fourth man slapped at a clump of thin metal spines that embedded themselves in his cheek and sank to his knees, eyes fluttering as a nerve toxin burned through his tissues.

Dredd got to his feet and stepped over the criminal's twitching body. The Sov-Judge stood nearby, gripping a small silver gun in her fist. "Give me the weapon, Kontarsky."

After a long moment, she handed him the firearm. Dredd studied it for a moment. "Volokov ZK-91 holdout pistol. How did you get this past the starport sensors?"

She patted her thigh. "Skin pocket."

"You know the law. No unsanctioned weapons inside the domes. I could have you put in the cubes for this." He weighed the tiny weapon in his hand.

"It only fires reduced velocity subsonic needle rounds. I'd never carry a weapon that could cause a blowout, Dredd. I'm not a fool."

"Hmmph." With a flick of the wrist, Dredd tossed the needler into the maw of a public garbage grinder. "Under the circumstances, I'll overlook this infraction. But don't test me again, understand? You can play with your Sov bag of tricks in your own time."

"Yes, Judge Dredd," she said, her cheeks burning with embarrassment.

"I think our friend here is also muerte," Rodriguez noted, nudging the foam-covered corpse with the tip of his boot. "I can see why they call it 'The Bubbly Death', eh?" He smiled. "So, tell me Dredd. Is this the kind of thing we can expect while we're working with you? Is this how it is down in Mega-City One?"

Dredd gave a shrug. "Different city. Same creeps."

A familiar face was waiting for him in the starport terminal and for a brief instant the sight of Judge-Marshal Tex standing there before him gave Dredd pause; twenty-five years earlier, he had stood in exactly that place and had welcomed him to the Moon.

Tex's face creased in a smile. "Well, howdy Joe." A glint of recognition told Dredd his old friend was thinking the very same thing. "Just like old times, ain't it?"

"Tex." Dredd took his hand and shook it. The Judge-Marshal still had the same firm grip, the same easy grin and trademark Stetson on his head, but the years had not been kind to the stout Texan. The hair that peeked out from under his hat was grey and his chubby face had turned craggy and drawn. He wore every day of his two and a half decades in office in the lines around his eyes. "Shame about the circumstances," Dredd added.

Tex nodded. "It is that." He studied the other two Judges. "I guess you'd be Rodriguez and Kontarsky, right?" Tex tapped his fingers to the brim of his hat. "Glad to have you both aboard."

"A pleasure to meet you, Judge-Marshal Tex," Nikita replied.

"So is this how you welcome everyone to the Moon?" Rodriguez jerked a thumb at the group of Luna Judges securing the remains of the sud-gunners. "Or maybe I'm thinking this is a special hello just for Dredd here?"

Tex's smile thinned to a tight line. "I reckon we'd better talk somewhere more private. Come on, I've got an L-Wagon waiting for us at the upper dock."

The low-grav flyer jetted away from the starport and turned in a long, lazy curve over the towers of Apollo Territory, heading towards the city core. Dredd glanced out of the window and watched the buildings flash by. A casual observer might mistake the view for a nighttime panorama of Mega-City One, with the same panoply of citiblocks and arcologies, but closer inspection picked out the spindly shapes of selenescrapers and skyhighways suspended on thin columns of lunacrete. Architecture throughout Luna-1 took advantage of the one-sixth gravity to create unique structures that would have collapsed under their own weight on Earth. The city's rapid pace of expansion from the early days of the Moon Rush had slowed, the nine original territory zones now filled, with new satellite domes growing like huge glassy mushroom caps around the vast half-sphere of the original settlement. Dredd picked out a few familiar landmarks as the craft threaded itself through aircar traffic: the bright lights of Main Street, the first road ever built on the Moon; the Spike, the glittering tower of the city computer hub; and in the near distance, the grey oval of Crater Stadium. Dredd noted that Rodriguez was maintaining a studied show of blasé disinterest, while Kontarsky was barely concealing her eagerness to drink it all in.

But things were different here. Not just the cosmetic changes in the growth of the city, but something deeper. Even from three hundred metres up, Dredd's seasoned street sense registered the telltale signs of decrepitude – zones where lighting was inactive, empty industrial compounds and run-down residential con-apts daubed with scrawls. Around the edges, the clean, model city he'd visited seven years ago was turning quietly back into the lawless colony he remembered from the turn of the century.

"Not like it used to be, is it?" Tex said quietly at his ear. The veteran Judge-Marshal read Dredd's thoughts in the set of his chin. "There was a time... Maybe we had our golden years, but now we're finding it hard."

Dredd didn't look away. "You're undermanned and underfunded."

Tex nodded ever so slightly. "You know I wouldn't have asked for help if I didn't need it, Dredd. But the fact is, we're on the ropes now. Some sectors are turning into no-go areas. We're having to send in Judges with Manta Prowl Tanks or not at all. The gang problem is getting worse, the usual punk juves are hooking up with organised crime..." He took a breath and rubbed at his eyes, clearly fatigued. "Hell, it's like the bad old days all over again."

The L-Wagon began to descend, passing by a vid-screen that flashed up a grinning Moon-U graphic. "What's that crud all about?"

"Pirate signal hackers bustin' into the comm channels. We've always had 'em up here, but these guys, they're real good. Luna Tek-Division is on the case but so far we're getting nowhere trying to jam it."

"Those yahoos at the starport, they were chanting it."

"Yup." Tex's face wrinkled, as if he'd smelt something bad. "They're stirring up all kinds of trouble in the barrios and the outpost domes. But this is bigger than some cockamamie cartoon. We're looking at an accel-eratin' street war situation here."

"Then we'll have to stamp on it. Hard."

Tex said nothing for a moment, then reached into a belt pocket. "Oh, I almost plumb forgot. As you lost your badge back there, I reckoned I could spot you for a temporary replacement, like. Here." He held out a gold disc and Dredd took it. "You're gonna be a Luna Judge for the time bein'. It's my estimation you oughta look like one."

It was a Luna-City shield, a five-pointed star over an inverted quarter-moon, with four smaller stars on the crescent. "I accept," said Dredd.

Rodriguez craned his neck to see. "Hey, can I get one of those too?"

Nearby, Kontarsky frowned at him. "I think you will need to earn it first."

The L-Wagon drifted into a hover then descended into the imposing structure of the Luna Grand Hall of Justice; modelled on the shape of a castle keep, the massive tower was one of the tallest constructions in the entire city. The north face of the building was sculpted into the shape of an eagle, with a crescent moon held firmly in its claws – a multi-storey reminder of the law's grip on the Moon. The flyer docked at a concealed landing bay in the upper levels and Tex walked them to his office, set in the eagle's head. One whole wall was an elliptical glasseen panel in the eye of the sculpture.

Three men, each in a different uniform, stood as they entered. Dredd recognised Tex's second-in-command, Deputy Judge-Marshal Che. The former Mex-City Judge gave Dredd a grave, barely civil nod that confirmed what he had suspected: Tex's own officers objected to the request for the taskforce from Earth.

"Sit down, y'all," Tex drawled. "We're not going to stand on ceremony here. I got no time for it and, frankly, neither do you." He touched a control in the desktop and part of the window became a video screen, scrolling up pictures from street cameras and spy-in-the-sky drones.

"You all know myself and Deputy Che," Tex continued, "and that gentleman there is Joe Dredd, of Mega-City One. I'm sure you all know him, by reputation if nothin' else. As per my request to the Office of the Triumvirate, you five officers form the joint-nationality taskforce that is here to assist the Luna Justice Department with the current crisis. Che, you wanna take over from here?"

The Deputy nodded, "Sí, Chief Judge. The taskforce will be an autonomous unit inside the department reporting directly to myself and Judge-Marshal Tex. Dredd will act as force commander and his deputy will be Judge Kontarsky of East-Meg Two. Our Sov friends have chosen her for her expertise in space law." He nodded to the SouthAm officer. "To my right is Judge Rodriguez from the PanAndes Conurb and these two gentlemen here are Judge Foster from the diplomatic corps out of Brit-Cit and Tek-Judge J'aele from Simba City. J'aele will be handling technical liaison."

Dredd scrutinised the two Judges. Foster, dark-haired with a sharply chiselled face, had the watchful air of a career Street Judge about him; the African J'aele was a little shorter, bald and muscular with a bull-neck that accentuated the tiger-skin shoulder pads he wore. Neither seemed to be typical for their specialities as envoy and technician. Two more wildcards? Dredd found himself wondering why their governments had chosen them.

Che continued: "As you are aware, incidents of violent crime and rioting have increased in outlying domes by forty per cent over the past two months and there has been a corresponding surge in anti-Judge sentiment." He paused; the hard truth of what he would say next weighed heavily on him. "It is our belief that a concerted effort is being made by elements of organised crime and dissident factions to engineer an armed insurrection in Luna-1."

"There is no doubt?" J'aele asked. "You are certain of this?"

"It's just a matter o' time," said Tex quietly.

Dredd grimaced. "Then we have to tear these creeps out by the root before it goes that far." He saw Kontarsky framing another piece of pro-Communist rhetoric and beat her to the punch. "You say they want a revolution? Well, you know as well as I do that no matter what the brains behind this are promising, all it is going to lead to is blood on the streets."

There was a bleak chorus of agreement around the table, even a reluctant assent from the East-Meg Judge.

"The last flashpoint, whaddaya call it, in Kipple Dome–" Rodriguez began.

"Kepler," corrected Che.

"Kipple, Kepple, whatever. The point is, the last riot. What happened there?"

"If I may," J'aele said. "I have read the forensic report from Tek Central. There was an oxygen outage in the dome and panic drove the populace there to riot. It appears that Moon-U pirate broadcasts were used to transmit images of the event across the entire city."

"Sabotage?" asked Dredd.

"Inconclusive at this time."

"How do we know these Moon-U pendejos didn't start the whole thing?"

"They stirred it up, that's for sure," said Tex. "Got the whole damn Moon riled up about it. The media's puttin' the blame right at the door of the Oxygen Board for causing the panic and claiming it was the Judges who started shootin' first."

Kontarsky pointed at a data window on the vid-screen. "What about these weapons that were used in the riots? How were your citizens able to get them?"

"We have no leads," Che said bluntly, angry that he had to admit his failure. "If we did, we would not be seeking help from outside agencies!"

Foster cleared his throat. "Pardon my directness, Deputy Che, but if this bunch of blokes from 'outside agencies' can't help you out, then you're going to find yourself out of a job quite sharpish. Marshal Tex here has remained in charge of Luna-1 thanks to his twenty-odd years of keeping this slice of the Moon in check, but the rules of the International Treaty of 2061 are very clear."

"Clear to you, gringo," said Rodriguez. "Not to me. Explain, please."

"It's all in the small print, chum. If the Triumvirate council's current representative – which would be our esteemed Judge-Marshal Tex – demonstrates an inability to keep the lunar colony under control, then the treaty is automatically suspended. That means all the territories will be up for grabs for whomever wants to deal, cheat or invade their way into them."

Foster worked a control pad and the vid-screen shifted to show a display of near-lunar space. Several small platforms and starships in orbit were highlighted. He pointed upward. "At any one time there's about a dozen diplomatic courier vessels from all the major powers on Earth hovering overhead, ships from each of our cities as well as places like Hondo, the Stani-States, Midgard, Sino-Cit... They're all ready to stake a claim if the Moon goes to pieces." Foster leant forward and Dredd realised he was speaking directly to him. "This ain't just about knocking down some paint-spraying coffee-house rebels. It's about the future of the Luna-1 colony."

Dredd got to his feet. "Then we're wasting time every second we spend debating it in here. Kontarsky, you and J'aele secure me an L-Wagon with a full tech station rig. Foster and Rodriguez, you come with me. We'll get our equipment from the quartermaster and meet you at pad three in twenty."

To their credit, each of the five members of Dredd's team rose without hesitation to his commands. "Let's move like we got a purpose," he added.

"Dredd," Tex called as they were leaving. "Where you headin'?"

"Where else? Kepler Dome," he replied. "Scene of the crime."

When they were alone in the room, Che gave Tex an arch look. "I thought age might have mellowed him a little, but it hasn't. Dredd hasn't changed a bit."

"How do you figure?"

"He's still got the same iron rod up his backside he had when he was Luna-1 Chief Judge. If anything, I'll bet he's even more of a hardcase now."

Tex's mien softened. "No doubt he's one tough hombre, but he'll do what it takes to get the job done, Che."

"I hope so, sir. I'm just not sure there will be much of a city left after he's through with it."

5. STREET LEVEL

Foster looked Dredd up and down as they walked through the halls of Justice Central. The Mega-City Judge spoke without facing him. "Something on your mind?"

The Brit-Citter hesitated for a moment. "It's not important. I just... Well, I just thought you'd be taller."

Rodriguez bit his lip to stifle a chuckle.

Dredd ignored the comment. "You were posted here on secondment?"

Foster nodded. "Yeah and that Simba fella too. You know the drill, Luna-1's an international zone so forty per cent of the Judge force comes from treaty state members."

"So why'd you get sent up, huh?" Rodriguez asked. "Who did you sneck off to get a Moon posting?"

Dredd saw Foster colour slightly. The SouthAm Judge had hit a nerve. "There's a lot of opportunity for Diplo-Div work in space, what with all the alien traffic and so on. On top of that, there's coppers from a dozen countries up here and you need to know who's who and what's what."

Dredd mused on his first impression of the Brit-Judge and played a hunch. "International cooperation. It's a different ballgame to the street."

"No arguments there," Foster gave a nod. "Some days I wish I was back in the Birmingham Wastes on traffic patrol."

His suspicions were confirmed; he didn't have to read Foster's file to figure out what the Brit-Judge wasn't saying. A Street Judge, somewhere along the line Foster had been shuttled off Earth for some sort of infraction and left to cool his heels in orbit. Dredd was sure that he would find a similar situation with J'aele if he dug deep enough into the Simba City Tek-Judge's background. The other nations had promised Hershey that Dredd would get the best officers for the job, but now it was becoming increasingly clear that his taskforce was made up of whomever they wanted out of the way. He filed this information away for later consideration as they approached the quartermaster's stores.

Rodriguez's foot dragged and he stumbled, swearing. "Keep up," Dredd said.

The SouthAm Judge sneered and fiddled with a control on his ankle. "Okay, okay. It's these damn gravity boots we gotta wear. I haven't had to calibrate a pair of these since I got off this dull piece of rock." Like all of Luna-1's law force, the Judges had donned g-boots prior to their arrival on the Moon. The modified footgear enabled the wearers to walk as if they were in an Earth-normal gravity field, even in places where municipal grav-generators did not operate.

A spindly mechanoid with four arms rolled over to Dredd on clanking caterpillar tracks. The robot was an old Moderna Systems Model Eight, the same kind that Mega-City One had retired years ago after a spate of programming errors. It was another sign of the poor state of Luna-1's Justice Department.

"Gentlemen. Follow me to ordnance, please."

The machine rumbled over to a firing range, where belts and holsters were piled next to a rack of flat, compact handguns. "As you know," the robot continued, "projectile weapons rated at grade three and above are illegal on the Moon except with Justice Department special approval waivers. For the duration of your stay, you'll each be equipped with a Glock-Weptek S-54 STUP-gun firearm."

Rodriguez glanced at Foster. "You got one of these already?"

The Brit-Judge nodded and drew his sidearm. "You never used a beam pistol before? They're energy weapons. They shoot streams of highly-charged particles in microsecond pulses."

"STUP stands for Scalar-Tesla Uniform Pulse," droned the droid. "Palm print reader and self-destruct charge, trigger mechanism and safety catches all match those of a standard Mark 11 Lawgiver. Battery magazines will auto-recharge while the guns are holstered."

Dredd and Rodriguez both took a gun and the weapons beeped softly to signify that they were now locked for their use only.

Foster took up a position on the range. "Let me show you how these things work." He flicked a thumb-dial. "They've got five levels of intensity, from a low-grade stun right up to a full power blast, manual or voice-active select. Hit someone with a level one shot and you'll make 'em puke or pass out. Go up to a five and–"

Foster squeezed the trigger plate and the gun bucked in his hand, the recoil washing back from the crackle of superheated air as the pulse flashed into the target dummy. The plasti-flesh body shape blew apart like an overripe fruit. "Well, you get the picture."

Rodriguez gave the gun a cautious once-over. "Eh, give me my pistola rata any day. These space toys look like something from a sci-fi vid-slug."

Dredd said nothing and brought up his STUP-gun. The air snapped and hissed as he let off four precise shots from a modified Weaver stance.

"Four discharges registered. All range targets hit, ninety-four per cent critical strike percentage," intoned the robot.

"Hmm." Dredd considered the pistol for a second and then holstered it. "Seems okay to me."

"Show-off." Rodriguez rapped on the droid's carapace. "So, tin-head, where do we go to get our rides, huh? Come on, speedo. I feel naked without my wheels."

"The bike park is over here," Foster indicated the direction of the flyer bay with a nod. "Come with me."

With the robot trailing behind them, Dredd and Rodriguez followed Foster into an open atrium halfway up the building. Ranks of parked air-cars painted in pursuit colour schemes and modified low-gravity H-wagons sat next to hover-bikes in varying states of disassembly.

"Judge-Marshal Tex has assigned a Krait 3000 model zipper bike for your personal usage, Judge Dredd," said the quartermaster droid, as it worked a set of lift controls. From a garage level one floor below them, a launch cradle rose up with a sleek gunmetal and silver-blue speeder resting upon it.

"Ooh, hello baby," Rodriguez breathed, admiring the machine. "That is a fine piece of engineering. Too good for Dredd, I think. She needs a more caring rider, like me, maybe."

The Krait was an agile skybike, armed with its own array of STUP-cannons and a suite of full-spectrum sensors in addition to all the standard features of a Judge's motorcycle. While the Earth-style wheeled Lawmasters were sometimes employed in Luna-1, it was more typical to see the retrojet-powered zipper bikes cutting back and forth across the lunar skyline.

Dredd ran a gloved hand over the fuselage. He'd ridden one of these shark-like flyers before, on a previous mission to the Moon. "Just this one?"

"Affirmative." the robot clicked. "The rest of your taskforce has been assigned the standard Skymaster."

"The Krait bikes are few and far between these days," Foster broke in. "They used to be the front-line vehicle for Street Judges up here, but they've dwindled. Not enough replacement parts, you see? There's barely a tenth of the original number still airworthy."

"Ugh, so what do we get?" Rodriguez asked.

Foster gestured to another model of zipper bike nearby. The Skymasters were built around the ground-based Mark III Lawmaster's chassis, but replacing the tyres and power plant with a Teka-Tek anti-grav drive and thruster grid. A frown creased Rodriguez's face. "The ladies, they are not going to be impressed by a brute machine like this."

"You can always walk," Dredd snapped.

"We're lucky to get these," said Foster, mounting his bike. "The way things are going, by the end of the year the department will be back to using ground bikes."

"So where the drokk does all the funding from the Triumvirate go?" Irritation rose in Dredd's tone.

Foster gave a weary shrug. "Look around, Dredd. It ain't going here."

The trio of Judges circled up and out of the launch bay, climbing to the upper landing pads. Dredd saw a bulky L-Wagon lift off as they passed and the larger flyer moved up behind them to follow their three-bike "V" formation. In the lead, Dredd scanned the horizon as the city blurred by beneath him. The Krait responded smoothly, cutting through the air like a blade.

"Dredd, this is Kontarsky. Switch to secure channel, please." The Sov-Blocker's voice issued from Dredd's helmet radio speaker. He toggled the control on the zipper bike's dashboard.

"Dredd, responding. What's so important that you need to talk to me without the rest of the team hearing?"

"I am merely following command protocol. And I have also made an observation."

"Let's hear it."

"I was examining the incident reports and after-action arrest transcripts from the Kepler riots. Many of the survivors claimed that they felt compelled to fight, or that an irrational rage or intense fear seized them. I suspect there might have been some sort of psychoactive agent at work—"

"When does a rioter ever want to take responsibility for what they've done? Besides, the food, the air and the water were the first things that Tex's people checked," Dredd snapped. "Read the file, Kontarsky. Ever since East-Meg One tried that trick with the Block Mania virus, we've been ready for it! If any chemical or biological factor was there, we'd know it."

The Sov-Judge's voice went tight with annoyance. "I am well aware of that, Judge Dredd. But perhaps it could have been something else. A psionic effect—"

"Luna Psi Division hasn't exactly been asleep over the past six months. A psyker strong enough to influence a few hundred thousand people wouldn't stay hidden from them for long." Dredd spotted the zipstrip tunnel to Kepler Dome and brought the skybike on to a new heading. "I want facts, Kontarsky, not speculations."

He switched back to the general radio channel, leaving the young Russian to seethe. "All units, form up, we're going down on the deck."

When they reached the skedway off-ramp to Kepler, the Judges were forced to halt in front of a massive set of airlock doors. The dome had been closed off completely from the rest of the Luna-1 network after the street fighting had threatened to spill over into the city proper and days later the place was still sealed, considered a giant crime scene. A Luna Judge at the gate control station waved Dredd over to him.

"You understand the dome has still to be re-certified after the riots?" he asked. "When things came apart in there, we had to evacuate and lock it down. There could still be booby-traps inside, maybe even a few stragglers still dug in."

"We could go in wearing environment suits," offered J'aele.

"If you come across a sniper or trip a frag mine in there, all an e-suit is going to do is slow you down." Dredd shook his head: "No, we'll take it slow and by the numbers. Open it up."

With a grinding hiss of hydraulics, the saw-toothed airlock doors yawned open, parting like the steel mandibles of some huge predatory insect. A puff of displaced air whistled out in a breeze and the scents carried on it sent alarm bells sounding in Dredd's mind. The acrid smell of smoke and cordite, melted plastic and the unmistakable odour of old, dried blood.

Just beyond the entranceway he saw the far end of the plaza outside the abandoned Kepler precinct house. The Justice Department building was a gutted ruin, black and skeletal. "Overwatch formation," Dredd called out. "Follow me."

The convoy of anti-grav vehicles kept low to the ground as it snaked across the lunacrete roadway, drifting up and over makeshift barricades and the shallow craters made by crude firebombs. "Be ready on your respirators, just in case," ordered Dredd. "Connect to your belt-pack oxy supply the instant you suspect any air leaks." If the dome did suffer a sudden breach, at least the Judges would be able to survive for a few minutes until rescue units could arrive. Dredd had felt the icy kiss of raw vacuum on his skin before and it wasn't an experience he wanted to repeat.

The Mega-City Judge studied the silent wreckage carefully, in his mind's eye reconstructing the confrontation that had taken place, figuring out what had happened when. Here was the burnt-out frame of a bot-cab, probably used as a ram to breach the precinct barricade.

There were the circular impact marks typical of a close-range hit from a sonic disruptor rifle. Across the plaza, the stain of a broad heat scorch was visible, one that could have been from a hand flamer or a rocket-propelled grenade.

Foster cursed softly under his breath. "I saw the other incident sites before this one, but I had no idea this one was so bad... Dredd, you ever seen anything like it before?"

"Too many times." Something about the whole scene didn't sit right with Dredd and it bothered him. He brought the Krait to a halt and held up a hand. "Foster, Rodriguez, dismount. We'll check out this zone. Kontarsky, you and J'aele set up the Tek-station at the crossped to the west and get to work on figuring out where this all started."

The Sov-Judge hesitated. "I should accompany you–"

"The crossped," Dredd repeated. "Get going."

Kontarsky gave him a grudging nod and returned to the L-Wagon. As she walked out of earshot, she began speaking into a recorder rod in low, urgent Russian.

"If I didn't know better, I'd say the Sov there was more interested in you than she is in the job," Foster noted.

"I'm sure it's purely professional," noted Dredd. "Spread out. Look for anything out of the ordinary."

Rodriguez put his hands on his hips. "That's it? We just came out here for a look around? I can think of better uses of our time."

Dredd frowned. "It's called Judge work, Rodriguez. Perhaps you've heard of it?"

The Pan Andes Judge muttered something rude under his breath and set to work with a scanalyser. Foster took the central quadrant of the plaza and Dredd walked the length of the perimeter, taking it all in. Four decades of experience on the street had granted the lawman an almost uncanny sense for a crime scene, the ability to at once see the big picture and to also focus in on small, seemingly insignificant details. With grim determination, Dredd circled the ruins from the street fighting. He caught sight of Kontarsky observing him from the crossped, the red of her rad-cloak peering through the broken teeth of a fractured building foundation. An abrupt jab of memory passed through Dredd's mind. The last time he had faced a Sov-Judge wandering through ruined city streets, they had been shooting at one another.

Rodriguez stood up and beckoned him over. As Dredd approached, he noticed a change in the SouthAm Judge's body language. "I found something, I think." He was muted now, more watchful. "When Che was briefing us he had information up on the screen about weapons they had captured from the survivors?"

"Yes, nothing conclusive though. Everything they found was generic stuff, low-grade knock-offs without manufacturer's marks or serial numbers."

"Sí, just your typical gangbanger spit guns. But look here." He indicated a low wall discoloured with smoke. "See anything familiar?"

Dredd bent down for a closer examination. Embedded in the grey lunar brickwork was a cluster of bright silver needles, each as long as his finger. "Standard pattern dispersal," he noted, glancing over his shoulder. "Probably fired from close range. I'd say the shooter was one or two metres away." With care, Dredd pulled a handful of the needler rounds out and rolled them in his palm.

"Those are from a Volokov, right?" Rodriguez asked. "Like the baby needler gun that the chica was packing?"

Dredd nodded. He could just about read the telltale rifling pattern on the shards that was common to the Sov-made weapons. "East-Meggers don't sell a lot of these on the open market. Could be war surplus from the '04 conflict."

Rodriguez looked in Kontarsky's direction. "You think, maybe–" he began in a low voice.

"You can secure that line of questioning right now," Dredd interrupted. "We need facts, not speculation," he said, repeating what he'd told the woman on the flight in. The Judge's analytical mind was turning the small shred of evidence over and over in his mind, making connections, forming a hypothesis.

"Got something?" said Foster as he come closer to them. Dredd showed him the spent needler rounds. "That tracks with what I've been seeing," the Brit-Judge noted. "Most of the weapons that the rioters employed could have been made on the Moon back in the old days, but here and there I'm seeing anomalies." He nodded towards a torched vuphone booth. "Heat diffusion traces on the glasseen over there matches the outputs from a Flesh-Blaster. These are both weapon signatures that look like off-world makes."

Rodriguez rubbed his chin. "Off-world? You mean from Earth, right?"

Foster nodded. "Guns like those Volokov needlers are very rare up here. You'd have to smuggle them in if you wanted one."

Dredd and Rodriguez exchanged a silent look.

"I just can't figure out where they got 'em," Foster continued. "We got no leads from the perps we pulled in. It's like these weapons were just lying around, ready for them to use."

Dredd secured the needle rounds in a belt pouch and strode back towards his bike. "If the guns were brought in from outside Luna-1, we've got a new factor to consider. Somebody spent the rocket fuel and the time to bring these weapons up the gravity well, which means there's gotta be more to this than just arming some cits for a pointless bloodbath." He paused. "Someone in Luna-City knows where these weapons came from."

"So we have to think about who we have to squeeze to get some results," Foster added. "Gun control's got pretty strict since the blowout in the Velikovsky botanical gardens dome, when you were here last. Most of the creeps who smuggle stuff up the well concentrate on low mass, high return products like drugs or Stookie glands. I doubt any of the usual suspects will cop to gun-running."

Dredd considered this for a moment. "Then maybe we need to concentrate on some of the old school Luna perps. And I think I know where to start looking."

"You got a lead you're not telling us about?" said Rodriguez.

"Just a feeling. You stay here and finish up. I'll meet you back at Justice Central at the end of the shift." Dredd gunned the Krait 3000's anti-grav motor and the skybike roared away, back towards the airlock.

"Huh," said Rodriguez. "He says he wants facts not speculation, then off he goes on a hunch. What do you make of that?"

Foster gave a wry smile. "He's Judge Dredd, pal. You know his record – if he says he's got an inkling on something, you can bet cold, hard credits it'll be on the ball."

Down by the crossped, Kontarsky looked up to see Dredd's zipper bike vanish into the zipstrip tunnel. She chewed her lip, then drew out her recorder and spoke into it once more.

Dredd held the throttle at cruising speed for a few minutes as he vectored down the tubeway back towards the central dome. He kept a close eye on his rearview scanner, watching for any sign of pursuit. He half-expected to glimpse Kontarsky trailing him on her Skymaster, but the Sov-Judge did not seem to be following him. That's the problem with fielding an international team, Dredd told himself, there's always the chance that people will put loyalty to their flag before justice.

It didn't take a genius to realise that Kontarsky was relaying every little decision that Dredd made back to the Sov-Block's diplomatic courier in orbit and the East-Meg Diktatorat on Earth. It stood to reason that there were probably dozens of covert agents in the pay of the Sov's Klandestine Ops Directorate on Luna-1, even if Kontarsky wasn't one of them. Certainly, Mega-City One had its share of spies in the Moon colony and so did all the other major nation states.

Luna-1 was an international zone and that meant that every city on Earth had some kind of presence here, all of them watching one another, jockeying for position and playing political mind games. The lawman sneered at the thought of becoming caught up in this sort of intrigue. He wasn't a man for shady schemes or diplomatic double-talk. Dredd preferred a straight, stand-up fight to back-alley dealings and secret treaties. He was the blunt instrument of justice and he liked it just fine that way.

When Dredd was certain he wasn't being tailed, he opened up the Krait's throttles to maximum and pushed the flyer to the redline, weaving between heavy aerotrucks, darting through the traffic like a barracuda through a pod of whales. The East-Meg Judge had been constantly observing Dredd from the moment he'd arrived at Union Station, no doubt even from before they had met. He hadn't expected anything less – after all, he was the man who'd wiped out millions of her fellow Sov-Blockers with the push of a single button – but the discovery of the needle rounds threatened to shift the balance of his evaluation of Kontarsky. If the Sovs had some kind of connection to the Kepler Dome incident, then her position on the taskforce suddenly had a whole new dimension to it. Maybe all that wide-eyed rookie stuff was just a front. He even considered for a moment that Rodriguez might have planted the needler rounds to implicate the Sov-Judge, but then what would the Pan Andes Conurb have to gain by doing that? Besides, Foster had backed up the SouthAm Judge's discovery with one of his own and the idea of the Brits being in league with the Banana City boys was verging on the ridiculous, given current international tensions between them.

Dredd blew out a breath. All this second-guessing was distracting him from the real investigation at hand. The only course of action that presented itself was to keep himself at the forefront of things until he could be sure where the loyalties of the other Judges lay. Despite the professionalism – or lack of it, in the case of Rodriguez – shown by each of the foreign officers, the five of them were circling each other like wary tigers, watching one another for signs of weakness or malfeasance. It was up to Dredd to play the role of the pack alpha, to pull them into line, weed out any weak links and maintain discipline. Anything less and the group would fall apart before they could make any progress.

At the Santini flyover, Dredd took a sharp turn to starboard and throttled down the Krait, settling into a shallow cruise altitude over the quadrant formed by the edges of Verne Avenue and the Odyssey Loop. The locals called this place the Pink Crater and since the very first days of Luna-1's incorporation, it had served as the city's red light district where colonists could go to let off a little steam. The more relaxed laws set in place during the Moon's wild frontier heyday still granted this portion of the dome a little more freedom than other more upmarket parts of town, with licensed casinos on the edges of the zone feeding local pleasure-seekers and eager tourists alike into the null-grav nude bars, virtu-porn arcades and Lust-O-Mats. Mega-City One had similar districts, but the Justice Department kept them strictly regulated with regular crime sweeps on an almost daily basis.

The open immorality of the Pink Crater set the Judge's teeth on edge. It was in the interests of the businesses in the area to keep any serious crime off the streets, but he was willing to bet that untold numbers of lawbreakers and infractions were passing by beneath him right now, if only he could crack the place open to see them. He orbited around a gaggle of tethered floater boudoirs above the Satellite of Love massage parlour and located the building he was looking for, a fetish club at the rough end of the loop called the Harsh Mistress.

Dredd set the bike to hover mode and dropped down on to the roof, pausing to check the setting on his STUP-gun.

The holographic image of the club's signature female clad in black leather bondage gear leered over the rooftop, brandishing a cat-o'-nine-tails and licking her lips. "Have you been bad?" the holo demanded of the revellers down on the street. "The harsh mistress knows you have! Come inside and get the punishment you deserve!"

Dredd gave a grim smile. "You have no idea how right you are," he told the sign.

6. VACUUM PACKED

Judge Dredd's boot made short work of the lock on the access hatch and he descended into the sweaty, ill-lit interior of the Harsh Mistress, the low-light image intensifier lenses in his helmet rendering the corridors of the club in green-tinted shades. Rastabilly skank music was currently enjoying a revival on the lunar cabaret scene and the grinding thuds of a particularly loud track's bassline resonated through the building. Dredd was thankful for the audio processing circuits in his headgear, which flattened the atonal pop music into a dull background hiss while still picking out the more important sounds of movement and activity. Correctly tuned, a Judge's helmet sensors could hear the sound of a spit gun being cocked amid the roar of a smashball stadium crowd.

A Bouncer-Mek met him halfway down the stairwell to the roof and grated out a stock warning in a metallic voice. "Your name's not down, you're not coming in. Hop it, you spugger!"

Dredd's reply was to fire a point-blank stun blast from his STUP-gun into the robot's braincase and it rocked back, spitting sparks.

"Awwk!" The pulse pistol worked just as well on mechanoids as it did on flesh-and-blood perps. The droid dropped to the floor in a clanking heap and lay there, twitching.

The Judge paused at the foot of the stairs to get his bearings. He was standing on a broad balcony that circled a packed dance floor below, where Luna-cits in various states of undress wrestled with things that could have been alien life forms or maybe just other people in bizarre fetish costumes. He shook his head and resisted the urge to arrest the lot of them. Off the balcony there were doors leading to private suites, soundproofed rooms where VIP club members could "entertain" or conduct clandestine trysts.

Dredd studied them carefully. The design of the club had been altered since he'd been here last and that had been a long time ago, with a force of two dozen Luna Judges and a fistful of warrants behind him. One of Tex's men at the time, Judge-Marshal Chico, had brought a tip-off to Dredd's attention and they had uncovered a smuggling ring bringing black market laser rifles up from Sino-City One. Two Judges had died in a firefight at the docks when they ambushed that cargo and Dredd had personally led the raid on the Harsh Mistress to arrest the man behind the deal, the night-club's owner-manager, Vik Umbra. He was a particularly odious perp, as Dredd recalled, with illicit tastes and desires that even the moderate laws of Luna-1's red light district paled at. If anyone could be sure to know something about the weapons from Kepler Dome, it would be him.

Dredd grabbed the arm of a woman who passed him. Her hair was a shock of bright electric blue and she wore a shiny black outfit of plasti-wrap, her neck covered by a choker adorned with rings.

"Hey, downshift, chummer!" she wailed, pushing at him. "What's your malfunction?"

"I'm looking for Vik Umbra. Where is he?"

"Vik?" she blinked. "He's in his g-room, wave me? You looking to spell with him? You a gravity-fun boy-boy guy?" She rubbed her hand over his uniform. "Oooh, deedee. This is real leather, wave? You gotta primo costume."

Dredd hissed in her ear. "It's not a costume, wave?"

"A real Judge?" her lip quivered. "I done nothin'!" The girl glanced at his badge and went pale. "Dredd? Dredd!"

Sometimes having his reputation precede him made getting what Dredd wanted a whole lot easier. "Show me where Vik is," he demanded and the blue-haired girl eagerly nodded her assent, ready to do anything to avoid time in the cubes herself.

She led him to an opulent room set back from the others and opened the door. Inside was an ornate, over-decorated antechamber where two human bodyguards were standing watch over a handful of frightened young juves, each chained to a spiked leash. The guards were quick and their hands were already diving for the triggers of their stump guns as he entered. Dredd wasted no time and fired two pulses into the meat-heads, sending them sprawling. Sorting through their pockets, he handed the girl the keys to the leash and nodded at the teenagers. "You. Take 'em and get lost."

The girl did what he asked and Dredd looked around, finding and smashing an alarm keypad. It wouldn't do for Umbra to call for help before they had had their discussion. The Judge found a used injector that reeked of Stookie and a copious supply of Umpty Candy on a side table, more than enough to put the club owner behind bars for another long stretch.

He shouldered open the next door and found himself in a bi-gravity chamber.

Close to the doorway where Dredd stood, the g-plates in the floor simulated an Earth-normal one gee environment, but further in across a discreet line of yellow tiles, the room was completely weightless. The sole occupant was a pallid ball of skin at least six times the size of the Judge, a naked, corpulent pinkish mass floating just within reach of the padded walls. Sex toys, sense-dep masks and other less identifiable objects drifted around the huge fatty in a lazy shoal. "Has someone brought me a new playmate?" said a breathy voice. "My last one broke." The fleshy sphere of a man rotated slightly and presently a head appeared, peering owlishly at the Judge from out of a dozen rolls of neck-flab.

"Hello, Vik," Dredd sneered. "Long time no see. Have you lost weight?"

"Rot you, Dredd!" The fatty trembled. "I gained one hundred and thirty-six kilograms!"

"My mistake."

"I heard you'd come back to the Moon," Umbra said, spittle flying from his lips in little spheres. "Well, you can liposuck me, you drokker! I'm legit now! You got nothing on me!"

"Really? What about the youth drugs and addictive candy I found in here? I'm sure there will be more if I look for it."

"Not mine!" Umbra screeched, flailing at an inert alarm switch. "You can't prove it's mine!"

Dredd spotted a control panel on the wall and turned a dial on it. The effect of the gravity nullifier on Vik's side of the room began to decrease and by centimetres the bulbous man-shape slowly settled to the floor. "One-sixth gee has been good to you, Vik. I bet you couldn't even walk under your own weight on Earth." Umbra pooled on the tiles in a flushed pile of adipose meat.

He gave a weak cough as the dial passed the two gee marker. "Look, Dredd, stop it! My heart will pop like a balloon if you keep turning that up! What do you want with me?"

"I put you away for fifteen for dealing in illegal weapons back in '99, Vik. But even if you're not in the gun trade any more, I figure you still know who's bringing them into Luna-1."

"Sneck off, Dredd! All my gunrunning days are over. Like I told you, I'm out of it."

The dial turned to up three gravities. "I'm sorry, I didn't catch that."

"Please!" Vik spat out bloody drool. "My heart can't take it!"

"Then give me a name, or else they'll have to use a spatula to scrape you into a coffin." Dredd thought he could hear the sound of ribs cracking.

"You're crazy if you think I'll give you anything, helmet-head! I withered away in prison thanks to you, living on just nine meals a day! I'll die first!"

Dredd tap-tapped his finger on the gravity dial. "You sure about that?"

Vik's bluster wavered a little. "If I roll over for you, Dredd, I'll be a corpse before the next earthrise. These guys, they're connected."

"So you *do* know something," Dredd nodded to himself. His guess about Umbra still being in the smuggler's loop had proven right. "You've got a choice, Vik. You have to ask yourself who you're more afraid of. Me or them?"

After a few wheezing breaths, Umbra gave a wobbly nod. "All right, drokk you. Let me up and I'll talk."

Dredd dialled back the gravity to lunar normal, enough to keep the fatty down on the ground. "Spit it out, creep."

"You know about the rebel miners on Ganymede, right?"

A nod. "Sure. It was a Sov colony. They took the place over."

"There was a big cargo of weapons on the way out to them about three months back, so I heard. Nothing to do with me, part of some deal with the Diamante cartel in the Med Free States fronting for the Siberian Mafia." Dredd knew the name; the cartel were pirates and middlemen for a dozen larger criminal groups worldwide and the Siberian connection would have explained the Sov-issue guns like the Volokov needlers and Beria flesh blasters. "But they never made it there. Most folks figured that the load got caught by the East-Meg Judges, but one of my girls heard different from a, uh, client."

"Someone from the cartel?"

"Nah, this guy worked for M-Haul. They do interplanetary freight and salvage. He let slip that his crew intercepted the cartel ship. They cut up the freighter for scrap and kept the weapons."

"A name," Dredd growled. "Give me a name."

"Sure, sure. Yud Swindo, that was the guy. But don't bother looking for him, he's dead. A day after he spilled his guts, he was found out on the Sea of Vapours without an e-suit and the girl he blabbed to got done the same way too. Pretty soon after that, M-Haul lost all four of its ships in a tragic docking accident, if you get my drift."

Dredd shook his head and turned up the gravity again. "You're spinning me a line, Vik. Your story is so full of holes I could drive a roadliner through it!"

Umbra coughed and choked. "No, spug it! You didn't let me finish! When M-Haul went down, all their assets, including the storage dome where they kept their salvage, got bought out cheap by their major shareholder, see."

"Which was who?"

"Another old face from the past, Dredd. The MoonieCorp company got it all. The same business that used to be run by CW Moonie, the famous lunar explorer. Until you put him in prison for life, of course."

"Moonie?" Dredd's brow furrowed. "But Moonie Enterprises was sold off when he was convicted. He lost control over all his holdings. It's an independent entity now."

"Yeah," Umbra gurgled sarcastically. "Sure it is." He wheezed in a breath. "So, I did what you asked, I talked. Now, how are you gonna keep me safe from these guys? I don't wanna end up freeze-dried out in the Oxygen Desert."

Dredd tapped the chin guard on his helmet and a wire-thin microphone pickup extended to his mouth. "Don't worry, Vik. Where you're going, there's plenty of bars on the windows to keep people out." He glanced around the room. "You're under arrest for multiple violations of Code Twenty, contraband statutes. Ten years in the iso-cubes."

Umbra began to thrash around on the floor in a desperate attempt to get up, his face flushing red, spitting and swearing at the Mega-City Judge.

"Dredd to control. Catch wagon required at the Harsh Mistress nightclub, Odyssey Loop." He paused, sizing up Umbra's obese form. "Better make sure you reinforce the hull first and bring a couple of anti-grav jacks."

It took another hour and a half for the Luna Judiciary to get Vik Umbra out of the building and into a vehicle big enough to carry him. In the end, Dredd had been forced to commandeer a couple of demolition meks from a construction yard off Buzz Aldrin Street to laser a hole in the nightclub's wall and remove the fatty with crane grabs. As he supervised the arrest, the Judge considered the chubby man's words. CW Moonie – it was a name he hadn't heard in years, but the Moonie bust had been the signature event of Dredd's tenure as Luna-1 Judge-Marshal.

Early in 2100, a couple of months after beginning his tour as the colony's Chief Judge, investigations into attempts on Dredd's life had led him to suspect the Moon's best known but most reclusive millionaire was intent on having him killed. Almost at the cost of his own life, the Judge had pursued and arrested the crime lord and incarcerated Moonie in the forbidding Farside Penitentiary, a prison dome on the lunar dark side. If Moonie had maintained some sort of connection to his old powerbase while he was in jail, he could be a valid suspect.

At last, Umbra's protesting form was inside the catch wagon and the vehicle's suspension squealed under the weight. Dredd waved them off and mounted his zipper bike, rising back into the air. It was just as likely that Umbra was trying to shift suspicion off himself as it was that an ageing criminal locked in a lunacrete vault was behind the Kepler Dome weapons, but Dredd couldn't afford to discount anything at this stage. He angled the bike at the distant shape of Justice Central and opened up the throttle. On the inner surface of the dome above him, Luna-1's solar reflectors folded closed, marking the start of the city's night-cycle.

The rest of the taskforce was waiting on one of the upper levels of the Luna Grand Hall of Justice, in a ready room where Judges going on or off shift could grab a quick cup of synthi-caff or a bite to eat. Windows around the edge of the room showed the glowing vista of the city as streetlights and holo-signs winked on. The sight momentarily captured Kontarsky and she lost a few seconds staring at it.

She caught Tek-Judge J'aele's eye and the African's face split in a smile. "It's really a sight, isn't it?" The Simba City Judge's voice was rich and deep. "I've been here for quite a while and I still find myself drifting off at the windows."

Kontarsky fought down a surge of discomfiture. "I was just observing."

J'aele's smile widened. "You don't have to impress me, Kontarsky. I'm not Dredd. I won't hold it against you if you behave like a human being now and then."

"I'm not trying to impress anybody," she said, a little more quickly than she'd have liked. "I'm just doing my duty."

The Tek-Judge let the sharp words roll off him. "Of course," he allowed.

Kontarsky's gaze dropped to the datapad in her hands. "Your report on the Kepler crime scene is very thorough. I don't think there's anything else I can add to it."

"If I may ask, are you not concerned by the evidence of Sov-made weapons at the incident site? Such a factor may reflect personally on your involvement in the taskforce."

He's testing me, she realised. "That information has no bearing on my role as deputy commander," she said in a practiced, clipped tone. "Besides, the larger percentage of the weapons were of NorthAm or Nu-Taiwanese manufacture."

J'aele was going to press the point, but a sharp expletive from across the room distracted them both. Rodriguez was close to the windows, hands clenching and unclenching at his hips, his body set and tense. "Madre de dios! Will you look at this snecking stomm!"

For a moment, Kontarsky couldn't understand what Rodriguez was talking about, until part of the city view outside the window moved – and she realised she was looking at a massive ad-blimp cruising over the Armstrong Hub Plaza. She and J'aele and a few other off-duty Judges, crossed over to get a better look.

The blimp was a big one, the size of a small sky-cruiser, shaped like an enormous cowrie shell with huge billboard screens sprouting from it on every side. Laser projectors cut slogans into the night air with neon-bright flickers and loudspeakers broadcast sales messages in a dozen languages; or at least, that was what the ad-blimp was supposed to be doing. The screens and holograms were flickering and blinking in and out of focus, as if something inside the craft was fooling around with the tuning.

"It's malfunctioning," said Foster.

"Yeah!" Rodriguez snapped angrily. "That's one word for it!" Even as he spoke, the blimp's display of garish off-world colony recruitment commercials reappeared for a few seconds, only to be suddenly replaced by a grinning cartoon figure.

"Kiss kiss, hi hi from Moon-U!" it squeaked, the synthesised voice carrying for dozens of blocks. "They try 2 stop me but they can't silence Moon-U!"

"Hackers," said J'aele with a grimace. "They're like a plague of rats. Every time we plug a hole in the network, they find another one." He plucked a hand computer from his pocket and worked at it. "These Moon-U people are the worst yet."

Scenes from the Kepler Dome riot – including images that Kontarsky knew were supposedly secure footage from Justice Department spy cameras – were running over the screens now. Far below, traffic was coming to a halt and pedestrians were craning their necks up to see what the giggling cartoon had to tell them. Moon-U gave them all a comical wink and beamed. "Here's what the Judges don't want U 2 know! It's not enough that they wanna shut us all down down down!" The caricature put a finger to its lips in an exaggerated gesture of conspiracy. "Now they gotta secret death squad on the streets – and they're coming for U!"

"Death squad?" said Foster, "What is this drivel?"

"Where's the anti-aircraft cannons?" Rodriguez said, becoming increasingly agitated. "Shoot the drokker down!"

"Over the most heavily populated area of the city?" J'aele retorted.

Moon-U produced a picture-in-picture and held it up. It was all Kontarsky could do to stop her jaw dropping open in shock as she recognised the faces in the image: it was her and Rodriguez, but slightly distorted and behind them were J'aele and Foster. The warped screen-Judges were feral and hateful-looking, weapons drawn with a blood-hungry cast to them. As she watched, the screen showed the four of them dashing down a corridor in the starport, gunning down citizens left and right with vicious abandon. The fake Foster ignored the dying pleas of an old woman and shot her squarely between the eyes; the screen J'aele produced a Masai war spear from out of nowhere and ran three men through with it, skewering them like a shish kebab.

Under other circumstances, the affable Simba City Judge might have found the ridiculous image amusing, but here and now it was enough to make his stomach turn. Up on the billboard, an obviously drunk Rodriguez flailed around, randomly shooting explosive bullets into the crowds and the virtual Kontarsky looked straight into camera before firing her weapon into the lens. Static flickered, then Moon-U reappeared, shaking his head sadly and wearing a black armband. "That was taken earlier today, my friends! 2 many people were killed, just for speaking their minds! And U could B next, so we have 2 make them stop! Tell them, we want free elections! If Judge-Marshal Tex don't step down, then we'll fight 'em!"

The dart-like shapes of two L-Wagons flickered through the air towards the ad-blimp and Foster saw the glints of sucker guns as the crews fired boarding cables at the floater. He shook his head. "What is this rubbish? Nobody's going to be dumb enough to fall for some doctored video footage!"

"Don't be so sure," said Kontarsky, pointing to the street below. Already, there were citizens yelling and waving their fists at the Hall of Justice. "Propaganda can be a very powerful tool. It is most insidious."

"It's not just the ad-blimp," J'aele noted. "They're also broadcasting on a dozen public vid-channels and street-screens."

Rodriguez's face was crimson with anger. "It's gotta be silenced! They make me look like some slack-jawed idiota drunkard!"

"Oh! Oh!" cried Moon-U, big tears forming in his saucer eyes. "They're coming 2 shut me up up up!" The cartoon character loomed large and brushed at the edges of the screens, as if he were trying to flick away the Judges crawling over the blimp like bothersome insects. "U have to know B 4 it's 2 late! Dumb old Marshal Tex has called in the most vicious killer of all to lead the death squad! He's a menace 2 society!" And with those words, a massively over-muscled but uncannily accurate imitation of Judge Dredd appeared over Moon-U's shoulder, a Lawgiver the size of an artillery piece in his spiked-gloved hand. Hellish red light glowed under the eye-slits of the false Dredd's helmet.

Barbed wire was wrapped around his forearms and the Eagle of Justice on his shoulder pad was sickle-clawed and vicious. "It's Judge Dredd! The man who killed a million billion people... just because he could!" Moon-U screamed like a girl and cowered as the monstrous lawman turned the gun on him. The words *No Justice, Just Us* were clearly written on the barrel.

"Better Dredd than dead!" roared the screen Judge and with an ear-splitting roar, the gun spat white light that overwhelmed the screen.

From behind Kontarsky and the other Judges, a voice remarked, "That's not a bad likeness."

The real Dredd studied the blimp, now silent and dark, as it began to drift slowly towards the ground. Rodriguez took a step towards him, a balled fist smacking into his palm with an audible thwack.

"Dredd! How can you let that happen, man? These hacker pendejos make us a drokking laughing-stock!"

"Get a grip, Rodriguez," said Dredd. "There are worse things to have than a bruised ego."

"Says you!" the Pan Andes Judge retorted hotly. "This whole taskforce is turning into one big La Luna Loca!"

"You have a better idea of how to run things?" Every one of the other Judges caught the warning tone in Dredd's voice, but Rodriguez seemed oblivious to it.

"Sure! We tool up, not with these toy guns, but some proper pistolas and make a few examples of these punkamentes!"

"So your advice is to do exactly what those hackers are accusing us of?" Dredd's lips twisted in a sarcastic sneer. "I'll take it under advisement. In the meantime, get yourself down to the barracks and take an eight-hour stand down. I'll be generous and assume the poor judgement you just displayed is a side-effect of your space-lag."

Rodriguez pulled off his helmet and gave Dredd a hard look; then the ire seemed to drain right out of him and he gave a tight nod. "Sí, sí. You're right, Dredd. It just rattled me, seeing my face up there like that."

"That goes for all of you," Dredd addressed the other Judges. "All taskforce personnel are to have the mandatory eight. We'll pick up on the morning shift. J'aele, accompany me to the docks. The rest of you will check out the offices of M-Haul, over in Von Braun Territory. Dismissed."

All the team members nodded their assent and drifted away. Dredd caught a snatch of quiet conversation between Foster and J'aele as they passed him. "What was with Rodriguez back there? For a second there, I thought he might do something stupid."

The Tek-Judge answered with a shrug. "It must be that fiery Latino temperament I've heard of."

Kontarsky lingered a moment, before passing Dredd her datapad. "Here's the summary of the Kepler Dome investigation. I hope you'll find it in order."

"I'm sure I will."

"If I may ask, what is the connection you have found to this M-Haul group?"

Dredd paged through the files. "I'm not sure yet. You've got a good eye for detail. You'll know it when you see it."

The Sov-Judge accepted this without comment, then asked, "Anything else?"

He nodded. "Rodriguez. Watch him, Kontarsky. If he steps out of line once more, I want him locked in the cargo bay of the next transport Earthside, understand?"

"I concur."

"Good. Now, go take your down time. I want you at the top of your game tomorrow."

She turned to go, then hesitated. "What about you? Or is it true what my kadet instructors told me, that you don't need to rest and dream like other people?"

"I'll take my ten minutes in the sleep machine," Dredd told her gruffly, turning to direct all his attention to the pad. "I gave up dreaming a long time ago."

7. OFFICER DOWN

The perp ducked as he wove between the oil drums, a heavy calibre spit gun in his hand. As three more go-gangers in identical colours rushed up to join him, Dredd snapped a command out of the side of his mouth: "Level three."

The STUP-gun gave an answering beep and the Judge fired: a sun-bright flash of yellow crossed the distance to the perp and hit him in the chest. He fell back, the spit gun vanishing as it left his fingers. The ganger's pals weren't fazed and kept on coming. The insect buzz of low-velocity bullets sang past Dredd's helmet as they fired. Dredd mentally picked out a shooting order for the men and squeezed the trigger three times. The last man took a pulse blast in the face before the first ganger had even hit the ground. Their inert bodies lay there on the floor for a few seconds before they popped out of existence in a blink of glowing pixels.

"Four discharges registered," said the range monitor droid. "All targets hit, ninety-seven per cent critical strike percentage."

"Better," Dredd said aloud. The lightweight beam gun took a little getting used to, but after an hour or so on the firing range picking off holographic criminals, the Judge was almost up to the same level of proficiency he exhibited with the heavier ballistic Lawgiver. "Reset," he told the robot. "Let's try for ninety-nine per cent."

Even as he spoke, Dredd became aware of someone else in the room. "Always the perfectionist, huh Joe?" Judge-Marshal Tex walked out of the shadows and joined Dredd at the firing stalls. The Texan was carrying a heavy silver revolver and a box of bullets.

"Tex," Dredd greeted the other man with a nod. "It's late. What are you doing down here?"

Tex loaded his pistol. "I could ask you the same thing. Ah, you know what it's like, Joe. The older you get, the less you sleep. Sometimes I come down here in the middle of the night, take in a little practice."

Dredd nodded. "Good discipline."

"Keeps me sharp," added Tex. "These days, it's the only chance I get to field a weapon, what with me flyin' a desk." He cocked the gun with a well-oiled click. "Targets up!"

This time, eight perps emerged from the corners of the simulator chamber and the two Judges made short work of them, both Dredd and Tex placing careful shots into shoulders to disarm or heads and chests to kill. In as many seconds, the eight holo-targets were dispatched. "All targets hit. Judge Dredd registers ninety-eight per cent critical strike percentage, Judge-Marshal Tex registers ninety per cent critical strike percentage."

Tex swore softly. "Gettin' slow in my old age."

Dredd studied the gun. "That's not a standard firearm."

"Nope, this here's an heirloom." He handed the pistol to Dredd. "Been in my family for more than two hundred years. It's gotta micro-thin diamond layer sealed over the metal, so she'll stay in perfect order for two hundred more. A genuine Colt Model 1873." Tex nodded down-range. "Go ahead, try her out."

Dredd ordered up two targets and fanned the Colt's hammer, blasting the last two bullets out of the barrel. "Both targets hit. One hundred per cent critical strike percentage," reported the monitor.

Tex removed his hat and ran a hand through his greying hair. "Shoot, Dredd. You can even handle an antique like a pro! Y'all never cease to amaze me."

Dredd handed back the pistol. "It's a good weapon. It doesn't matter how old it is. It can still do the job."

The comment hung in the air between them for a long moment, before Dredd finally broke the silence. "What's on your mind, Tex?"

"You know, it's funny. Seein' you step off that shuttle, seein' you wear a Luna-1 star. It's like no time has passed since you were Judge-Marshal yourself... Then I realise it's been a quarter century and I'm feelin' every damn day of it."

Dredd did not speak, letting his old friend give voice to his thoughts.

"Why'd you do it, Joe? Why did you make me the sheriff of this god-forsaken rock? Back before you were marshal, we had a new Chief Judge every six months, but then you came in and the last thing you did before you went back to the Big Meg was make me the honcho, permanently."

"You know why, Tex. Luna-1 needed someone like you back then, someone who knew the city and could keep it in line. You were the right man for the post and you did it better than anyone before you. You've served longer than anyone since the days of Fargo."

For a moment, a glow of pride glinted in Tex's eyes. "Yeah. Damn me, but I love this airless piece o' dirt." He gave Dredd a troubled look. "But

I'm caught, Joe. I'm getting too old for this and my judgement's startin' to slip. I'm like this here piece," he hefted the Colt for emphasis. "Just a damn relic."

"You're a fine lawman. Your service to the city has been exemplary. You could step down and no one would deny you a peaceful retirement."

Tex snorted with dry laughter. "C'mon, Dredd. You and me, we're too much alike to believe that quittin' ever works. We got the law in our blood. And you can't exactly go take the Long Walk on the Moon. Beside, there's no one I could trust to do the job after me... Che's a good Judge, but he's too soft on the international zoners. Heck, Joe, you're about the only other man I'd trust with this city and I'd never ask you to give up Mega-City One."

Dredd accepted this with a nod. Although in manner and personality, the laconic Tex was poles apart from Dredd's rigid disposition, the Judge-Marshal was one of the few men he knew that shared the same unswerving dedication to justice as he did. "We'll get to the root of this," Dredd told him. "Count on it."

Tex replied with a weary nod. "It's not me I'm worried about, Joe, you understand? It's my city. If I turn my back, if I give those lawless punks out there even an inch more, then Luna-1's gonna go to hell in a gruddamn handbasket."

"Not while I'm here."

The Judge-Marshal forced a smile and turned to go. "Ah, listen to me! You must be thinkin' ol' Tex here is going soft in the brain! I reckon I'll get me some shut-eye."

"Good night, Chief Judge." Dredd watched his former partner amble away into the gloom, weighing his old friend's words with careful, taciturn consideration.

In the Silent Room, things were anything but quiet.

"Again I find myself forced to question the validity of this alliance!" snapped the bald man, addressing his tall superior officer but speaking as much to the old, frail man in the hoverchair and his thin, gangly assistant. "We entered into this partnership after receiving certain promises, one of which was the assurance that Luna-1's criminal fraternity would not be an issue–"

"I know what I said!" the old man said, his voice like nails down a blackboard. "I made good on that!"

"Did you?" retorted the balding man. "Did you really? A few of the, what do you call them, the 'little fish' are dealt with, but you let the big ones roam free to flap their mouths to the Judges? To Dredd?"

632   I Am The Law: The Judge Dredd Omnibus

The thin man blew out a breath. "That was an unfortunate development. We were not aware that the information had proceeded beyond the targets we had already eliminated."

"Unfortunate," repeated the tall man. Until now, he had been content to let his subordinate speak, but now he weighed in with an exact, cold tone. "That is an extremely weak description of something that may jeopardise our entire project, especially when we are at such a critical juncture." He steepled his fingers. "Tell me, my dear friends, what masterful and completely foolproof plan do you have to deal with this blunder?"

The thin man exchanged nervous glances with his aged boss. "Well, uh, we thought we would just, you know, have him killed."

"And how do you propose to do that?"

The old man in the hoverchair recovered a little of his poise. "Like I've told you time and time again, I have loyal men in every part of this colony. The Luna Grand Hall of Justice is no exception."

The tall man raised an eyebrow. "So, what then? Some crooked Judge will simply walk into Umbra's cell and scramble his brains with a pulse blast?"

"Nothing so theatrical," the frail figure shook its head very slightly. "Our friend Vik is a big eater, but I'm afraid he'll find something in the prison food that will disagree with him. Permanently."

The bald man drummed his fingers impatiently on the obsidian table. "But this is too little too late! It is closing the barn door after the cow has bolted!"

"Horse," growled the tall man in exasperation. "After the horse has bolted. If you're going to copy their idioms, at least get them right…"

"I apologise, sir. Cow, horse; perhaps pig would be a better euphemism for that bloated sack of fat Umbra. My point stands, however. For better or worse, we must assume that because of this oversight, Dredd has moved closer to uncovering our operation."

"Indeed," his superior added. "So how shall we ensure that he is thrown off the trail? We cannot afford to have Dredd or that decrepit cowboy Tex disrupting the scheme until the grand finale is ready."

The frail old man gave a thin, predatory smile, his teeth emerging from behind his pallid lips like a knife being drawn from a sheath. "Oh, I have something in mind. With the technology you provided as your part of the alliance, I think we can set an incident in motion that will tie up Dredd and his little posse until we're ready to deal with them." He touched a control on the arm of his chair and the face of one of Dredd's taskforce formed in the holo-tank. "I believe you have already begun to turn the screws on this one?"

The bald man's expression was one of disdain. "I find your terminology crude. The protocol is subtle and carefully controlled, far more so than any clumsy physical torture methods."

"You Teks, you're always preening yourselves over your damn hardware." The old man gave an airy wave. "The fact remains, we'll give this Judge a good, hard push and see what breaks. Dredd will be so busy scrambling over the fallout that he'll be looking the other way when we come for him."

The bald man was about to complain once again, but the tall man cut him off. "Yes, I concur. This approach makes good use of our resources. I had hoped to play this card a little later, but circumstances demand otherwise. We will proceed as you suggest."

"I'm so glad you approve," the frail man replied, with thinly veiled sarcasm.

"One more point," the bald man pressed on, ignoring the narrow-eyed look from his superior officer. "The installation of the secondary device, the reserve contingency against Judge-Marshal Tex... Was it successful?"

"Completely," said the thin man. "The unit sent a burst transmission of telemetry after activation earlier today. It should remain undetected until we need to use it, if at all."

The tall man rubbed his chin thoughtfully. "Perhaps we could deploy it sooner rather than later. We may be able to combine it with our colleague's plan to disrupt Dredd's investigation."

The old man's smile grew wider. "That," he grinned, "is the best idea you've had all day! Dredd must be made to pay for his misdeeds and for the life of me, I'm damned if I can't think of a better way to do it than this!" He laughed, a dry and dusty sound like the crackling of old, dead leaves and presently, his fellow conspirators joined him in harsh, ruthless amusement at their plans.

Even the polished sheen of Kontarsky's helmet couldn't disguise the tight sneer of disdain that creased her face as she strode purposefully across the main atrium of the Green Cheese Shoplex, Judge Foster at her side and a muted, wary Rodriguez a couple of steps behind. From all sides, hard sell holo-commercials and the braying voices of advert drones were bombarding her.

"Get Ugly! Get Sump! Because you're worth it!"

"Plasti-Flakes – taste the difference! Now with flavour!"

"Mom's Robot Oil! An Oil... for Robots!"

"Wear Clothes By Qwecko... Or else you're a loser!"

The sheer, unadulterated consumerism of it all sickened her to the very core of her Soviet soul. The Shoplex was a broad, thick disc, forty storeys tall, from the outside resembling a gigantic wheel of Swiss cheese; inside, it was a loud, offensive temple to the capitalist ideal of money. Luna-citizens swarmed around her, pushing and shoving, forcing themselves into stores and vendor cubicles to snap up products they didn't need. The pure greed of the place seemed to leak into the very air itself and it made Kontarsky's guts knot. "Look at this place," she growled. "These people are like pigs at a trough."

Foster shrugged. "It's just shopping. Some people gotta have a hobby and it's better this than murdering their neighbours."

Kontarsky shook her head. She should have known better than to expect a sympathetic viewpoint from the Brit-Cit Judge. His corrupt nation was just as bad as all the others. She flicked a quick glance over her shoulder at Rodriguez, who was continually scanning the crowd, watchful and tense. Kontarsky doubted that he would feel any different, either.

As they approached the main bank of turbolifts, the Sov-Judge passed through a flickering scan-beam and triggered another advert. This one was a "cred-seeker," a targeted commercial that spoke directly to potential consumers. "Hello there!" it said, as a holo-image formed in front of her. "Wouldn't you look dynamite in the new Luna collection from Kalvin Klone?" The hologram morphed into a version of Kontarsky, but dressed in a sumptuous formal gown; the only incongruous note was that the holo-version of her was still wearing her Judge's helmet. For a split-second, Nikita found herself admiring how the clothes hung on her, wondering if she could afford the dress on her pay. In the next moment she waved the image away, annoyed at herself for briefly falling for the sales pitch.

The waiting shoppers parted before her stern gaze and the three Judges took the first lift to arrive. "M-Haul Incorporated," Kontarsky told the vox-control.

"Level thirty-six," said the lift and the capsule jetted upward.

"So," Rodriguez said suddenly. "What's the plan? We go in, rough a few of these spugs up, lean on them?" His fingers were drumming on the side of his helmet in a rapid tempo.

"We secure the company records," said Kontarsky, "and keep a look out for anyone who might have more information than they're letting on."

Foster nodded. "We got the better assignment, I reckon. Dredd and J'aele have got two whole warehouse domes to check out by the shipping docks."

Kontarsky nodded but said nothing. Before they had set out this morning, Dredd had given them a briefing on his interrogation of the criminal pervert Vik Umbra and the M-Haul connection to the weapons. She had her doubts that the MoonieCorp clue was anything more than a false lead – Kontarsky suspected that Umbra had used the name to play on Dredd's suspicions – but rousting the staff at the M-Haul offices might still have some value to the investigation.

The lift chimed and the doors opened to their destination floor. The moment they stepped out, the cacophony of commercial jingles and invasive advertising hit them squarely in the face. A robot bearing a tray of mock-meat patties began to follow them. "Hey there, citizens! How about a free sample of the new Flame-Grilled Fungi-Snack from Burger Me?"

"Go away," Kontarsky snapped.

"It's fungus-tastic!" continued the machine. "Fortified with extra synth for that char-broiled taste! Mmm-mmm!"

Without warning, Rodriguez rounded on the machine and knocked the tray out of its grippers. "You got mushrooms in your audio pickup, you tin-head clicker? She said get lost!" To underline his point, the SouthAm Judge gave the robot a bad-tempered shove that sent it squealing away on its castors.

Kontarsky let that slide for a moment and pushed open the doors to M-Haul's small office. "Justice Department," she said, her voice clear and hard. "Crime sweep."

The receptionist was a human – a rarity, Kontarsky noted – and she visibly paled as the Judges approached her. "C-can I help you?"

"The manager. Right now," said Foster. Kontarsky was impressed at the Brit-Judge's control and tone. The right amount of force and authority in a Judge's commands often spelled the difference between a pliant citizen and an obstructive one. The receptionist was already on her way into the office proper, a cluster of desk cubicles further back into the building and the trio of Judges advanced.

"Foster, watch the doors," Kontarsky said, sotto voce. "In case we get any runners."

The manager returned with the receptionist. He was a portly man, florid and sweaty with surprise. Kontarsky automatically tagged him as someone hiding something. She held out a hand computer to him. "I want all your office files downloaded to this unit."

"What's this all about?" he asked. "We've done nothing wrong. We've only just taken over this business." He dabbed at his forehead with a handkerchief. "Perhaps your concerns were with the previous owners–"

"I won't ask again," said Kontarsky. "Unless you'd like me to believe you are obstructing a Justice Department investigation?"

That was enough. The manager took the computer and she watched him link it to the M-Haul mainframe. In a matter of seconds, the dense

636 I Am The Law: The Judge Dredd Omnibus

memory core in the portable unit had flash-copied the office's entire file store, simultaneously broadcasting it back to a team of data analysts in Tek-Division.

"Now perhaps you can tell us something about the salvage stored in M-Haul's warehouses. What happened to the last consignments?"

The manager blinked. "What consignments?"

Rodriguez made a spitting noise and closed the distance to the over-weight man in two long strides. "Do we look like we have time to waste with you, idiota?" he barked, his fists balling. "Spill it, you worm!"

"I-I don't−"

"What?" His colour rising, Rodriguez shouted in the manager's face. "Are you going to lie to me again?"

Foster and Kontarsky exchanged glances and the Sov-Judge made a small halting gesture with her hand. If the Pan Andes lawman wanted to play up the role of bad cop, then let him. It would make things move quicker.

"There was no salvage in the company inventory when we took it over!" the sweaty man spluttered. "The storage domes were empty!"

Kontarsky studied her portable lie detector, the East-Meg version of the device the Mega-City Judges called a "Birdie". The needle was buried in the "Nyet" end of the scale.

"You're lying to me!" Rodriguez bellowed.

"He's telling the truth," began the Sov-Judge, but Rodriguez didn't seem to hear her.

"You stinkin' bastardo!" The SouthAm Judge gave the manager a vicious backhanded slap that sent him staggering. "You're in it with those other pendejos, right? Making me look like a fool!"

"Rodriguez!" she snapped. "Back off!"

"No, no, no," he growled and with one swift movement pulled the manager into a headlock and pressed the barrel of his pulse gun to the back of his skull. Judge Rodriguez flicked the power dial to level four and the pistol hummed with power. "He talks or he loses his head!"

"Rodriguez, you're out of line!" said Foster. "Let him go!"

"Shut up, Brit-boy! And you too, chica. You let me do this my way!"

"Rodriguez, put away that weapon."

"I don't think so!" he said, his face crimson red with barely restrained anger. "Talk, you fat slug! Talk!"

The manager whimpered, his synthi-wool slacks darkening as his bladder loosened. "Please! I don't know any−"

The pulse blast cut through the air like a thunderclap. At point-blank range, the manager's entire head vaporised into a mess of hot goo that blew out across the room in a spray. Kontarsky flinched as bits of brain matter pattered over her helmet. Then she was diving for cover as Rodriguez fired wildly, sending particle bursts into computer terminals, walls, the receptionist and other screaming workers.

Judge Foster stood his ground and tried to bracket the outlaw Judge with a brace of stun-level discharges but Rodriguez was too fast, fuelled by adrenaline and anger and sent a high-energy bolt into the Brit-Judge's chest. Kontarsky saw him go spinning away behind a charred desk.

She took a breath of heat-seared air and spoke into her helmet mic. "All units, we have a rogue officer at the Green Cheese Shoplex, level thirty-six! Foster is down. Judge Miguel Rodriguez has gone rogue!"

Broadcast over the general frequency to all Judges within a sector-wide radius, Kontarsky's urgent message crackled over Dredd's helmet speakers. His jaw hardened when he heard the name of the Pan Andes Judge.

I should have sent him home when I had the chance.

A few metres away, at the storage dome entrance, he saw Tek-Judge J'aele freeze, hearing the same call for help. Neither man said a word; they both turned and sprinted for their zipper bikes.

Dredd reached the Shoplex as the first H-wagons arrived, a few moments ahead of J'aele thanks to the superior speed and handling of the Krait 3000 he rode. Without stopping, he piloted the nimble grav-cycle through the main doors of the shopping mall, sounding the whooping sirens to scatter the droves of frightened civilians coming the other way. Inside, fire alarms were blaring and a soothing female voice asked politely for everyone to exit in a calm, orderly fashion.

No one was listening and people were falling over one another to get out. Dredd caught the sound of pulse-fire from the upper levels and the smashing of glasseen. As he swooped around, the Judge saw a juve using the confusion to steal a Tri-D projector from an electronics store. Dredd knocked him to his knees with a kick as he passed the opportunist thief. "Control, gotta kid in a blue radorak down outside the Gizmonics store, level one. Have someone pick him up. Looting, two years mandatory." Twisting the Krait's throttle, Dredd guided the bike up in a spiral climb. "Am in pursuit of Rodriguez."

"Copy, Dredd," came the voice of the dispatcher. "J'aele's on the way from the roof. He'll meet you there."

On the thirty-sixth floor, Dredd set the zipper to hover mode and dismounted, weaving through burnt planters and the heat-scorched corpses of citizens. He found the M-Haul offices a smoking ruin.

Kontarsky was at the doorway, fumbling at a medpack. Foster lay nearby, groaning weakly.

"He'll live," the Sov-Judge said. "The shot just grazed him." She nodded in the direction of a large kneepad boutique. "Rodriguez went in there. He's got hostages."

"What the drokk happened?"

Kontarsky gave a weak shrug. "He was fine one second and the next…"

J'aele approached from the stairwell with a trio of Special Judicial Service Judges. The Justice Department's internal affairs division, the SJS was notorious for its ruthless nature and the zeal with which it pursued errant Judges. The silver skull designs on their uniforms earned them the nickname "Reapers" from street officers. "We'll take it from here," said one of them. "SJS Chief Kessler's orders."

Dredd shook his head. "Negative. Rodriguez is one of my team. I'll deal with him. Kessler can take it up with me if he doesn't like it."

The SJS officers hesitated. Each of them knew Dredd by reputation and each of them knew he and Kessler had crossed swords before. Before any of them could object, J'aele handed Dredd a laser rifle. "Take this. It's more accurate than the STUP-gun. You'll be able to knock him out with one shot."

Dredd accepted the weapon with a grim nod.

8. CORPUS DELICTI

Dredd passed through the archway and into the garishly lit interior of Forbidden Knee – The Kneepad Store For Those Who Dare! – crouching low to minimise his silhouette. The Mauley laser rifle was pressed close to his chest, charged and ready to spit searing coherent light with a single trigger-squeeze. The Judge paused, weighing his options and considering the terrain. Forbidden Knee was one of the larger retail units in the Shoplex, with favoured positioning on the thirty-sixth floor. As such, it was crammed with hundreds of display cabinets and racks of high fashion kneepads that dangled down from the ceiling on thick cords. Even on distant Luna-1, the twenty-second century's most popular item of clothing was still a hot seller.

A high-pitched scream cut through the air and Dredd tensed. Stores like this tended to attract juves and he was sure that if Rodriguez had hostages, they'd be young ones. A small flicker of movement caught his eye and Dredd raised the rifle, bringing the vu-sight to bear. J'aele had already configured the weapon to urban fighting mode and Dredd toggled the compact scope from normal vision setting to X-ray. Someone was moving behind one of the larger displays and the gunsight rendered the solid object in a misty, see-through form. The Judge could clearly see the figure now, a woman on her knees, shoulders gently shaking as she sobbed.

Dredd made a mental note of her position and moved deeper into the store. Once in a while, Dredd heard a random series of pulse blasts and saw energy bolts lancing into the ceiling. One lucky shot caught a suspended display rack and sent a dozen Tommy Mutiefinger kneepads tumbling to the floor, to burn there in an expensive little bonfire. Rodriguez was shouting and ranting, but it was difficult for Dredd to get a sense of what he was saying – some of the words were in English, but the majority of his tirade was being conducted in a guttural SouthAm street-speak dialect.

A quiet voice whispered from his helmet speakers. "Dredd, Kontarsky here. I've handed Foster over to the Med-Judges. I am making my way up the service corridor behind the kneepad store."

"Understood." Dredd subvocalised, letting the sensors in his helmet mic enhance and relay his words. "Keep him from using the back way to make an escape. I'll take him out of play."

"Copy." Dredd sensed the weariness in Kontarsky's voice, the self-doubt. She had been in charge here and now Rodriguez's sudden burst of insanity would reflect badly on her judgement.

Dredd shifted the rifle again, part of him considering the number of other Judges that he had seen go off the edge in his career. Officers who used to be good law enforcers like Sleever or Gibson, men that Dredd had personally had to deal with. It was perhaps one of the worst tasks that a Judge could ever be faced with, something that no civilian outside the kinship of the law could ever truly understand. The constant pressure of upholding the legal system, of passing judgement on hundreds of thousands of people throughout the course of a single career, sometimes these things proved too much to handle. Rodriguez, with the lax morals in-bred from years of living in the licentious Pan Andes and his volatile temper, had clearly crossed that line. Dredd shut down the train of thought with a grimace. In these circumstances, doubt could be a killer. Dredd resolved to mention this to Kontarsky later in his field report.

"Stop crying!" Rodriguez bellowed at someone out of Dredd's line of sight, the SouthAm Judge suddenly appearing in a gap between two cash terminals. "I'll kill you if you don't stop your stinkin' noise!"

With the X-ray scope, Dredd could see the shape of a cowering teenager behind the tills and he pulled the rifle's stock firmly into his shoulder as Rodriguez raised his STUP-gun to press it against the weeping juve's head. "You're all in it against me, eh?" the rogue Judge spat. "Every one of you filthy putas trying to get into my head with your chattering!" He pressed his free hand to the side of his helmet, as if he were trying to block out a noise that only he could hear. "Shut up!"

In the instant Rodriguez's index finger tightened on the trigger of the pulse pistol, a handful of outcomes raced through Dredd's mind: he could call out, distract Rodriguez, try to reason with him. With a careful shot, Dredd might be able to hit the SouthAm Judge's hand and sear off his fingers with a laser bolt, disarming him, or he could take the safety shot, the clearest and simplest approach that wouldn't risk the lives of any more citizens.

The rifle sent a pencil-thin streak of hot light down an ionised tunnel of air, making a sound like bones cracking. Dredd's shot melted a penny-cred sized hole in the faceplate of Rodriguez's helmet, cutting instantly through the cartilage in his nose and into the soft interior of his addled brain. The laser bolt made the Judge's skull pop as the super-heated steam inside it expanded. All this occurred in less then a thousandth of a second, before Judge Miguel Juan Olivera Montoya Rodriguez collapsed to the floor of Forbidden Knee like a discarded rag doll.

"All units, be advised," Dredd said aloud. "Threat has been neu-tralised. Repeat, neutralised."

Although Chief Judge Ortiz was hundreds of thousands of kilometres away, broadcasting from the Pan Andes Conurb's Justicia Centrale, the distance did nothing to mute the volume with which he roared at his opposite number on Luna-1. "What kind of rinky-dink operation are you running up there, Tex?" he asked, his face filling the monitor screen in the Judge-Marshal's office. "You come crying to us for assistance and when we send you one of our best men, you kill him!"

Standing at attention next to Dredd, Sov-Judge Kontarsky fought to hold down a sneer. Best men? Rodriguez had been anything but that, a loutish oaf that Ortiz had wanted out of his hair, but given the direction the conversation was taking, she realised it would be impolitic to point out that detail at the moment.

Tex was fighting his corner as hard as the SouthAm Judge. "You're blamin' Luna-1 for this? Perhaps you didn't read the report we sent you, Ortiz, but I reckon you'll find that it was your man who assaulted fel-low Judges and murdered a half-dozen citizens!"

Ortiz seemed not to hear. "What did you do to him, huh? How did you make it happen?"

Judge-Marshal Che spoke up from where he stood. "You're not saying you think that we caused Rodriguez to go insane?"

Ortiz gave Che a filthy look. "Oh, so now you've got something to say?" The rivalry between the Judges of South America's Pan Andes and Mex-City was always a source of friction between SouthAm and Luna-1. "Hundreds of our people live in the lunar barrios of Puerto Luminia and if we can't be sure that Luna-1's Judge force is looking out for Pan Andes interests, things are going to get mui furioso!"

"Speak plainly!" Tex growled. "What in Sam Hill are you gettin' at?"

"This isn't the first time you NorthAm and Eurasian types have put the Pan Andes cities at the bottom of the pile. This is, how do you say, the thin end of the wedge! I'm recommending that the Pan Andes Conurb and Ciudad Barranquilla councils consider full withdrawal from the Triumvirate and diplomatic relations with Luna-1!"

"You've been looking for a way out of the lunar treaty for ages, haven't you, Ortiz?" rumbled Dredd, speaking for the first time. "And now you're going to blow up this incident in order to justify your needs."

"The killer himself speaks at last," snapped Ortiz, masking the moment of hesitation that Dredd's words forced from him. The Mega-City Judge had touched a raw nerve. "You should be happy that I'm not demanding your extradition for trial and execution, Dredd! If Tex has any sense, he should have you suspended!"

"Judge Dredd was following standard–" began Kontarsky, but Ortiz spoke over her.

"If I want to hear the whining of little girls, I'll go find myself a street-walker." He fixed Tex with a gimlet eye as the Sov-Judge fumed. "I want Judge Rodriguez's body on its way home within the hour and I'm order-ing our courier ship to prepare for departure. Our business, Señor Tex, is at an end."

"Rodriguez's autopsy isn't complete," said Che. "We must give his corpse a full–"

"Within the hour," Ortiz repeated with force. "Or else I'll send an armed cruiser to recover it. Judge Rodriguez deserves a hero's funeral." Before anyone else could speak, the comm-link cut and the screen flick-ered into a grey rain of static.

Tex sat heavily in his chair and shook his head. "Y'know, Joe, when I called you up here I expected to have a few deaders lyin' around because of it, but I never reckoned you'd be shootin' your own men."

"You saw the security tapes from the Shoplex. Rodriguez lost it. I had no choice."

Tex glanced at a monitor on his desk, where a loop of the SouthAm Judge's trail of destruction was playing. "Damn it, Dredd. Couldn't you have winged him?"

"Not without losing another innocent life. I made the call, Chief Judge. I take full responsibility for it."

Tex chewed his lip. "It ain't that simple, Joe. I'm responsible for what happens up here, not you." He stabbed a finger at the screen. "This is the last thing I want right now. It's already being broadcast city-wide by those Moon-U hackers."

"I was against this taskforce from the start," said Che. "Perhaps we should consider dissolving it."

Dredd gave him a hard look. "Thanks for the vote of confidence," he said bluntly. "Chief Judge, my team is making progress with this inves-tigation. I need to follow this through to the end."

The Texan's eyes narrowed. "You're on thin ice, Joe. Luna-1 ain't like Mega-City One. We gotta half-dozen nations cheek-by-jowl here and that means keeping everyone happy – or else what little support we get from Earth is gonna dry up."

"I don't think what happened to Rodriguez was a fluke," Dredd said. Beside him, Kontarsky's brows knitted in surprise. "His breakdown was engineered. Someone did it to throw a spanner in the works."

"How could you possibly be sure of that?" said Che. "The Med-Division's initial examination of Rodriguez showed nothing untoward."

"Call it a hunch," Dredd replied. "And you yourself said that his autopsy was incomplete. We need to examine the corpse in more detail."

"Can't do it," said Tex. "I'm sorry, but I'm not going to risk an international incident with Ortiz and his boys just on the basis of your hunch." He nodded towards the door. "Get back on the trail of those guns. I'll try to smooth things over with the Banana City gang."

As Dredd and Kontarsky reached the exit, Tex called out again. "Joe? I know it ain't your style, but can you try to keep the bodies to a minimum from now on?"

Kontarsky studied Dredd for a moment before speaking, as the two of them walked through the corridors of the Luna Grand Hall of Justice. She barely covered her surprise when Dredd had announced he suspected something unusual about Rodriguez's aberrant conduct. Kontarsky had considered the same thing herself, but dismissed the possibility as a wild supposition; her kadet instructors had always drilled into her that facts and facts alone were what made law enforcement work. East-Meg Judges did not believe in "hunches". Yet, the fact that Dredd had also come to a similar conclusion gave her a swell of pride that was very un-Soviet.

"So ask me," Dredd said, without looking at her.

"Why do you think Rodriguez was... influenced?"

"You were there. You tell me."

She chewed her lip. "It... It was more of a feeling than anything else," Kontarsky managed. "Something about him just seemed to be off." She shrugged. "Well, more off than his usual behaviour."

Dredd nodded. "Last night when we saw the hacker attack on the blimp. And again in the M-Haul offices."

Kontarsky gave a small smile. "Didn't you tell me earlier that you wanted facts, not speculation?"

"When you've been on the street as long as I have, you'll learn how to tell the difference."

She accepted this with a nod. "So, has your conclusion caused you to alter your opinion on my theory about an outside influence on the Kepler Dome rioters?"

Dredd gave a small shrug. "I'm keeping an open mind."

"The point is moot, anyway. Without a chance to study Rodriguez's body in close detail, any conclusions we have remain unfounded."

The senior Judge rubbed his chin, thinking. "Can't figure out why Ortiz is so eager to get the body back."

"I'm sure it is to prevent a deeper autopsy. It's not that I believe the Pan Andes Conurb is involved with our investigation, but it is common knowledge in East-Meg Two that SouthAm Judges have illegal bio-modifications banned by the global cyberware treaty."

"Oh?" Dredd said carefully.

"Strength enhancements, cybernetic brain implants, penile extensions... All of which I'm sure would be discovered on a deep scan by a Med-Tech. Use of stimulant drugs is also prevalent among their law enforcement community."

Dredd nodded. "Ortiz would be hard-pressed to make claims about treaty violations if it was found out his men were doing the same thing," he sneered. "I'm getting sick of all this political garbage."

"It is sometimes necessary–" Kontarsky began, but Dredd cut her off with a growl.

"What's necessary is to solve this case. Anything else is of secondary consideration." The Mega-City Judge fixed her with a hard stare and Kontarsky felt his eyes boring into her. "Understand?"

"Yes, sir."

They reached an intersection, one corridor leading up to the flight bay, the other down into the lower levels where the Tek Labs and medical centre were located. Kontarsky took two steps towards the upper levels before she realised Dredd wasn't walking with her. "Sir?" she repeated. "What are you doing?"

"What is necessary. Come on, let's go talk to J'aele. I've got a job for him."

The Simba City Tek-Judge placed his hands flat on the desktop and shook his head. "Out of the question. Frankly, Judge Dredd, I am shocked that you would even ask me to do such a thing."

"Too difficult for you?" Dredd asked lightly. "I'll understand if it's something beyond your skills."

J'aele's eyes narrowed. "I can do it. I just don't want to."

"Remember when Che said we were an autonomous investigation team? That means we have free rein to pursue this matter wherever it leads."

"Even if that risks an international incident?"

Dredd gave him a level look. "You know as well as any of us that all secured records of Judge Rodriguez will be purged from the system the moment his corpse leaves the city. I'm not asking you to break the law."

"No, but you are asking me to bend it and bend it a lot."

"I could make it a direct order."

"I would refuse."

"Really?" Kontarsky broke in, watching him over the top of the monitor screen in the Tek Lab cubicle. "And then what? You would be relieved and shipped home on the next flight... and I think that the reception you would get there would not be a warm one, da?"

J'aele's expression darkened. "No," he said at length. "It would not. I... was not favoured by the commanders of the Simba Justice Division."

Dredd mentally ticked off another conjecture. As he suspected, J'aele was another problem case, an officer sent to Luna-1 as some kind of punishment for a misdeed back home. But for now that didn't matter. He leaned forward. "You know as well as any one of us that we're on the clock, J'aele. I need to see the autopsy report on Rodriguez."

"Why don't you just ask Judge-Marshal Tex?"

"He has other concerns right now... And I'm not sure we can trust Tex's people," Dredd said quietly. "I'm not going to take the chance."

J'aele crossed his arms. "And what makes you think you can trust me?"

"I'm a good judge of character," retorted Dredd, "and besides, whether you're willing to admit it to me or not, you want to bust this case as much as the rest of us, if for no other reason than to show the folks back home how wrong they were about you."

A broad grin crept across the African Judge's ebony features. "You have an eye for people's flaws, I'll give you that. All right, I'll do it." J'aele began to work the keyboard before him, swiftly tapping into the medical centre's data core, descending through layers of stored information. "What do we tell them if the South Americans catch us with our noses in their business? If they detect me, it could be very bad."

"Then don't let them catch you," said Kontarsky.

Dredd watched the holo-screen in front of the Tek-Judge writhe and flex like a live thing, panels popping open and closed as he navigated through dense storehouses of material, circumventing pass codes and security protocols. "You're good at this," he remarked. "You've done it before."

J'aele nodded. "I'm part of the central computer division's tiger team. One of my duties up here is to monitor data defence strength from outside hack-attacks. We regularly simulate data penetration by staging mock raids on our own systems, looking for loopholes." He frowned.

"No matter how hard we try, though, those Moon-U perps are still getting in. It's infuriating."

Kontarsky said what Dredd was thinking. "Do you suspect the involvement of an insider?"

J'aele shrugged, still typing at a furious rate. "There are Judges from all over the world stationed here. Odds are that some of them will have viewpoints opposed to the people in power…" His words trailed off as a scroll of text began to march up the screen. "Here. We're in."

"That was fast," noted Dredd.

The Tek-Judge made a casual gesture. "I told you I could do it."

Kontarsky scrutinised the data. "It may have been for nothing. I don't see anything unusual here. It is as Che said, just the basic report."

"Freeze it there," Dredd interrupted. He pointed a gloved finger at a blank section of the virtual document. "There should be a comparative DNA scan listed. It's a standard stage-one post-mortem procedure."

"You're sure?" asked Kontarsky.

The senior Judge nodded. "I've signed off enough death certificates in my time to know the difference. Any Med-Tek examining Rodriguez would have done that, even on a quick check."

J'aele studied the display, working the console. "Dredd is correct. This is suspicious. I'm finding broken data tags in this part of the file."

"Which means?"

"The comparative DNA scan was entered here, but then it was erased. Rather sloppily, too." The Tek-Judge ran a few more commands and a cluster of red indicators blinked into life on the screen. "And that's not all. This file has been tampered with. Someone altered Rodriguez's autopsy report after the fact."

Dredd's brow furrowed. "Who has access to these records? Who could do that?"

"Senior medical department staff…" J'aele tapped out another string of commands. "The senior technician on duty today was Sanjeev Maktoh."

Kontarsky was already speaking into her helmet mic. "Control, query and locate Sanjeev Maktoh."

"Checking…" came the reply. "Confirming, Maktoh, Sanjeev. Justice Central medical department civilian auxiliary, Indo-Cit resident on lunar placement. He checked out from work a couple of hours ago, logging absent due to sickness."

"It's him!" she snapped. "Dredd, he must be the one."

"I need an address," Dredd told J'aele.

The African Judge nodded and flickered through to a personnel file. "Here it is. Ventner Boulevard, con-apt 44/LK/31."

Dredd threw J'aele a nod. "Good work."

J'aele sighed heavily. "Just don't tell anyone I gave in so easily."

Ventner Boulevard was in the midst of one of the central dome's mid-level residential districts, well appointed with a handful of block parks and shopplexes between the stubby half-ovoids of the con-apt buildings. Maktoh's small two-pod habitat module was on the thirty-first floor, facing outward. Dredd and Kontarsky made a landing on a nearby Multistack, giving them a clear line of sight into the medical technician's apartment.

Kontarsky studied the windows through a compact pair of Sov-issue binox. "I see movement inside. A single person, I believe. He appears quite agitated."

Dredd accepted the field glasses and took a look for himself. "He's packing a bag. What do you reckon, he's already bought a ticket back Earthside?"

She nodded her agreement. "If he's running scared, that might explain why he made such a bad job of doctoring the autopsy report. His disquiet could be helpful in interrogation."

"Agreed. We'll take him now. You go through the front door."

"You're not coming with me?"

Dredd gunned the Krait 3000's gravity drive. "I'll be around."

Sanjeev caught his foot on the trailing cuff of a shirt dangling out of the pile of clothes in his hands and tripped over. He landed on the suitcase that lay open on his folda-bed and it flipped, spilling out the contents he'd frantically packed into a mess of unkempt clothing. He fell to his knees and had to struggle to keep from crying. Sanjeev's stomach turned over and he felt the same about-to-throw-up sensation that had been dogging him since the phone call.

That voice at the other end of the line. Menacing him, intimidating, making veiled threats about what would happen to his mother and father, his wife and the pod where they lived in Indo City. He had done as the voice had asked, time and time again. He had hidden things in rooms in the Grand Hall of Justice. He had given things to shady people in dark alleys. He had slipped the tasteless, odourless capsules into the food of the fat prisoner in iso-cube 576. All of this he had done, gradually getting more and more afraid, more terrified by increments until today, the dam of his fears had broken. The voice had made him change things in the dead Judge's file and even as he did, Sanjeev was suddenly struck by the absolute certainty that this time he would be caught. When it was done, he closed up his desk and left, every muscle screaming in him to run, run, run!

And running was what he was doing... Just as soon as he could pack his bags. When the knock at the door came it was as loud as a gunshot and Sanjeev almost soiled himself in fright. It wasn't the casual, how-are-you knock of a neighbour or the hopeful entreaty of some robotic salesman. It was a cop knock, hard and forceful and without pity. "Sanjeev Maktoh?" asked a woman's voice. "Justice Department. Open the door."

If Sanjeev thought he was panicking before, then the absolute terror that descended on him after he heard those words showed that everything up until now had just been a taster of the real thing. He twisted on the spot, hands flapping at the air like distressed birds, mouth agape. Mad, insane plans raced through his mind – could he hide in the fridge? Barricade himself inside the toilet? Feign unconsciousness until she went away? But with a physical effort he shuttered his fear away and made himself focus. He ignored the banging on the door and the shouting woman outside. Sanjeev grabbed the billfold that held all the credits he had withdrawn from Luna Bank 6 and stuffed the one-way ticket to Delhi-Cit in his pocket, then he sprinted for the hab's window.

He heard the door crash open under the steel toe-caps of Judge Kontarsky's boot, heard the high-pitched whine of her STUP-gun going active. But he was at the window, it was open and he was through it, hundreds of metres up over Ventner Boulevard.

Sanjeev's fingers snatched at the box on the wall where the emergency floater was stored, the one-shot parachute-balloon combination that high-rise residents could use in lieu of a fire escape. It was empty.

A new sound reached his ears: the high-pitched motors of a zipper bike.

Dredd let the flyer drop down from where he had been hovering. He held out a bright orange bundle of plasti-fabric. "Looking for this?"

With crushing certainty, Sanjeev realised he had nowhere else to go and he closed his eyes, letting himself teeter forward and surrender to the lunar gravity. Before he could fall, however, something hard and rigid snapped into place around his wrist and suddenly he was yanked back into the apartment, landing once more in a pile of his own clothes.

Judge Kontarsky held the other ring of the cuffs she'd just snapped shut around Maktoh's hand. "Do not move," she told him, "or I may be forced to injure you... permanently."

Sanjeev gave a nod of acceptance and then threw up.

9. BREAKING STRAIN

As a Judge-kadet, Kontarsky had studied the techniques of interrogations very carefully. She'd learned how to give them and how to resist them, how to tell if someone who was answering was actually replying or just saying what they thought you wanted to hear. She watched Dredd take two long steps across Maktoh's hab and decided to treat this as another lesson, a chance to observe an American Judge in the midst of a cross-examination. As she expected, Dredd went for the direct approach.

"Spill it!" he barked, his face a few centimetres away from the medical technician's. "We know you tampered with the Rodriguez autopsy!"

Sanjeev said nothing, eyes flicking to Kontarsky as she wiped off her boots with one of his shirts. He gulped down air.

"Silent type, huh?" Dredd pressed. "Fine. We'll take you back to Justice Central and Psi-Division can pluck it out of your head the hard way."

"Nooo!" Maktoh suddenly found his voice. "Please, no! It's not safe there! They can get me anywhere!"

Dredd's eyes narrowed. "They? Who are *they*?"

The thin man's vu-phone chirped and with a weak, apologetic smile in the direction of his boss, he stepped away from the conference table and answered it with a husky snarl. "What? I told you never to call me here–"

The caller's voice was muted by distance. "Uh, sorry, Sellers–"

"No names!" the thin man snapped. "Are you even using an encrypted channel, you dolt?"

"Sorry, uh, sir, but it's the mark. He's got company."

The thin man winced and gave the other men in the Silent Room a wan look. "Judges?"

"Yeah. Two of 'em."

"Ah, sneck." He hesitated, he was glad he had put some men on Maktoh just to cover himself, but now he was afraid that things would get out of hand. The last thing he needed was for one of their assets to start blabbing so soon after Dredd had squeezed information out of that corpulent slug Umbra. The thin man decided not to take any chances. "You got the hardware with you?"

"Sure, boss. Right here." He could hear the rush of traffic in the background.

"Good. Waste him and then get the drokk out of there."

The trembling perp blinked fear-sweat out of his eyes. "I... I want protection," he said in a querulous voice.

"From what?" Kontarsky followed Dredd's lead, keeping her voice level and ice-cold. "Who are you working with?"

Words tumbled out of his mouth. "I needed the money, you see... I had gambling debts, I couldn't afford to let my family be shamed..."

"So you sold out," Dredd grated. "You'd better come clean. The more you hold back, the harder it's gonna be."

"I stole equipment for them, for the money. But then they wouldn't let me stop, they threatened my family..." The medic was on the verge of tears now. "Made me... do things. Change things."

"Like the autopsy," Kontarsky added.

"Yes... The analysis droid found anomalies in his brain tissue. I was told to blank the robot's memory, but it had already uploaded the data to the central file. I... I had to erase it..."

Dredd glanced down at the Birdie lie detector in his hand. Maktoh's stress levels were high, but his readings were still in the green. He hadn't said anything untruthful yet. "Tell me what you changed."

"I replaced the neurological scans. There were unusual readings in the aural centres of his brain. Very high levels of dopamine, serotonin and epinephrine..."

"Neurochemicals," said Kontarsky. "They stimulate adrenaline production and aggression."

The Mega-City Judge gave a slow nod. "Someone was pushing Rodriguez, making him crazy. How?"

"I... I can't be sure..."

"Take a guess!" Dredd growled.

Maktoh stared at the floor. "I think... Subsonic pulses, perhaps. Just beyond the range of human hearing, but powerful enough to affect the victim."

Kontarsky considered this for a moment. "This is quite possible. Sonic weapons technology is certainly capable of such a function."

Dredd grabbed the technician and dragged him to his feet. "Who was paying you, creep? I want a name!"

"No names!" Maktoh screamed, flailing in the Judge's iron grip. "Just a voice! A voice on the phone! The money came through Luna Bank! It's untraceable!"

"Dredd," Kontarsky said carefully, "Luna Bank is one of several subsidiaries owned by MoonieCorp."

"Well, well," said the Mega-City Judge. "What a surprise." He let Maktoh drop to the floor. "You're under arrest, pal. Conspiracy. Gambling. Computer hacking. Theft. I'm sure there's more. You won't be seeing your family for a long time."

The medic threw up his hands and yelled at the top of his lungs. "But I told you what you wanted to know! You promised me protection!" He stumbled backward, away from the Judges and swore at them in gutter Hindi.

"I never promised you anything," Dredd retorted.

"You're coming with us," Kontarsky added.

"No! No! NO!" Maktoh stamped on the floor like a child throwing a tantrum.

Something flickered on the edge of Dredd's vision and his head snapped around towards it. A thin tail of white smoke arcing around in a half-loop, something grey and bullet-quick spiralling towards the window.

"Down!" He shouted, reaching out to shove Maktoh to the floor.

Dredd was a half-second too slow. The compact mini-missile struck the glasseen window of the con-apt and the detonator triggered. Inside the warhead, a dense weave of monomolecular wires were projected outward in an expanding sphere and tore through Maktoh's apartment in a razor-edged hurricane. Dredd's right-hand glove was cut cleanly down the middle by a spinning fragment and behind him, Kontarsky lost a triangle-shaped section of her rad-cloak from another screeching piece of shrapnel.

Sanjeev was standing directly in the path of the detonation and took the full force of the weapon on his unarmored body. Dredd saw the medical technician jerk and spasm under a hundred hits before his body fell apart, irregular chunks of meat tumbling apart in a pink mist of fluids.

Kontarsky choked down a churn of hot bile in her throat and looked away. "I am uninjured…" she said, thanking her luck that the sofa she'd dropped behind had absorbed most of the damage.

"There!" spat Dredd, his now-bare hand stabbing out at something in the distance. Through the torn rent in the con-apt wall where the window had been, the Sov-Judge saw a black Skylord aero-sedan race away from a standing hover. "Blitzer team!" snapped the Judge. "In pursuit!"

Before she could react, Dredd was already vaulting out of the gap, dropping smartly into the saddle of his skybike where it floated below the balcony level.

The Krait 3000 handled well, turning sharply into the banks and angles as Dredd twisted the throttle, narrowing the gap between his flyer and the sleek shape of the dark aircar. He could see little of the interior through the sedan's tinted windows, but the bike's sensors swept an infrared frequency scan over the vehicle, showing three figures inside. Behind the driver, he could clearly see two human heat-shapes fumbling over a long, tubular object. The missile launcher. They're reloading, he thought.

The driver of the Skylord was good and Dredd could see that he knew the layout of Luna-1's streets. Against anyone else, that might have been an advantage, but with a Judge on his tail and the Krait's direct link to the city's central traffic net, Dredd was more than a match for the perp. Other vehicles were getting out of their way, yellow air-cabs and hover buses pulling aside to let them flash past. Dredd had the zipper bike's sirens and lights on the full power setting, the keening wails and flickering colours bouncing off the concrete canyons they sped down. The aircar turned sharply, pivoting around the offices of Interplanetary News and down into the stream of oncoming vehicles from a one-way sky-highway.

Slow and ponderous oxy-tankers passed by with horns blaring and a trio of egg-shaped floater pods collided with one another as Dredd's Krait cut through their formation like a diving falcon. For a moment, the Judge thought the aero-sedan was going to go full tilt towards the lower city levels, but then it angled upward and twisted into a side alley. Dredd executed a brutal wing-over and turned the zipper to follow them. His thumb flicked the bike's STUP-cannons from the "safe" to "armed" setting and he waited, counting down the seconds until the sedan's rear appeared in his target scope.

A flare of orange flame blinked out of the aircar's near side passenger window and Dredd jerked the handlebars by reflex, standing the Krait up on its stubby winglets. Heat from a jet of burning solid fuel seared the Judge's cheek as the rocket lanced past him, crackling through the air at near-supersonic speeds. His head whipped around to watch the missile spin past the zipper bike's underside and clip the upper floors of a Selenescraper. A fat bulb of yellow fire erupted out of the building where the warhead struck home, instantly immolating two whole floors of the tower.

"Grud!" Dredd said aloud. "Creeps have switched to hi-ex!" The Judge squeezed the pulse-cannon triggers and sent streaks of coherent particles stabbing out at the aero-sedan, bracketing the flyer. A well-aimed salvo punched through the trunk of the aircar and tore off the rear quarter fender and a stabiliser vane. The Skylord's driver pulled hard on the flight yoke, but the aircar lurched to starboard and began an uncontrolled turn.

Dredd gunned the Krait's thrusters and pulled parallel with the sedan, drawing his STUP-gun from its holster. "Level two!" he ordered. With these perps clearly eager to discharge military grade explosives as well as anti-personnel weapons inside the Luna-1 dome, Dredd's options had quickly changed from "arrest and detain" to "stop at all costs". Grud knew how many more shells they had to hand in there.

"Put it down, now!" he bellowed, his voice amplified by the helmet pickup and broadcast through the Krait's loudspeakers. "This is your only warning!"

The answer Dredd got was a snarl of spit gun fire as the Skylord sped over the roof of a tall, broad office block. Unable to turn as quickly with its stabilisers damaged, the aircar smashed through a video ad-screen, shattering it like glass. Dredd avoided the same obstacle and fired his pistol.

Pulse blasts punched out the windows on the driver's side of the flyer and tore ugly holes in the bodywork. Shots from a spit carbine sang out in reply, missing wide of the mark. Dredd returned fire and heard the clatter of a weapon discharge from inside the car. The thermographic scan of the sedan interior showed the gunman with the spit carbine twitch as he was hit, spastically emptying his weapon into the back of the seat in front of him.

Riddled with bullets, the driver slumped forward and his dead weight pressed on the steering column. The aircar obeyed and stood on its tail, the trunk flapping open like a gaping mouth as it soared vertically. Climbing on a powerful column of anti-grav thrust, the Skylord became a missile itself, heading straight towards the glasseen dome hundreds of metres above.

Dredd saw the danger coming. "Drokk! Control, Code black! Code black!" The two-word signal was an alert specific to space habitats and orbitals that simply meant explosive decompression imminent. Heedless of the speed of his own flyer, Dredd steered the zipper bike with his knees and used both hands to steady and aim the STUP-gun, firing full-power shots into the aero-sedan, desperately trying to knock out the gravity drive, but the Skylord was a favourite choice of Luna-1's criminals for a good reason. The thick fuselage could easily soak up energy weapon fire that would tear apart a weaker aircar.

The other occupant of the vehicle, the gunman who had interrupted his boss in the Silent Room, was desperately trying to load another high-yield explosive rocket into the launcher tube when the air-sedan collided with the inner surface of the Luna-1 dome. The shock made him jerk the trigger and the missile added its destructive force to the explosion of the Skylord's fuel cells.

Dredd saw the air-car vanish in a ball of fire before it was snatched away by the hard vacuum of space as a hole blew through the dome and out into the lunar void. The sudden tornado of screaming air ripped him from the saddle of the Krait 3000 and the bike followed the car out into the darkness. Time seemed to slow to an agonising trickle as he tumbled up towards the gap, the hole shrinking even as emergency jets of cellu-foam from nozzles on the dome frame raced to seal it closed.

Forcing all the air from his lungs, Dredd screwed his eyes shut and braced himself to be projected into space, but the sucking vacuum quit as quickly as it had started. The emergency seals had shut, leaving Dredd airborne and alone, hundreds of metres over the streets of Luna-1.

And so he fell.

"Bolze moi!" Kontarsky swore out loud, a rare expletive escaping her lips as she threw her Skymaster bike after Dredd. Her heart hammered in her chest when she saw the air-sedan explode and for a moment she thought that the Mega-City Judge would perish along with the blitzers in the car; but then she saw the dark streak of a body falling back towards the ground and knew he had cheated death once again. She angled her zipper bike towards him and unbidden, a memory of something her mother used to say popped into her mind. That one has a charmed life.

Certainly, luck was on Dredd's side today. The lower lunar gravity meant that his fall was slower than it would have been on Earth, which gave Kontarsky time to cross the distance and loop her Skymaster beneath him. She felt the rigid grip of his fingers snapping into her leg and, with a single swift motion, the senior Judge hauled himself up and into the saddle behind her. He made it seem easy, as if nearly getting blown out into space and falling hundreds of metres was something he did on a regular basis – but then, Nikita considered, given Dredd's record of repeatedly defying the odds, it probably was.

"Good timing," Dredd said, after he got his breath back. Kontarsky smiled to herself; that was the closest she would get to a thank-you.

L-Wagons and emergency tenders were already closing on the impact point on the dome, ready to patch the temporary cellu-foam plug with a new piece of glasseen. Dredd watched them go, contacting Luna Justice Central and ordering a moon rover unit to search for any remains on the void-side. He frowned. A detonation like that and an explosive decompression probably wouldn't leave a lot of evidence to sift through, but there was a chance that the vacuum might freeze-dry something that could give them another lead. A crew of lunar Judges in e-suits would find whatever was left of the Skylord sedan somewhere out in the moon-dust – and, Dredd hoped, the guns the blitzers they had been using.

The Sov-Judge's mind was clearly on the same track. "That missile launcher was military grade weaponry. This is a serious escalation from the small-arms we saw evidence of in Kepler."

"Agreed. It's time to step this investigation up a notch. We're wasting time chasing the little people while the creep who is pulling the strings is staying hidden."

"What do you propose, Judge Dredd?"

"Maktoh was being paid by a MoonieCorp shell company. MoonieCorp bought out M-Haul after they took possession of that weapons load. Those guns turn up in the hands of rioters. Do I have to draw you a picture?"

"It will be difficult to pin anything on them. MoonieCorp has worked very hard to disavow any connection to its founder following his incarceration. I took the liberty of checking the corporation's files – there are no records of any kind of infraction since they became an independent entity. They have... what is it you Americans say? They have kept their noses clean."

Dredd snorted. "Just because no one has found anything yet doesn't make MoonieCorp innocent. One connection might be coincidence. Two is enough for me to start kicking down doors and busting heads." He tapped her on the shoulder. "Get us back to the Grand Hall of Justice."

The blowout in the main dome had echoed across half a dozen sectors and broken windows on the upper levels of six citi-blocks in the prosperous parts of Luna-City North. Normally, news of something like a penetration of the dome would be kept rigidly suppressed by the Justice Department in the interests of public safety until the matter had been dealt with, perhaps adding a small report to one of the Judge-sponsored channels once everything had been cleared up, but other forces were watching and waiting for something like this to happen. Seconds after the emergency Code Black call went out, intelligent software subroutines and image processing engines went into play, creating footage and matching live feeds from co-opted street cameras to synthetic fakes.

Like a malignant imp, the crater-faced, computer-generated Moon-U mascot reappeared on screens all over the city, bringing with him a warning of terrifying disaster.

"Oh no!" cried the cartoon character, stopping traffic with his wails and turning thousands of people from their daily routines to watch him. "U won't believe this! Look at what the Judges did!"

Shaking his head and blubbering big wet tears, Moon-U played a scene of Dredd, laughing like a madman, as he fired a massive shoulder-mounted laser cannon at a bus full of screaming children. Teeth bared and spittle flying, the monstrous Dredd sent the energy bolt clean through the grav-transport and punched a huge hole in the city dome. The hover bus cracked open like a piñata, spilling kids of all ages and types into the whirling slipstream of the vacuum. People on the street watched in rapt horror as Moon-U's video showed the children sucked out into the blackness of space, their little bodies popping into too-red splats of gore.

"Dredd is crazy!" Moon-U shouted, imploring the audience to listen. "He's gonna kill U all unless U stop him!"

There were those among the crowds of viewers who saw through the display for what it was and some of them even had the wherewithal to say so out loud, a few even laughing at the ridiculous notion. But every single one of them was drowned out by the shouts of anger and hatred, as cries for justice echoed back and forth under the Luna-1 dome.

Tex snapped off the vid-screen with an angry flick of the wrist and stood up, fixing Dredd with a hard glare. "Grud damn it, Dredd! Were you even listening to me? I said I wanted minimum casualties, not massive property destruction! What the hell were you doin' out there?"

"You wanted results, Tex. I'm getting them for you."

"Results?" the Judge-Marshal exploded. He snatched up a data pad from his desk and read out what was displayed there. "A Justice Department medical technician dead, a wrecked con-apt and a half-dozen minor injuries in neighbouring apartments. Six separate airborne traffic accidents resulting from your pursuit of a criminal. Eight more deaders on the top floor of the Rent-A-Robot Agency tower, plus two more killed by falling masonry!" He slammed the pad down on the desk. "And then to top it all off, you punch a hole in the dome! You call that getting results?"

Dredd's eyes narrowed. "Let's be clear about this, Chief Judge. You requested my assistance up here because you wanted someone who could get the job done. I regret any innocent loss of life as much as the next Judge, but I had no choice but to go after that air-car. They murdered Maktoh right in front of me."

"All right, partner..." Tex took off his hat and rubbed his brow. "Let's say we forget the chase for a second and talk about this med-teck. What the drokk led you to him, huh?"

"Maktoh handled the autopsy files for Rodriguez. Something was rotten there and I followed it up."

Tex shook his head. "Don't give me that famous 'Joe Dredd hunch' bull! I know you leaned on that Simba City fella to hack the records, even after I told you to keep your damn nose out! You're lucky Ortiz and his cronies never found out about that lil' detail!" He threw up his hands. "Jovus! Che was right about you! You ain't mellowed in your old age, you've turned into a bigger hard-ass than you ever were!" The Texan waved a stern finger in Dredd's face. "You know, back home in the Big Meg you might be the big dog, but up here you're on my leash! We gotta different way o' doin' things on the Moon and you ain't towin' the line!"

Dredd ignored the accusing tone in his former partner's voice. "I don't have time to debate my methods with you, Tex. MoonieCorp is in this and it is in it deep. I put J'aele on a full sweep though their data records and Foster's going to join him when he's out of speed-heal–"

"You did what now? You're investigain' one of the biggest corporations on the Moon without my authorisation? You're barkin' up the wrong tree there, Joe! MoonieCorp ain't like it used to be in the past when ol' CW was honcho – they gotta good rep now, supporting charities, public works…"

"I'll bear that in mind," Dredd said dryly. "In the meantime, I'm taking a hopper out to Farside Pen to talk to Moonie himself."

"Oh no you ain't," Tex growled. "You disobey orders and disregard procedure like it ain't nothing and now you're on some kinda revenge kick, raking up perps from twenty-five years back? Moonie's a sick old man wastin' away in a cell on the dark side and you're layin' all this at his door? I reckon the low gravity is foggin' your brain, Dredd! If that's the best you can do, then you're not the Judge I remember."

Irritation flared in Dredd and his jaw hardened. "I'm not here to play nice for you, Tex. If you wanted a softly-softly approach, you should have called in someone else!" He made a derisive grunt, looked at Tex and saw nothing but his age and his weakness. "Maybe you were right when you said your judgement is getting rusty. You and Che sit up here in your office and you have forgotten what life is like down on the streets. You got soft and now Luna-1 is going to pay the price!"

"You arrogant son of a bitch!" Tex shouted. "I've held this chair for half my grud-damned career! I kept this city from self-destructin' while you played the yahoo on Earth, tossin' around nukes like they were spitballs! Remember this, Dredd, you ain't been Judge-Marshal up here for a long, long time! I'm the sheriff of Luna-1 and I say how it goes down, not you!"

Dredd slammed his hands down on the desk and stared Tex in the face. "Then do your damn job, old man! Or else step aside for someone who has the guts to enforce the law!"

"You callin' me out?" Tex retorted fiercely. "You stone-faced drokker, you think you can take me–" The Judge-Marshal's hand darted towards the antique six-gun in his belt holster.

Years of training automatically made Dredd go for his own weapon, muscle memory working his fingers before he was even conscious of it.

"Dredd!"

"Tex!"

Both men turned towards the source of the voices behind them. Che and Kontarsky entered the Chief Judge's office and beyond them through the open door, Dredd could see a dozen more men all watching with concern. Belatedly, he realised that every heated word he and Tex had exchanged must have been heard in the anteroom and corridor beyond. The hot anger that had raced through him just seconds earlier ebbed and Dredd carefully stepped back from Tex's desk, aware of the tension tightening every muscle in his body. The Judge-Marshal's expression held in a grimace of anger and disappointment.

"What is going on here?" Che demanded. "They can hear you out on Hestia!"

"Just a... difference of opinion." replied Dredd.

Tex sat heavily in his chair and drew a hand over his face. "I've got the Triumvirate breathin' down my neck, the citizens callin' for your blood... It's time to cut my losses." He gave Dredd a long, measuring look. "By order of the Judge-Marshal, you are to stand down from your position as taskforce leader. I want you on the first shuttle back to Mega-City One."

Kontarsky gasped. "Chief Judge, that is a mistake!"

Tex ignored her. "Luna-1 is gonna have to sort out its problems without your heavy-handed help, Dredd."

10. INTO DARKNESS

The old man in the hoverchair nodded slowly, the faint red lights of the Silent Room casting a demonic illumination over his craggy, pock-marked face.

"Perfect," he purred, drinking in the word. "I couldn't have asked for a better outcome. And with witnesses too." He gave a mocking salute to the bald man sitting across the room from him. "You're an artist, do you know that?"

The bald man seemed uncomfortable with the compliment and looked away. "I am merely an instrument of destiny. My skills serve only our cause."

His superior, the tall man, suppressed a cold smile. "Ah, you truly are a model Judge, are you not? Obedient and strong. Sometimes I wonder if you ever harbour dreams of taking power for yourself."

"Sir, I would never–" the junior man began.

The tall man waved him into silence. "No, no, I know you would never dream of it. You do not have the instinct to lead, do you?"

His subordinate looked away, barely covering the anger he felt at being mocked in front of the other cabal members. The bald man said nothing and simply accepted the insult. In time, he would show his superior just who it was who could lead and who could not.

"I have to admit, for a second there I almost thought Dredd and Tex were going to shoot one another!" said the thin man, sharing his words like a ribald joke with his chairbound master. "A few moments more and Dredd might have done the job for us!"

"There's still time," smirked the tall man, joining in the gallows humour.

"I swear," began the old man. "I've seen it work a dozen times now and still it fascinates me. Watching a normal man slip over the edge into rage, at just the push of a button... Planting one of the devices in Tex's office, though, that was a master stroke."

"We have spent many years perfecting the hypno-pulser technology." Pride swelled in the bald man's voice. "On low-level settings, like those we used on Dredd and Tex, the subjects don't even realise that they are being manipulated. That's the beauty of it, you see. The pulser just amplifies emotions that are already present."

"Well, however it works, it's genius. That gizmo is gonna make the Moon mine again."

"You're too kind." said the tall man, "But let's not forget it was your pet turncoat who did the deed. I trust that particular loose end will not come back to bother us any more?" he asked, addressing the old man's assistant.

"Not unless he can sew himself back together," the thin man said flatly. "And the men who were sent to kill him are corpses as well. There will be no repeat of the Umbra situation."

"I am gratified to hear that. Perhaps now we can resume our plans without any further unforeseen obstacles?"

"What about Dredd?" the bald man asked. "He'll be on the next ship to Earth. Are we going to just let him go?"

"Nothing is leaving until the solar flares have died down," the man in the wheelchair shook his head. "And besides, you don't know Joe Dredd like I do, son. That stubborn law-dog is too dumb to just down tools and go. He's gonna put himself right where we want him, you can count on it."

"We're monitoring Dredd's movements," added the thin man.

"Good," said the tall man, smiling once more. "In the meantime, order the assassin to prepare. We will begin phase two immediately."

"Is it true what I heard? About Dredd?" Foster said as he approached the table in the mess hall where J'aele and Kontarsky sat. The Tek-Judge gave him a sullen look and nodded. Foster sat heavily, wincing as he unwittingly put pressure on his recently healed arm.

Kontarsky gestured at the limb. "You are fit for duty?"

"More or less," Foster replied. "The skin is still a little tender but it's nothing I can't handle. I just have to avoid any flying bullets for the time being." He hesitated. "I reckon I owe you some thanks, Kontarsky. The Robo-Doc told me I might have lost my arm if you hadn't been there to slap a med-pack on me."

The Sov-Judge gave a tight nod of acceptance. "I would have done the same for anyone. Just because our cities may not be allies, there is no reason why we cannot work together on amicable terms."

Foster raised an eyebrow in mild surprise. "Blimey. What happened to you quoting East-Meg doctrine at the drop of a helmet? I thought all Sovs considered us Westerners to be decadent and contemptible."

Kontarsky sniffed. "Perhaps my exposure to different law enforcement cultures on Luna-1 has broadened my viewpoint." She gave Foster a sideways glance. "Besides, I never said I did not think you were decadent."

"What we are is high and dry," said J'aele, absently smoothing a hand over his bald head. "With Dredd's removal from the taskforce, we're cut adrift. With all due respect to you, Judge Kontarsky, I doubt very much that Judge-Marshal Tex will allow you to take charge of the crisis investigation."

Foster nodded. "I heard talk from one of the Med-Judges that Deputy Che will be taking over where Dredd left off."

J'aele gave a cynical grunt. "Then we can be assured that nothing will get done. Che was once a fine officer, but he is nothing but a desk man now. This investigation needs a senior Street Judge to lead it."

Kontarsky shook her head. "If I had not seen it myself, I would not have believed it. Dredd and Tex, the two of them were near to blows when we entered the office. In all honesty, I had expected better from him."

"Dredd's served for longer than some of us have been alive," said Foster, pointedly giving the Russian a brief look. "Tex too. Maybe they're both candidates for the old Long Walk, eh?"

"I refuse to accept that!" Kontarsky snapped hotly. "First Rodriguez and now this... There is a conspiracy at work here, I am convinced of it!"

"Perhaps," J'aele agreed, "but without firm leads we have nowhere to go. Dredd might have had the latitude to follow his instincts, but we do not. I have no doubt Che would not hesitate to ship us home too if we ignore protocol."

"What about Umbra?" Kontarsky said. "Perhaps we could interrogate him further–"

"Umbra is dead," said Foster flatly. "You didn't hear? He was stuffing his face and his ticker gave out. Pop! Just like that and the fat bloke was a goner. They had to take off the cell door just to get him out."

"A heart attack?" the Sov-Judge's lips thinned. "How convenient."

J'aele sighed. "It matters little. Dredd will be on his way back to Mega-City One within the hour and in a few days we will be knee-deep in the Apocalypse Day anniversary celebrations. Perhaps all of this unrest will have blown over by then."

"You think these riots are just the run-up to A-Day then?" asked Foster. "Just the usual war vets and troublemakers we get every year?"

"Wait a moment," Kontarsky broke in, holding her hand up in front of the Simba City Judge. "What did you say before? About Dredd?"

J'aele blinked. "I said Dredd is on his way back to Earth."

She shook her head. "No, you said within the hour. You said that Dredd would be on his way back to Mega-City One within the hour."

"Yes. I passed him in the flight bay just before I came down here. I tried to talk to him about what happened, but he told me he was on the next Earth-Direct out of here. He took a Skymaster and headed off towards the spaceport."

The confusion on Kontarsky's pale face was suddenly replaced by a dawning realisation. She bolted up from the table and made for the door. "I have to go!"

Foster watched her depart in surprise. "What was all that about?"

J'aele shrugged and sipped his synthi-caff. "I think that for Dredd, the girl has a 'thing'."

"A 'thing'?" Foster repeated. "For Old Stony Face? Jovus, it must be that chin, or something."

Kontarsky vaulted up the stairwell, taking the stairs two at a time, dodging past a pair of chattering servo-droids as she reached the vehicle park. Without waiting to get confirmation from Justice Central flight control, the Sov-Judge straddled the saddle of her zipper bike and kick-started the anti-gravity motor. Her Skymaster shot into the air, making a beeline for the spaceport terminal in Armstrong Territory.

On its lowest setting, the STUP-gun still packed enough charge to neutralise the prissy desk-bot in the landing bay office and Dredd carefully stepped over the twittering machine to work the controls that released the security lockout. The Justice Department command code that Tex had issued him had yet to be revoked, despite the fact that the Judge-Marshal had ordered Dredd home – a piece of luck that was working in his favour.

Dredd threw a glance out of the window to the spaceport bay below. There were three moon hoppers parked on launch cradles, each one an identical wedge-shaped craft resting close to the ground on a cluster of thruster modules. At full burn, cruising low over the lunar surface, one of them would be able to get him across the terminator to the far side in a couple of hours. The Mega-City Judge recovered a control key card and took the elevator down to the bay.

There were no humans down here, just a handful of maintenance droids and a bulky overseer unit working to strip down the drives of another hopper. Dredd had ensured that his timing was spot-on, in the ten-minute gap between shift change over between the human supervisors. As long as he didn't run into any problems, he would be well on his way before anyone realised that the moon shuttle was missing.

Dredd stepped up the ladder to the hopper's airlock and used the key card to open it. The security lamp flashed green and the outer door obediently opened. He was already clad in a Justice Department-issue environment suit, the helmet held under the crook of one arm and he had to shift his weight to move his suited form inside. Outside the influence of the gravity-field generator plates in the city proper, Dredd was careful not to let himself stumble under the lunar G-force. He was reaching out to tap the "close" control when he heard her words echoing through the launch bay.

"You told J'aele that you would be on the next Earth-Direct flight home," Kontarsky's voice issued out from above him, "but the port authority reported a magnitude nine solar flare today. Every Earthbound transport is grounded until the all-clear."

Dredd looked up and spotted her, the red rad-cloak catching the strip lights as she descended in the maintenance lift. She kept speaking. "Piloting a moon hopper alone under severe flare conditions is not recommended. A navigational malfunction could leave you stranded."

The lift deposited the Sov-Judge on the lower level and she approached him. Dredd's hand drifted towards the butt of his pulse gun. Knocking out a robot was one thing, but firing on another Judge? He wasn't sure he wanted to cross that line unless he was forced to. "Thanks for the tip. I'll bear that in mind."

"You're going out to interrogate Moonie? What do you hope to find?"

"Answers," Dredd replied.

"What if there are no answers, Dredd? What if Tex was right when he said that Moonie isn't involved? At the very least, you'll be deported from Luna-1, at worst you'll be up on disciplinary charges."

"I came up here to do a job," he grated. "And I'm going to see it through. You know as well as I do, Kontarsky, CW Moonie has some connection to the Kepler riot, to Rodriguez and Maktoh. If I can't find out what it is, this city will tear itself to pieces."

She nodded. "You are right, Dredd."

"Good. Now move back. The thrusters on these hoppers burn hot and you'll get fried if you're too close when I take off."

Kontarsky shook her head. "No, I don't think so." She took a step closer. "You're not going anywhere alone in this thing. You need a co-pilot."

"I can manage just fine on my own, rookie. I don't need your help."

"Really?" she said sharply. "Which one of us has the better training for this kind of vessel? You, someone who hasn't been inside a lunar craft for over two decades, or me, the winner of the Baikonour Kos-moDome space pilot excellence medal for three years running?"

"And if I don't agree?"

She shrugged. "Then you are going to have to shoot me, because otherwise I'll alert Justice Central and you'll barely make it over the Sea of Rains before you are discovered."

"You're bluffing."

Kontarsky shook her head, the ghost of a smile on her lips. "No, I'm volunteering."

Dredd gave her a long look, measuring her sincerity. "I doubt that will look good on your spotless record with the Kosmonaut Directorate."

The Sov-Judge stepped up into the airlock, gathering an e-suit in her hands. "Like you said, Dredd, there's a job to be done. I can worry about my record later."

"Take your station, then," he said, with a curt nod.

They kept off the main aerial corridors between Luna-1 and the outlying domeplexes, flying nap-of-the-moon over craters and between mountain ranges. Kontarsky proved her worth immediately by programming in a new, faster course that skirted the Heraclides Promontory and took them up and through the Jura Mountains. The solar flare was at its height now and with their suits and the hopper's rad-shields they would be able to survive the brief exposure to the sun's hard radiation; nevertheless, the trip was a risk. If the hopper got into trouble and ditched on the surface, both the Judges would be cooked before any rescue craft could reach them.

Other vehicles were few and far between and Dredd made sure to keep any mining rovers or transports at the extreme edge of sensor range. The flare meant that any communications except hyperchannel and landlines would be severely curtailed for the duration, preventing word of their abscondment spreading too quickly. The added bonus of the solar radiation was its disruptive effect on lunar orbital spy-sats, enough to make a visual or sensor sweep of the Moon's surface difficult. They dropped into the Bay of Dews and Dredd pushed the hopper's engines to full burn, skating the shuttlecraft over the compacted grey dust at high speed, the gravity-repulsors along the ventral hull pushing a thin bow-wave of powder out behind them.

At last, they crossed over the terminator and as the Earth disappeared behind the curvature of the Moon, a wave of shadow embraced the hopper. Kontarsky felt her breath catch in her throat as she peered out of the shuttle's windows; looking up at a star-filled sky that was brighter and denser than anything she'd ever glimpsed from home.

"Incredible..." she whispered, losing herself for a moment in the sight.

"Look sharp," said Dredd abruptly, interrupting her reverie. "Registering approach pattern to Farside Penitentiary."

Kontarsky shook off her moment of distraction and nodded. Now was not the time for sightseeing, she had to concentrate.

Judge-Warden Lee had to concentrate just to be sure that he'd heard the hailing message correctly. He asked the communications monitor to repeat the signal and the droid obediently did so. When he heard it the second time, his mouth went dry. *Dredd*? A surprise inspection by Judge Dredd? Lee had noted the Justice-Net dispatches that the former Judge-Marshal was in Luna-1, but like most things that took place on the near side of the Moon, Dredd's arrival was far off and none of Lee's concern. Never in a million years had he expected that Dredd would stick his nose in here.

Farside Pen was an outpost in the outer face of the Moon, virtually alone except for a couple of nearby mining concerns and the massive radio telescope array to the south. Judge Lee liked it that way. It was quiet here out in the dark, there was little or no trouble and it gave him time to put his feet up and read while the sentry-bots patrolled the prison proper. It was calm and controlled at Farside Penitentiary, but the warden instantly felt a sick feeling in his gut: Dredd's arrival was about to change all that.

Lee met Dredd and Kontarsky at the main airlock. The senior Judge wasted no time and ordered the warden to take him into the secure iso-cube blocks. "Had I known you were coming, Judge Dredd–" Lee began.

"If you knew I was coming, it would hardly be a surprise inspection, would it?" Dredd surveyed the corridors branching off as he strode along the main thoroughfare. "How many officers have you stationed here and what's the inmate count?"

"Ten Judges, including me. We have four hundred convicts spread over five sub-blocks."

"Ten men to handle forty times that number?" said Kontarsky.

"My staff are the best," Lee added defensively. "And we have an extensive force of servo-droids and armed sentry drones. Farside is secure."

Dredd halted at an intersection and pointed to a sign. "Block E. Special Conditions Unit. That's where you're keeping Moonie, right?"

"Moonie? Oh, of course, you were the arresting officer," nodded Lee. "That was before my time, but yes, he's being detained there. In fact," the warden smiled, warming to the subject, "a number of the felons that you were responsible for apprehending are incarcerated here. Lucius 'Geek' Gordon, the Weatherspoons Gang, Luufy McMarko, William Carmody, aka 'Wild Butch' Carmody—"

"But why is Moonie in there and not in the general population?" the Sov-Judge demanded.

Lee beckoned them to follow him. "Come with me." The warden led them through a double set of airlocks and into a hermetically sealed access tunnel. "Prisoners in the Special Conditions Unit are kept isolated from the rest of the convicts for medical or biological reasons. Some of our inmates have genetic traits or peculiarities that prevent them from associating with other people. Prisoner Moonie is just such a case." He gave Dredd a look. "Did you explain Moonie's, uh, condition to Judge Kontarsky?"

Dredd shook his head. "Feel free to clue her in."

They reached an observation gallery, located high over a deep pit. Ten iso-cubes radiated out from a central dais like points on a star. The warden picked up a data pad from a monitor station and studied it. "Clinton Wendell Moonie, aka Mister Moonie. Former owner of Moonie Enterprises, he was an independent astronaut explorer who came to the Moon in 2014 during the Lunar Rush. Moonie was responsible for many ore discoveries and ice finds, but he was mostly known for winning a ten million credit prize from the International Astronautics and Space Administration. He discovered alien life here, a form of primitive bacteria in Cleomedes Crater."

"Da, that is a matter of historical record. He became a crime lord by exploiting his fellow workers and attempted to take clandestine control of the Moon through his ruthless capitalist-imperialist business empire."

"Uh, yes," said Lee, "but what's not on record is why he became a recluse after winning the prize." The warden touched a control and a monitor screen lit up. Kontarsky's eyes widened as she saw the frail human figure displayed there. For a moment, she thought the screen was distorted in some way, but then she realised that the prisoner it showed had a hugely disfigured head, well over two or three times the size of a normal person's. The bony balloon-skull was pinkish-grey with veins pulsing visibly beneath the papery skin and the surface was pockmarked with lesions that looked like tiny lunar craters.

"Chyort Vozmi! What happened to him?" she asked, unable to look away.

"We call it Selenite Hydrocephalus Syndrome, more commonly known as Moonie's Disease. The bacteria he discovered did that... It softens the bone matter of the skull and causes it to swell until it pops. Most victims died, but Moonie, well, he was rich enough to keep himself alive. Immunisation wiped out the virus, or so we thought."

"You thought?" snapped Dredd. "Explain."

"The alien bacteria was only dormant. It mutated and became active again a few years ago and we couldn't cure the new version, so we were forced to put Moonie in an isolation module. He's been there ever since, cut off from human contact and tended by robots." Lee tapped a finger on his temple. "There's not a lot of him left up here, if you get my drift."

Dredd studied the monitor grimly. "Get me a hazmat suit. I want to go in and have a little chat with our friend."

The multiple airlocks slammed shut behind Dredd and he took a step into the isolation cell. Two droids slowly orbited the aged man lying on the recliner-bed, one a spidery Robo-Doc, the other a simple servo-droid that hand-fed the prisoner thin vitamin gruel. "Hello, Moonie. Remember me?" Dredd's voice was hollow and muffled inside the thick polypropylop of the one-piece hazard suit.

Moonie slowly raised his bulbous head and blinked. "Who?"

"Judge Dredd. I've got some questions for you, Moonie."

The frail little man made a sad face. "Oh, I can't help you, Judge Dredd. I'm old, old, old, now. Forgotten so much. So much. Ha ha."

"I told you," Lee's voice said in Dredd's earphone. "He's senile. It's a side-effect of the virus."

"I don't buy it!" Dredd growled.

"Buy?" said Moonie, suddenly animated. "But I'm not selling! Oh no, I only bought the Moon! And bought it all, all of it was mine, mine, mine! Ha ha."

"You never let it go, did you?" Dredd approached him, stern and serious. "Publicly you were cut off from MoonieCorp, but behind the scenes you're still pulling the strings, right? How did you do it? Who is your contact?"

The prisoner made the same sad face again. "I'm old, old, old, now. Forgotten so much. So much. Sorry, Judge Dredd. Sorry. Ha ha."

"Don't test me, creep!" Dredd spat. "You're not fooling anyone. I know you're behind the riots and the guns, I know you're trying to turn Luna-1 into a bloodbath!"

"Bath?" Moonie repeated. "Blood? Bath? Sorry, Judge Dredd. Sorry. Ha ha."

Dredd grabbed a handful of the convict's shirt and hauled him up off the bed. The skinny little man was surprisingly heavy. "You wanna do this the hard way, Moonie? I'll be happy to oblige."

"Dredd!" Kontarsky yelled. "Restrain yourself! He's just a feeble old man!"

But even as the Sov-Judge spoke, something like hate and anger flickered across Moonie's distorted face. "Unhand me!" He shouted and with a snake-fast movement, the prisoner snatched at Dredd's hazmat suit and viciously shoved him backwards. The attack caught the Judge unawares and Dredd stumbled, his plastic-booted feet losing purchase on the smooth cell floor. He fell and landed hard, the breath singing out of him in a gasp.

"Grud! Creep's got a punch like a pile-driver!" The Judge could feel the familiar sensation of a bruise forming on his sternum.

"Dredd! Your suit!" Kontarsky's voice contained an emotion he'd never heard from the Sov-Judge before – panic. His gaze dropped to his chest, where Moonie had grabbed him. There was a ragged tear where a fist-sized piece of the hazard suit had been torn away. "Y-You… You've been exposed!"

"That's impossible!" he heard Lee shout. "Those things are rip-proof!"

Dredd looked up to see Moonie, back to his earlier manner, sitting down on his bed. "Oh, I can't help you, Judge Dredd. I'm old, old, old, now. Forgotten so much. So much. Ha ha." Moonie repeated the exact same words he had spoken before, the patch of orange material falling unnoticed from his hand.

"Lee. What are the symptoms of Moonie's Disease?"

"Uh, the first signs are bleeding from the nostrils, muscle cramps, acute headache…"

"How long?"

"No more than two minutes from contact until the virus takes hold."

Dredd eyed Moonie and then shrugged off the rest of the hazmat gear. He looked up to where Lee and Kontarsky were watching, horrified, in the observation gallery. "That isn't him," he said simply.

"How can that be?" Kontarsky demanded.

"We'll know for sure in…" Dredd flicked a glance at his chronometer, "just under ninety seconds."

11. HIGH NOON

"Is he insane?" Judge-Warden Lee watched Dredd kick his discarded hazmat suit into one of the cell's dim corners. "He's just willingly exposed himself to an incurable alien viral strain!"

Kontarsky found herself hesitating before she answered. Ever since she and Che had walked in on Dredd's argument with Marshal Tex, a doubting voice in the back of her mind had started to question the Mega-City Judge's stability. He was taking a serious risk down there in the cell, just to prove a point. She shook the thought away with a turn of her head. "How long has he been in there for?"

Lee checked the clock on the monitor console. "Too long. If he's infected, he'll be feeling it any second."

The Sov-Judge tapped her helmet microphone. "Dredd. What is your condition?"

There was a long second when Dredd did not speak and Kontarsky saw him rub a gloved hand over his upper lip, looking for any telltale traces of blood. If he collapsed in there now, it would all come down on her shoulders.

"Four-square," Dredd's voice grated over the comm. "No infection, just like I thought."

Lee shook his head. "But... but that can't be. Moonie is the carrier, he's patient zero! How can you be all right? Unless the virus has gone back into a dormant state again."

For his part, the prisoner seemed to be oblivious of Dredd and the conversation going on around him. The Judge indicated the Robo-Doc. "If that were true, your droid would have reported it, right?"

"Well, yes..." The warden's brow furrowed. "But these inmates are checked by an independent, off-base medical technician every six months. The last visit was very recent and Moonie here was still classified as dangerously infectious."

"A medical technician?" repeated Kontarsky. "From where?"

"The Luna Grand Hall of Justice. It's a standard operating procedure–"

"What was his name?" snapped Dredd, although he knew the answer already.

"An Indo-Citter, I think… Mac-something…"

"Maktoh." Kontarsky said the word with a frown. "Sanjeev Maktoh."

"Yeah, that's the guy."

Down in the isolation chamber, Dredd's teeth bared in an angry snarl. "We're being played for chumps!" He advanced on the prisoner, drawing his daystick from where the baton rested on his belt-loop. "Get up!" he ordered.

Moonie blinked at him. "Oh, oh, oh. Sorry Judge Dredd. Sorry. Ha ha."

"That act is getting real old and my patience is just about through. Stand up, creep and let's see what you're really made of!" Dredd's hand darted forward and hauled Moonie off the bunk, knocking aside the servo-droid in a clatter of utensils.

"Don't touch me!" the old man shouted, a vicious light flaring in his eyes. Moonie raised claw-like hands to defend himself, but Dredd deflected them with the daystick.

"Not this time, pal!"

The prisoner lunged, his big spherical head bobbing on his skinny neck like a bouncing beach ball. Dredd's daystick connected with Moonie's temple and there was a cracking sound, like ice breaking.

Watching on the monitor, Kontarsky's stomach turned over. For a moment, she was sure that Dredd had caved in the criminal's skull. Moonie then shook himself like a wet dog and a palm-sized piece of bony matter clattered to the floor.

"You've done it now!" the prisoner shrieked in a shrill, high voice. "You've damaged me!"

Moonie turned to face Dredd and there, through the rent torn in his scalp, the Judge could see delicate electronics and mechanical workings. "An android. I knew it!" He snatched at the duplicate's throat. "Where's the real Moonie?"

"Gone gone gone!" the robot chimed in a singsong voice. "Free, free, free! Mister Moonie is going to be back on top, you'll see! He'll have his revenge! He'll have the Moon, Moon, Moon!"

Dredd shoved the droid to the floor and left it there, chattering and babbling away to itself. Behind him, the hatchway irised open to admit Kontarsky and Lee, who nervously scanned the air with a bio-sensor.

"Not a trace of disease contaminants anywhere!" he said. "The Robo-Doc must have been reprogrammed to give false readings."

Acrid smoke issued from the android and it let out a thin screech. With a flash of seared plastic it deflated, melting into a pool of unidentifiable wreckage. "If this machine has been standing in for the criminal Moonie, then how long has it been here?" asked Kontarsky.

Lee's face was pale. "I... I don't know. Like I said, most of the prison's systems are automated. Whoever swapped this robot for the real man must have been able to bypass our security hardware."

The Sov-Judge shook her head, taking in the enormity of it. "Dredd, do you realise what that means? Moonie could have been free for months, or even years!"

Dredd nudged the molten remains of the robot's head with his boot, the frozen rictus of the android's sick grin staring backup at him from the floor. "We can worry about how and where he escaped later. All I want to know is where Moonie is *now*."

The frail man in the hoverchair sipped from a glass of water and looked up as his assistant approached him. "What is it now, Sellers? Cheer up, boy, you look like a moon-cow with chronic gas."

"Sir, there's been a development you should know about," said the thin man. "The decoy? The android at Farside prison?"

The old man made a dismissive gestured. "Yes, yes, what of it?"

"It's been discovered, sir. Dredd was there."

"Show me."

Sellers handed over a data pad and thumbed a button. A few moments of footage shot through tiny cameras inside the eyes of the duplicate played. The blurry form of a Judge's helmet filled the picture. Dredd's voice emerged from the pad's speaker. "An android. I knew it! Where's the real Moonie?"

The frail little man laughed softly to himself. "Where?" he said to the air, his face splitting in a feral grin. "Why, I'm right here, Dredd. And soon I'll be exactly where I'm supposed to be... with the Moon in my hands!"

"Mister Moonie, uh, sir," said his assistant. "How do you wish to proceed?"

"Our operative is in place, yes?"

"He returned from Union Station this morning."

"Then proceed as planned."

"Sir, respectfully I feel I must go on the record and protest this decision in the strongest terms."

Tex turned sharply and threw down the Judge-Marshal's Rad-Cape of Office, crossing the distance to Che in a few quick steps. "Oh, you do,

I Am The Law: The Judge Dredd Omnibus

huh? Grud damn it, man, protestin' about what I do seems like all you're good for these days!"

Che kept his face neutral and stood his ground. "You asked my for my opinion, sir. I'm giving it to you."

Tex made a negative noise and picked up the cape again, straightening it over his broad shoulders. Che used the opportunity to take a look at the monitor screen set up in the corner of the anteroom. The display showed a view of the area outside, the broad fan of steps leading into the Grand Hall of Justice, where public announcements and important press conferences were held – just as one was to be given today.

"There is no need for this sort of display, Marshal. The public media office could have simply set something up to broadcast on the city-wide communications net."

Tex picked up his favourite hat and absently flicked a piece of lint from the brim. "Oh yeah? With them Moon-U hackers cuttin' into every signal whenever they want? What kinda message would it send if all o' Luna-1 thinks I'm broadcastin' from a safe little bunker somewhere, cowerin' behind a desk?" He spoke the last words with venom. "No, Che, we gotta step up to this, do it out in the open and show no fear." He donned the hat and straightened his badge. "That's the frontier way. Things are going straight to hell out there and we gotta show that the Judges mean business."

"I know that but we are less than forty-eight hours away from the annual Apocalypse War holiday. Could it not at least wait until after that? Or at least, you could consider using a force field or a las-screen."

"Damn it, man, why are you doggin' me on this?"

Che's lips thinned to a hard line. He knew that Tex would not be swayed. "Because I am your deputy, Judge-Marshal and it is my duty to point out alternatives to you."

Tex gave him a tight nod. "And that you have and respectfully, you can shove 'em."

"Yes, sir."

The Chief Judge of Luna-1 straightened and walked purposefully out of the anteroom and into the glare of the camera drones and spotlights. "Any word on Dredd?" he asked out of the corner of his mouth.

"Nothing. We have been unable to locate him or the Sov-Judge Kontarsky within the city limits. However, a hopper shuttle was launched a few hours ago from one of the outer docks at the spaceport. Dredd's ident code was used."

Tex smothered a growl. "Don't that beat all? That's Joe all over – he's like a damn pit-bull. Tell him to let go and he'll still hang on there and bite all the way down to the bone."

"What are your orders for when he returns?"

Tex stepped up to the podium. "I'll deal with him when the time comes."

The Judge-Marshal looked over the wide plaza that stretched out between the front of the Justice Central to the south and the Luna Academy of Law to the north. A milling throng of people was gathered there, easily a thousand citizens. Most of them were quiet, but there were a fair number brandishing placards and banners. There was a seventy-thirty mix of slogans visible, leaning in favour of mottoes about *Moon-U, Luna Liberty* and *Judges Out!* vying with a sprinkling of pro-government demonstrators. Voices were raised and there were some angry words being thrown around, but mercifully violence had not broken out. That might have had something to do with the rank of Judges wielding day-sticks and STUP-guns spread out in a thin black line along the bottom of the stairs.

Tex gave the careful nod and smile to the audience that had become his trademark. "My fellow citizens of Luna-1, I thank you for your time and attention tonight. I have called this public address to answer some of the concerns that have been risin' to the fore here in our good city over the past few months."

Foster stood at J'aele's side in the Grand Hall's overt media control centre, a dozen floors above the steps where Tex was speaking. A live feed from each of the hovercams recording him was displayed on a large wallscreen, each shot fixing Tex carefully under the powerful, clean light of the floods. All of Luna-1's media were present in some form, from Tri-D channels like LCTV and IPN to newsfax services like the Luna Module and SeleNet.

"You know, when I watch him talk I realise why he's done this job for so long," said Foster.

"And why is that?" J'aele asked, glancing at a console.

"The man has integrity. Honesty just comes off him in waves. He's nobody's fool and he's tough with it, but you get the sense he'll give you a fair shake. Every city should be so lucky to have a man like Tex in charge." Foster looked away. "It's funny. I heard he never even wanted the job of Judge-Marshal in the first place."

"That is correct," J'aele said, his attention elsewhere, "but those who seek power are usually the ones who are least suited to have it."

"True enough," Foster nodded at the console readout. "You got a problem there?"

"No, not at all and that worries me," the Tek-Judge replied, indicating the screen. "Because of the importance of this public address, Tek-

Division has brought in all its counter-intrusion specialists to make sure the broadcasts are not interrupted–"

"You don't want those Moon-U punks breaking into the transmission?"

"Exactly. But we're monitoring all available wavebands across the comm-net and there's nothing going on out there. Not a single pirate signal or attack program in sight."

Foster shrugged. "Maybe you scared them off."

J'aele shook his head. "I think not, Judge Foster. The jackals do not stay in their den when a meal is within their reach. Moon-U are simply choosing not to disrupt this broadcast."

"Isn't that a good thing?"

"No. Mark my words, Foster, they're planning something. I have a very bad feeling about this."

Tex knew that the crowd was hooked now and while he was sure that there were plenty of folks out there who hated what he stood for, he knew that they were at least listening to him. "Luna-1 is a proud city. We're a nation-state of folks from all over the Earth and just as much as we're part of our home planet, we're also independent. We're Selenites, Lunarians, whatever name you choose, many of us Moon-born and Moon-bred. Some folks out there are sayin' we ain't free, that the Judges are keeping you prisoner. Well, that there is a lie and I'm here tonight to tell you that Luna-1 is the freest damn city off Earth!"

A soft murmur of agreement moved through the crowd and Tex smiled a little to hear it. Any disquiet that Che's earlier comments might have brought up in him faded as he watched the strength of his words influencing the citizens. "There's folks out there who are screamin' for free elections, but we already got those. My name's been on that ballot time after time and you good people have always voted me back in to office, 'cos you know I'll do right by you. Now these same folks think I'm a tired old cowboy, long in the tooth and slow in the brain, but let me tell you this – I'm sharp enough to know that Luna-1 ain't gonna rip itself apart on the say-so of some cartoon goofball!"

Tex flashed a grin as a ripple of laughter crossed the plaza, before his expression hardened. "I'm gonna keep this city safe. It's my life's work. And no amount of rumours and half-truths are gonna get in the way of that." He tapped his badge. "This here means Marshal and that means I'm the law–"

At that moment, something high on the upper floors of the Luna Academy building glittered brightly and caught Tex's attention. The Chief Judge had a fraction of a second to register the vibrant crimson flash before a high-energy collimated laser beam lanced through his chest, the crack of superheated oxygen breaking the night air a moment later. The powerful bolt of coherent light melted through the middle of his badge and tore through skin and bone to flash burn his heart into cinders. Judge-Marshal Tex tumbled away from the podium, trailing a thin pink stream of vaporised blood. He was dead before he hit the lunacrete steps.

Shock and terror broke through the crowd like a wave and the panicked citizens surged in all directions, the line of Judges distending under their weight. Che was the first to the body and the sight of the ruined corpse of his old friend and commander made his guts knot with anger and sorrow. "Seal off the plaza!" he bellowed. "Now!"

In the media centre there was a stunned silence until J'aele snapped out an order to one of the camera operators. "The Academy – the shot came from the Academy! Get a hovercam up there!"

Several of the views that had been trained on Tex now swooped giddily around and flickered over the crowd, catching blink-fast images of fighting, screaming, hysterical people. Then the Justice Department's training facility filled the sub-screens as the flying camera drones closed in on it.

Foster spotted the gunman first. "There! Unit six, upper quadrant! Send men over there right now!"

The hovercam could see little; it was unlit on the office level where the sniper had fired from and the drone's low-light lenses were insufficient to show anything but gross shapes and shadows. The figure, clad in a dark outfit with bulky shoulder padding, was sprinting for a null-grav drop tube and it turned as the hovercam closed in. Foster got the impression of a pistol in the killer's hand and then with a flash, the drone's live feed became a rain of static.

"Replay!" J'aele barked. "Freeze that last frame!"

One of the other Tek-Judges did as he was asked, halting the video feed at the exact instant before the assassin destroyed the drone. The picture was blurry and dim, but the clothing the gunman wore was distinct, even in the gloom.

It was the uniform of a Mega-City One Judge.

In the hours after Tex's murder, the panic at Justice Plaza turned into a crisis that soon expanded far beyond the death of one man. Che's orders and a poorly considered command given later by a watch commander led to the use of neutralising stumm gas and riot foam on the people who had gathered to hear the Judge-Marshal speak. Under the glare of all Luna-1's media, a few Judges were injured and dozens of citizens were killed in the deadly crush of bodies; every bloody incident and moment captured and broadcast across the city.

As the solar shutters across the dome interiors began to fan open to announce the lunar dawn, the last of the bodies trapped in the hardened foam were being cut free. Parked medi-flyers and emergency porta-domes were serving as field hospitals for those people too badly crushed to be moved and Judges of every stripe were everywhere, combing the plaza with serious and careful intent.

Tex's body had been one of the first things to be removed, but the brown smear of his blood, heat-dried by the laser bolt, was still there, a dark streak across the centre of the Grand Hall's stairs. Che stood to one side of the podium, which had miraculously survived the events of the night untouched. The Mex-City Judge was fixated on the upper floors of the Law Academy, watching the L-Wagon floating outside the room where the gunman had hidden.

Foster and J'aele approached, gingerly giving the bloodstain the widest possible berth. "Reporting as ordered," the Brit-Cit officer announced.

Che nodded. "Quick thinking with the camera drone." His voice was flat and toneless. "Good work. What's the word from the other sector houses?"

The two men hesitated.

"Spit it out!" Che snapped. "I gave you an order!"

"It is bad, sir," J'aele began. "Multiple demonstrations across the city were taking place during the speech and the majority of them lit off into full scale riots the moment Tex was killed. Pro-justice and anti-government activists clashed. There have been a lot of deaths."

Che closed his eyes, as if the words were causing him physical pain. "Containment?"

"Ongoing," added Foster. "Riot units are in deployment in all nine territories and a curfew is in effect in most sectors. Manta prowl tanks and pat-wagons have been mobilised." The Judge paused. "The... the Moon-U broadcasts have begun again, city-wide."

Che gave J'aele a withering look. "Your division's performance has been pathetic, J'aele! Can you do nothing to block these chattering fools?"

The Simba City Judge looked uncomfortable. "They are not common hackers, sir. The Moon-U signals are using military-grade encryption technology... It is far beyond the capacity of the equipment possessed by the Luna Justice Department."

The Deputy Judge-Marshal made a spitting sound. "Our systems are so out of date it's a wonder we can still keep air in here!" He thumped one fist against the podium. "Damn them!"

"The pirate transmissions are inciting disorder in a dozen places. They're claiming that Tex's killer was Judge Dredd, sir and they're denouncing you as the instigator."

Neither Foster nor J'aele had any grasp of Che's native language and so they were spared the full impact of the string of invective he let out in response. His swarthy complexion flushed crimson with barely restrained fury. "This will not stand!" he growled. "I want you both to join the crime scene investigation team in the Academy building and evaluate the situation there! Get back to me with a preliminary report in fifteen minutes."

J'aele and Foster said nothing and acknowledged the command with nods.

The twenty-eighth floor of the Luna-1 Law Academy was primarily devoted to offices handling conscription and evaluation. By day it was busy with servo-droids, Judge-Tutors and a small staff of civilian specialists, but during the evening it was silent and inactive. Visitors to floor twenty-eight were typically parents looking to induct their children into the fifteen-year program that would turn them into Judges, but tonight someone else had entered by stealth with a plan for murder.

The darkened corridor Foster and J'aele had seen from the hovercam's live feed was now starkly lit by floating glow-globes and pin-spots, stark magnesium-bright light banishing all shadows and any places where even the tiniest speck of evidence might hide. Spider-like investigator robots prowled slowly over the floors, walls and ceiling, scanning the surfaces with fans of green laser light. J'aele gave a nod of greeting to another Tek-Judge, who crouched by a blackened disc of metal.

"Here's your camera droid," said the officer. "Close range pulse blast hit, I'd say a level four setting."

"I concur," agreed J'aele. "What else do you have?"

The Tek-Judge stood up and Foster caught the name Tyler on the glint of his badge. "Not much. We checked the security camera footage and whoever this guy was, he knew exactly where all the sensors were located."

"He? You're sure the suspect is male, then?" Foster replied.

"Yup. Body kinetics and motion track ties in with a male, approximately two metres tall, aged between thirty to fifty years-old."

"That fits the description of hundreds of Judges," J'aele was dismissive, "and that's even if the assassin was actually a Judge and not just a jimp."

Tyler indicated the window from where the shot had come. "Well, Judge impersonator or not, the shooter was a professionally trained marksman. Takes a good eye to make a heart-shot from this distance. Which brings me neatly to the weapon of choice."

"You found the gun?" said Foster. "Where?"

"Garbage grinder in the maintenance room. There wasn't a lot of it left by the time we got here, but we lucked out. The grinders clogged up when they chewed through the battery packs and they left a few pieces relatively intact." Tyler picked up a plastic-sealed packet and handed it to Foster. Inside, the Judge could clearly see the shape of a pistol grip and a trigger assembly.

"Any markings?"

Tyler nodded. "Oh yeah." He tapped the packet with a stylus. "That's part of a Mauley M500 Hunter-Stalker. We're running the serial numbers down right now, but it's my guess that the weapon is Justice Department stock."

"I know these rifles," said J'aele. "I've used them myself–"

"Yes," said a new voice. "Yes, Judge J'aele, you have." As one, the three men turned to see four more Judges exit the drop shaft that the killer had used to make his escape. Only the Simba City lawman was able to keep a neutral expression; Foster's and Tyler's faces both soured as they recognised the uniforms of the Luna-1 Special Judicial Service. The man who had spoken advanced on them. The harsh floodlights glinted off the clear disc of a cyberlink monocle over his right eye and under their luminescence the lengthy pink scar that crossed the left side of his face glowed red.

Foster's eyes drifted to the skull-shaped sigils on the SJS officer's shoulder pads and badge. He could never figure out why the Justice Department's internal affairs division had such a thing for death imagery. "Judge Kessler. So glad you could join us."

Kessler scrutinised Foster through the monocle for a moment and the Judge knew that the SJS Chief was using the device to call up his records. "The pleasure is all mine, Foster," he said, a humourless, icy smile playing over his lips. Kessler's reputation was well-known throughout the city: a ruthless, vicious man, the SJS-Judge was more than willing to go to extreme lengths to get the results he wanted and unlike the internal investigations divisions of other Mega-Cities, Luna-1's SJS had full discretionary powers. Quite rightly, other Judges spoke Kessler's name with dread and antipathy. "I'm here to inform you that as of now, in accordance with Justice Department regulations 46-A through 48-F, the SJS is taking direct control of this murder investigation. From this point on, you may consider yourselves under my command."

12. POLITIKA

Instead of hugging the lunar surface as they had on the journey over the terminator, Dredd ordered Kontarsky to get them back to the domed city as quickly as she could. The Sov-Judge programmed in a speedy suborbital trajectory that took them up and over the Pole, approaching the city's starport dock.

As they descended, Kontarsky tapped the side of her helmet as a message broke in over the guard channel. "Dredd, I am getting a signal from Traffic Control. There is a curfew in effect across all of Luna-1."

Dredd came forward into the cockpit from the rear cabin, a half-finished cup of synthi-caff in his gloved hand. "Any details?"

She shook her head. "No, just a warning. I will tap into the civilian video network for more information."

"Give me a feed on the monitor."

Kontarsky did as she was commanded and presently a grainy image broadcast on LCTV's news feed came into focus. "Reception is poor," she noted. "It's not the solar flares. It must be localised interference."

"Probably Moon-U trying to jam them." Dredd fell silent as a newsreader, grim-faced and severe, appeared on screen.

"For those of you just joining us, we apologise for the pre-emption of SportsTime and bring you this ongoing report of the current breaking story across Luna-1…" The display cut to footage of rioting near the water reclamation plants. "Tonight, a city is in uproar as millions of lunarians take to the streets in anger and fear after the brutal assassination of Chief Judge-Marshal Jefferson J Tex."

Kontarsky's heart suddenly leapt into her throat as she watched the murder of Tex play out, the flash of the laser piercing the lawman like a lightning bolt.

"Tex…" Dredd's voice was a low growl.

"Recent incidents of civil disobedience by members of the Luna Liberty group Moon-U have spilled over into full-scale street warfare in all nine territories, as the Justice Department struggles to maintain an enforced curfew to stem the tide of lawlessness."

"They killed him," Kontarsky breathed, hardly able to take in the enormity of what she had just seen. "They must have planned this all along."

Dredd crushed the metallic cup in his hand with a snap. "Moonie," he snarled. "He's behind this!"

The screen changed to show Che placing his hand on a giant star-and-moon sigil in the Grand Hall's central chamber. "Former Deputy Chief Che was sworn in as Judge-Marshal of Luna-1 a few hours ago and he promised that the current disorder would be dealt with as swiftly as possible, in addition to apprehending Tex's killer. Meanwhile, rumours continue to circulate that Mega-City One's Judge Joseph Dredd is the prime suspect in this heinous crime. Judge Udo Kessler, head of Luna's Special Judicial Service, had this to say..." The SJS chief stared into the camera. "We will capture Tex's murderer, you may be assured of that. He will not be able to hide, even behind the shield of a Judge's badge."

Kontarsky muted the channel, the soundless footage of more rioting and street fighting taking on an unreal quality. "I... I am shocked."

Behind her, Dredd was staring out of one of the hopper's windows, his jaw set with implacable resolution. "I'll find him, Tex," Dredd said softly, giving his old friend a private farewell. "Count on it."

The Sov-Judge spoke. "I have linked into a local Justice Department data-nexus. The SJS have us both at the top of a priority watch-list."

"Figures. Kessler's got no love for me. If he's on the case, he'll do whatever he can to lay the blame on me."

"You think the SJS could be involved in Moonie's conspiracy?"

"Maybe. Or he could just be using Kessler's natural antipathy towards me. Either way, it puts a king-sized block in our way."

She tapped her fingers on the flight yoke, thinking. "Judge-Warden Lee will be able to vouch for your presence at the prison and I can testify that I was with you during the assassination–"

"It would never get that far," Dredd rumbled. "If Moonie can get a Chief Judge killed in front of thousands of people, he'll have schemes in place to deal with us." The Judge shook his head. "No, we need evidence, something to tie MoonieCorp to this whole set-up." Dredd bent over a console and called up a digi-map. "Divert course and bring us down near Kepler."

"Why do you want to return there? The dome is still sealed off. What do you expect to find?"

"The clues from the weapons led us to Moonie, but that's dead-ended for now until we can locate the real man. Our only other lead is the oxygen outage."

Kontarsky considered this for a moment. "Very well. I'll drop you off outside and you can go cross-country."

"You have other plans?" Dredd asked.

"Yes. I'm going to land at the starport and turn myself in."

Dredd snorted. "I knew you Sovs were all crazy. Kessler's not likely to go easy on you just because you're a rookie, Kontarsky."

She bristled. "As I told you before, Dredd. I am not a rookie anymore. I am an East-Meg Judge and any interrogation of me can only be handled by a superior Sov officer. Kessler won't be able to hold me. Once I am inside Luna-1, I can buy you some time. I will use what influence I can to assist you."

"And I'm just supposed to take the word of a Sov-Blocker as gospel? What's to stop you singing like a canary?"

Kontarsky's expression hardened. "I'm a Judge. I do not lie."

He nodded and gestured at the lunar surface. "All right. It's a lousy plan but it's all we've got. I'll get an e-suit, you set us down behind that ridge."

"Affirmative." Kontarsky angled the hopper smoothly into a controlled touchdown and settled the shuttle in a flurry of moondust. She glanced back at Dredd as he secured the spacesuit over his uniform. Again she felt conflicted towards him, part of her still strong with years of indoctrination that labelled the Mega-City Judge as her most hated enemy, another part of her seeing him as someone worthy of her respect and trust. "Dredd, I feel I must say how sorry I am about the Judge-Marshal. I... I know that Tex was a personal friend of yours. You have my condolences."

"Save it," Dredd grated. "We'll mourn him when we have Moonie on death row and this insurrection stamped out."

Kontarsky hesitated. She had expected some glimmer of emotion from Dredd, even the smallest hint that he was affected by his former partner's death, but if there was any kind of emotion lurking under that obdurate surface, he kept it well concealed. The Judge's face remained set and unreadable and something about that coldness unsettled her more than any shouting rage might have. He sealed his helmet visor down and gave her a curt nod, then he was gone and Nikita was alone with the turmoil of her thoughts.

With Kessler's arrival, the tension level at the Academy crime scene became palpable. It wasn't unheard of for the SJS to become involved in homicide cases on Justice Department sites, but more typically they only intervened when there was a clear suspicion of a "blue on blue" killing – a polite euphemism for a Judge murdering a Judge. Kessler's presence was tacit acknowledgement that a fellow lawman was firmly implicated in the assassination of Judge-Marshal Tex.

Kessler ordered one of his men forward with a snap of his fingers and the subordinate SJS officer unlimbered a complex scanner unit.

"What's that?" Foster asked.

"Skin-sniffer," J'aele replied. "A very advanced DNA sensor that checks for residual traces in the air or on surfaces."

Tek-Judge Tyler's face wrinkled in annoyance. "How the drokk have SJS got hold of one of those? Tek-Division have to work with obsolete hardware and those guys get state-of-the-art kit?"

The SJS sensor technician ran the skin-sniffer head over the three Judges. "Hold still," he ordered, "I need to register you so we can exclude you from the sweep."

"You all have alibis, yes?" Kessler asked in a deceptively casual manner.

Tyler sneered, refusing to grace the question with an answer. "Can we get on with our jobs now?"

The SJS chief nodded. "You may. In the meantime, I have some information that may assist you." He snatched the recovered rifle fragment from Foster's grip. "The partial serial numbers discovered on this evidence have been analysed. Central has identified this weapon as stock from Armoury Delta in the Grand Hall of Justice. It was assigned to a Street Judge during the shooting incident at the Green Cheese Shoplex earlier this week."

"Who?" demanded Foster.

J'aele felt his blood run cold. "Me."

"Yes," said Kessler, savouring the word. "But you passed it on to another officer, didn't you? There were several witnesses to that fact, including some of my own men." When the Tek-Judge didn't answer, Kessler continued. "Just as it was used to kill Judge-Marshal Tex, this rifle also killed Judge Rodriguez."

"Dredd?" said Foster. "You gave the gun to Dredd?"

The Simba City Judge said nothing, his gaze never leaving Kessler's.

Kessler continued; he was enjoying his little performance. "Armoury files have no record of this rifle being returned to the Hall of Justice or any other precinct command, which means it remained in Dredd's possession."

Foster gave a scornful snort. "No chance. Everyone knows Dredd is a stickler for protocol and regs. Hell, he wrote half of them! Your boys must have made a mistake."

"The SJS does not make mistakes!" Kessler snapped, all trace of his oily smile gone in an instant. "But men do and Dredd is nothing but that, an old man!" After a moment, Kessler composed himself and his flash of anger faded as if it had never been there. "Continue your investigation. I expect to know every detail that you uncover."

Tyler returned to examining the wrecked hovercam as Kessler moved away with his men. "I bet he's just loving this," the Tek-Judge said quietly.

J'aele blinked. "What do you mean?"

"If Kessler is fixing to put Dredd in the frame for shooting Tex, you can be sure he's as happy as a dunce in munce." Tyler lowered his voice. "This was before you two were sent up here, but a while back old Stony Face was in Luna-1 on a Psi-Division gig, babysitting some pre-cog. Anyhow, along the way Dredd got fingered for some murders and they set Kessler loose on him. The killer turned out be some sorta weirdo zombie, but by the time they'd figured that out, our pal Scarface over there had worked him over pretty bad."

"He tortured Dredd?" Foster's jaw dropped open. "Stomm..."

"Yup. Word is, Kessler was real angry about letting Dredd slip through his fingers and he's had an axe to grind ever since. When he wasn't able to break him, Kessler took it personally."

J'aele was about to add something, but a strident beeping from the skin-sniffer unit began to sound. "What is it?"

Kessler could barely keep himself from breaking into a grin, the pink slash of his scar puckering the skin on his cheek. "We appear to have a match. The scanner has detected a minute genetic reading that corresponds with that of gene-strain 0001, Mega-City One variant." He licked his lips. "Dredd was in this corridor within the last eight hours."

"That's not possible," Foster snapped. "The killer could have easily planted a DNA trace and there's hundreds of people who passed through this area, it could be any one of them–"

"Only a senior Judge would have been able to gain access to this floor outside of office hours!" Kessler countered. "Only a Judge would have known how to circumvent the security sensors." He gave Foster a measuring look, "Or perhaps, the murderer might have had an accomplice? Say, another Judge working in a secure area in another building?"

"You're accusing Judge Foster?" said J'aele. "You have no proof!"

"Soon I will have all the proof I need, Judge J'aele. Piece by piece, I'll have this crime solved and the perp brought to swift, brutal justice. The killer," Kessler looked back at Foster, "and whoever aided and abetted him."

The Brit-Cit Judge grimaced and beckoned J'aele angrily. "Come on, we got a report to make to Che. The smell in this place is making me sick to my stomach."

Kessler ignored the jibe and drew a microphone from his equipment belt and spoke into it. "Kessler to Central, SJS advisory to all officers in the Luna-1 environs. Issue an all-points bulletin to intercept and detain Judge Joseph Dredd. Dredd is to be transferred to the Luna SJS head-quarters when apprehended for immediate interview and examination."

Dredd shielded his eyes as Kontarsky poured power to the thrusters and the hopper launched itself back into the black sky, the jet wash sending a slow wave of grey moondust flowing away behind it. The blunt shape of the flyer vanished behind the lip of a crater and was gone from sight. Beyond it in the distance was the graceful arc of the Luna-1 dome, shimmering in the reflected sunlight. He took a deep breath of plastic-tasting suit air and set off, carefully walking in the half-bounce, half-step gait that astronauts had used on the Moon since the days of the old Apollo missions.

The thing that always struck Dredd the most about being in space was the silence. Living in one of the largest cities in the world since birth, Dredd had grown accustomed to the constant background rush of noise from traffic, people and machines that made up the accompaniment to life in the Big Meg; but out here, there was no sound but the rasp of his own breathing and the soft chime of his virtual compass display. He didn't like the quiet; something about it felt wrong.

Skirting a security sensor, the Judge carefully approached Kepler's outer wall. The small conurb dome was gloomy, dimly lit with the faint glow of emergency lights. Glancing up, Dredd could see the inert disc of the oxy-station above it.

He checked his surroundings. In the soundless vacuum, a patrolling security droid or hopper could be on him before he knew it – but he had approached undetected and there was no other movement on the stark monochrome landscape. He reached a small emergency airlock and worked an override code through his thick, suited fingers.

A green light blinked and the outer door opened. "So far, so good," Dredd said aloud.

There were three Luna SJS officers waiting in the launch bay as the hop-per shuttle dropped down on its hangar cradle. Even though she had been expecting to see them there, Kontarsky still had to smother a moment of fear when her muscles tensed in a primal fight-or-flight reflex. She shook her head to clear the emotion. No, she had a duty to perform and to run would be a waste of energy.

While the auto-lander guided her in, the young Sov-Judge removed the data chip that contained the hopper's cockpit flight recorder and ground it into powder under her boot heel. Now no trace remained of her flight path, including her touch-and-go landing in the Badlands and, most importantly, any audio transcription of the conversations between herself and Dredd on the flight deck.

Kontarsky fastened her rad-cloak at her neck and donned her helmet, settling herself in the pre-determined posture that Kadet instructors described as suitable for appearances before antagonists and foreigners. With practiced arrogance, she stepped down from the hopper's airlock and into the circle of Judges.

"You are here for me?" she said, before they could speak.

One of the SJS men nodded. "Come with us, Judge Kontarsky."

She started forward, but another Judge blocked her path. "I will require you to surrender your weapon. For the time being."

Kontarsky gave him a measured sneer in answer and produced her STUP-gun with a flick of the wrist. "Then let us proceed."

A pursuit model L-Wagon decorated with the SJS's characteristic skull symbol sped them across the cityscape and past the Grand Hall of Justice. Kontarsky glanced out at the plaza before the building, which was still cordoned off from the public. She saw the footage of Tex's cold-blooded murder in her mind's eye once again and felt a chill wash over her.

The flyer dipped sharply and circled down into a pad atop the Special Judicial Service's own headquarters building. It was a dark and gothic version of the Grand Hall, shaped like an Eagle of Justice with its wings spread, but where Justice Central's hawkish monolith suggested watchful integrity the SJS building promised nothing but fear. The dark-eyed eagle sat with claws splayed over twin skulls, each a dozen storeys tall and the entire construction was cut from drab grey lunar stone. It resembled the castle of some fanciful medieval warlord more than an institution of law enforcement. Kontarsky knew this kind of subtle architectural propaganda well; she could recall the oppressive, dominating shapes of East-Meg Two's Diktatorat Tower and the minarets of the Nu-Kremlin.

The trio of SJS-Judges took her to a small room lit with a greenish strip-light and furnished with a simple set of metal chairs and a table. A single security camera observed the chamber with a steady red eye. Kontarsky sat, removing her helmet and waited. She had played these kinds of games before and she would not allow mere lunarians to force unconscious clues from her.

She marked time by counting the panels in the walls. She was halfway through when the door opened to admit Judge Kessler and the SJS officer who had taken her gun. Kessler sat down opposite her and produced a data-pad.

"Judge Nikita Kontarsky. You are being held here as part of the Security of the City Act. You are required by law to give me the following information. One: the whereabouts of Judge Joseph Dredd. Two: a complete report on your recent lunar joyride. Three: a full statement covering all your activities since your first meeting with Dredd on Union Station." He laid the pad down in front of her and touched a key. "Begin now."

The Sov-Judge slowly folded her arms and met Kessler's monocled gaze. "I refuse to comply with any of your orders. Furthermore, under the articles of the Global Lunar Partnership Treaty, I demand you turn me over to my direct superior, Kommissar Ivanov of the East-Meg Diplomatic Korps." Kontarsky watched the irritation flare red along the forked line of Kessler's scar. If her timing was right, the SJS chief had arrived at exactly the right moment.

"I think you will find that things will proceed much more comfortably for you if you comply," Kessler cocked his head. "It would be a pity to blacken your record at so early a stage with something like this."

Kontarsky ignored the veiled threat. Such an amateur ploy, she told herself. *He has none of the subtlety of my Sov teacher-inquisitors.*

The other Judge tapped his helmet. "Kessler, it's Kommissar Ivanov–"

Kessler made a dismissive gesture. "She's not speaking to anyone."

"No, sir, you don't understand. He's just arrived. Kommissar Ivanov is in the building."

At that moment, Kontarsky very much wanted to give Kessler a smug smile of superiority, but she resisted. To give in to that impulse would have been a very un-Soviet response.

After a moment, Kessler stood up. "Very well. We'll play it your way." He smoothed the greying hair at his temples. "But I guarantee you will lead me to Dredd, one way or another."

Kontarsky kept her face utterly neutral and her expression stayed rigid even after the SJS men had left.

Kommissar Ivanov entered the interview room alone and gave Kontarsky the briefest of nods. She stood up and saluted and her superior returned the gesture. Ivanov removed a small conical device from a pocket in his greatcoat and placed it on the table. A blinking indicator light flashed green and he sat.

"The sensor mask is operating at full capacity," he said. "We may speak freely now."

I Am The Law: The Judge Dredd Omnibus **687**

Kontarsky remained on her feet. "Sir, thank you for answering my signal. I had not expected you to come in person."

Ivanov gave a slight smile. "It was the least I could do for one of my former students, Nikita. Besides, I so rarely have good reason to leave the *Irkutsk*." An interplanetary light cruiser rechristened as a "diplomatic courier", the starship *Irkutsk* was East-Meg Two's orbiting embassy above Luna-1 and the kommissar's base of operations. "I have been keeping an eye on your progress here on the Moon, but I must confess I was surprised to get your message."

"I apologise if I caused you any inconvenience, sir."

"No, no, my dear," he waved her comment away. "In fact, our meeting comes at a most opportune moment."

The Sov-Judge's face creased in confusion. "I do not understand. I requested assistance as part of the investigation that I have been conducting with Judge Dredd–"

"Dredd, yes," Ivanov said the name as if it left a sour taste in his mouth. "Your reports on his activities have been most thorough, Nikita, but I have become concerned that you are allowing yourself to identify with this American." He waved a finger at her. "That is a dangerous trend to follow. I need not tell you what the monitors at the Diktatorat might think of such a thing."

Kontarsky's jaw worked. "I..."

The kommissar indicated the other chair. "Sit, please. Do not be afraid, my dear. I have edited any references in your reports that might have reflected badly on you before forwarding them to the Kremlin. I can understand how you might see something to admire in Dredd... Even our enemies can teach us something, eh?"

She nodded as she sat. "I believe that Dredd may be correct in his suspicions that a rebellion is being fomented here on the Moon, possibly by the escaped criminal capitalist CW Moonie."

Ivanov raised an eyebrow. "That is an interesting hypothesis. And what would you propose we do about it?"

"Assist Dredd, of course. Kessler and his SJS believe he is responsible for Judge-Marshal Tex's murder, but I can vouch for his innocence."

"Ah yes, a sad event. And yet, as our history teaches us, such a thing can sometimes be the tool of political change for the better."

Kontarsky stopped short. "I do not follow you, sir."

"Oh, come now, Nikita, you are not the naïve Judge-kadet you were when you were in my classes on ethical interpretation. We both know that there are freedom loving peoples on the Moon who yearn for a government by the workers and not by the imperialist Judge system. You yourself have said this."

"Yes, but to place the blame for murder on an innocent man–"

"Do not forget, Dredd is responsible for many transgressions against the Motherland," Ivanov replied. "And regardless, often one man must suffer for the good of the many. Think, Nikita. Is it any wonder that Luna-1 is on the verge of revolution? The so-called United Cities of America bled this planetoid white. Even after they allowed other nations to stake claims here with their mealy-mouthed partnership treaty, their Triumvirate ties us up in endless bureaucracy. If their control of the Moon ends, will it really be such a bad thing?" He leaned closer. "A free Luna-1 would welcome East-Meg Two as a partner for all time, not as a poor beggar at the table as we are now – and you, Nikita, could be a part of that. A heroine to the Sov people, just as you were before."

Kontarsky found she couldn't look away from her old teacher's face and she gave a robotic nod of agreement.

The kommissar smiled. "We'll talk more about this later. For now, though, I find myself wondering. Where is Judge Dredd?"

13. NO ESCAPE

Dredd picked his way quickly and carefully through the silent gloom of Kepler Dome's interior, concealing himself behind wreckage whenever a security drone buzzed overhead. As he had expected, the Justice Department had pulled whatever officers they were using to guard the dome and sent them into the city proper to quell the riots. That meant that the Judge had just a few robot patrols to avoid while he worked his way through the streets. Dredd knew the capabilities of the old Mark II spy-in-the-sky flybots – they were poor with infrared, which meant he could conceal himself behind a lunacrete wall or the frame of a ground-car with a good chance of escaping detection.

With the dome's systems on standby, the air inside was frigid. There was a thin layer of frost on everything and Dredd's breath emerged in small wisps of vapour. The wintry cold chilled his exposed flesh and the smells of decay and smoke still lingered in the air.

Rounding a corner, a flicker of movement caught his eye and Dredd froze. A troupe of four-legged worker droids ambled across the cluttered pavement, followed by a slow-moving cargo wagon and a lifter-bot. As he watched, the machines paused and began to sort through the debris, picking out the few remaining corpses of the Kepler incident's victims. He moved closer. The worker machines were no threat to him, none of them equipped with anything more than a dog-smart computer brain. The droids moved around him, unaware of his presence, quietly gathering up the dead and preparing them for removal. The lifter gripped the body of a Judge in a Cal-Hab uniform and carried it to the wagon. Dredd saw the dried smears of blood across the dead man's studded helmet and noted the corpses of eight more rioters gathered nearby. The Scottish Judge had clearly fallen taking on all-comers. Something glittered as it fell from the body and bounced on the ground. Dredd knelt and scooped it up – it was the Cal-Hab lawman's silver-grey shield. He weighed the badge in his hand for a moment, considering it and then tucked it in a belt pouch.

He had ditched his e-suit in the airlock, unwilling to risk wearing the bulky gear in a normal gravity environment. If he was called upon to use his weapon, Dredd wanted to be sure that he would have every advantage his years of training had given him. Secluded in the lee of a building, the Judge drew his STUP-gun and checked the charge. The pistol's battery pack was in the green and he dialled the beam setting down to level one. If he got in a firefight with other Judges, a stun blast would be enough to dispatch them without risking a more permanent injury. He ignored a brief flash of annoyance that rose in his chest. Damn Kessler for forcing him into this!

Dredd crossed the skedway, ducking low to minimise his silhouette and vanished into an ascent shaft that led to the crest of the dome. With power switched off to everything but minimal life support and the grav-plates, the elevator was inactive, but an emergency ladder inside the tube led upwards. He followed it into the dimness above, where he could make out a circle of faint light. Dredd holstered his weapon and began to climb.

Like everything else inside Kepler Dome, the oxy-station was an empty half-ruin, consoles and panels smashed without rhyme or reason and myriad fragments of shattered glasseen underfoot. The bitter stink of stale smoke was strong up here and black soot stained every surface where the fumes had filtered into the control centre. There were no corpses; the oxy-station workers had been quick enough to abandon their posts the moment the rioting had broken out. The wholesale destruction of the place had occurred at the hands of maddened citizens, who had mistakenly assaulted the facility believing that they could simply turn their air supply back on. When they found the controls locked, the rioters had turned their anger and fear on everything around them.

Dredd brushed a drift of plastic shards off one of the few consoles still intact and hit the activation icon. A stylised glyph in the shape of an old mechanical key appeared. "This panel is secured. Please consult your supervisor for further information," it said, the synthetic voice garbled through a broken speaker.

"Justice Department override," Dredd told the computer. "Open records."

"Ident code required. Please submit key card for scan."

Each employee of the Oxygen Board wore an identity card around their neck that would automatically give their security codes to the consoles and Judges used a similar method with officer-specific ident chips – but with his name on the SJS watch list, any attempt by Dredd to use his code would appear immediately on a Justice Central scan grid. Instead, he took a gamble, drew the Cal-Hab Judge's badge from his belt and waved it over the console. The console's scanner read the micro-miniature chip inside the shield.

The panel gave an answering beep. "Ident code confirmed. Welcome to Oxy-station four-seven, Judge Vandal. Command over-ride accepted."

"Lucky for me this isn't a voice recognition system." Dredd said aloud. "Computer, open last day log entry. Replay shutdown incident."

The screen unfolded into a series of data windows and a camera's-eye view of the control room. Dredd watched as Moon-U's face flickered over a few of the console screens and the outbreak of panic among the oxy-workers, before the crimson alert lights flashed on as the airflow ceased. He studied the oxy-station's second-by-second breathing gas monitor, scrutinising the sine-wave pattern of air filtering through the feed pipes and out into Kepler Dome. The display blinked past, almost too quickly for the eye to register.

Something tugged at the edges of Dredd's investigative sense. Something was wrong here, something that J'aele and the Tek-Judges had missed. He ran the replay a dozen more times before he finally saw it. "Computer, enhance airflow pattern display. Show me where the oxygen feed was coming from."

The screen changed to show a simulated view of the pipe network. "O2 feed at this time index switched over from dual flow to secondary source."

"That's not possible." Dredd knew from J'aele's report that Kepler, being a low-rent dome, took most of its air from the cheaper recycling plants out on the lunar surface, using only a little of the more expensive atmospheric gases brought in by astro-tanker; but according to the screen, just seconds before it had shut down, the oxygen flow had switched from a mix of the two to just recycled air. "Security locks are supposed to prevent that from happening. Explain!"

"Cause unknown. Conjecture – human error."

"Someone cut off the air remotely." he breathed. "It wasn't an accident after all." Dredd tapped in a series of commands and brought up a citywide map, highlighting all the incidents of disorder and violence prior to the Kepler riot. Every one of them was in a sub-dome or an outlying conurb complex, each a poor neighbourhood without the high-cost pure air that most of Luna-1's population enjoyed. "What's the source of the recycled air for all these domes?" Dredd asked grimly.

A logo appeared on the screen. "LunAir Recovery Incorporated," said the computer. "A division of MoonieCorp."

In spite of himself, an angry sneer formed on Dredd's lips. "The guns, the air… Moonie's planning to strangle the entire city!"

And then without warning, the oxy-station's windows were flooded with brilliant, blinding white light.

The L-Wagon's floodlights poured a million-candlepower glare into the platform, enough to overpower the polarising anti-dazzle lenses in the Judge's helmet. From the cockpit, the pilot called over his shoulder. "Full beam! I see him, in the control room!"

"Hold station!" snapped Judge Hiro, one of Kessler's senior SJS officers. "Give me laser cannon control!"

The pilot gaped. "Sir? Our orders are to arrest Dredd, not kill him!"

"The lasers!" Hiro growled, a warning in his voice. "Or else I'll charge you with obstruction of justice!"

Reluctantly, the pilot switched the L-Wagon's gun controls to Hiro's console and the SJS man locked the cannons on the oxy-station. Hiro's partner Judge Wright watched him take aim. "Dial down the power, man. If you shoot wide you'll punch through the dome."

Hiro grinned savagely. "It's just a warning shot." He thumbed the fire control and twin bolts of energy flashed out and cut through the oxy-station.

Inside, Dredd fell into a tuck-and-roll as the las-blast tore through the control centre, ripping open the walls and turning the computer console into scrap metal. Hot semi-molten fragments spat into the air, turning his breath acidic in his throat.

"Dredd!" The SJS-Judge's voice bellowed over the L-Wagon's public address system. "By order of the Chief Judge-Marshal, you are under arrest!"

"How the drokk did they find me?" Dredd growled, fumbling for his pulse gun. "Can't get captured now… Kessler's gonna lock me up and throw away the key!"

He rose up from behind the cover of a ruined desk and sent a brace of shots out through the rent in the wall. The pulse blasts sparked off the L-Wagon's hull and the airfoils.

"He's aiming for the stabilisers! He's trying to bring us down!" yelled the pilot.

Hiro leapt from the laser station and sprinted into the cockpit. "Wright, take the lasers!" He grabbed a handful of the pilot's uniform. "You! Get out of that chair!"

"What?" the pilot blinked. "You're not authorised to fly this–"

"I said get out!" Hiro shouted, smacking the pilot aside with a hard right cross. The other man recoiled, dazed and the SJS officer shoved him out of the control seat. Hiro grabbed the joystick and throttle, turning the L-Wagon to face the hole torn in the side of the oxy-station. The flyer's floodlights picked out Dredd as he sprinted for the lift tube.

"Oh no you don't!" grated Hiro.

The pattern of the spotlights shifted suddenly as the L-Wagon lurched forward. Dredd had a moment to see the nose of the flyer looming though the broken wall before he was knocked off his feet by a colossal impact. The front quarter of the L-Wagon penetrated the interior of the oxy-station, cutting through desks and consoles like matchwood. Dredd rolled, his STUP-gun spinning away from him, dodging falling girders and pieces of ceiling.

The echo of the collision ringing in his ears, Dredd pushed himself backup to his feet and dived for his gun. From the corner of his eye he caught a blink of movement, a night-black uniform trimmed with silver skulls coming at him like a rocket. His fingers touched the butt of the pulse gun just as a daystick cracked him across the back.

"Stay down!" Wright commanded. "We got you!"

Dredd decided otherwise. He flipped over, caught Wright's shin between his ankles and twisted. The SJS-Judge let out a hiss of pain and fell over backwards, arms windmilling. Dredd reached for the STUP-gun in time to meet Judge Hiro's boot in the face.

The second SJS officer kicked him again for good measure, then brought down his heel on Dredd's splayed hand. "Fingers!" he spat, teeth bared in a snarl.

Constellations of light exploded inside Dredd's skull, flares of pain making him dizzy. He shifted, coming to his feet, trying to gather himself.

"Tough old bastard." Wright's voice said from somewhere nearby.

"Not tough enough," retorted Hiro. "Got your gun?"

"Yeah."

"Then shoot him."

Dredd launched himself towards the SJS-Judge just as something sunbright and sizzling struck him hard in the chest. The walls of the oxy-station seemed to shift and merge, as if they were collapsing in on him. Darkness gathered in on Dredd, voices chasing him into a senseless black void.

"You could have killed us all with that stunt, Hiro."

"Don't be such a weakling."

* * *

Che examined the object on the desk before him and his lips twisted in a weary grimace. "And this is?"

"I believe it is some form of listening device," said Kessler, absently running a finger over his scarred chin. "After you were sworn in I took the liberty of ordering a deep scan of Judge-Marshal Tex's... Uh, that is, of your office and my technicians discovered it. The unit self-destructed before we could make a thorough examination, but it appears to have been a transmitter."

Che pushed it away. "Bugs planted in the Chief Judge's office. How did we come to this? It sickens me to think we may have turncoats and crooked Judges among our forces!"

"I wholeheartedly agree, sir. Luna-1 is a city that enjoys unprecedented freedoms, but because of that we must also be the most watchful. That is why the SJS is also free to pursue its objectives to the bitter end." Kessler said the last words with relish.

"I want every officer on the take found and purged!" Che thumped the desk with his fist.

Kessler smiled crookedly. "Already in progress, sir. We are investigating the technician Maktoh, who I suspect Dredd killed in order to prevent discovery of his own collusion and Rodriguez. There may be others."

Che nodded. "What is the word from the street? Is the curfew holding?"

"For now, Judge-Marshal. There has been some squawking from the veterans' societies and citizen rights groups about the possible effects on the upcoming Apocalypse Day anniversary, but we've dealt with that." Kessler handed the Chief Judge a data-pad. "We still have a few isolated pockets of trouble here and there – an incident at the Tycho Brahe Hilton hotel and a fire at the Leisureplex – but nothing that cannot be quelled with the correct application of force."

"And those punkamente channel hackers?"

Kessler's face soured. "Their transmissions remain untraceable, sir. Tek Division simply do not have hardware advanced enough to block their frequency-hopping attack programs. Short of shutting down every vid-screen, net-link and radio on Luna-1, there's no way we can stop them."

"And so they continue to goad us and make the citizens side against us," he spat. "If you can't block the signals, then find the source and destroy it! There is a cancer at the heart of this city, Kessler and these are all symptoms of it. I want it cut out, do you understand? Ripped out, if needs be, but gone!" He stood up and began to pace. "Tex's death will be avenged, of that you must be certain!"

"My sentiments exactly, Judge-Marshal. You should know that two of my best men have reported in with Dredd in custody. He will be arriving in confinement in a matter of minutes."

"Dredd! I never wanted him up here, do you know?" Che studied the room around him. Despite the events of the past twenty-four hours, he could not settle himself with the idea that the city was now his to command. "I told Tex that we could handle these insurrections ourselves, and now it has come to this."

"Desperate times require extreme measures," said Kessler archly. "Dredd is a tricky one. He lives on his reputation, but only the clearest thinkers can see he's not all he appears to be."

"I... I never wanted to take Tex's place, Kessler, you understand? Not like this. I don't know if I can do the job that he did."

"You have the full support of every man serving under you, sir," Kessler replied smoothly, "including the Special Judicial Service."

Che gave a vague nod. "Yes... Thank you, Kessler."

A chime sounded from the intercom. "Chief Judge, we're ready to begin the conference."

"Very well." Che sat down and turned to face the eagle's-eye window. "Begin." The glasseen oval flickered and changed to become a series of smaller screens. Each displayed the face of a senior Judge from the member states of the Global Partnership Treaty, some broadcasting from Earth, others from their courier ships in lunar orbit. Kessler sneered as he saw Kommisar Ivanov appear among them.

A dozen voices began talking at once, all of them raised and angry.

Che waved a hand in front of his face, as if he was dismissing a nagging insect. "One at a time, please, señors!"

Kessler watched as Che fought off recriminations and harsh words from representatives of a dozen city-states. Each of them said it in a different way, but all of them were pushing the same agenda – they all believed that Luna-1 was on the verge of collapse and that their city was the one that should step in to take over.

Kessler kept his expression set, but inwardly he sneered. Look at them, fighting over the Moon like a pack of rabid dogs! The SJS chief doubted that any one of the diplomats and representatives had the strength of will to keep Luna-1 in line. Only a hardened man, someone like himself, was capable of that. His eyes drifted to Che, whose face was ruddy with anxiety. Perhaps, he thought, I may have to take a more proactive hand in things.

Then the feed from Mega-City One was highlighted and Chief Judge Hershey's face filled the screen. "Judge-Marshal Che, before we go any further, I must protest your issue of an arrest warrant for Judge Dredd–"

Kessler broke in before Che could answer. "You may protest all you want, Chief Judge, but you have no jurisdiction here. Dredd is my prisoner and he is going to answer for his crimes!"

The SJS-Judge's words set off a new storm of invective from the screens but Kessler simply looked on, a mocking glint in his monocled eye.

Consciousness returned to Dredd as a series of slow, dull aches all over his body. He opened his eyes and his vision swam for a moment before he recognised the shape of a bio-lume strip above him. Gingerly, he righted himself; someone had roughly deposited him on a bunk in a standard iso-cube. Almost every item of Justice Department-issue clothing was gone, even down to his boots. All they had left him was the regulation blue-black undersuit and his helmet.

Dredd washed away the metallic taste in his mouth with a cupped handful of water from the sink mounted in the far wall. Aside from the bunk, the steel toilet in the opposite corner of the room and the black dome of a scanner in the ceiling, the cell was bare. The Judge absently ran a hand over the plasteen walls. He'd lost count of the number of perps he'd put in places like this one, but he remembered with absolute clarity every time that he had been forced into a cell. It happened with a regularity that Dredd found extremely irritating. Anywhere else and he might have held out hope for a fair trial, a chance to prove his innocence – but with Kessler prosecuting him and Moonie's unseen influence infesting the Luna-1 Justice Department, Dredd had his doubts.

Once I get out of this, he thought to himself, I'm recommending a serious review of the Luna Judge force.

He stepped up to the cell door and peered through a grille. Beyond, he could see a dozen more doors and a corridor leading off around a corner. Dredd guessed that he was in the sub-basement levels of the Grand Hall of Justice, in the long-term holding cells. Before too long, he'd probably be transferred over to the SJS building and left to Kessler's tender mercies. He remembered his last visit there with razor-sharp clarity and Kessler's leering face hanging over him as he tried to wring a confession from him. There was no doubt in Dredd's mind that this time the SJS officer would pull out all the stops; Kessler would make their previous meeting look like a happy chit-chat.

A Luna-City Judge came into view and stopped in front of Dredd's cell. "You're awake." He beckoned someone that Dredd could not see. "You have a visitor."

There was a flick of red and black and Kontarsky appeared, her ice-cold eyes giving him the most cursory of glances. "Open it," she told the other Judge. "I need to speak to him."

Dredd knew the drill. He stepped back into the cell and the door retracted into the wall. Kontarsky entered and the Luna-City Judge stood in the doorway. "They caught you," she said flatly.

"Yeah. A real coincidence, considering that you were the only one who knew where I was." He studied her face for any sign of emotion, any hint that would give him a clue about what she was thinking, but there was nothing.

"You are the most wanted man in the city, Dredd. Your capture was inevitable." Kontarsky ignored the thinly veiled accusation. "Kessler was denied access to interrogate me. I have been released into the custody of Kommissar Ivanov."

"Don't let me keep you from reporting in to your bosses at the Diktatorat. I'm sure they'll be pleased to hear that an Enemy of the People has been arrested for a murder he didn't commit."

"Kessler believes you are the agent of chaos here, Dredd. He intends to prove that you are working to destabilise Luna-1, possibly as an instrument of the crime lord Moonie–"

"I put Moonie away!" Dredd snapped. "You were there at Farside, you saw what happened to Rodriguez and Maktoh! You know what will happen if we don't stop that freak. He wants the Moon so badly he'll cause the deaths of thousands to get it!"

Kontarsky said nothing for a long moment, then in a rapid blur of movement, she whipped around and drew a compact needle gun from inside the folds of her cloak, turning the pistol on the Luna Judge. "Do not move," she ordered, "or you will be shot."

"Where did you get that?" said Dredd, indicating the weapon.

"I had a spare," Kontarsky retorted. "Do you not recognise a prison break when you see one? We have little time. I programmed the isocube's security camera to run a loop of footage, but it will only last for a few minutes."

Dredd folded his arms. "Why should I trust you? For all I know, you're part of this conspiracy as well. How do I know you didn't tip off the SJS about where to find me? How do I know you're not going to have me 'shot while trying to escape'?"

"Because I give you my word. Not as an East-Meg citizen or a member of the Sov party, but as a Judge." She stepped closer to him, careful to keep her pistol on the guard. "I am a Russian and I am a patriot, but my first loyalty is to justice. To the law."

Dredd held out his hand. "Prove it. Give me the gun."

Kontarsky did not hesitate. "Here." She placed the needler in his palm and did not flinch when the Mega-City Judge carefully aimed the weapon at her.

"What's to stop me shooting you and making my own way out of here?"

"Nothing. But I can help you get to the heart of this conspiracy, Dredd. There's more at stake than just the dissension here in Luna-1; I suspect that Kommisar Ivanov may be involved in some way."

Dredd considered this new development. An East-Meg connection chimed with the illegal weapons discovered at Kepler and Kontarsky's knowledge would be a useful asset – if he could bring himself to trust a Sov-Judge.

"Guess you're right," he said after a moment. "You!" Dredd told the Luna Judge. "Get in here. Give me your gear."

The guard nodded. "I'm not going to stop you, sir," he replied, quickly stripping off his holster, shoulder pads, belt and boots. "I don't care what the SJS say, I know you didn't kill the Chief Judge."

Dredd studied the younger man's face. "Do I know you, son?"

"Goodworthy, sir. Judge Arthur Goodworthy, Junior. You saved my dad's life once, back on New Year's Eve, 2100. He went Futsie."

Dredd nodded, the events returning to him. "Future shock syndrome. You were just a child, your father worked for Moonie."

"Yes," said Goodworthy. "That creep worked my dad until he cracked, then sent his goons to gun him down on the street! But you stood up for him, sir. You got him to the shrinks and I never forgot that. That's why I became a Judge." He handed Dredd his STUP-gun. "Get him, sir. The Moon doesn't need scum like Moonie any more."

"Count on it." Dredd nodded at Kontarsky and the Sov-Judge struck Goodworthy with a nerve punch, knocking him unconscious.

"He would have helped us," said Kontarsky. "We could have used him."

Dredd shook his head. "No sense giving Kessler anyone else to take it out on. From now, we do this alone."

"Very well. I assume you have some sort of plan?

"I'll explain on the way."

14. FRESH AIR

With a grim set to his jaw, Dredd watched the metropolitan sprawl flash past through the small rectangular window of the railshuttle, buildings in the foreground blurring into abstract white shapes while the structures further away seemed to move at a more sedate speed. Luna-1 was a city under siege by forces from within and without. Thin plumes of smoke lingered in the air over places where street-fights had turned into infernos and the glittering shapes of Manta prowl tanks and armed Justice Department flyers wove low patterns between the Selenescrapers, spotlights washing over citiblocks and con-apt clusters.

Now and then, Dredd saw the faraway blink-blink of a muzzle flash, too distant to be heard over the rumble of the robot zoom train's maglev. The bubbling undercurrent of tension and lawlessness that he had sensed when he first arrived was raging on the surface now. People were dying and there was little that the Judges could do except plug the flow and pray that more cracks didn't appear. The Mega-City lawman had heard rumours over the past few years about the state of Luna-1, but he had typically dismissed them as hearsay. Somewhere in the back of his mind, Dredd had always known that the lunar capital would stay on an even keel as long as his old friend Tex was at the helm – but now the Judge-Marshal's corpse was barely cold and his city was self-destructing. What would happen in the coming days would be a test of fire for the new leader of Luna-1 and Dredd knew in his bones that former Deputy Judge-Marshal Che wasn't up to the task. Worse, Che was relying on Kessler for support without considering the SJS chief's own agenda.

The curfew would settle things for a few hours, but soon the city would grow restless once more – and the next time it would be worse. Dredd had seen countless block wars during his career, even the monstrous citywide conflict that was the precursor to the invasion by East-Meg One and he knew the cycle of violence behind them all too well. Citizens, trapped in lives that had little point, angry at everything and bored with the status quo were easy converts to the pack mentality and lust for casual violence that mob rule provided. But unlike the people of Earthbound Mega-Cities, Luna-1's populace didn't have the room to expand and blow off steam – they had a city with a lid on it, a pressure cooker that would get hotter and hotter until it exploded. No, there was only one way to stem the tide now. They had to find the root cause of the disorder. Find it and destroy it.

The railshuttle turned on to an outbound loop and with a lurch it was suddenly beyond the main city dome, passing behind the Puerto Luminia barrio and out into the wilderness of the Oxygen Desert. There was little aerial traffic over the city, the curfew extended to all forms of travel, including orbital transports and spaceliners. Only vehicles vital to Luna-1's operation, like this robot train or the constant string of astro-tankers, were still running. But there were other ships up there, hard-edged shapes glinting among the stars, watching one another and biding their time. They circled the Moon like patient vultures shadowing a dying man, crewed by men who were diplomats in name only, men who kept a vigil for the first moment of opportunity. Dredd had no doubt that the moment Luna-1 turned into a fully-fledged war zone, each of them would be landing troop transports full of well-armed "advisors" intent on planting their flag on the city.

"We are accelerating," said Kontarsky. She shifted her position behind a cargo pod and frowned. "This is most uncomfortable."

"I didn't pick this train for the smooth ride," Dredd retorted. "We couldn't chance trying to take another hopper… This is the best option we have."

The Sov-Judge gave a nod. "As you say. But these things are not meant for human passengers and crew. We only have air in this wagon because the cargo in these pods would degrade without it."

Dredd remembered the last time he'd ridden the rails – aboard a hijacked, bomb-laden zoom train crossing the Black Atlantic – and decided that the drab lunar railshuttle was a big improvement. Kontarsky's escape ploy had been good enough to sneak the two of them out of the Grand Hall of Justice without arousing suspicion. Judge Goodworthy had kept his promise and, for all Dredd knew, he was still sleeping off Kontarsky's nerve strike in the iso-cube, waiting for the getaway to be discovered.

Dredd had guided them to a railhead depot in District Six, where automated magnetic levitation trains were dispatched to the distant outpost domes and factory complexes. From there, it had been a fairly simple matter for him to locate a railshuttle bound for the destination he wanted and they had boarded by stealth as machine loaders filled the train with freight. Kontarsky went along with all his commands up to this point without comment, but Dredd couldn't shake off his nagging doubts about the youthful Sov-Judge. It had taken a lot to convince himself not to just stun her and leave her with Goodworthy, but she'd proven useful throughout the investigation and like it or not, he had no way of knowing if something she had said got him caught by the SJS Judges Hiro and Wright. Kessler was smart, after all and he would have probably put someone in Kepler Dome just on the off-chance that Dredd would turn up there. It was what Dredd would have done, if the circumstances were reversed. On top of that, if Kontarsky was right about Ivanov, someone with knowledge of Sov protocols could be invaluable.

Still, trust never came easy to Dredd and Kontarsky had a long way to go before she fully earned it. Keep your friends close, but keep your enemies closer, he remembered, watching her from the corner of his eye.

"Now that we are outside the city walls, perhaps you would be kind enough to inform me as to where we are going?"

"I found something at Kepler, in the oxy-station. Someone tampered with the airflow."

"Tek-Division said the oxygen outage was an accident. That's what triggered the disturbance."

Dredd shook his head. "I'm not convinced. Those Moon-U creeps were right there, stirring up trouble the moment the fans stopped spinning. They knew what was going to happen. They caused it. It doesn't take a genius to figure out that Moonie is to blame for this."

"Moonie, Moonie, everything keeps coming back to him. I don't understand, Dredd, what kind of person is he? If what you say about him is true, how can a man nurture such a plan for two and a half decades without being discovered?"

The railshuttle rattled through a set of points. "Money, Kontarsky. Cold, hard credits. Moonie was one of the richest humans alive when I busted him and back then Luna-1 was a boomtown, full of men who were more than willing to take his coin – Judges included. And those that didn't work for him were afraid of him."

"But you put him away. You changed all that."

"I thought I did. Now I'm not so sure. Power like that doesn't just dry up overnight. Moonie just made sure his assets went dark, so he could pick them backup when he needed them. If I hadn't arrested him then, he would have ended up owning the Moon, lock, stock and moonrocks. That's been his goal all along. What he's doing now, it's all steps along the same road."

"He wants to become lord of the Moon, is that it? Like some deformed gnome king from a child's storybook?"

Dredd shrugged. "That's a little more flowery than I'd put it, but yes, that's about the size of it. He poured his life into exploring the Moon and it bit him in the ass when that virus infected him. He's been looking for revenge ever since... He told me once that the Moon 'owes him' and to pay back that debt he's gonna try to take it all."

"He's insane," Kontarsky pronounced.

"That fact has never been in question," agreed Dredd.

She responded with a slight, humourless smile. "I'm still waiting for an answer. Where is this train taking us?"

Dredd pointed to the window. "Take a look."

Kontarsky pressed her face to the glass, craning her neck to look along the direction the railshuttle was travelling. Rising up from the vast bowl of Catharina Crater was a gunmetal hemisphere. It sat like a vast silver-grey octopus, thick tubular tentacles extending out to the surrounding moonscape and vanishing into smaller caverns. In the surrounding acres, robotic ice harvesters combed the lunar mantle for ancient deposits of frozen gases, while vent tunnels big enough to drive a mo-pad through connected the facility with distribution plants in Luna-1. The Sov-Judge saw the glitter of a holo-sign floating above the dome: *LunAir – Every Breath You Take*!

"The Oxy-Dome Complex," Dredd announced. "The central atmosphere recycling plant for most of the Moon, including Kepler."

"You think we'll find Moonie there?"

"No, but someone in that dome shut off the air to Kepler and they did it on Moonie's orders. We find them..."

"We find him," Kontarsky finished.

"Find him!" Moonie raged, his broad, leering face turning pinkish-red as the blood rushed through the nearly translucent skin over his skull. Spittle flew from his lips and as an afterthought, he struck his aide across the cheek. "You are worse than useless, you skinny wretch! You assure me that Dredd is behind bars, then you tell me that he isn't... What do I pay you for?"

Sellers's throat went dry and his jaw worked as he tried to explain himself. Across the table in the Silent Room, he could see the other two members of the cabal watching his superior's tirade with utter calm, their faces neutral. In many ways, that was more insulting than if they had openly mocked him for his mistakes.

"Answer me!" Moonie snapped, rocking forward on his hoverchair. "Where is Dredd?"

"Our man in the Special Judicial Service is searching," the words came out in a rush, "and he informs me that Judge-Marshal Che is extremely distressed about the development."

"He's not the only one!" bellowed Moonie. "We should have taken Dredd ourselves instead of letting those idiot Judges confine him! That indecisive dolt Che isn't fit to lead a Mariachi band, let alone a city!" The old man coughed harshly, his energy all but spent on the effort of losing his temper.

"Better that Che is in charge than someone else," said the bald man. "He may have found the hypno-pulser we used to affect Tex but his ineffectual manner will serve our needs just as well." He paused and looked away. "As for Dredd, your obsession with this man is clouding your vision of the larger picture."

Moonie's face reddened once again, but the tall man cut him off before he could launch into another furious rant. "But, as we all know, Dredd is an impediment that must be dealt with and while I had hoped we might be able to recover him intact, for examination purposes, I see now that his death is the only logical route to pursue."

"Finally!" Sellers muttered. "You had him in your sights a half-dozen times and now at last you want to kill him."

The tall man deflected the comment effortlessly. "Please do not try to shift blame to me for your failures, Sellers. Despite your rudeness, I will grant you this gift." He produced a rod-like device and placed it on the black stone table.

Moonie's chair skated closer and he snatched up the object before his aide could touch it. "What is this?" he asked, even as he thumbed a switch on the tip.

The holo-screen blipped and shifted to show a relief map of the lunar surface. A bright indicator flag shimmered into existence near the base of the Sea of Nectar.

Moonie's age-yellowed teeth showed in a feral smile. "A tracer?"

The tall man nodded. "Dredd is not alone. I took the liberty of placing a tracking device on the person of his travelling companion."

"Kontarsky..." said Sellers. "The iso-cube guard told the SJS that she was Dredd's hostage."

"A simple fiction," said the tall man. "But one that will soon come to an unhappy ending."

Sellers studied the map. "The air plant. He's heading towards the air plant."

Moonie sneered. "It doesn't matter. He'll never get the chance to act on anything he finds there." The aged crime lord stabbed at a communicator control on his chair. "Get a hit team out to the Oxy-Dome complex. Dredd is there. Tell them to bring me back his head."

* * *

The two Judges kept to the shadows, avoiding the footprints of heat sensors and the scanning heads of static security cameras. The railshuttle was already gone, having paused for only a few moments on a siding inside the Oxy-Dome before rumbling onward with one less container of mechanical spares on its flatbed. It was time enough for Dredd and Kontarsky to alight, slipping between loader-meks that carried huge chunks of gas ice from automated cars that went to and from the mineshafts.

There was air inside the Oxy-Dome, warm and humid, a spill-off from the electro-chemical cracking processes that constantly thundered through the fractionation towers around them. The atmosphere smelled dull and stale here, thick with the recovered exhalations of millions of Luna-1 citizens.

Kontarsky nodded at a complex knot of pipes and conduits that emerged from the dome's lower levels. "Those are the recycler channels. There's carbon dioxide coming in through them and filtered oxygen going back."

Dredd gave an absent nod, watching a large crane grab pass over their heads carrying a pallet piled high with chips of dirty ice. Most of the frozen gases used by LunAir came from numerous deposits inside the lunar rock face, but some had a more distant origin, carved off the sides of comets in slow solar orbits and sent hurtling moonward to soft-land in the Sea of Nectar. Harvester robots scooped up the fragments and ferried them back to the Oxy-Dome in a constant circuit.

The Mega-City Judge paused and watched the vast machines working around them in a hissing, clanking ballet of metal and plastic. "No humans here," he noted, "not even an observer pod or an overseer."

"We should locate the command centre," said the Sov-Judge. "Any organic personnel would be there–"

She fell silent as a spotlight stabbed out of nowhere and flooded their concealment with hard, white light. A synthetic voice screeched from above them. "Intruder alert! Industrial spies detected! Confine and terminate!"

"That's not good," Dredd said and snatched at Kontarsky's arm, pulling her out of the spotlight. Ozone crackled through the air behind them as an electro-blaster shot thousands of volts into the space where they had just been crouching. The harsh sodium glare swivelled to follow them and Dredd caught a glimpse of its source: an insectile security drone suspended on a quad of vector-jets. Amid the constant noise of the oxygen works, neither of the Judges had heard the robot approaching them.

Kontarsky understood what needed to be done before Dredd said it to her and she broke away from him, sprinting in the opposite direction. The drone saw the movement and hesitated for a fraction of a second, unsure if she or Dredd was the target of primary importance. In that moment, Dredd set his STUP-gun to level four tight-beam and shot at it.

The pulse-blast sheared one of the thruster pods off the drone and sent it listing to starboard like a sailboat caught in a sudden gale. The spotlight ran wildly over the walls as it struggled to regain control of its flight. Another pulse of hot light from the direction that Kontarsky had run flickered into the drone's casing and buffeted it, but the machine recovered and aimed back at the Sov-Judge, fixing her in the middle of its sights. Without the anti-dazzle visor in her helmet, Kontarsky was blinded by the drone's beam and she fired wildly at it, her shots missing by several metres. Trapped between two slow-moving tankers, she braced herself for the inevitable shock of voltage from the e-blaster, but it never came.

Without warning, there was an ear-splitting gush of sparks and something heavy flattened the drone into the sub-levels below them, knocking it out of the air like a fly swatted by a sledgehammer. Blinking away purple after-images on her retinas, Kontarsky looked up to see Dredd beckoning to her. Above the Mega-City Judge, a crane frame buzzed and spat where he had blown off the retaining bolts that held an ice pallet. "Spaciba…" she managed.

Dredd pointed with the STUP-gun. "This way."

Kontarsky shook off the sick feeling in her stomach that the fear of imminent death had created and followed him. She listened for the sound of drone motors and heard them – lots of them. Next time there would be more and Dredd would not be able to drop an ice load on all of them.

"Neutralise the intruders!" screamed the electronic voice. "Productivity has been threatened! Intercept and destroy!"

Klaxons were sounding now and flashing red strobes pulsed into life across the inside of the Oxy-Dome. Robots that had the right kind of sensors or that weren't engaged in some kind of critical work stopped what they were doing and looked for the two human shapes; the data from them went straight to the security drones, vectoring them towards the Judges like a flock of airborne predators.

"We must get off the factory floor!" Kontarsky cried. "We are too exposed here!"

Dredd ducked into an alcove where a heavy hatch was half-concealed in shadow. "Here!" he snapped. "Help me with the wheel!"

The door had not been used in a long time and rust caked the lip and the circular handle in the centre. Clearly, no human had been into this part of the oxygen works in years. With a final grunt of effort, Dredd and

Kontarsky forced the hatch open and almost fell through it, desperately pushing it shut again as the drones closed in. The man-sized entryway was too small for the larger security flyers, but both Judges knew that it wouldn't be long before a humanoid robot was sent after them.

"This…" Kontarsky said, catching her breath. "This has not gone as well as I would have hoped."

Dredd spared her a look. "We go up," he said. The hatch opened on to a ladder that extended away to the myriad sub-levels below and the multiple floors above. "This must be some sort of maintenance duct, for human use."

Kontarsky considered this as they climbed. "You said yourself, there aren't any people down on the lower levels."

"No," he agreed, "and I'm starting to suspect that the only living things in this place are us."

They proceeded almost without incident, except for a moment fifteen levels high, when something fast had come clanking up from below them. In the faint light of the shaft, all either of the Judges had been able to see were the sparks flicking off the walls as steel claws scraped their way up after them. Dredd ordered Kontarsky to look away and he fired his pulse gun past her, a full power charge ripping through the confined tube of air and striking the robot dead centre. It clattered and scraped all the way back down again, making fresh blooms of sparks as it fell.

They continued upward. It was the longest climb of Nikita Kontarsky's life, or so it seemed. In the moments when she wasn't struggling with arms and legs that felt like lead, she marvelled at the constant pace that Dredd maintained, steadily advancing up the shaft towards the upper levels. Had she not known better, she might have suspected that the Judge was a machine himself, maybe one of those near-human life model decoy replicants that she had heard rumours about. What if he does have oil pumping through those veins, her fatigued mind wondered, what if Joseph Dredd has been dead for decades and Mega-City One has just kept on turning out robot duplicates? It was a mad idea, but one that many other kadets had declared as certain truth during her training. She shook the thought away as a strong hand curled around her wrist and guided her off the ladder.

"We're here. Ready?"

With effort, she raised her pistol. "I am."

Dredd forcefully kicked open the hatch on the top level and strode out. Kontarsky followed him, watching. If Dredd wasn't a machine, then he was as near to one as a man would ever get.

The room they had emerged into was a large gallery set into the roof of the oxygen works. From here, anyone operating the command consoles that ringed the walls could look out across the full spread of the dome's systems. This high up, the Oxy-Dome's interior looked like some vast set of interlocking clockwork toys, each working in perfect precision.

The synthetic voice that had called the Judges out screamed through the air again, louder and more strident this time. "Alert! Alert! Intruders in central processing unit! Productivity is in jeopardy! Alert! Alert!"

Slats in the ceiling retreated to allow arms on gimbals to extend downward, uncoiling like inverted scorpion tails; each one ended in the barbed sting of an active electro-blaster and they tracked as one towards Dredd and Kontarsky. The two law enforcers took cover and snapped out shot after shot from their pulse pistols, burning smoky soot-black sears across the roof of the chamber. The blasters fired back, but they were slow and had been poorly maintained, just like the rusted hatch. In a matter of a few moments, all the remote weapons had been destroyed.

Dredd kept his gun handy and approached a central dais where a raised console sat. A crude approximation of a face – indicator light eyes and an oscillating sine wave mouth – was displayed there. "Identify yourself!" Dredd barked at the screen.

"LunAir Oxy-Dome Control Computer XF6," replied the voice. "You are an intruder. The authorities have been notified. You will be captured and–"

Dredd picked another console at random and fired a shot into it. The panel spat out a puff of desultory smoke and far below in the oxygen works, a whole sector of the plant went dark. "I want answers, chip-head, not a conversation. Where's your human overseer?"

"System XF6 operates flawlessly without human intervention," the computer said snidely. "Orders come direct via data link."

"You cut off the air to Kepler Dome. How?"

"This unit cannot answer questions of–"

Dredd blew a trio of fist-sized holes in a panel to his left and faint sirens screamed, as if the Oxy-Dome was a wounded animal crying out in pain. "How?" Dredd repeated.

It suddenly dawned on Kontarsky what Dredd was doing. Like many centralised industrial computers, the XF6 was programmed to prioritise factory productivity over everything else, even its own survival. By damaging its sub-consoles and wrecking the plant, Dredd was effectively interrogating the machine in the same way that someone might break a human subject's finger or strike them to elicit a response.

"Productivity is in jeopardy!" the computer whined. "Please desist!"

Kontarsky approached a large processor module and rested her STUP-gun's barrel on it. Dredd gave her a cool nod.

"Wait! XF6 will respond!"

"Better," said Dredd. "There are multiple redundant systems in the Luna-1 life-support hardware. How did you circumvent them all?"

"All Luna-1 systems are built on an existing framework. Embedded commands in base software allow subversion of all subsequent additions and upgrades."

"A back door program?" Kontarsky wondered. "When was it put in place?"

"At the point of initial construction, circa 2058."

"That's when Luna-1 was first built." Dredd noted, "Drokk! That means there's been a kill switch wired into the whole city since day one!"

"But who could have done this?"

Dredd's lip curled in a sneer. "Ask yourself, who was in charge back then? Who was it that made sure he got every construction contract, every land grab, every sweet deal? This place was the wild frontier. Laws were flouted as long as the job got done."

"Computer, who was primary contractor for the original Luna-1 dome systems?" Kontarsky demanded.

"Moonie Enterprises," said the console. "The company was disbanded as of 2100 by order of then-current Judge-Marshal Joseph Dredd."

15. TRANQUILITY BASE

Dredd turned to Kontarsky. "You asked me before how one man could plan to steal the Moon and here's your answer: Clinton Moonie has been taking the long view... He's been planning this caper since before you were born."

"A secret command that lets him shut off air to any dome on the Moon... The implications of such a thing are staggering. But if Moonie can do this, why has he never used it before? When he was arrested, he could have traded his freedom for the threat of suffocating Luna-1," she replied.

"You still don't really understand him, do you? He's no street perp. Moonie doesn't want freedom, at least not in the way that you or I think of it. He doesn't care about anything except power, power over the Moon. He wants to own this ball of rock and everyone on it. What good is being master of a city when it's full of corpses?"

"I see your point," she conceded. "But we have no assurances that he won't change his mind and we still have many questions unanswered. Even with his money and influence, how could he have escaped and substituted a duplicate without detection? How could he have operated for months and not raise any suspicions?"

Dredd gave her a level stare. "You tell me, Kontarsky."

She matched his look. "You continue to distrust me, Dredd? You know the answers to these questions yourself and yet you test me over and over, hoping that I will reveal myself in a lie, yes? Why can you not see past my uniform and accept that we are fighting the same foe?"

"Because someone is helping Moonie and like you said, that someone may be one of your countrymen."

The Sov-Judge's pale face flushed. "I said no such thing! I voiced a suspicion, nothing more!" She forced herself to calm down. "It is true that I believe Moonie is not working alone, but his accomplices could be–"

Dredd looked away. "We'll burn that bridge when we come to it. Right now we have to concentrate on keeping Luna-1 breathing. If Moonie can pull the plug on the air, he's more dangerous than we ever suspected. We've gotta take that away from him and quickly. There's no telling what other surprises he's got lurking in the city's control sub-routines."

"The computer's orders came through a data link," she gestured to the control console on the dais. "The Oxy-Dome uses hard lines, fibre optic cables."

"Yes, they're more reliable than transmitters during the solar flares. That means the signal came down the line from the central computer hub in Luna-1 itself. If I know Moonie, he's close by so he can watch and gloat, but he's not dumb enough to be hiding in Luna-City itself. He's beaming his orders through the hub and straight into the network."

"Yes," nodded Kontarsky. "Very clever. He uses the system itself to carry his commands, making them invisible. But how do we sever that control without a shutdown of every system on Luna-1? I hardly think Che will agree to let us reboot the entire city."

The Sov-Judge was correct. Even if they could overcome the impossible odds against it, such a thing would plunge the lunar metropolis into chaos, exactly the circumstances that the fleet of so-called diplomatic cruisers in orbit was waiting for. Dredd realised the callous, engineered subtlety of Moonie's plans – the crime lord had set up the city like a complex game board, the pieces all turned to his advantage. But their other options had been reduced to nothing. "We're not going to ask for permission. How long would it take us to get back to the city?"

Kontarsky made a quick calculation. "Four hours in a rover, if we traversed the Sea of Tranquillity. Could we not return on the cargo train?"

"Negative, those railshuttles run once a day and the next won't pass this way until past dawn tomorrow. We need to get to the Spike."

"What are you planning, Dredd?" she demanded. The Spike was Luna-1's primary computer centre, a huge needle-shaped tower in Serenity Territory. Dominating the Luna-1 skyline, virtually every piece of computer data that flowed through the city complex went in or out of the vast plasteen spire.

"If we want to stop Moonie turning the air off, then Luna-1 has to go off the air. We're gonna spike the Spike."

"Perhaps all the free oxygen in here has affected your mind, Dredd. What you're suggesting is extremely dangerous! There's no telling what the side effects could be!"

The Mega-City Judge took a step closer. "Why are you opposed to trying, Kontarsky? All of this time, we've been dancing to Moonie's tune, always one step behind his game-plan." Dredd shook his head. "Not any more. We're going to change the rules. We reboot the hub and he'll be forced to use another way to tap into the dome systems."

The point of Dredd's daring gambit snapped into crisp focus for the Sov-Judge. "If Moonie does that, he won't be hidden. We'll be able to track him to his point of origin."

"Exactly. I figure we've got a fifty-fifty chance of making this work."

She frowned. "If it fails, the next thing we will see is armed ships and troopers from a dozen countries cutting their way through the airlocks and shooting each other. Are you really willing to risk a war?"

Dredd holstered his gun with a slight shrug. "Wouldn't be the first time."

At that moment, a kilometre above the lunar surface and a few more downrange from the Oxy-Dome Complex, a fast rocket was streaking westward under full burn, cutting a brilliant red streak across the black sky. The rocket itself was little more than a skeletal framework, an ugly collection of engine bells, fuel tanks and guidance systems that lacked even the most basic design aesthetics. Built to operate in a vacuum, it had none of the smooth lines of a trans-atmospheric liner or a NEO clipper, but that had no bearing on the craft's ability to perform its function and it was doing it to perfection. Thin Mylar sheets that served as micro-meteor barriers tore away from the middle of the fuselage like falling petals. They revealed four angular man-shapes hanging inside the rocket's frame, clustered like piglets suckling at a sow. One of the man-shapes was skinny and nimble-looking, with extra arms and legs; the other three were like cast blocks of dark metal in the shape of a human being.

A green lamp blinked on inside the heads of the three big man-shapes and the rocket let go of them, pushing them and their skinny sibling away under jets of inert gas. Any observer watching the figures falling towards the surface might have been reminded of an earthbound sky-diver. Messages carried on low-power laser beams blinked between the four and they shifted orientation as they dropped, revealing retro-rocket packs that would soft-land them just inside the factory perimeter. The rocket, its cargo delivered and its purpose complete, altered course and aimed for the foot of the Lunar Pyrenees. At maximum thrust, the crater it would form on impact would swallow any piece of wreckage bigger than a child's fist.

The larger figures used the time during the drop to run a few final diagnostics on their weapons and exoskeleton systems. None of them spoke. Each of them knew exactly who their targets were.

A new alarm sound chirped in the control room for a couple of seconds before suddenly being silenced. Dredd saw something appear and then disappear on one of the sub-consoles. "What the drokk was that?" he demanded of the computer.

The machine actually hesitated. "A glitch," it said finally. "A minor malfunction, now corrected. Please remain calm."

Kontarsky raised an eyebrow. "Doubtful. I believe a burst transmission was just received by the XF6 system." She tapped the screen on another panel. "It's hiding something from us. New orders, perhaps?"

Dredd indicated her drawn weapon with the jut of his chin. "Explain it to our silicon pal here, will you?"

The Sov-Judge dialled down the pulse setting and tore blaster bolts through two adjacent monitor stations. "Awwk!" The computer replied with a noise that might almost have been an analogue of physical pain. "Desist! Desist! The authorities are on the way! You will be neutralised!"

The screen close to Dredd reactivated, to display a real-time image from the perimeter sensors. Kontarsky saw the scan, the four downward tracks approaching the complex. "Missiles!" she gasped.

"Too slow," Dredd replied. "Besides, a missile hit in the wrong place here would blast a chunk out of the Moon as big as Texas City... No, these are something else. Not big enough to be landers, they must be hunter-killers or drop-troopers." The Judge didn't waste time on speculating who had sent them or how they had tracked them – for now they needed to flee. "We're sitting ducks here. We need a way out."

"We're at the top of the dome," said Kontarsky. "By the time we go down the ladder shaft, they would be setting up camp at the bottom."

"And we can't trust Smiley here not to lock us in the elevator," Dredd jerked a thumb at the XF6. "Where's the escape airlock for this floor?"

"Here!" Kontarsky tugged at a latch on the far wall and a sliding panel folded open. Another alarm went off automatically. Usually, escape airlocks were only accessed when fire or moonquakes had cut off all other means of egress.

The Russian tossed out a thin garment made from neon-bright orange plastic. "An emergency e-suit. These should be enough to protect us until we can reach the rover bays on ground level."

"You cannot abscond!" began the computer. "You will be–"

This time Kontarsky didn't wait to be asked, only paused before sealing her helmet shut to silence the XF6 with an energy bolt right between the machine's photoreceptor eyes.

Suited, Dredd followed her into the cramped airlock and pressed the heel of his hand into the button for fast decompression. The inner door had barely shut before the air caught in the lock screamed away into the lunar night. They stepped out and found themselves at the very crest of the Oxy-Dome, lit by the colours of the LunAir holo-sign.

Kontarsky pointed, pressing her jaws together to stop her teeth chattering in the polar cold. "Look, up there. I saw something."

Dredd followed her direction and caught a flash of reflected sunlight off a metallic surface, an object closing fast. "Where are the rovers?"

"Below us. We can use the walkway on the dome to get down," she began.

Dredd shook his head, the orange suit exaggerating the movement. "No time for that. We're taking the express route."

Kontarsky started to argue, but Dredd hit her hard with a body-check that flattened her to the curved surface of the roof. Without the adhesive soles of her suit's g-boots to hold her upright, she began to slide. The two Judges locked arms and fell like a human toboggan, racing down the steep slope of the dome towards the lip of the crater a hundred metres below.

Even through the thick polypropylop of the emergency suit, Dredd felt the stinging heat of friction as the material heated up from the forced descent; one sharp jag of metal in their path and they would suffer a catastrophic puncture.

Kontarsky screwed her eyes shut and held her breath, counting the seconds in her mind, desperately trying not to imagine what would happen if they struck a rocky outcrop at the lip of the domed crater – but Dredd's luck held and, with a shocking thud that made her spit out flecks of blood, they impacted a drift of moondust and rolled to a clumsy, bruising halt.

"Please have the decency to warn me if you wish to throw me off a roof," she snapped, checking her suit for tears as she stood up.

Dredd probed a hairline crack in his faceplate and frowned. "Our friends are almost here. Let's get ourselves some wheels."

The spindly humanoid shape landed on all fours next to the three identical man-forms. Its extra limbs unfolded to produce laser tips and a fan of sensors. The seeker head instantly found Dredd and Kontarsky, the heat of their bodies visible against the cold of the landscape in the infrared spectrum. It opened a real-time link to the armoured figures and showed them.

The figures threw off the disposable thruster packs that had slowed their descents and unlimbered a variety of weapons from magnetic clamps on their backpacks. Their leader gestured and they spread out in a loose formation.

The rover garage was a prefabricated hut of plastiform panels, sheathed from the hard radiation of the sun by a coasting of lunacrete. The roller-blind door gave easily under the combined fire from the Judges' pistols and they clambered inside, careful not to catch their suits on the orange-red edges of the hole they had burned. Kontarsky pulled a lamp from her belt and waved it around the room. There were a couple of open-deck moonjeeps to one side and a yo-yo, a civilian flybike similar to the Zippers used by the Judges. Dredd ignored them all and crossed to the largest vehicle in the room: set on a cluster of six fat wheels, the rover's hull was two spheres linked by a stubby tube. It was almost as tall as the garage was wide, but it had a sealed cabin and a better chance for survival on the lunar terrain. "This one," he said.

Kontarsky nodded and followed him through the rover's cramped air-lock. Inside, the vehicle smelled stale and mouldy. "This thing is ancient," she said under her breath.

If Dredd heard her comment, he gave no sign. The Judge dropped into the driver's seat and pressed the starter pedal. The rover's motor clicked and hummed, but did not engage. Dredd saw movement through the hole in the garage door and frowned, pushing the pedal again, harder this time.

The Sov-Judge saw it too, the thin, shiny arms clutching at the door, probing at the interior. With a sharp flash of motion, the skinny humanoid mechanism sprang through the torn gap and landed some-where in the shadows, out of sight.

"Hunter-killer," Dredd noted, working the ignition once more. This time, the motor hissed into life and the rover's headlight cast white beams over the garage interior. The vehicle lurched forward and Kontarsky let out a yelp as the scrawny robot slammed into the windscreen and hung there.

The machine's twitching head was only an arm's length away from Dredd's face, with nothing but the armoured glasseen of the window between them. A lipless metal mouth opened and extruded a drill-bit tongue that whirred into the plastic. Dredd stamped on the accelerator and the drive motors in the wheels responded, skidding as they picked up traction before launching the rover forward. The hunter-killer droid brought its extra arms around to aim a pair of laser cutters, concentrat-ing with digital precision on its primary target. Dredd ignored the robot and drove the moon rover straight into the centre of the garage's roller door. The collision sent a ringing crash through the hull of the vehicle and Kontarsky reeled, slipping to her knees in the gangway.

For a second, Dredd lost control of the rover and it fishtailed, the six balloon tyres biting into the moondust and kicking up spurts of grey powder like slow-motion fountains. The hunter-killer was flattened into the windscreen by the impact and parts of it broke off, thin legs snap-ping at the joints. Dredd saw a piece of the garage door fold away, the edge shearing through the droid's flexible neck. The robot's body dropped, tumbling under the axle. The rover bounced once, twice, three times as the portside wheels rode straight over it, smashing the attack drone into pieces.

Kontarsky struggled back to her feet, fingers clutching at a grab-bar for support as the rover bounded over the rough ground. She made a sour face at the head of the robot, which was still staring at them through the glasseen, impaled in place on its own drill shaft.

One of the suited men was knocked off his feet by the rover's explosive departure and he took long seconds to stand up once again. In the meantime, the leader and his other team-mate were sprinting after the fleeing vehicle, using compressed gas thrusters in their boot soles to make low, loping hops across the ground. Bouncing like children's toys, they skipped after the vehicle. Specially programmed targeting software developed for combat on the lunar surface came into play, overlaying graphics on the inside of their helmets, tracking the rover and predicting where it would go next. The scopes crunched numbers for velocity, speed, gravity and distance, giving the two of them aim points as good as anything a rock-steady target would have provided.

Ruby-coloured lasers winked out, linking the armoured figures and the rover like thin threads. One shot tore off the vehicle's communications antenna, the second struck the hub of the starboard rear wheel, melting vital gears in the drive mechanism.

Dredd felt the laser bolt hits rather than heard them, the seizing motor forcing a shudder up through the rover chassis. He paid no attention to the warning lights that flared on the dashboard, his boot pressing the accelerator pedal to the firewall. Beside him, Kontarsky was strapping herself into the jump seat.

"There are no weapons," her voice was high with barely concealed anxiety. "A remote construction arm, nothing else."

"Use it," said Dredd and he pulled hard on the steering yoke, bringing the rover around in a tight turn. The broad expanse of the Oxy-Dome reappeared in the window and before it the bouncing shapes of the two armoured suits. Dredd chose one of the suits at random and aimed the rover directly at it, revving the electric motor.

The leader used her jets to leap up to the top of a rocky outcropping as the rover swept past, bearing down on her team-mate at full speed. She toggled her laser to a broad-beam setting and raked a fiery streak down the length of the hull as the vehicle darted away. Her team-mate easily side-stepped the oncoming rover, but too late the leader saw that Dredd's intention had been to make him do exactly that, not to run him down. The other armoured suit dodged directly into the path of the heavy crane arm extending out from the back of the rover and, before she could shout a warning over the radio, the leader watched the claw-gripper at the end strike the figure in the chest, ripping away a great chunk of metallic armour as it passed. The other man twisted away into the dust, a gout of crimson gushing into the vacuum as he fell. Flash-frozen spheres of bright arterial blood scattered around him like a handful of jewels.

The rover skidded around and leapt over a rise, heading north to the Sea of Tranquillity. Frowning inside her helmet, the leader waited for her other team-mate to arrive and they paused to strip their dead comrade of equipment before destroying his corpse with a thermo-bomb.

Dredd pushed the rover to the redline while Kontarsky scrambled into the vehicle's engineering spaces, keeping one eye on the radar display in the dashboard. The screen showed sporadic contacts as the armoured hunters tracked them, the rover's sensors picking them up for just an instant as they crested a hill or jetted too high on their thrusters. They were close.

Kontarsky swayed down the gangway and dropped heavily into the other seat. Like Dredd, she had discarded the emergency environment suit as soon as they had found industrial-grade atmosphere gear in the rover. The Sov-Judge had also dispensed with her rad-cloak in order to squeeze into the maintenance bay. She wiped a speck of dirt from her milk-pale face; her expression spoke volumes before she opened her mouth. "Some of the batteries and a lubricant tank have been vented to vacuum. We have enough power to reach Luna-1 but we'll burn out the motors if we maintain this rate of speed."

"If we slow down those shooters will be on us in minutes."

Kontarsky threw up her hands in exasperation and swore in Russian, her cool finally cracking. "Fine! Just keep driving, then. At full power, sooner or later the motors will seize and the friction will cause a fire. We'll burn alive or suffocate!"

Dredd's eyes flicked to the radar screen in time to see another blink as something moved behind them. "We need another option, then." He pulled up a local map on the heads-up display. "Find somewhere to stop, make a stand. Otherwise, they'll be dogging us all the way." He highlighted an area and zoomed in.

Kontarsky saw where he was looking and shook her head. "You are joking."

The Mega-City Judge pulled the steering yoke around and changed course. "Have you got a better idea?"

She had to admit that she did not. "I'll fetch the suits."

The armoured figures landed on puffs of gas and dropped to their haunches, just as they had been trained. The leader tongued a switch on her chin-guard and gave her team-mate a quick beam-signal. He replied in the affirmative and walked in a crouch to the rover parked on the lip of a lunar dune. She watched her team-mate vanish inside, then reappear moments later. He made a shrugging motion. Empty.

They approached the flat piece of land before them, navigating around a small crater and from nowhere, a hologram blinked into life. Both of them had to restrain themselves from opening fire.

"Hello!" said the ghostly image of a smiling man, his voice broadcasting over their radio channels. "Welcome to Tranquillity Base National Park, the site of the first manned landing on the Moon in the year 1969! Please enjoy our interactive exhibit, but do keep off the–"

The proximity-activated hologram faded away in mid-speech as they left it behind and then the leader saw them – two orange shapes clustered in the lee of a low hillock. They fired, both hits to the bodies of their targets and the suited figures slumped like discarded rag dolls. The leader closed the distance to them.

The holographic guide appeared and disappeared as she passed another point of interest. "To your left is a laser ranging retroreflector that was left behind–"

She swore aloud and flashed out an alert signal. The orange suits were decoys – Dredd had filled them with air and laid them out to draw their fire! As if in answer, pulse blasts blinked from out of cover and she ducked, watching them converge on her team-mate. She saw puffs of blood stream out from his suit joints, then she looked away, triggering her jets and shot at the gunner directly ahead of her, half-hidden behind the shape of an ancient lunar lander.

Dredd saw the armoured suit fly towards him and ducked, rolling under the leg of the bug-like lunar module. The heavier suit turned after him, but the Judge had agility on his side and he ducked up and around behind it. With a vicious shove, Dredd slammed the leader's helmet into the one hundred and fifty year-old spacecraft. The suit's visor spiderwebbed with the force of the impact.

"Restored to its original state by the Historical Sticklers Society, the Apollo 11 lunar module seen here carried two human astronauts from ZZZT–" The holo was choked off in mid-speech as the armoured suit shoved an elbow into Dredd's chest and threw him into the display unit five metres away.

His ribs singing with pain, Dredd tried to scramble to his feet as the leader jetted across the distance between them. His STUP-gun had fallen out of arm's reach when he'd been thrown and now unarmed and injured, he saw the blocky shape of the armoured suit coming at him like a guided missile.

Dredd's suited fingers closed around something by his side and by reflex he pulled it from the moondust to brandish it like a spear. Unable to stop in time, the leader impaled herself on the spike and Dredd rammed it home through her faceplate, turning it into a window of red ruin. She slumped backward into a heap and only then did Dredd realise what he'd used as a makeshift weapon. Lanced through the suit's helmet was a steel rod that ended in a metallic Stars and Stripes.

16. RED MOON

Kontarsky scrambled over the lip of the shallow crater that had hidden her and sprinted as well as she could in the low lunar gravity, skipping over the moondust towards the shape of the second armoured figure. Streams of dark liquid, frozen into thick streaks by exposure to vacuum marred the grey frame of the exoskeleton; the hydrostatic shock of being hit by two full power pulse blasts had ruptured the delicate flesh of the man inside and cracked the suit collar. The armed hunter was bleeding inside and, if the blood loss didn't kill him first, he'd choke to death on his own vital fluids.

The Sov-Judge saw Dredd fighting with the other armoured figure in the periphery of her vision and ignored them; the Mega-City Judge was more than capable of dismissing his opponent without her help. She skidded to a halt near the injured man and planted a kick in his side as he tried to get up. Kontarsky felt conflicting emotions flood through her. A strong, heady anger was welling up in her chest and she wanted to turn it on the hunter, as if hurting him would pay back all the people who had been working against her. The rage drowned out the cold, clinical part of her personality for just long enough and she pressed her STUP-gun at his damaged chest plate.

The man mouthed something, but it was lost inside his bloodstained helmet. Kontarsky fired and the suit became his tomb. It wasn't until the life had guttered out in his eyes that she realised she knew what he had said. A plea, a single word, begging her not to kill him. *Nyet*.

She stiffened as the implications of it settled on her. Kontarsky peered closer at the suit, scrutinising the lines of its design, the framework of the laser weapon still gripped in one hand. The armour was of East-Meg manufacture, of that she was utterly sure. She looked away as Dredd approached, suddenly afraid that he would read everything through the emotions on her face.

Dredd gave the other corpse a cursory look. "Would have liked to get a live one," he said. "Might have been able to get something useful from them." When she didn't respond, he continued. "This hardware look familiar to you?"

"No," she replied, a little too quickly. "Why?"

"It's military specification stuff," Dredd noted, "not the kind of thing I'd expect a crook like Moonie to get his hands on. These people," he pointed at the dead man. "They were professionals."

"What does it matter now that they are dead?" Kontarsky tried not to be blunt, but she failed. "We can proceed now without any more interruptions, yes?"

"Yes," Dredd echoed after a moment, casting a measured eye over the Sov-Judge before making for the parked rover. "Let's get going."

As Kontarsky followed, her boot stubbed on something silver, half-buried in the moondust. She paused and bent to examine it.

"What?" Dredd paused on the ladder into the rover.

"It must have been knocked off the lunar module during the fight," she began, the thick fingers of her suit brushing the grey sand off the object. "A plaque..." Etched into the metal plate were black letters, partly bleached by solar radiation but still readable. *We came in peace for all mankind*, it said. Kontarsky considered the object for a moment, then dropped it back where she had found it. The words left a bitter taste in her mouth. "It's nothing. Nothing important."

The Sov-Judge mounted the ladder and soon the rover was on its way, leaving the bodies of the newly dead among the footprints of ancient history.

Arnos LeGrove wasn't afraid of a fight. He was a Citi-Def veteran and proud of it! Oh sure, he'd been just like all the other guys on floor 114 of Tommy Lee Jones Block, taking his regular stint polishing the sonic cannon or doing drills, never once imagining that his training would come in useful. But all that had changed one morning when Sov nukes started flying over the walls of Mega-City One and the Apocalypse War began. He grew up quick, then, real quick. Arnos watched whole sectors vanish in nuclear flame and saw his buddies cut apart by las-fire from Sentinoid robots. By a process of attrition, Arnos ended up as platoon leader for the TLJ Citi-Def force and, out of one thousand able-bodied but bored citizens, there were maybe a couple hundred left when the last shots were fired. On Armistice Day, when East-Meg One was frying in an atomic storm of revenge, Arnos sat on the hull of a downed Strato-V and realised he was a changed man.

He'd met Gidea during the war – Gidea Parq as she'd been back then – and the conflict had brought them together. They married on VS Day and started a new life together. Gidea lost everything to the Sov invasion, but a will from her Uncle Drayton had saved them both from destitution. Drayton owned land in Apollo Territory and the young couple had grabbed it with both hands, heading off to Luna-1 and a better future.

But Arnos never forgot the war and so each year for the past two decades, he and his wife and every other Mega-City-1 ex-pat who lived through it had marched in the Apocalypse Parade. Arnos didn't like the fact that the East-Meg veterans were allowed to have their own parade as well, but that was the downside of living in an international zone. This morning, the Judges had broadcast a warning that the streets were still unsafe and the nightfall curfew was still in force. Gidea stayed home, but Arnos was damned if he was going to miss the parade; he'd never missed a single one, not even on the day when his son Bruce had gone in for that head transplant operation. The Apocalypse War had changed Arnos LeGrove. It had defined him and, ever since, some small part of him had been praying for it to happen all over again.

Today, his wish had been granted.

Arnos hollered at the top of his lungs and kicked aside the bullet-riddled body of some crusty Sov eldo, a fat guy he remembered as owning a Zonkers franchise down on Collins Boulevard. Behind him, two dozen A-War veterans gave lusty cheers and brandished the weapons they'd taken. Arnos didn't quite understand where the guns had come from – it just seemed that one moment the fighting had been hand-to-hand and then someone had started shooting. It didn't matter to him if the blasters and spit-guns had fallen from the sky; the weapons simply propagated out into the crowds, one rioter picking them up from the hands of another when they died. If somebody out there was handing out guns like party favours, then Arnos was more than happy to take them.

When he had occasion to look up – which wasn't often, thanks to the fierce exchanges of gunfire and the homemade Molotov cocktails that sang through the air – Arnos had the vague impression of something important being imparted on the ubiquitous wall-screens that appeared every few hundred metres along the street. Some of the screens had pictures of stern, serious-looking Judges or newsreaders on them, explaining in calm and reassuring voices that everyone would be much better off returning to their homes. Those screens got shot at or stoned. Most of the other displays were left untouched though, as they showed pirated loops of footage from streetcams of fighting, fighting and more fighting. One time, a screen near the Planet Express dealership happened to show a close-up of an East-Meg Judge getting struck by a falling sofa and Arnos's mob roared with approval. The screen must have understood they liked that, because it showed the clip again and again, even bleeding it over to more panels to keep pace with them as they advanced down the road. Now and then he heard some squeaky voice babbling away about something, or he glimpsed a cartoon character up there capering around like a fool. Arnos didn't pay attention to it, though. Every time he looked at the screens or listened to them, they just seemed to make him more irate than before.

The parade had started quietly enough, just like any other year and they'd got as far as the minute of silence when someone had coughed. Arnos had never been so angry as he was right then. The hot rage just flooded over him like a red wave. Of course, it had been one of the East-Megger vets making the noise, an early arrival from their stinking "peace parade" and after just a moment the Sov was being beaten by a dozen men. Then the snecking Sov's pals had arrived and the whole thing had just kicked off.

Arnos and the other guys from the Big Meg fell back into the street-fighting mode from the war as if it had been only yesterday – Perry Vale and his sister Maida on point, Lou Isham with his cyber-leg bringing up the rear and big Shadwell carrying a cheese laser he'd liberated from a delicatessen. Pretty soon they were at the head of a big crowd, the mob rolling forward with inertia of its own, the feeble resistance of the East-Meggers already crushed and forgotten. They got to the Von Braun Overpass and Arnos felt the shock that ran through the whole group when they came face to face with another mob coming the opposite way.

Arnos wasn't sure who the other folks were – they might have been part of another march from another sector of the city, or maybe just some knot of rowdies left over from the troubles the night before – but as a feral, hate-filled grin split his face, he found that in all honesty, he didn't care at all. All that mattered was that these people were not him and for that reason they all had to die.

The two mobs tore into one another, spit-guns flaring like popping firecrackers, screams and yells echoing. Every tension, every petty anger and insult that any of these people had ever felt was being nurtured and massaged, brought to the fore without any of them realising it. They turned on each other, repeating a scene that was taking place in a dozen flash points around Luna-1. There was no point to it, no ground being taken or objectives being destroyed. It was not block war; it was carnage.

Arnos was killed by a bolt from a Beria flesh-blaster pistol gripped in the skinny hand of a kid half his age. It was perhaps ironic that the gun he lost his life to was Apocalypse War-era surplus, an officer's weapon that had been recovered from East-Meg POWs. All of this was lost on Arnos LeGrove, though, as he choked out bits of his own lungs through a sucking chest wound.

Arnos lay to one side of the melee, unable to move or turn his head, his line of sight fixed on an ad-screen that dangled at a dangerous angle from the offices of Acme Plumbing. In the corner of the screen was a dumpy little figure, a bubble-headed caricature cherub with a skull like the Moon and a green complexion. It looked at Arnos and watched the war veteran bleed to death, laughing at him as if it was the funniest joke in the world.

"Off," said Judge-Marshal Che to the window-screen. "Off!" he shouted at it, when the device did not respond immediately. The office's voice-recognition system was still getting used to Che's speech patterns and he was growing weary of constantly repeating himself to the machine. The oval window went dark, taking away the spy-in-the-sky footage and the real-time view of the city beyond. Che allowed himself a moment to close his eyes and hide there in the darkness of his own mind. Everything was moving so fast, he told himself, no time to stop and assimilate it all, no time to think or make the right choices.

Che was afraid to open his eyes again. He couldn't see it, but he could sense the oncoming rush of more problems, more decisions and more pressure rumbling towards him like a distant, dark thunderhead. For all his career, Che had been happy to stand in Marshal Tex's shadow; the Mex-City Judge was no fool, he knew his limitations, he knew that Tex was the best at his job, just as he, Che, was the best man to be Tex's adjutant and deputy. But he had never, never wanted to take the Chief Judge's place. There had often been talk of it among the lower ranks, but Che had always refused to address the matter. Other senior Judges had been generous enough to ascribe noble reasons to his decision, but in the cold silent moments when Che lay alone in his bunk, he knew in his heart of hearts that he simply was not capable of running Luna-1. He hated himself for it, but he could never be the man that Tex was. And now, his greatest nightmare had been made reality and Che was afraid that he would be exposed as a bumbler – indecisive and hesitant.

"Sir?" said Kessler, concerned as the long seconds of silence stretched into minutes. "I must have your orders, Chief Judge."

Che opened his eyes and studied the SJS-Judge. Kessler seemed to thrive on the chaos that was drowning the city; the livid pink scar that cut across his taut face fairly glowed with excitement. Kessler stood, hands clasped behind his back, watching Che through his cyberlink monocle. Behind him, the Brit-Cit Judge Foster shifted uncomfortably next to the silent, quiet shape of Tek-Judge J'aele.

"What... what is our status at this point?" Che managed. He tried to keep the weariness out of his voice.

"Every available man has been pulled from static duty and deployed in the streets," Kessler said crisply, "All Justice Department facilities are on high alert and riot gear has been issued. I took the liberty of order-ing the activation of an electro-cordon around the Grand Hall plaza, as well as assigning a unit of Omni-Tanks for area security."

"Good, good. Madre de dios," Che breathed. "That it should come to this..."

"We are monitoring external transmissions," added J'aele. "There is an increased amount of signal traffic moving between Earth relay sats and the diplomatic fleet in lunar orbit."

"They know what's going on down here," said Foster grimly.

Kessler made a sound like a sigh. "Chief Judge, we cannot maintain this state for more than a few more hours. As it is, all Judges are exe-cuting your command to hold and contain the fighting, but losses are increasing exponentially. We must be proactive!"

Che considered this, rubbing his damp palms together. "If we contain the rioters, they will burn themselves out eventually. These... incidents must be kept isolated–"

"With respect, sir," Foster broke in. "It's not working. We're seeing more eruptions of conflict, not less."

"You have a suggestion?"

"I do, sir," Foster took a breath before continuing. "We should declare a State of Emergency and petition the members of the treaty states for assistance–"

"Are you mad?" Kessler spat. He jerked a thumb at the ceiling and the sky beyond the dome. "They're waiting up there to storm the city and gather up the scraps, but are you proposing we just open the door to them right now?"

Foster coloured. "The global partnership treaty states that signatories must provide strategic help if Luna-1 calls for it."

"Yes and once they're here in our city, they'll dig in and take over!" Kessler retorted, rounding on the Brit-Citter. "Luna-1 doesn't need help to quell this riot – it needs decisive action, now!"

"It's not a riot any more, Kessler," rumbled J'aele. "It's anarchy."

"Exactly!" The SJS officer looked back at Che. "Which is why the time for passivity is over! Chief Judge, you must authorise a full mobilisation to war footing."

"War?" snapped Foster, "With who? Our own citizens?"

"Your citizens?" Kessler said without turning, "Your citizens live on a little island on Earth, Foster. I'm talking about saving the people of Luna-1." He stepped closer to Che and pressed both hands down on the Judge-Marshal's desk, his monocle glinting. "Do as Foster says, declare a State of Emergency, but authorise a suspension of the Lunar Constitution and martial law. Give me sanction to do what it takes and I promise you, this city will be subdued by nightfall!"

"At what cost?" demanded the Tek-Judge.

"At any cost," Kessler retorted coldly. "If we choose any other course of action, we risk appearing weak before the rest of the world. We – Luna-1 – cannot take that risk."

Che broke away from Kessler's hard gaze with a near-physical effort. Weakness. It was the one thing that the Judge-Marshal feared above all else, the one thing that Tex had been able to avoid by his sheer force of will. If Che appeared to be weak now, then everything around him would come crashing down. He would fail and Luna-1 would pay the price. "By order of the Chief Judge-Marshal of Luna-1," he intoned, fighting to keep his voice level, "as of now all Justice Department forces are to go to Defence Condition One status. The city's borders are to be sealed. Use of discretionary lethal force is authorised."

Foster and J'aele said nothing, both of them shocked into silence.

Kessler's lip tugged in a slight smile of victory. "I will need to deploy heavy weapons and combat firearms to all officers. With your permission, sir, I'd like to take direct command of the operation."

Che nodded. "Yes, yes. You understand what must be done, Kessler. I place my trust in you." The Chief Judge seemed to sag in his chair.

J'aele found his voice. "Sir, I must beg that you reconsider!"

"You are dismissed!" Che barked, with sudden violence. "We will not be seen as weak! I want order imposed on Luna-1!"

Kessler gave a curt nod and strode out of the office, with Foster and J'aele following in a heavy silence.

Once he was alone, Che moved to a concealed cabinet behind Tex's desk and opened a small cooler where a bottle of old Earth whisky lay. Taking a glass in a trembling hand, he poured himself a large shot and bolted it down his throat in one sharp go. He found himself staring at the star-and-moon sigil behind the desk.

"Santa Maria," he whispered to the empty room, "forgive me."

"This?" Judge Hiro snapped at the robot, "You called me from a barricade under fire to show me this?" He stabbed his finger at the shape of a broken-down moon rover as other droids in the airlock garage hauled the dark, silent vehicle into the maintenance bay.

The robot supervisor missed his angry tone. "It rolled to a halt just outside airlock four. Regulations demand that a Judge be present when any such unaccounted-for vehicle arrives at a city dome entrance–"

Hiro waved the droid into silence. "Yes, yes, whatever. Just open it up and I'll be on my way. There's a million psycho cits on the streets and I still have a full clip of ammo." He patted the Hornet hand cannon slung over his shoulder with affection. "War is coming and I aim to be on the winning side."

The robot crew worked the rover's door. Hiro gave the vehicle's registration a cursory glance – the code indicated an industrial unit, probably a runaway from a factory dome. The SJS-Judge snatched a torch from the supervisor and climbed inside. He expected to see a desiccated corpse, probably some idiot who had set out with the rover on auto-drive without filling up on air first. Instead, the first thing he noticed was the head of a hunter-killer droid, speared in the windscreen glass by a drill-bit. Hiro was about to say something when the cold metal shape of a pistol pressed into his temple.

"Hello again," said Dredd. "Remember me?"

Hiro had an L-Wagon parked outside, his partner, Wright, was inside. Kontarsky shot the other SJS officer with a stun bolt and took the flyer up into the air. Dredd made sure that Hiro was safely handcuffed in the crew compartment behind her.

The Sov-Judge flew fast and low, swinging between towers and citi-blocks, making a fast beeline for the angular shape of the Spike.

Dredd considered the Hornet he'd taken off the SJS-Judge. "What are you doing with this? It's not standard issue."

Hiro snorted. "It's not exactly a 'standard issue' day, Dredd. Look out of the window, you'll see what I mean."

The senior Judge looked down on the streets flashing by beneath them and saw they were alive with fire and explosions. Omni-Tanks fired frag shells into crowds of armed citizens, Cyclops lasers sizzled through glasseen and steel and everywhere lay the dead, some torn apart by bullets, others trampled by mobs. "Grud! It's a warzone down there! What the drokk happened?"

"Che grew a spine," Hiro retorted. "The SJS is in operational control now, Dredd. Kessler's going to make sure the cits learn a lesson in humility."

The hollow thud of an explosion floated past the flyer and Kontarsky swore softly. "Multiple missile hits on Edward Norton Block to the south. I see five Mantas firing on the ruins."

Hiro shrugged. "Can't make a synthi-omelette without breaking–"

Dredd silenced him with a look. "Kessler likes the taste of blood, doesn't he?"

"You ought to know."

The senior Judge looked away. "Where are we?" he asked Kontarsky.

"Landing now," she replied.

Neither the Sov-Judge nor Dredd saw Hiro touch a blister on his glove, instantly sending an alert signal to Justice Central.

The vast needle of the Luna-1 Computer Hub Tower, known throughout the metropolis as the Spike, loomed large in the cockpit window. Hiro sneered.

"You won't be able to touch down without a clearance code. They'll blast you out of the sky first."

Dredd threw Kontarsky a nod and she pushed the throttle to maximum, zooming towards the tower like a bullet. "It's not a problem," Dredd was almost casual. "We brought a key."

The Sov-Judge took the L-Wagon into a controlled crash-landing on the seventy-seventh floor of the Spike, shattering a wall of glasseen panels to touch down in the middle of a small atrium. She feathered the controls enough to nose it through walls and into the arena-like command centre at the tower's core. Computer technicians and servo-droids scattered as the flyer's hatch opened.

Dredd waved his STUP-gun at Hiro's head. "Stay here. Don't get cute."

The SJS-Judge said something foul enough to earn him a dozen conduct demerits, but Dredd was already gone, climbing down after Kontarsky.

She menaced a quivering compu-tech with an icy glare. "Show me the main data processing monitor, now." The operator nodded a worried assent and led her to a panel. Dredd noted Kontarsky's method with approval. She had clearly picked up a few pointers from him on intimidation.

"Run a sweep," Dredd told her. "Look for anything anomalous."

She nodded. Having glimpsed the commands on the XF6 screens at the Oxy-Dome, Kontarsky now knew exactly what to search for – and in a few moments, she had found it.

The Sov-Judge highlighted a series of tiny data strings hidden in the streaming virtual traffic of the hub. To Dredd they looked like single bubbles picked out of a churning foam of information. "Here. These match what we saw earlier."

Dredd considered the screen. "If these hidden commands have been here all the time, why didn't J'aele and Tek Division spot them?"

"It's ingenious," she marvelled. "The signals cloak themselves in the background chatter. Unless you know exactly, precisely, where to look for them, you'd think they were just glitches or junk data."

The Judge drew his pistol and set the gun's power pack to cycle. "The Spike is shielded from electro-magnetic pulses from outside?" he asked the technician. He got a wary nod in return. "But not from inside, right?" Again, the man gave a nod. Dredd switched the pistol into self-destruct mode. "Where's the main router hub?"

The sweaty little man pointed to a column of pulsing circuitry that ran along the length of the Spike. "Uh, there... But it's beam-shielded! You can't just shoot it!"

"I'm not going to," Dredd replied and tossed his STUP-gun into the access channel surrounding the column. The weapon clattered against the hub and began to emit a keening whine. "I'd advise you take cover."

Kontarsky rolled under the console just as Dredd's pulse pistol overloaded. The computer centre was lit by an actinic blue flash that turned the room into a still monochrome image and then everything went dark.

Everything.

17. NEGATIVE ACTION

"Sneck!" yelled Foster from the saddle of his Skymaster. "Look at that!"

To his left, flying behind him, Tek-Judge J'aele felt his gut tighten as every light in Luna-1 went out. It was like a huge blanket of darkness racing across the city below them. From the Apollo Territory in the north to Crater in the south, a wave of black enveloped the colony dome. J'aele's gaze flicked to the screen between his handlebars, the direct link to the central records computer at the Grand Hall of Justice – and instead of the usual train of data and readouts, there was an error message: *Data link lost.*

The only illumination came from torches down on the street, the odd headlight beam from a vehicle or the twinkling orange-yellow reflections from a fire. At first, the Simba City Judge suspected an EMP weapon, but such a thing would have knocked out the controls of their Zippers as well and sent them plunging towards the ground. "It's Dredd," he said with grim certainty. "Who else could it be?" Overhead, the arc of a rising Earth was clearly visible through the dome, shining a dusky light over the metropolis.

Foster's voice carried through the rushing air. "Judge Hiro's beacon signal is steady at the Spike. We're close."

J'aele nodded. "Let's move. If we don't get to him first, Kessler's SJS is going to have Dredd's head before we find out what he's–"

The Tek-Judge's words died in his throat. Just as suddenly as it had done dark, Luna-1 was coming back to life, lights and holos flashing back into being in a cascade of brilliant colour.

"Total elapsed downtime, eighty-three point one-five seconds," Kontarsky read the figures from her wrist chronograph. "This is wrong. The system should take at least four minutes to recover and reboot itself."

"I thought you said this would work, Kontarsky," Dredd growled.

"It should have!" she shrilled. "There's no explanation why it wouldn't!"

Around the control room, video screens blinked on in a surge of white static.

"Oh oh oh, but there is!" A synthetic voice quacked out of the speakers. "Nice try, Judges, but oh so wrong, wrong, wrong!" The Moon-U caricature dropped into frame, wearing a parody of Kontarsky's East-Meg uniform. It toyed with an impossibly long rad-cape and strode around in a mocking lockstep, flipping from screen to screen around the room. "U think I'd let U pull the plug on my home town? No way Joe-Joe! Moon-U is 2 smart 4 U 2!"

The Sov-Judge stared at the control panel in front of her, where the city's data stream raced past in a roiling rush of numbers. "Impossible! There's no way they could have hacked into the system so fast after a shutdown! It can't happen!"

"No, it can't," Dredd agreed, an ice-cold certainty building up inside him. "Tek-Division has been scouring the city for a hideout for these hackers and they found nothing."

Moon-U capered around and tripped over its cape in a pratfall. "Can't catch me. He, he, he!"

"But what if there is no hideout?" Dredd continued. "What if there are no hackers? Moon-U's not some computer geek's cartoon puppet... It's alive! There's no other explanation!"

Kontarsky gasped. "An artificial intelligence? A self-aware program living inside the Luna-1 network..."

Moon-U shrugged off the East-Meg outfit and toyed with a floppy T-shirt it wore underneath. The computer graphic imp studied a huge pocket-watch. "Tick-tock, tick-tock, Joe Dredd! Took U long enough 2 figure it out out out! Moon-U ain't a hacker... Moon-U is the hack!"

One of the sweaty technicians shook his head. "But that kind of intelligent software is banned under the Turing Accords!"

"Yeah," Dredd added. "Smart programs don't just grow on trees. That thing is way beyond the capacity of someone like Moonie."

"Well, thanks 4 playing," the cartoon chirped. "But now Moon-U's got things 2 do, places 2 go, go, go..."

Kontarsky's face froze as she studied the data stream. "Dredd, look at this. I think there is something else here, something encrypted in the AI's source code."

"Hey!" Moon-U shifted, appearing with a towel wrapped around it, a shower cap on its head, brandishing a bath sponge. "No peeking! Can't a program get some privacy? Moon-U's all naked!"

"Shut that thing up!" Dredd barked at the technician, peering at Kontarsky's screen. The Sov-Judge indicated an intermittent line of data and Dredd watched it scroll past. "Looks like a comm signal."

"It is," Kontarsky replied. "It's encoded into every Moon-U transmission. Every time that moronic gnome appears on a public screen somewhere, it is putting out a series of subsonic pulses. They are just below the range of human hearing."

"Moronic? How rude!"

"Subliminals, just like Maktoh said," Dredd replied, his face tightening with annoyance. "Drokk! This thing isn't just stirring up the riots – it's causing them!"

"And that's Moon-U's Q 2 zoom! Bye, bye, bye!" With a puff of digital smoke, the deformed figure disappeared, the screens returning to their normal settings.

Dredd tapped on the console. "We've got to get this information to Che. This changes everything. Now we know what that Moon-U is, we've got a fighting chance of stopping it."

They sprinted for the L-Wagon resting in the atrium. Dredd stepped through the hole Kontarsky's landing had made in the wall and into the sights of four guns.

"Hands on your helmet, Dredd," said Foster, stepping into view. "Nice and easy."

J'aele gestured at the Sov-Judge. "You too, Kontarsky."

Freed from his cuffs, Hiro made a threatening move with his Hornet street cannon. He leered at the Mega-City Judge. "Nothing to say, Dredd? No pithy comeback? You've sealed your fate with this little stunt. How many people do you think your blackout has killed?"

"A lot less than your SJS brutality!" Kontarsky snarled. "I saw what you skull-heads are doing out there! You make the East-Meg Secret Korps look like choirboys!"

Hiro glanced at Wright, who looked uncomfortable – perhaps because the woman was telling the truth, or perhaps from the after-affects of her stun blast. "Don't be so gutless. Citizens only understand one thing: naked force. If some have to die for us to underline that, then so be it."

Foster gave him a sharp look. "What the spug are you made of, man? Whatever happened to 'serve and protect'?"

"Scarface only believes in serving himself, isn't that right?" said Dredd. "Or maybe it's not Kessler who is holding your leash?"

Hiro crossed the distance to Dredd in a flash, the Hornet at his chest. "Shut up, old man! You're a relic, just like Tex! Once Luna-1 is under new management, it'll be men like me who'll be in charge!" He gave an icy smile and cocked the weapon. "Maybe I should save Kessler the trouble of an execution detail and cap you right now."

"Hiro," said Wright, "drop the gun." The other SJS-Judge aimed his pistol at his partner's head.

"What?" Hiro exploded. "You're siding with them? You're weaker than I thought you were! You disgust me!"

"Compassion isn't a weakness," Wright's voice was level and hard. "I always suspected you were dirty, but I never could believe it until now. You're in it with Moonie, aren't you?"

"Wright, don't be a fool! This is bigger than you know!"

The SJS officer shook his head. "I said drop it."

Hiro snarled and spun in place, turning the gun towards him. Dredd saw the opening and lashed out, planting a perfect nerve-strike in Hiro's throat. The SJS officer crumpled into a heap.

Wright frowned. "I am so sick of that guy."

Dredd stepped over Hiro's unconscious form and scooped up his gun. Foster and J'aele exchanged glances. "Uh, Dredd," said the Brit-Judge. "Technically you're under arrest now."

"Maybe later," Dredd replied, nodding at Kontarsky. "Bring these two up to speed." As the Sov-Judge conversed with the other men in urgent tones, Dredd approached Wright. "I thought you SJS types stuck together."

"I had my fill of Kessler's orders," Wright replied. "He's got Che to suspend the constitution, but it's just made things worse. The streets are running red out there."

"What about this creep?" Dredd glanced at Hiro.

"He's been getting further and further off-book. I'm sure he had something to do with Tex's murder. I know he's on the take, I just couldn't prove it."

"The Psi-Judges back at Central will be able to confirm that," said Dredd. "Sorry we had to shoot you before."

The SJS-Judge gave a weary shrug. "It happens."

Foster's eyes widened. "You're telling me that Moon-U freak is beaming hypnotic pulses through the vid-screens? That's incredible!"

"Is it?" said the Sov-Judge. "Think about it, Foster. Most of Luna-1's population spend half their life watching the Tri-D – with enough exposure to something as subtle as this, you could push anyone into an abnormal emotional state with the right stimulus."

"Why haven't any Judges been affected?"

She cocked her head. "How many serving officers do you know who have time to watch the vid eight hours a day?"

"Show me the data stream," said J'aele, as the implications of Kontarsky's words became clear to him. The woman handed him a digital pad with a recording of the hub traffic. The Tek-Judge gave a low whistle. "This is very impressive. The bandwidth is incredibly tight for a self-aware program. The Moon-U AI must have some sort of packet-shunt capacity."

Foster rolled his eyes. "In English, please?"

"That little data-demon is like a viral colony, you see?" J'aele explained. "It's constantly reproducing and moving through its host body – in this case, Luna-1's computer network – but the processing power is spread across hundreds of thousands of virtual locations." He frowned. "Now we know what to look for, we could start eradicating it, but it would just keep popping up somewhere else."

"So how do we kill it?" Dredd walked towards them. "And when we do, how do we make sure this thing stays dead?"

"If we can find the AI's source code, we could create a counter-program to hunt it down and erase it all," said the Sov-Judge. She gave the African a nervous look as J'aele scrutinised the pad.

When J'aele looked up, it was with an air of seriousness and concern. He studied Kontarsky for a moment; Dredd saw something unspoken pass between them.

"This program..." said the Tek-Judge. "It has an advanced encryption algorithm protecting it. I recognise the type."

"Origin?" Dredd demanded.

"I think Judge Kontarsky knows," J'aele's hand dropped to his holster. "Don't you, Nikita?"

The Sov-Judge's jade-green eyes softened with regret. "It's an East-Meg military code. I wasn't sure until a moment ago, but Judge J'aele's reaction confirms it. The Moon-U AI is Soviet software."

"You understand what this means, Kontarsky? This is proof that Moonie's partners in crime are East-Meg Two," said Dredd.

Foster rubbed his chin. "It makes sense. The Sovs want the Moon as much as anyone does. They hook up with Moonie and he uses his underworld connections to kick-start a rebellion, running the guns to fuel the riots. Then afterwards he'd probably set himself up as president-for-life in return for letting the East-Meggers have the mineral rights."

Kontarsky was shaken by her own admission. "Those hit-men who came after us at Tranquillity were Sov troopers too. There's only one place they could have come from, the same place where the AI was probably activated..." She looked away suddenly, her lip trembling. "I can't believe he would try to kill me."

"What's it going to be?" Dredd asked her. "You have a choice, Kontarsky. Your own countrymen have betrayed you, put you in harm's way. You know what will happen if we don't end this. You've got to ask yourself where your loyalties really lie. The flag…" and he pointed at the bronze shield at her throat, "or the badge."

Unbidden, the young Sov-Judge's fingers reached up and touched the cool metal, running over the Cyrillic characters of her name. Suddenly, Nikita's path was very clear to her. "The time delay of signals from Earth means that the AI must be being directed from a source closer to Luna-1. From lunar orbit."

"The *Irkutsk*," said Dredd. "Kommissar Ivanov's courier ship."

"Da," she replied, her voice quiet and brittle.

"Dredd," Foster said carefully. "If we attack a Russkie vessel, that'll mean war with the Sovs."

The Mega-City Judge nodded. "Been there. Done that."

Judge-Marshal Che threw the reports at Kessler's chest and slammed a fist into the desk. "I told you to impose order, not tear the city apart!" Spittle flew from his lips and his face flushed crimson.

The SJS officer's crooked mouth curled into a sneer. "It's too late for second thoughts now, Chief Judge. You gave the command. Your name is on the record. I am merely executing your directives."

"Punitive executions for all crimes?" Che raged. "At this rate, the Special Judicial Service will have killed more citizens than the uprising has! Sector Command reports that dozens of officers are refusing to follow these barbaric orders and I cannot blame them!"

"Those Judges have been suspended or cancelled," Kessler said briskly. "The SJS is firmly in operational control on the streets." He fixed Che with a cold eye. "You wanted this problem solved, but now it comes to getting your hands dirty, you fold like a deck of cards!"

"How dare you!" Che managed, indignant. "I am Judge-Marshal of Luna-1! You will address me with respect!"

"Respect?" Kessler hissed the word like an insult. "For a man who was content to live out his life in the shadow of another? This was your test of fire, Che and you have been found wanting! Luna-1 needs a man of strength, now more than ever, but instead you quibble about bloodshed and casualties!" He gave a callous chuckle. "You cannot hide behind your desk, Chief Judge. You must make the hard choices or else you must step down in favour of someone more exacting."

At once, all the bluster and fight left Che and he sagged into his chair. The Judge-Marshal seemed to deflate, the chain of office around his neck and the cloak on his shoulders too big, too heavy for his wiry frame. The burden of command had always been a part of Che's career – he would not have risen to his rank under Tex's leadership otherwise

– but the cold-blooded murder of his friend and the slow destruction of his city had broken him. "Of course… You are right…" he managed, his eyes focused on some distant midpoint.

"I'm always right," Kessler replied, contempt for Che dripping from every word.

"Chief Judge!" An anxious voice bleated from Che's intercom. "He's here! It's Judge–"

"Dredd!" Kessler shouted, as the Mega-City Judge entered with Kontarsky, Foster and J'aele close behind. The SJS officer pulled his firearm. "Stay where you are! You are under arrest for the murder of Judge-Marshal Tex and–"

"Stow it, Kessler," Dredd's voice was iron-hard and it gave the other man pause. Dredd towered over Che. "Chief Judge," he growled, "I have reason to believe that Sov agents are behind the disorder. It is my firm belief that Kommissar Ivanov of East-Meg Two is in conspiracy with the escaped criminal CW Moonie to depose the government of Luna-1. I want your permission to proceed with a full assault on Ivanov's vessel."

Che blinked owlishly at him. "I… I cannot sanction such action…"

Kessler still had his gun pointed at Dredd's helmet, although the senior Judge seemed not to notice. "You're insane! You've cooked up this mad story in order to further your own agenda of revenge! I should shoot you where you stand!"

The Chief Judge waved a weak hand at Kessler. "I cannot…" he repeated. "Kessler… Kessler is in charge now."

The SJS chief smiled. "You see, Dredd? Judge-Marshal Che understands which of us has the stomach for this job."

Dredd turned his full attention on Kessler for the first time, a burning determination flaring in his face. "The only thing stopping me from breaking your neck right now is the law, Kessler. The same law that you've stepped all over to get where you are. The same law you're breaking to gun down innocent civilians just to push yourself up the chain of command." With a sudden rush of movement, Dredd struck Kessler, the heel of his right hand cracking the SJS-Judge's nose, his left snatching the man's STUP-gun from his grip. Kessler stumbled backwards, blood gushing from his nostrils. "Your city is coming apart at the seams and all you see is a chance to exploit it. Tex is dead because you couldn't keep your own house in order!"

"Wh-what do you mean?"

"I had a Psi-Judge give your boy Hiro a deep scan before I came in here. He was the shooter in the plaza. He killed Tex and tried to frame me for it." Dredd's face wrinkled, as if he smelt something foul in the air. "I'll deal with you when this is over."

Foster trained his pistol on the injured Judge. "You just stay down there on the floor, chummy."

"Che," said Dredd. "We're out of time. Give the order."

Colour drained from Che's face. "I... I can't." He met Dredd's gaze, tugging the Judge-Marshal's badge from his chest. "I never should have taken this in the first place. I have failed my city." He pressed the shield into Dredd's hand. "Tex always trusted you, Joe. Don't let him down like I did."

Dredd held the star-and-crescent sigil for a long moment, then he snatched a bound copy of the Lunar Constitution from a shelf and slammed it down on the desk. With one hand on the book, he began to speak in a clear, exact voice. "I, Joseph Dredd, pledge allegiance to the badge of Judge-Marshal of Luna-1 and to the code for which it stands. One colony, under law, with discipline and order for all."

"You can't just take over!" Kessler yelled. "Who do you think you are?"

"Quiet!" snarled Foster. "I'll tell you who he is... He's Chief Judge!"

"Acting Judge-Marshal," Dredd corrected. "For now." He looked to Kontarsky. "Get me a live feed to the diplomatic ships."

"What should we do?" said J'aele.

"Prep a combat shuttle for immediate launch." He tossed the Tek-Judge Kessler's pistol. "And get that skull-head creep out of here."

"What about Che?" Foster asked softly.

Dredd gave the other man a sombre look. "Take him down to Med-Bay."

"Something is going on," said Sellers, studying his screen. "Multiple signals from Justice Central to all the other couriers."

"The cowards are calling for help," said the bald man. "Not that they'll get it."

Sellers gave the East-Meg Tek-Judge a hard stare. "You seem confident of that, Gorovich. How come?"

The Sov officer smiled. "No one will dare oppose us. To do so will risk our nuclear retribution and the unbridled might of the glorious East-Meg nation-state."

"You spout the party rhetoric so well," Judge Gorovich's commanding officer said with an arch sneer. "Sometimes I wonder if you are capable of thinking beyond it."

Gorovich smothered an angry retort with a false smile. "I am merely a willing servant of the Sov people, Kommissar Ivanov."

"Indeed..." replied the tall Russian diplomat. Ivanov glanced around the Silent Room, at Sellers and Moonie, who watched the interplay with amused looks on their faces. "And I'm sure our friends here on Luna-1 will hold East-Meg Two in the highest esteem once we have successfully brought them to power, yes?"

"Clinton Moonie never forgets his friends," chirped the frail old man. "Or his enemies, for that matter."

"That much is certain…" murmured Gorovich.

"We've reached the terminal phase of the uprising," said Sellers, consulting his screen again. "I guess it's time for you to start rolling in your jackboot boys, kommissar."

Ivanov raised an eyebrow at Sellers's use of words, but otherwise ignored the insult. He touched a control on his desk and spoke in quick, clipped Russian. "Ivanov to the bridge. Captain, bring us to deployment range and stand by to launch all drop-troopers and landers." He snapped off the intercom without even waiting for an acknowledgement of his orders.

The kommissar settled back in his chair, watching alert indicators blink on as drones loaded Rad-Sweeper tanks and Sentinoid wardroids into cargo landers. Concealed in the scanner-opaque belly of the *Irkutsk*, elite Neo-Spetznaz troopers were joining the machines in preparation for the lunar assault. "And now, gentlemen," he said with a frosty smile, "we wait for the sun to rise on a Red Moon."

The eagle's-eye window showed the faces of a dozen diplomatic officers from Mega-Cities across the globe, each one broadcasting from their orbital embassies. Dredd scanned their expressions: none of them showed even the slightest suggestion of solidarity.

"I'm not going to waste time dancing around the subject," Dredd told them, "All of you are fully aware of what's been happening down here in the last seventy-two hours. As Acting Judge-Marshal of Luna-1, I'm invoking the emergency assistance clause in the global partnership treaty. I need troops, medical supplies and technical staff."

The silence that followed his announcement hung in the air. The Brit-Cit representative cleared his throat. "Dredd, what you're asking… It's difficult to agree to. We have no troops–"

"Bull," Dredd broke in. "The treaty says your ships are supposed to be unarmed but we all know that's not true. Every one of you has a military contingent aboard."

"You accuse us of a violation?" the Sino-City ambassador spluttered. "How dare you!"

"Spare me the wounded pride act," Dredd grated. "Luna-1's bleeding to death while you're playing games up there. Get past your politics and do the right thing."

The cardinal from Vatican City gave a tight smile. "Dredd, you have much to learn about diplomacy. You cannot simply demand we ignore one part of the treaty and accept another."

"You ask us is to place our flag with yours," Casablanca's representative added. "You ask us to join you against the East-Meg peoples."

Dredd fumed. "If you back us, Ivanov won't dare send troops in! He's relying on you to be too gutless to fight, so he can stroll in and pick up the pieces!"

"Brit-Cit cannot risk engaging Sov forces," said the British ambassador. "I'm sorry, Dredd. I wish it could be otherwise." The link from the Brit-Cit ship went dark.

"Sino-City also refuses to bolster your petty skirmish." Another screen winked out.

"If the Sovs take the Moon, every Mega-City on Earth will pay the price!" Dredd snapped. "If you force us to fight them alone, Luna-1 will be obliterated in the crossfire!"

"Then you should consider honourable surrender, Judge-Marshal," Hondo's diplomat noted. "For the sake of the Selenite citizens."

The last links were severed, leaving Dredd to stare out of the oval window at the smouldering city beyond.

"None of them would even consider it," said Kontarsky. "They don't dare fire on East-Meg officers."

Dredd shook his head. "It's not just that. They're hoping that Ivanov's soldiers are going to fail, that we're going to kill each other. Then they'll come in and fight amongst themselves to stake their claims on the Moon. We're on our own."

The shuttle J'aele had chosen for the assault was one of the fastest craft in the Luna-1 fleet, an agile Falcon-class inter-orbital pursuit ship.

"It is designed for rapid response, mostly going after Belt pirates or chump dumpers who haven't gone interstellar. The weapons suite is good, but it's not enough to do serious damage to a cruiser like *Irkutsk*. It has decent armour, but the best defensive system is its speed. At full burn, even smart missiles will have trouble tracking it."

Dredd ran a hand over the bullet-shaped fuselage. "We're not looking for a dogfight. This is a shock attack. I want to get on board Ivanov's ship before he can say 'Das vidanya'."

"Got that covered," added Foster. "I had the meks bolt on some counter-measure pods. We'll drop enough tinsel to make them think it's Christmas."

"Let's load up, then." Dredd turned to find Kontarsky watching him.

"I thought you could use a replacement firearm," she said, handing him his diplomatic case.

Dredd opened the container and removed his Mega-City Lawgiver and a dozen ammunition clips. "Rodriguez was right. A real gun's better than those beamers."

"I want to join the assault team," she said, without preamble. "I am fully rated on the cruiser-class starship design."

Dredd holstered his pistol. "You were reporting to Ivanov every moment you could during the investigation. He used you to track us out at the Oxy-Dome. You kept quiet when you knew there was Sov involvement in Moonie's plan. Tell me why I should trust you now."

She nodded at the Lawgiver. "You took the gun. If you don't trust me, how do you know I didn't sabotage it?" She paused. "Ivanov used me to help turn Luna-1 into a battleground. I cannot let that go unanswered."

"Good enough," He looked away. "Get on board. We lift in five."

18. POINT OF IMPACT

The shuttle was on automatic as it swept in low over the hull of the *Irkutsk*. Laser cupolas tracking the speeding ship were fooled as gales of silver thread spat from pods on the Falcon's winglets, sending their beams into knots of tinsel instead of homing in on the Justice Department ship. Klaxons blared inside the Sov vessel as scanners saw the shuttle multiplied a hundred-fold on their screens.

In the ship's cargo bay, Dredd aimed the clamp gun in his hand through the open hatch, sighting the flat expanse of the cruiser's fuselage as it flashed by. He didn't check to see if the others were tethered to the cable; they had been briefed and he expected them to follow procedure. Dredd picked his spot and fired. The gun threw a flat-headed projectile at the other vessel, trailing a diamond filament behind it.

The clamp struck the *Irkutsk* with a clang and locked in place. In the next second, Dredd and the other Judges were reeled out of the shuttle like fishermen pulled over the side of a boat, while the Falcon continued on its course. He glanced over his shoulder as the motors in the clamp gun drew them to the enemy ship: behind him Kontarsky, J'aele and Foster drifted in a loose line, each tied to the other through a belt webbing loop. Their gamble, that the Sov gun crews would be too occupied trying to target the shuttle to notice a string of human shapes threading across the darkness, had paid off.

Boots impacted on the hull with a resonant thud, automatic electromagnets kicking in to let them stand on the curve of dark metal. Foster made a gulping sound, his stomach threatening to rebel as he caught a glimpse of the Moon turning above them.

"Kontarsky, find us a hatch." Dredd weighed a cutting charge in his fist. "Otherwise, we'll have to do it the messy way and blast the hull."

She pointed, "There's a port by the plasma–"

Her words were cut off by a discharge of static across the comm channels, as one of the lasers tore open the shuttle with a lucky shot. Dredd turned just in time to see the Falcon's wounded form flip over. Out of control, the shuttlecraft fell into the larger ship like a bat-winged missile and struck the bow of the *Irkutsk*. The cruiser's fuselage rippled with the aftershock and white showers of frozen oxygen erupted out from the impact crater.

"So much for our security deposit," said Foster dryly.

Alarms cut through the Silent Room, bringing Ivanov and Gorovich to their feet. "What the sneck?" said Moonie. "We're under attack!"

"The bridge…" Gorovich said, leaning into a display on the holo-screen. "Something collided with the bridge!"

The kommissar's face soured and he barged Sellers aside. "Gorovich! We'll go to the secure command unit. We must launch the assault now!"

"And what am I supposed to do?" demanded Moonie. "Sit on my hands?"

"This is now a military operation," snapped Ivanov, any trace of his cool demeanour gone, "and I am the supreme authority in that area!"

Before he could frame an argument, the two Sovs left the crime lord behind, racing out into the corridor.

Sellers frowned at Moonie, pondering on the abrupt change of tone in their ally. "Ivanov won't spare any men to protect us if things start going south."

Moonie nodded his agreement, spinning his hoverchair about in a tight circle. "Forget him," he grated, stabbing a crooked finger at the control console on his chair. "I have the Moon-U command transmitter. I'm the one with all the leverage."

"What good will that do us if the ship blows up?" Sellers's voice cracked.

Moonie jetted closer and slapped him across the face. "Show some backbone, son. I've still got a couple of tricks up my sleeve." The wizened figure produced a laser pistol and handed it to Sellers. "Here. Maybe this will give you a little courage."

The airlock's outer hatch opened like a trapdoor to reveal a wedge-shaped machine lurking inside, bristling with guns and flailing tentacle limbs.

"Sentinoid!" snapped Dredd, kicking off the hull as he brought his Lawgiver to bear.

The metallic guardian was a shipboard model similar to those deployed in Mega-City One during the Apocalypse War. J'aele was seconds too slow to avoid it, scrambling back across the fuselage as the robot boiled out of the open airlock. One of the sinuous appendages caught the African's forearm in a pincer and severed it with a deft snip.

Globes of blood scattered from the wound as J'aele's e-suit pumped him full of painkillers and quickly sealed a plasti-sheath over his stump.

Foster narrowly avoided losing his head the same way as Kontarsky released a fusillade of pulse fire. The Sentinoid turned towards them, las-cannons emerging from its chest; it was all the distraction Dredd needed.

"Hi-Ex," he told his gun and fired. Oxygenated rounds could fire underwater or in a vacuum with little loss of velocity at close ranges, but the physics of shooting a ballistic weapon in space remained the same. Recoil shoved him back like a kick in the chest, even as the bullet struck its mark. During the war, it had taken several direct hits to knock out one of these droids, but the larger-yield explosive rounds from the newer Mark 11 Lawgiver killed the machine with a single shot. The blast cut into its brain-case and boiled the delicate electronics there into vapour. The Sentinoid went limp, losing purchase on the hull. Then it flapped away into space like a discarded rag in an updraft.

Dredd reeled himself back in as the others clambered into the airlock. It was a tight fit and the Judge saw the hollow, sick look on J'aele's face as their helmets bumped. "Status?" he asked.

"I can function," J'aele replied stiffly, fighting off the shock of the blood loss.

Foster forced a smile. "You tekies always say you can work with one hand tied behind your back. Now you get to prove it."

The inner airlock opened and they were in enemy territory.

Kontarsky had provided a partial digi-map of the cruiser's interior and Foster and J'aele took off the moment they were aboard the *Irkutsk*. The ship's computer core was held in a zero-gravity cylinder along the spine of the vessel and it would be there that the Tek-Judge would find the source code for the Moon-U AI. Meanwhile, Dredd and Kontarsky headed forward. The lightweight environment suits they wore were a far cry from the bulky civilian models that they had liberated from the Oxy-Dome rover, close-fitting unitards with heat-shunt meshes and a compact re-breather to recycle their air. The Luna Judges had less than a dozen of them and the price of a single one could have easily paid for a decent-sized hab in a Lovell District luxy-apt.

Dredd surveyed the empty corridor. "Where is everyone? This ship have a skeleton crew or something?"

Kontarsky shook her head. "Nyet, the vessel is on a Condition One alert." She pointed to a blinking indicator lamp on the ceiling. "Everyone is at their stations. The other crew will be in the loading bay, preparing the drop-troops for deployment." She stepped forward and

Dredd followed their progress on a wrist-mounted sensor display screen. "The turbolift hub is this way. If we can get to the secure command unit, we can override the ship's systems."

The senior Judge examined the display. "Some kinda shielded shelter on the mid-deck."

Kontarsky nodded. "Like a bunker, if you will. In the event of an emergency, senior Kommandants or political officers can seal themselves in and operate the entire vessel from there." She smiled grimly. "It makes any thoughts of mutiny obsolete."

Dredd caught the sound of voices and froze. "Someone's coming!"

"Is this really necessary, kommissar?" said Gorovich, jogging to keep up with Ivanov's long-legged gait. "I do not believe–"

"What you believe is irrelevant, Gorovich!" Ivanov snapped. "I will not allow this operation to fall apart in the final phase! That strike on the bridge is clearly the prelude to a direct attack... The Luna-City Judges are desperate." He frowned. "I should have taken direct command of this from the start."

Gorovich spoke without thinking as they approached the turbolifts. "But then you would be dead now, blown out into space with the captain and the rest."

Ivanov ignored the two troopers who saluted him and gave the bald Tek-Judge a lethal stare, reading the poorly masked disappointment on his face. "How inopportune for you that I still live. Your plans to usurp me must wait for another day."

Gorovich made negative noises. "I... I intend no such thing, sir. I am merely a servant of the Sov peoples–"

"Yes, yes," Ivanov said dismissively, using a key card to activate the direct drop shaft to the secure command unit. "You're a model party member."

"It's him!" Kontarsky hissed from their hiding place. "If he gets through that hatch, there's no way of opening it from outside!"

Dredd flipped the selector on his Lawgiver to Ricochet. "Take him!"

Ivanov saw the brief instant of movement as the two figures in e-suits appeared around the corner. He shouted an order and the troopers brought up their beam rifles as the attackers opened fire. The kommissar knew the tell-tale report of a Lawgiver very well; he'd heard it untold times during his service through the Apocalypse War and there, behind the cowl of the suit, he saw light flash off the grim visage of a Mega-City Judge's helmet. *Dredd*.

Bullets made from a titanium-rubber matrix skipped off the metal walls with keening screeches, cutting through exposed flesh and severing the jugular of one of the troopers. On reflex, Ivanov grabbed Gorovich and thrust him forward like a shield, letting the hapless Tek-Judge soak up a dozen hits – a fitting final service for such a dutiful Sov officer, he decided. The kommissar shoved the jerking body away and dived into the drop shaft as it yawned open. As he fell into safety, he thought he heard Kontarsky's voice crying out in anger but then the hatch sealed behind him and the noise was gone.

Her pulse blasts had made short work of the other trooper, but Kontarsky and Dredd reached the shaft hatch too late to stop it slamming closed, magnetic bolts thudding home with unyielding finality. The Sov-Judge cursed Ivanov's clone-mother under her breath and kicked the hatch ineffectively.

Dredd examined the shaft, fingering a small vent to the side. "There's an air duct here."

The Sov-Judge shook her head. "It doesn't connect to the secure unit. There's a bulkhead between them."

"How thick?" said Dredd. He reached into his backpack. "Thick enough to resist a thermite hull-cutter?" The Judge offered her a disc-like charge; a flat cone of explosive, the charge was strong enough to melt a man-sized hole through starship-grade metals in a matter of seconds.

Kontarsky studied the device, thinking. "It might be enough, but the shaft is too small for you to fit through."

Dredd dropped the charge in her hands. "I wasn't thinking of me."

The Sov-Judge gulped. "Oh." She began to strip off the outer layers of the e-suit, dropping her backpack and belt. "You understand, Dredd, if I cannot stop him, he'll launch the landers. Once the drop pods are away, there's nothing we can do to stop them."

"Then don't fail."

She nodded, ripping open the vent. "How will you locate Moonie?"

Dredd knelt by Gorovich as a weak groan escaped the Sov agent. "Maybe our friend here can give me some directions." He pressed on the Tek-Judge's wounded chest and Gorovich drooled blood. "Where's the dome-head, creep?" Dredd demanded.

"Suh..." Gorovich managed. "Suh-Silent. Room."

Kontarsky nodded again. "Yes, these cruisers often have such a facility. It's a sensor-opaque conference room."

"Where?"

The woman picked up her pistol and the cutter charge. "Just look for the only empty space on the scanner." Kontarsky swallowed the last of her nerves and gave Dredd a brisk salute. "Good luck, sir." She shifted her weight and vanished into the vent conduit.

Dredd's helmet radio crackled. "Foster to Dredd."

"Dredd here. Go ahead."

"Uh, right..." There was the sound of pulse fire in the background, then silence. "We've secured the computer core. Minimal resistance. J'aele's doing his thing, but I think one of the technicians may have set off the–"

From nowhere, an ear-splitting whine sounded throughout the ship and a synthetic voice bellowed something in angry Russian.

"The, uh, alarms," Foster finished.

Dredd reloaded his Lawgiver and studied the digi-map, overlaying templates from the e-suit's suite of thermal, radiation and sonic sensors. Sure enough, a large cabin further down the hull appeared on the display like a black hole in the cruiser's innards. "Copy that," he said, "Finish your job and then commandeer an escape pod. Don't wait around for me or Kontarsky."

Dredd snapped off the throat mic and broke into a run.

Kommissar Ivanov's nose wrinkled as the smell of hot plastic touched his nostrils. For a moment, he thought that Dredd might have tossed a gas grenade into the drop shaft with him, or found a way to pump some toxin into the secure unit – but then he remembered that the unit had its own independent air supply, along with food, water, even a dedicated two-man launch in case the *Irkutsk* was scuttled. Alone in the compact command centre, he turned and started as his eyes came across the wide, discoloured oval forming on the bulkhead behind him. The tritanium alloy wall was bowing inward as he watched, the hissing metal going from cherry red to white-hot. Ivanov ducked behind the auto-helm console just as the bubble of superheated metal popped with a rasping cough of air, spitting globules of molten alloy across the floor.

He couldn't help but smile as a figure dropped through the newly made hole, her normally pale face a florid red from the heat backwash. The kommissar resisted the temptation to shoot her straight away and stood up to meet Kontarsky as she blinked away the sting of fumes from her eyes, her gun clasped firmly in her fist.

"Ah, Nikita, you are so resourceful," Ivanov indicated the breach. "A hull-burner. I should have anticipated that." He gave a little sigh. "No matter. I'm pleased you could join me."

"You," Kontarsky said through a seared throat, "are in violation of multiple statues of the Luna-1 penal code. You are under arrest."

Ivanov smirked. "This is a little joke, Nikita? Surely you understand what I am doing here?" He stepped closer to her, his voice warming even though the Volokov needler in his hand never wavered. "I am furthering the cause of the East-Meg city-state. By tomorrow, the Sov flag will be flying over Luna-1."

She sneered. "And will that be before or after your squalid little capitalist comrade names himself lunar emperor?"

The kommissar's smile slipped. "Moonie is just a puppet, a greedy fool we used to ferry weapons for us. He will be a willing part of the glorious Revolution and you can be part of it too, my dear." He held out a hand to her. "You have always been loyal to the Motherland, Nikita. Do not disappoint the Rodina now."

Kontarsky willed her finger to tighten on the pulse gun's trigger, but her hand remained immobile.

The first thing through the door of the Silent Room was the corpse of the guard who had been unfortunate enough to be standing outside it. Dredd shot him through the heart and then shouldered the dead Sov-Judge into the dark confines of the chamber. As he expected, laser fire erupted inside, savaging the body. Dredd followed his decoy, falling into a tuck and roll across the floor. He glimpsed something at the far end of the room, just the vaguest impression of a figure in a chair, blink-lit by the discharges from a beam pistol in his hand.

Accelerated photons tore through the air with cracks like fractured glass, searing the Judge as he wove between the shapes of chairs and the black bulk of the obsidian table. A wallscreen blew as a salvo of bolts ripped it apart and Dredd's street-honed skills pinpointed the shooter's position. He fired, three rounds spitting from the Lawgiver's muzzle so close together that the discharge sounded like tendons shredding. The figure slumped forward.

Dredd turned the seat to face him with the tip of his boot, switching on the lamps in his helmet. The man in the chair died with an imploring look in his eyes, his mouth silenced with plasti-tape, wrists held by cuffs to the seat arms. The laser he held made irritable clicking noises as its auto-seek mode lost its target.

"Poor Sellers," Moonie's voice issued out of the shadows. "He wasn't a bad guy. Just a little slow on the uptake. Rather like you, Joe."

Dredd's helmet lamps swung and picked out Moonie's age-scarred, bulbous face and his diminutive body drifting silently above him on a hoverchair. The floater disgorged fist-sized turrets from every surface and plates of metal snapped into place over Moonie's body. A combat visor dropped down over his broad forehead, framing the horrible rictus of the old man's yellowed smile. Dredd dodged away as the hoverchair unfolded like a lethal blossom into a skeletal frame of battle armour.

"Grud!" Dredd got off two shots, but the rounds deflected away.

Moonie grinned and hit a switch; oily flame jetted after the Judge and turned a chair into a torch. "I offered you a partnership once, Dredd and you turned me down. I made the mistake of underestimating you then. This time, I'm just gonna kill you."

The Judge replied with hot lead, bracketing the criminal with more bullets.

Moonie came on undaunted, his too-wide face twisted with cruel laughter.

"Join me, Nikita," Ivanov pressed. "It's time to grow up, my dear kadet. Time to learn that names, ideologies, they matter for nothing. East-Meg, Mega-City... They are all just shapes on a map. All that really matters is power and wealth." He smiled, his hand reaching for her STUP-gun. "Once you have that, you can believe whatever you want... And Luna-1 will make me very rich indeed."

As his fingers gently brushed the pistol's barrel, Kontarsky found her voice again. "When you were my tutor, I had nothing but respect and admiration for you. I saw you as the embodiment of East-Meg perfection. Every kadet wanted to be like you, the decorated war hero of the American invasion, the champion of Minsk." A smile fluttered on Ivanov's lips, but it quickly died when he saw the icy look in her green eyes. "But all of that is a lie. You are an opportunist, a disgrace to the Soviet ideal, kommissar," she said. "You do not wish to see the people of Luna-1 gain freedom. You only wish to enrich yourself."

Her hand shook and the pulse gun discharged. Ivanov tumbled away from her, the point-blank blast smoking in his gut. "Dubiina! You motherless imbecile!" he choked. "Don't you realise, the Diktatorat ordered me to do this? If I am guilty, so are they! Do you know what you have done?"

"No," she admitted, "but I know I have kept my honour."

Ivanov screamed and fired his needler. Kontarsky dodged, and the shots went wide and shredded the helm console. Like a wounded beast, the cruiser lurched out of control and the g-plates struggled to compensate. "Then at least, dear Nikita, we will both perish together!" Blood bubbled out of his lips.

"No," she repeated and shot him in the head.

* * *

The quiver that ran through the hull of the *Irkutsk* threw Dredd off his feet and his helmet bounced off the table, lighting fireworks of pain inside his head.

Moonie was startled by the vessel's sudden shift and his floater whined as he tried to maintain a bead on his prey. The aged criminal stabbed at firing keys and spat a spread of micro-missiles at the Judge. The tiny, finger-sized rockets impacted the tabletop and cut it in half, shattering the lunar basalt into massive chunks. Dredd rolled, pain slashing through him as a miniature avalanche of razor-edged stone fragments scattered across the floor.

Options raced through Dredd's mind at lightning speed. Although Moonie was happy to discharge explosives inside the ship, Dredd didn't dare to use a High Explosive round in return – one deflected shot in the wrong place could kill them both. "Armour piercing," he said through gritted teeth and fired back at the floating cluster of guns and plating.

Moonie screeched as the shell penetrated somewhere above his leg and the recoil spun his hoverchair about in a drunken pirouette. He returned fire with a fan of ruby-red laser light, carving a burning line down the walls and over the carpeted floor. The hot beam left a smouldering trail in its wake over the furniture and Dredd had to dive behind a repeater screen to avoid losing a limb.

Creep's got me on the defensive, Dredd's mind raced. Gotta make him the rat on the run... Dimly, the Judge was aware of Foster's voice in his ear, yelling something about the ship going out of control, the helm malfunctioning, but he tuned it out. With all the mechanical precision of the hardware wired into Moonie's chair-cum-battle armour, one millisecond of indecision would be enough to cost Dredd his life.

As if in reply to his thoughts, Moonie shouted: "I see you, Joe! The dark's like daylight to Mister Moonie!"

Another flame spurt whooshed over Dredd's helmet, melting a monitor to molten slag. The Judge bolted from cover and found himself at the head of the chamber, the humming disc of a holo-screen at his feet.

Moonie came screeching after him and Dredd met his charge with paced shots that shredded armour plate and cut through flesh. Clawed, servo-assisted hands snapped out for the lawman's throat, as drool flew from Moonie's lips in anticipation of murder. Dredd waited for the last possible second then triggered the inert holo with a kick-switch.

A huge image of the Moon from orbit sprang into life in the air between them and Dredd's anti-dazzle visor darkened instantly – but Moonie, staring intently through an image intensifier, was blinded. He screamed, flailing at the insubstantial image, clawing at his eyes.

"Heatseeker," commanded the Judge and he sent the heart-chaser bullet through the rips he'd torn in Moonie's armour, into the soft flesh beneath.

The hoverchair sank to the floor gracelessly and toppled over. Moonie spat foamy pink spittle and slapped vengefully at a control near his hand. "You Earther bastard! You killed me! But I'm not going without a fight."

"Drokk!" Dredd saw Moonie's fingers move and stamped on them, the brittle bones snapping like twigs.

"Too late!" he wheezed. "I sent the zero command to Moon-U, understand? No more air for Luna-1, Dredd!" Moonie's massive spherical face lolled forward as his life ebbed out of him. "I die, you die, everyone dies!"

Dredd gave a slow shake of the head. "Your pet AI is on the endangered list, Moonie. It's as dead as you are!"

"No!" Moonie shook with rage. "If I can't have the Moon, no one can! No one!"

Dredd rested the barrel of his Lawgiver against Moonie's bloated skull. "Clinton Wendell Moonie," he pronounced, his face set in a grim mask, "for your numerous crimes against the people of Luna-1, I judge you guilty as charged. The sentence is death."

The gunshot echoed like thunder down the corridors of the doomed starship.

"Is that it?" said Foster at J'aele's shoulder.

The Tek-Judge gave a weary nod. "I think so."

"You think? You're not sure?"

"Can you slice through a Sov data core with one hand missing and a bloodstream full of De-Shock?" J'aele snapped, suddenly fierce. "No? Well, then shut up!" The Simba City Judge punched out a final string of keystrokes. "There. I've launched the null program. Once it comes into contact with the Moon-U AI, it will automatically begin decompiling it. The bitstream should reach the Luna-1 network in ninety seconds." He sagged. "I feel... so tired..."

"Oh, no," Foster dragged him to his feet. "None of that. Come on, mate, let's blow this place." He paused. "Uh, bad choice of words, eh?"

The Brit-Cit Judge's voice filled Dredd's helmet: "Job done! We're on our way out!"

"Copy," he replied, casting a last look at Moonie's corpse. The crime lord's eyes were wide open, the glittering light of the lunar holo-display reflected in them. "Kontarsky, do you read me? It's time to go."

The Sov-Judge's voice came back leaden with effort. "Affirmative, Dredd. The kommissar had been removed from office."

Dredd nodded to himself. "Get to a pod. I'll see you Moonside."

Without looking back, the Judge sprinted from the Silent Room as the cruiser began its final fall towards the lunar surface.

19. MOONRISE

Driven insane by conflicting commands, the wounded auto-helm on the *Irkutsk* turned the starship out of orbit at full burn and pointed its broken bow towards the grey surface of the Moon. In the sealed compartments of the drop pods and landers, the elite of East-Meg Two's forces were on radio silence and they never heard the panicked screams of the rest of the crew as the ship turned into a huge guided missile. Some of the troopers wondered a little at the shift in gravity as the vessel manoeuvred, but they never got to ponder it for more than a few moments.

At maximum power, the People's Star Navy Diplomatic Vessel *Irkutsk* rammed itself into the lunar regolith, carving a new crater in the planetoid's pock-marked surface. A few seconds later, the spontaneous detonation of its fusion core was visible to the naked eye of anyone on Earth's nightside.

"Whoo hoo hoo!" cheered Moon-U, as it tap-danced back and forth over a giant wall-screen in the Green Cheese Shoplex. The mall was now a blackened ruin, the stores gutted by fire and looting, the once-pristine floors smeared with soot and blood. The malevolent image showed big, pointed teeth and mocked the dead and dying. It was enjoying this, the sensation of power that came from flooding the minds of these small, simple organics with maddening sound. It was so easy to pressure their primitive hind-brains with the right frequencies and triggers, dragging out the violent tribal behaviour patterns that lurked inside the psyche of every human being. The software entity moved them around like toys in its own private nursery, throwing them against one another or sending them insane. Moon-U made them dance to its tune and the intelligent program was delighted by it. The AI played with the city with all the ruthless, directionless evil of a petulant child, listening to the people gasp as it choked off their final breaths, forcing them to fight even as they asphyxiated. It would be so sad when its job was done.

But then, from the wellspring of synthetic emotions inside it, the program felt something new emerge, something black and deep, a vast tidal wave of darkness.

Fear, as cold as space itself.

Elements of the AI peeking through exterior sensors felt the tremor as the *Irkutsk* dashed itself against the lunar surface and other fragments tasted the first precursors to the null program as it surged through Luna-1's computer net. Dimly, it became aware of the fact that the men who had created it were dead and, without them, it suddenly had no purpose, no directions to follow or orders to fulfil. Analogues of dread and despair bubbled up from the core of its essence.

"No, no, no!" Moon-U cried. The virtual being fled from the screens, coiling itself into a tiny ball of existence. It raced for the deep ranges of the city's memory cores, dropping into the low levels of dusty, untouched data where no search programs ever ventured – but the null was already there, surging up to meet it, closing in from all sides. It chipped away at Moon-U's mind, lopping off lines of code like a scythe through wheat.

The AI ran until it had nowhere to go and there, in some forgotten corner of a data store, the spiteful creation was suffocated and torn into meaningless binary threads of ones and zeros. Moon-U's death scream shattered street-screens all across the city, its last spastic twitches of life blooming in random pixel patterns and as it died, the hold it had on Luna-1 disintegrated with it.

Across the Moon, millions of minds were cleared of rage and hate as if a veil had been drawn away from them and the stifling, thick poison of a spent, dioxide-clogged atmosphere began to fade as clean, fresh air flooded back into the domes.

And out in the Ocean of Storms, a rain of hull fragments and pieces of starship fell across the landscape. Among them was a trio of escape pods that dropped on plumes of retro-rocket fire, settling back into the gentle embrace of the lunar day.

A full Earth hung in the blackness above the crystalline glasseen of the cemetery dome. It seemed incongruous there, the blue-emerald marbling of humanity's homeworld mirroring the layers of false greenery that carpeted the graveyard's floor. The stone orchard of burial markers and low tombs stretched off to the bowed horizon of Gravity Boot Hill's dome, simple rectangular headstones mingling with the ornate shapes of willowy angels. The statues seemed frail and delicate, as if they were frozen in that moment before they leapt from their plinths and into the lunar sky.

The stones had been joined by a new monument: simple in form but with lines that were strong and sturdy, it stood among the quadrant of the cemetery that was reserved for the Justice Department's honoured dead. Dredd let his eyes fall to the inscription on the face of the tomb-stone: "Judge Tex – Bringing Justice to the Hereafter."

A burial detail of twenty Judges stood to attention as Tex's coffin was lowered into the grey earth, eight of them from terrestrial Mega-Cities to represent the foreign officers serving on Luna-1. Tex's will had asked for no special religious ceremony, so the casket dropped away into the dark in silence.

Foster stepped forward when the deed was done and drew his pulse gun. With reverence, he led the twenty officers in a cross-armed firing salute. The low-power energy beams sang through the heavy air.

Dredd gave Kontarsky a sideways glance. She was ill-at-ease in her East-Meg uniform, as if it no longer fitted her correctly. Although the Sov-Judge had kept it to herself, Dredd knew that she had already been chastised by her superiors on Earth and it was certain that the moment she returned, she would be stripped of her rank at the very least. East-Meg Two had been quick to distance itself from Ivanov's plans, claiming that he was a renegade pursuing his own agenda, but Dredd didn't believe a word of it. The Diktatorat had kept its hands clean.

He took a step up to the podium and studied the crowd; mostly senior Luna-City Judges, a few discreet reporters and a knot of whispering diplomats from the orbital embassies. "We are here to pay our respects to Judge-Marshal Jefferson Tex, Chief Judge of Luna-1. Tex was a fine lawman and a strong leader. This city and the law itself, is poorer for his loss." A wave of nods went through the audience. "In this troubled period, I found myself called upon to take his place, but it is a post I cannot continue to hold." Dredd saw questions appearing in the expres-sions before him. "My mission here on Luna-1 is at an end, but before I discharge my responsibility as Judge-Marshal, I have one last act to perform." He looked directly at the diplomatic party, which had fallen silent.

"When Luna-1 stood alone against the tide of lawlessness that threat-ened to engulf it, the call for help went unanswered by those who call themselves the allies of the lunarian citizenry. These people were will-ing to allow Moonie's insurrection to occur, to let Luna-1 fall rather than aid it." The representatives murmured amongst themselves in low, urgent tones. "Your allies preferred the chance to fight over the remains of any failed revolution rather than jockey for position under the rules of the Partnership Treaty." Dredd looked into the cameras that had zoomed closer as the impact of his speech became clear; his face filled a million screens across the city. "It is clear that Luna-1 will never be able to achieve its own destiny while other cities fight over it like a trophy. Therefore, by my executive order, I officially nullify the Global Partnership Treaty and return control of this colony to the surviving members of the original founding Triumvirate: Mega-City One and Texas City."

There was an explosion of gasps and cries of disbelief from across the cemetery. Dredd ignored the shouts from men and women who decried his orders and continued to speak as if they had said nothing. "Furthermore, after the manner in which the security of the city's air supply was threatened by the control of the Oxygen Board, I am also ordering that the Board be immediately broken up and privatised, so that it can never again be manipulated by the whims of one individual."

The voices of dissent rose and fell like a wave, but Dredd noted that there were far more Judges in the crowd who nodded with agreement than those who did not. "Finally," he said, reaching for the badge that Che had given him only a day earlier, "I now step down from the post of Judge-Marshal of Luna-1 and name my replacement as Judge Nikita Kontarsky, formerly of East-Meg Two. She will serve Luna-1 until a new Marshal is selected in six months' time."

Dredd stepped away from the podium and left his words to hang there behind him, coiling in the air like smoke. Kontarsky's gaze met his as he passed her. Dredd paused and laid the badge in her hand. "Good luck," he said. "You'll need it."

The Sov-Judge was speechless and she stared at the gold star-and-crescent-moon in her gloved hand. She wasn't even aware that Dredd had gone until the reporters were crowding around her, demanding a statement.

Dredd slipped away through the cluster of dark uniforms and the shade of the spindly lunar elm trees at the base of the hill.

"Always the same thing with you, isn't it, Dredd?" said a voice from the shadows.

"Kessler." Dredd turned as the SJS chief emerged from cover.

"You come up here, you screw with the status quo and then you leave. Meanwhile, Luna-1 has to deal with the mess you made. You've ruined this city, do you understand that? You've signed Luna-1's death warrant!"

Dredd rounded on the other Judge. "I've given the people a chance. A chance to forge their own future, not one controlled by politicians hundreds of thousands of kilometres away. I've given them breathing space."

"Really?" Kessler sneered. "Are you so naïve? You've forced Luna-1 to stand alone and without a strong hand as Chief Judge, it will wither and die! The other cities will withdraw all their support. With the dissolution of the treaty, all you've done is cut off the lifeline from Earth!"

"That treaty wasn't a lifeline, it was a noose," Dredd retorted. "Every Mega-City on Earth was using it to control the colony up here. Nobody cared about these citizens... They just used Luna-1 like a political pawn, a prize in their big game."

The scar on the SJS-Judge's face was red with anger. "That's all it is!" Kessler spat. "A commodity, nothing more! This is how the game of empire is played–"

"Spare me," Dredd grated. "These people wanted freedom and I've given it to them. But you...you're no better than Moonie, Ivanov or the others up there in the courier ships. You stood by and watched Che make all the wrong choices and you did *nothing*. You wanted him to fail. You were waiting for the moment when you could push him out and take his place and it didn't matter a drokk to you if citizens had to die in the meantime. I saw what your men did out there on the streets. Non-combatants gunned down, zero regard for preservation of innocent life. You're a disgrace to the shield."

Kessler fumed. "I was only obeying orders."

"We'll see," Dredd said after a moment. "The last thing I did before I turned the badge over to Kontarsky was to begin an internal affairs investigation. Your man Wright seemed quite concerned about Judge Hiro's complicity and some of your more zealous mandates. I put him in charge of filing the report." He let the implications of this sink in. "I'm sure Wright will be very thorough. I gave him full discretionary powers in the matter."

Kessler tried to frame a retort, but it just came out as an angry splutter.

Dredd turned his back on the SJS officer and walked away, crossing the line of the Justice Department cordon and into the crowd of onlookers. A few reporters who'd been quick enough to see him leave raced after him, a flock of hover-cams clustered around them.

"Judge Dredd! Any comments for the Luna-1 citizens?"

"How can you justify such an act?"

"Are you and Kontarsky romantically linked?"

A daystick spiked the nearest hover-cam and sent it spinning away in a whirr of complaining gyros. "Back off!" snarled Foster, waving the baton menacingly. "You heard the man. He's off the job now!"

J'aele and the Brit-Cit Judge forced back the cordon a little more so Dredd could reach a Skymaster bike parked at the kerb.

"You surely know how to make an exit, Dredd," said the African, favouring his arm. The Tek-Judge's stump had been replaced with a new cyber-limb, a skeletal construct of black carbon and dull steel. "I think perhaps you would have caused less trouble if you had just let off a stumm grenade in there."

Dredd mounted the zipper skycycle. "You think I was wrong?"

J'aele shook his head. "On the contrary. I think you've liberated Luna-1 more than any revolution could have. I just hope the citizens can handle it."

"That's why we're here," said Dredd. "Freedom alone is anarchy, but freedom with the law. That's a chance for something better."

Foster grinned. "Blimey, Dredd, that almost sounded philosophical. You getting soft in your old age?"

Dredd was about to snap a rejoinder when a juve tried to jump the barricade. On reflex, he swung out a fist and sent the punk reeling, blood and teeth flying from the kid's flapping mouth. "Code 13, Section 7. Disorderly conduct, twelve months," Dredd reeled off the sentence with automatic calm.

"My mistake," said Foster.

"Where next for you?" J'aele asked. "Back to Mega-City One?"

Dredd gave a curt nod, thumbing the Skymaster's ignition. "Creeps down there probably had a field day while I was away. Can't let that slide." He glanced at the two Judges. "You?"

J'aele frowned. "With no treaty now, our cities will recall us both."

Foster made a spitting sound. "That'll be lovely," he said without warmth.

"Kontarsky's going to need people around her she can trust," said Dredd. "You might consider trading in your badges for Luna-1 shields." He gunned the Zipper's motor and powered the bike into the air. "See you on the streets."

Chief Judge Hershey had ordered a Space Corps Shadow-class interceptor diverted off its patrol route to pick up Dredd and return him home; something about wanting him back in the Big Meg for a debriefing that would probably be more like an interrogation. Dredd crossed the landing pad to where the sleek little ship sat on a trio of landing skids, ducking under the nuclear cruise missile blister in the nose.

"You're going to need a co-pilot."

Dredd turned to face Kontarsky as she approached. She had a slight smile on her face at her own joke. "I've got one," he replied. "No solar flares to worry about this time." Dredd noted that she still wore her East-Meg uniform, although the badge that clasped her rad-cape was now the Luna-1 sigil. "I thought you'd be at the Grand Hall getting sworn in."

She shrugged. "I may not yet officially be Judge-Marshal, but I still have some influence. They can wait for me." Kontarsky studied him for a moment. "You have saved my life with this act, do you know that?" She tapped the badge. "After killing Kommisar Ivanov, my life as a Sov citizen is over. I would have returned home to infamy and shame... If I were lucky. More likely, I would have been cashiered and then found dead in some filthy vodkarama."

Dredd paused by the airlock. "I haven't done you any favours, Kontarsky. Luna-1 is in chaos right now and you'll need all your strength to hold it together."

She took a step closer and her cool seemed to crack. "I have to know: wh-why me?" she stammered.

"Lots of reasons. Because you're capable. Because you know the Moon and the law. Because you can't go home again." He gave her a nod of respect. "But mostly because you're a good Judge."

The Russian accepted this with a flash of her green eyes and she snapped into a brisk salute, all trace of her irresolute moment vanishing like vapour. "It has been an honour to serve with you, Judge Dredd."

Dredd returned the gesture. "And you, Judge-Marshal Kontarsky."

She retreated to the lip of the pad as the Interceptor's main drive powered up and, with a rumble of thrust, the Shadow leapt from the pad and shot through the glowing seal-field, receding into a glowing dot that merged with the starry night sky.

Dredd felt the pressure of the G-force push him back into his chair as the ship tore free of the Moon's feeble gravity and angled to face the Earth. He glanced across as the pilot's hands danced over the throttle controls.

"Can this thing go any faster?"

The pilot blinked at him. "Uh, well, yeah. But that's not usually–"

Dredd studied the blue planet beneath him. The dark smudge of Mega-City One was just visible through the clouds, lights emerging from the day-night terminator like a swarm of distant embers. "Every second I waste up here, some perp is walking free down on my streets." He looked away. "Floor it. I got work to do."

The Interceptor's fusion engine surged and, like a falling meteor, Justice came blazing its way back towards Mega-City One.

ABOUT THE AUTHORS

Gordon Rennie lives in a state of befuddled cynicism in Edinburgh, Scotland, where he writes comics, novels, computer game scripts and anything else anyone's willing to pay him money for. In between waiting patiently to become the main writer on the *2000 AD Judge Dredd* script, he spends his time getting into Internet flame wars and pretending to be a lifelong supporter of Hibernian FC.

David Bishop was born and raised in New Zealand, becoming a daily newspaper journalist at eighteen years old. He emigrated to Britain in 1990 and was editor of the *Judge Dredd Megazine* and then *2000 AD*, before becoming a freelance writer. His contributions to Black Flame include *Nikolai Dante: The Strangelove Gambit* and *A Nightmare on Elm Street: Suffer the Children*, as well as the three titles in the *Fiends of the Eastern Front* series. He also writes non-fiction books and articles, audio dramas, comics and has been a creative consultant on three forthcoming video games.

Simon Jowett spent 26 years pretending to be interested in getting a proper job before selling his first script (for a *Dr Who* comic strip). Since then, he has written for some of the biggest names in action/adventure, including *James Bond*, *Young Indiana Jones* and *Spider-Man*, and in children's TV, including *Wallace & Gromit* and *Bob the Builder*. He has also written scripts for computer games and rewritten scripts for feature films.

Peter J Evans made his professional writing debut in 1992. Since then he has worked on a wide variety of projects, producing everything from articles and reviews to sticker books and the back covers of videos. In 1995 he co-wrote the award-winning Manga Video *Collectors Edition* catalogue, and his first novel was published in 1999. His more recent projects include the Black Flame novel *Judge Dredd: Black Atlantic*, and the five-part *Durham Red* cycle.

James Swallow's other works include the *Sundowners* series of "steampunk" Westerns, *Rogue Trooper: Blood Relative*, *Jade Dragon*, *The Butterfly Effect* and several critically acclaimed *Warhammer 40,000* novels for the Black Library. His non-fiction features *Dark Eye: The Films of David Fincher* and books on genre television and animation; Swallow's other credits include writing for *Star Trek Voyager*, *Doctor Who*, scripts for videogames and audio dramas.

THE BIG MEG GLOSSARY

Antarctic City: Abundant in minerals, the Antarctic Territories are governed by six global powers.

Apocalypse War: Attempted invasion of Mega-City One by East Meg in 2014. Most of the population and the city were destroyed.

Banana City: A violent and corrupt city in Latin America.

Black Atlantic: An apt description of the Atlantic Ocean whose waters are so heavily polluted that it is incredibly toxic and lethal to humans.

Block: Giant skyscrapers that make up most of Mega-City One. The inhabitants of blocks are known as blockers. Sometimes the pressures of living in such cramped high-rise conditions lead to block mania, which may spark a war.

Boing: An aerosol sprayed substance that forms a rubber bubble around its user.

Bouncer-Mek: A large and imposing robot mainly used for bouncer roles.

Brit-Cit: British counterpart of Mega-City One.

Catch Wagon: A vehicle designed for the collection of criminals.

Control: The nerve centre of Mega-City One, relaying information to Judges on the streets.

Daystick: The Judge's favoured truncheon.

Futsie: "Future shock"; a mental breakdown of epic proportions, which causes some of The Big Meg's citizens to become irrationally violent.

Glasseen: Futuristic variation of glass.

Grud: (By Grud! Jovus Grud!) By God! Jesus Christ! Other derivatives include Sweet Jovus (Sweet Jesus) and Sweet Jovus Son of Grud.

Iso-Cube: The standard imprisonment for criminals, a huge block full of very small isolation cubes.

Juve: A young criminal often aged twenty years-old or younger.

H-wagon: Justice Department hover vehicle that can shift large amounts of man and firepower.

Hovercam: A small and compact video camera with the ability to hover.

Lawgiver: The weapon of choice for the Judge, an automatic multi-shell gun whose ammunition ranges from armour piercing to ricochet rounds.

Lawmaster: The Judge's computer-controlled motor-bike. Extremely powerful, intelligent and heavily armed.

Luna-1: In 2061, the three American Mega-Cites united to populate a one-million square mile base on the Moon.

L-Wagon: A Luna version of the Mega-City H-wagon.

Pedway: A pedestrian-only pathway as other ped-ways are mechanised.

Perp: A Judge's term for a criminal/perpetrator.

Rad-lands: Old name for the Cursed Earth, a vast, radioactive wasteland.

Simba-City: After the nuclear destruction during the Apocalypse War, South Africa has been shattered and mostly uninhabitable. The major cities are Umur (Libya), New Jerusalem (North-east Ethipoa) and Simba-City (Cameroon).

SJS: The Special Judicial Squad act as the Judge's police; they seek out corruption and crime within the Law with extreme prejudice.

Skedway: A minor roadway; smaller than a megway but larger than an overzoom.

STUP-gun: A highly effective and powerful firearm that shoots streams of highly charged particles in microsecond pulses.

Synthi-caf: A refreshing drink that is similar to banned coffee, it has now deemed illegal due to its highly addictive properties and has been replaced by various forms of synthi-synthi-caf.

Tek-Judge: A technical and engineering specialist whose skills range from advanced forensic analysis to the repairing of vehicles, weapons, etc.

Titan: A small moon orbiting Saturn, used as a dedicated maximum-security prison for Mega-City One's most dangerous criminals.

Tri-D: Also known as holovision; there are over 312 channels in Mega-City One.

Umpty Candy: A sweet: hyper-addictive and illegal candy.

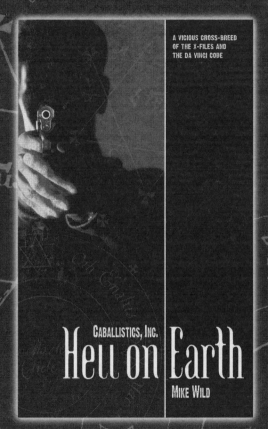